OPENING NIGHT
SPINSTERS IN JEOPARDY
SCALES OF JUSTICE

Dame Ngaio Marsh was born in New Zealand in 1895 and died in February 1982. She wrote over 30 detective novels and many of her stories have theatrical settings, for Ngaio Marsh's real passion was the theatre. Both actress and producer, she almost single-handedly revived the New Zealand public's interest in the theatre. It was for this work that she received what she called her 'damery' in 1966.

'The finest writer in the English language of the pure, classical puzzle whodunit. Among the crime queens, Ngaio Marsh stands out as an Empress.'   *The Sun*

'Ngaio Marsh transforms the detective story from a mere puzzle into a novel.'   *Daily Express*

'Her work is as nearly flawless as makes no odds. Character, plot, wit, good writing, and sound technique.'   *Sunday Times*

'She writes better than Christie!'   *New York Times*

'Brilliantly readable . . . first class detection.'   *Observer*

'Still, quite simply, the greatest exponent of the classical English detective story.'   *Daily Telegraph*

'Read just one of Ngaio Marsh's novels and you've got to read them all . . . '   *Daily Mail*

BY THE SAME AUTHOR

NGAIO MARSH

Opening Night

Spinsters in Jeopardy

Scales of Justice

AND

The Hand in the Sand

HARPER

HARPER
an imprint of HarperCollins*Publishers*
77-85 Fulham Palace Road
Hammersmith, London W6 8JB
www.harpercollins.co.uk

This omnibus edition 2009
1

Opening Night first published in Great Britain by Collins 1951
Spinsters in Jeopardy first published in Great Britain by Collins 1954
Scales of Justice first published in Great Britain by Collins 1955
The Hand in the Sand first published in Great Britain in
Death on the Air and Other Stories by HarperCollins*Publishers* 1995

Ngaio Marsh asserts the moral right to
be identified as the author of these works

ISBN 978 0 00 732874 1
Printed and bound in Great Britain by
Clays Ltd, St Ives plc

Mixed Sources
Product group from well-managed
forests and other controlled sources
www.fsc.org Cert no. SW-COC-1806
© 1996 Forest Stewardship Council

FSC is a non-profit international organisation established to promote the
responsible management of the world's forests. Products carrying the FSC
label are independently certified to assure consumers that they come
from forests that are managed to meet the social, economic and
ecological needs of present and future generations.

Find out more about HarperCollins and the environment at
www.harpercollins.co.uk/green

CONTENTS

Opening Night

*To The Management and Company of The New Zealand
Student Players of 1949 in love and gratitude*

Contents

Cast of Characters

CHAPTER 1

Martyn at the Vulcan

As she turned into Carpet Street the girl wondered at her own obstinacy. To what a pass it had brought her, she thought. She lifted first
one foot and then the other, determined not to drag them. They felt
now as if their texture had changed: their bones, it seemed, were
covered by sponge and burning wires.

A clock in a jeweller's window gave the time as twenty-three
minutes to five. She knew, by the consequential scurry of its second-
hand, that it was alive. It was surrounded by other clocks that made
mad dead statements of divergent times as if, she thought, to set
before her the stages of that day's fruitless pilgrimage. Nine o'clock,
the first agent. Nine thirty-six, the beginning of the wait for auditions at the Unicorn; five minutes past twelve, the first dismissal.
'Thank you, Miss–ah–Thank you, dear. Leave your name and
address. Next, please.' No record of her flight from the smell of
restaurants but it must have been about ten-to-two, a time regis-
tered by a gilt carriage-clock in the corner, that she had climbed the
stairs to Garnet Marks' Agency on the third floor. Three o'clock
exactly at the Achilles where the auditions had already closed, and
the next hour in and out of film agencies. 'Leave your picture if you
like, dear. Let you know if there's anything.' Always the same. As
punctual as time itself. The clocks receded, wobbled, enlarged themselves and at the same time spread before their dials a tenuous veil.
Beneath the arm of a bronze nude that brandished an active swinging dial, she caught sight of a face: her own. She groped in her bag
and presently in front of the mirrored face, a hand appeared and

5

made a gesture at its own mouth with the stub of a lipstick. There
was a coolness on her forehead, something pressed heavily against
it. She discovered that this was the shop-window.

Behind the looking-glass was a man who peered at her from the
shop's interior. She steadied herself with her hand against the window, lifted her suitcase and turned away.

The Vulcan Theatre was near the bottom of the street. Although
she did not at first see its name above the entry, she had, during the
past fortnight, discovered a sensitivity to theatres. She was aware of
them at a distance. The way was downhill: her knees trembled and
she resisted with difficulty an impulse to break into a shamble.
Among the stream of faces that approached and sailed past there
were now some that, on seeing hers, sharpened into awareness and
speculation. She attracted notice.

The stage-door was at the end of an alleyway. Puddles of water
obstructed her passage and she did not altogether avoid them. The
surface of the wall was crenellated and damp.

'She knows,' a rather shrill uncertain voice announced inside the
theatre, 'but she *mustn't* be told.' A second voice spoke unintelligibly.
The first voice repeated its statement with a change of emphasis:
'She *knows* but she mustn't be *told*,' and after a further interruption
added dismally: 'Thank you very much.'

Five women came out of the stage-door and it was shut behind
them. She leant against the wall as they passed her. The first two
muttered together and moved their shoulders petulantly, the third
stared at her and at once she bent her head. The fourth passed by
quickly with compressed lips. She kept her head averted and heard,
but did not see, the last girl halt beside her.

'Well, for God's sake!' She looked up and saw, for the second time
that day, a too-large face, over-painted, with lips that twisted downwards, tinted lids, and thickly mascaraed lashes.

She said: 'I'm late, aren't I?'

'You've had it, dear. I gave you the wrong tip at Marks's. The
show here, with the part I told you about, goes on this week. They
were auditioning for a tour: 'That'll be all for today, ladies, thank
you. What's the hurry, here's your hat. For what it's worth, it's all
over.'

'I lost my way,' she said faintly.

'Too bad.' The large face swam nearer. 'Are you all right?' it demanded.

She made a slight movement of her head. 'A bit tired. All right, really.'

'You look shocking. Here: wait a sec. Try this.'

'No, no. Really. Thank you so much but – '

'It's OK. A chap who travels for a French firm gave it to me. It's marvellous stuff: cognac. Go *on*.'

A hand steadied her head. The cold mouth of the flask opened her lips and pressed against her teeth. She tried to say: 'I've had nothing to eat,' and at once was forced to gulp down a burning stream. The voice encouraged her: 'Do you a power of good. Have the other half.'

She shuddered, gasped and pushed the flask away. 'No, please!'

'Is it doing the trick?'

'This is wonderfully kind of you. I am so grateful. Yes, I think it must be doing the trick.'

'Gra-a-a-nd. Well, if you're sure you'll be OK . . .'

'Yes, indeed. I don't even know your name.'

'Trixie O'Sullivan.'

'I'm Martyn Tarne.'

'Look nice in the programme, wouldn't it? If there's nothing else I can do . . .'

'Honestly. I'll be fine.'

'You look better,' Miss O'Sullivan said doubtfully. 'We may run into each other again. The bloody round, the common task.' She began to move away. 'I've got a date, actually, and I'm running late.'

'Yes, of course. Goodbye, and thank you.'

'It's open in front. There's a seat in the foyer. Nobody'll say anything. Why not sit there for a bit?' She was halfway down the alley. 'Hope you get fixed up,' she said. 'God, it's going to rain. What a life!'

'What a life,' Martyn Tarne echoed and tried to sound gay and ironic.

'I hope you'll be all right. 'Bye.'

'Goodbye and thank you.'

The alley was quiet now. Without moving she took stock of herself. Something thrummed inside her head and the tips of her fingers tingled but she no longer felt as if she was going to faint. The brandy glowed at the core of her being, sending out ripples of comfort. She tried to think what she should do. There was a church, back in the Strand: she ought to know its name. One could sleep there, she had been told, and perhaps there would be soup. That would leave two and eightpence for tomorrow: all she had. She lifted her suitcase, it was heavier than she had remembered, and walked to the end of the alleyway. Half a dozen raindrops plopped into a puddle. People hurried along the footpath with upward glances and opened their umbrellas. As she hesitated, the rain came down suddenly and decisively. She turned towards the front of the theatre and at first thought it was shut. Then she noticed that one of the plate-glass doors was ajar.

She pushed it open and went in.

The Vulcan was a new theatre, fashioned from the shell of an old one. Its foyer was an affair of geranium-red leather, chromium steel and double glass walls housing cacti. The central box-office marked 'Reserved Tickets Only' was flanked by doors and beyond them, in the corners, were tubular steel and rubber-foam seats. She crossed the heavily carpeted floor and sat in one of these. Her feet and legs, released from the torment of supporting and moving her body, throbbed ardently.

Facing Martyn, on a huge easel, was a frame of photographs under a printed legend: 'Opening at this Theatre on Thursday, May 11th: *Thus to Revisit*, a New Play by John James Rutherford.' She stared at two large familiar faces and four strange smaller ones. Adam Poole and Helena Hamilton: those were famous faces. Monstrously enlarged, they had looked out at the New Zealand and Australian public from hoardings and from above cinema entrances. She had stood in queues many times to see them, severally and together. They were in the centre and surrounding them were Clark Bennington with a pipe and stick and a look of faded romanticism in his eyes, J. G. Darcey with pince-nez and hair en brosse, Gay Gainsford, young and intense, and Parry Percival, youngish and dashing. The faces swam together and grew dim.

It was very quiet in the foyer and beginning to get dark. On the other side of the entrance doors the rain drove down slantways half blinding her vision of homeward-bound pedestrians and the traffic of the street beyond them. She saw the lights go on in the top of a bus, illuminating the passive and remote faces of its passengers. The glare of headlamps shone pale across the rain. A wave of loneliness, excruciating in its intensity, engulfed Martyn and she closed her eyes. For the first time since her ordeal began, panic rose in her throat and sickened her. Phrases drifted with an aimless rhythm on the tide of her desolation: 'You're sunk, you're sunk, you're utterly sunk, you asked for it, and you've got it. What'll happen to you now?'

She was drowning at night in a very lonely sea. She saw lights shine on some unattainable shore. Pieces of flotsam bobbed indifferently against her hands. At the climax of despair, metallic noises, stupid and commonplace, set up a clatter in her head.

Martyn jerked galvanically and opened her eyes. The whirr and click of her fantasy had been repeated behind an obscured-glass wall on her left. Light glowed beyond the wall and she was confronted by the image of a god, sand-blasted across the surface of the glass and beating at a forge under the surprising supervision, it appeared, of Melpomene and Thalia. Farther along, a notice in red light: 'Dress Circle and Stalls', jutted out from an opening. Beyond the hammer-blows of her heart a muffled voice spoke peevishly.

'. . . Not much use to *me*. What? Yes, I know, old boy, but that's not the point.'

The voice seemed to listen. Martyn thought: 'This is it. In a minute I'll be turned out.'

'. . . Something pretty bad,' the voice said irritably. 'She's gone to hospital. . . . They *said* so but nobody's turned up. . . . Well, you know what she's like, old boy, don't you? We've been snowed under all day and *I* haven't been able to do anything about it . . . auditions for the northern tour of the old piece . . . yes, yes, that's all fixed but . . . Look, another thing: *The Onlooker* wants a story and pictures for this week . . . yes, on stage. In costume. Nine-thirty in the morning and everything still in the boxes. . . . Well, can't you think of *anyone*? . . . Who? . . . O, God, I'll give it a pop. All right, old boy, thanks.'

To Martyn, dazed with brandy and sleep, it was a distortion of a daydream. Very often had she dreamt herself into a theatre where all was confusion because the leading actress had laryngitis and the understudy was useless. She would present herself

modestly: 'I happen to know the lines. I could perhaps . . . ' The
sudden attentiveness, when she began to speak the lines . . . the
opening night . . . the grateful tears streaming down the boiled
shirts of the management . . . the critics . . . no image had been
too gross for her.

'Eileen?' said the voice. 'Thank God! Listen, darling, it's Bob
Grantley here. Listen, Eileen, I want you to do something terribly
kind. I know it's asking a hell of a lot but I'm in trouble and you're
my last hope. Helena's dresser's ill. Yes, indeed, poor old Tansey. Yes,
I'm afraid so. Just this afternoon, and we haven't been able to raise
anybody. First dress-rehearsal tomorrow night and a photograph call
in the morning and nothing unpacked or anything. I know what a
good soul you are and I wondered . . . O, God! I see. Yes, I see. No,
of course. Oh, well, never mind. I know you would. Yes. 'Bye.'

Silence. Precariously alone in the foyer, she meditated an advance
upon the man beyond the glass wall and suppressed a dreadful
impulse in herself towards hysteria. This was her daydream in
terms of reality. She must have slept longer than she had thought.
Her feet were sleeping still. She began to test them, tingling and
pricking, against the floor. She could see her reflection in the front
doors, a dingy figure with a pallid face and cavernous shadows for
eyes.

The light behind the glass wall went out. There was, however, still
a yellow glow coming through the box-office door. As she got to her
feet and steadied herself, the door opened.

'I believe,' she said, 'you are looking for a dresser.'

II

As he had stopped dead in the lighted doorway she couldn't see the
man clearly but his silhouette was stocky and trim.

He said with what seemed to be a mixture of irritation and relief:
'Good Lord, how long have you been here?'

'Not long. You were on the telephone. I didn't like to interrupt.'

'Interrupt!' he ejaculated as if she talked nonsense.

He looked at his watch, groaned, and said rapidly: 'You've come
about this job? From Mrs Greenacres, aren't you?'

She wondered who Mrs Greenacres could be? An employment agent? She hunted desperately for the right phrase, the authentic language.

'I understood you required a dresser and I would be pleased to apply.' Should she have added 'sir'?

'It's for Miss Helena Hamilton,' he said rapidly. 'Her own dresser who's been with her for years – for a long time – has been taken ill. I explained to Mrs Greenacres. Photograph call for nine in the morning and first dress-rehearsal tomorrow night. We open on Thursday. The dressing's heavy. Two quick changes and so on. I suppose you've got references?'

Her mouth was dry. She said: 'I haven't brought – ' and was saved by the telephone bell. He plunged back into the office and she heard him shout 'Vulcan' into the receiver. 'Grantley, here,' he said. 'Oh, hallo, darling. Look, I'm desperately sorry, but I've been held up or I'd have rung you before. For God's sake apologize for me. Try and keep them going till I get there. I know, I know. Not a smell of one until – ' the voice became suddenly muffled. She caught isolated words. 'I think so . . . yes, I'll ask . . . yes . . . Right. 'Bye, darling.'

He darted out, now wearing a hat and struggling into a raincoat. 'Look,' he said, 'Miss – '

'Tarne.'

'Miss Tarne. Can you start right away? Miss Hamilton's things are in her dressing-room. They need to be unpacked and hung out tonight. There'll be a lot of pressing. The cleaners have been in but the room's not ready. You can finish in the morning but she wants the things that can't be ironed – I wouldn't know – hung out. Here are the keys. We'll see how you get on and fix up something definite tomorrow if you suit. The night-watchman's there. He'll open the room for you. Say I sent you. Here!'

He fished out a wallet, found a card and scribbled on it. 'He is a bit of a stickler: you'd better take this.'

She took the card and the keys. 'Tonight?' she said. 'Now?'

'Well, can you?'

'I – yes. But – '

'Not worrying about after-hours, are you?'

'No.'

For the first time he seemed, in the darkish foyer, to be looking closely at her. 'I suppose,' he muttered, 'it's a bit – ' and stopped short.

Martyn said in a voice that to herself sounded half-choked: 'I'm perfectly trustworthy. You spoke of references. I have – '

'Oh, yes, yes,' he said. 'Good. That'll be OK then. I'm late. Will you be all right? You can go through the house. It's raining outside. Through there, will you? Thank you. Goodnight.'

Taking up her suitcase, she went through the door he swung open and found herself in the theatre.

She was at the back of the stalls, standing on thick carpet at the top of the ramp and facing the centre aisle. It was not absolutely dark. The curtain was half-raised and a bluish light filtered in from off-stage through some opening – a faintly-discerned window – in the scenery. This light was dimly reflected on the shrouded boxes. The dome was invisible, lost in shadow, and so far above that the rain, hammering on the roof beyond it, sounded much as a rumour of drums to Martyn. The deadened air smelt of naphthalene and plush.

She started off cautiously down the aisle. 'I forgot,' said Mr Grantley's voice behind her. She managed to choke back a yelp. 'You'd better get some flowers for the dressing-room. She likes roses. Here's another card.'

'I don't think I've – '

'Florian's at the corner,' he shouted. 'Show them the card.'

The door swung to behind him and, a moment later, she heard a more remote slam. She waited for a little while longer, to accustom herself to the dark. The shadows melted and the shape of the audi-torium filtered through them like an image on a film in the dark-room. She thought it beautiful: the curve of the circle, the fan-like shell that enclosed it, the elegance of the proscenium and modesty of the ornament – all these seemed good to Martyn, and her grow-ing sight of them refreshed her. Though this encouragement had an unreal, rather dream-like character, yet it did actually dispel some-thing of her physical exhaustion so that it was with renewed heart that she climbed a little curved flight of steps on the prompt side of the proscenium, pushed open the pass-door at the top and arrived back-stage.

She was on her own ground. A single blue working-light, thick with dust, revealed a baize letter-rack and hinted at the baton and canvas backs of scenery fading upwards into yawning blackness. At her feet a litter of flex ran down into holes in the stage. There were vague, scarcely discernible shapes that she recognized as stacked flats, light bunches, the underside of perches, a wind machine and rain box. She smelt paint and glue-size. As she received the assurance of these familiar signs she heard a faint scuffling noise, a rattle of paper, she thought. She moved forward.

In the darkness ahead of her a door opened on an oblong of light which widened to admit the figure of a man in an overcoat. He stood with bent head, fumbled in his pocket and produced a torch. The beam shot out, hunted briefly about the set and walls and found her. She blinked into a dazzling white disc and said: 'Mr Grantley sent me round. I'm the dresser.'

'Dresser?' the man said hoarsely. He kept his torchlight on her face and moved towards her. 'I wasn't told about no dresser,' he said.

She held Mr Grantley's card out. He came closer and flashed his light on it without touching it. 'Ah,' he said with a sort of grudging cheerfulness, 'that's different. Now I know where I am, don't I?'

'I hope so,' she said, trying to make her voice friendly. 'I'm sorry to bother you. Miss Hamilton's dresser has been taken ill and I've got the job.'

'*Aren't* you lucky,' he said with obvious relish and added: 'Not but what she isn't a lady when she takes the fit for it.'

He was eating something. The movement of his jaws, the succulent noises he made and the faint odour of food were an outrage. She could have screamed her hunger at him. Her mouth filled with saliva.

'He says to open the star room,' he said. 'Come on froo while I get the keys. I was 'avin' me bitter supper.'

She followed him into a tiny room choked with junk. A kettle stuttered on a gas-ring by a sink clotted with dregs of calcimine paint and tea leaves. His supper was laid out on a newspaper: bread and an open tin of jam. He explained that he was about to make a cup of tea and suggested she should wait while he did so. She leant against the door and watched him. The fragrance of freshly brewed tea rose above the reek of stale size and dust. She thought: 'If he drinks it now I'll have to go out.'

'Like a drop of char?' he said. His back was turned to her.

'Very much.'

He rinsed out a stained cup under the tap.

Martyn said loudly: 'I've got a tin of meat in my case. I was saving it. If you'd like to share it and could spare some of your bread . . .'

He swung round and for the first time she saw his face. He was dark and thin and his eyes were brightly impertinent. Their expression changed as he stared at her.

''Allo, 'allo!' he said. 'Who gave *you* a tanner and borrowed 'alf a crahn? What's up?'

'I'm all right.'

'*Are* you? Your looks don't flatter, you, then.'

'I'm a bit tired and – ' Her voice broke and she thought in terror that she was going to cry. 'It's nothing,' she said.

''Ere!' He dragged a box out from under the sink and not ungently pushed her down on it. 'Where's this remarkable tin of very perticerlar meat? Give us a shine at it?'

He shoved her suitcase over and while she fumbled at the lock busied himself with pouring out tea. 'Nothing to touch a drop of the old char when you're browned off,' he said. He put the reeking cup of dark fluid beside her and turned away to the bench.

'With any luck,' Martyn thought folding back the garments in her case, 'I won't have to sell these now.'

She found the tin and gave it to him. 'Coo!' he said, 'looks lovely, don't it? Tongue and veal and a pitcher of sheep to show there's no deception. Very tempting.'

'Can you open it?'

'Can I open it? Oh, dear.'

She drank her scalding tea and watched him open the tin and turn its contents out on a more than dubious plate. Using his clasp knife he perched chunks of meat on a slab of bread and held it out to her. 'You're in luck,' he said. 'Eat it slow.'

She urged him to join her but he said he would set his share aside for later. They could both, he suggested, take another cut at it tomorrow. He examined the tin with interest while Martyn consumed her portion. She had never before given such intense concentration to a physical act. She would never have believed that eating could bring so fierce a satisfaction.

'Comes from Australia, don't it?' her companion said, still contemplating the tin.

'New Zealand.'

'Same thing.'

Martyn said: 'Not really. There's quite a big sea in between.'

'Do you come from there?'

'Where?'

'Australia.'

'No. I'm a New Zealander.'

'Same thing.'

She looked up and found him grinning at her. He made the gesture of wiping the smile off his face. 'Oh, dear,' he said.

Martyn finished her tea and stood up. 'I must start my job,' she said.

'Feel better?'

'Much, much better.'

'Would it be quite a spell since you ate anything?'

'Yesterday.'

'I never fancy drinking on an empty stomach, myself.'

Her face burnt against the palms of her hands. 'But I don't . . . I mean, I know. I mean I was a bit faint and somebody . . . a girl . . . she was terribly kind . . .'

'Does your mother know you're aht?' he asked ironically and took a key from a collection hung on nails behind the door. 'If you *must* work,' he said.

'Please.'

'Personally escorted tour abaht to commence. Follow in single file and don't talk to the guide. I thank you.'

She followed him to the stage and round the back of the set. He warned her of obstructions by bobbing his torchlight on them and, when she stumbled against a muffled table, took her hand. She was disquieted by the grip of his fingers, calloused, and wooden, and by the warmth of his palm which was unexpectedly soft. She was oppressed with renewed loneliness and fear.

'End of the penny section,' he said, releasing her. He unlocked a door, reached inside and switched on a light.

'They call this the greenroom,' he said. 'That's what it was in the old days. It's been done up. Guvnor's idea.'

It was a room without a window, newly painted in green. There were a number of armchairs in brown leather, a round table littered with magazines, a set of well-stocked bookshelves and a gas-fire. Groups of framed Pollock's prints decorated the walls: 'Mr Dale as Claude Amboine', 'Mr T. Hicks as Richard I', 'Mr S. French as Harlequin'. This last enchanted Martyn because the diamonds of Mr French's costume had been filled in with actual red and green sequins and he glittered in his frame.

Above the fireplace hung a largish sketch – it was little more than that – of a man of about thirty-five in medieval dress, with a hood that he was in the act of pushing away from his face. The face was arresting. It had great purity of form being wide across the eyes and heart shaped. The mouth, in particular, was of a most subtle character, perfectly masculine but drawn with extreme delicacy. It was well done: it had both strength and refinement yet it was not these qualities that disturbed Martyn. Reflected in the glass that covered the picture she saw her own face lying ghost-wise across the other; their forms intermingled like those in a twice-exposed photograph. It seemed to Martyn that her companion must be looking over her shoulder at this double image and she moved away from him and nearer to the picture. The reflection disappeared. Something was written faintly in one corner of the sketch. She drew closer and saw that it was a single word: 'Everyman'.

'Spitting image of him, ain't it?' said the doorkeeper behind her.

'I don't know,' she said quickly; 'is it?'

'*Is* it! Don't you know the guvnor when you see 'im?'

'The governor?'

'Streuth, you're a caution and no error. Don't you know who owns this show? That's the great Mr Adam Poole, that is.'

'Oh,' she murmured after a pause and added uneasily, 'I've seen him in the pictures, of course.'

'Go on!' he jeered. 'Where would that be? Australia? Fancy!'

He had been very kind to her but she found his remorseless vein of irony exasperating. It would have been easier and less tedious to have let it go but she found herself embarked on an explanation. Of course she knew all about Mr Adam Poole, she said. She had seen his photograph in the foyer. All his pictures had been shown in New Zealand. She knew he was the most distinguished of the younger contemporary actor-managers. She was merely startled by the paint-ing, because . . . But it was impossible to explain why the face in the painting disturbed her and the unfinished phrase trailed away into an embarrassed silence.

Her companion listened to this rigmarole with an equivocal grin and when she gave it up merely remarked: 'Don't apologize. It's the same with all the ladies: 'E fair rocks 'em. Talk about 'aving what it takes.'

'I don't mean that at all,' she shouted angrily.

'You should see 'em clawing at each other to get at 'im rahnd the stage-door, first nights. Something savage! Females of the speeches? Disgrace to their sexes more like. There's an ironing-board etceterer in the wardrobe-room farther along. You can plug in when you're ready. 'Er Royal 'Ighness is over the way.'

He went out, opened a further door, switched on a light and called to her to join him.

III

As soon as she crossed the threshold of the star dressing-room she smelt greasepaint. The dressing-shelf was bare, the room untenanted, but the smell of cosmetics mingled with the faint reek of gas. There were isolated dabs of colour on the shelves and the looking-glass; the lamp-bulbs were smeared with cream and red where sticks of greasepaint had been warmed at them and on a shelf above the wash-basin somebody had left a miniature frying-pan of congealed mascara in which a hair-pin was embedded.

It was a largish room, windowless and dank, with an air of sub-merged grandeur about it. The full-length cheval-glass swung from a gilt frame. There was an Empire couch, an armchair and an ornate stool before the dressing-shelf. The floor was carpeted in red with a florid pattern that use had in part obliterated. A number of dress-boxes bearing the legend 'Costumes by Pierrot et Cie' were stacked in the middle of the room and there were two suitcases on the shelf. A gas-heater stood against one wall and there was a caged jet above the wash-basin.

'Here we are,' said the doorkeeper. 'All yer own.'

She turned to thank him and encountered a speculative stare. 'Cosy,' he said, 'ain't it?' and moved nearer. 'Nice little hidey-hole, ain't it?'

'You've been very kind,' Martyn said. 'I'll manage splendidly now. Thank you very much indeed.'

'Don't mention it. Any time.' His hand reached out clumsily to her. 'Been aht in the rain,' he said thickly. 'Naughty girl.'

'I'll soon dry off. I'm quite all right.'

She moved behind the pile of dress-boxes and fumbled with the string on the top one. There was a hissing noise. She heard him strike a match and a moment later was horribly jolted by an explosion from the gas-heater. It forced an involuntary cry from her.

''Allo, 'allo!' her companion said. 'Ain't superstitious, are we?'

'Superstitious?'

He made an inexplicable gesture towards the gas-fire. '*You* know,' he said, grinning horridly at her.

'I'm afraid I don't understand.'

'Don't tell me you never 'eard abaht the great Jupiter case! Don't they learn you nothing in them anti-podes?'

The heater reddened and purred.

'Come to think of it,' he said, 'it'd be before your time. I wasn't here myself when it occurred, a-course, but them that was don't give you a chance to forget it. Not that they mention it direct-like but it don't get forgotten.'

'What was it?' Martyn asked against her will.

'Sure yer not superstitious?'

'No, I'm not.'

'You ain't been long in this business, then. Nor more am I. Shake 'ands.' He extended his hand so pointedly that she was obliged to put her own in it and had some difficulty in releasing herself.

'It must be five years ago,' he said, 'all of that. A bloke in number four dressing-room did another bloke in, very cunning, by blowing dahn the tube of 'is own gas-fire. Like if I went nex' door and blew dahn the tube, this fire'd go aht. And if you was dead drunk like you might of been if this girl friend of yours'd been very generous with 'er brandy you'd be commy-toes and before you knew where you was you'd be dead. Which is what occurred.

It made a very nasty impression and the theatre was shut dahn for a long time until they 'ad it all altered and pansied up. The guvnor won't 'ave it mentioned. 'E changed the name of the 'ouse when 'e took it on. But call it what you like the memory, as they say, lingers on. Silly, though, ain't it? You and me don't care. That's right, isn't it? We'd rather be cosy. Wouldn't we?' He gave a kind of significance to the word 'cosy'. Martyn unlocked the suitcases. Her fingers were unsteady and she turned her back in order to hide them from him. He stood in front of the gas-fire and began to give out a smell of hot dirty cloth. She took sheets from the suitcase, hung them under the clothes pegs round the walls, and began to unpack the boxes. Her feet throbbed cruelly and, with a surreptitious manipulation, she shuffled them out of her wet shoes.

'That's the ticket,' he said. 'Dry 'em orf, shall we?'

He advanced upon her and squatted to gather up the shoes. His hand, large and prehensile, with a life of its own, darted out and closed over her foot. ''Ow abaht yer stockings?'

Martyn felt not only frightened but humiliated and ridiculous: wobbling, dead tired, on one foot. It was as if she were half caught in some particularly degrading kind of stocks.

She said: 'Look here, you're a good chap. You've been terribly kind. Let me get on with the job.'

His grip slackened. He looked up at her without embarrassment, his thin London face sharp with curiosity. 'OK,' he said. 'No offence meant. Call it a day, eh?'

'Call it a day.'

'You're the boss,' he said and got to his feet. He put her shoes down in front of the gas-fire and went to the door. 'Live far from 'ere?' he asked. A feeling of intense desolation swept through her and left her without the heart to prevaricate.

'I don't know,' she said. 'I've got to find somewhere. There's a women's hostel near Paddington, I think.'

'Broke?'

'I'll be all right, now I've got this job.'

His hand was in his pocket: ''Ere,' he said.

'No, no. Please.'

'Come orf it. We're pals, ain't we?'

'No, really. I'm terribly grateful but I'd rather not. I'm all right.'

'You're the boss,' he said again, and after a pause: 'I can't get the idea, honest I can't. The way you speak and be'ave and all. What's the story? 'Ard luck or what?'

'There's no story, really.'

'Just what you say yourself. No questions asked.' He opened the door and moved into the passage. 'Mind,' he said over his shoulder, 'it's against the rules but I won't be rahnd again. My mate relieves me at eight ack emma but I'll tip 'im the wink if it suits you. Them chairs in the greenroom's not bad for a bit of kip and there's the fire. I'll turn it on. Please yerself a-course.'

'Oh,' she said, 'could I? *Could* I?'

'Never know what you can do till you try. Keep it under your tifter, though, or I'll be in trouble. So long. Don't get down'earted. It'll be all the same in a fahsand years.'

He had gone. Martyn ran into the passage and saw his torchlight bobbing out on the stage. She called after him:

'Thank you – thank you so much. I don't know your name – but thank you and goodnight.'

'Badger's the name,' he said, and his voice sounded hollow in the empty darkness. 'Call me Fred.'

The light bobbed out of sight. She heard him whistling for a moment and then a door slammed and she was alone.

With renewed heart she turned back to her job.

IV

At ten o'clock she had finished. She had traversed with diligence all the hazards of fatigue: the mounting threat of sleep, the clumsiness that makes the simplest action an ordeal, the horror of inertia and the temptation to let go the tortured muscles and give up, finally and indifferently, the awful struggle.

Five carefully ironed dresses hung sheeted against the walls, the make-up was laid out on the covered dressing-shelf. The boxes were stacked away, the framed photographs set out. It only remained to buy roses in the morning for Miss Helena Hamilton. Even the vase was ready and filled with water.

Martyn leant heavily on the back of a chair and stared at two photographs of the same face in a double leather case. They were not theatre photographs but studio portraits and the face looked younger than the face in the greenroom: younger and more formidable, with the mouth set truculently and the gaze withdrawn. But it had the same effect on Martyn. Written at the bottom of each of these photographs, in a small incisive hand, was 'Helena from Adam. 1950'. 'Perhaps,' she thought, 'he's married to her.'

Hag-ridden by the fear that she had forgotten some important detail, she paused in the doorway and looked round the room. No, she thought, there was nothing more to be done. But as she turned to go she saw herself, cruelly reflected in the long cheval-glass. It was not, of course, the first time she had seen herself that night; she had passed before the looking-glasses a dozen times and had actually polished them, but her attention had been ruthlessly fixed on the job in hand and she had not once focused her eyes on her own image. Now she did so. She saw a girl in a yellow sweater and dark skirt with black hair that hung in streaks over her forehead. She saw a white, heart-shaped face with smudges under the eyes and a mouth that was normally firm and delicate but now drooped with fatigue. She raised her hand, pushed the hair back from her face and stared for a moment or two longer. Then she switched off the light and blundered across the passage into the greenroom. Here, collapsed in an armchair with her overcoat across her, she slept heavily until morning.

CHAPTER 2

In a Glass Darkly

Martyn slept for ten hours. A wind got up in the night and found its way into the top of the stagehouse at the Vulcan. Up in the grid old back-cloths moved a little and, since the Vulcan was a hemp-house, there was a soughing among the forest of ropes. Flakes of paper, relics of some Victorian snowstorm, were dislodged from the top of a batten and fluttered down to the stage. Rain, driven fitfully against the theatre, ran in cascades down pipes and dripped noisily from ledges into the stage-door entry. The theatre mice came out, explored the contents of paste-pots in the sink-room and scuttled unsuccessfully about a covered plate of tongue and veal. Out in the auditorium there arose at intervals a vague whisper and in his cubby-hole off the dock Fred Badger dozed and woke uneasily. At one o'clock he went on his rounds. He padded down corridors, flicking his torchlight on framed sketches for décor and costumes, explored the foyer and examined the locked doors of the offices. He climbed the heavily carpeted stairs and, lost in meditation, stood for a long time in the dress-circle among shrouded rows of seats and curtained doorways. Sighing dolorously he returned back-stage and made a stealthy entrance on to the set. Finally he creaked to the greenroom door and impelled by who knows what impulse furtively opened it.

Martyn lay across the chair, her knees supported underneath by one of its arms and her head by the other. The glow from the gas-fire was reflected in her face. Fred Badger stood for quite a long time eyeing her and scraping his chin with calloused fingers. At last he backed out, softly closed the door and tiptoed to his cubby-hole, where he telephoned the fire-station to make his routine report.

At dawn the rain stopped and cleaning vans swept the water down Carpet Street with their great brushes. Milk carts clinked past the Vulcan and the first bus roared by. Martyn heard none of them. She woke to the murmur of the gas-fire, and the confused memory of a dream in which someone tapped gently at a door. The window-less room was still dark but she looked at her watch in the fire-glow and found it was eight o'clock. She got up stiffly, crossed the room and opened the door on grey diffused daylight. A cup of tea with a large sandwich balanced on it had been left on the floor of the passage. Underneath it was a torn scrap of paper on which was scrawled: 'Keep your pecker up matey see you some more.'

With a feeling of gratitude and timid security she breakfasted in the greenroom, and afterwards explored the empty passage, finding at the far end an unlocked and unused dressing-room. To this room she brought her own suitcase and here, with a chair propped under the door handle, she stripped and washed in icy water. In clean clothes, with her toilet complete, and with a feeling of detachment, as if she herself looked on from a distance at these proceedings, she crossed the stage and went out through the side door and up the alleyway into Carpet Street.

It was a clean sunny morning. The air struck sharply at her lips and nostrils and the light dazzled her. A van had drawn up outside the Vulcan and men were lifting furniture from it. There were clean-ers at work in the foyer and a telegraph boy came out whistling. Carpet Street was noisy with traffic. Martyn turned left and walked quickly downhill until she came to a corner shop called Florian. In the window a girl in a blue overall was setting out a large gilt basket of roses. The door was still locked, but Martyn, emboldened by fresh air and a sense of freedom and adventure, tapped on the window and when the girl looked up, pointed to the roses and held up Mr Grantley's card. The girl smiled and, leaving the window, came to let her in.

Martyn said: 'I'm sorry to bother you but Mr Grantley at the Vulcan told me to get some roses for Miss Helena Hamilton. He didn't give me any money and I'm afraid I haven't got any. Is this all very irregular and tiresome?'

'That will be quayte OK,' the girl said in a friendly manner. 'Mr Grantley has an account.'

'Perhaps you know what sort of rose I should get,' Martyn suggested. She felt extraordinarily light and rather loquacious. 'You see, I'm Miss Hamilton's dresser but I'm new and I don't know what she likes.'

'Red would be quayte in order, I think. There are some lovely Bloody Warriors just in.' She caught Martyn's eye and giggled. 'Well, they do think of the weirdest names, don't they? Look: aren't they lovelies?'

She held up a group of roses with drops of water clinging to their half-opened petals. 'Gorgeous,' she said, 'aren't they? Such a colour.'

Martyn, appalled at the price, took a dozen. The girl looked curiously at her and said: 'Miss Hamilton's dresser. Fancy! Aren't you lucky?' and she was vividly reminded of Fred Badger.

'I feel terribly lucky this morning,' she said and was going away when the girl, turning pink under her makeup, said: 'Pardon me asking but I don't suppose you could get me Miss Hamilton's autograph. I'd be ever so thrilled.'

'I haven't even seen her yet but I'll do my best.'

'You *are* a ducks. Thanks a million. Of course,' the girl added, 'I'm a real fan. I never miss any of her pictures and I do think Adam Poole – pardon me, Mr Poole – is simply mawvellous. I mean to say I just think he's mawvellous. They're so mawvellous together. I suppose he's crazy about her in real life, isn't he? I always say they couldn't ect together like that – you know – so gorgeously – unless they had a pretty hot clue on the sayde. Don't you agree?'

Martyn said she hadn't had a chance of forming an opinion as yet and left the florist in pensive contemplation of the remaining Bloody Warriors.

When she got back to the theatre its character had completely changed; it was alive and noisy. The dock-doors were open and sunlight lay in incongruous patches on painted canvas and stacked furniture. Up in the grid there was a sound of hammering. A back-cloth hung diagonally in mid-air and descended in jerks, while a man in shirt sleeves shouted, 'Down on yer long. Now yer short. Now bodily. Right-oh. Dead it. Now find yer Number Two.'

A chandelier lay in a heap in the middle of the stage and, above it, was suspended a batten of spotlights within reach of an elderly mechanist who fitted pink and straw-coloured mediums into their frames. Near the stage-door a group of men stared at a small empire desk from which a stage-hand had removed a cloth wrapping. A tall young man in spectacles, wearing a red pullover and corduroy trousers, said irritably: 'It's too bloody chi-chi. Without a shadow of doubt, he'll hate its guts.'

He glanced at Martyn and added: 'Put them in her room, dear, will you?'

She hurried to the dressing-room passage and found that here, too, there was life and movement. A vacuum-cleaner hummed in the greenroom, a bald man in overalls was tacking cards on the doors, somewhere down the passage an unseen person sang cheerfully and the door next to Miss Hamilton's was open. These signs of preparation awakened in Martyn a sense of urgency. In a sudden fluster she unwrapped her roses and thrust them into the vase. The stalks were too long and she had nothing to cut them with. She ran down the passage to the empty room, and reflected as she rootled in her suitcase that she would be expected to having sewing materials at hand. Here was the housewife an aunt had given her when she left New Zealand but it was depleted and in a muddle. She ran back with it, sawed at the rose stems with her nail-scissors and when someone in the next room tapped on the wall, inadvertently jammed the points into her hand.

'And how,' a disembodied voice inquired, 'is La Belle Tansey this morning?'

Sucking her left hand and arranging roses with her right, Martyn wondered how she should respond to this advance. She called out, tentatively: 'I'm afraid it's not Miss Tansey.'

'What's that?' the voice said vaguely, and a moment later she heard the brisk sound of a clothes-brush at work.

The roses were done at last. She stood with the ends of the stalks in her hand and wondered why she had become so nervous.

'Here we go again,' a voice said in the doorway. She spun round to face a small man in an alpaca coat with a dinner jacket in his hands. He stared at her with his jaw dropped. 'Pardon me,' he said. 'I thought you was Miss Tansey.'

Martyn explained.

'Well!' he said. 'That'll be her heart, that will. She ought to have given up before this. I warned her. In hospital, too? T'ch, t'ch, t'ch.' He wagged his head and looked, apparently in astonishment, at Martyn. 'So that's the story,' he continued, 'and you've stepped into the breach? Fancy that! Better introduce ourselves, hadn't we? The name's Cringle but Bob'll do as well as anything else. I'm 'is lordship's dresser. How are you?'

Martyn gave him her name and they shook hands. He had a pleasant face covered with a cobweb of fine wrinkles. 'Been long at this game?' he asked and added: 'Well, that's a foolish question, isn't it? I should have said: will this be your first place or are you doing it in your school holidays or something of that sort.'

'Do you suppose,' Martyn said anxiously, 'Miss Hamilton will think I'm too young?'

'Not if you give satisfaction she won't. She's all right if you give satisfaction. Different from my case. Slave meself dizzy, I can, and if 'is lordship's in one of 'is moods, what do I get for it? Spare me days, I don't know why I put up with it and that's a fact: But *she's* all right if she likes you.' He paused and added tentatively: 'but you know all about that, I dare say.' Martyn was silent and felt his curiosity reach out as if it was something tangible. At last she said desperately: 'I'll try. I want to give satisfaction.'

He glanced round the room. 'Looks nice,' he said. 'Are you pressed and shook out? Yes, I can see you are. Flowers too. Very nice. Would you be a friend of hers? Doing it to oblige, like?'

'No, no. I've never seen her. Except in the pictures, of course.'

'Is that a fact?' His rather bird-like eyes were bright with speculation. 'Young ladies,' he said, 'have to turn their hands to all sorts of work these days, don't they?'

'I suppose so. Yes.'

'No offence, I hope, but I was wondering if you come from one of these drama schools. Hoping to learn a bit, watching from the side, like.'

A kind of sheepishness that had hardened into obstinacy prevented her from telling him in a few words, why she was there. The impulse of a fortnight ago to rush to somebody – the ship's captain, the High Commissioner for her own country, anyone – and unload her burden of disaster, had given place almost at once to a determined silence. This mess was of her own making, she had decided, and she herself would see it out. And throughout the loneliness and panic of her ordeal, to this resolution she had stuck. It had ceased to be a reasoned affair with Martyn: the less she said, the less she wanted to say. She had become crystallized in reticence.

So she met the curiosity of the little dresser with an evasion. 'It'd be wonderful,' she said, 'if I did get the chance.'

A deep voice with an unusually vibrant quality called out on the stage. 'Bob! Where the devil have you got to? Bob!'

'Cripes!' the little dresser ejaculated. 'Here we are *and* in one of our tantrums. *In here, sir! Coming, sir.*'

He darted towards the doorway but before he reached it a man áppeared there, a man so tall that for a fraction of a second he looked down over the dresser's head directly into Martyn's eyes.

'This young lady,' Bob Cringle explained with an air of discovery, 'is the new dresser for Miss Hamilton. I just been showing her the ropes, Mr Poole, sir.'

'You'd much better attend to your own work. I want you.' He glanced again at Martyn. 'Good morning,' he said and was gone. 'Look at this!' she heard him say angrily in the next room. 'Where *are* you!'

Cringle paused in the doorway to turn his thumbs down and his eyes up. 'Here we are, sir. What's the little trouble?' he said pacifically, and disappeared.

Martyn thought: 'The picture in the greenroom is more like him than the photographs.' Preoccupied with this discovery she was only vaguely aware of a fragrance in the air and a new voice in the passage. The next moment her employer came into the dressing-room.

II

An encounter with a person hitherto only seen and heard on the cinema screen is often disconcerting. It is as if the two-dimensional and enormous image had contracted about a living skeleton and in taking on substance had acquired an embarrassing normality. One is not always glad to change the familiar shadow for the strange reality.

Helena Hamilton was a blonde woman. She had every grace. To set down in detail the perfections of her hair, eyes, mouth and complexion, her shape and the gallantry of her carriage would be to reiterate merely that which everyone had seen in her innumerable pictures. She was, in fact, quite astonishingly beautiful. Even the circumstance of her looking somewhat older than her moving shadow could not modify the shock of finding her its equal in everything but this.

Coupled with her beauty was her charm. This was famous. She could reduce press conferences to a conglomerate of eager, even naïve, males. She could make a curtain-speech that every leading woman in every theatre in the English-speaking world had made before her and persuade the last man in the audience that it was original. She could convince bit-part actresses playing maids in first acts that there, but for the grace of God, went she.

On Martyn, however, taken off her balance and entirely by surprise, it was Miss Hamilton's smell that made the first impression. At ten guineas a moderately sized bottle, she smelt like Master Fenton, all April and May. Martyn was very much shorter than Miss Hamilton but this did not prevent her from feeling cumbersome and out of place, as if she had been caught red-handed with her own work in the dressing-room. This awkwardness was in part dispelled by the friendliness of Miss Hamilton's smile and the warmth of her enchanting voice.

'You've come to help me, haven't you?' she said. 'Now, that *is* kind. I know all about you from Mr Grantley and I fully expect we'll get along famously together. The only thing I *don't* know, in fact, is your name.'

Martyn wondered if she ought to give only her Christian name or only her surname. She said: 'Tarne. Martyn Tarne.'

'But what a charming name!' The brilliant eyes looked into Martyn's face and their gaze sharpened. After a fractional pause she repeated: 'Really charming,' and turned her back.

It took Martyn a moment or two to realize that this was her cue to remove Miss Hamilton's coat. She lifted it from her shoulders – it was made of Persian lamb and smelt delicious – and hung it up. When she turned round she found that her employer was looking at her. She smiled reassuringly at Martyn and said: 'You've got everything arranged very nicely. Roses, too. Lovely.'

'They're from Mr Grantley.'

'Sweet of him but I bet he sent you to buy them.'

'Well – ' Martyn began and was saved by the entry of the young man in the red sweater with a dressing-case for which she was given the keys. While she was unpacking it the door opened and a middle-aged, handsome man with a raffish face and an air of boldness came in. She remembered the photographs in the foyer. This was Clark Bennington. He addressed himself to Miss Hamilton.

'Hallo,' he said, 'I've been talking to John Rutherford.'

'What about?' she asked and sounded nervous.

'About that kid. Young Gay. He's been at her again. So's Adam.'

He glanced at Martyn. 'I wanted to talk to you,' he added discontentedly.

'Well, so you shall. But I've got to change, now, Ben. And, look, this is my new dresser, Martyn Tarne.'

He eyed Martyn with more attention. 'Quite a change from old Tansey,' he said. 'And a very nice change, too.' He turned away. 'Is Adam down?' He jerked his head at the wall.

'Yes.'

'I'll see you later, then.'

'All right, but – yes, all right.'

He went out, leaving a faint rumour of alcohol behind him.

She was quite still for a moment after he had gone. Martyn heard her fetch a sigh, a sound half-impatient, half-anxious. 'Oh well,' she said, 'let's get going, shall we?'

Martyn had been much exercised about the extent of her duties. Did, for instance, a dresser undress her employer? Did she kneel at her feet and roll down her stockings? Did she unhook and unbutton? Or did she stand capably aside while these rites were performed by the principal herself. Miss Hamilton solved the problem by removing her dress, throwing it to Martyn and waiting to be inserted into her dressing-gown. During these operations a rumble of male voices sounded at intervals in the adjoining room. Presently there was a tap at the door. Martyn answered it and found the little dresser with a florists' box in his hands. 'Mr Poole's compliments,' he said and winked broadly before retiring.

Miss Hamilton by this time was spreading a yellow film over her face. She asked Martyn to open the box and, on seeing three orchids that lay, crisp and fabulous on their mossy bed, sang 'Darling!' on two clear notes.

The voice beyond the wall responded. 'Hallo?'

'They're quite perfect. Thank you, my sweet.'

'Good,' the voice said. Martyn laid the box on the dressing-table and saw the card: 'Until tomorrow. Adam.'

She got through the next half-hour pretty successfully, she hoped. There seemed to be no blunders and Miss Hamilton continued charming and apparently delighted. There were constant visitors. A tap on the door would be followed by a head looking round and always by the invitation to come in. First there was Miss Gay Gainsford, a young and rather intense person with a pretty air of deference who seemed to be in a state of extreme anxiety.

'Well, darling,' Miss Hamilton said, glancing at her in the glass: 'Everything under strict control?'

Miss Gainsford said unevenly: 'I suppose so. I'm trying to be good and sort of *biddable*, do you know, but underneath I realize that I'm seething like a cauldron. Butterflies the size of *bats* in the stomach.'

'Well, of course. But you mustn't be terrified really, because whatever happens we all know John's written a good play, don't we?'

'I suppose we do.'

'We do indeed. And Gay – you're going to make a great personal success in this part. I want you to tell yourself you are. Do you know? *Tell* yourself.'

'I wish I could believe it.' Miss Gainsford clasped her hands and raised them to her lips. 'It's not very easy,' she said, 'when he – John – Dr Rutherford – so obviously thinks I'm a misfit. Everybody keeps telling me it's a marvellous part but for me it's twenty sides of hopeless hell. Honestly, it is.'

'Gay, what *nonsense*. John may seem hard – '

'*Seem?*'

'Well, he may *be* hard, then. He's famous for it, after all. But you'll get your reward, my dear, when the time comes. Remember,' said Miss Hamilton with immense gravity, 'we all have faith in you.'

'Of course,' said Miss Gainsford with an increased quaver in her voice, 'it's too marvellous your feeling like that about it. You've been so miraculously kind. And Uncle Ben, of course. Both of you. I can't get over it.'

'But, my dear, that's utter nonsense. You're going to be one of our rising young actresses.'

'You do *really* think so!'

'But yes. We all do.' Her voice lost a little colour and then freshened. 'We all do,' she repeated firmly and turned back to her glass.

Miss Gainsford went to the door and hesitated there. 'Adam doesn't,' she said loudly.

Miss Hamilton made a quick expressive gesture toward the next dressing-room and put her fingers to her lips. 'He'll be *really* angry if he hears you say that,' she whispered and added aloud with somewhat forced casualness: 'Is John down this morning?'

'He's on-stage. I think he said he'd like to speak to you.'

'I want to see him particularly. Will you tell him, darling?'

'Of course, Aunty Ella,' Miss Gainsford said rather miserably and added, 'I'm sorry. I forgot. Of course, Ella, darling.' With a wan smile she was gone.

'Oh, dear!' Miss Hamilton sighed and catching Martyn's eye in the looking-glass made a rueful face. 'If only – ' she began and stopped unaccountably, her gaze still fixed on Martyn's image. 'Never mind,' she said.

There was a noisy footfall in the passage followed by a bang on the door, and, with scarcely a pause for permission, by the entry of a large, florid and angry-looking man wearing a sweater, a leather waistcoat, a muffler and a very old duffel coat.

'Good morning, John darling,' said Miss Hamilton gaily and extended her hand. The newcomer planted a smacking kiss on it and fixed Martyn with a china-blue and bulging pair of eyes. Martyn turned away from this embarrassing regard.

'What have we here?' he demanded. His voice was loud and rumbling.

'My new dresser. Dr Rutherford, Martyn.'

'Stay me with flagons!' said Dr Rutherford. He turned on Miss Hamilton. 'That fool of a wench Gainsford said you wanted me,' he said. 'What's up?'

'John, *what* have you been saying to that child?'

'I? Nothing. Nothing to what I could, and, mark you, what I ought to say to her. I merely asked if, for the sake of my sanity, she'd be good enough to play the central scene without a goddam simper on her fat and wholly unsuitable dial.'

'You're frightening her.'

'She's terrifying me. She may be your niece, Ella – '

'She's not my niece. She's Ben's niece.'

'If she was the Pope's niece she'd still be a goddam pain in the neck. I wrote this part for an intelligent actress who could be made to look reasonably like Adam. What do you give me? A moronic amateur who looks like nothing on God's earth.'

'She's extremely pretty.'

'Lollypops! Adam's too damn easy on her. The only hope lies in shaking her up. Or kicking her out and I'd do that myself if I had my way. It ought to have been done a month back. Even now – '

'Oh, my *dear* John! We open in two days you might remember.'

'An actress worth her salt'd memorize it in an hour. I told her – '

'I do beg you,' she said, 'to leave her to Adam. After all, he is the producer, John, and he's very wise.'

Dr Rutherford pulled out of some submerged pocket a metal box. From this he extracted a pinch of snuff which he took with loud and uncouth noises.

'In a moment,' he said, 'you'll be telling me the author ought to keep out of the theatre.'

'That's utter nonsense.'

'Let them try to keep *me* out,' he said and burst into a neighing laugh.

Miss Hamilton slightly opened her mouth, hardened her upper lip, and with the closest attention, painted it a purplish red. 'Really,' she said briskly, 'you'd much better behave prettily, you know. You'll end by having her on your hands with a nervous breakdown.'

'The sooner the better if it's a good one.'

'Honestly, John, you are the rock *bottom* when you get like this. If you didn't write the plays you do write – if you weren't the greatest dramatist since – '

'Spare me the raptures,' he said, 'and give me some actors. And while we're on the subject I may as well tell you that I don't like the way Ben is shaping in the big scene. If Adam doesn't watch him he'll be up to some bloody leading-man hocus-pocus and by God if he tries that on I'll wring his neck for him.'

She turned and faced him. 'John, he *won't*. I'm sure he won't.'

'No, you're not. You can't be sure. Nor can I. But if there's any sign of it tonight, and Adam doesn't tackle him, I will. I'll tickle his catastrophe, by God I will. As for that Mongolian monstrosity, that discard from the waxworks, Mr Parry Percival; what devil – will you answer me – what inverted sadist foisted it on my play?'

'Now, look here, John – ' Miss Hamilton began with some warmth and was shouted down.

'Have I not stipulated from the beginning of my disastrous association with this ill-fated playhouse that I would have none of these abortions in my works? These Things. These foetid Growths. These Queers.'

'Parry isn't one.'

'Yah! He shrieks it. I have an instinct, my girl. I nose them as I go into the lobby.'

She made a gesture of despair: 'I give up,' she said.

He helped himself to another pinch of snuff. 'Hooey!' he snorted. 'You don't do anything of the sort, my sweetiepie. You're going to rock 'em, you and Adam. Think of that and preen yourself. And leave all the rest – to *me*.'

'Don't quote from Macbeth. If Gay Gainsford heard you doing that she really would go off at the deep end.'

'Which is precisely where I'd like to push her.'

'Oh, go away,' she cried out impatiently but with an air of good nature. 'I've had you. You're wonderful and you're hopeless. Go away.'

'The audience is concluded?' He scraped the parody of a regency bow.

'The audience is concluded. The door, Martyn.'

Martyn opened the door. Until then, feeling wretchedly in the way, she had busied herself with the stack of suitcases in the corner of the room and now, for the first time, came absolutely face to face with the visitor. He eyed her with an extraordinary air of astonishment.

'Here!' he said. 'Hi!'

'No, John,' Miss Hamilton said with great determination. 'No!'

'*Eureka!*'

'Nothing of the sort. Good morning.'

He gave a shrill whistle and swaggered out. Martyn turned back to find her employer staring into the glass. Her hands trembled and she clasped them together. 'Martyn,' she said, 'I'm going to call you Martyn because it's such a nice name. You know, a dresser is rather a particular sort of person. She has to be as deaf as a post and as blind as a bat to almost everything that goes on under her very nose. Dr Rutherford is, as I expect you know, a most distinguished and brilliant person. Our Greatest English Playwright. But like many brilliant people,' Miss Hamilton continued in what Martyn couldn't help thinking a rather too special voice, 'he is *eccentric*. We all understand and we expect you to do so too. Do you know?'

Martyn said she did.

'Good. Now, put me into that pink thing and let us know the worst about it, shall we?'

When she was dressed she stood before the cheval-glass and looked with cold intensity at her image. 'My God,' she said, 'the lighting had better be good.'

Martyn said: 'Isn't it right? It looks lovely to me.'

'My poor girl!' she muttered. 'You run to my husband and ask him for cigarettes. He's got my case. I need a stimulant.'

Martyn hurried into the passage and tapped at the next door. 'So they are married,' she thought. 'He must be ten years younger than she is but they're married and he still sends her orchids in the morning.'

The deep voice shouted impatiently: 'Come in!' and she opened the door and went in.

The little dresser was putting Poole into a dinner jacket. Their backs were turned to Martyn. 'Yes?' Poole said.

'Miss Hamilton would like her cigarette-case, if you please.'

'I haven't got it,' he said and shouted: 'Ella!'

'Hallo, darling?'

'I haven't got your case.'

There was a considerable pause. The voice beyond the wall called: 'No, no. Ben's got it. Mr Bennington, Martyn.'

'I'm so sorry,' Martyn said, and made for the door, conscious of the little dresser's embarrassment and of Poole's annoyance.

Mr Clark Bennington's room was on the opposite side of the passage and next to the greenroom. On her entrance Martyn was abruptly and most unpleasantly transported into the immediate past – into yesterday with its exhaustion, muddle and panic, to the moment of extreme humiliation when Fred Badger had smelt brandy on her breath. Mr Bennington's flask was open on his dressing-shelf and he was in the act of entertaining a thickset gentleman with beautifully groomed white hair, wearing a monocle, in a strikingly handsome face. This person set down his tumbler and gazed in a startled fashion at Martyn.

'It's not,' he said, evidently picking up, with some difficulty, the conversation she had interrupted, 'it's not that I would for the world interfere, Ben, dear boy. Nor do I enjoy raising what is no doubt a delicate subject in these particular circumstances. But I feel for the child damnably, you know. Damnably. Moreover, it does rather appear that the doctor never loses an opportunity to upset her.'

'I couldn't agree more, old boy, and I'm bloody angry about it. Yes, dear, wait a moment, will you?' Mr Bennington rejoined, running his speeches together and addressing them to no one in particular. 'This is my wife's new dresser, J.G.'

'Really?' Mr J. G. Darcey responded and bowed politely to Martyn. 'Good morning, child. See you later, Ben, my boy. Thousand thanks.'

He rose, looked kindly at Martyn, dropped his monocle, passed his hand over his hair and went out, breaking into operatic song in the passage.

Mr Bennington made a half-hearted attempt to put his flask out of sight and addressed himself to Martyn.

'And what,' he asked, 'can I do for the new dresser?' Martyn delivered her message. 'Cigarette-case? Have I got my wife's cigarette-case? God, I don't know. Try my overcoat, dear, will you? Behind the door. Inside pocket. No secrets,' he added obscurely. 'Forgive my asking you. I'm busy.'

But he didn't seem particularly busy. He twisted round in his chair and watched Martyn as she made a fruitless search of his overcoat pockets. 'This is your first job?' he asked. She said it was not and he added: 'As a dresser, I mean.'

'I've worked in the theatre before.'

'And where was that?'

'In New Zealand.'

'*Really?*' he said as if she had answered some vitally important question.

'I'm afraid,' Martyn went on quickly, 'it's not in the overcoat.'

'God, what a bore! Give me my jacket then, would you? The grey flannel.'

She handed it to him and he fumbled through the pockets. A pocket-book dropped on the floor, spilling its contents. Martyn gathered them together and he made such a clumsy business of taking them from her that she was obliged to put them on the shelf. Among them was an envelope bearing a foreign stamp and postmark. He snatched it up and it fluttered in his fingers. 'Mustn't lose track of that one, must we?' he said and laughed. 'All the way from Uncle Tito.' He thrust it at Martyn. 'Look,' he said and steadied his hand against the edge of the shelf. 'What d'you think of *that?* Take it.'

Troubled at once by the delay and by the oddness of his manner Martyn took the envelope and saw that it was addressed to Bennington.

'Do you collect autographs?' Bennington asked with ridiculous intensity – 'or signed letters?'

'No, I'm afraid I don't,' she said and put the letter face down on the shelf.

'There's someone,' he said with a jab of his finger at the envelope, 'who'd give a hell of a lot for *that* one in there. A hell of a lot.'

He burst out laughing, pulled a cigarette-case out of the jacket and handed it to her with a flourish. 'Purest gold,' he said. 'Birthday present but not from me. I'm her husband you know. What the hell! Are you leaving me? Don't go.'

Martyn made her escape and ran back to Miss Hamilton's room where she found her in conference with Adam Poole and a young man of romantic appearance whom she recognized as the original of the last of the photographs in the foyer – Mr Parry Percival. The instinct that makes us aware of a conversation in which we ourselves have in our absence been involved, warned Martyn that they had been talking about her and had broken off on her entrance. After a moment's silence, Mr Percival, with far too elaborate a non-chalance, said: 'Yes: well there you have it,' and it was obvious that there was a kind of double significance in this remark. Miss Hamilton said: 'My poor Martyn, where *have* you been?' with a lightness that was not quite cordial.

'I'm sorry,' Martyn said: 'Mr Bennington had trouble in finding the case.' She hesitated for a moment and added, 'Madam.'

'That,' Miss Hamilton rejoined, looking at Adam Poole, 'rings dismally true. Would you believe it, darling, I became so furious with him for taking it that, most reluctantly, I gave him one for himself. He lost it instantly of course and now swears he didn't and mine is his. If you follow me.'

'With considerable difficulty,' Poole said, 'I do.'

Parry Percival laughed gracefully. He had a winning, if not altogether authentic air of ingenuousness, and at the moment seemed to be hovering on the edge of some indiscretion. 'I am afraid,' he said ruefully to Miss Hamilton, 'I'm rather in disgrace myself.'

'With me, or with Adam?'

'I hope not with either of you. With Ben.' He glanced apologetically at Poole, who did not look at him. 'Because of the part, I mean. I suppose I spoke out of turn, but I really did think I could play it – still do for a matter of that, but there it is.'

It was obvious that he was speaking at Poole. Martyn saw Miss Hamilton look from one man to the other before she said lightly, 'I think you could too, Parry, but as you say, there it is. Ben *has* got a flair, you know.'

Percival laughed. 'He has indeed,' he said, 'he has had it for twenty years. Sorry. I shouldn't have said that. Honestly, I *am* sorry.'

Poole said, 'I dislike post-mortems on casting, Parry.'

'I know, I *do* apologize.' Percival turned ingratiatingly, and the strong light caught his face sideways. Martyn saw with astonishment that under the thin film of greasepaint there was a system of incipient lines, and she realized that he was not, after all, a young man. 'I know,' he repeated, 'I'm being naughty.'

Poole said, 'We open on Thursday. The whole thing was thrashed out weeks ago. Any discussion now is completely fruitless.'

'That,' said Miss Hamilton, 'is what I have been trying to tell the doctor.'

'John? I heard him bellowing in here,' Poole said. 'Where's he gone? I want a word with him. And with you, Parry, by the way. It's about that scene at the window in the second act. You're not making your exit line. You must top Ben there. It's most important.'

'Look, old boy,' Mr Percival said with agonized intensity, 'I *know*. It's just another of those things. Have you *seen* what Ben does? Have you seen that business with my handkerchief? He won't take his hands off me. The whole exit gets messed up.'

'I'll see what can be done.'

'John,' said Miss Hamilton, 'is worried about it too, Adam.'

Poole said: 'Then he should talk to me.'

'You know what the doctor is.'

'We all do,' said Parry Percival, 'and the public, I fear, is beginning to find out. God, there I go again.'

Poole looked at him. 'You'll get along better, I think, Parry, if you deny yourself these cracks against the rest of the company. Rutherford has written a serious play. It'd be a pity if any of us should lose faith in it.'

Percival reddened and made towards the door. 'I'm just being a nuisance,' he said. 'I'll take myself off and be photographed like a good boy.' He made an insinuating movement of his shoulders towards Miss Hamilton, and fluttered his hand at her dress. 'Marvellous,' he said, 'a triumph, if the bit-part actor may be allowed to say so.'

The door shut crisply behind him, and Miss Hamilton said: 'Darling, aren't you rather high and grand with poor Parry?'

'I don't think so. He's behaving like an ass. He couldn't play the part. He was born to be a feed.'

'He'd *look* it.'

'If all goes well Ben will *be* it.'

'If all goes well! Adam, I'm terrified. He's – '

'Are you dressed, Ella? The cameras are ready.'

'Shoes, please, Martyn,' said Miss Hamilton. 'Yes, darling. I'm right.'

Martyn fastened her shoes and then opened the door. Miss Hamilton swept out, lifting her skirts with great elegance. Martyn waited for Poole to follow, but he said: 'You're meant to be on-stage. Take make-up and a glass and whatever Miss Hamilton may need for her hair.'

She thanked him and in a flurry gathered the things together. Poole took the Persian lamb coat and stood by the door. She hesitated, expecting him to precede her, but found that he was looking at the cheval-glass. When she followed his gaze it was to be confronted by their images, side by side in the glass.

'Extraordinary,' he said abruptly, 'isn't it?' and motioned her to go out.

III

When Martyn went out on the stage she was able for the first time to see the company assembled together, and found it consisted, as far as the players were concerned, of no more than the six persons she had already encountered: first in their fixed professional poses in the show-frame at the front of the house, and later in their dressing-rooms. She had attached mental tags to them and found herself thinking of Helen Hamilton as the Leading Lady, of Gay Gainsford as the Ingénue, of J. G. Darcey as the Character Actor, of Parry Percival as the Juvenile, of Clark Bennington regrettably, perhaps unjustly, as the Drunken Actor, and of Adam Poole – but as yet she had found no label for Poole, unless it was the old-fashioned one of 'Governor', which pleased her by its vicarious association with the days of the Victorian actor-managers.

To this actual cast of six she must add a number of satellite figures – the author, Dr John Rutherford, whose eccentricities seemed to surpass those of his legend, with which she was already acquainted, the man in the red sweater who was the stage-manager, and was called Clem Smith, his assistant, a morose lurking figure, and the crew of stage-hands who went about their business or contemplated the actors with equal detachment.

The actors were forming themselves now into a stage 'picture', moving in a workmanlike manner, under the direction of Adam Poole, and watched with restless attentiveness by an elderly, slack-jointed man, carrying a paint pot and brushes. This man, the last of all the figures to appear upon the stage that morning, seemed to have no recognizable job but to be concerned in all of them. He was dressed in overalls and a tartan shirt, from which his long neck emerged, bird-like and crapulous, to terminate in a head that wobbled slightly as if its articulation with the top of the spine had loosened with age. He was

constantly addressed with exasperated affection as Jacko. Under his
direction, bunches of lights were wheeled into position, cameramen
peered and muttered, and at his given signal the players, by an easy
transition in behaviour and appearance, became larger than life. A gap
was left in the middle of the group, and into this when all was ready
floated Helena Hamilton, ruffling her plumage, and becoming at once
the focal point of the picture.

'Darling,' she said, it's not going to be a flash, is it, with all of you
looking like village idiots, and me like the Third Witch on the morning after the cauldron scene?'

'If you can hold it for three seconds,' Adam Poole said, 'it needn't
be a flash.'

'I can hold anything, if you come in and help me.'

He moved in beside her. 'All right,' he said, 'let's try it. The end of
the first act,' and at once she turned upon him a look of tragic and
burning intensity. The elderly man wandered across and tweaked at
her skirts. Without changing pose or expression, she said, 'Isn't it
shameful the way Jacko can't keep his hands off me.' He grinned
and ambled away. Adam Poole said 'Right,' the group froze in pos-
tures of urgency that led the eye towards the two central figures and
the cameras clicked.

Martyn tried, as the morning wore on, to get some idea of the
content of the play but was unable to do so. Occasionally the players would speak snatches of dialogue leading up to the moment
when a photograph was to be taken, and from these she gathered
that the major conflict of the theme was between the characters
played by Adam Poole and Clark Bennington and that this conflict
was one of ideas. About a particular shot there was a great deal of
difficulty. In this Poole and Gay Gainsford confronted each other and
it was necessary that her posture, the arrested gesture of her hand
and even her expression should be an exact reflection of his.

To Martyn, Poole had seemed to be a short-tempered man, but
with Gay Gainsford he showed exemplary patience. 'It's the old
story, Gay,' he said, 'you're overanxious. It's not enough for you to
look like me. Let's face it,' he hesitated for a moment and said quickly,
'we've had all this, haven't we – but it's worth repeating – you can't
look strikingly like me, although Jacko's done wonders. What
you've got to do is to *be* me. At this moment, don't you see, you're

my heredity, confronting me like a threat. As far as the photograph is concerned, we can cheat – the shot can be taken over your shoulder, but in the performance there can be no cheating, and that is why I'm making such a thing of it. Now let's take it with the line. Your head's on your arms, you raise it slowly to face me. Ready now. Right, up you come.'

Miss Gainsford raised her face to his as he leaned across the writing-desk and whispered: *'Don't you like what you see?* At the same moment there was a cascade of laughter from Miss Hamilton. Poole's voice cracked like a whiplash, 'Helena, please,' and she turned from Parry Percival to say, 'Darling, I'm so sorry,' and in the same breath spoke her line of dialogue: *'But it's you, don't you see, you can't escape from it, it's you.'* Gay Gainsford made a hopeless little gesture and Poole said: 'Too late, of course. Try again.'

They tried several times, in an atmosphere of increasing tension. The amiable Jacko was called in to make an infinitesimal change in Gay's make-up, and Martyn saw him blot away a tear. At this juncture a disembodied voice roared from the back of the circle: *'Sister, have comfort. All of us have cause to wail the dimming of our shining star.'*

Poole glanced into the auditorium. 'Do shut up like a good chap, John,' he said.

> *'Pour all your tears! I am your sorrows nurse*
> *And I will pamper it with la-men-ta-ti-ons.'*

The man called Jacko burst out laughing and was instantly dismissed to the dressing-rooms by Poole.

There followed a quarter of an hour of mounting hysteria on the part of Gay Gainsford and of implacable persistence from Adam Poole. He said suddenly, 'All right, we'll cheat. Shift the camera.'

The remaining photographs were taken with a great deal of trouble. Miss Gainsford, looking utterly miserable, went off to her dressing-room. The man called Jacko reappeared and ambled across to Miss Hamilton. There was an adjustment in make-up while Martyn held up the mirror.

'Maybe it's lucky,' he said, 'you don't have to look like somebody else.'

'Are you being nice or beastly, Jacko?'

He put a cigarette between her lips and lit it. 'The dresses are good,' he said. He had a very slight foreign accent.

'You think so, do you?'

'Naturally. I design them *for you*.'

'Next time,' she said gently, 'you'd better write the play as well.'

He was a phenomenally ugly man but a smile of extraordinary sweetness broke across his face.

'All these agonies!' he murmured, 'and on Thursday night everyone will be kissing everyone else and at the Combined Arts Ball we are in triumph and on Friday morning you will be purring over your notices. And you must not be unkind about the play. It is a good play.' He grinned again, more broadly. His teeth were enormous and uneven. 'Even the little niece of the great husband cannot entirely destroy it.'

'Jacko!'

'You may say what you like, it is not intelligent casting.'

'Please, Jacko.'

'All right, all right. I remind you instead of the Combined Arts Ball, and that no one has decided in what costume we go.'

'Nobody has any ideas. Jacko, you must invent something marvellous.'

'And in two days I must also create out of air eight marvellous costumes.'

'Darling Jacko, how beastly we are to you. But you know you love performing your little wonders.'

'I suggest then, that we are characters from Chekhov as they would be in Hollywood. You absurdly gorgeous, and the little niece still grimly ingénue. Adam perhaps as Vanya if he were played by Boris Karloff. And so on.'

'Where shall I get my absurdly gorgeous dress?'

'I paint the design on canvas and cut it out and if I were introduced to your dresser I would persuade her to sew it up.' He took the glass from Martyn and said, 'No one makes any introductions in this theatre, so we introduce ourselves to each other. I am Jacques Doré, and you are the little chick whom the stork has brought too late, or dropped into the wrong nest. Really,' he said, rolling his eyes at Miss Hamilton, 'it is the most remarkable coincidence, if it is a coincidence. I am dropping bricks,' he added. 'I am a very privileged person but one day I drop an outsize brick, and away I go.' He made a circle of his thumb and forefinger and looked through it, as though it were a quizzing glass, at Martyn. 'All the same,' he said, 'it is a pity you are a little dresser and not a little actress.'

IV

Between the photograph call and the dress-rehearsal, which was timed for seven o'clock, a state of uneven ferment prevailed at the Vulcan. During the rare occasions on which she had time to reflect, Martyn anticipated a sort of personal zero hour, a moment when she would have to take stock, to come to a decision. She had two and fourpence and no place of abode, and she had no idea when she would be paid, or how much she would get. This moment of reckoning, however, she continually postponed. The problem of food was answered for the moment by the announcement that it would be provided for everyone whose work kept them in the theatre throughout the play. As Miss Hamilton had discovered a number of minor alterations to be made in her dresses, Martyn was of this company. Having by this time realized the position of extraordinary ubiquity held by Jacko, she was not surprised to find him cooking a mysterious but savoury mess over the gas-ring in Fred Badger's sink-room.

This concoction was served in enamel mugs, at odd intervals, to anyone who asked for it and Martyn found herself eating her share in company with Bob Cringle, Mr Poole's dresser. From him she learnt more about Mr Jacques Doré. He was responsible for the décor and dressing of all Poole's productions. His official status was that of assistant to Mr Poole but in actual fact he seemed to be a kind of superior odd-job man. 'General dogsbody,' Cringle gossiped, 'that's what Mr Jacko is. "Poole's Luck" people call him, and if the guvnor was superstitious about anything, which 'e is *not*, it would be about Mr Jacko. The lady's the same. Can't do without 'im. As a matter of fact it's on 'er account 'e sticks it out. You might say 'e's 'er property, a kind of pet, if you like to put it that way. Joined up with 'er and 'is nibs when they was in Canada and the guvnor still doing the child-wonder at 'is posh college. 'E's a Canadian-Frenchy, Mr Jacko is. Twenty years ago that must 'ave been, only don't say I said so. It's what they call dog-like devotion, and that's no error. To 'er, *not* to 'is nibs.'

'Do you mean Mr Bennington?' Martyn ventured.

'Clark Bennington, the distinguished character actor, that's right,' said Cringle drily. Evidently he was not inclined to elaborate this theme. He entertained Martyn, instead, with a lively account of the eccentricities of Dr John Rutherford. 'My oaff,' he said, 'what a daisy! Did you 'ear 'im chi-ikeing from the front this morning? Typical! We done three of 'is pieces up to date and never a dull moment. Rows and ructions, ructions and rows from the word go. The guvnor puts up with it on account he likes the pieces and what a time 'e has with 'im, oh, dear. It's something shocking the way doctor cuts up. Dynamite! This time it's the little lady and 'is nibs and Mr Parry Profile Percival 'e's got it in for. Can't do nothing to please 'im. You should 'ear 'im at rehearsals. "You're bastardizing my play," 'e 'owls. "Get the 'ell aht of it," 'e shrieks. You never seen such an exhibition. Shocking! Then the guvnor shuts 'im up, 'e 'as an attack of the willies or what-have-you and keeps aht of the theaytre for a couple of days. Never longer, though, which is very unfortunate for all concerned.'

To Martyn, held as she was in a sort of emotional suspension, the lives and events enclosed within the stage walls and curtain of the Vulcan Theatre assumed a greater reality than her own immediate problem. Her existence since five o'clock the previous afternoon when she had walked into the theatre, had much of the character and substance of a dream with all the shifting values, the passages of confusion and extreme clarity which make up the texture of a dream. She was in a state of semi-trauma and found it vaguely agreeable. Her jobs would keep her busy all the afternoon and tonight there was the first dress-rehearsal.

She could, she thought, tread water indefinitely, half in and half out of her dreams, as long as she didn't come face to face with Mr Adam Poole in any more looking-glasses.

CHAPTER 3

First Dress-Rehearsal

'I wish,' Martyn said, 'I knew what the play was about. Is it really a modern morality and do you think it good?'

'All good plays are moralities,' said Jacko sententiously, and he leant so far back on the top of his step-ladder that Martyn hurriedly grasped it. 'And this is a good play with a very old theme.' He hesitated for a moment and she wondered if she only imagined that he looked worried. 'Here is a selected man with new ideas in conflict with people who have very old ones. Adam plays the selected man. He has been brought up on an island by a community of idealists; he represents the value of environment. By his own wish he returns to his original habitat, and there he is confronted by his heredity, in the persons of his great uncle, who is played by J. G. Darcey, his brilliant but unstable cousin, who is played by Clark Bennington, this cousin's wife, who is Helena, and with whom he falls in love, and their daughter who is freakishly like him, but vicious and who represents therefore his inescapable heredity. This wretched girl,' Jacko continued with great relish, looking at Martyn out of the corner of his eyes, 'is engaged to a nonentity but finds herself drawn by a terrible attraction to Adam himself. She is played by Gay Gainsford. Receive again from me the pink pot, and bestow upon me the brown. As I have recited it to you so baldly, without nuance and without detail, you will say perhaps if Ibsen or Kafka or Brecht or even Sartre had written this play it would have been a good one.'

Inexplicably, he again seemed to be in some sort of distress. 'It has, in fact,' he said, 'a continental flavour. But for those who have ears to hear and eyes to see, it has a wider implication than I have suggested. It is a tale, in point of fact, about the struggle of the human being in the detestable situation in which from the beginning he has found himself. Now I descend.' He climbed down his step-ladder, groaning lamentably. 'And now,' he said, 'we have some light and we see if what I have done is good. Go out into the front of the house and in a moment I join you.'

By the time Martyn reached the sixth row of the stalls the stage was fully illuminated, and for the first time she saw the set for Act II as Jacko had intended it.

It was an interior, simple in design and execution, but with an air of being over-civilized and stale. 'They are,' Jacko explained, slumping into a seat beside her, 'bad people who live in it. They are not bad of their own volition, but because they have been set down in this place by their heredity and cannot escape. And now you say, all this is pretentious nonsense, and nobody will notice my set except perhaps a few queers who come to first nights and in any case will get it all wrong. And now we wash ourselves and go out to a place where I am known, and we eat a little, and you tell me why you look like a puppy who has found his tail but dare not wag it. Come.'

The restaurant where Jacko was known turned out to be hard by the theatre, and situated in a basement. He insisted on paying for a surprisingly good meal, and Martyn's two and fourpence remained in her pocket. Whereas the curiosity of Fred Badger and Bob Cringle, and in some degree of the actors, had been covert and indirect, Jacko's was unblushing and persistent.

'Now,' he said, over their coffee, 'I ask you my questions. If there is a secret you tell me so, and with difficulty I shut myself up. If not, you confide in me, because everybody in the Vulcan makes me their confidant and I am greatly flattered by this. In any case we remain friends, no bones broken, and we repeat our little outings. How old do you think I am?'

With some embarrassment, Martyn looked at his scrawny neck, at the thin lichen-like growth of fuzz on his head, and at his heavily scored and indented face. 'Fifty-seven,' she ventured.

'Sixty-two,' said Jacko complacently. 'I am sixty-two years old, and a bit of a character. I have not the talent to make a character of myself for the people who sit in front, so instead I play to actors.

A wheel within wheels. For twenty years I have built up my role of confidant and now, if I wanted to, I couldn't leave off. For example I can speak perfect English, but my accent is a feature of the role of Papa Jacko, and must be sustained. Everybody knows it is a game and, amiably, everyone pretends with me. It is all rather ham and *jejune*, but I hope that you are going to play too.'

Martyn thought, 'It would be pleasant to tell him: I'm sure he's very nice and so why don't I do it? I suppose it's because he looks so very old.' And whether with uncanny prescience or else by a queer coincidence, he said, 'I'm not nearly as peculiar as I look.'

Martyn said tentatively, 'But I honestly don't know what you want me to tell you.'

On the opposite wall of the restaurant there was a tarnished looking-glass, upon the surface of which someone had half-heartedly painted a number of water-lilies and leaves. Among this growth, as if drowned in Edwardiana, Jacko's and Martyn's faces were reflected. He pointed to hers.

'See,' he said. 'We rehearse a play for which it is necessary a secondary-part actress should resemble, strikingly, the leading man. We have auditions, and from the hundreds of anxious ingénues we select the one who is least unlike him, but she is still very unlike him. Incidentally,' Jacko continued, looking Martyn very hard in the eye, 'she is the niece of Clark Bennington. She is not very like him either which is neither here nor there and perhaps fortunate for her. It is her unlikeness to Adam that we must deplore. Moreover, although I am a genius with make-up, there is very little I can do about it. So we depend instead on reflected emotions and echoed mannerisms. But although she is a nice little actress with a nice small talent, she cannot do this very well either. In the meantime our author who is a person of unbridled passion where his art is in question, becomes incensed with her performance and makes scenes and everybody except her Uncle Bennington retires into corners and tears pieces of their hair out. The little actress also retires into corners and weeps and is comforted by her Uncle Bennington, who never the less knows she is no good.

'Upon this scene there enters, in the guise of a dresser,' he jabbed his finger at the fly-blown glass, 'this. Look at it. If I set out to draw the daughter or the young sister of the leading man, that is what I should draw. Everybody has a look at her and retires again into corners to ask what it is about. Because obviously, she is not a dresser. Is she perhaps – and there are many excited speculations. "A niece for a niece?" we ask ourselves, and there is some mention of Adam's extreme youth, you must excuse me, and the wrong side of the rose bush, and everybody says it cannot be an accident and waits to see, except Papa Jacko whose curiosity will not permit him to wait.'

Martyn cried out, 'I've never seen him before, except in films in New Zealand. He knows nothing about me at all. Nothing. I came here from New Zealand a fortnight ago and I've been looking for a job ever since. I came to the Vulcan looking for a job, that's all there is about it.'

'Did you come looking for the job of dresser to Miss Hamilton?'

'For any job,' she said desperately. 'I heard by accident about the dresser.'

'But it was not to be a dresser that you came all the way from New Zealand, and yet it was to work in the theatre, and so perhaps after all you hoped to be an actress.'

'Yes,' Martyn said, throwing up her hands, 'all right, I hoped to be an actress. But please let's forget all about it. You can't imagine how thankful I am to be a dresser, and if you think I'm secretly hoping Miss Gainsford will get laryngitis or break her leg, you couldn't be more mistaken. I don't believe in fairy tales.'

'What humbugs you all are.'

'Who?' she demanded indignantly.

'All you Anglo-Saxons. You humbug even yourselves. Conceive for the moment the *mise en scène*, the situation, the coincidence, and have you the cheek to tell me again that you came thirteen thousand miles to be an actress and yet do not wish to play this part. Are you a good actress?'

'Don't,' Martyn said, 'don't. I've got a job and I'm in a sort of a trance. It makes everything very simple and I don't want to come out of it.'

Jacko grinned fiendishly. 'Just a little touch of laryngitis?' he suggested.

Martyn got up. 'Thank you very much for my nice dinner,' she said. 'I ought to be getting on with my job.'

'Little hypocrite. Or perhaps after all you know already you are a very bad actress.'

Without answering she walked out ahead of him, and they returned in silence to the Vulcan.

II

Timed to begin at seven, the dress-rehearsal actually started at ten-past eight. Miss Hamilton had no changes in the first act, and told Martyn she might watch from the front. She went out and sat at the back of the stalls near the other dressers.

Suddenly the lights went up along the fringe of the curtain. Martyn's flesh began to creep. Throughout the auditorium other little flames sprang up, illuminating from below, like miniature foot-lights, the faces of the watchers in front. A remote voice said, 'OK. Take it away,' a band of gold appeared below the fringe of the cur-tain, widened and grew to a lighted stage. Parry Percival spoke the opening line of Dr Rutherford's new play.

Martyn liked the first act. It concerned itself with the group of fig-ures Jacko had already described – the old man, his son, his son's wife, their daughter and her fiancé. They were creatures of conven-tion, the wife alone possessed of some inclination to reach out beyond her enclosed and aimless existence.

Gay Gainsford's entry as the daughter was a delayed one, and try as she might not to anticipate it, Martyn felt a sinking in her midriff when at last towards the end of the act Miss Gainsford came on. It was quite a small part but one of immense importance. Of the entire group the girl represented the third generation, the most completely lost, and in the writing of her part Rutherford displayed the influ-ence of Existentialism. It was clear that with a few lines to carry her she must make her mark, and clever production was written over everything she did. Agitated as she was by Jacko's direct attack, Martyn wondered if she only imagined that there was nothing more than production there, and if Miss Gainsford was really as ill at ease as she herself supposed. A specific gesture had been introduced and was evidently important, a sudden thrust of her fingers through her short hair, and she twice used a phrase: 'That was not what I meant' where in the context it was evidently intended to plant a barb of attention in the minds of the audience. When this moment came, Martyn sensed uneasiness among the actors. She glanced at Poole and saw him make the specific gesture he had given Miss Gainsford, a quick thrust of his fingers through his hair.

At this juncture the voice in the circle ejaculated: 'Boo!'

'Quiet!' said Poole.

Miss Gainsford hesitated, looked wretchedly into the auditorium, and lost her words. She was twice prompted before she went on again. Bennington crossed the stage, put his arm about her shoulder and glared into the circle. The prompter once more threw out a line, Miss Gainsford repeated it and they were off again. Poole got up and went back-stage through the pass-door. The secretary leant forward and shakily lit one cigarette from the butt of another. For the life of her, Martyn couldn't resist glancing at Jacko. He was slumped back in his stall with his arms folded – deliberately imperturbable, she felt – putting on an act. The light from the stage caught his emu-like head and as if conscious of her attention, he rolled his eyes round at her. She hastily looked back at the stage.

With Gay Gainsford's exit, Martyn could have sworn, a wave of relaxation blessed the actors. The dialogue began to move forward compactly with a firm upward curve towards some well-designed climax. There was an increase in tempo corresponding with the rising suspense. Martyn's blood tingled and her heart thumped. Through which door would the entrance be made? The players began a complex circling movement accompanied by a sharp crescendo in the dialogue. Up and up it soared. 'Now,' she thought, 'now!' The action of the play was held in suspense, poised and adjusted, and into the prepared silence, with judgement and precision, at the head of Jacko's twisted flight of steps, came Adam Poole.

'Is that an entrance,' thought Martyn, pressing her hands together, 'or is it an entrance?'

The curtain came down almost immediately. The secretary gathered his notes together and went backstage.

Dr Rutherford shouted: 'Hold your horses,' thundered out of the circle, reappeared in the stalls, and plunged through the pass-door to back-stage where he could be heard cruelly apostrophizing the

Almighty and the actors. Jacko stretched elaborately and slouched down the centre aisle, saying into the air as he passed Martyn, 'You had better get round for the change.'

Horrified, Martyn bolted like a rabbit. When she arrived in the dressing-room she found her employer, with a set face, attempting to unhook an elaborate back fastening. Martyn bleated an apology which was cut short.

'I hope,' said Miss Hamilton, 'you haven't mistaken the nature of your job, Martyn. You are my dresser and as such are expected to be here, in this dressing-room, whenever I return to it. Do you understand?'

Martyn, feeling very sick, said that she did, and with trembling fingers effected the complicated change. Miss Hamilton was completely silent, and to Martyn, humiliated and miserable, the necessary intimacies of her work were particularly mortifying.

A boy's voice in the passage chanted: 'Second Act, please. Second Act,' and Miss Hamilton said, 'Have you got everything on-stage for the quick change?'

'I think so, madam.'

'Very well.' She looked at herself coldly and searchingly in the long glass and added, 'I will go out.'

Martyn opened the door. Her employer glanced critically at her. 'You're as white as a sheet,' she said, 'what's the matter?'

Martyn stammered, 'Am I? I'm sorry, madam. It must have been the first act.'

'Did you like it?'

'*Like it?*' Martyn repeated. 'Oh, yes, I liked it.'

'As much as that?' As easily as if she had passed from one room into another, Miss Hamilton re-entered her mood of enchantment. 'What a ridiculous child you are,' she said. 'It's only actresses who are allowed to have temperaments.'

She went out to the stage, and as Martyn followed her she was surprised to feel in herself a kind of resistance to this woman who could so easily command her own happiness or misery.

An improvised dressing-room had been built on the stage for the quick change, and in or near it Martyn spent the whole of the second act. She was not sure when the quick change came, and didn't like to ask anybody. She therefore spent the first quarter of an hour on tenterhooks, hearing the dialogue, but not seeing anything of the play.

After a short introductory passage the act opened with a long scene between Helena Hamilton and Adam Poole in which their attraction to each other was introduced and established, and her instinctive struggle against her environment made clear and developed. The scene was admirably played by both of them, and carried the play strongly forward. When Miss Hamilton came off she found her dresser bright eyed and excited. Martyn effected the change without any blunders and in good time. Miss Hamilton's attention seemed to be divided between her clothes and the scene which was now being played between J. G. Darcey, Poole and her husband. This scene built up into a quarrel between Poole and Bennington which at its climax was broken by Poole saying in his normal voice, 'I dislike interrupting dress-rehearsals, Ben, but we've had this point over and over again. Please take the line as we rehearsed it.'

There was complete silence, perhaps for five seconds, and then, unseen, so that Martyn formed no picture of what he was doing or how he looked, Bennington began to giggle. The sound wavered and bubbled into a laugh. Helena Hamilton whispered: 'Oh, my *God*!' and went out to the stage. Martyn followed. A group of stage-hands who had been moving round the set stopped dead as if in suspended animation. Parry Percival, waiting off-stage, turned with a look of elaborate concern to Miss Hamilton and mimed bewilderment.

Bennington's laughter broke down into ungainly speech. 'I always say,' he said, 'there is no future in being an actor-manager unless you arrange things your own way. I want to make this chap a human being. You and John say he's to be a monster. All right, all right, dear boy, I won't offend again. He shall be less human than Caliban, and far less sympathetic.'

Evidently Poole was standing inside the entrance nearest to the dressing-room, because Martyn heard Bennington cross the stage and when he spoke again he was quite close to her, and had lowered his voice. 'You're grabbing everything, aren't you?' the voice wavered. 'On – and off-stage, as you might say – domestically and professionally. The piratical Mr Poole.'

Poole muttered, 'If you are not too drunk to think, we'll go on,' and pitching his voice, threw out a line of dialogue: '*If you knew what you wanted, if there was any object, however silly, behind anything you say or do, I could find some excuse for you – '*

Martyn heard Helena Hamilton catch her breath in a sob. The next moment she had flung open the door and made her entrance.

III

Through the good offices of Jacko, Martyn was able to watch the rest of the act from the side. Evidently he was determined she should see as much as possible of the play. He sent her round a list, scribbled in an elaborate hand, of the warnings and cues for Miss Hamilton's entrances and exits and times when she changed her dress. 'Stand in the OP corner,' he had written across the paper, 'and think of your sins.' She wouldn't have dared to follow his advice if Miss Hamilton, on her first exit, had not said with a sort of irritated good nature: 'You needn't wait in the dressing-room perpetually. Just be ready for me: that's all.'

So she stood in the shadows of the OP corner and saw the one big scene between Adam Poole and Gay Gainsford. The author's intention was clear enough. In this girl, the impure flower of her heredity, the most hopelessly lost of all the group, he sought to show the obverse side of the character Poole presented. She was his twisted shadow, a spiritual incubus. In everything she said and did the audience must see a distortion of Poole himself, until at the end they faced each other across the desk, as in the scene that had been photographed, and Helena Hamilton re-entered to speak the line of climax: *'But it's you, don't you see? You can't escape it. It's you,'* and the curtain came down.

Gay Gainsford was not good enough. It was not only that she didn't resemble Poole closely; her performance was too anxious, too careful a reproduction of mannerisms without a flame to light them. Martyn burnt in her shadowy corner. The transparent covering in which, like a sea-creature, she had spent her twenty-four hours' respite, now shrivelled away and she was exposed to the inexorable hunger of an unsatisfied player.

She didn't see Bennington until he put his hand on her arm as the curtain came down, and he startled her so much that she cried out and backed away from him.

'So you think you could do it, dear, do you?' he said.

Martyn stammered: 'I'm sorry. Miss Hamilton will want me,' and dodged past him towards the improvised dressing-room. He followed and with a conventionally showy movement, barred her entrance.

'Wait a minute, *wait* a minute,' he said. 'I want to talk to you.'

She stood there, afraid of him, conscious of his smell of grease-paint and alcohol and thinking him a ridiculous as well as an alarming person.

'I'm *so* angry,' he said conversationally, 'just literally *so* angry that I'm afraid you're going to find me quite a difficult man. And now we've got that ironed out perhaps you'll tell me who the bloody hell you are.'

'You know who I am,' Martyn said desperately. 'Please let me go in.'

'M'wife's dresser?'

He took her chin in his hand and twisted her face to the light. Poole came round the back of the set. Martyn thought: 'He'll be sick of the sight of me. Always getting myself into stupid little scenes.' Bennington's hand felt wet and hot round her chin.

'M'wife's dresser,' he repeated. 'And m'wife's lover's little by-blow. That the story?'

The edge of Poole's hand dropped on his arm. 'In you go,' he said to Martyn, and twisted Bennington away from the door. Martyn slipped through and he shut it behind her. She heard him say: 'You're an offensive fellow in your cups, Ben. We'll have this out after rehearsal. Get along and change for the third act.'

There was a moment's pause. The door opened and he looked in.

'Are you all right?' he asked.

'Perfectly, thank you,' Martyn said and in an agony of embarrassment added, 'I'm sorry to be a nuisance, sir.'

'Oh, don't be an ass,' he said with great ill-humour. The next moment he had gone.

Miss Hamilton, looking desperately worried, came in to change for the third act.

IV

The dress-rehearsal ended at midnight in an atmosphere of acute tension. Because she had not yet been paid, Martyn proposed to sleep again in the greenroom. So easily do our standards adjust themselves to our circumstances that whereas on her first night at the Vulcan the greenroom had been a blessed haven, her hours of precarious security had bred a longing for a bed and ordered cleanliness, and she began to dread the night.

In groups and singly, the actors and stage-staff drifted away. Their voices died out in the alley and passages, and she saw, with dismay, that Fred Badger had emerged from the door of his cubby-hole and now eyed her speculatively. Desolation and fear possessed Martyn. With a show of preoccupation, she hurried away to Miss Hamilton's dressing-room which she had already set in order. Here she would find a moment's respite. Perhaps in a few minutes she would creep down the passage and lock herself in the empty room and wait there until Fred Badger had gone his rounds. He would think she had found a lodging somewhere and left the theatre. She opened the door of Miss Hamilton's room and went in.

Adam Poole was sitting in front of the gas-fire.

Martyn stammered, 'I'm sorry,' and made for the door.

'Come in,' he said and stood up. 'I want to see you for a moment.'

'Well,' Martyn thought sickly, 'this is it. I'm to go.'

He twisted the chair round and ordered rather than invited her to sit in it. As she did so she thought: 'I won't be able to sleep here tonight. When he's sacked me I'll get my suitcase and ask my way to the nearest women's hostel. I'll walk alone through the streets and when I get there the hostel will be shut.'

He had turned his back to her and seemed to be examining something on the dressing-shelf.

'I would very much rather have disregarded this business,' he said irritably, 'but I suppose I can't. For one thing, someone should apologize to you for Bennington's behaviour. He's not likely to do it for himself.'

'It really didn't matter.'

'Of course it mattered,' he said sharply. 'It was insufferable. For both of us.'

She was too distressed to recognize as one of pleasure the small shock this last phrase gave her.

'You realize, of course, how this nonsense started,' he was saying. 'You've seen something of the play. You've seen me. It's not a matter for congratulation, I dare say, but you're like enough to be my daughter. You're a New Zealander, I understand. How old are you?'

'Nineteen, sir.'

'You needn't bother to pepper your replies with this "sir" business. It's not in character and it's entirely unconvincing. I'm thirty-eight. I toured New Zealand in my first job twenty years ago, and Bennington was in the company. That, apparently, is good enough for him. Under the circumstances I hope you won't mind my asking you who your parents are and where you were born.'

'I've no objection whatever,' said Martyn with spirit. 'My father was Martyn Tarne. He was the son and grandson of a high-country run-holder – a sheep-farmer – in the South Island. He was killed on Crete.'

He turned and looked directly at her for the first time since she had come into the room.

'I see. And your mother?'

'She's the daughter of a run-holder in the same district?'

'Do you mind telling me her maiden name, if you please?'

Martyn said: 'I don't see what good this will do.'

'Don't you, indeed? Don't you, after all, resent the sort of conjecture that's brewing among these people?'

'I certainly haven't the smallest desire to be thought your daughter.'

'And I couldn't agree more. Good Lord!' he said. 'This is a fat-headed way for us to talk. Why don't you want to tell me your mother's maiden name? What was the matter with it?'

'She always thought it sounded silly. It was Paula Poole Passington.'

He brought the palm of his hand down crisply on the back of her chair. 'And why in the world,' he asked, 'couldn't you say so at once?' Martyn was silent. 'Paula Poole Passington,' he repeated. 'All right. An old cousin of my father's – cousin Paula – married someone called Passington and disappeared. I suppose to New Zealand. Why didn't she look me up when I went out there?'

'I believe she didn't care for theatricals,' said Martyn. 'She was my grandmother. The connection is really quite distant.'

'You might at least have mentioned it.'

'I preferred not to.'

'Too proud?'

'If you like,' she said desperately.

'Why did you come to England?'

'To earn my living.'

'As a dresser?' She was silent. 'Well?' he said.

'As best I could.'

'As an actress? Oh, for God's sake,' he added, 'it's damnably late and I'll be obliged if you'll behave reasonably. I may tell you I've spoken to Jacko. Don't you think you're making an ass of yourself? All this mystery act!'

Martyn got up and faced him. 'I'm sorry,' she said. 'It's a silly business but it's not an act. I didn't want to make a thing of it. I joined an English touring company in New Zealand a year ago and they took me on with them to Australia.'

'What company was this? What parts did you play?'

She told him.

'I heard about the tour,' he said. 'They were a reasonably good company.'

'They paid quite well and I did broadcasting too. I saved up enough to keep me in England for six months and got a job as an assistant children's minder in a ship. Perhaps I should explain that my father lost pretty well everything in the slump, and we are poor people. I had my money in traveller's cheques and the day we landed they were stolen out of my bag, together with my letters of introduction. The bank will probably be able to stop them and let me have it back but until they decide, I'm hard up. That's all.'

'How long have you been here?'

'A fortnight.'

'Where have you tried?'

'Agencies. All the London theatres, I think.'

'This one last? Why?'

'One of them had to be last.'

'Did you know of this – connection – as you call it?'

'Yes. My mother knew of it.'

'And the resemblance?'

'I – we saw your pictures – people sometimes said – ' They looked at each other, warily, with guarded interest.

'And you deliberately fought shy of this theatre because you knew I was playing here?'

'Yes.'

'Did you know about this piece? The girl's part?'

Martyn was beginning to be very tired. A weariness of spirit and body seeped up through her being in a sluggish tide. She was near to tears and thrust her hand nervously through her short hair. He made some kind of ejaculation and she said at once: 'I didn't mean to do that.'

'But you knew about the part when you came here?'

'There's a lot of gossip at the agencies when you're waiting. A girl I stood next to in the queue at Garnet Marks' told me they wanted someone at the Vulcan who could be made up to look like you. She'd got it all muddled up with yesterday's auditions for the touring company in another piece.'

'So you thought you'd try?'

'Yes. I was a bit desperate by then. I thought I'd try.'

'Without, I suppose, mentioning this famous "connection"?'

'Yes.'

'And finding there was nothing for you in the piece you applied for the job of dresser?'

'Yes.'

'Well,' he said, 'it's fantastic, but at least it's less fantastic than pure coincidence would have been. One rather respects you by the way, if it's not impertinent in a second cousin once removed to say so.'

'Thank you,' she said vaguely.

'The question is: What are we going to do about it?'

Martyn turned away to the ranks of dresses and with business-like movements of her trembling hands, tweaked at the sheets that covered them. She said briskly: 'I realize of course that I'll have to go. Perhaps Miss Hamilton – '

'You think you ought to go?' his voice said behind her. 'I suppose you're right. It's an awkward business.'

'I'm sorry.'

'But I'd like to – it's difficult to suggest – '

'I'll be perfectly all right,' she said with savage brightness. 'Please don't give it another thought.'

'Why, by the way, are you still in the theatre?'

'I was going to sleep here,' Martyn said loudly. 'I did last night. The night-watchman knows.'

'You would be paid on Friday.'

'Like the actors?'

'Certainly. How much is there in the exchequer between now and Friday?' Martyn was silent and he said with a complete change of voice: 'My manners, you will already have been told, are notoriously offensive but I don't believe I was going to say anything that would have offended you.'

'I've got two and fourpence.'

He opened the door and shouted: 'Jacko!' into the echoing darkness. She heard the greenroom door creak and in a moment or two Jacko came in. He carried a board with a half-finished drawing pinned to it. This he exhibited to Poole. 'Crazy, isn't it?' he said. 'Helena's costume for the ball. What must I do but waste my beauty-sleep concocting it. Everybody will have to work very hard if it is to be made. I see you are in need of my counsel. What goes on?'

'Against my better judgement,' Poole said, 'I'm going to follow your advice. You always think you're indispensable at auditions. Give me some light out there and then sit in front.'

'It is past midnight. This child has worked and worried herself into a complete *bouleversement*. She is as pale as a pierrot.'

Poole looked at her. 'Are you all right?' he asked her. 'It won't take ten minutes.'

'I don't understand, but I'm all right.'

'There you are, Jacko,' Poole said and sounded pleased. 'It's over to you.'

Jacko took her by the shoulders and gently pushed her down on the chair. 'Attention,' he said. 'We make a bargain. I live not so far from here in an apartment house kept by a well-disposed French couple. An entirely respectable house, you understand, with no funny business. At the top one finds an attic room as it might be in a tale for children, and so small, it is but twice the size of its nice little bed. The rental is low, within the compass of a silly girl who gets herself into equivocal situations. At my recommendation she will be accommodated in the attic which is included in my portion of the house and will pay me the rent at the end of a week. But in exchange for my good offices she does for us a little service. Again, no funny business.'

'Oh, dear!' Martyn said. She leant towards the dressing-shelf and propped her face in her hands. 'It sounds so wonderful,' she said and tried to steady her voice, 'a nice little bed.'

'All right, Jacko,' Poole said. She heard the door open and shut. 'I want you to relax for a few minutes,' his voice went on. 'Relax all over like a cat. Don't think of anything in particular. You're going to sleep sound tonight. All will be well.'

The gas-fire hummed, the smell of roses and cosmetics filled the warm room. 'Do you smoke?' Poole asked.

'Sometimes.'

'Here you are.'

She drew in the smoke gratefully. He went into the passage and she watched him light his own cigarette. Her thoughts drifted aimlessly about the bony structure of his head and face. Presently a stronger light streamed down the passage. Jacko's voice called something from a great distance.

Poole turned to her. 'Come along,' he said.

On the stage, dust-thickened rays from pageant-lamps settled in a pool of light about a desk and two chairs. It was like an island in a vague region of blueness. She found herself seated there at the desk, facing him across it. In response to a gesture of Poole's she rested her arms on the desk and her face in her arms.

'Listen,' he said, 'and don't move. You are in the hall of an old house, beautiful but decaying. You are the girl with the bad heredity. You are the creature who goes round and round in her great empty cage like a stoat filled with a wicked desire. The object of your desire is the man on the other side of the desk who is joined to you in blood and of whose face and mind you are the ill reflection. In a moment you will raise your face to his. He will make a gesture and you will make the same gesture. Then you will say: "Don't you like what you see?" It must be horrible and real. Don't move. Think of it. Then raise your head and speak.'

There was a kind of voluptuousness in Martyn's fatigue. Only the chair she sat on and the desk that propped her arms and head prevented her, she felt, from slipping to the floor. Into this defencelessness Poole's suggestions entered like those of a mesmerist, and that perfection of duality for which actors pray and which they are so rarely granted now fully invested her. She was herself and she was the girl in the play. She guided the girl and was aware of her and she governed the possession of the girl by the obverse of the man in the play. When at last she raised her face and looked at him and repeated his gesture it seemed to her that she looked into a glass and saw her own reflection and spoke to it.

'*Don't you like what you see?*' Martyn said.

In the pause that followed, the sound of her own breathing and Poole's returned. She could hear her heart beat.

'Can you do it again?' he said.

'I don't know,' she said helplessly. 'I don't know at all.' She turned away and with a childish gesture hid her face in the crook of her arm. In dismay and shame she set loose the tears she had so long denied herself.

'There now!' he said, not so much as if to comfort her as to proclaim some private triumph of his own. Out in the dark auditorium Jacko struck his hands together once.

Poole touched her shoulder. 'It's nothing,' he said. 'These are growing pains. They will pass.' From the door in the set he said: 'You can have the understudy. We'll make terms tomorrow. If you prefer it, the relationship can be forgotten. Goodnight.'

He left her alone and presently Jacko returned to the stage carrying her suitcase.

'Now,' he said, 'we go home.'

CHAPTER 4

Second Dress-Rehearsal

When Martyn opened her eyes on the second morning of her adventure it was with the sensation of having come to rest after a painful journey.

She lay quiet and looked about her. It was a bright morning and the sun came in at the attic window above her bed. The room had an air of great cleanliness and freshness. She remembered now that Jacko had told her he occasionally made use of it and indeed, tiny as it was it bore his eccentric imprint. A set of designs for *Twelfth Night* was pinned to a wall-board. Ranged along the shelf were a number of figures dressed in paper as the persons in this play and on the wall facing her bed hung a mask of the fool, Feste, looking very like Jacko himself.

There never was such a little room,' Martyn sighed and began to plan how she would collect and stow away her modest belongings. She was filled with gratitude and with astonished humility.

The bathroom was on the next floor and as she went downstairs she smelt coffee and fresh bread. A door on the landing opened and Jacko's clownish head looked out.

'Breakfast in ten minutes,' he said. 'Speed is essential.'

Of all the amenities, it seemed to Martyn, a hot bath was the most beneficent and after that a shower under which one could wash one's hair quickly. 'Lucky it's short,' she thought and rubbed it dry with her towel.

She was out again in eight minutes to find Jacko on the landing.

'Good,' he said. 'In your woollen gown you are entirely respectable. A clean school child. In.'

He marshalled her into a largish room set out in an orderly manner as a workshop. Martyn wondered why Jacko, who showed such exquisite neatness in his work, should in his person present such a wild front to the world. He was dressed now in faded cotton trousers, a paint-stained undervest and a tattered dressing-gown. He was unshaven and uncombed and his prominent eyes were slightly bloodshot. His manner, however, was as usual, amiable and disarming.

'I propose,' he said, 'that we breakfast together as a general rule. A light breakfast and supper are included in the arrangement. You will hand me your ration book and I shall shop with discretion. Undoubtedly I am a better cook than you and will therefore make myself responsible for supper. For luncheon you may return if you wish and forage ineffectually for yourself or make what other arrangement seems good to you. Approved?'

Martyn said carefully: 'If you please, Jacko, I'm so grateful and so muddled I can't think at all sensibly. You see, I don't know what I shall be earning.'

'For your dual and unusual role of understudy and dresser, I imagine about eight pounds a week. Your rental, *demi-pension*, here, is two.'

'It seems so little,' Martyn said timidly. 'The rent, I mean.'

Jacko tapped the side of the coffee-pot with a spoon.

'*Attention*,' he said. 'How often must I repeat. You will have the goodness to understand I am not a dirty old man. It is true that I am virile,' he continued with some complacency, 'but you are not my type. I prefer the more mature, the more *mondaine*, the – ' He stopped short, the spoon with which he had been gesticulating, still held aloof. His eyes were fixed on the wall behind Martyn. She turned her head to see a sketch in watercolour of Helena Hamilton. When she faced Jacko again, he was grinning desperately.

'Believe me,' he said, 'you are in no danger of discomfort from the smallest whisper of scandal. I am notoriously pure. This morning there are eggs and therefore an omelette. Let us observe silence while I make it.'

He was gay, in his outlandish fashion, from then onwards. When they had finished their admirable breakfast she helped him wash up and he gave her what he called her orders for the day. She was to go down to the theatre with him, set about her work as a dresser and at three o'clock she would be given a formal rehearsal as under-study. At night, for the second dress-rehearsal, she would again take up her duties as Miss Hamilton's dresser.

'An eccentric arrangement,' Jacko said. He groped in the bosom of his undervest and produced a somewhat tattered actor's 'part', type-written and bound in paper. 'Only thirteen sides,' he said. 'A bit-part. You will study the lines while you press and stitch and by this after-noon you are word perfect, isn't it? You are, of course, delighted?'

'Delighted,' Martyn said, 'is not exactly the word. I'm flabbergasted and excited and grateful for everything and I just can't believe it's true. But it is a bit worrying to feel I've sort of got in on a fluke and that everybody's wondering what it's all about. They are, you know.'

'All that,' Jacko said with an ungainly sweep of his arm, 'is of no importance. Gay Gainsford is still to play the part. She will not play it well but she is the niece of the leading lady's husband and she is therefore in a favourable position.'

'Yes, but her uncle – '

He said quickly: 'Clark Bennington was once a good actor. He is now a stencil. He drinks too much and when he is drunk he is offen-sive. Forget him.' He turned away and with less than his usual deft-ness began to set out his work-table. From an adjoining room he said indistinctly: 'I advise that which I find difficult to perform. Do not allow yourself to become hag-ridden by this man. It is a great mis-take. I myself – ' His voice was lost in the spurt of running water. Martyn heard him shout: 'Run off and learn your lines. I have a job in hand.'

With a feeling of unease she returned to her room. But when she opened her part and began to read the lines this feeling retreated until it hung like a very small cloud over the hinterland of her mind. The foreground was occupied entirely by the exercise of memorizing and in a few minutes she had almost, but not quite, forgotten her anxiety.

II

She was given her moves that afternoon by the stage-manager and, at three o'clock, rehearsed her scenes with the other two understudies.

The remaining parts were read from the script. Jacko pottered about back-stage intent on one of his odd jobs; otherwise the theatre seemed to be deserted. Martyn had memorized her lines but inevitably lost them from time to time in her effort to associate them with physical movement. The uncompromising half-light of a working-stage, the mechanical pacing to and fro of understudies, the half-muted lines raised to concert pitch only for cues, and the dead sound of voices in an empty house: all these workaday circumstances, though she was familiar enough with them, after all, laid a weight upon her: she lost her belief in the magic of the previous night. She was oppressed by this anticlimax, and could scarcely summon up the resources of her young experience to meet it.

The positions and moves had been planned with a vivid understanding of the text and seemed to spring out of it. She learnt them readily enough. Rather to her surprise, and, she thought, that of the other understudies, they were finally taken through her scenes at concert pitch so that by the end of the rehearsal the visual and aural aspects of her part had fused into a whole. She had got her routine. But it was no more than a routine: she spoke and paused and moved and spoke and there was no reality at all, she felt, in anything she did. Clem Smith, the stage-manager, said nothing about interpretation but, huddled in his overcoat, merely set the moves and then crouched over the script. She was not even a failure, she was just another colourless understudy and nothing had happened.

When it was over, Clem Smith shut the book and said: 'Thank you, ladies and gentlemen. Eleven in the morning if you please.' He lit a cigarette and went down into the auditorium and out through the front of the house.

Left alone on the stage, Martyn struggled with an acute attack of deflation. She tried to call herself to order. This in itself was a humiliating if salutary exercise. If, she thought savagely, she had been a Victorian young lady, she would at this juncture have locked herself away with a plush-bound journal and after shedding some mortified tears, forced a confession out of herself. As it was, she set her jaw and worked it out there and then. The truth was, she told herself, she had been at her old tricks again: she had indulged in the most blatant kind of day-dream. She had thought up a success story and dumped herself down in the middle of it with half a dozen pageant-lamps bathing her girlish form. Because she looked like Poole and because last night she had had a mild success with one line by playing it off her nerves she had actually had the gall to imagine – here Martyn felt her scalp creep and her face burn. 'Come on,' she thought, 'out with it.'

Very well, then. She had dreamed up a further rehearsal with Poole. She had seen herself responding eagerly to his production, she had heard him say regretfully that if things had been different . . . She had even . . . At this point overtaken with self-loathing Martyn performed the childish exercise of throwing her part across the stage, stamping violently and thrusting her fingers through her hair.

'*Damn and blast and hell*,' said Martyn, pitching her voice to the back row of the gallery.

'Not quite as bad as all that.'

Adam Poole came out of the shadowed pit and down the centre aisle of the stalls. He rested his hands on the rail of the orchestral well. Martyn gaped at him.

'You've got the mechanics,' he said. 'Walk through it again by yourself before tomorrow. Then you can begin to think about the girl. Get the layout of the house into your head. Know your environment. What has she been doing all day before the play opens? What has she been thinking about? Why does she say the things she says and do the things she does? Listen to the other chaps' lines. Come down here for five minutes and we'll see what you think about acting.'

Martyn went down into the house. Of all her experiences during these three days at the Vulcan Theatre, she was to remember this most vividly. It was a curious interview. They sat side by side as if waiting for the rise of curtain. Their voices were deadened by the plush stalls. Jacko could be heard moving about behind the set and in some distant room, back-stage, somebody in desultory fashion hammered and sawed. At first Martyn was ill at ease, unable to dismiss or to reconcile the jumble of distracted notions that beset her. But Poole was talking about theatre and about problems of the actor. He talked well, without particular emphasis but with penetration and authority. Soon she listened with single hearing and with all her attention to what he had to say. Her nervousness and uncertainty were gone and presently she was able to speak of matters that had exercised her in her own brief experience of the stage. Their conver-

sation was adult and fruitful. It didn't even occur to her that they
were getting on rather well together.

Jacko came out on the stage. He shielded his eyes with his hand
and peered into the auditorium.

'Adam?' he said.

'Hallo? What is it?'

'It is Helena on the telephone to inquire why have you not rung her
at four, the time being now five-thirty. Will you take it in the office?'

'Good Lord!' he ejaculated and got up. Martyn moved into the
aisle to let him out.

He said: 'All right, Miss Tarne. Work along the lines we've been
talking about and you should be able to cope with the job. We take
our understudies seriously at the Vulcan and like to feel they're an
integral part of the company. You'll rehearse again tomorrow morning and – ' He stopped unaccountably and after a moment said hurriedly: 'You're all right, aren't you? I mean you feel quite happy
about this arrangement?'

'Yes,' she said. 'Very happy.'

'Good.' He hesitated again for a second and then said: 'I must go,'
and was off down the aisle to the front of the house. He called out:
'I'll be in the office for some time, Jacko, if anyone wants me.' A
door banged. There was a long silence.

Jacko advanced to the footlights. 'Where are you?' he asked.

'Here,' said Martyn.

'I see you. Or a piece of you. Where is the rest? Reassemble yourself. There is work to be done.'

The work turned out to be the sewing together of a fantastic garment
created and tacked up by Jacko himself. It had a flamboyant design,
stencilled in black and yellow, of double-headed eagles and was made,
in part, of scenic canvas. There was an electric sewing-machine in
the wardrobe-room which was next to Mr J. G. Darcey's at the end of
the passage. Here Jacko sat Martyn down and here, for the next hour,
she laboured under his exacting direction while he himself crawled
about the floor cutting out further garments for the Combined Arts
Ball. At half-past six he went out, saying he would return with food.

Martyn laboured on. Sometimes she repeated the lines of her
part, her voice drowned by the clatter of the machine. Sometimes,
when engaged in hand-work it would seem, in the silent room, that

she had entered into a new existence, as if she had at that moment been born and was a stranger to her former self. And since this was rather a frightening sensation, though not new to Martyn, she must rouse herself and make a conscious effort to dispel it. On one of these occasions, when she had just switched off the machine, she felt something of the impulse that had guided her first attempt at the scene with Poole. Wishing to retain and strengthen this experience she set aside her work and rested her head on her arms as the scene required. She waited in this posture, summoning her resources, and when she was ready, raised her head to confront her opposite.

Gay Gainsford stood on the other side of the table, watching her.

III

Martyn's flesh leapt on her bones. She cried out and made a sweeping gesture with her arms. A pair of scissors clattered to the floor.

I'm sorry I startled you,' said Miss Gainsford. 'I came in quietly. I thought you were asleep but I realize now – you were doing that scene. Weren't you?'

'I've been given the understudy,' Martyn said.

'You've had an audition and a rehearsal, haven't you?'

'Yes. I was so frightful at rehearsal, I thought I'd have another shot by myself.'

'You needn't,' Miss Gainsford said, 'try to make it easy for me.'

Martyn, still shaken and bewildered, looked at her visitor. She saw a pretty face that, under its make-up, was sodden with tears. Even as she looked the large photogenic eyes hooded and the small mouth quivered.

'I suppose,' Miss Gainsford said, 'you know what you're doing to me.'

'Good Lord!' Martyn ejaculated, 'what *is* all this? What have I done? I've got your understudy. I'm damn thankful to have it and so far I've made a pretty poor showing.'

'It's no good taking that line with me. I know what's happening.'

'Nothing's happening. Oh, *please*,' Martyn implored, torn between pity and a rising fear, '*please* don't cry. I'm nothing. I'm just any old understudy.'

'That's pretty hot, I must say,' Miss Gainsford said. Her voice wavered grotesquely between two registers like an adolescent boy's; 'to talk about any old understudy when you've got that appearance. What's everyone saying about you when they think I'm not about? "She's got the appearance!" It doesn't matter to them that I've had to dye my hair because they don't like wigs. I still haven't got the appearance. I'm a shoulder-length natural ash-blonde and I've had to have an urchin cut and go black and all I get is insults. In any other management,' she continued wildly, 'the author wouldn't be allowed to speak to the artistes like that man speaks to me. In any other management an artiste would be protected against that kind of treatment. Adam's worse if anything. He's so bloody patient and persistent and half the time you don't know what he's talking about.'

She drew breath, sobbed and hunted in her bag for her handkerchief.

Martyn said: 'I'm so terribly sorry. It's awful when things go badly at rehearsals. But the worst kind of rehearsals *do* have a way of turning into the best kind of performances. And it's a grand play, isn't it?'

'I loathe the play. To me it's a lot of highbrow hokum and I don't care who knows it. Why the hell couldn't Uncle Ben leave me where I was, playing leads and second leads in fortnightly rep? We were a happy family in fortnightly rep; everyone had fun and games and there wasn't this ghastly graveyard atmosphere. I was miserable enough, God knows, before you came but now it's just *more* than I can stand.'

'But I'm not going to play the part,' Martyn said desperately. 'You'll be all right. It's just got you down for the moment. I'd be no good, I expect, anyway.'

'It's what they're all saying and thinking. It's a pity, they're saying, that you came too late.'

'Nonsense. You only imagine that because of the likeness.'

'Do I? Let me tell you I'm not imagining *all* the things they're saying about you. And about Adam. How you *can* stay here and take it! Unless it's true. *Is* it true?'

Martyn closed her hands on the material she had been sewing. 'I don't want to know what they're saying. There's nothing unkind that's true for them to say.'

'So the likeness is purely an accident? There's no relationship?'

Martyn said: 'It seems that we are very distantly related: so distantly that the likeness is a freak. I didn't want to tell anyone about it. It's of no significance at all. I haven't used it to get into the theatre.'

'I don't know how and why you got in but I wish to God you'd get out. How you *can* hang on knowing what they think, if it isn't true! You can't have any pride or decency. It's so cruel. It's so *damnably* cruel.'

Martyn looked at the pretty tear-blubbered face and thought in terror that if it had been that of Atropos it could scarcely have offered a more dangerous threat. 'Don't!' she cried out. 'Please don't say that, I need this job so desperately. Honestly, *honestly* you're making a thing of all this. I'm not hurting you.'

'Yes, you are. You're driving me completely frantic. I'm nervously and emotionally exhausted.' Miss Gainsford sobbed with an air of quoting somebody else. 'It just needed you to send me over the border-line. Uncle Ben keeps on and on and on about it until I think I'll go mad. This is a beastly unlucky theatre anyway. Everyone knows there's something wrong about it and then you come in like a Jonah and it's the rock *bottom*. If,' Miss Gainsford went on, developing a command of histrionic climax of which Martyn would scarcely have suspected her capable, 'if you have *any* pity at all, *any* humanity, you'll spare me this awful ordeal.'

'But this is all nonsense. You're making a song about nothing. I won't be taken in by it,' Martyn said and recognized defeat in her own voice.

Miss Gainsford stared at her with watery indignation and through trembling lips uttered her final cliché. 'You can't,' she said, 'do this thing to me,' and broke down completely.

It seemed to Martyn that beyond a façade of stock emotionalism she recognized a real and a profound distress. She thought confusedly that if they had met on some common and reasonable ground she would have been able to put up a better defence. As it was they merely floundered in a welter of unreason. It was intolerably distressing to her. Her precarious happiness died, she wanted to escape: she was lost. With a feeling of nightmarish detachment she heard herself say: 'All right. I'll speak to Mr Poole. I'll say I can't do the understudy.'

Miss Gainsford had turned away. She held her handkerchief to her face. Her shoulders and head had been quivering but now they were still. There was a considerable pause. She blew her nose fussily, cleared her throat, and looked up at Martyn.

'But if you're Helena's dresser,' she said 'you'll still be *about*.'

'You can't mean you want to turn me out of the theatre altogether.'

'There's no need,' Miss Gainsford mumbled, 'to put it like that.'

Martyn heard a voice and footsteps in the passage. She didn't want to be confronted with Jacko. She said: 'I'll see if Mr Poole's still in the theatre. I'll speak to him now if he is.'

As she made for the door Miss Gainsford snatched at her arm. 'Please!' she said. 'I *am* grateful. But you will be really generous won't you? Really big? You won't bring me into it will you? With Adam I mean. Adam wouldn't underst – '

Her face set as if she had been held in suspension like a motion picture freezing into a still. She didn't even release her hold on Martyn's arm.

Martyn spun round and saw Poole, with Jacko behind him in the passage. To her own astonishment she burst out laughing.

'No really!' she stammered, 'it's too much! This is the third time. Like the demon king in pantomime.'

'What the devil to you mean?'

'I'm sorry. It's just your flair for popping up in crises. Other people's crises. Mine in fact.'

He grimaced as if he gave her up as a bad job. 'What's the present crisis?' he said and looked at Miss Gainsford who had turned aside and was uneasily painting her mouth.

'What is it, Gay?'

'Please!' she choked. 'Please let me go. I'm all right, really. Quite all right. I just rather want to be alone.'

She achieved a tearful smile at Poole and an imploring glance at Martyn. Poole stood away from the door and watched her go out with her chin up and with courageous suffering neatly portrayed in every inch of her body.

She disappeared into the passage and a moment later the door of the greenroom was heard to shut.

'It is a case of miscasting,' said Jacko, coming into the room. 'She should be in Hollywood. She has what it takes in Hollywood. What an exit! We have misjudged her.'

'Go and see what's the matter.'

'She wants,' said Jacko, making a dolorous face, 'to be alone.'

'No, she doesn't. She wants an audience. You're it. Get along and do your stuff.'

Jacko put several parcels on the table. 'I am the dogsbody,' he said, 'to end all dogsbodies.' And went out.

'Now, then,' Poole said.

Martyn gathered up her work and was silent.

'What's the matter? You're as white as a sheet. Sit down. What is all this?'

She sat behind the machine.

'Come on,' he said.

'I'm sorry if it's inconvenient for you but I'm afraid I've got to give notice.'

'Indeed? As dresser or as understudy?'

'As both.'

'It's extremely inconvenient and I don't accept it.'

'But you must. Honestly, you must. I can't go on like this: it isn't fair.'

'Do you mean because of that girl?'

'Because of her and because of everything. She'll have a breakdown. There'll be some disaster.'

'She doesn't imagine you're going to be given the part over her head, does she?'

'No, no, of course not. It's just that she's finding it hard anyway and the – the sight of me sort of panics her.'

'The likeness?'

'Yes.'

'She needn't look at you. I'm afraid she's the most complete ass, that girl,' he muttered. He picked up a fold of the material Martyn had been sewing, looked absently at it and pushed the whole thing across the table. 'Understand,' he said. 'I won't for a second entertain the idea of your going. For one thing Helena can't do without you and for another I will not be dictated to by a minor actress in my own company. Nor,' he added with a change of tone, 'by anyone else.'

'I'm so terribly sorry for her,' Martyn said. 'She feels there's some sort of underground movement against her. She really feels it.'

'And you?'

'I must admit I don't much enjoy the sensation of being in the theatre on sufferance. But I was so thankful – ' she caught her breath and stopped.

'Who makes you feel you're on sufferance? Gay? Bennington? Percival?'

'I used a silly phrase. Naturally, they all must think it a bit queer, my turning up. It *looks* queer.'

'It'd look a damn sight queerer if you faded out again. I can't think,' he said impatiently, 'how you could let yourself be bamboozled by that girl.'

'But it's *not* all bamboozle. She really is at the end of her tether.'

Martyn waited for a moment. She thought inconsequently how strange it was that she should talk like this to Adam Poole who two days ago, had been a celebrated name, a remote legend, seen and heard and felt through a veil of characterization in his films.

'Oh, well,' she thought and said aloud: 'I'm thinking of the show. It's such a good play. She mustn't be allowed to fail. I'm thinking about that.'

He came nearer and looked at her with a sort of incredulity. 'Good Lord,' he said, 'I believe you are! Do you mean to say you haven't considered your own chance if she did crack up? Where's your wishful thinking?'

Martyn slapped her palm down on the table. 'But of course I have. Of course I've done my bit of wishful thinking. But don't you see – '

He reached across the table and for a brief moment his hand closed over hers. 'I think I do,' he said. 'I'm beginning, it seems, to get a taste of your quality. How do you suppose the show would get on if you had to play?'

'That's unfair,' Martyn cried.

'Well,' he said, 'don't run out on me. That'd be unfair, if you like. No dresser. No understudy. A damn shabby trick. As for this background music, I know where it arises. It's a more complex business than you may suppose. I shall attend to it.' He moved behind her chair, and rested his hand on its back. 'Well,' he said, 'shall we "clap hands and a bargain"? How say you?'

Martyn said slowly: 'I don't see how I can do anything but say yes.'

'There's my girl.' His hand brushed across her head and he moved away.

'Though I must say,' Martyn added, 'you do well to quote Petruchio. And Henry V, if it comes to that.'

'A brace of autocratic male animals? Therefore it must follow, you are "Kate" in two places. And – shrewd Kate, French Kate, kind Kate but never curs't Kate – you will rehearse at eleven tomorrow, hold or cut bowstrings. Agreed?'

'I am content.'

'Damned if you look it, however. All right. I'll have a word with that girl. Good day to you, Kate.'

'Good day, sir,' said Martyn.

IV

That night the second dress-rehearsal went through as for performance, without, as far as Martyn knew, any interruption during the action.

She stayed throughout in one or the other of Miss Hamilton's dressing-rooms and, on the occasions when she was in transit, contrived to be out of the way of any players. In the second act, her duties kept her in the improvised dressing-room on the stage and she heard a good deal of the dialogue.

There is perhaps nothing that gives one so strong a sense of theatre from the inside as the sound of invisible players in action. The disembodied and remote voices, projected at an unseen mark, the uncanny quiet off-stage, the smells and the feeling that the walls and the dust listen, the sense of a simmering expectancy; all these together make a corporate life so that the theatre itself seems to breathe and pulse and give out a warmth. This warmth communicated itself to Martyn and, in spite of all her misgivings, she glowed and thought to herself. 'This is my place. This is where I belong.'

Much of the effect of the girl's part in this act depended, not so much on what she said, which was little, but on mime and on that integrity of approach, which is made manifest in the smallest gesture, the least movement. Listening to Miss Gainsford's slight uncoloured voice Martyn thought: 'But perhaps if one watched her it would be better. Perhaps something is happening that cannot be heard; only seen.'

Miss Hamilton, when she came off for her changes, spoke of nothing but the business in hand and said little enough about that. She was indrawn and formal in her dealings with her dresser. Martyn wondered uneasily how much Poole had told her of their interviews, whether she had any strong views or prejudices about her husband's niece or shared his resentment that Martyn herself had been cast as an understudy.

The heat radiated by the strong lights of the dressing-rooms intensified their characteristic smells. With business-like precision Miss Hamilton would aim an atomizer at her person and spray herself rhythmically with scent while Martyn, standing on a chair, waited to slip a dress over her head. After the end of the second act when she was about this business in the star-room, Poole came in: 'That went very nicely, Ella,' he said.

Martyn paused with the dress in her hands. Miss Hamilton extended her whitened arms and, with a very beautiful movement, turned to him.

'Oh, darling,' she said. 'Did it? Did it really?'

Martyn thought she had never seen anyone more lovely than her employer was then. Hers was the kind of beauty that declared itself when most simply arrayed. The white cloth that protected her hair added a Holbein-like emphasis to the bones and subtly turning planes of her face. There was a sort of naïvety and warmth in her posture: a touching intimacy. Martyn saw Poole take the hands that were extended to him and she turned her head away, not liking, with the voluminous dress in her arms, to climb down from her station on the chair. She felt suddenly desolate and shrunken within herself.

'Was it *really* right?' Miss Hamilton said.

'You were, at least.'

'But – otherwise?'

'Much as one would expect.'

'Where's John?'

'In the circle, under oath not to come down until I say so.'

'Pray God he keep his oath,' she quoted sombrely.

'Hallo, Kate,' Poole said.

'Kate?' Miss Hamilton asked. 'Why, Kate?'

'I suspect her,' said Poole, 'of being a shrew. Get on with your job, Kate. What are you doing up there?'

Miss Hamilton said, 'Really, darling!' and moved away to the chair. Martyn slipped the dress over her head, jumped down and began to fasten it. She did this to a running accompaniment from Poole. He whispered to himself anxiously as if he were Martyn, muttered and grunted as if Miss Hamilton complained that the dress was tight, and thus kept up a preposterous dialogue, matching his words to their actions. This was done so quaintly and with so little effort that Martyn had much ado to keep a straight face and Miss Hamilton was moved to exasperated laughter. When she was dressed she took him by the arms. 'Since when, my sweet, have you become a dressing-room comedian?'

'Oh, God, your only jig-maker!'

'Last act, please, last act,' said the call-boy in the passage.

'Come on,' she said, and they went out together.

When the curtain was up, Martyn returned to the improvised dressing-room on the stage and there, having for the moment no duties, she listened to the invisible play and tried to discipline her most unruly heart.

Bennington's last exit was followed in the play by his suicide, off-stage. Jacko, who had, it seemed, a passion for even the simplest of off-stage stunts, had come round from the front of the house to supervise the gunshot. He stood near the entry into the dressing-room passage with a stage-hand who carried an effects-gun. This was fired at the appropriate moment and as they were stationed not far from Martyn in her canvas room, she leapt at the report which was nerve-shatteringly successful. The acrid smell of the discharge drifted into her roofless shelter.

Evidently Bennington was standing nearby. His voice, carefully lowered to a murmur, sounded just beyond the canvas wall. 'And that,' he said, 'takes me *right* off, thank God. Give me a cigarette, Jacko, will you?' There was a pause. The stage-hand moved away. A match scraped and Bennington said: 'Come to my room and have a drink.'

'Thank you, Ben, not now,' Jacko whispered. 'The curtain comes down in five minutes.'

'Followed by a delicious post-mortem conducted by the Great Producer and the Talented Author. Entrancing prospect! How did I go, Jacko?'

'No actor,' Jacko returned, 'cares to be told how he goes in anything but terms of extravagant praise. You know how clever you always are. You are quite as clever tonight as you have always been. Moreover you showed some discretion.'

Martyn heard Bennington chuckle. 'There's still tomorrow,' he said. 'I reserve my fire, old boy. I bide my time.'

There was a pause. Martyn heard one of them fetch a long sigh: Jacko, evidently, because Bennington as if in answer to it said: 'Oh, nonsense.' After a moment he added: The kid's all right,' and when Jacko didn't answer: 'Don't you think so?'

'Why, yes,' said Jacko.

On the stage the voices of Helena Hamilton and Adam Poole built towards a climax. The call-boy came round behind the set and went down the passage chanting: 'All on for the Curtain please. All on.'

Martyn shifted the chair in the dressing-room and moved noisily. There was a brief silence.

'I don't give a damn if she can hear,' Bennington said more loudly. 'Wait a moment. Stay where you are. I was asking you what you thought of Gay's performance. She's all right. Isn't she?'

'Yes, yes. I must go.'

'Wait a bit. If the fools left her alone she'd go tremendously. I tell you what, old boy. If our Eccentric Author exercises his talent for wisecracking on that kid tonight I'll damn well take a hand.'

'You will precipitate a further scene, and that is to be avoided.'

'I'm not going to stand by and hear her bullied. By God, I'm not. I understand you've given harbourage, by the way, to the Mystery Maiden.'

'I must get round to the side. By your leave, Ben.'

'Plenty of time.'

And Martyn knew that Bennington stood in the entry to the passage, barring the way.

'I'm talking,' he said, 'about this understudy-cum-dresser. Miss X.'

'You are prolific in cryptic titles.'

'Call her what you like, it's a peculiar business. What is she? You may as well tell me, you know. Some ancient indiscretion of Adam's adolescence come home to roost?'

'Be quiet, Ben.'

'For twopence I'd ask Adam himself. And that's not the only question I'd like to ask him. Do you think I relish my position?'

'They are getting near the tag. It is almost over.'

'Why do you suppose I drink a bit? What would you do in my place?'

'Think before I speak,' said Jacko, 'for one thing.'

A buzzer sounded. 'There's the curtain,' said Jacko. 'Look out.'

Martyn heard a kind of scuffle followed by an oath from Bennington. There were steps in the passage. The curtain fell with a giant whisper. A gust of air swept through the region back-stage.

'All on,' said the stage-manager distantly. Martyn heard the players go on and the curtain rise and fall again.

Poole, on the stage, said: 'And that's all of that. All right, everyone. Settle down and I'll take the notes. John will be round in a moment. I'll wait for you, Ella.'

Miss Hamilton came into the improvised room. Martyn removed her dress and put her into her gown.

'I'll take my make-up off out there,' she said. 'Bring the things, Martyn, will you? Grease, towels and my cigarettes?'

Martyn had them ready. She followed Miss Hamilton out and for the first time that night went on to the set.

Poole, wearing a dark dressing-gown, stood with his back to the curtain. The other five members of the cast sat, relaxed but attentive, about the stage. Jacko and Clem Smith waited by the prompt corner with papers and pencils. Martyn held a looking-glass before Miss Hamilton who said: 'Adam, darling, you don't mind, do you? I mustn't miss a word but I *do* rather want to get on,' and began to remove her make-up.

Upon this scene Dr John James Rutherford erupted. His arrival was prefaced in his usual manner by slammed doors, blundering footsteps and loud ejaculations. He then appeared in the central entrance, flame-headed, unshaven, overcoated, and grasping a sheaf of papers.

'Roast me,' he said, 'in sulphur. Wash me in steepdown gulfs of liquid fire ere I again endure the loathy torment of a dress-rehearsal. What have I done, ye gods, that I should – '

'All right, John,' Poole said. 'Not yet. Sit down. On some heavy piece of furniture and carefully.'

Clem Smith shouted: 'Alf! The doctor's chair.'

A large chair with broken springs was brought on and placed with its back to the curtain. Dr Rutherford hurled himself into it and produced his snuff-box. 'I am a child to chiding,' he said. 'What goes on, chums?'

Poole said: 'I'm going to take my stuff. If anything I have to say repeats exactly any of your own notes you might leave it out for the sake of saving time. If you've any objections, be a good chap and save them till I've finished. Agreed?'

'Can't we cut the flummery and get down to business.'

'That's just what I'm suggesting.'

'Is it? I wasn't listening. Press on then, my dear fellow. Press on.'

They settled down. Jacko gave Poole a block of notes and he began to work through them. 'Nothing much in Act I,' he said, 'until we get to –' His voice went on evenly. He spoke of details in timing, of orchestration and occasionally of stage-management. Sometimes a player would ask a question and there would be a brief discussion. Sometimes Clem Smith would make a note. For the scenes where Poole had been on, Jacko, it appeared, had taken separate notes. Martyn learnt for the first time that Jacko's official status was that of assistant to Poole and thought it characteristic of him that he made so little of his authority.

From where she stood, holding the glass for Helena Hamilton, she could see all the players. In the foreground was the alert and beautiful face of her employer, a little older now with its make-up gone, turning at times to the looking-glass and at times, when something in his notes concerned her, towards Poole. Beyond Miss Hamilton sat J. G. Darcey alone and thoughtfully filling his pipe. He glanced occasionally, with an air of anxious solicitude, at Miss Gainsford. At the far side Parry Percival lay in an armchair looking fretful. Bennington stood near the centre with a towel in his hands. At one moment he came behind his wife. Putting a hand on her shoulder he reached over it, helped himself to a dollop of grease from a jar in her case and slapped it on his face. She made a slight movement of distaste and immediately afterwards a little secret grimace as if she had caught herself out in a blunder. For a moment he retained his hold of her shoulder. Then he looked down at her, dragged his clean fingers across her neck and, smearing the grease over his face, returned to his former position and began to clean away his make-up.

Martyn didn't want to look at Gay Gainsford but was unable altogether to avoid doing so. Miss Gainsford sat, at first alone, on a smallish sofa. She seemed to have herself tolerably well in hand but her eyes were restless and her fingers plaited and replaited the folds of her dress. Bennington watched her from a distance until he had done with his towel. Then he crossed the stage and sat beside her, taking one of the restless hands in his. He looked hard at Martyn who was visited painfully by a feeling of great compassion for both of them and by a sensation of remorse. She had a notion, which she tried to dismiss as fantastic, that Poole sensed this reaction. His glance rested for a moment on her and she thought: 'This is getting too complicated. It's going to be too much for me.' She made an involuntary movement and at once Miss Hamilton put out a hand to the glass.

When Poole had dealt with the first act he turned to Dr Rutherford who had sat throughout with his legs extended and his chin on his chest, directing from under his brows a glare of extreme malevolence at the entire cast.

'Anything to add to that, John?' Poole asked.

'Apart from a passing observation that I regard the whole thing as a *tour de force* of understatement and with reservations that I keep to myself – ' Here Dr Rutherford looked fixedly at Parry Percival. 'I am mum. I reserve my fire.'

'Act Two, then,' said Poole and began again.

Martyn became aware after a few minutes that Dr Rutherford, like Bennington, was staring at her. She was as horribly fascinated as birds are said to be by the unwinking gaze of a snake. Do what she could to look elsewhere about the stage, she must after a time steal a glance at him only to meet his speculative and bloodshot regard. This alarmed her profoundly. She was persuaded that a feeling of tension had been communicated to the others and that they, too, were aware of some kind of impending crisis. This feeling grew in intensity as Poole's voice went steadily on with his notes. He had got about half-way through the second act when Dr Rutherford ejaculated, 'Hi! Wait a bit!' and began a frenzied search through his own notes which seemed to be in complete disorder. Finally he pounced on a sheet of paper, dragged out a pair of spectacles and, with a hand raised to enjoin silence, read it to himself with strange noises in his breathing. Having scattered the rest of his notes over his person and the floor he now folded this particular sheet and sat on it.

'Proceed,' he said. The cast stirred uneasily. Poole continued. He had come to the scene between himself and Miss Gainsford and beyond a minor adjustment of position said nothing about it. Miss Hamilton, who had arrived at the final stage of her street make-up, dusted her face with powder, nodded good-humouredly at Martyn and turned to face Poole. Martyn thankfully shut the dressing-case and made for the nearest exit.

At the same moment Poole reached the end of his notes for the second act and Dr Rutherford shouted: 'Hold on! Stop that wench!'

Martyn, with a sensation of falling into chaos, turned in the doorway.

She saw nine faces lifted towards her own. They made a pattern against the smoke-thickened air. Her eyes travelled from one to the other and rested finally on Poole's.

'It's all right,' he said. 'Go home.'

'No, you don't,' Dr Rutherford shouted excitedly.

'Indeed she does,' said Poole. 'Run away home, Kate. Goodnight to you.'

Martyn heard the storm break as she fled down the passage.

CHAPTER 5

Opening Night

From noon until half-past six on the opening night of Dr Rutherford's new play, the persons most concerned in its birth were absent from their theatre. Left to itself the Vulcan was possessed only by an immense expectancy. It waited. In the auditorium, rows of seats, stripped of their dust-cloths, stared at the curtain. The curtain itself presented its reverse side to Jacko's set, closing it in with a stuffy air of secrecy. The stage was dark. Battalions of dead lamps, focused at crazy angles, overhung it with the promise of light. Cue-sheets fixed to the switchboard awaited the electrician, the prompt-script was on its shelf, the properties were ranged on trestle-tables. Everything abided its time in the dark theatre.

To enter into this silent house was to feel as if one surprised a poised and expectant presence. This air of suspense made itself felt to the occasional intruders: to the boy who from time to time came through from the office with telegrams for the dressing-rooms, to the girl from Florian's and the young man from the wig-maker's, and to the piano-tuner who, for an hour, twanged and hammered in the covered well. And to Martyn Tarne who, alone in the ironing-room, set about the final pressing of the dresses under her care.

The offices were already active and behind their sandblasted glass walls typewriters clattered and telephone bells rang incessantly. The blacked-out box-plan lay across Bob Grantley's desk and stacked along the wall were rectangular parcels of programmes, fresh from the printer.

And at two o'clock the queues for the early doors began to form up in Carpet Street.

II

It was at two o'clock that Helena Hamilton, after an hour's massage, went to bed. Her husband had telephoned, with a certain air of opulence which she had learnt to dread, that he would lunch at his club and return to their flat during the afternoon to rest.

In her darkened room she followed a practised routine and, relaxing one set of muscles after another, awaited sleep. This time, however, her self-discipline was unsuccessful. If only she could hear him come in it would be better: if only she could see into what sort of state he had got himself. She used all her formulae for repose but none of them worked. At three o'clock she was still awake and still miserably anxious.

It was no good trying to cheer herself up by telling over her rosary of romantic memories. Usually this was a successful exercise. She had conducted her affairs of the heart, she knew, with grace and civility. She had almost always managed to keep them on a level of enchantment. She had simply allowed them to occur with the inconsequence and charm of self-sown larkspurs in an otherwise correctly ordered border. They had hung out their gay little banners for a season and then been painlessly tweaked up. Except, perhaps, for Adam. With Adam, she remembered uneasily, it had been different. With Adam, so much her junior, it had been a more deeply-rooted affair. It had put an end, finally, to her living with Ben as his wife. It had made an enemy of Ben. And at once her thoughts were infested with worries about the contemporary scene at the theatre. 'It's such a muddle!' she thought, 'and I hate muddles.' They had had nothing but trouble all through rehearsals. Ben fighting with everybody and jealous of Adam. The doctor bawling everybody out. And that wretchedly unhappy child Gay (who, God knew, would never be an actress as long as she lived) first pitchforked into the part by Ben and now almost bullied out of it by the doctor. And, last of all, Martyn Tarne.

She had touched the raw centre of her anxieties. Under any other conditions, she told herself, she would have welcomed the appearance out of a clear sky and, one had to face it, under very odd circumstances, of this little antipodean: this throw-back to some forebear that she and Adam were supposed to have in common. Helena would have been inclined to like Martyn for the resemblance instead of feeling so uncomfortably disturbed by it. Of course she accepted Adam's explanation but at the same time she thought it rather naïve of him to believe that the girl had actually kept away from the theatre because she didn't want to make capital out of the relationship. That, Helena thought, turning restlessly on her bed, was really too simple of Adam. Moreover he had stirred up the already exacerbated nerves of the company by giving this girl the understudy without, until last night, making public the relationship.

There she went, thinking about last night's scene: John Rutherford demanding that even at this stage Martyn should play the part, Gay imploring Adam to release her, Ben saying he would walk out on the show if Gay went, and Adam . . . Adam had done the right thing of course. He had come down strongly with one of his rare thrusts of anger and reduced them to complete silence. He had then described the circumstances of Martyn's arrival at the theatre and had added in a voice of ice that there was and could be no question of any change in the cast. He finished his notes and left the theatre, followed by Jacko.

This had been the signal for an extremely messy row in which everybody seemed to come to light with some deep-seated grudge. Ben had quarrelled almost simultaneously with Parry Percival (on the score of technique), with Dr Rutherford (on the score of casting), with his niece (on the score of humanity) and, unexpectedly, with J. G. Darcey (on the score of Ben bullying Gay). Percival had responded to a witticism of the doctor's by a stream of shrill invective which astonished everybody, himself included, and Gay had knitted the whole scene into a major climax by having a fit of hysterics from which she was restored with brutal efficiency by Dr Rutherford himself.

The party had then broken up. J.G. sustained his new role of knightly concern by taking Gay home. Parry Percival left in a recrudescence of fury occasioned by the doctor flinging after him a composite Shakespearian epithet ('Get you gone, you dwarf; your minimus of hind'ring knot-grass made; you bead, you acorn'). She herself had retired into the wings. The stage-staff had already disappeared. The doctor and Ben finding themselves in undisputed possession of the stage had squared up to each with the resolution of all-in wrestlers and she, being desperately tired, had taken the car home and asked their man to return to the theatre for her husband. When she woke late in the morning she was told he had already gone out.

'I wish,' a voice cried out in her mind, 'I wish to God he'd never come back.'

And at that moment she heard him stumble heavily upstairs.

She expected him to go straight to his room and was dismayed when he came to a halt outside her door and, with a clumsy sound that might have been intended for a knock, opened it and came in. The smell of brandy and cigars came in with him and invaded the whole room. It was more than a year since that had happened.

He walked uncertainly to the foot of the bed and leant on it – and she was frightened of him.

'Hallo,' he said.

'What is it, Ben? I'm resting.'

'I thought you might be interested. There'll be no more nonsense from John about Gay.'

'Good,' she said.

'He's calmed down. I got him to see reason.'

'He's not so bad, really – old John.'

'He's had some good news from abroad. About the play.'

'Translation rights?'

'Something like that.' He was smiling at her, uncertainly. 'You look comfy,' he said. 'All tucked up.'

'Why don't you try and get some rest yourself?' He leant over the foot of the bed and said something under his breath. 'What?' she said anxiously. 'What did you say?'

'I said it's a pity Adam didn't appear a bit sooner, isn't it? I'm so extraneous.'

Her heart thumped like a fist inside her ribs. 'Ben, *please*,' she said.

'And another thing. Do you both imagine I don't see through this dresser-cum-understudy racket? Darling, I don't much enjoy playing the cuckold in your restoration comedy but I'm just bloody well furious when you so grossly underestimate my intelligence. When was it? On his New Zealand tour in 1930?'

'What is this nonsense!' she said breathlessly.

'Sorry. How are you managing tonight? You and Adam?'

'My dear Ben!'

'I'll tell you. You're making shift with me for once in a blue moon. And I'm not talking about tonight.'

She recognized this scene. She had dreamt it many times. His face had advanced upon her while she lay inert with terror, as one does in a nightmare. For an infinitesimal moment she was visited by the hope that perhaps after all she had slept and if she could only scream, would awaken. But she couldn't scream. She was quite helpless.

III

Adam Poole's telephone rang at half-past four. He had gone late to rest and was awakened from a deep sleep. For a second or two he didn't recognize her voice and she spoke so disjointedly that even when he was broad awake he couldn't make out what she was saying.

'What is it?' he said: 'Ella, what's the matter? I can't hear you.'

Then she spoke more clearly and he understood.

IV

At six o'clock the persons in the play began to move towards the theatre. In their lodgings and flats they bestirred themselves after their several fashions: to drink tea or black coffee, choke down pieces of bread and butter that tasted like sawdust, or swallow aspirin and alcohol. This was their zero hour: the hour of low vitality when the stimulus of the theatre and the last assault of nerves was yet to come. By a quarter past six they were all on their way. Their dressers were already in their rooms and Jacko prowled restlessly about the darkened stage. Dr John James Rutherford, clad in an evening-suit and a boiled shirt garnished with snuff, both of which dated from some distant period when he still attended the annual dinners of the BMA, plunged into the office and made such a nuisance of himself that Bob Grantley implored him to go away.

At twenty past six the taxi carrying Gay Gainsford and J. G. Darcey turned into Carpet Street. Darcey sat with his knees crossed elegantly and his hat perched on them. In the half light his head and profile looked like those of a much younger man.

'It *was* sweet of you to call for me, J.G.,' Gay said unevenly.

He smiled, without looking at her, and patted her hand. 'I'm always petrified myself,' he said, 'on first nights.'

'Are you? I suppose a true artiste must be.'

'Ah, youth, youth!' sighed J.G., a little stagily perhaps, but, if she hadn't been too preoccupied to notice it, with a certain overtone of genuine nostalgia.

'It's worse than the usual first-night horrors for *me*,' she said. 'I'm just boxing on in a private hell of my own.'

'My poor child.'

She turned a little towards him and leant her head into his shoulder. 'Nice!' she murmured and after a moment: 'I'm so frightened of him, J.G.'

With the practised ease of a good actor, he slipped his arm round her. 'I won't have it,' he said. 'By God, I won't! If he worries you again, author or no author – '

'It's not *him*,' she said. 'Not the doctor. Oh, I know he's simply filthy to work with and he does fuss me dreadfully but it's not the doctor *really* who's responsible for all my misery.'

'No? Who is then?'

'Uncle Ben!' She made a small wailing noise that was muffled by his coat. He bent his head attentively to listen. 'J.G., I'm just plain *terrified* of Uncle Ben.'

V

Parry Percival always enjoyed his arrival at the theatre when there was a gallery queue to be penetrated. One raised one's hat and said: 'Pardon me. Thanks so much,' to the gratified ladies. One heard them murmur one's name. It was a heartening little fillip to one's self-esteem.

On this occasion the stimulant didn't work with its normal magic. He was too worried to relish it wholeheartedly.

Ben, he thought hotly, was insufferable. Every device by which a second-leading man could make a bit-part actor look foolish had been brought into play during rehearsals. Ben had upstaged him, had flurried him by introducing new business, had topped his lines and, even while he was seething with impotent fury, had reduced him to nervous giggles by looking sideways at him. It was the technique with which a schoolmaster could torture a small boy, and it revived in Parry hideous memories of his childhood.

Only partially restored by the evidence of prestige afforded by the gallery queue he walked down the stage-door alley and into the theatre. He was at once engulfed in its warmth and expectancy.

He passed into the dressing-room passage. Helena Hamilton's door was half-open and the lights were on. He tapped, looked in and was greeted by the smell of greasepaint, powder, wet-white and flowers. The gas-fire groaned comfortably. Martyn, who was spreading towels, turned and found herself confronted by his deceptively boyish face.

'Early at work?' he fluted.

Martyn wished him good evening.

'Helena not down yet?'

'Not yet.'

He hung about the dressing-room, fingering photographs and eyeing Martyn.

'I hear you come from Down Under,' he said. 'I nearly accepted an engagement to go out there last year but I didn't really like the people so I turned it down. Adam played it in the year dot, I believe. Well, more years ago than he would care to remember, I dare say. Twenty, if we're going to let our back hair down. Before you were born, I dare say.'

'Yes,' Martyn agreed. 'Just before.'

Her answer appeared to give him extraordinary satisfaction. 'Just before?' he repeated. 'Really?' and Martyn thought: 'I mustn't let myself be worried by this.'

He seemed to hover on the edge of some further observation and pottered about the dressing-room examining the great mass of flowers. 'I'll swear,' he said crossly, 'those aren't the roses I chose at Florian's. Honestly that female's an absolute menace.'

Martyn, seeing how miserable he looked, felt sorry for him. He muttered: 'I do so *abominate* first nights,' and she rejoined: 'They are pretty ghastly, aren't they?' Because he seemed unable to take himself off, she added with an air of finality: 'Anyway, may I wish you luck for this one?'

'Sweet of you,' he said. 'I'll need it. I'm the stooge of this piece. Well, thanks, anyway.'

He drifted into the passage, halted outside the open door of Poole's dressing-room and greeted Bob Cringle. 'Governor not down yet?'

'We're on our way, Mr Percival.'

Parry inclined his head and strolled into the room. He stood close to Bob leaning his back against the dressing-shelf, his legs elegantly crossed.

'Our little stranger,' he murmured, 'seems to be new-brooming away next door.'

'That's right, sir,' said Bob. 'Settled in very nice.'

'Strong resemblance,' Parry said invitingly.

'To the guvnor, sir?' Bob rejoined cheerfully. 'That's right. Quite a coincidence.'

'A coincidence!' Parry echoed. 'Well, not precisely, Bob. I understand there's a distant relationship. It was mentioned for the first time last night. Which accounts for the set-up, one supposes. Tell me, Bob, have you ever before heard of a dresser doubling as understudy?'

'Worked-out very convenient, hasn't it, sir?'

'Oh, very,' said Parry discontentedly. 'Look, Bob. You were with the governor on his New Zealand tour in '30, weren't you?'

Bob said woodenly: 'That's correct, sir. 'E was just a boy in them days. Might I trouble you to move, Mr Percival. I got my table to lay out.'

'Oh, sorry. I'm in the way. As usual. Quite! Quite!' He waved his hand and walked jauntily into the passage.

'Good luck for tonight, sir,' said Bob and shut the door after him.

Parry moved on to J. G. Darcey's room. He tapped, was answered, and went in. J.G. was already embarked on his make-up.

'Bob,' said Parry, 'refused to be drawn.'

'Good evening, dear boy. About what?'

'Oh, *you* know. The New Zealand tour and so on.'

'Did you see her?'

'I happened to look in.'

'What's she like?'

Parry lit a cigarette. 'As you have seen,' he said, 'she's fantastically like *him*. Which is really the point at issue. But *fantastically* like.'

'Can she give a show?'

'Oh *yes*,' said Parry. He leaned forward and hugged his knees boyishly. 'Oh, yes indeed. Indeed she can, my dear J.G. You'd be surprised.'

J.G. made a noncommittal sound and went on with his make-up.

'This morning,' Parry continued, 'the doctor was there. And Ben. Ben, quite obviously devoured with chagrin. I confess I couldn't help rather gloating. As I remarked, it's getting under his skin. Together, no doubt, with vast potations of brandy and soda.'

'I hope to God he's all right tonight.'

'It appears that Gay was in the back of the house, poor thing, while it was going on.'

'She didn't tell me that,' J.G. said anxiously and, catching Parry's sharpened glance, he added: 'I didn't really hear anything about it.'

'It was a repetition of last night. Really, one feels quite dizzy. Gay rushed weeping to Adam and again implored him to let her throw in the part. The doctor, of course, was all for it. Adam was charming but Uncle Ben produced another temperament. He and the doctor left simultaneously in a silence more ominous, I assure you, than last night's dog fight. Ben's not down, yet.'

'Not yet,' J.G. said and repeated: 'I hope to God he's all right.'

For a moment the two men were united in a common anxiety. J.G. said: 'Christ, I wish I didn't get nervous on first nights.'

VI

Clark Bennington's dresser, a thin melancholy man, put him into his gown and hovered, expressionless, behind him. 'I shan't need you before the change,' said Bennington. 'See if you can help Mr Darcey.'

The man went out. Bennington knew he had guessed the reason for his dismissal. He wondered why he could never bring himself to have a drink in front of his dresser. After all there was nothing in taking a nip before the show. Adam, of course, chose to make a great thing of never touching it. And at the thought of Adam Poole he felt resentment and fear stir at the back of his mind. He got his flask out of his overcoat pocket and poured a stiff shot of brandy.

'The thing to do,' he told himself, 'is to wipe this afternoon clean out. Forget it. Forget everything except my work.' But he remembered, unexpectedly, the way, fifteen years ago, he used to prepare himself for a first night. He used to make a difficult and intensive approach to his initial entrance so that when he walked out on the stage he was already possessed by a life that had been created in the dressing-room. Took a lot of concentration: Stanislavsky and all that. Hard going: but in those days it had seemed worth the effort. Helena had encouraged him. He had a notion she and Adam still went in for it. But now he had mastered the easier way: the repeated mannerism, the trick of pause and the unexpected flattening of the voice: the technical box of tricks.

He finished his drink quickly and began to grease his face. He noticed how the flesh had dropped into sad folds under the eyes, had blurred the jaw-line and had sunk into grooves about the nostrils and the corners of the mouth. All right for this part, of course, where he had to make a sight of himself, but he had been a fine-looking man. Helena had fallen for him in a big way until Adam cut him out. At the thought of Adam he experienced a sort of regurgitation of misery and anger. 'I'm a haunted man,' he thought suddenly.

He had let himself get into a state, he knew, because of this afternoon. Helena's face, gaping with terror, like a fish, almost, kept rising up in his mind and wouldn't be dismissed. Things always worked like that with him: remorse always turned into nightmare.

It had been a bad week altogether. Rows with everybody: with John Rutherford in particular and with Adam over that blasted little dresser. He felt he was the victim of some elaborate plot. He was fond of Gay: she was a nice friendly little thing: his own flesh and blood. Until he had brought her into this piece she had seemed to like him. Not a bad little artiste either and good enough, by God, for the artsy-craftsy part they had thrown at her. He thought of her scene with Poole and of her unhappiness in her failure and how, in some damned cock-eyed way, they all, including Gay, seemed to

blame him for it. He supposed she thought he had bullied her into
hanging on. Perhaps in a way he had, but he felt so much that he
was the victim of a combined assault. 'Alone,' he thought, 'I'm so
desperately *alone*,' and he could almost hear the word as one would
say it on the stage, making an echo, forlorn and hopeless and
extremely effective.

'I'm giving myself the jim-jams,' he thought. He wondered if
Helena had told Adam about this afternoon. By God, that would
rock Adam, if she had. And at once a picture rose up to torture him,
a picture of Helena weeping in Adam's arms and taking solace there.
He saw his forehead grow red in the looking-glass and told himself
he had better steady up. No good getting into one of his tempers
with a first performance ahead of him and everything so tricky with
young Gay. There he was, coming back to that girl, that phoney
dresser. He poured out another drink and began his make-up.

He recognized with satisfaction a familiar change of mood and he
now indulged himself with a sort of treat. He brought out a little
piece of secret knowledge he had stored away. Among this company
of enemies there was one over whom he exercised almost complete
power. Over one, at least, he had, overwhelmingly, the whip-hand
and the knowledge of his sovereignty warmed him almost as comfortably as the brandy. He began to think about his part. Ideas, brand
new and as clever as paint, crowded each other in his imagination.
He anticipated his coming mastery.

His left hand slid towards the flask. 'One more,' he said, 'and I'll
be fine.'

VII

In her room across the passage, Gay Gainsford faced her own reflection and watched Jacko's hands pass across it. He dabbed with his
fingertips under the cheekbones and made a droning sound behind
his closed lips. He was a very good make-up; it was one of his many
talents. At the dress-rehearsals the touch of his fingers had soothed
rather than exacerbated her nerves but tonight, evidently, she found
it almost intolerable.

'Haven't you finished?' she asked.

'Patience, patience. We do not catch a train. Have you never observed the triangular shadows under Adam's cheekbones? They are yet to be created.'

'Poor Jacko!' Gay said breathlessly, 'this must be such a bore for you. Considering everything.'

'Quiet, now. How can I work?'

'No, but I mean it must be so exasperating to think that two doors away there's somebody who wouldn't need your help. Just a straight make-up, wouldn't it be? No trouble.'

'I adore making-up. It is my most brilliant gift.'

'But she's your find in a way, isn't she? You'd like her to have the part, wouldn't you?'

He rested his hands on her shoulders. '*Ne vous dérangez pas,*' he said. 'Shut up, in fact. Tranquillize yourself, idiot girl.'

'But I want you to tell me.'

'Then I tell you. Yes, I would like to see this little freak play your part because she is in fact a little freak. She has dropped into this theatre like an accident in somebody else's dream and the effect is fantastic. But she is well content to remain off-stage and it is you who play and we have faith in you and wish you well with all our hearts.'

'That's very nice of you,' Gay said.

'What a sour voice! It is true. And now reflect. Reflect upon the minuteness of Edmund Kean, upon Sarah's one leg and upon Irving's two, upon ugly actresses who convince their audiences they are beautiful and old actors who persuade them they are young. It is all in the mind, the spirit and the preparation. What does Adam say? Think in, and then play out. Do so.'

'I can't,' Gay said between her teeth. 'I can't.' She twisted in her chair. He lifted his fingers away from her face quickly, with a wide gesture. 'Jacko,' she said. 'There's a jinx on this night. Jacko, did you know? It was on the night of the Combined Arts Ball that it happened.'

'What is this foolishness?'

'You know. Five years ago. The stage-hands were talking about it. I heard them. The gas-fire case. The night that man was murdered. Everyone knows.'

'Be silent!' Jacko said loudly. 'This is idiocy. I forbid you to speak of it. The chatter of morons. The Combined Arts Ball has no fixed

date and if it had, shall an assembly of British bourgeoisie in bad
fancy-dress control our destiny? I am ashamed of you. You are altogether too stupid. Master yourself.'

'It's not only that. It's everything. I can't face it.'

His fingers closed down on her shoulders. 'Master yourself,' he
said. 'You must. If you cry I shall beat you and wipe your make-up
across your face. I defy you to cry.'

He cleaned his hands, tipped her head forward and began to massage the nape of her neck. 'There are all sorts of things,' he said, 'that
you must remember and as many more to forget. Forget the little freak
and the troubles of today. Remember to relax all your muscles and also
your nerves and your thoughts. Remember the girl in the play and the
faith I have in you, and Adam and also your Uncle Bennington.'

'Spare me my Uncle Bennington, Jacko. If my Uncle Bennington
had left me where I belong, in fortnightly rep, I wouldn't be facing
this hell. I know what everyone thinks of Uncle Ben and I agree with
them. I never want to see him again. I hate him. He's made me go
on with this. I wanted to throw the part in. It's not my part. I loathe
it. No, I don't loathe it, that's not true. I loathe myself for letting
everybody down. Oh, God, Jacko, what am I going to do.'

Across the bowed head Jacko looked at his own reflection and
poked a face at it.

'You shall play this part,' he said through his teeth, 'mouse-heart,
skunk-girl. You shall play. Think of nothing. Unbridle your infinite
capacity for inertia and be dumb.'

Watching himself, he arranged his face in an unconvincing glower
and fetched up a Shakespearian belly-voice.

'*The devil damn thee black thou creamfaced loon. Where gottest thou that
goose-look?*'

He caught his breath. Beneath his fingers, Gay's neck stiffened. He
began to swear elaborately, in French and in a whisper.

'Jacko. *Jacko.* Where does that line come?'

'I invented it.'

'You didn't. You *didn't*. It's Macbeth,' she wailed. '*You've quoted
from Macbeth!*' and burst into a flurry of terrified weeping.

'Great suffering and all-enduring Saints of God,' apostrophized
Jacko, 'give me some patience with this Quaking Thing.'

But Gay's cries mounted in a sharp crescendo. She flung out her arms and beat with her fists on the dressing-table. A bottle of wet-white rocked to and fro, over-balanced, rapped smartly against the looking-glass and fell over. A neatly splintered star frosted the surface of the glass.

Gay pointed to it with an air of crazy triumph, snatched up her towel, and scrubbed it across her make-up. She thrust her face, blotched and streaked with black cosmetic, at Jacko.

'*Don't you like what you see?*' she quoted, and rocketed into genuine hysteria.

Five minutes later Jacko walked down the passage towards Adam Poole's room leaving J.G., who had rushed to the rescue in his shirt-sleeves, in helpless contemplation of the screaming Gay. Jacko disregarded the open doors and the anxious painted faces that looked out at him.

Bennington shouted from his room:

'What the hell goes on? Who *is* that?'

'Listen,' Jacko began, thrusting his head in at the door. He looked at Bennington and stopped short. 'Stay where you are,' he said and crossed the passage to Poole's room.

Poole had swung round in his chair to face the door. Bob Cringle stood beside him twisting a towel in his hands.

'Well?' Poole said. 'What is it? Is it Gay?'

'She's gone up. Sky high. I can't do anything nor can J.G. and I don't believe anyone can. She refuses to go on.'

'Where's John. Is this his doing?'

'God knows. I don't think so. He came in an hour ago and said he'd be back at five-to-seven.'

'Has Ben tried?'

'She does nothing but scream that she never wants to see him again. In my opinion, Ben would be fatal.'

'He must be able to hear all this.'

'I told him to stay where he is.'

Poole looked sharply at Jacko and went out. Gay's laughter had broken down in a storm of irregular sobbing that could be heard quite clearly. Helena Hamilton called out, 'Adam, shall I go to her?' and he answered from the passage, 'Better not I think.'

He was some time with Gay. They heard her shouting. 'No. No. I won't go on. No,' over and over again like an automaton.

When he came out he went to Helena Hamilton's room. She was dressed and made-up. Martyn, with an ashen face, stood inside the doorway.

'I'm sorry, darling,' Poole said, 'but you'll have to do without a dresser.'

The call-boy came down the passage chanting:

'Half-hour. Half-hour, please.'

Poole and Martyn looked at each other.

'You'll be all right,' he said.

CHAPTER 6

Performance

At ten-to-eight Martyn stood by the entrance.

She was dressed in Gay's clothes and Jacko had made her up very lightly. They had all wished her luck: J.G., Parry Percival, Helena Hamilton, Adam Poole, Clem Smith and even the dressers and stagehands.

There had been something real and touching in their way of doing this so that, even in her terror, she had felt they were good and very kind. Bennington alone had not wished her well but he had kept right away and this abstention, she thought, showed a certain generosity.

She no longer felt sick but the lining of her mouth and throat was harsh as if, in fact, she had actually vomited. She thought her sense of hearing must have become distorted. The actors' voices on the other side of the canvas wall had the remote quality of voices in a nightmare whereas the hammer-blows of her heart and the rustle of her dress that accompanied them sounded exceeding loud.

She saw the frames of the set, their lashings and painted legends, 'Act I, P. 2' and the door which she was to open. She could look into the prompt corner where the ASM followed the lighted script with his finger and where, high above him, the electrician leaned over his perch, watching the play. The stage-lights were reflected into his face. Everything was monstrous in its preoccupation. Martyn was alone.

She tried to command the upsurge of panic in her heart, to practise an approach to her ordeal, to create, in place of these implacable realities, the reality of the house in the play and that part of it in which now, out of sight of the audience, she must already have her being. This attempt went down before the clamour of her nerves. 'I'm going to fail,' she thought.

Jacko came round the set. She hoped he wouldn't speak to her and as if he sensed this wish, he stopped at a distance and waited.

'I must listen,' she thought. 'I'm not listening. I don't know where they've got to. I've forgotten which way the door opens. I've missed my cue.' Her inside deflated and despair griped it like a colic.

She turned and found Poole beside her.

'You're all right,' he said. 'The door opens on. You can do it. Now, my girl. On you go.'

Martyn didn't hear the round of applause with which a London audience greets a player who appears at short notice.

She was on. She had made her entry and was engulfed in the play.

II

Dr Rutherford sat in the OP box with his massive shoulder turned to the house and his gloved hands folded together on the balustrade. His face was in shadow but the stage-lights just touched the bulging curve of his old-fashioned shirt-front. He was monumentally still. One of the critics, an elderly man, said in an aside to a colleague, that Rutherford reminded him of Watt's picture of the Minotaur.

For the greater part of the first act he was alone, having, as he had explained in the office, no masochistic itch to invite a guest to a Roman holiday where he himself was the major sacrifice. Towards the end of the act, however, Bob Grantley came into the box and stood behind him. Grantley's attention was divided. Sometimes he looked down through beams of spot-lights at the stalls, cobbled with heads, sometimes at the stage and sometimes, sideways and with caution, at the doctor himself. Really, Grantley thought, he was quite uncomfortably motionless. One couldn't tell what he was thinking and one hesitated, the Lord knew, to ask him.

Down on the stage Clark Bennington and Parry Percival and J.G. Darcey had opened the long crescendo leading to Helena's entrance.

Grantley thought suddenly how vividly an actor's nature could be exposed on the stage: there was for instance a kind of bed-rock nice-ness about old J.G., a youthfulness of spirit that declaimed itself through the superimposed make-up, the characterization and J.G.'s indisputable middle-age. And Bennington? And Percival? Grantley had begun to consider them in these terms when Percival, speaking one of his colourless lines, turned down-stage. Bennington moved centre, looked at Darcey and neatly sketched a parody of Percival's somewhat finicking movement. The theatre was filled with laughter. Percival turned quickly, Bennington smiled innocently at him, pro-longing the laugh.

Grantley looked apprehensively at the doctor.

'Is that new?' he ventured in a whisper. 'That business?'

The doctor didn't answer and Grantley wondered if he only imag-ined that the great hands on the balustrade had closed more tightly over each other.

Helena Hamilton came on to a storm of applause and with her entrance the action was roused to a new excitement and was inten-sified with every word she uttered. The theatre grew warm with her presence and with a sense of heightened surprise.

'Now they're all on,' Grantley thought, 'except Adam and the girl.'

He drew a chair forward stealthily and sat behind Rutherford.

'It's going enormously,' he murmured to the massive shoulder. 'Terrific, old boy.' And because he was nervous he added: 'This brings the girl on, doesn't it?'

For the first time, the doctor spoke. His lips scarcely moved. A submerged voice uttered within him. 'Hence,' it said, 'heap of wrath, foul indigested lump.'

'Sorry, old boy,' whispered Grantley and began to wonder what hope in hell there was of persuading the distinguished author to have a drink in the office during the interval with a hand-picked number of important persons.

He was still preoccupied with this problem when a side door in the set opened and a dark girl with short hair walked out on the stage.

Grantley joined in the kindly applause. The doctor remained immovable.

The players swept up to their major climax, Adam came on and five minutes later the curtain fell on the first act. The hands of the audience filled the house with a storm of rain. The storm swelled prodigiously and persisted even after the lights had come up.

'Ah, good girl,' Bob Grantley stammered, filled with the sudden and excessive emotion of the theatre. 'Good old Adam. Jolly good show!'

Greatly daring, he clapped the doctor on the shoulders.

The doctor remained immovable.

Grantley edged away to the back of the box. 'I must get back,' he said. 'Look, John, there are one or two people coming to the office for a drink who would be – '

The doctor turned massively in his seat and faced him.

'No,' he said, 'thank you.'

'Well, but look, dear boy, it's just one of those things. You know how it is, John, you know how – '

'Shut up,' said the doctor, without any particular malice. 'I'm going back-stage,' he added. He rose and turned away from the audience. 'I have no desire to swill tepid spirits with minor celebrities among the backsides of sandblasted gods. Thank you, however. See you later.'

He opened the pass-door at the back of the box.

'You're pleased, aren't you?' Grantley said. 'You *must* be pleased.'

'Must I? Must I indeed?'

'With the girl, at least? So far?'

'The wench is a good wench. So far. I go to tell her so. By your leave, Robert.'

He lumbered through the pass-door and Grantley heard him plunge dangerously down the narrow stairway to the stage.

III

Dr Rutherford emerged in a kaleidoscopic world: a world where walls fell softly apart, landscapes ascended into darkness and stairways turned and moved aside. A blue haze rose from the stage which was itself in motion. Jacko's first set revolved bodily, giving way to a new and more distorted version of itself which came to rest, facing the curtain. Masking pieces were run forward to frame it in. The doctor started off for the dressing-room passage and was at once involved with moving flats. 'If you please, sir.' 'Stand aside, there, *please*.' 'Clear stage, *by* your leave.' His bulky shape was screened and exposed again and again plunged forward confusedly. Warning bells rang, the call-boy began to chant: 'Second Act beginners, please. Second Act.'

'Lights,' Clem Smith said.

The shifting world stood still. Circuit by circuit the lights came on and bore down on the acting area. The last toggle-line slapped home and was made fast and the sweating stage-hands walked disinterestedly off the set. Clem Smith, with his back to the curtain, made a final check. 'Clear stage,' he said and looked at his watch. The curtain-hand climbed an iron ladder.

'Six minutes,' said the ASM. He wrote it on his chart. Clem moved into the prompt corner. 'Right,' he said. 'Actors, please.'

J. G. Darcey and Parry Percival walked on to the set and took up their positions. Helena Hamilton came out of her dressing-room. She stood with her hands clasped lightly at her waist at a little distance from the door by which she must enter. A figure emerged from the shadows near the passage and went up to her.

'Miss Hamilton,' Martyn said nervously, 'I'm not on for your quick change. I can do it.'

Helena turned. She looked at Martyn for a moment with an odd fixedness. Then a smile of extraordinary charm broke across her face and she took Martyn's head lightly between her hands.

'My dear child,' she murmured, 'my ridiculous child.' She hesitated for a moment and then said briskly: 'I've got a new dresser.'

'A new dresser?'

'Jacko. He's most efficient.'

Poole came down the passage. She turned to him and linked her arm through his. 'She's going to be splendid in her scene,' she said. 'Isn't she?'

Poole said: 'Keep it up, Kate. All's well.' And in the look he gave Helena Hamilton there was something of comradeship, something of compassion and something, perhaps, of gratitude.

Dr Rutherford emerged from the passage and addressed himself to Martyn: 'Here!' he said. 'I've been looking for you, my pretty. You might be a lot worse, considering, but you haven't done anything yet. When you play this next scene, my poppet, these few precepts in thy – '

'No, John,' Poole and Helena Hamilton said together. 'Not now.'

He glowered at them. Poole nodded to Martyn who began to move away but had not got far before she heard Rutherford say: 'Have you tackled that fellow? Did you see it? Where is he? By God, when I get at him – '

'Stand by,' said Clem Smith.

'Quiet, John,' said Poole imperatively. 'Back to your box, sir.'

The curtain rose on the second act.

For the rest of her life the physical events that were encompassed by the actual performance of the play were to be almost lost for Martyn: indeed she could not be perfectly certain that they had happened at all. She might have been under hypnosis or some partial anaesthesia for all the reality they afterwards retained.

This odd condition which was perhaps the result of some kind of physical compensation for the extreme assault on her nerves and emotion, persisted until she made her final exit in the last act. It happened some time before the curtain. The character she played was the first to relinquish its hold and to fade out of the picture. She came off and returned to her corner near the entry into the passage. The others were all on, the dressers and stage-staff, drawn by the hazards of a first night watched from the side and Jacko was near the prompt corner. The passage and dressing-rooms seemed deserted and Martyn was quite alone. She began to emerge from her trance-like suspension. Parry Percival and J.G. Darcey came off and, in turn, spoke to her.

Parry said incoherently: 'Darling, you were perfectly splendid. I'm just *so* angry at the moment I can't *speak* but I do congratulate you.'

Martyn saw that he actually trembled with an emotion that was, she must suppose, fury. Out of the dream from which she was not yet fully awakened there came a memory of gargantuan laughter and she thought she associated it with Bennington and with Percival. He said: 'This settles it. I'm taking action. God, this settles it!' and darted down the passage.

Martyn thought, still confusedly, that she should go to the dressing-room and tidy her make-up for the curtain call. But it was not her dressing-room, it was Gay's and she felt uneasy about it. While she hesitated J. G. Darcey came off.

He put his hand on Martyn's shoulder. 'Well done, child,' he said. 'A very creditable performance.'

Martyn thanked him and, on an impulse, added: 'Mr Darcey, is Gay still here? Should I say something to her? I'd like to but I know how she must feel and I don't want to be clumsy.'

He waited for a moment, looking at her. 'She's in the greenroom,' he said. 'Perhaps later. Not now, I think. Nice of you.'

'I won't unless you say so, then.'

He made her a little bow. 'I am at your service,' he said and followed Percival down the passage.

Jacko came round the set with the stage-hand who was to fire the effects gun. When he saw Martyn his whole face split in a grin. He took her hands in his and kissed them and she was overwhelmed with shyness.

'But your face,' he said, wrinkling his own into a monkey's grimace. 'It shines like a good deed in a naughty world. Do not touch it yourself. To your dressing-room. I come in two minutes. Away, before your ears are blasted.'

He moved down-stage, applied his eye to a secret hole in the set through which he could watch the action and held out his arm in warning to the stage-hand who then lifted the effects gun. Martyn went down the passage as Bennington came off. He caught her up: 'Miss Tarne. Wait a moment, will you?'

Dreading another intolerable encounter Martyn faced him. His make-up had been designed to exhibit the brutality of the character and did so all too successfully. The lips were painted a florid red, the pouches under the eyes and the sensual drag from the nostrils to the mouth had been carefully emphasized. He was sweating heavily through the greasepaint and his face glistened in the dull light of the passage.

'I just wanted to say'– he began and at that moment the gun was fired and Martyn gave an involuntary cry; he went on talking – 'when I see it,' he was saying, 'I suppose you aren't to be blamed for that. You saw your chance and took it. Gay and Adam tell me you offered to get out and were not allowed to go. That may be fair enough: I wouldn't know. But I'm not worrying about that.' He spoke disjointedly. It was as if his thoughts were too disordered for any coherent expression. 'I just wanted to tell you that you needn't suppose what I'm going to do – you needn't think – I mean – '

He touched his shining face with the palm of his hand. Jacko came down the passage and took Martyn by the elbow. 'Quick,' he said, 'into your room. You want powdering, Ben. Excuse me.'

Bennington went into his own room. Jacko thrust Martyn into hers, and leaving the door open followed Bennington. She heard him say: 'Take care with your upper lip. It is dripping with sweat.' He darted back to Martyn, stood her near the dressing-shelf and, with an expression of the utmost concentration effected a number of what he called running repairs to her make-up and her hair. They heard Percival and Darcey go past on their way to the stage. A humming noise caused by some distant dynamo made itself heard, the tap in the wash-basin dripped, the voices on the stage sounded intermittently. Martyn looked at Gay's make-up box, at her dressing-gown and at the array of mascots on the shelf and wished very heavily that Jacko would have done. Presently the call-boy came down the passage with his summons for the final curtain. 'Come,' said Jacko.

He took her round to the prompt side.

Here she found a group already waiting: Darcey and Percival, Clem Smith, the two dressers and, at a distance, one or two stage-hands. They all watched the final scene between Helena Hamilton and Adam Poole. In this scene Rutherford tied up and stated finally the whole thesis of his play. The man was faced with his ultimate decision. Would he stay and attempt, with the woman, to establish a sane and enlightened formula for living in place of the one he himself had destroyed or would he go back to his island community and attempt a further development within himself and in a less complex environment? As throughout the play, the conflict was set out in terms of human and personal relationships. It could be played like many another love scene, purely on those terms. Or it could be so handled that the wider implications could be felt by the audience and in the hands of these two players that was what happened. The play ended with them pledging themselves to each other and to an incredible task. As Poole spoke the last lines the electrician, with one eye on Clem below, played madly over his switchboard. The entire set changed its aspect, seemed to dissolve, turned threadbare, a skeleton, a wraith, while beyond it a wide stylized landscape was flooded with light and became as Poole spoke the tag, the background upon which the curtain fell.

'Might as well be back in panto,' said the electrician leaning on his dimmers, 'we got the transformation scene. All we want's the bloody fairy queen.'

It was at this moment, when the applause seemed to surge forward and beat against the curtains, when Clem shouted: 'All on,' and Dr Rutherford plunged out of the OP pass-door, when the players walked on and linked hands, that Poole, looking hurriedly along the line, said: 'Where's Ben?'

One of those panic-stricken crises peculiar to the theatre boiled up on the instant. From her position between Darcey and Percival on the stage Martyn saw the call-boy make some kind of protest to Clem Smith and disappear. Above the applause they heard him hare down the passage, yelling: 'Mr Bennington! Mr Bennington! Please! You're on!'

'We can't wait,' Poole shouted. 'Take it up, Clem.'

The curtain rose and Martyn looked into a sea of faces and hands. She felt herself led forward into the roaring swell, bowed with the others, felt Darcey's and Percival's hands tighten on hers, bowed again and with them retreated a few steps up-stage as the first curtain fell.

'Well?' Poole shouted into the wings. The call-boy could be heard beating on the dressing-room door.

Percival said: 'What's the betting he comes on for a star call?'

'He's passed out,' said Darcey. 'Had one or two more since he came off.'

'By God, I wouldn't cry if he never came to.'

'Go on, Clem,' said Poole.

The curtain rose and fell again, twice. Percival and Darcey took Martyn off and it went up again on Poole and Helena Hamilton, this time to those cries of 'bravo' that reach the actors as a long open sound like the voice of a singing wind. In the wings, Clem Smith with his eyes on the stage was saying repeatedly: 'He doesn't answer. He's locked in. The b—— doesn't answer.'

Martyn saw Poole coming towards her and stood aside. He seemed to tower over her as he took her hand. 'Come along,' he said. Darcey and Percival and the group offstage began to clap.

Poole led her on. She felt herself resisting and heard him say: 'Yes, it's all right.'

So bereft was Martyn of her normal stage-wiseness that he had to tell her to bow. She did so and wondered why there was a warm sound of laughter in the applause. She looked at Poole, found he was bowing to her and bent her head under his smile. He returned her to the wings.

They were all on again. Dr Rutherford came out from the OP corner. The cast joined in the applause. Martyn's heart had begun to sing so loudly that it was like to deafen every emotion but a universal gratitude. She thought Rutherford looked like an old lion standing there in his out-of-date evening-dress, his hair ruffled, his gloved hand touching his bulging shirt, bowing in an unwieldy manner to the audience and to the cast. He moved forward and the theatre was abruptly silent: silent, but for an obscure and intermittent thudding in the dressing-room passage. Clem Smith said something to the ASM and rushed away, jingling keys.

'Hah,' said Dr Rutherford with a preliminary bellow. 'Hah – thankee. I'm much obliged to you, ladies and gentlemen and to the actors. The actors are much obliged, no doubt, to you but not necessarily to me.' Here the audience laughed and the actors smiled. 'I am not able to judge,' the doctor continued with a rich roll in his voice, 'whether you have extracted from this play the substance of its argument. If you have done so we may all felicitate each other with the indiscriminate enthusiasm characteristic of these occasions: if you have not, I for my part am not prepared to say where the blame should rest.'

A solitary man laughed in the audience. The doctor rolled an eye at him and, with this clownish trick, brought the house down. 'The prettiest epilogue to a play that I am acquainted with,' he went on, 'is (as I need perhaps hardly mention to so intelligent an audience) that written for a boy-actor by William Shakespeare. I am neither a boy nor an actor but I beg leave to end by quoting to you. "If it be true that good wine needs no bush – "'

'Gas!' Parry Percival said under his breath. Martyn, who thought the doctor was going well, glanced indignantly at Parry and was astonished to see that he looked frightened.

'"– therefore",' the doctor was saying arrogantly, '"to beg will not become me – "'

'Gas!' said an imperative voice off-stage and someone else ran noisily round the back of the set.

And then Martyn smelt it. Gas.

IV

To the actors it seemed afterwards as if they had been fantastically slow to understand that disaster had come upon the theatre. The curtain went down on Dr Rutherford's last word. There was a further outbreak of applause. Someone off-stage shouted: 'The King, for God's sake,' and at once the anthem rolled out disinterestedly in the well. Poole ran off the stage and was met by Clem Smith who had a bunch of keys in his hand. The rest followed him.

The area back-stage reeked of gas.

It was extraordinary how little was said. The players stood together and looked about them with the question in their faces that they were unable to ask.

Poole said: 'Keep all visitors out, Clem. Send them to the foyer.' And at once the ASM spoke into the prompt telephone. Bob Grantley burst through the pass-door, beaming from ear to ear.

'*Stupendous!*' he shouted. 'John! Ella! Adam! My God, chaps, you've done it – '

He stood, stock-still, his arms extended, the smile dying on his face.

'Go back, Bob,' Poole said. 'Cope with the people. Ask our guests to go on and not wait for us. Ben's ill. Clem: get all available doors open. We want air.'

Grantley said: 'Gas?'

'Quick,' Poole said. 'Take them with you. Settle them down and explain. He's ill. Then ring me here. But quickly, Bob. Quickly.'

Grantley went out without another word.

'Where is he?' Dr Rutherford demanded.

Helena Hamilton suddenly said: 'Adam?'

'Go on to the stage, Ella. It's better you shouldn't be here, believe me. Kate will stay with you. I'll come in a moment.'

'Here you are, Doctor,' said Clem Smith.

There was a blundering sound in the direction of the passage. Rutherford said, 'Open the dock doors,' and went behind the set.

Poole thrust Helena through the prompt entry and shut the door behind her. Draughts of cold air came through the side entrances.

'Kate,' Poole said, 'go in and keep her there if you can. Will you? And, Kate – '

Rutherford reappeared and with him four stage-hands bearing with difficulty the inert body of Clark Bennington, the head swinging upside down between the two leaders, its mouth wide open.

Poole moved quickly but he was too late to shield Martyn.

'Never mind,' he said. 'Go in with Helena.'

'Anyone here done respiration for gassed cases?' Dr Rutherford demanded. 'I can start but I'm not good for long.'

'I can,' said the ASM. 'I was a warden.'

'I can,' said Jacko.

'And I,' said Poole.

'In the dock then. Shut these doors and open the outer ones.'

Kneeling by Helena Hamilton and holding her hand, Martyn heard the doors roll back and the shambling steps go into the dock. The doors crashed behind them.

Martyn said: 'They're giving him respiration, Dr Rutherford's there.'

Helena nodded with an air of sagacity. Her face was quite without expression, and she was shivering.

'I'll get your coat,' Martyn said. It was in the improvised dressing-room on the OP side. She was back in a moment and put Helena into it as if she was a child, guiding her arms and wrapping the fur about her.

A voice off-stage – J. G. Darcey's – said: 'Where's Gay? Is Gay still in the greenroom?'

Martyn was astonished when Helena, behind the mask that had become her face, said loudly: 'Yes. She's there. In the greenroom.'

There was a moment's silence and then J.G. said: 'She mustn't stay there. Good God – '

They heard him go away.

Parry Percival's voice announced abruptly that he was going to be sick. 'But where?' he cried distractedly. 'Where?'

'In your dressing-room for Pete's sake,' Clem Smith said.

'It'll be full of gas. Oh, *really*!' There was an agonized and not quite silent interval. 'I couldn't be more sorry,' Percival said weakly.

'I want,' Helena said, 'to know what happened. I want to see Adam. Ask him to come, please.'

Martyn made for the door but before she reached it Dr Rutherford came in, followed by Poole. Rutherford had taken off his coat and was a fantastic sight in boiled shirt, black trousers and red braces.

'Well, Ella,' he said, 'this is not a nice business. We're doing everything that can be done. I'm getting a new oxygen thing in as quickly as possible. There have been some remarkable saves in these cases. But I think you ought to know it's a thinnish chance. There's no pulse and so on.'

'I want,' she said, holding out her hand to Poole, 'to know what happened.'

Poole said gently: 'All right, Ella, you shall. It looks as if Ben locked himself in after his exit and then turned the gas-fire off – and on again. When Clem unlocked the door and went in he found Ben on the floor. His head was near the fire and a coat over both. He could only have been like that for quite a short time.'

'This theatre,' she said. 'This awful theatre.'

Poole looked as if he would make some kind of protest but after a moment's hesitation he said: 'All right, Ella. Perhaps it did suggest the means but if he had made up his mind he would, in any case, have found the means.'

'Why?' she said. 'Why has he done it?'

Dr Rutherford growled inarticulately and went out. They heard him open and shut the dock doors. Poole sat down by Helena and took her hands in his. Martyn was going but he looked up at her and said: 'No, don't. Don't go, Kate,' and she waited near the door.

'This is no time,' Poole said, 'to speculate. He may be saved. If he isn't, then we shall of course ask ourselves just why. But he was in a bad way, Ella. He'd gone to pieces and he knew it.'

'I wasn't much help,' she said, 'was I? Though it's true to say I did try for quite a long time.'

'Indeed you did. There's one thing you must be told. If it's no go with Ben, we'll have to inform the police.'

She put her hand to her forehead as if she was puzzled. 'The police?' she repeated and stared at him. 'No, darling, no!' she cried and after a moment whispered. 'They might think – oh, darling, darling, darling, the Lord knows what they think!'

The door up-stage opened and Gay Gainsford came in, followed by Darcey.

She was in her street clothes and at some time during the evening had made extensive repairs to her face which wore, at the moment, an expression oddly compounded of triumph and distraction. Before she could speak she was seized with a paroxysm of coughing.

Darcey said: 'Is it all right for Gay to wait here?'

'Yes, of course,' said Helena.

He went out and Poole followed him saying he would return.

'Darling,' Miss Gainsford gasped. 'I knew. I knew as soon as I smelt it. There's a Thing in this theatre. Everything pointed to it. I just sat there and *knew*.' She coughed again. 'Oh I do feel so sick,' she said.

'Gay for pity's sake what are you talking about?' Helena said.

'It was Fate, I felt. I wasn't a bit surprised. I just knew something had to happen tonight.'

'Do you mean to say,' Helena murmured, and the wraith of her gift for irony was on her mouth, 'that you just sat in the greenroom with your finger raised, telling yourself it was Fate?'

'Darling Aunty – I'm sorry. I forgot – darling, Ella, wasn't it amazing?'

Helena made a little gesture of defeat. Miss Gainsford looked at her for a moment and then, with the prettiest air of compassion, knelt at her feet. 'Sweet,' she said, 'I'm so terribly, terribly sorry. We're together in this, aren't we? He was my uncle and your husband.'

'True enough,' said Helena. She looked at Martyn over the head bent in devoted commiseration, and shook her own helplessly. Gay Gainsford sank into a sitting posture and leant her cheek against Helena's hand. The hand, after a courteous interval, was withdrawn.

There followed a very long silence. Martyn sat at a distance and wondered if there was anything in the world she could do to help. There was an intermittent murmur of voices somewhere off-stage. Gay Gainsford, feeling perhaps that she had sustained her position long enough, moved by gradual degrees away from her aunt by marriage, rose and, sighing heavily, transferred herself to the sofa.

Time dragged on, mostly in silence. Helena lit one cigarette from the butt of another, Gay sighed with infuriating punctuality and Martyn's thoughts drifted sadly about the evaporation of her small triumph.

Presently there were sounds of arrival. One or two persons walked round the set from the outside entry to the dock and were evidently admitted into it.

'Who can that be, I wonder?' Helena Hamilton asked idly, and after a moment, 'Is Jacko about?'

'I'll see,' said Martyn.

She found Jacko off-stage with Darcey and Parry Percival. Percival was saying: 'Well, naturally, nobody wants to go to the party but I must say that as one is quite evidently useless here I don't see why one can't go home.'

Jacko said: 'You would be recalled by the police, I dare say, if you went.'

He caught sight of Martyn who went up to him. His face was beaded with sweat. 'What is it, my small?' he asked. 'This is a sad epilogue to your success story. Never mind. What is it?'

'I think Miss Hamilton would like to see you?'

'Then, I come. It is time, in any case.'

He took her by the elbow and they went in together. When Helena saw him she seemed to rouse herself. 'Jacko?' she said.

He didn't answer and she got up quickly and went to him. 'Jacko! What is it? Has it happened?'

Jacko's hands, so refined and delicate that they seemed like those of another man, touched her hair and her face.

'It has happened,' he said. 'We have tried very hard but nothing is any good at all and there is no more to be done. He has taken wing.'

Gay Gainsford broke into a fit of sobbing but Helena stooped her head to Jacko's shoulder and when his arms had closed about her said: 'Help me to feel something, Jacko. I'm quite empty of feeling. Help me to be sorry.'

Above her head, Jacko's face, glistening with sweat, grotesque and primitive, had the fixed inscrutability of a classic mask.

CHAPTER 7

Disaster

Clem Smith rang up the police as soon as Dr Rutherford said that Bennington was beyond recovery and within five minutes a constable and sergeant had appeared at the stage-door. They went into the dock with Rutherford and then to Bennington's dressing-room where they remained alone for some time. During this period an aimless discussion developed among the members of the company about where they should go. Clem Smith suggested the greenroom as the warmest place and added, tactlessly, that the fumes had probably dispersed and if so there was no reason why they shouldn't light the fire. Both Parry Percival and Gay Gainsford had made an outcry against this suggestion on the grounds of delicacy and susceptibility. Darcey supported Gay, the ASM suggested the offices and Jacko the auditorium. Doctor Rutherford, who appeared to be less upset than anyone else, merely remarked that 'all places that the eye of Heaven visits, are to a wise man, ports and happy havens,' which, as Percival said acidly, got them nowhere.

Finally Poole asked if the central-heating couldn't be stoked up and a stage-hand was dispatched to the underworld to find out. Evidently he met with success as presently the air became less chilled. With only a spatter of desultory conversation, the players sat about the stage and cleaned their faces. And they listened.

They heard the two men come back along the passage and separate. Then the central door opened and the young constable came in.

He was a tall good-looking youth with a charming smile.

'The sergeant,' he said, 'has asked me to explain that he's tele-phoning Scotland Yard. He couldn't be more sorry but he's afraid he'll have to ask everybody to wait until he gets his instructions. He's sure you'll understand that it's just a matter of routine.'

He might have been apologizing for his mother's late arrival at her own dinner-party.

He was about to withdraw when Dr Rutherford said: 'Hi! Sonny!'

'Yes, sir?' said the young constable obligingly.

'You intrigue me. You talk, as they say, like a book. *Non sine dis animosus infans.* You swear with a good grace and wear your boots very smooth, do you not?'

The young constable was, it seemed, only momentarily taken aback. He said: 'Well, sir, for my boots they are after the Dogberry fashion and for my swearing, sir, it goes by the book.'

The doctor who, until now, had seemed to share the general feel-ing of oppression and shock, appeared to cheer up with indecent haste. He was, in fact, clearly enchanted: 'Definite, definite, well-educated infant,' he quoted exultantly.

'I mean that in court, sir, we swear by the Book. But I'm afraid, sir,' added the young constable apologetically, 'that I'm not much of a hand at "Bardinage". My purse is empty already. If you'll excuse me,' he concluded, with a civil glance round the company, 'I'll just – '

He was again about to withdraw when his sergeant came in at the OP entrance.

'Good evening, ladies and gentlemen,' the sergeant said in what Martyn, for one, felt was the regulation manner. 'Very sorry to keep you, I'm sure. Sad business. In these cases we have to do a routine check-up as you might say. My superior officers will be here in a moment and then, I hope, we shan't be long. Thank you.'

He tramped across the stage, said something inaudible to the con-stable and was heard to go into the dock. The constable took a chair from the prompt corner, placed it in the proscenium entrance and, with a modest air, sat on it. His glance fell upon Martyn and he smiled at her. They were the youngest persons there and it was as if they signalled in a friendly manner to each other. In turning away from this pleasant exchange, Martyn found that Poole was watching her with fixed and, it seemed, angry glare. To her fury she found that she was very much disturbed by this circumstance.

They had by this time all cleaned their faces. Helena Hamilton with an unsteady hand put on a light street make-up. The men looked ghastly in the cold working lights that bleakly illuminated the stage.

Parry Percival said fretfully: 'Well, I must say I do *not* see the smallest point in our hanging about like this.'

The constable was about to answer when they all heard sounds of arrival at the stage-door. He said: 'This will be the party from the Yard, sir,' and crossed to the far exit. The sergeant was heard to join him there.

There was a brief conversation off-stage. A voice said: 'You two go round with Gibson then, will you? I'll join you in a moment.'

The young constable reappeared to usher in a tall man in plain clothes.

'Chief Detective-Inspector Alleyn,' he said.

II

Martyn, in her weary pilgrimage round the West End, had seen men of whom Alleyn at first reminded her. In the neighbourhood of the St James's Theatre, they had emerged from clubs, from restaurants and from enchanting and preposterous shops. There had been something in their bearing and their clothes that gave them a precise definition. But when she looked more closely at Inspector Alleyn's face, this association became modified. It was a spare and scholarly face with a monkish look about it.

Martyn had formed the habit of thinking of people's voices in terms of colour. Helena Hamilton's voice, for instance, was for Martyn golden, Gay Gainsford's pink, Darcey's brown and Adam Poole's violet. When Alleyn spoke she decided that his voice was a royal blue of the clearest sort.

Reminding herself that this was no time to indulge this freakish habit of classification she gave him her full attention.

'You will, I'm sure,' he was saying, 'realize that in these cases, our job is simply to determine that they are, on the face of it, what they appear to be. In order to do this effectively we are obliged to make a fairly thorough examination of the scene as we find it.

This takes a little time always but if everything's quite straightforward, as I expect it will be, we won't keep you very long. Is that
clear?'

He looked round his small audience. Poole said at once: 'Yes, of
course. We all understand. At the same time, if it's a matter of taking statements, I'd be grateful if you'd see Miss Hamilton first.'

'Miss Hamilton?' Alleyn said and after a moment's hesitation,
looked at her.

'I'm his wife,' she said. 'I'm Helena Bennington.'

'I'm so sorry. I didn't know. Yes, I'm sure that can be managed.
Probably the best will be for me to see you all together. If everything
seems quite clear there may be no excuse for further interviews. And
now, if you'll excuse me, I'll have a look round and then rejoin you.
There is a doctor among you, isn't there? Dr Rutherford?' Dr
Rutherford cleared his throat portentously. 'Are you he, sir? Perhaps
you'll join us.'

'Indubitably,' said the doctor. 'I had so concluded.'

'Good,' Alleyn said and looked faintly amused. 'Will you lead the
way?'

They were at the door when Jacko suddenly said: 'A moment, if
you please, Chief Inspector.'

'Yes?'

'I would like permission to make soup. There is a filthy small
kitchen-place inhabited only by the night-watchman where I have a
can of prepared soup. Everyone is very cold and fatigued and entirely
empty. My name is Jacques Doré. I am dogsbody-in-waiting in this
theatre and there is much virtue in my soup.'

Alleyn said: 'By all means. Is the kitchen-place that small sink-
room near the dock with the gas-jet in it?'

'But you haven't looked at the place yet!' Parry Percival ejaculated.

'I've been here before,' said Alleyn. 'I remember the theatre. Shall
we get on, Dr Rutherford?'

They went out. Gay Gainsford, whose particular talent, from now
onwards, was to lie in the voicing of disquieting thoughts which her
companions shared but decided to leave unspoken, said in a distracted
manner: '*When* was he here before?' And when nobody answered
she said dramatically: 'I can see it all! He must be the man they sent
that other time.' She paused and collected their reluctant attention.

She laid her hand on J.G.'s arm and raised her voice: 'That's why he's come again,' she announced.

'Come now, dear,' J.G. murmured inadequately and Poole said quickly: 'My *dear* Gay!'

'But I'm all right!' she persisted. 'I'm sure I'm right. Why else should he know about the sink-room?' She looked about her with an air of terrified complacency.

'*And last time,*' she pointed out, '*it was Murder.*'

'Climax,' said Jacko. 'Picture and Slow Curtain! Put your hands together, ladies and gentlemen, for this clever little artiste.'

He went out with his eyes turned up.

'Jacko's terribly hard, isn't he?' Gay said to Darcey. 'After all Uncle Ben *was* my uncle.' She caught sight of Helena Hamilton. 'And your husband,' she said hurriedly, 'of course, darling.'

III

The stage-hands had set up in the dock one of the trestle-tables used for properties. They had laid Clark Bennington's body on it and had covered it with a sheet from the wardrobe-room. The dock was a tall echoing place, concrete floored, with stacks of old flats leaning against the walls. A solitary unprotected lamp bulb, dust-encrusted, hung above the table.

A group of four men in dark overcoats and hats stood beside this improvised bier and it so chanced they had taken up their places at the four corners and looked therefore as if they kept guard over it. Their hats shadowed their faces and they stood in pools of shadow. A fifth man, bareheaded, stood at the foot of the bier and a little removed from it. When the tallest of the men reached out to the margin of the sheet, his arm cast a black bar over its white and eloquent form. His gloved hand dragged down the sheet and exposed a rigid gaping face encrusted with grease-paint. He uncovered his head and the other three, a little awkwardly, followed his example.

'Well, Curtis?' he asked.

Dr Curtis, the police-surgeon, bent over the head, blotting it out with his shadow. He took a flashlamp from his pocket and the face, in this changed light, started out with an altered look as if it had secretly rearranged its expression.

'God!' Curtis muttered. 'He looks pretty ghastly doesn't he. What an atrocious make-up.'

From his removed position Dr Rutherford said loudly: 'My dear man, the make-up was required for My Play. It should, in point of fact, be a damn sight more repellent. But *vanitas vanitatum*. Also: *Mit der Dummheit kämpfen Götter selbst vergebens*. I didn't let them fix him up at all. Thought you'd prefer not.' His voice echoed coldly round the dock.

'Quite so,' Curtis murmured. 'Much better not.'

'Smell very noticeable still,' a thick-set grizzled man observed. 'Always hangs about in these cases,' rejoined the sergeant, 'doesn't it, Mr Fox?'

'We worked damn hard on him,' Dr Rutherford said. 'It never looked like it from the start. Not a hope.'

'Well,' said Curtis, drawing back, 'it all seems straightforward enough, Alleyn. It doesn't call for a very extensive autopsy but of course we'll do the usual things.'

'Lend me your torch a moment,' Alleyn said, and after a moment: 'Very heavy make-up, isn't it? He's so thickly powdered.'

'He needed it. He sweated,' Dr Rutherford said, 'like a pig. Alcohol and a dicky heart.'

'Did you look after him, sir?'

'Not I. I don't practise nowadays. The alcohol declared itself and he used to talk about a heart condition. Valvula trouble, I should imagine. I don't know who his medical man was. His wife can tell you.'

Dr Curtis replaced the sheet. 'That,' he said to Rutherford, 'might account for him going quickly.'

'Certainly.'

'There's a mark under the jaw,' Alleyn said. 'Did either of you notice it. The make-up is thinner there. Is it a bruise?'

Curtis said: 'I saw it, yes. It might be a bruise. We'll see better when we clean him up.'

'Right. I'll look at the room,' Alleyn said. 'Who found him?'

'The stage-manager,' said Rutherford.

'Then perhaps you wouldn't mind asking him to come along when you rejoin the others. Thank you, so much, Dr Rutherford.

We're glad to have had your report. You'll be called for the inquest, I'm afraid.'

'Hell's teeth, I suppose I shall. So be it.' He moved to the doors. The sergeant obligingly rolled them open and he muttered: 'Thankee,' and with an air of dissatisfaction went out.

Dr Curtis said: 'I'd better go and make professional noises at him.'

'Yes, do,' Alleyn said.

On their way to Bennington's room they passed Jacko and a stage-hand bearing a fragrant steaming can and a number of cups to the stage. In his cubby-hole, Fred Badger was entertaining a group of stage-hands and dressers. They had steaming pannikins in their hands and they eyed the police party in silence.

'Smells very tasty, doesn't it?' Detective-Inspector Fox observed rather wistfully.

The young constable, who was stationed by the door through which Martyn had made her entrance, opened it for the soup-party and shut it after them.

Fox growled: 'Keep your wits about you.'

'Yes, sir,' said the young constable and exhibited his note-book.

Clem Smith was waiting for them in Bennington's room. The lights were full on and a white glare beat on the dressing-shelf and walls. Bennington's street clothes and his suit for the first act hung on coat-hangers along the walls. His make-up was laid out on a towel and the shelf was littered with small objects that in their casual air of usage suggested that he had merely left the room for a moment and would return to take them up again. On the floor, hard by the dead gas-fire, lay an overcoat from which the reek of gas, which still hung about the room, seemed to arise. The worn rug was drawn up into wrinkles.

Clem Smith's face was white and anxious under his shock of dark hair. He shook hands jerkily with Alleyn and then looked as if he wondered if he ought to have done so. 'This is a pretty ghastly sort of party,' he muttered, 'isn't it?'

Alleyn said: 'It seems that you came in for the worst part of it. Do you mind telling us what happened?'

Fox moved behind Clem and produced his note-book. Sergeant Gibson began to make a list of the objects in the room. Clem watched him with an air of distaste.

'Easy enough to tell you,' he said. 'He came off about eight minutes before the final curtain and I suppose went straight to this room. When the boy came round for the curtain-call, Ben didn't appear with the others. I didn't notice. There's an important light-cue at the end and I was watching for it. Then, when they all went on, he just wasn't there. We couldn't hold the curtain for long. I sent it up for the first call and the boy went back and hammered on this door. It was locked. He smelt gas and began to yell for Ben and then ran back to tell me what was wrong. I'd got the doctor on for his speech by that time. I left my ASM in charge, took the bunch of extra keys from the prompt corner and tore round here.'

He wetted his lips and fumbled in his pocket. 'Is it safe to smoke,' he asked.

'I'm afraid we'd better wait a little longer,' Alleyn said. 'Sorry.'

'OK. Well, I unlocked the door. As soon as it opened the stink hit me in the face. I don't know why but I expected him to be sitting at the shelf. I don't suppose, really, it was long before I saw him but it seemed fantastically long. He was lying there, by the heater. I could only see his legs and the lower half of his body. The rest was hidden by that coat. It was tucked in behind the heater, and over his head and shoulders. It looked like a tent. I heard the hiss going on underneath it.' Clem rubbed his mouth. 'I don't think,' he said, 'I was as idiotically slow as all this makes me out to be. I don't think honestly, it was more than seconds before I went in. Honestly, I don't think so.'

'I expect you're right about that. Time goes all relative in a crisis.'

'Does it? Good. Well, then: I ran in and hauled the coat away. He was on his left side – his mouth – it was – The lead-in had been disconnected and it was by his mouth, hissing. I turned it off and dragged him by the heels. He sort of stuck on the carpet. Jacko – Jacques Doré bolted in and helped.'

'One moment,' Alleyn said. 'Did you knock over that box of powder on the dressing-table? Either of you?'

Clem Smith stared at it. 'That? No, I didn't go near it and I'd got him half-way to the door when Jacko came in. He must have done it himself.'

'Right. Sorry. Go on.'

'We lifted Ben into the passage and shut his door. At the far end of the passage there's a window, the only one near. We got it open and carried him to it. I think he was dead even then. I'm sure he was. I've seen gassed cases before; in the blitz.'

Alleyn said: 'You seem to have tackled this one like an old hand, at all events.'

'I'm damn glad you think so,' said Clem, and sounded it.

Alleyn looked at the Yale lock on the door. 'This seems in good enough shape,' he said absently.

'It's new,' Clem said. 'There were pretty extensive renovations and a sort of general clean up when Mr Poole took the theatre over. It's useful for the artistes to be able to lock up valuables in their rooms and the old locks were clumsy and rusted up. In any case – ' He stopped and then said uncomfortably: 'The whole place has been repainted and modernized.'

'Including the gas installations?'

'Yes,' said Clem, not looking at Alleyn. 'That's all new too.'

'Two of the old dressing-rooms have been knocked together to form the greenroom?'

'Yes.'

'And there are new dividing walls? And ventilators, now, in the dressing-rooms?'

'Yes,' said Clem unhappily and added: 'I suppose that's why he used his coat.'

'It does look,' Alleyn said without stressing it, 'as if the general idea was to speed things up, doesn't it? All right, Mr Smith, thank you. Would you explain to the people on the stage that I'll come as soon as we've finished our job here? It won't be very long. We'll probably ask you to sign a statement of the actual discovery as you've described it to us. You'll be glad to get away from this room, I expect.'

Inspector Fox had secreted his note-book and now ushered Clem Smith out. Clem appeared to go thankfully.

'Plain sailing, wouldn't you say, Mr Alleyn?' said Fox, looking along the passage. 'Nobody about,' he added. 'I'll leave the door open.'

Alleyn rubbed his nose. 'It looks like plain sailing, Fox, certainly. But in view of the other blasted affair we can't take a damn thing for granted. You weren't on the Jupiter case, were you, Gibson?'

'No, sir,' said Gibson looking up from his note-book. 'Homicide dressed up to look like suicide, wasn't it?'

'It was, indeed. The place has been pretty extensively chopped up and rehashed but the victim was on this side of the passage and in what must have been the room now taken in to make the green-room. Next door there was a gas-fire backing on to his own. The job was done by blowing down the tube next door. This put out the fire in this room and left the gas on, of course. The one next door was then relit. The victim was pretty well dead-drunk and the trick worked. We got the bloke on the traces of crepe-hair and greasepaint he left on the tube.'

'Very careless,' Fox said. 'Silly chap, really.'

'The theatre,' Alleyn said, 'was shut up for a long time. Three or four years at least. Then Adam Poole took it, renamed it the Vulcan and got a permit for renovation. I fancy this is only his second production here.'

'Perhaps,' Fox speculated, 'the past history of the place played on the deceased's mind and led him to do away with himself after the same fashion.'

'Sort of superstitious?' Gibson ventured.

'Not precisely,' said Fox majestically. 'And yet something after that style of thing. They're a very superstitious mob, actors, Fred. Very. And if he had reason, in any case, to entertain the notion of suicide – '

'He must,' Alleyn interjected, 'have also entertained the very nasty notion of throwing suspicion of foul play on his fellow-actors. If there's a gas-fire back to back with this –'

'And there is,' Fox said.

'The devil there is! So what does Bennington do? He recreates as far as possible the whole set-up, leaves no note, no indication, as far as we can see, of his intention to gas himself, and – who's next door, Fox?'

'A Mr Parry Percival.'

'All right. Bennington pushes off, leaving Mr Parry Percival ostensibly in the position of the Jupiter murderer. Rotten sort of suicide that'd be, Br'er Fox.'

'We don't know anything yet, of course,' said Fox.

'We don't and the crashing hellish bore about the whole business lies in the all too obvious fact that we'll have to find out. What's on your inventory, Gibson?'

Sergeant Gibson opened his note-book and adopted his official manner.

'Dressing-table or shelf,' he said. 'One standing mirror. One cardboard box containing false hair, rouge, substance labelled "nose-paste", seven fragments of greasepaint and one unopened box of powder. Shelf. Towel spread out to serve as table-cloth. On towel – one tray containing six sticks of greasepaint. To right of tray, bottle of spirit-adhesive. Bottle containing what appears to be substance known as liquid powder. Open box of powder overturned. Behind box of powder, pile of six pieces of cotton-wool and a roll from which these pieces have been removed.' He looked up at Alleyn. 'Intended to be used for powdering purposes, Mr Alleyn.'

'That's it,' Alleyn said. He was doubled up, peering at the floor under the dressing-shelf. 'Nothing there,' he grunted. 'Go on.'

'To left of tray: cigarette-case with three cigarettes and open box of fifty. Box of matches. Ash-tray. Towel, stained with greasepaint. Behind mirror: Flask: one-sixth full; and used tumbler smelling of spirits.'

Alleyn looked behind the standing glass. 'Furtive sort of cache,' he said. 'Go on.'

'Considerable quantity of powder spilt on shelf and on adjacent floor area. Considerable quantity of ash. Left wall. Clothes. I haven't been through the pockets yet, Mr Alleyn. There's nothing on the floor but powder and some paper ash, original form indistinguishable. Stain as of something burnt on hearth.'

'Go ahead with it then. I wanted,' Alleyn said with a discontented air, 'to *hear* whether I was wrong.'

Fox and Gibson looked placidly at him. 'All right,' he said, 'don't mind me. I'm broody.'

He squatted down by the overcoat. 'It really is the most obscene smell, gas,' he muttered. 'How anybody *can* always passes my comprehension.' He poked in a gingerly manner at the coat. 'Powder over everything,' he grumbled. 'Where had this coat been? On the empty hanger near the door presumably. That's damned rum. Check it with his dresser. We'll have to get Bailey along, Fox. And Thompson. Blast!'

'I'll ring the Yard,' said Fox and went out.

Alleyn squinted through a lens at the wing-taps of the gas-fire. 'I can see prints clearly enough,' he said, 'on both. We can check with

Bennington's. There's even a speck or two of powder settled on the taps.'

'In the air, I dare say,' said Gibson.

'I dare say it *was*. Like the gas. We can't go any further here until the dabs and flash party has done its stuff. Finished, Gibson?'

'Finished, Mr Alleyn. Nothing much in the pockets. Bills. Old racing card. Cheque-book and so on. Nothing on the body, by the way, but a handkerchief.'

'Come on, then. I've had my bellyful of gas.'

But he stood in the doorway eyeing the room and whistling softly.

'I wish I could believe in you,' he apostrophized it, 'but split me and sink me if I can. No, by all that's phoney, not for one credulous second. Come on, Gibson. Let's talk to these experts.'

IV

They all felt a little better for Jacko's soup which had been laced with something that as J. G. Darcey said (and looked uncomfortable as soon as he had said it) went straight to the spot marked X.

Whether it was this potent soup or whether extreme emotional and physical fatigue had induced in Martyn its familiar compliment, an uncanny sharpening of the mind, she began to consider for the first time the general reaction of the company to Bennington's death. She thought: 'I don't believe there's one of us who really minds very much. How lonely for him! Perhaps he felt the awful isolation of a child that knows itself unwanted and thought he'd put himself out of the way of caring.'

It was a shock to Martyn when Helena Hamilton suddenly gave voice to her own thoughts. Helena had sat with her chin in her hand, looking at the floor. There was an unerring grace about her and this fireside posture had the beauty of complete relaxation. Without raising her eyes she said: 'My dears, my dears, for pity's sake don't let's pretend. Don't let me pretend. I didn't love him. Isn't that sad? We all know and we try to patch up a decorous scene but it won't do. We're shocked and uneasy and dreadfully tired. Don't let's put ourselves to the trouble of pretending. It's so useless.'

Gay said: 'But I *did* love him!' and J.G. put his arm about her.

'Did you?' Helena murmured. 'Perhaps you did, darling. Then you must hug your sorrow to yourself. Because I'm afraid nobody really shares it.'

Poole said: 'We understand, Ella.'

With that familiar gesture, not looking at him, she reached out her hand. When he had taken it in his, she said: 'When one is dreadfully tired, one talks. I do, at all events. I talk much too easily. Perhaps that's a sign of a shallow woman. You know, my dears, I begin to think I'm only capable of affection. I have a great capacity for affection but as for my loves, they have no real permanency. None.'

Jacko said gently: 'Perhaps your talent for affection is equal to other women's knack of loving.'

Gay and Parry Percival looked at him in astonishment but Poole said: 'That may well be.'

'What I meant to say,' Helena went on, 'only I do sidetrack myself so awfully, is this. Hadn't we better stop being muted and mournful and talk about what may happen and what we ought to do? Adam, darling, I thought perhaps they might all be respecting my sorrow or something. What should we be talking about? What's the situation?'

Poole moved one of the chairs with its back to the curtain and sat on it. Dr Rutherford returned and lumped himself down in the corner. 'They're talking,' he said, 'to Clem Smith in the – they're talking to Clem. I've seen the police-surgeon, a subfusc exhibit but one that can tell a hawk from a hernshaw if they're held under his nose. He agrees that there was nothing else I could have done which is no doubt immensely gratifying to me. What are you all talking about? You look like a dress-rehearsal.'

'We were about to discuss the whole situation,' said Poole. 'Helena feels it should be discussed and I think we all agree with her.'

'What situation pray? Ben's? Or ours? There is no more to be said about Ben's situation. As far as we know, my dear Ella, he has administered to himself a not too uncomfortable and effective anaesthetic which, after he had become entirely unconscious, brought about the end he had in mind. For a man who had decided to shuffle off this mortal coil he behaved very sensibly.'

'Oh, *please*,' Gay whispered. '*Please!*'

Dr Rutherford contemplated her in silence for a moment and then said: 'What's up, Misery?' Helena, Darcey and Parry Percival made expostulatory noises. Poole said: 'See here, John, you'll either pipe down or preserve the decencies.'

Gay, fortified perhaps by this common reaction, said loudly: 'You might at least have the grace to remember he was my uncle.'

'Grace me no grace,' Dr Rutherford quoted inevitably. 'And uncle me no uncles.' After a moment's reflection, he added: 'All right, Thalia, have a good cry. But you must know, if the rudiments of seasoned thinking are within your command, that your Uncle Ben did you a damn shabby turn. A scurvy trick, by God. However, I digress. Get on with the post-mortem, Chorus. I am dumb.'

'You'll be good enough to remain so,' said Poole warmly. 'Very well, then. It seems to me, Ella, that Ben took this – this way out – for a number of reasons. I know you want me to speak plainly and I'm going to speak very plainly indeed, my dear.'

'Oh, yes,' she said. 'Please, but – ' For a moment they looked at each other. Martyn wondered if she imagined that Poole's head moved in the faintest possible negative. 'Yes,' Helena said, 'very plainly, please.'

'Well, then,' Poole said, 'we know that for the last year Ben, never a very temperate man, has been a desperately intemperate one. We know his habits undermined his health, his character and his integrity as an actor. I think he realized this very thoroughly. He was an unhappy man who looked back at what he had once been and was appalled. We all know he did things in performance tonight that, from an actor of his standing, were quite beyond the pale.'

Parry Percival ejaculated: 'Well, I mean to say – oh, well. Never mind.'

'Exactly,' Poole said. 'He had reached a sort of chronic state of instability. We all know he was subject to fits of depression. I believe he did what he did when he was at a low ebb. I believe he would have done it sooner or later by one means or another. And, in my view for what it's worth, that's the whole story. Tragic enough, God knows, but, in its tragedy, simple. I don't know if you agree.'

Darcey said: 'If there's nothing else, I mean,' he said diffidently, glancing at Helena, 'if nothing has happened that would seem like a further motive.'

Helena's gaze rested for a moment on Poole and then on Darcey.
'I think Adam's right,' she said. 'I'm afraid he was appalled by a sudden realization of himself. I'm afraid he was insufferably lonely.'

'Oh, my God!' Gay ejaculated and having by this means collected
their unwilling attention, she added: 'I shall never forgive myself:
never.'

Dr Rutherford groaned loudly.

'I failed him,' Gay announced. 'I was a bitter, bitter disappointment to him. I dare say I turned the scale.'

'Now in the name of all the gods at once,' Dr Rutherford began and
was brought to a stop by the entry of Clem Smith.

Clem looked uneasily at Helena Hamilton and said: 'They're in
the dressing-room. He says they won't keep you waiting much
longer.'

'It's all right, then?' Parry Percival blurted out and added in a flurry:
'I mean there won't be a whole lot of formalities. I mean we'll be
able to get away. I mean – '

'I've no idea about that,' Clem said. 'Alleyn just said they'd be
here soon.' He had brought a cup of soup with him and he withdrew
into a corner and began to drink it. The others watched him anxiously but said nothing.

'What did he ask you about?' Jacko demanded suddenly.

'About what we did at the time.'

'Anything else?'

'Well, yes. He – well in point of fact, he seemed to be interested in
the alterations to the theatre.'

'To the dressing-rooms in particular?' Poole asked quickly.

'Yes,' Clem said unhappily. 'To them.'

There was a long silence broken by Jacko.

'I find nothing remarkable in this,' he said. 'Ella has shown us the
way with great courage and Adam has spoken his mind. Let us all
speak ours. I may resemble an ostrich but I do not propose to imitate its behaviour. Of what do we all think? There is the unpleasing
little circumstance of the Jupiter case and we think of that. When
Gay mentions it she does so with the air of one who opens a closet
and out tumbles a skeleton. But why? It is inevitable that these gentlemen, who also remember the Jupiter case, should wish to inspect
the dressing-rooms. They wish, in fact, to make very sure indeed

that this is a case of suicide and not of murder. And since we are all quite certain that it is suicide we should not disturb ourselves that they do their duty.'

'Exactly,'Poole said.

'It's going,' Darcey muttered, 'to be damn bad publicity.'

'Merciful Heavens!' Parry Percival exclaimed. 'The Publicity! None of us thought of that!'

'Did we not?' said Poole.

'I must say,' Parry complained, 'I *would* like to know what's going to happen, Adam. I mean – darling Ella, I know you'll understand – but I mean, about the piece. Do we go on? Or what?'

'Yes,' Helena said. 'We go on. Please, Adam.'

'Ella, I've got to think. There are so many – '

'We go on. Indeed, indeed we do.'

Martyn felt rather than saw the sense of relief in Darcey and Percival.

Darcey said, 'I'm the understudy, Lord help me,' and Percival made a tiny ambiguous sound that might have been one of satisfaction or of chagrin.

'How are you for it, J.G.?' Helena asked.

'I *know* it,' he said heavily.

'I'll work whenever you like. We've got the weekend.'

'Thank you, Ella.'

'Your own understudy's all right,' said Clem.

'Good.'

It was clear to Martyn that this retreat into professionalism was a great relief to them and it was clear also that Poole didn't share in their comfort. Watching him, she was reminded of his portrait in the greenroom: he looked withdrawn and troubled.

A lively and almost cosy discussion about recasting had developed. Clem Smith, Jacko and Percival were all talking at once when, with her infallible talent for scenes, Gay exclaimed passionately:

'I can't bear it! I think you're all awful!'

They broke off. Having collected their attention she built rapidly to her climax. 'To sit round and talk about the show as if nothing had happened! How you can! When beyond those doors, he's lying there forgotten. Cold and forgotten! It's the most brutal thing I've ever heard of and if you think I'm coming near this horrible, fated, *haunted* place again, I'm telling you, here and now, that wild horses wouldn't drag me inside the theatre once I'm away from it. I suppose someone will find time to tell me when the funeral is going to be. I happen to be just about his only relation.'

They all began to expostulate at once but she topped their lines with the determination of a robust star. 'You needn't bother to explain,' she shouted. 'I understand only too well, thank you.' She caught sight of Martyn and pointed wildly at her. 'You've angled for this miserable part, and now you've got it. I think it's extremely likely you're responsible for what's happened.'

Poole said: 'You'll stop at once, Gay. Stop.'

'I won't! I won't be gagged! It drove my Uncle Ben to despair and I don't care who knows it.'

It was upon this line that Alleyn, as if he had mastered one of the major points of stage technique, made his entrance up-stage and centre.

V

Although he must have heard every word of Gay's final outburst, Alleyn gave no sign of having done so.

'Well, now,' he said. 'I'm afraid the first thing I have to say to you all won't be very pleasant news. We don't look like getting through with our side of this unhappy business as quickly as I hoped. I know you are all desperately tired and very shocked and I'm sorry. But the general circumstances aren't quite as straightforward as, on the face of it, you have probably supposed them to be.'

A trickle of ice moved under Martyn's diaphragm. She thought: 'No, it's not fair. I can't be made to have two goes of the jim-jams in one night.'

Alleyn addressed himself specifically to Helena Hamilton.

'You'll have guessed – of course you will – that one can't overlook the other case of gas-poisoning that is associated with this theatre. It must have jumped to everybody's mind, almost at once.'

'Yes, of course,' she said. 'We've been talking about it.'

The men looked uneasily at her but Alleyn said at once: 'I'm sure you have. So have we. And I expect you've wondered, as we have, if the memory of that former case could have influenced your husband.'

'I'm certain it did,' she said quickly. 'We all are.'

The others made small affirmative noises. Only Dr Rutherford was silent. Martyn saw with amazement that his chin had sunk on his rhythmically heaving bosom, his eyes were shut and his lips pursed in the manner of a sleeper who is just not snoring. He was at the back of the group and, she hoped, concealed from Alleyn.

'Have you,' Alleyn asked, 'any specific argument to support this theory?'

'No *specific* reason. But I know he thought a lot of that other dreadful business. He didn't *like* this theatre. Mr Alleyn, actors are sensitive to atmosphere. We talk a lot about the theatres we play in and we get very vivid – you would probably think absurdly vivid – impressions of their "personalities". My husband felt there was a – an unpleasant atmosphere in this place. He often said so. In a way I think it had a rather horrible fascination for him. We'd a sort of tacit understanding in the Vulcan that its past history wouldn't be discussed among us but I know he did talk about it. Not to us but to people who had been concerned in the other affair.'

'Yes, I see.' Alleyn waited for a moment. The young constable completed a note. His back was now turned to the company. 'Did anyone else notice this preoccupation of Mr Bennington's?'

'Oh, yes!' Gay said with mournful emphasis. '*I* did. He talked to me about it, but when he saw how much it upset me – because I'm so stupidly sensitive to atmosphere – I just can't help it – it's one of those things – but I *am* – because when I first came – into the theatre I just knew – you may laugh at me but these things can't be denied – '

'When,' Alleyn prompted, 'he saw that it upset you?'

'He stopped. I was his niece. It was rather a marvellous relationship.'

'He stopped,' Alleyn said. 'Right.' He had a programme in his hand and now glanced at it. 'You must be Miss Gainsford I think. Is that right?'

'Yes, I am. But my name's really Bennington. I'm his only brother's daughter. My father died in the war and Uncle Ben really felt we were awfully *near* to each other, do you know? That's why it's so devastating for me because I sensed how wretchedly unhappy he was.'

'Do you mind telling us why you thought him so unhappy?'

J. G. Darcey interposed quickly: 'I don't think it was more than a general intuitive sort of thing, was it, Gay? Nothing special.'

'Well – ' Gay said reluctantly and Helena intervened.

'I don't think any of us have any doubt about my husband's unhappiness, Mr Alleyn. Before you came in I was saying how most *most* anxious I am that we should be very frank with each other and of course with you. My husband drank so heavily that he had ruined his health and his work quite completely. I wasn't able to help him and we were not – ' The colour died out of her face and she hesitated. 'Our life together wasn't true,' she said, 'it had no reality at all. Tonight he behaved very badly on the stage. He coloured his part at the expense of the other actors and I think he was horrified at what he'd done. He was very drunk indeed tonight. I feel he suddenly looked at himself and couldn't face what he saw. I feel that very strongly.'

'One *does* sense these things,' Gay interjected eagerly, 'or I do at any rate.'

'I'm sure you do,' Alleyn agreed politely. Gay drew breath and was about to go on when he said: 'Of course, if any of you can tell us any happenings or remarks or so on, that seem to prove that he had this thing in mind, it will be a very great help.'

Martyn heard her voice, acting, it seemed, of its own volition: 'I think, perhaps – '

Alleyn turned to her and his smile reassured her. 'Yes,' he said. 'Forgive me, but I don't yet know all your names.' He looked again at his programme and then at her. Gay gave a small laugh. Darcey put his hand over hers and said something undistinguishable.

Poole said quickly: 'Miss Martyn Tarne. She is, or should be, our heroine tonight. Miss Gainsford was ill and Miss Tarne, who was the understudy, took her part at half an hour's notice. We'd all be extremely proud of her if we had the wits to be anything but worried and exhausted.'

Martyn's heart seemed to perform some eccentric gyration in the direction of her throat and she thought: 'That's done it. Now my voice is going to be ungainly with emotion.'

Alleyn said: 'That must have been a most terrifying and exciting adventure,' and she gulped and nodded. 'What had you remembered,' he went on after a moment, 'that might help us?'

'It was something he said when he came off in the last act.'

'For his final exit in the play?'

'Yes.'

'I'll be very glad to hear it.'

'I'll try to remember exactly what it was,' Martyn said carefully. 'I was in the dressing-room passage on my way to my – to Miss Gainsford's room and he caught me up. He spoke very disjointedly and strangely, not finishing his sentences. But one thing he said – I think it was the last – I do remember quite distinctly because it puzzled me very much. He said: "I just wanted to tell you that you needn't suppose what I'm going to do – " and then he stopped as if he was confused and added, I think: "you needn't suppose – " and broke off again. And then Jacko – Mr Doré – came and told me to go into the dressing-room to have my make-up attended to and, I think, said something to Mr Bennington about his.'

'I told him he was shining with sweat,' said Jacko. 'And he went into his room.'

'Alone?' Alleyn asked.

'I just looked in to make sure he had heard me. I told him again he needed powder and then went at once to this infant.'

'Miss Tarne, can you remember anything else Mr Bennington said?'

'Not really. I'm afraid I was rather in a haze myself just then.'

'The great adventure?'

'Yes,' said Martyn gratefully. 'I've an idea he said something about my performance. Perhaps I should explain that I knew he must be very disappointed and upset about my going on instead of Miss Gainsford but his manner was not unfriendly and I have the impression that he meant to say he didn't bear for me, personally, any kind of resentment. But that's putting it too definitely. I'm not at all sure what he said, except for that one sentence. Of that I'm quite positive.'

'Good,' Alleyn said. 'Thank you. Did you hear this remark, Mr Doré?'

Jacko said promptly: 'But certainly. I was already in the passage and he spoke loudly as I came up.'

'Did you form any opinion as to what he meant?'

'I was busy and very pleased with this infant and I did not concern myself. If I thought at all it was to wonder if he was going to make a scene because the niece had not played. He had a talent for scenes. It appears to be a family trait. I thought perhaps he meant that this infant would not be included in some scene he planned to make or be scolded for her success.'

'Did he seem to you to be upset?'

'Oh, yes. Yes. Upset. Yes.'

'Very much distressed, would you say?'

'*All his visage wanned?*' inquired a voice in the background. '*Tears in his eyes. Distraction in's aspect?*'

Alleyn moved his position until he could look past Gay and Darcey at the recumbent doctor. 'Or even,' he said, '*his whole function suiting with forms to his conceit?*'

'Hah!' the doctor ejaculated and sat up. 'Upon my soul the whirligig of time brings in his revenges. Even to the point where the dull detection apes at artifice, inspectors echo with informéd breath their pasteboard prototypes of fancy wrought. I am amazed and know not what to say.' He helped himself to snuff and fell back into a recumbent position.

'Please don't mind him,' Helena said, smiling at Alleyn. 'He is a very foolish vain old man and has read somewhere that it's clever to quote in a muddled sort of way from the better known bits of the Bard.'

'We encourage him too much,' Jacko added gloomily.

'We have become too friendly with him,' said Poole.

'A figo for your friendship,' said Dr Rutherford.

Parry Percival sighed ostentatiously and Darcey said: 'Couldn't we get on?' Alleyn looked good-humouredly at Jacko and said: 'Yes, Mr Doré?'

'I wouldn't agree,' Jacko said, 'that Ben was very much upset but that was an almost chronic condition of late with poor Ben. I believe now with Miss Hamilton that he had decided there was little further enjoyment to be found in observing the dissolution of his own character and was about to take the foolproof way of ending it. He wished to assure Martyn that the decision had nothing to do with chagrin over Martyn's success or the failure of his niece. And that, if I am right, was nice of Ben.'

'I don't think we need use the word "failure",' J.G. objected. 'Gay was quite unable to go on.'

'I hope you are better now, Miss Gainsford,' Alleyn said.

Gay made an eloquent gesture with both hands and let them fall in her lap. 'What does it matter?' she said. 'Better? Oh, yes, I'm better.' And with the closest possible imitation of Helena Hamilton's familiar gesture she extended her hand, without looking at him to J.G. Darcey. He took it anxiously. 'Much better,' he said, patting it.

Martyn thought: 'Oh, dear, he *is* in love with her. *Poor* J.G.!'

Alleyn looked thoughtfully at them for a moment and then turned to the others.

'There's a general suggestion,' he said, 'that none of you was very surprised by this event. May I just – sort of tally-up – the general opinion as far as I've heard it? It helps to keep things tidy, I find. Miss Hamilton, you tell us that your husband had a curious, an almost morbid interest in the Jupiter case. You and Mr Doré agree that Mr Bennington had decided to take his life because he couldn't face the "dissolution of his character". Miss Gainsford, if I understand her, believes he was deeply disturbed by the *mise en sène* and also by her inability to go on tonight for this part. Miss Tarne's account of what was probably the last statement he made suggests that he wanted her to understand that some action he had in mind had nothing to do with her. Mr Doré supports this interpretation and confirms the actual words that were used. This, as far as it goes, is the only tangible bit of evidence as to intention that we have.'

Poole lifted his head. His face was very white and a lock of black hair had fallen over his forehead turning him momentarily into the likeness, Martyn thought inconsequently, of Michelangelo's 'Adam'. He said: 'There's the fact itself, Alleyn. There's what he did.'

Alleyn said carefully: 'There's an interval of perhaps eight minutes between what he said and when he was found.'

'Look here – ' Parry Percival began and then relapsed. 'Let it pass,' he said. '*I* wouldn't know.'

'Pipe up, Narcissus,' Dr Rutherford adjured him, 'the inspector won't bite you.'

'Oh, shut up!' Parry shouted and was awarded a complete and astonished silence. He rose and addressed himself to the players. 'You're all being *so* bloody frank and sensible about this suicide,' he said. 'You're *so* anxious to show everybody how honest you are. The doctor's *so* unconcerned he can even spare a moment to indulge in his favourite pastime of me-baiting. I know what the doctor thinks of me and it doesn't say much for his talents as a diagnostician. But if it's Queer to feel desperately sorry for a man who was miserable enough to choke himself to death at a gas-jet, if it's Queer to be physically and mentally sick at the thought of it then, by God, I'd rather be Queer than normal. Now!'

There followed a silence broken only by the faint whisper of the young constable's pencil.

Doctor Rutherford struggled to his feet and lumbered down to Parry.

'Your argument, my young coxcomb,' he said thoughtfully, 'is as seaworthy as a sieve. As for my diagnosis, if you're the normal man you'd have me believe, why the hell don't you show like one? You exhibit the stigmata of that waterfly whom it is a vice to know, and fly into a fit when the inevitable conclusion is drawn.' He took Parry by the elbow and addressed himself to the company in the manner of a lecturer. 'A phenomenon,' he said, 'that is not without its dim interest. I invite your attention. Here is an alleged actor who, an hour or two since, was made a public and egregious figure of fun by the deceased. Who was roasted by the deceased before an audience of a thousand whinnying nincompoops? Who allowed his performance to be prostituted by the deceased before this audience? Who before his final and most welcome exit suffered himself to be tripped up contemptuously by the deceased, and who fell on his painted face before this audience? Here is this phenomenon, ladies and gents, who now proposes himself as Exhibit A in the Compassion Stakes. I invite your – '

Poole said: '*Quiet!*' and when Dr Rutherford grinned at him added: 'I meant it, John. You will be quiet if you please.'

Parry wrenched himself free from the doctor and turned on Alleyn. 'You're supposed to be in charge here – ' he began and Poole said quickly: 'Yes, Alleyn, I really do think that this discussion is getting quite fantastically out of hand. If we're all satisfied that this case of suicide – '

'Which,' Alleyn said, 'we are not.'

They were all talking at once: Helena, the doctor, Parry, Gay and Darcey. They were like a disorderly chorus in a verse play. Martyn, who had been watching Alleyn, was terrified. She saw him glance at the constable. Then he stood up.

'One moment,' he said. The chorus broke off inconsequently as it had begun.

'We've reached a point,' Alleyn said, 'where it's my duty to tell you I'm by no means satisfied that this is, in fact, a case of suicide.'

Martyn was actually conscious, in some kind, of a sense of relief. She could find no look either of surprise or anger in any of her fellow-players. Their faces were so many white discs and they were motionless and silent. At last Clem Smith said with an indecent lack of conviction: 'He was horribly careless about things like that – taps – I mean – ' His voice sank to a murmur. They heard the word 'accident'.

'Is it not strange,' Jacko said loudly, 'how loath one is to pronounce the word that is in all our minds. And truth to tell, it has a soft and ugly character.' His lips closed over his fantastic teeth. He used the exaggerated articulation of an old actor. 'Murder,' he said. 'So beastly, isn't it?'

It was at this point that one of the stage-hands, following, no doubt, his routine for the night, pulled up the curtain and exhibited the scene of climax to the deserted auditorium.

CHAPTER 8

After-Piece

When Martyn considered the company as they sat about their own working stage, bruised by anxiety and fatigue, Jacko's ugly word sounded not so much frightening as preposterous. It was unthinkable that it could kindle even a bat-light of fear in any of their hearts. 'And yet,' thought Martyn, 'it has done so. There are little points of terror, burning in all of us like match-flames.'

After Jacko had spoken there was a long silence broken at last by Adam Poole who asked temperately: 'Are we to understand, Alleyn, that you have quite ruled out the possibility of suicide?'

'By no means,' Alleyn rejoined. 'I still hope you may be able, among you, to show that there is at least a clear enough probability of suicide for us to leave the case as it stands until the inquest. But where there are strong indications that it may *not* be suicide we can't risk waiting as long as that without a pretty exhaustive look round.'

'And there are such indications?'

'There are indeed.'

'Strong?'

Alleyn waited a moment. 'Sufficiently strong,' he said.

'What are they?' Dr Rutherford demanded.

'It must suffice,' Alleyn quibbled politely, 'that they are sufficient.'

'An elegant sufficiency, by God!'

'But, Mr Alleyn,' Helena cried out, 'what can we tell you? Except that we all most sincerely believe that Ben did this himself. Because we know him to have been bitterly unhappy. What else is there for us to say?'

'It will help, you know, when we get a clear picture of what you were all doing and where you were between the time he left the stage and the time he was found. Inspector Fox is checking now with the stage-staff. I propose to do so with the players.'

'I see,' she said. She leant forward and her air of reasonableness and attention was beautifully executed. 'You want to find out which of us had the opportunity to murder Ben?'

Gay Gainsford and Parry began an outcry but Helena raised her hand and they were quiet. 'That's it, isn't it?' she said.

'Yes,' Alleyn said, 'that really is it. I fancy you would rather be spared the stock evasions about routine inquiries and all the rest of it.'

'Much rather.'

'I was sure of it,' Alleyn said. 'Then shall we start with you, if you please?'

'I was on the stage for the whole of that time, Mr Alleyn. There's a scene, before Ben's exit between J.G. – that's Mr Darcey, over there – Parry, Adam, Ben and myself. Then J.G. and Parry go off and Ben follows a moment later. Adam and I finish the play.'

'So you, too,' Alleyn said to Poole, 'were here, on the stage, for the whole of this period?'

'I go off for a moment after his exit. It's a strange, rather horridly strange, coincidence that in the play he – the character he played, I mean – does commit suicide offstage. He shoots himself. When I hear the shot I go off. The two other men have already made their exits. They remain off but I come on again almost immediately. I wait outside the door on the left from a position where I could watch Miss Hamilton and I re-enter on a "business" cue from her.'

'How long would this take?'

'Shall we show you?' Helena suggested. She got up and moved to the centre of the stage. She raised her clasped hands to her mouth and stood motionless. She was another woman.

As if Clem had called: 'Clear stage,' and indeed he looked about him with an air of authority, Martyn, Jacko and Gay moved into the wings. Parry and J.G. went to the foot of the stairs and Poole crossed to above Helena. They placed themselves thus in the business-like manner of a rehearsal. The doctor however remained prone on his sofa breathing deeply and completely disregarded by everybody. Helena glanced at Clem Smith who went to the book.

'From Ben's exit, Clem,' Poole said and after a moment Helena turned and addressed herself to the empty stage on her left.

'*I've only one thing to say, but it's between the three of us.*' She turned to Parry and Darcey. '*Do you mind?*' she asked them.

Parry said: '*I don't understand and I'm past minding.*'

Darcey said: '*My head is buzzing with a sense of my own inadequacy. I shall be glad to be alone.*'

They went out, each on his own line, leaving Helena, Adam, and the ghost of Bennington, on the stage.

Helena spoke again to vacancy. '*It must be clear to you, now. It's the end, isn't it?*'

'*Yes,*' Clem's voice said. '*I understand you perfectly. Goodbye, my dear.*'

They looked at the door on the left. Alleyn took out his watch. Helena made a quick movement as if to prevent the departure of an unseen person and Poole laid his hand on her arm. They brought dead Ben back to the stage by their mime and dismissed him as vividly. It seemed that the door must open and shut for him as he went out.

Poole said: '*And now I must speak to you alone.*' There followed a short passage of dialogue which he and Helena played *a tempo* but with muted voices. Jacko, in the wings, clapped his hands and the report was as startling as a gun shot. Poole ran out through the left-hand door.

Helena traced a series of movements about the stage. Her gestures were made in the manner of an exercise but the shadow of their significance was reflected in her face. Finally she moved into the window and seemed to compel herself to look out. Poole re-rentered.

'Thank you,' Alleyn said, shutting his watch. 'Fifty seconds. Will you all come on again, if you please?'

When they had assembled in their old positions, he said: 'Did anyone notice Mr Poole as he waited by the door for his re-entry?'

'The door's recessed,' Poole said. 'I was more or less screened.'

'Someone off-stage may have noticed, however.' He looked from Darcey to Percival.

'We went straight to our rooms,' said Parry.

'Together?'

'I was first. Miss Tarne was in the entrance to the passage and I spoke to her for a moment. J.G. followed me, I think.'

'Do you remember this, Miss Tarne?'

It had been at the time when Martyn had begun to come back to earth. It was like a recollection from a dream. 'Yes,' she said. 'I remember. They both spoke to me.'

'And went on down the passage?'

'Yes.'

'To be followed in a short time by yourself and Mr Bennington?'

'Yes.'

'And then Mr Doré joined you and you went to your rooms?'

'Yes.'

'So that after Mr Bennington had gone to his room, you, Mr Percival, were in your dressing-room which is next door to his, Mr Darcey was in his room which is on the far side of Mr Percival's and Miss Tarne was in her room – or more correctly, perhaps, Miss Gainsford's – with Mr Doré, who joined her there after looking in on Mr Bennington. Right?'

They murmured an uneasy assent.

'How long were you all in these rooms?'

Jacko said: 'I believe I have said I adjusted this infant's make-up and returned with her to the stage.'

'I think,' said Martyn, 'that the other two went out to the stage before we did. I remember hearing them go up the passage together. That was before the call for the final curtain. We went out after the call, didn't we, Jacko?'

'Certainly, my infant. And by that time you were a little more awake, isn't it? The pink clouds had receded a certain distance?'

Martyn nodded, feeling foolish. Poole came behind her and rested his hands on her shoulders. 'So there would appear at least to be an alibi for the Infant Phenomenon,' he said. It was the most natural and inevitable thing in the world for her to lean back. His hands moved to her arms and he held her to him for an uncharted second while a spring of well-being broke over her astounded heart.

Alleyn looked from her face to Poole's and she guessed that he wondered about their likeness to each other. Poole, answering her thoughts and Alleyn's unspoken question, said: 'We are remotely related, but I am not allowed to mention it. She's ashamed of the connection.'

'That's unlucky,' Alleyn said with a smile, 'since it declares itself so unequivocally.'

Gay Gainsford said loudly to Darcey: 'Do you suppose, darling, they'd let me get my cigarettes?'

Helena said: 'Here you are, Gay.' Darcey had already opened his case and held it out to her in his right hand. His left hand was in his trouser pocket. His posture was elegant and modish, out of keeping with his look of anxiety and watchfulness.

'Where are your cigarettes?' Alleyn asked and Gay said quickly: 'It doesn't matter, thank you. I've got one. I won't bother. I'm sorry I interrupted.'

'But where are they?'

'I don't really know what I've done with them.'

'Where were you during the performance?'

She said impatiently: 'It *really* doesn't matter. I'll look for them later or something.'

'Gay,' said Jacko, 'was in the greenroom throughout the show.'

'Lamprey will see if he can find them.'

The young constable said: 'Yes, of course, sir,' and went out.

'In the greenroom?' Alleyn said. 'Were you there all the time, Miss Gainsford?'

Standing in front of her with his back to Alleyn, Darcey held a light to her cigarette. She inhaled and coughed violently. He said: 'Gay didn't feel fit enough to move. She curled up in a chair in the greenroom. I was to take her home after the show.'

'When did you leave the greenroom, Miss Gainsford?'

But it seemed that Gay had half-asphyxiated herself with her cigarette. She handed it wildly to Darcey, buried her face in her handkerchief and was madly convulsed. PC Lamprey returned with a packet of cigarettes, was waved away with vehemence, gave them to Darcey and on his own initiative fetched a cup of water.

'If the face is congested,' Dr Rutherford advised from the sofa, 'hold her up by the heels.' His eyes remained closed.

Whether it was the possibility of being subjected to this treatment or the sip of water that Darcey persuaded her to take or the generous thumps on her back, administered by Jacko, that effected a cure, the paroxysm abated. Alleyn, who had watched this scene thoughtfully, said: 'If you are quite yourself again, Miss Gainsford, will you try to remember when you left the greenroom?'

She shook her head weakly and said in an invalid's voice: 'Please, I honestly don't remember. Is it very important?'

'Oh, for pity's sake, Gay!' cried Helena with every sign of the liveliest irritation. 'Do stop being such an unmitigated ass. You're not choking: if you were your eyes would water and you'd probably dribble. Of course it's important. You were in the greenroom and next door to Ben. Think!'

'But you can't imagine – ' Gay said wildly. 'Oh, Aunty – I'm sorry, I mean, Ella – I do think that's a frightful thing to suggest.'

'My dear Gay,' Poole said, 'I don't suppose Ella or Mr Alleyn or any of us imagines you went into Ben's room, knocked him sense-less with a straight left to the jaw and then turned the gas on. We merely want to know what you did do.'

J.G. who had given a sharp ejaculation and, half-risen from his chair, now sank back.

Alleyn said: 'It would also be interesting, Mr Poole, to hear how you knew about the straight left to the jaw.'

II

Poole was behind Martyn and a little removed from her. She felt his stillness in her own bones. When he spoke it was a shock rather than a relief to hear how easy and relaxed his voice sounded.

'Do you realize, Alleyn,' he said, 'you've given me an opportunity to use, in reverse, a really smashing detective's cliché. I didn't know. You have just told me!'

'And that,' Alleyn said with some relish, 'as I believe you would say in the profession, takes me off with a hollow laugh and a faint hiss. So you merely guessed at the straight left?'

'If Ben was killed, and I don't believe he was, it seemed to me to be the only way this murder could be brought about.'

'Surely not,' Alleyn said without emphasis. 'There is the method that was used before in this theatre with complete success.'

'I don't know that I would describe as completely successful, a method that ended with the arrest of its employer.'

'Oh,' Alleyn said lightly, 'that's another story. He underestimated our methods.'

'A good enough warning to anyone else not to follow his plan of action.'

'Or perhaps merely a hint that it could be improved upon,' Alleyn said. 'What do you think, Mr Darcey?'

'I?' J.G. sounded bewildered. 'I don't know. I'm afraid I haven't followed the argument.'

'You were still thinking about the straight-left theory perhaps?'

'I believe with the others that it was suicide,' said J.G. He had sat down again beside Gay. His legs were stretched out before him and crossed at the ankles, his hands were in his trouser pockets and his chin on his chest. It was the attitude of a distinguished MP during a damaging speech from the opposite side of the House.

Alleyn said: 'And we still don't know when Miss Gainsford left the greenroom.'

'Oh, *lawks*!' Parry ejaculated. 'This is *too* tiresome, J.G., you looked in at the greenroom door when we came back for the curtain call, don't you remember? Was she there then? Were you there, then, Gay darling?'

Gay opened her mouth to speak but J.G. said quickly: 'Yes, of course I did. Stupid of me to forget. Gay was sound asleep in the armchair, Mr Alleyn. I didn't disturb her.' He passed his right hand over his beautifully groomed head. 'It's a most extraordinary thing,' he said vexedly, 'that I should have forgotten this. Of course she was asleep. Because later, when – well, when, in point of fact the discovery had been made – I asked where Gay was and someone said she was still in the greenroom and I was naturally worried and went to fetch her. She was still asleep and the greenroom, by that time, reeking with gas. I brought her back here.'

'Have you any idea, Miss Gainsford,' Alleyn asked, 'about when you dropped off?'

'I was exhausted, Mr Alleyn. Physically and emotionally exhausted. I still am.'

'Was it, for instance, before the beginning of the last act?'

'N-n-no. No. Because J.G. came in to see how I was in the second interval. Didn't you, darling? And I was exhausted, wasn't I?'

'Yes, dear.'

'And he gave me some aspirins and I took two. And I suppose, in that state of utter exhaustion, they work. So I fell into a sleep – an exhausted sleep, it was.'

'Naturally,' Helena murmured with a glance at Alleyn. 'It would be exhausted.'

'Undoubtedly,' said Jacko, 'it was exhausted.'

'Well, it was,' said Gay crossly. 'Because I was. Utterly.'

'Did anyone else beside Mr Darcey go into the greenroom during the second interval?'

Gay looked quickly at J.G. 'Honestly,' she said, 'I'm *so* muddled about times it really isn't safe to ask me. I'm sure to be wrong.'

'Mr Darcey?'

'No,' J.G. said.

'Well, my dearest J.G.,' Parry said, 'I couldn't be more reluctant to keep popping in like one of the Eumenides in that utterly incomprehensible play but I do assure you that you're at fault here. Ben went into the greenroom in the second interval.'

'Dear Heaven!' Helena said, on a note of desperation. 'What has happened to us all!'

'I'm terribly sorry, Ella darling,' Parry said and sounded it.

'But why should you be sorry? Why shouldn't Ben go and see his niece in the interval? He played the whole of the third act afterwards. Of course you should say so, Parry, if you know what you're talking about. Shouldn't he, Adam? Shouldn't he, Mr Alleyn?'

Poole was looking with a sort of incredulous astonishment at Darcey. 'I think he should,' he said slowly.

'And you, Mr Darcey?' asked Alleyn.

'All right, Parry,' said J.G., 'go on.'

'There's not much more to be said and anyway I don't suppose it matters. It was before they'd called the third act. Helena and Adam and Martyn had gone out. They begin the act, I come on a bit later and Ben after me and J.G. later still. I wanted to see how the show was going and I was on my way in the passage when Ben came out of his room and went into the greenroom next door. The act was called soon after that.'

'Did you speak to him?' Alleyn asked.

'I did not,' said Parry with some emphasis. 'I merely went out to the stage and joined Jacko and the two dressers and the call-boy who were watching from the prompt side, and Clem.'

'That's right,' Clem said. 'I remember telling you all to keep away from the bunches. The boy called J.G. and Ben about five minutes later.'

'Were you still in the greenroom when you were called, Mr Darcey?'

'Yes.'

'With Mr Bennington?'

'He'd gone to his room.'

'Not for the life of me,' Helena said, wearily, 'can I see why you had to be so mysterious, J.G.'

'Perhaps,' Alleyn said, 'the reason is in your left trouser pocket, Mr Darcey.'

J.G. didn't take his hand out of his pocket. He stood up and addressed himself directly to Alleyn.

'May I speak to you privately?' he asked.

'Of course,' Alleyn said. 'Shall we go to the greenroom?'

III

In the greenroom and in the presence of Alleyn and of Fox who had joined them there, J.G. Darcey took his left hand out of his trouser pocket and extended it palm downwards for their inspection. It was a well-shaped and well-kept hand but the knuckles were grazed. A trace of blood had seeped out round the greasepaint and powder which had been daubed over the raw skin.

'I suppose I've behaved very stupidly,' he said. 'But I hoped there would be no need to come out. It has no bearing whatever on his death.'

'In that case,' Alleyn said, 'it will not be brought out. But you'll do well to be frank.'

'I dare say,' said J.G. wryly.

'There's a bruise under the deceased's jaw on the right side that could well have been caused by that straight left Mr Poole talked about. Now, we could ask you to hold your left fist to this bruise and

see if there's any correspondence. If you tell me you didn't let drive
at him we'll ask you if you are willing to make this experiment.'

'I assure you that rather than do any such thing I'd willingly
admit that I hit him,' J.G. said with a shudder.

'And also why you hit him?'

'Oh, yes, if I can. If I can,' he repeated and pressed his hand to his
eyes. 'D'you mind if we sit down, Alleyn? I'm a bit tired.'

'Do.'

J.G. sat in the leather armchair where Martyn and, in her turn,
Gay Gainsford had slept. In the dim light of the greenroom his face
looked wan and shadowed. 'Not the chicken I was,' he said and it
was an admission actors do not love to make.

Alleyn faced him. Fox sat down behind him, flattened his note-
book on the table and placed his spectacles across his nose. There
was something cosy about Fox when he took notes. Alleyn remembered absently that his wife had once observed that Mr Fox was a
cross between a bear and a baby and exhibited the most pleasing
traits of both creatures.

The masked light above Jacko's sketch of Adam Poole shone
down upon it and it thus was given considerable emphasis in an otherwise shadowed room.

'If you want a short statement,' J.G. said, 'I can give it to you in
a sentence. I hit Ben under the jaw in this room during the second
act wait. I didn't knock him out but he was so astonished he took
himself off. I was a handy amateur welter-weight in my young days
but it must be twenty years or more since I put up my hands. I must
say I rather enjoyed it.'

'What sort of condition was he in?'

'Damned unpleasant. Oh, you mean drunk or sober? I should say
ugly-drunk. Ben was a soak. I've never seen him incapacitated but
really I've hardly ever seen him stone-cold either. He was in his second degree of drunkenness: offensive, outrageous and incalculable.
He'd behaved atrociously throughout the first and second acts.'

'In what way?'

'As only a clever actor with too much drink in him can behave.
Scoring off other people. Playing for cheap laughs. Doing unre-
hearsed bits of business that made nonsense of the production. Upon
my word,' said J.G. thoughtfully, 'I wonder Adam or the doctor or

poor little Parry, if he'd had the guts, didn't get in first and give him what he deserved. A perfectly bloody fellow.'

'Was it because of his performance that you hit him?'

J.G. looked at his fingernails and seemed to ponder. 'No,' he said at last. 'Or not directly. If I thought you'd believe me I'd say yes, but no doubt you'll talk to her and she's so upset anyway – '

'You mean Miss Gainsford?'

'Yes,' said J.G. with the oddest air of pride and embarrassment. 'I mean Gay.'

'Was it on her account you dotted him one?'

'It was. He was damned offensive.'

'I'm sorry,' Alleyn said, 'but you'll realize that we do want to be told a little more than that about it.'

'I suppose so.' He clasped his hands and examined his bruised knuckles. 'Although I find it extremely difficult and unpleasant to go into the wretched business. It's only because I hope you'll let Gay off, as far as possible, if you know the whole story. That's why I asked to see you alone.' He slewed round and looked discontentedly at Fox.

'Inspector Fox,' Alleyn said, 'is almost pathologically discreet.'

'Glad to hear it. Well, as you've heard, I'd managed to get hold of a bottle of aspirins and I brought them to her, here, in the second interval. Gay was sitting in this chair. She was still terribly upset. Crying. I don't know if you've realized why she didn't go on for the part?'

'No. I'd be glad to have the whole story.'

J.G. embarked on it with obvious reluctance but as he talked his hesitancy lessened and he even seemed to find some kind of ease in speaking. He described Gay's part and her struggle at rehearsals. It was clear that, however unwillingly, he shared the general opinion of her limited talent. 'She'd have given a reasonable show,' he said, 'if she'd been given a reasonable chance but from the beginning the part got her down. She's a natural ingénue and this thing's really "character". It was bad casting. Adam kept the doctor at bay as much as possible but she knew what he thought. She didn't *want* the part. She was happy where she was in repertory but Ben dragged her in. He saw himself as a sort of fairy-godfather-uncle and when she found the part difficult he turned obstinate and wouldn't let her throw it in.

Out of vanity really. He was very vain. She's a frail little thing, you know, all heart and sensitivity, and between them they've brought her to the edge of a breakdown. It didn't help matters when Miss Martyn Tarne appeared out of a clear sky, first as Helena Hamilton's dresser and then as Gay's understudy and then – mysteriously as some of the cast, Ben in particular, thought – as Adam's distant cousin. You noticed the uncanny resemblance but you may not know the part in the play requires it. That was the last straw for Gay. She'd been ill with nerves and fright and tonight she cracked up completely and wouldn't – couldn't go on. When I saw her in the first interval she was a bit quieter but in the second act little Miss Tarne did very well indeed. Quite startling, it was. Incidentally, I suppose her success infuriated Ben. And Gay heard everybody raving about her as they came off. Naturally that upset her again. So she was in tears when I came in.'

He leant forward and rested his head in his hands. His voice was less distinct. 'I'm fond of her,' he said. 'She's got used to me being about. When I came in she ran to me and – I needn't go into the way I felt. There's no explaining these things. She was sobbing in my arms, poor bird, and God knows my heart had turned over. Ben came in. He went for her like a pick-pocket. He was crazy. I tried to shut him up. He didn't make a noise – I don't mean that – matter of fact what he said streamed out of him in a whisper. He was quite off his head and began talking about Helena – about his wife. He used straight-out obscenities. There'd been an episode that afternoon and – well he used the sort of generalization that Lear and Othello and Leontes use, if you remember your Shakespeare.'

'Yes.'

'Gay was still clinging to me and he began to talk the same sort of stuff about her. I'm not going into details. I put her away from me and quite deliberately gave him what was coming to him. I don't remember what I said. I don't think any of us said anything. So he went out nursing his jaw and they called me for the last act and I went out too. During this last act, when we were on together, I could see the bruise coming out under his make-up.'

'What was his general behaviour like during the final act?'

'As far as I was concerned he behaved in the way people do when they play opposite someone they've had a row with off-stage. He

didn't look me in the eye. He looked at my forehead or ears. It does-
n't show from the front. He played fairly soundly until poor Parry
got out of position. Parry is his butt in the piece but of course what
Ben did was outrageous. He stuck out his foot as Parry moved and
brought him down. That was not long before his own exit. I never
saw him again after that until he was carried out. That's all. I don't
know if you've believed me but I hope you'll let Gay off any more
of this stuff.'

Alleyn didn't answer. He looked at the young-old actor for a
moment. J.G. was lighting a cigarette with that trained economy and
grace of movement that were part of his stock-in-trade. His head was
stooped and Alleyn saw how carefully the silver hair had been dis-
tributed over the scalp. The hands were slightly tremulous. How old
was J.G. Fifty? Fifty-five? Sixty? Was he the victim of that Indian
summer that can so unmercifully visit an ageing man?

'It's the very devil, in these cases,' Alleyn said, 'how one has to
plug away at everyone in turn. Not that it helps to say so. There's
one more question that I'm afraid you won't enjoy at all. Can you
tell me more specifically what Bennington said about – I think you
called it an episode – of the afternoon, in which his wife was concerned?'

'No, by God I can't,' said J.G. hotly.

'He spoke about it in front of Miss Gainsford, didn't he?'

'You can't possibly ask Gay about it. It's out of the question.'

'Not, I'm afraid, for an investigating officer,' said Alleyn, who
thought that J.G.'s sense of delicacy, if delicacy was in question, was
possibly a good deal more sensitive than Miss Gainsford's. 'Do you
suppose Bennington talked about this episode to other people?'

'In the condition he was in I should think it possible.'

'Well,' Alleyn said, 'we shall have to find out.'

'See here, Alleyn. What happened, if he spoke the truth, was
something entirely between himself and his wife and it's on her
account that I can't repeat what he said. You know she and Poole
were on-stage at the crucial time and that there's no sense in thinking of motive if that's what you're after, where they are concerned.'

Alleyn said: 'This episode might constitute a motive for suicide,
however.'

J.G. looked up quickly. 'Suicide? But – why?'

'Shame?' Alleyn suggested. 'Self-loathing if he sobered up after you hit him and took stock of himself? I imagine they've been virtually separated for some time.'

'I see you have a talent,' said J.G., 'for reading between the lines.'

'Let us rather call it an ugly little knack. Thank you, Mr Darcey, I don't think I need bother you any more for the moment.'

J.G. went slowly to the door. He hesitated for a moment and then said: 'If you're looking for a motive, Alleyn, you'll find it in a sort of way all over the place. He wasn't a likeable chap and he'd antagonized everyone. Even poor little Parry came off breathing revenge after the way he'd been handled but, my God, actors do that kind of thing only too often. Feeling runs high, you know, on first nights.'

'So it would seem.'

'Can I take that child home?'

'I'm sorry,' Alleyn said, 'not yet. Not just yet.'

IV

'Well,' Alleyn said when J.G. had gone. 'What have you got at your end of the table, Br'er Fox?'

Fox turned back the pages of his note-book.

'What you might call negative evidence on the whole, Mr Alleyn. Clearance for the understudies who watched the show from the back of the circle and then went home. Clearance for the two dressers (male), the stage-manager and his assistant and the stage-hands. They were all watching the play or on their jobs. On statements taken independently, they clear each other.'

'That's something.'

'No female dresser,' Mr Fox observed. 'Which seems odd.'

'Miss Tarne was the sole female dresser and she'd been promoted overnight to what I believe I should call starletdom. Which in itself seems to me to be a rum go. I've always imagined female dressers to be cups-of-tea in alpaca aprons and not embryo actresses. I don't think Miss Tarne could have done the job but she comes into the picture as the supplanter of Uncle Ben's dear little niece whom I find an extremely irritating ass with a certain amount of low cunning. Miss Tarne, on the other hand, seems pleasant and intelligent and looks nice. You must allow me my prejudices, Br'er Fox.'

'She's Mr Poole's third cousin or something.'

'The case reeks with obscure relationships – blood, marital and illicit, as far as one can see. Did you get anything from Bennington's dresser?'

'Nothing much,' said Fox, sighing. 'It seems the deceased didn't like him to hang about on account of being a silent drinker. He was in the dressing-room up to about 7 p.m. and was then told to go and see if he could be of any use to the other gentlemen and not to come back till the first interval when the deceased changed his clothes. I must say that chap earns his wages pretty easily. As far as I could make out the rest of his duties for the night consisted in tearing off chunks of cotton-wool for the deceased to do up his face with. I checked his visits to the dressing-room by that. The last time he looked in was after the deceased went on the stage in the third act. He cleared away the used cotton-wool and powdered a clean bit. In the normal course of events I suppose he'd have put Mr Bennington into the fancy-dress he was going to wear to the ball and then gone home quite worn out.'

'Was he at all talkative?'

'Not got enough energy, Mr Alleyn. Nothing to say for himself barring the opinion that the deceased was almost on the DT mark. The other dresser, Cringle, seems a bright little chap. He just works for Mr Poole.'

'Have you let him go?'

'Yes, sir, I have. And the stage-hands. We can look them out again if we want them but for the moment I think we've just about cleaned them up. I've let the assistant stage-manager – ASM they call him – get away, too. Wife's expecting any time and he never left the prompting book.'

'That reduces the mixed bag a bit. You've been through all the rooms, of course, but before we do anything else, Br'er Fox, let's have a prowl.'

They went into the passage. Fox jerked his thumb at Bennington's room. 'Gibson's doing a fly-crawl in there,' he said. 'If there's anything, he'll find it. That dresser-chap didn't clear anything up except his used powder-puffs.'

They passed Bennington's room and went into Parry Percival's next door. Here they found Detective-Sergeants Thompson and Bailey, the one a photographic and the other a fingerprint expert. They were packing up their gear.

'Well, Bailey?' Alleyn asked.

Bailey looked morosely at his superior. 'It's there all right, sir,' he said grudgingly. 'Complete prints, very near, and a check-up all over the shop.'

'What about next door?'

'Deceased's room, sir? His prints on the wing-tap and the tube. Trace of red greasepaint on the rubber connection at the end of the tube. Matches paint on deceased's lips.'

'Very painstaking,' said Alleyn. 'Have you tried the experiment?'

'Seeing the fires are back to back, sir,' Fox said, 'we have. Sergeant Gibson blew down this tube and deceased's fire went out. As in former case.'

'Well,' Alleyn said, 'there you are. Personally I don't believe a word of it, either way.' He looked, without interest, at the telegrams stuck round the frame of Parry's looking-glass and at his costume for the ball. '*Very fancy*,' he muttered. 'Who's in the next room?'

'Mr J.G. Darcey,' said Thompson.

They went into J.G.'s room which was neat and impersonal in character and contained nothing, it seemed, of interest, unless a photograph of Miss Gainsford looking *insouciante* could be so regarded.

In the last room on this side of the passage they saw the electric-machine, some rough sketches, scraps of material and other evidences of Martyn's sewing-party for Jacko. Alleyn glanced round it, crossed the passage and looked into the empty room opposite. 'Dismal little cells when they're unoccupied, aren't they?' he said and moved on to Gay Gainsford's room.

He stood there, his hands in his pockets, with Fox at his elbow. 'This one suffers from the fashionable complaint, Fox,' he said. 'Schizophrenia. It's got a split personality. On my left a rather too smart overcoat, a frisky hat, chichi gloves, a pansy purse-bag, a large bottle of one of the less reputable scents, a gaggle of mascots, a bouquet from the management and orchids from – who do you suppose?' He turned over the card. 'Yes. Alas, yes, with love and a thousand good wishes from her devoted J.G. On my right a well-worn and modest little topcoat, a pair of carefully tended shoes and gloves that remind one of the White Rabbit, a grey skirt and beret and a yellow jumper. A handbag that contains, I'm sure, one of those rather heart-rending little purses and – what else?' He explored the bag. 'A New Zealand passport issued this year in which one finds Miss Tarne is nineteen years old and an actress. So the dresser's job was – what? The result of an appeal to the celebrated third cousin? But why not give her the understudy at once? She's fantastically like him and I'll be sworn he's mightily catched with her. What's more, even old Darcey says she's a damn good actress.' He turned the leaves of the passport. 'She only arrived in England seventeen days ago. Can that account for the oddness of the set-up? Anyway, I don't suppose it matters. Let's go next door, shall we?'

Cringle had left Poole's room in exquisite order. Telegrams were pinned in rows on the wall. A towel was spread over the make-up. A cigarette had been half-extracted from a packet and a match left ready on the top of its box. A framed photograph of Helena Hamilton stood near the glass. Beside it a tiny clock with a gay face ticked feverishly. It stood on a card. Alleyn moved it delicately and read the inscription. 'From Helena. Tonight and tomorrow and always: bless you.'

'The standard for first night keepsakes seems to be set at a high level,' Alleyn muttered. 'This is a French clock, Fox, with a Sevres face encircled with garnets. What do you suppose the gentleman gave the lady?'

'Would a tiara be common?' asked Fox.

'Let's go next door and see.'

Helena's room smelt and looked like a conservatory. A table had been brought in to carry the flowers. Jacko had set out the inevitable telegrams and had hung up the dresses under their dust sheets. 'Here we are,' Alleyn said. 'A sort of jeroboam of the most expensive scent on the market. Price, I should say, round about thirty pounds. "From Adam." Why don't you give me presents when we solve a petty larceny, Foxkin? Now, I may be fanciful but this looks to me like the gift of a man who's at his wits' end and plumps for the expensive, the easy and the obvious. Here's something entirely different. Look at this, Fox.'

It was a necklace of six wooden medallions strung between jade rings. Each plaque was most delicately carved in the likeness of a head in profile and each head was a portrait of one of the company of players. The card bore the date and the inscription: 'From J.'

'Must have taken a long time to do,' observed Fox. 'That'll be the foreign gentleman's work, no doubt, Mr Doré.'

'No doubt. I wonder if love's labour has been altogether lost,' said Alleyn. 'I hope she appreciates it.'

He took up the leather-case with its two photographs of Poole. 'He's a remarkable looking chap,' he said. 'If there's anything to be made of faces in terms of character, and I still like to pretend there is, what's to be made of this one? It's what they call a heart-shaped face, broad across the eyes with a firmly moulded chin and a generous but delicate mouth. Reminds one of a Holbein drawing. Doré's sketch in the greenroom is damn good. Doré crops up all over the place, doesn't he? Designs their fancy dresses. Paints their faces, in a double sense. Does their décor and with complete self-effacement, loves their leading lady.'

'Do you reckon?'

'I do indeed, Br'er Fox,' Alleyn said and rubbed his nose vexedly. 'However. Gibson's done all the usual things in these rooms, I suppose?'

'Yes, Mr Alleyn. Pockets, suitcases and boxes. Nothing to show for it.'

'We may as well let them come home to roost, then. We'll see them separately. They can change into their day clothes. The Gainsford has already, of course, done so. Blast! I suppose I'll have to check Darcey's statement with the Gainsford. She gives me the horrors, that young woman.'

'Shall I see her, Mr Alleyn?'

'You can stay and take your notes. I'll see her in the greenroom. No, wait a bit. You stay with the others, Fox, and send young Lamprey along with her. Tell them they can change in their rooms, fan them before they go, and make sure they go singly. I don't want them talking together. And you might try again if you can dig up anything that sounds at all off-key with Bennington over the last few days. Anything that distressed or excited him.'

'He seems to have been rather easily excited.'

'He does, doesn't he, but you never know. I don't believe it was suicide, Fox, and I'm not yet satisfied that we've unearthed anything that's good enough for a motive for murder. Trip away, Foxkin. Ply your craft.'

Fox went out sedately. Alleyn crossed the passage and opened the door of Bennington's room. Sergeant Gibson was discovered, squatting on his haunches before the dead gas-fire.

'Anything?' Alleyn asked.

'There's this bit of a stain that looks like a scorch on the hearth, sir.'

'Yes, I saw that. Any deposit?'

'We-ll.'

'We may have to try.'

'The powder-pads the deceased's dresser cleared away were in the rubbish bin on the stage where he said he put them. Nothing else in the bin. There's this burnt paper on the floor but it's in small flakes – powder almost.'

'All right. Seal the room when you've finished. And Gibson, don't let the mortuary van go without telling me.'

'Very good, sir.'

Alleyn returned to the greenroom. He heard Miss Gainsford approaching under the wing of PC Lamprey. She spoke in a high grand voice that seemed to come out of a drawing-room comedy of the twenties.

'I think you're *too* intrepid,' she was saying, 'to start from rock bottom like this. It must be so devastatingly boring for you, though I will say it's rather a comfort to think one is in the hands of, to coin a phrase, a gent. Two gents in fact.'

'Chief Inspector Alleyn' said PC Lamprey, 'is in the greenroom I think, Miss.'

'My dear, you do it quite marvellously. You ought, again to coin a phrase, to go on the stage.'

Evidently Miss Gainsford lingered in the passage. Alleyn heard his subordinate murmur: 'Shall I go first?' His regulation boots clumped firmly to the door which he now opened.

'Will you see Miss Gainsford, sir?' asked PC Lamprey, who was pink in the face.

'All right, Mike,' Alleyn said. 'Show her in and take notes.'

'Will you come this way, Miss?'

Miss Gainsford made her entrance with a Mayfairish gallantry that was singularly dated. Alleyn wondered if she had decided that her first reading of her new role was mistaken. 'She's abandoned the brave little woman for the suffering mondaine who goes down with an epigram,' he thought and sure enough Miss Gainsford addressed herself to him with staccato utterance and brittle highhandedness.

'Ought one to be terribly flattered because one is the first to be grilled?' she asked. 'Or is it a sinister little hint that one is top of the suspect list?'

'As you don't have to change,' Alleyn said, 'I thought it would be convenient to see you first. Will you sit down, Miss Gainsford?'

She did so elaborately, gave herself a cigarette, and turned to PC Lamprey: 'May one ask The Force for a light?' she asked. 'Or would that be against the rules?'

Alleyn lit her cigarette while his unhappy subordinate retired to the table. She turned in her chair to watch him. 'Is he going to take me down and use it all in evidence against me?' she asked. Her nostrils dilated, she raised her chin and added jerkily: 'That's what's called the Usual Warning, isn't it?'

'A warning is given in police practice,' Alleyn said as woodenly as possible, 'if there is any chance that the person under interrogation will make a statement that is damaging to himself. Lamprey will note down this interview and if it seems advisable you will be asked, later on, to give a signed statement.'

'If that was meant to be reassuring,' said Miss Gainsford, 'I can't have heard it properly. Could we get cracking?'

'Certainly. Miss Gainsford, you were in the greenroom throughout the performance. During the last interval you were visited by Mr J. G. Darcey and by your uncle. Do you agree that as the result of something the deceased said, Mr Darcey hit him on the jaw?'

She said: 'Wasn't it too embarrassing! I mean the Gorgeous Primitive Beast is one thing but one old gentleman banging another about is so utterly another. I'm afraid I didn't put that very clearly.'

'You agree that Mr Darcey hit Mr Bennington?'

'But madly. Like a sledge-hammer. I found it so difficult to know what to say. There just seemed to be no clue to further conversation.'

'It is the conversation before rather than after the blow that I should like to hear about, if you please.'

Alleyn had turned away from her and was looking at Jacko's portrait of Poole. He waited for some moments before she said sharply,

'I suppose you think because I talk like this about it I've got no feeling. You couldn't be more at fault.' It was as if she called his attention to her performance.

He said, without turning: 'I assure you I hadn't given it a thought. What did your uncle say that angered Mr Darcey?'

'He was upset,' she said sulkily, 'because I was ill and couldn't play.'

'Hardly an occasion for hitting him.'

'J.G. is very sensitive about me. He treats me like a piece of china.'

'Which is more than he did for your uncle, it seems.'

'Uncle Ben talked rather wildly.' Miss Gainsford seemed to grope for her poise and made a half-hearted return to her brittle manner. 'Let's face it,' she said, 'he was stinking, poor pet.'

'You mean he was drunk?'

'Yes, I do.'

'And abusive?'

'I didn't care. I understood him.'

'Did he talk about Miss Hamilton?'

'Obviously J.G.'s already told you he did, so why ask me?'

'We like to get confirmation of statements.'

'Well, you tell me what he said and I'll see about confirming it.'

For the first time Alleyn looked at her. She wore an expression of rather frightened impertinence. 'I'm afraid,' he said, 'that won't quite do. I'm sure you're very anxious to get away from the theatre, Miss Gainsford, and we've still a lot of work before us. If you will give me your account of this conversation I shall be glad to hear it; if you prefer so to do I'll take note of your refusal and keep you no longer.'

She gaped slightly, attempted a laugh and seemed to gather up the rags of her impersonation.

'Oh, but I'll tell you,' she said. 'Why not? It's only that there's so pathetically little to tell. I can't help feeling darling auntie – she likes me to call her Ella – was *too* Pinero and Galsworthy about it. It appears that poorest Uncle Ben came in from his club and found her in a suitable setting and – well, there you are, and – well, really even after all these years of segregation you couldn't call it a seduction. Or could you? Anyway she chose to treat it as such and raised the most piercing hue and cry and he went all primitive and when he came in here he was evidently in the throes of a sort of hangover and see-ing J.G. was being rather sweet to me put a sinister interpretation on it and described the whole incident and was rather rude about women generally and me and auntie in particular. And J.G. took a gloomy view of his attitude and hit him. And, I mean, taking it by and large, one couldn't help feeling: *what* a song and dance about nothing in particular. Is that all you wanted to know?'

'Do you think any other members of the company know of all this?'

She looked genuinely surprised. 'Oh yes,' she said. 'Adam and Jacko, anyway. I mean Uncle Ben appeared to have a sort of nation-wide hook-up idea about it but even if *he* didn't mention it, *she'd* naturally tell Adam, wouldn't you think? And Jacko, because every-body tells Jacko everything. And he was doing dresser for her. Yes, I'd certainly think she'd tell Jacko.'

'I see. Thank you, Miss Gainsford. That's all.'

'Really?' She was on her feet. 'I can go home?'

Alleyn answered her as he had answered J.G. 'I'm sorry: not yet. Not just yet.'

PC Lamprey opened the door. Inevitably, she paused on the threshold. 'Never tell *me* there's nothing in atmosphere,' she said. 'I *knew* when I came into this theatre. As if the very walls screamed it at me. I *knew*.'

She went out.

'Tell me, Mike,' Alleyn said, 'are many young women of your generation like that?'

'Well, no sir. She's what one might call a composite picture, don't you think?'

'I do, indeed. And I fancy she's got her genres a bit confused.'

'She tells me she's been playing in *Private Lives, The Second Mrs Tanqueray* and *Sleeping Partners* in the provinces.'

'That may account for it,' said Alleyn.

An agitated voice – Parry Percival's – was raised in the passage to be answered in a more subdued manner by Sergeant Gibson's.

'Go and see what it is, Mike,' Alleyn said.

But before Lamprey could reach the door it was flung open and Parry burst in, slamming it in Gibson's affronted face. He addressed himself instantly and breathlessly to Alleyn.

'I'm sorry,' he said, 'but I've just remembered something. I've been so *hideously* upset, I just simply never gave it a thought. It was when I smelt gas. When I went back to my room I smelt gas and I turned off my fire. I ought to have told you. I've just realized.'

'I think perhaps what you have just realized,' Alleyn said, 'is the probability of our testing your gas-fire for fingerprints and finding your own.'

CHAPTER 9

The Shadow of Otto Brod

Parry stood inside the door and pinched his lips as if he realized they were white and hoped to restore their colour.

'I don't know anything about fingerprints,' he said. 'I never read about crime. I don't know anything about it. When I came off after my final exit I went to my room. I was just going back for the call when I smelt gas. We're all nervous about gas in this theatre and anyway the room was frightfully hot. I turned the thing off. That's all.'

'This was after Bennington tripped you up?'

'I've told you. It was after my last exit and before the call. It wasn't – '

He walked forward very slowly and sat down in front of Alleyn. 'You can't think that sort of thing about me,' he said and sounded as if he was moved more by astonishment than by any other emotion. 'My God, *look* at me. I'm so hopelessly harmless. I'm not vicious. I'm not even odd. I'm just harmless.'

'Why didn't you tell me at once that you noticed the smell of gas?'

'Because, as I've tried to suggest, I'm no good at this sort of thing. The doctor got me all upset and in any case the whole show was so unspeakable.' He stared at Alleyn and, as if that explained everything, said: 'I saw him. I saw him when they carried him out. I've never been much good about dead people. In the blitz I sort of managed but I never got used to it.'

'Was the smell of gas very strong in your room?'

'No. Not strong at all. But in this theatre – we were all thinking about that other time and I just thought it was too bad of the management to have anything faulty in the system considering the history of the place. I don't know that I thought anything more than that: I smelt it and remembered, and got a spasm of the horrors. Then I felt angry at being given a shock and then I turned my fire off and went out. It was rather like not looking at the new moon through glass. You don't really believe it can do anything but you avoid it. I forgot all about the gas as soon as I got on-stage. I didn't give it another thought until I smelt it again during the doctor's speech.'

'Yes, I see.'

'You do, really, don't you? After all, suppose I – suppose I had thought I'd copy that other awful thing: well, I'd scarcely be fool enough to leave my fingerprints on the tap, would I?'

'But you tell me,' Alleyn said, not making too much of it, 'that you don't know anything about fingerprints.'

'God!' Parry whispered, staring at him, 'you do frighten me. It's not fair. You frighten me.'

'Believe me, there's no need for an innocent man to be frightened.'

'How can you be so sure of yourselves? Do you never make mistakes?'

'We do indeed. But not,' Alleyn said, 'in the end. Not nowadays on these sorts of cases.'

'What do you mean these sort of cases!'

'Why, I mean on what may turn out to be a capital charge.'

'I can't believe it!' Parry cried out. 'I shall never believe it. We're not like that. We're kind, rather simple people. We wear our hearts on our sleeves. We're not complicated enough to kill each other.'

Alleyn said with a smile: 'You're quite complicated enough for us at the moment. Is there anything else you've remembered that you think perhaps you ought to tell me about?'

Parry shook his head and dragged himself to his feet. Alleyn saw, as Martyn had seen before him, that he was not an exceedingly young man. 'No,' he said. 'There's nothing I can think of.'

'You may go to your dressing-room now, if you'd like to change into – what should I say? – into plain clothes?'

'Thank you. I simply loathe the thought of my room after all this but I shall be glad to change.'

'Do you mind if Lamprey does a routine search before you go? We'll ask this of all of you.'

Parry showed the whites of his eyes but said at once: 'Why should I mind?'

Alleyn nodded to young Lamprey who advanced upon Parry with an apologetic smile.

'It's a painless extraction, sir,' he said.

Parry raised his arms in a curve with his white hands held like a dancer's above his head. There was a silence and a swift efficient exploration. 'Thank you so much, sir,' said Mike Lamprey. 'Cigarette-case, lighter, and handkerchief, Mr Alleyn.'

'Right. Take Mr Percival along to his room, will you?'

Parry said: 'There couldn't be a more fruitless question but it would be nice to know, one way or the other, if you have believed me.'

'There couldn't be a more unorthodox answer,' Alleyn rejoined, 'but at the moment I see no reason to disbelieve you, Mr Percival.'

When Lamprey came back he found his senior officer looking wistfully at his pipe and whistling under his breath.

'Mike,' Alleyn said. 'The nastiest cases in our game are very often the simplest. There's something sticking out under my nose in this theatre and I can't see it. I know it's there because of another thing that, Lord pity us all, Fox and I *can* see.'

'Really, sir? Am I allowed to ask what it is?'

'You're getting on in the service, now. What have you spotted on your own account?'

'Is it something to do with Bennington's behaviour, sir?'

'It is indeed. If a man's going to commit suicide, Mike, and his face is made up to look loathsome, what does he do about it? If he's a vain man (and Bennington appears to have had his share of professional vanity), if he minds about the appearance of his own corpse, he cleans off the greasepaint. If he doesn't give a damn, he leaves it as it is. But with time running short he does *not* carefully and heavily powder his unbecoming make-up for all the world as if he meant to go on and take his curtain-call with the rest of them. Now, does he?'

'Well, no sir,' said Mike. 'If you put it like that, I don't believe he does.'

II

By half-past twelve most of the company on the stage seemed to be asleep or dozing. Dr Rutherford on his couch occasionally lapsed into bouts of snoring from which he would rouse a little, groan, take snuff and then settle down again. Helena lay in a deep chair with her feet on a stool. Her eyes were closed but Martyn thought that if she slept it was but lightly. Clem had made himself a bed of some old curtains and was curled up on it beyond the twisting stairway. Jacko, having tucked Helena up in her fur coat, settled himself on the stage beside her, dozing, Martyn thought, like some eccentric watch-dog at his post. J.G. and Gay Gainsford were summoned in turn and in turn came back, J.G. silently, Gay with some attempt at conversation. In the presence of the watchful Mr Fox this soon petered out. Presently she too, fell to nodding. Immediately after her return Parry Percival suddenly made an inarticulate ejaculation and, before Fox could move, darted off the stage. Sergeant Gibson was heard to accost him in the passage. Fox remained where he was and there was another long silence.

Adam Poole and Martyn looked into each other's faces. He crossed the stage to where she sat, on the left side which was the farthest removed from Fox. He pulled up a small chair and sat facing her.

'Kate,' he muttered, 'I'm so sorry about all this. There are hare's-foot shadows under your eyes, your mouth droops, your hands are anxious and your hair is limp though not at all unbecoming. You should be sound asleep in Jacko's garret under the stars and there should be the sound of applause in your dreams. Really, it's too bad.'

Martyn said: 'It's nice of you to think so but you have other things to consider.'

'I'm glad to have my thoughts interrupted.'

'Then I still have my uses.'

'You can see that chunk of a man over there. Is he watching us?'

'Yes. With an air of absent-mindedness which I'm not at all inclined to misunderstand.'

'I don't think he can hear us though it's a pity my diction is so good. If I take your hand perhaps he'll suppose I'm making love to you and feel some slight constabular delicacy.'

'I hardly think so,' Martyn whispered and tried to make nothing of his lips against her palm.

'Will you believe, Kate, that I am not in the habit of making passes at young ladies in my company?'

Martyn found herself looking at the back of Helena's chair.

'Oh, yes,' Poole said. 'There's that, too. I make no bones about that. It's another and a long and fading story. On both parts. Fading, on both parts, Kate. I have been very much honoured.'

'I can't help feeling this scene is being played at the wrong time, in the wrong place and before the wrong audience. And I doubt,' Martyn said, not looking at him, 'if it should be played at all.'

'But I can't be mistaken. It has happened for us, Martyn. Hasn't it? Suddenly, preposterously, almost at first sight we blinked and looked again and there we were. Tell me it's happened. The bird under your wrist is so wildly agitated. Is that only because you are frightened?'

'I am frightened. I wanted to ask your advice and now you make it impossible.'

'I'll give you my advice. There. Now you are alone again. But for the sake of the law's peace of mind as well as my own you must take a firm line about your blushing.'

'It was something he said to me that morning,' she murmured in the lowest voice she could command.

'Do you mean the morning when I first saw you?'

'I mean,' Martyn said desperately, 'the morning the photographs were taken. I had to go to his dressing-room.'

'I remember very well. You came into mine too.'

'He said something, then. He was very odd in his manner. They've asked us to try and remember anything at all unusual.'

'Are you going to tell me what it was?'

In a few words and under her breath she did so.

Poole said: 'Perhaps you should tell them. Yes, I think you should. In a moment I'll do something about it but there's one thing more I must say to you. Do you know I'm glad this scene has been played so awkwardly – inaudible, huddled up, inauspicious and uneffective. Technically altogether bad. It gives it a kind of authority, I hope. Martyn, are you very much surprised? Please look at me.'

She did as he asked and discovered an expression of such doubt and anxiety in his face that to her own astonishment she put her hand against his cheek and he held it there for a second. 'God!' he said. 'What a thing to happen!' He got up abruptly and crossed the stage.

'Inspector,' he said, 'Miss Tarne has remembered an incident three days old which we both think might possibly be of some help. What should we do about it?'

The others stirred a little. J.G. opened his eyes.

Fox got up. 'Thank you very much, sir,' he said. 'When Mr Alleyn is disengaged I'm sure he'll – Yes? What is it?'

PC Lamprey had come in. He delivered his message about the dressing-rooms being open for the use of their occupants. At the sound of his brisk and loudish voice they all stirred. Helena and Darcey got to their feet. Jacko sat up. Clem, Gay and Dr Rutherford opened their eyes, listened to the announcement and went to sleep again.

Fox said: 'You can take this young lady along to the chief in three minutes, Lamprey. Now, ladies and gentlemen, if you'd care to go to your rooms.'

He shepherded Helena and the two men through the door and looked back at Poole. 'What about you, sir?'

Poole with his eyes on Martyn, said: 'Yes, I'm coming.' Fox waited stolidly at the door for him and after a moment's hesitation Poole followed the others. Fox went with them.

Mike Lamprey said: 'We'll let them get settled, Miss Tarne, and then I'll take you along to Mr Alleyn. You must be getting very bored with all this hanging about.'

Martyn, whose emotional processes were in a state of chaos, replied with a vague smile. She wondered disjointedly if constables of PC Lamprey's class were a commonplace in the English force. He glanced good-humouredly at Gay and the three dozing men and evidently felt obliged to make further conversation.

'I heard someone say,' he began, 'that you are a New Zealander. I was out there as a small boy.'

'Were you, really?' Martyn said and wondered confusedly if he could have been the son of a former governor-general.

'We had a place out there on a mountain. Mount Silver it was. Would that be anywhere near your part of the world?'

Something clicked in Martyn's memory. 'Oh, yes!' she said. 'I've heard about the Lampreys of Mount Silver, I'm sure and – ' Her recollections clarified a little. 'Yes, indeed,' she added lamely.

'No doubt,' said Mike with a cheerful laugh, 'a legend of lunacy has survived us. We came home when I was about eight and soon afterwards my uncle happened to get murdered in our flat and Mr Alleyn handled the case. I thought at the time I'd like to go into the Force and the idea sort of persisted. And there you are, you know. Potted autobiography. Shall we go along and see if he's free?'

He escorted her down the passage to the greenroom door past Sergeant Gibson who seemed to be on guard there. Mike chatted freely as they went, rather as if he was taking her into supper after a successful dance. The star-bemused Martyn found herself brightly chatting back at him.

This social atmosphere was not entirely dispelled, she felt, by Alleyn himself, who received her rather as a distinguished surgeon might greet a patient.

'Come in, Miss Tarne,' he said cordially. 'I hear you've thought of something to tell us about this wretched business. Do sit down.'

She sat in her old chair, facing the gas-fire and with her back to the table. Only when she looked up involuntarily at the sketch of Adam Poole did she realize that young Lamprey had settled himself at the table and taken out a note-book. She could see his image reflected in the glass.

Inspector Fox came in and went quietly to the far end of the room where he sat in a shadowed corner and appeared to consult his own note-book.

'Well,' Alleyn said, 'what's it all about?'

'You'll probably think it's about nothing,' Martyn began, 'and if you do I shall be sorry I've bothered you with it. But I thought – just in case – '

'You were perfectly right. Believe me, we are "conditioned", if that's the beastly word, to blind alleys. Let's have it.'

'On my first morning in this theatre,' Martyn said. 'which was the day before yesterday . . . no, if it's past midnight, the day before that.'

'Tuesday?'

'Yes. On that morning I went to Mr Bennington's room to fetch Miss Hamilton's cigarette-case. He was rather strange in his manner but at first I thought that was because – I thought he'd noticed my likeness to Mr Poole. He couldn't find the case and in hunting through the pockets of a jacket, a letter dropped to the floor. I picked it up and he drew my attention to it in the oddest sort of way. I'd describe his manner almost as triumphant. He said something about autographs. I think he asked me if I collected autographs or auto-graphed letters. He pointed to the envelope which I still had in my hand and said there was somebody who'd give a hell of a lot for that one. Those, I'm almost sure, were his exact words.'

'Did you look at the letter?'

'Yes, I did, because of what he said. It was addressed to him and it had a foreign stamp on it. The writing was very bold and it seemed to me foreign looking. I put it on the shelf face downwards and he drew my attention to it again by stabbing at it with his finger. The name of the sender was written on the back.'

'Do you remember it?'

'Yes, I do, because of his insistence.'

'Good girl,' said Alleyn quietly.

'It was "Otto Brod" and the address was a theatre in Prague. I'm afraid I don't remember the name of the theatre or the street. I *ought* to remember the theatre. It was a French name, Théâtre de – something. *Why* can't I remember!'

'You haven't done badly. Was there something in the envelope?'

'Yes. It wasn't anything fat. One sheet of paper I should think.'

'And his manner was triumphant?'

'I thought so. He was just rather odd about it. He'd been drinking – brandy I thought – the tumbler was on the dressing-shelf and he made as if to put the flask behind his looking-glass.'

'Did you think he was at all the worse for wear?'

'I wondered if it accounted for his queer behaviour.'

'Can you tell me anything else he said? The whole conversation if you remember it.'

Martyn thought back and it seemed she had journeyed half a life-time in three days. There was the room. There was J.G. going out and leaving her with Bennington and there was Bennington staring at her and talking about the cigarette-case. There was also some-thing else, buried away behind her thoughts of which the memory now returned. She was made miserable by it.

'He said, I think, something about the cigarette-case. That he himself hadn't given it to Miss Hamilton.'

'Did he say who gave it to her?'

'No,' Martyn said. 'I don't think he said that. Just that *he* didn't.'

'And was his manner of saying this strange?'

'I thought his manner throughout was – uncomfortable and odd. He seemed to me to be a very unhappy man.'

'Yet you used the word triumphant?'

'There can be unhappy victories.'

'True for you. There can, indeed. Tell me one thing more. Do you connect the two conversations? I mean do you think what he said about the cigarette-case had anything to do with what he said about the letter?'

'I should say nothing. Nothing at all.'

'Oh, Lord!' Alleyn said resignedly and called out: 'Have you got all that, Mike?'

'Coming up the straight, sir.'

'Put it into longhand, now, will you, and we'll ask Miss Tarne to have a look at it and see if she's been misrepresented. Do you mind waiting a minute or two, Miss Tarne? It'll save you coming back.'

'No, of course not,' said Martyn whose ideas of police investigation were undergoing a private revolution. Alleyn offered her a cigarette and lit it for her. The consultation, she felt, was over and the famous surgeon was putting his patient at her ease.

'I gather from Lamprey's far-reaching conversation that you are a New Zealander,' he said. 'If I may say so, you seem to have dropped out of a clear sky into your own success story. Have you been long at the Vulcan, Miss Tarne?'

'A night and three days.'

'Good Lord! And in that time you've migrated from dresser to what sounds like minor stardom. Success story, indeed!'

'Yes, but – ' Martyn hesitated. For the first time since she walked into the Vulcan she felt able to talk about herself. It didn't occur to her that it was odd for her confidant to be a police officer.

'It's all been very eccentric,' she said. 'I only reached England a little over a fortnight ago and my money was stolen in the ship so I had to get some sort of job rather quickly.'

'Did you report the theft to the police?'

'No. The purser said he didn't think it would do any good.'

'So much,' said Alleyn with a wry look, 'for the police!'

'I'm sorry – ' Martyn began and he said: 'Never mind. It's not an uncommon attitude. I'm afraid. So you had a rather unhappy arrival. Lucky there was your cousin to come to your rescue.'

'But – no – I mean – ' Martyn felt herself blushing and plunged on. 'That's just what I didn't want to do. I mean I didn't want to go to him at all. He didn't know of my existence. You see – '

It was part of Alleyn's professional equipment that something in his make-up invited confidence. Mr Fox once said of his superior that he would be able to get himself worked up over the life story of a mollusc provided the narrative was obtained first-hand. He heard Martyn's story with the liveliest interest up to the point where she entered the theatre. He didn't seem to think it queer that she should have been anxious to conceal her relationship to Poole or that she was stupid to avoid the Vulcan in her search for a job. She was describing her interview with Bob Grantley on Wednesday night when Sergeant Gibson's voice sounded in the passage. He tapped on the door and came in.

'Excuse me, sir,' he said, 'but could you see the night-watchman. He seems to think it's important.'

He had got as far as this when he was elbowed aside by Fred Badger who came angrily into the room.

''Ere!' he said. 'Are you the guvnor of this 'owd'yerdo?'

'Yes,' said Alleyn.

'Well, look. You can lay orf this young lady, see? No call to get nosy on account of what she done, see? I don't know nothink abaht the law, see, but I'm in charge 'ere of a night and what she done she done wiv my permission. Nah!'

'Just a moment – ' Alleyn began and was roared down.

'Suppose it was an offence! What abaht it! She never done no 'arm. No offence taken where none was intended, that's correct ain't it! Nah ven!'

'What,' Alleyn said turning to Martyn, 'is this about?'

'I'm afraid it's about me sleeping in the theatre that first night. I'd nowhere to go and it was very late. Mr Badger very kindly – didn't turn me out.'

'I see. Where did you sleep?'

'Here. In this chair.'

'Like a charld,' Fred Badger interposed. 'Slep' like a charld all night. I looked in on me rahnds and seen 'er laying safe in the arms of Morpus. Innercent. And if anyone tells you different you can refer 'im to me. Badger's the name.'

'All right, Badger.'

'If you put me pot on with the management for what I done, leaving 'er to lay – all right. Aht! Finish! There's better jobs rahnd the corner.'

'Yes. All right. I don't think we'll take it up.'

'Awright. Fair enough.' He addressed himself to Martyn. 'And what was mentioned between you and me in a friendly manner needn't be mentioned no more. Let bygones be bygones.' He returned to Alleyn. 'She's as innercent as a babe. Arst 'is nibs.'

Alleyn waited for a moment and then said: 'Thank you.' Gibson succeeded in removing Fred Badger but not before he had directed at Martyn that peculiar clicking sound of approval which is accompanied by a significant jerk of the head.

When he had gone Alleyn said: 'I think I'd better ask you to interpret. What *was* his exquisite meaning?'

Martyn felt a dryness in her mouth. 'I think,' she said, 'he's afraid he'll get into trouble for letting me sleep in here that night and I think he's afraid I'll get into trouble if I tell you that he showed me how the murder in the Jupiter case was accomplished.'

'That seems a little far-fetched.'

Martyn said rapidly: 'I suppose it's idiotic of me to say this but I'd rather say it. Mr Bennington very naturally resented my luck in this theatre. He tackled me about it and he was pretty truculent. I expect the stage-hands have gossiped to Badger and he thinks you might – might – '

'Smell a motive?'

'Yes,' said Martyn.

'Did Bennington threaten you?'

'I don't remember exactly what he said. His manner was threatening. He frightened me.'

'Where did this happen?'

'Off-stage, during the first dress-rehearsal.'

'Was anyone present when he tackled you?'

The image of Poole rose in Martyn's memory. She saw him take Bennington by the arm and twist him away from her.

'There were people about,' she said. 'They were changing the set. I should think it very likely – I mean it was a very public sort of encounter.'

He looked thoughtfully at her and she wondered if she had changed colour. 'This,' he said, 'was before it was decided you were to play the part?'

'Oh, yes. That was only decided half an hour before the show went on.'

'So it was. Did he do anything about this decision? Go for you, again?'

'He didn't come near me until I'd finished. And knowing how much he must mind, I was grateful for that.'

Alleyn said: 'You've been very sensible to tell me this, Miss Tarne.'

Martyn swallowed hard. 'I don't know,' she said, 'that I would have told you if it hadn't been for Fred Badger.'

'Ah, well,' Alleyn said, 'one mustn't expect too much. How about that statement, Mike?'

'Here we are, sir. I hope you can read my writing, Miss Tarne.'

When she took the paper, Martyn found her hands were not steady. Alleyn moved away to the table with his subordinate. She sat down again and read the large schoolboyish writing. It was a short and accurate résumé of the incident of the letter from Prague.

'It's quite right,' she said. 'Am I to sign it?'

'If you please. There will be statements for most of the others to sign later on but yours is so short I thought we might as well get it over now.'

He gave her his pen and she went to the table and signed. PC Lamprey smiled reassuringly at her and escorted her to the door.

Alleyn said: 'Thank you so much, Miss Tarne. Do you live far from here?'

'Not very far. A quarter of an hour's walk.'

'I wish I could let you go home now but I don't quite like to do that. Something might crop up that we'd want to refer to you.'

'Might it?'

'You never know,' he said. 'Anyway you can change now.' Lamprey opened the door and she went to the dressing-room.

When she had gone Alleyn said: 'What did you make of her, Mike?'

'I thought she was rather a sweetiepie, sir,' said PC Lamprey. Fox, in his disregarded corner, snorted loudly.

'That was all too obvious,' said Alleyn. 'Sweetness apart, did you find her truthful?'

'I'd have said so, sir, yes.'

'What about you, Br'er Fox? Come out of cover and declare yourself.'

Fox rose, removed his spectacles and advanced upon them. 'There was something,' he observed, 'about that business of when the deceased went for her.'

'There was indeed. Not exactly lying, wouldn't you think, so much as leaving something out?'

'Particularly in respect of whether there was a witness.'

'She had her back to you but she looked at this portrait of Adam Poole. I'd make a long bet, Poole found Bennington slanging that child and ordered him off.'

'Very possibly, Mr Alleyn. He's sweet on the young lady. That's plain to see. *And* she on him.'

'Good Lord!' Mike Lamprey ejaculated. 'He must be forty! I'm sorry, sir.'

Mr Fox began a stately reproof but Alleyn said: 'Go away, Mike. Go back to the stage. Wake Dr Rutherford and ask him to come here. I want a change from actors.'

III

Dr Rutherford, on his entry into the greenroom, was a figure of high fantasy. For his greater ease in sleeping he had pulled his boiled shirt from its confinement and it dangled fore and aft like a crumpled tabard. Restrained only by his slackened braces, it formed a mask, Alleyn conjectured, for a free adjustment of the doctor's trouser buttoning. He had removed his jacket and assumed an overcoat. His collar was released and his tie dangled on his bosom. His hair was tousled and his face blotched.

He paused in the doorway while Lamprey announced him and then, with a dismissive gesture, addressed himself to Alleyn and Fox.

'Calling my officers about me in my branched velvet gown,' he shouted, 'having come from a day-bed where I left Miss Gainsford sleeping, I present myself as a brand for the constabular burning. What's cooking, my hearties?'

He stood there, puffing and blowing, and eyed them with an expression of extreme impertinence. If he had been an actor, Alleyn thought, he would have been cast, and cast ideally, for Falstaff. He fished under his shirt tail, produced his snuff-box, and helped himself, with a parody of regency deportment, to a generous pinch. 'Speak!' he said. 'Propound! I am all ears.'

'I have nothing, I'm afraid, to propound,' Alleyn said cheerfully, 'and am therefore unable to pronounce. As for speaking, I hope you'll do most of that yourself, Dr Rutherford. Will you sit down?'

Dr Rutherford, with his usual precipitancy, hurled himself into the nearest armchair. As an afterthought he spread his shirt tail with ridiculous finicking movements across his lap. 'I am a thought down-gyved,' he observed. 'My points are untrussed. Forgive me.'

'Tell me,' Alleyn said. 'Do you think Bennington was murdered?'

The doctor opened his eyes very wide, folded his hands on his stomach, revolved his thumbs and said: 'No.'

'No?'

'No.'

'We do.'

'Why?'

'I'll come to that when I'm quite sure you may be put into the impossible class.'

'Am I a suspect, by all that's pettifogging?'

'Not if you can prove yourself otherwise.'

'By God!' said Dr Rutherford deeply, 'if I'd thought I could get away with it, be damned if I wouldn't have had a shot. He was an unconscionable rogue, was Ben.'

'In what way?'

'In every way, by Janus. A drunkard. A wife-terrorist. An exhibitionist. And what's more,' he went on with rising intensity, 'a damned wrecker of plays. A yeaforsooth knavish pander, by heaven! I tell you this, and I tell you plainly, if I, sitting in my OP box, could have persuaded the Lord to stoop out of the firmament and drop a tidy thunderbolt on Ben, I would have done it with bells on. Joyously!'

'A thunderbolt,' Alleyn said, 'is one of the few means of dispatch that we have not seriously considered. Would you mind telling me where you were between the time when he made his last exit and the time when you appeared before the audience?'

'Brief let me be. In my box. On the stairs. Off-stage. On the stage.'

'Can you tell me exactly when you left your box?'

'While they were making their initial mops and mows at the audience.'

'Did you meet anyone or notice anything at all remarkable during this period?'

'Nothing, and nobody whatever.'

'From which side did you enter for your own call?'

'The OP, which is actors' right.'

'So you merely emerged from the stairs that lead from the box to the stage and found yourself hard by the entrance?'

'Precisely.'

'Have you any witness to all this, sir?'

'To my knowledge,' said the doctor, 'none whatever. There may have been a rude mechanical or so.'

'As far as your presence in the box is concerned there was the audience. Nine hundred of them.'

'In spite of its mangling at the hands of two of the actors, I believe the attention of the audience to have been upon My Play. In any case,' the doctor added, helping himself to a particularly large pinch of snuff and holding it poised before his face, 'I had shrunk in modest confusion behind the curtain.'

'Perhaps someone visited you?'

'Not after the first act. I locked myself in,' he added, taking his snuff with uncouth noises, 'as a precautionary measure. I loathe company.'

'Did you come back-stage at any other time during the performance?'

'I did. I came back in both intervals. Primarily to see the little wench.'

'Miss Tarne?' Alleyn ventured.

'She. A tidy little wench it is and will make a good player. If she doesn't allow herself to be debauched by the sissies that rule the roost in our lamentable theatre.'

'Did you, during either of these intervals, visit the dressing-rooms?'

'I went to the usual office at the end of the passage if you call that a dressing-room.'

'And returned to your box – when?'

'As soon as the curtain went up.'

'I see.' Alleyn thought for a moment and then said: 'Dr Rutherford, do you know anything about a man called Otto Brod?'

The doctor gave a formidable gasp. His eyes bulged, his nostrils wrinkled and his jaw dropped. The grimace turned out to be the preliminary spasm of a gargantuan sneeze. A handkerchief not being at his disposal, he snatched up the tail of his shirt, clapped it to his face and revealed a state of astonishing disorder below the waist.

'Otto Brod?' he repeated looking at Alleyn over his shirt tail as if it was an improvised yashmak. 'Never heard of him.'

'His correspondence seems to be of some value,' Alleyn said vaguely but the doctor merely gaped at him. 'I don't,' he said flatly, 'know what you're talking about.'

Alleyn gave up Otto Brod. 'You'll have guessed,' he said, 'that I've already heard a good deal about the events of the last few days: I mean as they concerned the final rehearsals and the change in casting.'

'Indeed? Then you will have heard that Ben and I had one flaming row after another. If you're looking for motive,' said Dr Rutherford with an expansive gesture, 'I'm lousy with it. We hated each other's guts, Ben and I. Of the two I should say, however, that he was the more murderously inclined.'

'Was this feeling chiefly on account of the part his niece was to have played?'

'Fundamentally it was the fine flower of a natural antipathy. The contributive elements were his behaviour as an actor in My Play and the obvious and immediate necessity to return his niece to her squalid little *métier* and replace her by the wench. We had at each other on that issue,' said Dr Rutherford with relish, 'after both auditions and on every other occasion that presented itself.'

'And in the end, it seems, you won?'

'Pah!' said the doctor with a dismissive wave of his hand. 'Cat's meat!'

Alleyn looked a little dubiously at the chaotic disarray of his garments. 'Have you any objection,' he asked, 'to being searched?'

'Not I,' cried the doctor and hauled himself up from his chair. Fox
approached him.

'By the way,' Alleyn said. 'As a medical man, would you say that
a punch on the jaw such as Bennington was given, could have been
the cause of his fainting some time afterwards? Remembering his
general condition?'

'Who says he had a punch on the jaw? It's probably a hypostatic
discoloration. What do *you* want?' Dr Rutherford demanded of Fox.

'If you wouldn't mind your taking your hands out of your pockets, sir,' Fox suggested.

The doctor said: 'Let not us that are squires of the night's body be
called thieves of the day's beauty,' and obligingly withdrew his
hands from his trouser pockets. Unfortunately he pulled the linings
out with them. A number of objects fell about his feet–pencils, his
snuffbox, scraps of paper, a pill-box, a programme, a notebook and
a half-eaten cake of chocolate. A small cloud of snuff floated above
this collection. Fox bent down and made a clucking sound of disapproval. He began to collect the scattered objects, inhaled snuff and
was seized with a paroxysm of sneezing. The doctor broke into a fit
of uncouth laughter and floundered damagingly among the exhibits.

'Dr Rutherford,' Alleyn said with an air of the liveliest exasperation, 'I would be immensely obliged to you if you'd have the goodness to stop behaving like a pantaloon. Get off those things, if you
please.'

The doctor backed away into his chair and examined an unlovely
mess of chocolate and cardboard on the sole of his boot. 'But, blast
your lights my good ass,' he said, 'there goes my spare ration. An
ounce of the best rapee, by heaven!' Fox began to pick the fragments
of the pill-box from his boot. Having collected and laid aside the
dropped possessions, he scraped up a heap of snuff. 'It's no good
now, Dogberry,' said the doctor with an air of intense disapproval.
Fox tipped the scrapings into an envelope.

Alleyn stood over the doctor. 'I think,' he said, 'you had better
give this up, you know.'

The doctor favoured him with an antic grimace but said nothing.
'You're putting on an act, Dr Rutherford, and I do assure you it's not

at all convincing. As a red-herring it stinks to high heaven. Let me tell you this. We now know that Bennington was hit over the jaw. We know when it happened. We know that the bruise was afterwards camouflaged with make-up. I want you to come with me while I remove this make-up. Where's your jacket?'

'*Give me my robe. Put on my crown. I have immortal longings in me.*'

Fox went out and returned with a tail-coat that was in great disorder. 'Nothing in the pockets, Mr Alleyn,' he said briefly. Alleyn nodded and he handed it to Dr Rutherford who slung it over his shoulder.

Alleyn led the way down the passage where Gibson was still on guard and round the back of the stage to the dock. PC Lamprey came off the set and rolled the doors back.

Bennington had stiffened a little since they last looked at him. His face bore the expression of knowledgeable acquiescence that is so often seen in the dead. Using the back of a knife-blade, Alleyn scraped away the greasepaint from the left jaw. Fox held a piece of card for him and he laid smears of greasepaint on it in the manner of a painter setting his palette. The discoloured mark on the jaw showed clearly.

'There it is,' Alleyn said, and stood aside for Dr Rutherford.

'A tidy buffet, if buffet it was. Who gave it him?'

Alleyn didn't answer. He moved round to the other side and went on cleaning the face.

'The notion that it could have contributed to his death,' the doctor said, 'is preposterous. If, as you say, there was an interval between the blow and the supposed collapse. Preposterous!'

Fox had brought cream and a towel with which Alleyn now completed his task. The doctor watched him with an air of impatience and unease. 'Damned if I know why you keep me hanging about,' he grumbled at last.

'I wanted your opinion on the bruise. That's all, Fox. Is the mortuary van here?'

'On its way, sir,' said Fox who was wrapping his piece of card in paper.

Alleyn looked at the doctor. 'Do you think,' he said, 'that his wife will want to see him?'

'She won't want to. She may think she ought to. Humbug, in my opinion. Distress herself for nothing. What good does it do anybody?'

'I think, however, I should at least ask her.'

'Why the blazes you can't let her go home, passes my comprehension. And where do *I* go, now? I'm getting damn bored with Ben's company.'

'You may wait either on the stage or, if you'd rather, in the unoccupied dressing-room. Or the office, I think, is open.'

'Can I have my snuff back?' Dr Rutherford asked with something of the shamefaced air of a small boy wanting a favour.

'I think we might let you do that,' Alleyn said. 'Fox, will you give Dr Rutherford his snuff-box?'

Dr Rutherford lumbered uncertainly to the door. He stood there with his chin on his chest and his hands in his pockets.

'See here, Alleyn,' he said, looking from under his eyebrows at him. 'Suppose I told you it was I who gave Ben that wallop on his mug. What then?'

'Why,' Alleyn said, 'I shouldn't believe you, you know.'

CHAPTER 10

Summing Up

Alleyn saw Helena Hamilton in her dressing-room. It was an oddly exotic setting. The scent of banked flowers, of tobacco smoke and of cosmetics was exceedingly heavy, the air hot and exhausted. She had changed into her street clothes and sat in an armchair that had been turned with its back to the door so that when he entered he saw nothing of her but her right hand trailing near the floor with a cigarette between her fingers. She called: 'Come in, Mr Alleyn,' in a warm voice as if he was an especially welcome visitor. He would not have guessed from this greeting that when he faced her he would find her looking so desperately tired.

As if she read his thoughts she put her hands to her eyes and said: 'My goodness, this is a long night, isn't it?'

'I hope that for you, at least, it is nearing its end,' he said. 'I've come to tell you that we are ready to take him away.'

'Does that mean I ought to – to look at him?'

'Only if you feel you want to. I can see no absolute need at all; if I may say so.'

'I don't want to,' she whispered and added in a stronger voice: 'It would be a pretence. I have no real sorrow and I have never seen the dead. I should only be frightened and confused.'

Alleyn went to the door and looked into the passage where Fox waited with Gibson. He shook his head and Fox went away. When Alleyn came back to her she looked up at him and said: 'What else?'

'A question or two. Have you ever known or heard of a man called Otto Brod?'

Her eyes widened. 'But what a strange question!' she said. 'Otto Brod? Yes. He's a Czech or an Austrian, I don't remember which. An intellectual. We met him three years ago when we did a tour of the Continent. He had written a play and asked my husband to read it. It was in German and Ben's German wasn't up to it. The idea was that he should get someone over here to look at it but he was dreadfully bad at keeping those sorts of promises and I don't think he ever did anything about it.'

'Have they kept in touch, do you know?'

'Oddly enough, Ben said a few days ago that he'd heard from Otto. I think he'd written from time to time for news of his play but I don't suppose Ben answered.' She pressed her thumb and fingers on her eyes. 'If you want to see the letter,' she said, 'it's in his coat.'

Alleyn said carefully: 'You mean the jacket he wore to the theatre? Or his overcoat?'

'The jacket. He was always taking my cigarette-case in mistake for his own. He took it out of his breast-pocket when he was leaving for the theatre and the letter was with it.' She waited for a moment and then said: 'He was rather odd about it.'

'In what way?' Alleyn asked. She had used Martyn's very phrase and now when she spoke again it was with the uncanny precision of a delayed echo: 'He was rather strange in his manner. He held the letter out with the cigarette-case and drew my attention to it. He said, I think, "That's my trump card." He seemed to be pleased in a not very attractive way. I took my case. He put the letter back in his pocket and went straight out.'

'Did you get the impression he meant it was a trump card he could use against somebody?'

'Yes. I think I did.'

'And did you form any idea who that person could be?'

She leant forward and cupped her face in her hands. 'Oh, yes,' she said. 'It seemed to me that it was I myself he meant. Or Adam. Or both of us. It sounded like a threat.' She looked up at Alleyn. 'We've both got alibis, haven't we? If it was murder.'

'*You* have, undoubtedly,' Alleyn said and she looked frightened.

He asked her why she thought her husband had meant that the letter was a threat to herself or to Poole but she evaded this question, saying vaguely that she had felt it to be so.

'You didn't come down to the theatre with your husband?' Alleyn said.

'No. He was ready before I was. And in any case – ' She made a slight expressive gesture and didn't complete her sentence.

Alleyn said: 'I think I must tell you that I know something of what happened this afternoon.'

The colour that flooded her face ebbed painfully and left it very white. She said: 'How do you know that? You can't know.' She stopped and seemed to listen. They could just hear Poole in the next room. He sounded as if he was moving about irresolutely. She caught her breath and after a moment she said loudly: 'Was it Jacko? No, no, it was never Jacko.'

'Your husband himself – ' Alleyn began and she caught him up quickly. 'Ben? Ah, I can believe that. I can believe he would boast of it. To one of the men. To J.G.? Was it J.G.? Or perhaps even to Gay?'

Alleyn said gently: 'You must know I can't answer questions like these.'

'It was never Jacko,' she repeated positively and he said: 'I haven't interviewed Mr Doré yet.'

'Haven't you? Good.'

'Did you like Otto Brod?'

She smiled slightly and lifted herself in her chair. Her face became secret and brilliant. 'For a little while,' she said, 'he was a fortunate man.'

'Fortunate?'

'For a little while I loved him.'

'Fortunate indeed,' said Alleyn.

'You put that very civilly, Mr Alleyn.'

'Do you think there was some connection here? I mean between your relationship with Brod and the apparent threat when your husband showed you the letter?'

She shook her head. 'I don't know. I don't think Ben realized. It was as brief as summer lightning, our affair.'

'On both parts?'

'Oh, no,' she said as if he had asked a foolish question. 'Otto was very young, rather violent and dreadfully faithful, poor sweet. You are looking at me in an equivocal manner, Mr Alleyn. Do you disapprove?'

Alleyn said formally: 'Let us say that I am quite out of my depth with – '

'Why do you hesitate? With what?'

'I was going to say with a *femme fatale*,' said Alleyn.

'Have I been complimented again?'

He didn't answer and after a moment she turned away as if she suddenly lost heart in some unguessed-at object she had had in mind.

'I suppose,' she said, 'I may not ask you why you believe Ben was murdered?'

'I think you may. For one reason: his last act in the dressing-room was not consistent with suicide. He refurbished his make-up.'

'That's penetrating of you,' she said. 'It was an unsympathetic make-up. But I still believe he killed himself. He had much to regret and nothing in the wide world to look forward to. Except discomfiture.'

'The performance tonight, among other things, to regret?'

'Among all the other things. The change in casting, for one. It may have upset him very much. Because yesterday he thought he'd stopped what he called John's nonsense about Gay. And there was his own behaviour, his hopeless, *hopeless* degradation. He had given up, Mr Alleyn. Believe me he had quite given up. You will find I'm right, I promise you.'

'I wish I may,' Alleyn said. 'And I think that's all at the moment. If you'll excuse me, I'll get on with my job.'

'Get on with it, then,' she said and looked amused. She watched him go and he wondered after he had shut the door if her expression had changed.

II

Adam Poole greeted Alleyn with a sort of controlled impatience. He had changed and was on his feet. Apparently Alleyn had interrupted an aimless promenade about the room.

'Well?' he said. 'Are you any further on? Or am I not supposed to ask?'

'A good deal further, I think,' Alleyn said. 'I want a word with you, if I may have it, and then with Mr Doré. I shall then have something to say to all of you. After that I think we shall know where we are.'

'And you're convinced, are you, that Bennington was murdered?'

'Yes, I'm quite convinced of that.'

'I wish to God I knew why.'

'I'll tell you,' Alleyn said, 'before the night is out.'

Poole faced him. 'I can't believe it,' he said, 'of any of us. It's quite incredulous.' He looked at the wall between his own room and Helena's. 'I could hear your voices in there,' he said. 'Is she all right?'

'She's perfectly composed.'

'I don't know why you wanted to talk to her at all.'

'I had three things to say to Miss Hamilton. I asked her if she wanted to see her husband before he was taken away. She didn't want to do so. Then I told her that I knew about an event of yesterday afternoon.'

'What event!' Poole demanded sharply.

'I mean an encounter between her husband and herself.'

'How the hell did you hear about that?'

'You knew of it yourself, evidently.'

Poole said: 'Yes, all right. I knew,' and then, as if the notion had just come to him and filled him with astonishment, he exclaimed: 'Good God, I believe you think it's a motive for *me*.' He thrust his hand through his hair. 'That's about as ironical an idea as one could possibly imagine.' He stared at Alleyn. An onlooker coming into the room at that moment would have thought that the two men had something in common and a liking for each other. 'You can't imagine,' Poole said, 'how inappropriate *that* idea is.'

'I haven't yet said I entertain it, you know.'

'It's not surprising if you do. After all, I suppose I could, fantastically, have galloped from the stage to Ben's room, laid him out, turned the gas on and doubled back in time to re-enter! Do you know what my line of re-entry is in the play?'

'No.'

'I come in, shut the door, go up to Helena, and say: "*You've guessed, haven't you? He's taken the only way out. I suppose we must be said to be free.*" It all seems to fit so very neatly, doesn't it? Except that for us it's a year or more out of date.' He looked at Alleyn. 'I really don't know,' he added, 'why I'm talking like this. It's probably most injudicious. But I've had a good deal to think about the last two days and Ben's death has more or less put the crown on it.

What am I to do about this theatre? What are we to do about the show? What's going to happen about – ' He broke off and looked at the wall that separated his room from Martyn's. 'Look here, Alleyn,' he said. 'You've no doubt heard all there is to hear and more about my private life. And Helena's. It's the curse of this job that one is perpetually in the spotlight.'

He seemed to expect some comment on this. Alleyn said lightly: 'The curse of greatness?'

'Nothing like it, I'm afraid. See here, Alleyn. There are some women who just can't be fitted into any kind of ethical or sociological pigeon-hole. Ellen Terry was one of them. It's not that they are above reproach in the sense most people mean by the phrase, but that they are outside it. They behave naturally in an artificial set-up. When an attachment comes to an end, it does so without any regrets or recrimination. Often, with an abiding affection on both sides. Do you agree?'

'That there are such women? Yes?'

'Helena is one. I'm not doing this very well but I do want you to believe that she's right outside this beastly thing. It won't get you any further and it may hurt her profoundly if you try to establish some link between her relationship with her husband or anyone else and the circumstances of his death. I don't know what you said to each other but I do know it would never occur to her to be on guard for her own sake.'

'I asked her to tell me about Otto Brod.'

Poole's reaction to this was surprising. He looked exasperated. 'There you are!' he said. 'That's exactly what I mean. Otto Brod! A fantastic irresponsible affair that floated out of some midsummer notion of Vienna and Strauss waltzes. How the devil you heard of it I don't know, though I've no doubt that at the time she fluttered him like a plume in her bonnet for all to see. I never met him but I understand he was some young intellectual with a pale face, no money and an over-developed faculty for symbolic tragedy. Why bring him in?'

Alleyn told him that Bennington, when he came down to the theatre, had had a letter from Brod in his pocket and Poole said angrily: 'Why the hell shouldn't he? What of it?'

'The letter is not to be found.'

'My dear chap, I suppose he chucked it out or burnt it or something.'

'I hardly think so,' said Alleyn. 'He told Miss Hamilton it was his trump card.'

Poole was completely still for some moments. Then he turned away to the dressing-shelf and looked for his cigarettes.

'Now what in the wide world,' he said with his back to Alleyn, 'could he have meant by a trump card?'

'That,' said Alleyn, 'is what, above everything else, I should very much like to know.'

'I don't suppose it means a damn thing, after all. It certainly doesn't to me.'

He turned to offer his cigarettes but found that Alleyn had his own case open in his hands. 'I'd ask you to have a drink,' Poole said, 'but I don't keep it in the dressing-room during the show. If you'd come to the office – '

'Nothing I'd like more but we don't have it in the working hours either.'

'Of course not. Stupid of me.' Poole glanced at his dress for the ball and then at his watch. 'I hope,' he said, 'that my business-manager is enjoying himself with my guests at my party.'

'He rang up some time ago to inquire. There was no message for you.'

'Thank you.' Poole leant against the dressing-shelf and lit his cigarette.

'It seems to me,' Alleyn said, 'that there is something you want to say to me. I've not brought a witness in here. If what you say is likely to be wanted as evidence I'll ask you to repeat it formally. If not, it will have no official significance.'

'You're very perceptive. I'm damned if I know why I should want to tell you this but I do. Just out of earshot behind these two walls are two women. Of my relation with the one, you seem to have heard. I imagine it's pretty generally known. I've tried to suggest that it has come to its end as simply, if that's not too fancy a way of putting it, as a flower relinquishes its petals. For a time I've pretended their colour had not faded and I've watched them fall with regret. But from the beginning we both knew it was that sort of affair. She didn't pretend at all. She's quite above any of the usual subterfuges and it's some weeks ago that she let me know it was almost over for her. I think we both kept it up out of politeness more than anything else. When she told me of Ben's unspeakable behaviour yesterday, I felt as one must feel about an outrage to a woman whom one knows very well and likes very much. I was appalled to discover in myself no stronger emotion than this. It was precisely this discovery that told me the last petal had indeed fallen and now – ' He lifted his hands. 'Now, Ben gets himself murdered, you say, and I've run out of the appropriate emotions.'

Alleyn said: 'We are creatures of convention and like our tragedies to take a recognizable form.'

'I'm afraid this is not even a tragedy. Unless – ' he turned his head and looked at the other wall. 'I haven't seen Martyn,' he said, 'since you spoke to her. She's all right, isn't she?' Before Alleyn could answer he went on: 'I suppose she's told you about herself – her arrival out of a clear sky and all the rest of it?'

'Everything, I think.'

'I hope to God – I want to see her, Alleyn. She's alone in there. She may be frightened. I don't suppose you understand.'

'She's told me of the relationship between you.'

'The *relationship* – ' he said quickly. 'You mean – '

'She's told me you are related. It's natural that you should be concerned about her.'

Poole stared at him. 'My good ass,' he said, 'I'm eighteen years her senior and I love her like a boy of her own age.'

'In that case,' Alleyn remarked. 'You can *not* be said to have run out of the appropriate emotions.'

He grinned at Poole in a friendly manner, and accompanied by Fox, went to his final interview – with Jacques Doré.

III

It took place on the stage. Dr Rutherford elected to retire into the office to effect, he had told Fox, a few paltry adjustments of his costume. The players, too, were all in their several rooms and Clem Smith had been wakened, re-examined by Fox, and allowed to go home.

So Jacko was alone in the tortured scene he had himself designed.

'What do we talk about?' he asked and began to roll himself a cigarette.

'First of all,' Alleyn said, 'I must tell you that I am asking for a general search through the clothes that have been worn in the theatre. We have no warrant at this stage but so far no one has objected.'

'Then who am I to do so?'

Fox went through his pockets and found a number of curious objects – chalk, pencils, a rubber, a surgeon's scalpel which Jacko said he used for wood carving, and which was protected by a sheath, a pocket-book with money, a photograph of Helena Hamilton, various scraps of paper with drawings on them, pieces of cotton-wool and an empty bottle smelling strongly of ether. This, he told Alleyn, had contained a fluid used for cleaning purposes. 'Always they are messing themselves and always I am removing the mess. My overcoat is in the junk room. It contains merely a filthy handkerchief, I believe.'

Alleyn thanked him and returned the scalpel, the pocket-book and drawing-materials. Fox laid the other things aside, sat down and opened his note-book.

'Next,' Alleyn said, 'I think I'd better ask you what your official job is in this theatre. I see by the programme – '

'The programme,' Jacko said, 'is euphemistic. "Assistant to Adam Poole" is it not? Let us rather say: Dogsbody in Ordinary to the Vulcan Theatre. Henchman Extraordinary to Mr Adam Poole. At the moment, dresser to Miss Helena Hamilton. Confidant to all and sundry. Johannes Factotum and not without bells on. *Le* Vulcan, *c'est moi*, in a shabby manner of speaking. Also: *j'y suis, j'y reste*. I hope.'

'Judging by this scenery,' Alleyn rejoined, 'and by an enchanting necklace which I think is your work, there shouldn't be much doubt about that. But your association with the management goes further back than the Vulcan, doesn't it?'

'Twenty years,' Jacko said, licking his cigarette paper, 'for twenty years I improvise my role of Pantaloon for them. Foolishness, but such is my deplorable type. The eternal doormat. What can I do for you?'

Alleyn said: 'You can tell me if you still think Bennington committed suicide?'

Jacko lit his cigarette. 'Certainly,' he said. 'You are wasting your time.'

'Was he a vain man?'

'Immensely. And he knew he was artistically sunk.'

'Vain of his looks?'

'But yes, *yes!* ' Jacko said with great emphasis, and then looked very sharply at Alleyn. 'Why, of his looks?'

'Did he object to his make-up in this play? It seemed to me a particularly repulsive one.'

'He disliked it, yes. He exhibited the vanity of the failing actor in this. Always, always he must be sympathetic. Fortunately Adam insisted on the make-up.'

'I think you told me that you noticed his face was shiny with sweat before he went for the last time to his room?'

'I did.'

'And you advised him to remedy this? You even looked into his room to make sure?'

'Yes,' Jacko agreed after a pause, 'I did.'

'So when you had gone he sat at his dressing-table and carefully furbished up his repellent make-up as if for the curtain call. And then gassed himself?'

'The impulse perhaps came very suddenly.' Jacko half-closed his eyes and looked through their sandy lashes at his cigarette smoke. 'Ah, yes,' he said softly. 'Listen. He repairs his face. He has a last look at himself. He is about to get up when his attention sharpens. He continues to stare. He sees the ruin of his face. He was once a coarsely handsome fellow, was Ben, with a bold rake-helly air. The coarseness has increased but where, he asks himself, are the looks? Pouches, grooves, veins, yellow eyeballs and all emphasized most hideously by the make-up. This is what he has become, he thinks, he has become the man he has been playing. And his heart descends into his belly. He knows despair and he makes up his mind. There is hardly time to do it. In a minute or two he will be called. So quickly, quickly he lies on the floor, with trembling hands he pulls his coat over his head and puts the end of the gas-tube in his mouth.'

'You knew how he was found then?'

'Clem told me. I envisaged everything. He enters a world of whirling dreams. And in a little while he is dead. I see it very clearly.'

'Almost as if you'd been there,' Alleyn said lightly. 'Is this, do you argue, his sole motive? What about the quarrels that had been going

on? The change of cast at the last moment? The handing over of
Miss Gainsford's part to Miss Tarne? He was very much upset by
that, wasn't he?'

Jacko doubled himself up like an ungainly animal and squatted
on a stool. 'Too much has been made of the change of casting,' he
said. 'He accepted it in the end. He made a friendly gesture. On
thinking it over I have decided we were all wrong to lay so much
emphasis on this controversy.' He peered sideways at Alleyn. 'It was
the disintegration of his artistic integrity that did it,' he said. 'I now
consider the change of casting to be of no significance.'

Alleyn looked him very hard in the eye. 'And that,' he said, 'is
where we disagree. I consider it to be of the most complete significance: the key, in fact, to the whole puzzle of his death.'

'I cannot agree,' said Jacko. 'I am sorry.'

Alleyn waited for a moment and then – and for the last time – asked
the now familiar question.

'Do you know anything about a man called Otto Brod?'

There was a long silence. Jacko's back was bent and his head
almost between his knees.

'I have heard of him,' he said at last.

'Did you know him?'

'I have never met him. Never.'

'Perhaps you have seen some of his work?'

Jacko was silent.

'*Können Sie Deutsch lesen?*'

Fox looked up from his notes with an expression of blank surprise. They heard a car turn in from Carpet Street and come up the
side lane with a chime of bells. It stopped and a door slammed.

'*Jawohl,*' Jacko whispered.

The outside doors of the dock were rolled back. The sound resembled stage-thunder. Then the inner and nearer doors opened heavily
and someone walked round the back of the set. Young Lamprey
came through the prompt entrance. 'The mortuary van, sir,' he said.

'All right. They can go ahead.'

He went out again. There was a sound of voices and of boots on
concrete. A cold draught of night air blew in from the dock and set
the borders creaking. A rope tapped against canvas and a sighing
breath wandered about the grid. The doors were rolled together. The

engine started up and, to another chime of bells, Bennington made his final exit from the Vulcan. The theatre settled back into its night-watch.

Jacko's cigarette had burnt his lips. He spat it out and got slowly to his feet.

'You have been very clever,' he said. He spoke as if his lips were stiff with cold.

'Did Bennington tell you how he would, if necessary, play his trump card?'

'Not until after he had decided to play it.'

'But you had recognized the possibility?'

'Yes.'

Alleyn nodded to Fox who shut his note-book, removed his spectacles and went out.

'What now?' Jacko asked.

'All on,' Alleyn said. 'A company call. This is the curtain speech, Mr Doré.'

IV

Lamprey had called them and then retired. They found an empty stage awaiting them. It was from force of habit, Martyn supposed, that they took up, for the last time, their after-rehearsal positions on the stage. Helena lay back in her deep chair with Jacko on the floor at her feet. When he settled himself there, she touched his cheek and he turned his lips to her hand. Martyn wondered if he was ill. He saw that she looked at him and made his clown's grimace. She supposed that, like everybody else, he was merely exhausted. Darcey and Gay Gainsford sat together on the small settee and Parry Percival on his upright chair behind them. At the back, Dr Rutherford lay on the sofa with a newspaper spread over his face. Martyn had returned to her old seat near the prompt corner and Poole to his central chair facing the group. 'We have come out of our rooms,' Martyn thought, 'like rabbits from their burrows.' Through the prompt entrance she could see Fred Badger, lurking anxiously in the shadows.

Alleyn and his subordinates stood in a group near the dock doors. On the wall close by them was the baize rack with criss-crossed tapes in which two receipts and a number of commercial cards were exhibited. Fox had read them all. He now replaced the last and looked through the prompt corner to the stage.

'Are they all on?' Alleyn asked.

'All present and correct, sir.'

'Do you think I'm taking a very risky line, Br'er Fox?'

'Well, sir,' said Fox uneasily. 'It's a very unusual sort of procedure, isn't it?'

'It's a very unusual case,' Alleyn rejoined and after a moment's reflection he took Fox by the arm. 'Come on, old trooper,' he said. 'Let's get it over.'

He walked on to the stage almost as if, like Poole, he was going to sum up a rehearsal. Fox went to his old chair near the back entrance. Martyn heard the other men move round behind the set. They took up positions, she thought, outside the entrances and it was unpleasant to think of them waiting there, unseen.

Alleyn stood with his back to the curtain and Poole at once slewed his chair round to face him. With the exception of Jacko who was rolling a cigarette, they all watched Alleyn. Even the doctor removed his newspaper, sat up, stared, groaned and returned ostentatiously to his former position.

For a moment, Alleyn looked round the group and to Martyn he seemed to have an air of compassion. When he began to speak his manner was informal but extremely deliberate.

'In asking you to come here together,' he said, 'I've taken an unorthodox line. I don't myself know whether I am justified in taking it and I shan't know until those of you who are free to do so have gone home. That will be in a few minutes, I think.

'I have to tell you that your fellow-player has been murdered. All of you must know that we've formed this opinion and I think most of you know that I was first inclined to it by the circumstance of his behaviour on returning to his dressing-room. His last conscious act was to repair his stage make-up. While that seemed to me to be inconsistent with suicide it was, on the other hand, much too slender a thread to tie up a case for homicide. But there is more conclusive evidence and I'm going to put it before you. He powdered his face. His dresser had already removed the pieces of cotton-wool that had been used earlier in the evening and put out a fresh pad. Yet after his death there was no used pad of cotton-wool anywhere in the room. There is, on the other hand, a fresh stain near the gas-fire which may, on analysis, turn out to have been caused by such a pad having been burnt on the hearth. The box of powder has been overturned on the shelf and there is a deposit of powder all over that corner of the room. As you know, his head and shoulders were covered, tentwise, with his overcoat. There was powder on this coat and over his fingerprints on the top of the gas-fire. The coat had hung near the door and would, while it was there, have been out of range of any powder flying about. The powder, it is clear, had been scattered after and not before he was gassed. If he was, in fact, gassed.'

Poole and Darcey made simultaneous ejaculations. Helena and Gay looked bewildered, and Percival incredulous. Jacko stared at the floor and the doctor groaned under his newspaper.

'The post-mortem,' Alleyn said, 'will of course settle this one way or the other. It will be exhaustive. Now, it's quite certain that the dresser didn't go into the room after Mr Bennington entered it this last time and it is equally certain that the dresser left it in good order – the powder-pad prepared, the clothes hung up, the fire burning and the door unlocked. It is also certain that the powder was not overturned by the men who carried Mr Bennington out. It was spilt by someone who was in the room after he was on the floor with the coat over his head. This person, the police will maintain, was his murderer. Now, the question arises, doesn't it, how it came about that he was in such a condition – comatose or unconscious – that it was possible to get him down on the floor, put out the gas-fire, and then disengage the connecting tube, put the rubber end in his mouth and turn the gas on again, get his fingerprints on the wing-tap and cover him with his own overcoat. There is still about one sixth of brandy left in his flask. He was not too drunk to make up his own face and he was more or less his own man, though not completely so, when he spoke to Miss Tarne just before he went into his room. During the second interval Mr Darcey hit him on the jaw and raised a bruise. I suppose it is possible that his murderer hit him again on the same spot – there is no other bruise – and knocked him out. A close examination of the bruise may show if this was so. In that case the murderer would need to pay only one visit to the room: he would simply walk in, a few minutes before the final curtain, knock his victim out and set the stage for apparent suicide.

'On the other hand it's possible that he was drugged.'

He waited for a moment. Helena Hamilton said: 'I don't believe in all this. I don't mean, Mr Alleyn, that I think you're wrong: I mean it just sounds unreal and rather commonplace like a case reported in a newspaper. One knows that probably it's all happened but one doesn't actively believe it. I'm sorry I interrupted.'

'I hope,' Alleyn said. 'You will all feel perfectly free to interrupt at any point. About this possibility of drugging. If the brandy was drugged, then of course we shall find out. Moreover it must have been tinkered with after he went on for his final scene. Indeed, any use of a drug, and one cannot disregard the possibility of even the most fantastic methods, must surely have been prepared while he was on the stage during the last act. We shall, of course, have a chemical analysis made of everything he used – the brandy, his tumbler, his cigarettes, his make-up and even the greasepaint on his face. I tell you, quite frankly, that I've no idea at all whether this will get us any further.'

Fox cleared his throat. This modest sound drew the attention of the company upon him but he merely looked gravely preoccupied and they turned back to Alleyn.

'Following out this line of thought it seems clear,' he said, 'that two visits would have to be made to the dressing-room. The first, during his scene in the last act and the second, after he had come off and before the smell of gas was first noticed: by Mr Parry Percival.'

Percival said in a high voice: 'I knew this was coming.' Gay Gainsford turned and looked at him with an expression of the liveliest horror. He caught her eye and said: 'Oh, don't be fantastic, Gay darling. *Honestly!*'

'Mr Percival,' Alleyn said, 'whose room is next to Mr Bennington's and whose fire backs on his, noticed a smell of gas when he was about to go out for the curtain-call. He tells us he is particularly sensitive to the smell because of its association in this theatre and that he turned his own fire off and went out. Thus his fingerprints were found on the tap.'

'Well, naturally they were,' Parry said angrily. 'Really, Gay!'

'This, of course,' Alleyn went on, 'was reminiscent of the Jupiter case but in that case the tube was not disconnected because the murderer never entered the room. He blew down the next-door tube and the fire went out. In that instance the victim was comatose from alcohol. Now, it seems quite clear to us that while this thing was planned with one eye on the Jupiter case, there was no intention to throw the blame upon anyone else and that Mr Percival's reaction to the smell was not foreseen by the planner. What the planner hoped to emphasize was Mr Bennington's absorption in the former case. We were to suppose that when he decided to take his own life he used the method by which he was obsessed. On the other hand,' Alleyn said, 'suppose this hypothetical planner was none other than Bennington himself?'

V

Their response to this statement had a delayed action. They behaved as actors do when they make what is technically known as a 'double take'. There were a few seconds of blank witlessness followed by a sudden and violent reaction. Darcey and Percival shouted together that it would be exactly like Ben: Helena cried out inarticulately and Poole gave a violent ejaculation. The doctor crackled his newspaper and Martyn's thoughts tumbled about in her head like dice. Jacko, alone, stared incredulously at Alleyn.

'Do you mean,' Jacko asked, 'that we are to understand that Ben killed himself in such a way as to throw suspicion of murder upon one of us? Is that your meaning?'

'No. For a time we wondered if this might be so but the state of the dressing-room, as I'd hoped I'd made clear, flatly contradicts any such theory. No. I believe the planner based the method on Bennington's preoccupation with the other case and hoped we would be led to some such conclusion. If powder had not been spilt on the overcoat we might well have done so.'

'So we are still – in the dark,' Helena said and gave the common-place phrase a most sombre colour.

'Not altogether. I needn't go over the collection of near-motives that have cropped up in the course of our interviews. Some of them sound far-fetched, others at least possible. It's not generally recog-nized that, given a certain temperament, the motive for homicide can

be astonishingly unconvincing. Men have been killed from petty cov-
etousness, out of fright, vanity, jealousy, boredom, or sheer hatred.
One or other of these motives lies at the back of this case. You all, I
think, had cause to dislike this man. In one of you the cause was
wedded to that particular kink which distinguishes murderers from
the rest of mankind. With such beings there is usually some – shall I
say, explosive agency, a sort of fuse – which, if it is touched off, sets
them going as murder-machines. In this case I believe the fuse to
have been a letter written by Otto Brod to Clark Bennington. This letter has disappeared and was probably burnt in his dressing-room. As
the powder-pad may have been burnt. By his murderer.'

Poole said: 'I can't begin to see the sense of all this,' and Helena
said drearily: 'Dark. In the dark.'

Alleyn seemed to be lost in thought. Martyn, alone of all the company, looked at him. She thought she had never seen a face as withdrawn and – incongruously the word flashed up again – compassionate.
She wondered if he had come to some crucial point and she watched
anxiously for the sign of a decision. But at this moment she felt
Poole's eyes upon her and when she looked at him they exchanged
the delighted smiles of lovers. 'How *can* we,' she thought, and tried
to feel guilty. But she hadn't heard Alleyn speak and he was half-
way through his first sentence before she gave him her attention.

'. . . So far about opportunity,' he was saying. 'If there were two
visits to the dressing-room during the last act I think probably all of
you except Miss Hamilton could have made the earlier one. But for
the second visit there is a more restricted field. Shall I take you in the
order in which you are sitting? Miss Tarne, in that case, comes first.'

Martyn thought: 'I ought to feel frightened again.'

'Miss Tarne has told us that after she left the stage, and she was
the first to leave it, she stood at the entry to the dressing-room passage. She was in a rather bemused state of mind and doesn't remember much about it until Mr Percival, Mr Darcey and Mr Bennington
himself came past. All three spoke to her in turn and went on down
the passage. It is now that the crucial period begins. Mr Doré was
nearby and after directing the gunshot, took her to her dressing-
room. On the way, he looked in for a few seconds on Mr Bennington
who had just gone to his own room. After Miss Tarne and Mr Doré
had both heard Mr Darcey and Mr Percival return to the stage, they

followed them out. They give each other near alibis up to this point and the stage-hands extend Miss Tarne's alibi to beyond the crucial time. She is, I think, out of the picture.'

Gay Gainsford stared at Martyn. 'That,' she said, 'must be quite a change for you.'

'Miss Gainsford comes next.' Alleyn said as if he had not heard her. 'She was in the greenroom throughout the crucial period and tells us she was asleep. There is no witness to this.'

'George!' said Gay Gainsford wildly and turned to Darcey, thus revealing for the first time in this chronicle, his Christian name. 'It's all right, dear,' he said. 'Don't be frightened. It's all right.'

'Mr Percival and Mr Darcey are also in the list of persons without alibis. They left the stage and returned to it together, or nearly so. But they went of course to separate rooms. Mr Percival is the only one who noticed the smell of gas. Dr Rutherford,' Alleyn went on, moving slightly in order to see the doctor, 'could certainly have visited the room during this period, as at any other stage of the performance. He could have come down from his box, passed unobserved round the back of the scenery, taken cover and gone in after these four persons were in their own rooms.'

He waited politely but the doctor's newspaper rose and fell rhythmically. Alleyn raised his voice slightly. 'He could have returned to his OP stairs when the rest of you were collected on the prompt side and he could have made an official entry in the character of Author.' He waited for a moment. The others looked in a scandalized manner at the recumbent doctor but said nothing.

'Mr Poole has himself pointed out that he could have darted to the room during his brief period off-stage. He could not, in my opinion, have effected all that had to be done and if he had missed his re-entry he would have drawn immediate attention to himself.

'Mr Doré is in a somewhat different category from the rest,' Alleyn said. 'We know he came from her dressing-room with Miss Tarne but although he was seen with the others on the prompt side, he was at the back of the group and in the shadows. Everyone's attention at this period was riveted on the stage. The call-boy checked over the players for the curtain-call and noticed Mr Bennington had not yet appeared. Neither he nor anyone else had reason to check Mr Doré's movements.'

Jacko said: 'I remind you that Parry said he smelt gas while I was still with Miss Tarne in her room.'

'I have remembered,' Alleyn answered, 'what Mr Percival said.' He looked at Helena Hamilton. 'And while all this was happening,' he concluded, 'Miss Hamilton was on the stage holding the attention of a great cloud of witnesses in what I think must have been a most remarkable play.'

There was a long silence.

'That's all I have to say,' Alleyn's voice changed its colour a little. 'I'm going to ask you to return to your rooms. You'll want to do so in any case to collect your coats and so on. If you would like to talk things over among yourselves you are quite free to do so. We shall be in the greenroom. If each of you will come in and leave us an address and telephone number I'll be grateful.' He looked round them for a moment. Perhaps deliberately he repeated the stage-manager's customary dismissal: 'Thank you, ladies and gentlemen. That will be all.'

CHAPTER 11

Last Act

Alleyn stood in front of Adam Poole's portrait and looked at his little group of fellow-policemen.

'Well,' he said. 'I've done it.'

'Very unusual,' said Fox.

Bailey and Thompson stared at the floor.

Gibson blew out a long breath and wiped his forehead.

PC Lamprey looked as if he would like to speak but knew his place too well. Alleyn caught his eye. 'That, Mike,' he said, 'was an almost flawless example of how an investigating officer is not meant to behave. You will be good enough to forget it.'

'Certainly, sir.'

'What do you reckon, Mr Alleyn?' Fox asked. 'A confession? Brazen it out? Attempt to escape? Or what?'

'There'll be no escape, Mr Fox,' Gibson said. 'We've got the place plastered outside. No cars without supervision within a quarter of a mile and a full description.'

'I said "attempt", Fred,' Mr Fox pointed out majestically.

'If I've bungled,' Alleyn muttered, 'I've at least bungled in a big way. A monumental mess.'

They looked uneasily at him. Bailey astonished everybody by saying to his boots, with all his customary moroseness: 'That'll be the day.'

'Don't talk Australian,' Mr Fox chided immediately but he looked upon Bailey with approval.

A door in the passage opened and shut.

'Here we go,' said Alleyn.

A moment later there was a tap at the greenroom door and Parry Percival came in. He wore a dark overcoat, a brilliant scarf, yellow gloves and a green hat.

'If I'm still under suspicion,' he said, 'I'd like to know but I suppose no one will tell me.'

Fox said heartily: 'I shouldn't worry about that if I were you, sir. If you'd just give me your address and phone number. Purely as a reference.'

Parry gave them and Lamprey wrote them down.

'Thank you, Mr Percival,' Alleyn said. 'Goodnight.' Parry walked to the door. 'They all seem to be going home in twos except me,' he said. 'Which is rather dreary. I hope no one gets coshed for his pains. Considering one of them seems to be a murderer it's not too fantastic a notion though I suppose you know your own business. Oh, well. Goodnight.'

Evidently he collided with Gay Gainsford in the passage. They heard her ejaculation and his fretful apology. She came in followed by Darcey.

'I couldn't face this alone,' she said and looked genuinely frightened. 'So George brought me.'

'Perfectly in order, Miss Gainsford,' Fox assured her.

Darcey, whose face was drawn and white, stood near the door. She looked appealingly at him and he came forward and gave their addresses and telephone numbers. His voice sounded old. 'I should like to see this lady home,' he said and was at once given leave to do so. Alleyn opened the door for them and they went out, arm in arm.

Poole came next. He gave a quick look round the room and addressed himself to Alleyn. 'I don't understand all this,' he said, 'but if any member of my company is to be arrested, I'd rather stay here. I'd like to see Martyn Tarne home – she lives only ten minutes away – but if it's all right with you, I'll come back.' He hesitated and then said quickly, 'I've spoken to Jacques Doré.'

Alleyn waited for a moment. 'Yes,' he said at last, 'I'd be glad if you'd come back.'

'Will you see Helena now? She's had about all she can take.'

'Yes, of course.'

'I'll get her,' Poole said and crossed the passage. They heard him call: 'Ella?' and in a moment he reopened the door for her.

She had put a velvet beret on her head and had pulled the fullness forward so that her eyes were shadowed. Her mouth drooped with fatigue but it had been carefully painted. Fox took her address and number.

'Is the car here?' she asked and Fox said: 'Yes, Madam, in the yard. The constable will show you out.'

'I'll take you, Ella,' Poole said. 'Are you sure you'd rather be alone?'

She turned to Alleyn. 'I thought,' she said, 'that if I'm allowed, I'd rather like to take Jacko. If he's still about. Would you mind telling him? I'll wait in the car.'

'There's no one,' Alleyn asked, 'that you'd like us to send for? Or ring up?'

'No, thank you,' she said. 'I'd just rather like to have old Jacko.'

She gave him her hand. 'I believe,' she said, 'that when I can think at all sensibly about all this, I'll know you've been kind and considerate.'

Poole went out with her and Lamprey followed them.

A moment later, Martyn came in.

As she stood at the table and watched Fox write out her address she felt how little she believed in herself here, in this quietly fantastic setting. Fox and his two silent and soberly dressed associates were so incredibly what she had always pictured plain-clothes detectives to be, and Alleyn, on the contrary, so completely unlike. She was much occupied with this notion and almost forgot to give him her message.

'Jacko,' she said, 'asked me to say his address is the same as mine. I have a room in the house where he lodges.' She felt there might be some ambiguity in this statement and was about to amend it when Alleyn asked: 'Has Mr Doré gone?'

'I think he's waiting for Miss Hamilton in her car.'

'I see,' Alleyn said. 'And I believe Mr Poole is waiting for you. Goodbye, Miss Tarne, and good luck.'

Her face broke into a smile. 'Thank you *very* much,' said Martyn.

Poole's voice called in the passage. 'Where are you, Kate?'

She said goodnight and went out.

Their steps died away down the passage and across the stage. A door slammed and the theatre was silent.

'Come on,' said Alleyn.

He led the way round the back of Jacko's set to the prompt corner.

Only the off-stage working lights were alive. The stage itself was almost as shadowy as it was when Martyn first set foot on it. A dust-begrimed lamp above the letter rack cast a yellow light over its surface.

In the centre, conspicuous in its fresh whiteness, was an envelope, that had not been there before.

It was addressed in a spidery hand to Chief Detective-Inspector Alleyn.

He took it from the rack. 'So he did it this way,' he said and without another word, led them on to the stage.

Jacko's twisted stairway rose out of the shadows like a crazy ejaculation. At its base, untenanted chairs faced each other in silent communion. The sofa was in the darkest place of all.

Young Lamprey began to climb the iron steps to the switchboard. The rest used their flashlamps. Five pencils of light interlaced, hovered and met at their tips on a crumpled newspaper. They advanced upon the sofa as if it housed an enemy but when Alleyn lifted the newspaper and the five lights enlarged themselves on Dr Rutherford's face, it was clearly to be seen that he was dead.

II

The little group of men stood together in the now fully-lit stage while Alleyn read the letter. It was written on official theatre paper and headed: 'The Office. 1.45 am.'

Dear Alleyn,

I cry you patience if this letter is but disjointedly patched together. Time presses and I seem to hear the clink of constabular bracelets.

Otto Brod wrote a play which he asked Clark Bennington to vet. Ben showed it to the two persons of his acquaintance who could read German and had some judgement. I refer to Doré and myself. The play we presented last night was my own free adaptation of Brod's piece made without his consent or knowledge. Base is the slave that pays. In every way mine is an improvement. Was it George Moore who said that the difference between his quotation and those of the next man was that he left out the inverted commas? I am in full agreement with this attitude and so, by the way, was Will Shakespeare. Doré, however, is a bourgeois where the arts are in question. He recognized the source, disapproved, but had the grace to remain mum. The British critics, like Doré, would take the uncivilized view and Ben knew it. He suspected the original authorship, wrote to Brod and three days ago got an answer confirming his suspicions. This letter he proposed to use as an instrument of blackmail. I told Ben, which was no more than the truth, that I intended to make things right with Brod who, if he's not a popinjay, would be well-content with the honour I've done him and the arrangement I proposed. Ben would have none of this. He threatened to publish Brod's letter if a certain change was made in the casting. The day before yesterday, under duress, I submitted and no longer pressed for this change. However, owing to Miss G's highstrikes, it was, after all, effected. Five minutes before the curtain went up on the first act, Ben informed me, with, Ho, such bugs and goblins in my life, that at the final curtain, he intended to advance to the footlights and tell the audience I'd pinched the play. Knowing Ben meant business, I acted: in a manner which, it appears, you have rumbled and which will be fully revealed by your analysis of the greasepaint on his unlovely mug.

He powdered his face with pethidine-hydrochloride, an effective analgesic drug, now in fashion, of which the maximum therapeutic dose is 100 mg. Ben got about 2 gm on his sweaty upper lip. I loaded his prepared powder-pad with pethidine (forgive the nauseating alliteration) while he was on in the last act and burnt the pad when I returned, immediately before the curtain-call. He was then comatose and I doubt if the gassing was necessary. However, I wished to suggest suicide. I overturned his powder box in opening out his overcoat. My own vestment being habitually besprinkled with snuff was none the worse but the powder must have settled on his coat after I had covered his head. Unfortunate. I fancy that with unexpected penetration, you have in all respects hit on the *modus operandi*. Pity we couldn't share the curtain-call.

It may interest you to know that I have formed the habit of pepping up my snuff with this admirable drug and had provided myself with a princely quantity in the powder form used for dispensing purposes. One never knew which way the cat would jump with Ben. I have been equipped for action since he threatened to use his precious letter. By the way it would amuse me to know if you first dropped to it when I trampled on my pethidine box in the greenroom. Dogberry, I perceived, collected the pieces.

My other spare part is secreted in the groove of the sofa. I shall now return to the sofa, listen to your oration and if, as I suspect, it comes close to the facts, will take the necessary and final step. I shall instruct the moronic and repellent Badger to place this letter in the rack if I am still asleep when the party breaks up. Pray do not attempt artificial respiration. I assure you I shall be as dead as a door-nail. While I could triumphantly justify my use of Brod's play I declined the mortification of the inevitable publicity, more particularly as it would reflect upon persons other than myself. If you wish to hang a motive on my closed file you may make it vanity.

Let me conclude with a final quotation from my fellow-plagiarist.

> *Sometimes we are devils to ourselves*
> *When we will tempt the frailty of our powers*
> *Presuming on their changeful potency.'*

I hear the summons to return. Moriturus, to coin as Miss G would say, a phrase, te saluto, Caesar.

Your etc on the edge of the viewless winds.

John James Rutherford

III

Alleyn folded the letter and gave it to Fox. He walked back to the sofa and stood looking down at its burden for some time.

'Well, Fox,' he said at last, 'he diddled us in the end, didn't he?'

'Did he, Mr Alleyn?' asked Fox woodenly.

Bailey and Thompson moved tactfully off-stage. Young Lamprey came on with a sheet from one of the dressing-rooms. Fox took it and dismissed him with a jerk of his head. When the sheet was decently bestowed, Alleyn and Fox looked at each other.

'Oh, let us still be merciful!' Alleyn said, and it is uncertain whether this quotation from the doctor's favourite source was intended as an epitaph or an observation upon police procedure.

IV

Poole switched off his engine outside Jacko's house. Martyn stirred and he said: 'Do you want to go in at once? We haven't said a word to each other. Are you deadly tired?'

'No more than everybody else but – yes. Aren't you? You must,' she said drowsily, 'be so dreadfully puzzled and worried.'

'I suppose so. No. Not really. Not now. But you must sleep, Martyn. "Martyn." There, now, I've used your Christian name again. Do you know that I called you Kate because I felt it wasn't time yet, for the other? That astonished me. In the theatre we be-darling and be-Christian name each other at the drop of a hat. But it wouldn't do with you.'

He looked down at her. She thought: 'I really must rouse myself,' but bodily inertia, linked with a sort of purification of the spirit flooded through her and she was still.

'It isn't fair,' Poole said, 'when your eyelids are so heavy, to ask you if I've made a mistake. Perhaps tomorrow you will think you dreamed this, but Martyn, before many more days are out, I shall ask you to marry me. I do love you so very much.'

To Martyn his voice seemed to come from an immensely long way but it brought her a feeling of great content and refreshment. It was as if her spirit burgeoned and flowered into complete happiness. She tried to express something of this but her voice stumbled over a few disjointed words and she gave it up. She heard him laugh and felt him move away. In a moment he was standing with the door open. He took her keys from her hand.

'Shall I carry you in? I must go back to the theatre.'

The cold night air joined with this reminder of their ordeal to awaken her completely. She got out and waited anxiously beside him while he opened the house door.

'Is it awful to feel so happy?' she asked. 'With such a terror waiting? Why must you go to the theatre?' And after a moment. 'Do you *know?*'

'It's not awful. The terrors are over. Alleyn said I might return. And I think I do know. There. Goodnight. Quickly, quickly, my darling heart, goodnight and good morning.'

He waited until the door shut behind her and then drove back to the theatre.

The pass-door into the foyer was open and the young policeman stood beside it.

'Mr Alleyn is in here, sir,' he said.

Poole went in and found Alleyn with his hands in his pockets in front of the great frame of photographs on their easel.

'I'm afraid I've got news,' he said, 'that may be a shock to you.'

'I don't think so,' Poole said. 'Jacko spoke to me before I left. He knew about the play: I didn't. And we both thought John's sleep was much too sound.'

They stood side by side and looked at the legend over the photographs.

'Opening at this Theatre on Thursday, May 11
"THUS TO REVISIT"
A New Play by John James Rutherford.'

Spinsters in Jeopardy

For
Anita and Val Muling
with my thanks

Contents

Cast of Characters

Roderick Alleyn — *Chief Detective-Inspector, CID, New Scotland Yard*

Agatha Troy — *His Wife*

Miss Truebody — *Their fellow-passenger*

Dr Claudel — *A French physician*

Raoul Mllano — *Of Roqueville. Owner-driver*

Dr Ali Baradi — *A surgeon*

Mahomet — *His servant*

Mr Oberon — *Of the Château de la Chèvre d'Argent*

Ginny Taylor
Robin Herrington
Carbury Glande — *His guests*
Annabella Wells

Teresa — *The fiancée of Raoul*

M. Dupont — *Of the Sûreté. Acting Commissaire at the Préfecture, Roqueville*

M. Callard — *Managing Director of the Compagnie Chimique des Alpes Maritimes*

M. & Madame Milano — *The parents of Raoul*

Marie — *A maker of figurines*

M. Malaquin — *Proprietor of the Hôtel Royal*

P. E. Garbel — *A chemist*

Prologue

Without moving his head, Ricky slewed his eyes round until he was able to look slantways at the back of his mother's easel.

'I'm getting pretty bored, however,' he announced.

'Stick it a bit longer, darling, I implore you, and look at Daddy.'

'Well, because it's just about as boring a thing as a person can have to do. Isn't it Daddy?'

'When I did it,' said his father, 'I was allowed to look at your mama, so I wasn't bored. But as there are degrees of boredom,' he continued, 'so there are different kinds of bores. You might almost say there are recognizable schools.'

'To which school,' said his wife, stepping back from her easel, 'would you say Mr Garbel belonged? Ricky, look at Daddy for five minutes more and then I promise we'll stop.'

Ricky sighed ostentatiously and contemplated his father.

'Well, as far as we know him,' Alleyn said, 'to the epistolary school. There, he's a classic. In person he's undoubtedly the sort of bore that shows you things you don't want to see. Snapshots in envelopes. Barren conservatories. Newspaper cuttings. He's relentless in this. I think he carries things on his person and puts them in front of you without giving you the smallest clue about what you're meant to say. You're moving, Ricky.'

'Isn't it five minutes yet?'

'No, and it never will be if you fidget. How long is it, Troy, since you first heard from Mr Garbel?'

'About eighteen months. He wrote for Christmas. All told I've had six letters and five postcards from Mr Garbel. This last arrived this morning. That's what put him into my head.'

'Daddy, who is Mr Garbel?'

'One of Mummy's admirers. He lives in the Maritime Alps and writes love letters to her.'

'Why?'

'He says it's because he's her third cousin once removed, but I know better.'

'What do you know better?'

With a spare paint-brush clenched between her teeth, Troy said indistinctly:'Keep like that, Ricky darling, I *implore* you.'

'OK. Tell me properly, Daddy, about Mr Garbel.'

'Well, he suddenly wrote to Mummy and said Mummy's great-aunt's daughter was his second cousin, and that he thought Mummy would like to know that he lived at a place called Roqueville in the Maritime Alps. He sent a map of Roqueville, marking the place where the road he lived in ought to be shown, but wasn't, and he told Mummy how he didn't go out much or meet many people.'

'Pretty dull, however.'

'He told her about all the food you can buy there that you can't buy here and he sent her copies of newspapers with bus timetables marked and messages at the side saying: "I find this bus convenient and often take it. It leaves the corner by the principal hotel every half-hour." Do you still want to hear about Mr Garbel?'

'Unless it's time to stop, I might as well.'

'Mummy wrote to Mr Garbel and said how interesting she found his letter.'

'Did you, Mummy?'

'One has to be polite,' Troy muttered and laid a thin stroke of rose on the mouth of Ricky's portrait.

'And he wrote back sending her three used bus tickets and a used train ticket.'

'Does she collect them?'

'Mr Garbel thought she would like to know that they were his tickets punched by guards and conductors all for him. He also sends her beautifully coloured postcards of the Maritime Alps.'

'What's that? May I have them?'

' . . . with arrows pointing to where his house would be if you could see it and to where the road goes to a house he sometimes visits, only the house is off the postcard.'

'Like a picture puzzle, sort of?'

'Sort of. And he tells Mummy how, when he was young and doing chemistry at Cambridge, he almost met her great-aunt who was his second cousin, once removed.'

'Did he have a shop?'

'No, he's a special kind of chemist without a shop. When he sends Mummy presents of used tickets and old newspapers he writes on them: 'Sent by P.E. Garbel, 16 Rue des Violettes, Roqueville, to Mrs Agatha Alleyn (née Troy) daughter of Stephen and Harriet Troy (née Baynton.)''

'That's you, isn't it, Mummy? What else?'

'Is it possible, Ricky,' asked his wondering father, 'that you find this interesting?'

'Yes,' said Ricky. 'I like it. Does he mention me?'

'I don't think so.'

'Or you?'

'He suggests that Mummy might care to read parts of his letter to me.'

'May we go and see him?'

'Yes,' said Alleyn. 'As a matter of fact I think we may.'

Troy turned from her work and gaped at her husband. 'What can you mean?' she exclaimed.

'Is it time, Mummy? Because it must be, so may I get down?'

'Yes, thank you, my sweet. You have been terribly good and I must think of some exciting reward.'

'Going to see Mr Garbel, frinstance?'

'I'm afraid,' Troy said, 'that Daddy, poor thing, was being rather silly.'

'Well then – ride to Babylon?' Ricky suggested and looked out of the corners of his eyes at his father.

'All right,' Alleyn groaned, parodying despair, 'OK. *All right.* Here we go!'

He swung the excitedly squealing Ricky up to his shoulders and grasped his ankles.

'Good old horse,' Ricky shouted and patted his father's cheek. 'Non-stop to Babylon. Good old horse.'

Troy looked dotingly at him. 'Say to Nanny that I said you could ask for an extra high tea.'

'Top highest with strawberry jam?'

'If there is any.'

'Lavish!' said Ricky and gave a cry of primitive food-lust. 'Giddy-up horse,' he shouted. The family of Alleyn broke into a chant:

How many miles to Babylon?
Five score and ten.
Can I get there by candle-light?

'*Yes! and back again!*' Ricky yelled and was carried at a canter from the room.

Troy listened to the diminishing rumpus on the stairs and looked at her work.

'How happy we are!' she thought and then, foolishly, 'touch wood!' And she picked up a brush and dragged a touch of colour from the hair across the brow. 'How lucky I am,' she thought, more soberly and her mood persisted when Alleyn came back with his hair tousled like Ricky's and his tie under his ear.

He said: 'May I look?'

'All right,' Troy agreed, wiping her brushes, 'but don't say anything.'

He grinned and walked round to the front of the easel. Troy had painted a head that seemed to have light as its substance. Even the locks of dark hair might have been spun from sunshine. It was a work in line rather than in mass but the line flowed and turned with a subtlety that made any further elaboration unnecessary. 'It needs another hour,' Troy muttered.

'In that case,' Alleyn said, 'I can at least touch wood.'

She gave him a quick grateful look and said, 'What is all this about Mr Garbel?'

'I saw the A.C. this morning. He was particularly nice, which generally means he's got you pricked down for a particularly nasty job. On the face of it this one doesn't sound so bad. It seems MI5 and the Sureté are having a bit of a party with the Narcotics Bureau, and our people want somebody with fairly fluent French to go over for talks and a bit of field-work. As it *is* MI5 we'd better observe the usual rule of airy tact on your part and phony inscrutability on mine. But it turns out that the field-work lies, to coin a coy phrase, not a hundred miles from Roqueville.'

'Never!' Troy ejaculated. 'In the Garbel country?'

'Precisely. Now it occurs to me that what with war, Ricky and the atrocious nature of my job, we've never had a holiday abroad together. Nanny is due for a fortnight at Reading. Why shouldn't you and Ricky come with me to Roqueville and call on Mr Garbel?'

Troy looked delighted but she said: 'You can't go round doing top-secret jobs for MI5 trailing your wife and child. It would look so amateurish. Besides, we agreed never to mix business with pleasure, Rory.'

'In this case the more amateurish I look, the better. And I should only be based on Roqueville. The job lies outside it, so we wouldn't really be mixing business with pleasure.'

He looked at her for a moment. 'Do come,' he said, 'you know you're dying to meet Mr Garbel.'

Troy scraped her palette. 'I'm dying to come,' she amended, 'but not to meet Mr Garbel. And yet: I don't know. There's a sort of itch, I confess it, to find out just how deadly dull he is. Like a suicidal tendency.'

'You must yield to it. Write to him and tell him you're coming. You might enclose a bus ticket from Putney to the Fulham Road. How do you address him: 'Dear Cousin – ' but what is his Christian name?'

'I've no idea. He's just P.E. Garbel. To his intimates, he tells me, he is known as Peg. He adds inevitably, a quip about being square in a round hole.'

'Roqueville being the hole?'

'Presumably.'

'Has he a job, do you think?'

'For all I know he may be writing a monograph on bicarbonate of soda. If he is he'll probably ask us to read the manuscript.'

'At all events we must meet him. Put down that damn' palette and tell me you're coming.'

Troy wiped her hands on her smock. 'We're coming,' she said.

II

In his château outside Roqueville Mr Oberon looked across the nighted Mediterranean towards North Africa and then smiled gently upon his assembled guests.

'How fortunate we are,' he said. 'Not a jarring note. All gathered together with one pure object in mind.' He ran over their names as if they composed a sort of celestial roll-call. 'Our youngest disciple,' he said beaming on Ginny Taylor. 'A wonderful field of experience awaits her. She stands on the threshold of ecstasy. It is not too much to say, of ecstasy. And Robin too.' Robin Herrington, who had been watching Ginny Taylor, looked up sharply. 'Ah, youth, youth,' sighed Mr Oberon ambiguously and turned to the remaining guests, two men and a woman. 'Do we envy them?' he asked and answered himself. 'No! No, for ours is the richer tilth. We are the husbandmen, are we not?'

Dr Baradi lifted his dark, fleshy and intelligent head. He looked at his host. 'Yes, indeed,' he said. 'We are precisely that. And when Annabella arrives – I think you said she was coming?'

'Dear Annabella!' Mr Oberon exclaimed. 'Yes. On Tuesday. Unexpectedly.'

'Ah!' said Carbury Glande, looking at his paint-stained finger-nails. 'On Tuesday. Then she will be rested and ready for our Thursday rites.'

'Dear Annabella!' Dr Baradi echoed sumptuously.

The sixth guest turned her ravaged face and short-sighted eyes towards Ginny Taylor.

'Is this your first visit?' she asked.

Ginny was looking at Mr Oberon. She wore an expression that was unbecoming to her youth, a look of uncertainty, excitement and perhaps fear.

'Yes,' she said. 'My first.'

'A neophyte,' Baradi murmured richly.

'Soon to be so young a priestess,' Mr Oberon added. 'It is very touching.' He smiled at Ginny with parted lips.

A tinkling crash broke across the conversation. Robin Herrington had dropped his glass on the tessellated floor. The remains of his cocktail ran into a little pool near Mr Oberon's feet.

Mr Oberon cut across his apologies. 'No, no,' he said. 'It is a happy symbol. Perhaps a promise. Let us call it a libation,' he said. 'Shall we dine?'

CHAPTER 1

Journey to the South

Alleyn lifted himself on his elbow and turned his watch to the blue light above his pillow. Twenty minutes past five. In another hour they would be in Roqueville.

The abrupt fall of silence when the train stopped must have woken him. He listened intently but, apart from the hiss of escaping steam and the slam of a door in a distant carriage, everything was quiet and still.

He heard the men in the double sleeper next to his own exchange desultory remarks. One of them yawned loudly.

Alleyn thought the station must be Douceville. Sure enough, someone walked past the window and a lonely voice announced to the night: *'Douce-v-i-ll-e.'*

The engine hissed again. The same voice, apparently continuing a broken conversation, called out: *'Pas ce soir, par exemple!'* Someone else laughed distantly. The voices receded to be followed by the most characteristic of all stationary-train noises, the tap of steel on steel. The taps tinkered away into the distance.

Alleyn manoeuvred himself to the bottom of his bunk, dangled his long legs in space for a moment and then slithered to the floor. The window was not completely shuttered. He peered through the gap and was confronted by the bottom of a poster for Dubonnet and the lower half of a porter carrying a lamp. The lamp swung to and fro, a bell rang and the train clanked discreetly. The lamp and poster were replaced by the lower halves of two discharged passengers, a pile of luggage, a stretch of empty platform and a succession of swiftly moving pools of light. Then there was only the night hurrying past with blurred suggestions of rocks and olive trees.

The train gathered speed and settled down to its perpetual choriambic statement: 'What a to-*do*. What a to-*do*.'

Alleyn cautiously lowered the window-blind. The train was crossing the seaward end of a valley and the moon in its third quarter was riding the westward heavens. Its radiance emphasized the natural pallor of hills and trees and dramatized the shapes of rocks and mountains. With the immediate gesture of a shutter, a high bank obliterated this landscape. The train passed through a village and for two seconds Alleyn looked into a lamplit room where a woman watched a man intent over an early breakfast. What occupation got them up so soon? They were there, sharp in his vision, and were gone.

He turned from the window wondering if Troy, who shared his pleasure in train journeys, was awake in her single berth next door. In twenty minutes he would go and see. In the meantime he hoped that, in the almost complete darkness, he could dress himself without making a disturbance. He began to do so, steadying himself against the lurch and swing of this small, noisy and unstable world.

'Hallo.' A treble voice ventured from the blackness of the lower bunk. 'Are we getting out soon?'

'Hallo,' Alleyn rejoined. 'No, go to sleep.'

'I couldn't be wakier. Matter of fac' I've been awake pretty well all night.'

Alleyn groped for his shirt, staggered, barked his shin on the edge of his suitcase and swore under his breath.

'Because,' the treble voice continued, 'if we aren't getting out why are you dressing yourself?'

'To be ready for when we are.'

'I see,' said the voice. 'Is Mummy getting ready for getting out too?'

'Not yet.'

'Why?'

'It's not time.'

'Is she asleep?'

'I don't know, old boy.'

'Then how do you know she's not getting ready?'

'I don't know, really. I just hope she's not.'

'Why?'

'I want her to rest, and if you say why again I won't answer.'

'I see.' There was a pause. The voice chuckled. 'Why?' it asked.

Alleyn had found his shirt. He now discovered that he had put it on inside out. He took it off.

'If,' the voice pursued, 'I said a sensible why, would you answer, Daddy?'

'It would have to be entirely sensible.'

'Why are you getting up in the dark?'

'I had hoped,' Alleyn said bitterly, 'that all little boys were fast asleep and I didn't want to wake them.'

'Because now you know, they aren't asleep so why – ?'

'You're perfectly right,' Alleyn said. The train rounded a curve and he ran with some violence against the door. He switched on the light and contemplated his son.

Ricky had the newly-made look peculiar to little boys in bed. His dark hair hung sweetly over his forehead, his eyes shone and his cheeks and lips were brilliant. One would have said he was so new that his colours had not yet dried.

'I like being in a train,' he said, 'more lavishly than anything that's ever happened so far. Do you like being in a train, Daddy?'

'Yes,' said Alleyn. He opened the door of the washing-cabinet which lit itself up. Ricky watched his father shave.

'Where are we now?' he said presently.

'By a sea. It's called the Mediterranean and it's just out there on the other side of the train. We shall see it when it's daytime.'

'Are we in the middle of the night?'

'Not quite. We're in the very early morning. Out there everybody is fast asleep,' Alleyn suggested, not very hopefully.

'Everybody?'

'Almost everybody. Fast asleep and snoring.'

'All except us,' Ricky said with rich satisfaction, 'because we are lavishly wide awake in the very early morning in a train. Aren't we Daddy?'

'That's it. Soon we'll pass the house where I'm going tomorrow. The train doesn't stop there, so I have to go on with you to Roqueville and drive back. You and Mummy will stay in Roqueville.'

'Where will you be most of the time?'

'Sometimes with you and sometimes at this house. It's called the Château de la Chèvre d'Argent. That means the House of the Silver Goat.'

'Pretty funny name, however,' said Ricky.

A stream of sparks ran past the window. The light from the carriage flew across the surface of a stone wall. The train had begun to climb steeply. It gradually slowed down until there was time to see nearby objects lamplit, in the world outside: a giant cactus, a flight of steps, part of an olive grove. The engine laboured almost to a standstill. Outside their window, perhaps a hundred yards away, there was a vast house that seemed to grow out of the cliff. It stood full in the moonlight and shadows, black as ink, were thrown by buttresses across its recessed face. A solitary window, veiled by a patterned blind, glowed dully yellow.

'*Somebody* is awake out there,' Ricky observed. ' "Out" "In"?' he speculated. 'Daddy, what are those people? "Out" or "In"?'

'Outside for us, I suppose, and inside for them.'

'Ouside the train and inside the house,' Ricky agreed. 'Suppose the train ran through the house, would they be "in" for us?'

'I hope,' his father observed glumly, 'that you won't grow up a metaphysician.'

'What's that? Look, there they are in their house. We've stopped, haven't we?'

The carriage window was exactly opposite the lighted one in the cliff-like wall of the house. A blurred shape moved in the room on the other side of the blind. It swelled and became a black body pressed against the window.

Allyen made a sharp ejaculation and a swift movement.

'Because you're standing right in front of the window,' Ricky said politely, 'and it would be rather nice to see out.'

The train jerked galvanically and with a compound racketing noise, slowly entered a tunnel, emerged, and gathering pace, began a descent to sea-level.

The door of the compartment opened and Troy stood there in a woollen dressing-gown. Her short hair was rumpled and hung over her forehead like her son's. Her face was white and her eyes dark with perturbation. Alleyn turned quickly. She looked from him to Ricky. 'Have you seen out of the window?' she asked.

'*I* have,' said Alleyn. 'And so, by the look of you, have you.'

Troy said, 'Can you help me with my suitcase?' and to Ricky: 'I'll come back and get you up soon, darling.'

'Are you both going?'

'We'll be just next door. We shan't be long,' Alleyn said.

'It's only because it's in a train.'

'We know,' Troy reassured him. 'But it's all right. Honestly. OK?'

'OK,' Ricky said in a small voice and Troy touched his cheek.

Alleyn followed her into her own compartment. She sat down on her bunk and stared at him. 'I can't believe that was true,' she said.

'I'm sorry you saw it.'

'Then it was true. Ought we to do anything? Rory, ought you to do anything? Oh *dear*, how tiresome.'

'Well, I can't do much while moving away at sixty miles an hour. I suppose I'd better ring up the Préfecture when we get to Roqueville.'

He sat down beside her. 'Never mind, darling,' he said, 'there may be another explanation.'

'I don't see how there can be, unless – Do you mind telling me what you saw?'

Alleyn said carefully. 'A lighted window, masked by a spring blind. A woman falling against the blind and releasing it. Beyond the woman, but out of sight to us, there must have been a brilliant lamp and in its light, farther back in the room and on our right, stood a man in a white garment. His face, oddly enough, was in shadow. There was something that looked like a wheel, beyond his right shoulder. His right arm was raised.'

'And in his hand – ?'

'Yes,' Alleyn said, 'that's the tricky bit, isn't it?'

'And then the tunnel. It was like one of those sudden breaks in an old-fashioned film, too abrupt to be really dramatic. It was there and then it didn't exist. No,' said Troy, 'I won't believe it was true. I won't believe something is still going on inside that house. And what a house too! It looked like a Gastave Doré, really bad romantic'

Alleyn said: 'Are you all right to get dressed? I'll just have a word with the car attendant. He may have seen it, too. After all, we may not be the only people awake and looking out, though I fancy mine was the only compartment with the light on. Yours was in darkness, by the way.'

'I had the window shutter down, though. I'd been thinking how strange it is to see into other people's lives through a train window.'

'I know,' Alleyn said. 'There's a touch of magic in it.'

'And then – to see that! Not so magical.'

'Never mind. I'll talk to the attendant and then I'll come back and get Ricky up. He'll be getting train-fever. We should reach Roqueville in about twenty minutes. All right?'

'Oh, I'm right as a bank,' said Troy.

'Nothing like the Golden South for a carefree holiday,' Alleyn said. He grinned at her, went out into the corridor and opened the door of his own sleeper.

Ricky was still sitting up in his bunk. His hands were clenched and his eyes wide open. 'You're being a pretty long time, however,' he said.

'Mummy's coming in a minute. I'm just going to have a word with the chap outside. Stick it out, old boy.'

'OK,' said Ricky.

The attendant, a pale man with a dimple in his chin, was dozing on his stool at the forward end of the carriage. Alleyn, who had already discovered that he spoke very little English, addressed him in diplomatic French that had become only slightly hesitant through disuse. Had the attendant, he asked, happened to be awake when the train paused outside a tunnel a few minutes ago? The man seemed to be in some doubt as to whether Alleyn was about to complain because he was asleep or because the train had halted. It took a minute or two to clear up this difficulty and to discover that he had, in point of fact, been asleep for some time.

'I'm sorry to trouble you,' Alleyn said, 'but can you, by any chance tell me the name of the large building near the entrance to the tunnel?'

'Ah, yes, yes,' the attendant said. 'Certainly, monsieur, since I am a native of these parts. It is known to everybody, this house, on account of its great antiquity. It is the Château de la Chèvre d'Argent.'

'I thought it might be,' said Alleyn.

II

Alleyn reminded the sleepy attendant that they were leaving the train at Roqueville and tipped him generously. The man thanked him with that peculiarly Gallic effusiveness that is at once too logical and too adroit to be offensive.

'Do you know,' Alleyn said, as if on an afterthought, 'who lives in the Château de la Chèvre d'Argent?'

The attendant believed it was leased to an extremely wealthy gentleman, possibly an American, possibly an Englishman, who entertained very exclusively. He believed the *ménage* to be an excessively distinguished one.

Alleyn waited for a moment and then said, 'I think there was a little trouble there tonight. One saw a scene through a lighted window when the train halted.'

The attendant's shoulders suggested that all things are possible and that speculation is vain. His eyes were as blank as boot buttons in his pallid face. Should he not perhaps fetch the baggage of Monsieur and Madame and the little one in readiness for their descent at Roqueville. He had his hand on the door of Alleyn's compartment when from somewhere towards the rear of the carriage, a woman screamed twice.

They were short screams, ejaculatory in character, as if they had been wrenched out of her, and very shrill. The attendant wagged his head from side to side in exasperation, begged Alleyn to excuse him, and went off down the corridor to the rearmost compartment. He tapped. Alleyn guessed at an agitated response. The attendant went in and Troy put her head out of her own door.

'What now, for pity's sake?' she asked.

'Somebody having a nightmare or something. Are you ready?'

'Yes. But what a rum journey we're having!'

The attendant came back at a jog-trot. Was Alleyn perhaps a doctor? An English lady had been taken ill. She was in great pain: the abdomen, the attendant elaborated, clutching his own in pantomime. It was evidently a formidable seizure. If Monsieur, by any chance –

Alleyn said he was not a doctor. Troy said, 'I'll go and see the poor thing, shall I? Perhaps there's a doctor somewhere in the train. You get Ricky up, darling.'

She made off down the swaying corridor. The attendant began to tap on doors and to inquire fruitlessly of his passengers if they were doctors. 'I shall see my comrades of the other *voitures*,' he said importantly. 'Evidently one must organize.'

Alleyn found Ricky sketchily half-dressed and in a child's panic.

'Where have you been, however?' he demanded. 'Because I didn't know where everyone was. We're going to be late for getting out. I can't find my pants. Where's Mummy?'

Alleyn calmed him, got him ready and packed their luggage. Ricky, white-faced, sat on the lower bunk with his gaze turned on the door. He liked, when travelling, to have his family under his eye. Alleyn, remembering his own childhood, knew his little son was racked with an illogical and bottomless anxiety, an anxiety that vanished when the door opened and Troy came in.

'Oh golly, Mum!' Ricky said and his lip trembled.

'Hallo, there,' Troy said in the especially calm voice she kept for Ricky's panics. She sat down beside him, putting her arm where he could lean back against it and looked at her husband.

'I think that woman's very ill,' she said. 'She looks frightful. She had what she thought was some kind of food poisoning this morning and dosed herself with castor-oil. And then, just now she had a violent pain, really awful, she says, in the appendix place and now she hasn't any pain at all and looks ghastly. Wouldn't that be a perforation, perhaps?'

'Your guess is as good as mine, my love.'

'Rory, she's about fifty and she comes from the Bermudas and has no relations in the world and wears a string bag on her head and she's never been abroad before and we can't just let her be whisked on into the Italian Riviera with a perforated appendix if that's what it is.'

'Oh, damn!'

'Well, can we? I said,' Troy went on, looking sideways at her husband, 'that you'd come and talk to her.'

'Darling, what the hell can I do?'

'You're calming in a panic, isn't he, Rick?'

'Yes,' said Ricky, again turning white. 'I don't suppose you're both going away, are you, Mummy?'

'You can come with us. You could look through the corridor window at the sea. It's shiny with moonlight and Daddy and I will be just on the other side of the poor thing's door. Her name's Miss Truebody and she knows Daddy's a policeman.'

'Well, I must say . . . ' Alleyn began indignantly.

'We'd better hurry, hadn't we?' Troy stood up holding Ricky's hand. He clung to her like a limpet.

At the far end of the corridor their own car attendant stood with two of his colleagues outside Miss Truebody's door. They made dubious grimaces at one another and spoke in voices that were drowned by the racket of the train. When they saw Troy, they all took off their silver-braided caps and bowed to her. A doctor, they said, had been discovered in the *troisième voiture* and was now with the unfortunate lady. Perhaps Madame would join him. Their own attendant tapped on the door and with an ineffable smirk at Troy, opened it. 'Madame!' he invited.

Troy went in and Ricky feverishly transferred his hold to Alleyn's hand. Together, they looked out of the corridor window.

The railway, on this part of the coast, followed an embankment a few feet above sea level and as Troy had said, the moon shone on the Mediterranean. A long cape ran out over the glossy water and near its tip a few points of yellow light showed in early-rising households. The stars were beginning to pale.

'That's Cap St Gilles,' Alleyn said. 'Lovely, isn't it, Rick?'

Ricky nodded. He had one ear tuned to his mother's voice which could just be heard beyond Miss Truebody's door.

'Yes,' he said, 'it is lovely.' Alleyn wondered if Ricky was really as pedantically-mannered a child as some of their friends seemed to think.

'Aren't we getting a bit near?' Ricky asked. 'Bettern't Mummy come now?'

'It's all right. We've ten minutes yet and the train people know we're getting off. I promise it's all right. Here's Mummy now.'

She came out followed by a small bald gentleman with waxed moustaches, wearing striped professional trousers, patent leather boots and a frogged dressing-gown.

'Your French is badly needed. This is the doctor,' Troy said and haltingly introduced her husband.

The doctor was formally enchanted. He said crisply that he had examined the patient who almost certainly suffered from a perforated appendix and should undoubtedly be operated upon as soon as possible. He regretted extremely that he himself had an urgent professional appointment in St Celeste and could not, therefore, accept responsibility. Perhaps the best thing to do would be to discharge Miss Truebody at Roqueville and send her back by the evening train to St Christophe where she could go to hospital. Of course, if there was a surgeon in Roqueville the operation might be performed there. In any case he would give Miss Truebody an injection of morphine. His shoulders rose. It was a position of extreme difficulty. They must hope, must they not, that there would be a medical man and suitable accommodation available at Roqueville? He believed he had understood Madame to say that she and Monsieur l'Inspecteur-en-Chef would be good enough to assist their compatriot.

Monsieur l'Inspecteur-en-Chef glared at his wife and said they would, of course, be enchanted. Troy said in English that it had obviously comforted Miss Truebody and impressed the doctor to learn of her husband's rank. The doctor bowed, delivered a few definitive compliments and lurching in a still dignified manner down the swinging corridor, made for his own carriage, followed by his own attendant.

Troy said: 'Come and speak to her, Rory. It'll help.'

'Daddy?' Ricky said in a small voice.

'We won't be a minute,' Troy and Alleyn answered together, and Alleyn added, 'We know how it feels, Rick, but one has got to get used to these things.' Ricky nodded and swallowed.

Alleyn followed Troy into Miss Truebody's compartment. 'This is my husband, Miss Truebody,' Troy said. 'He's had a word with the doctor and he'll tell you all about it.'

Miss Truebody lay on her back with her knees a little drawn up and her sick hands closed vice-like over the sheet. She had a rather blunt face that in health probably was rosy but now was ominously blotched and looked as if it had shrunk away from her nose. This effect was heightened by the circumstance of her having removed her teeth. There were beads of sweat along the margin of her grey hair and her upper lip and the ridges where her eyebrows would have been if she had possessed any; the face was singularly smooth and showed none of the minor blemishes characteristic of her age. Over her head she wore, as Troy had noticed, a sort of net bag made of pink string. She looked terrified. Something in her eyes reminded Alleyn of Ricky in one of his travel-panics.

He told her, as reassuringly as might be, of the doctor's pronouncement. Her expression did not change and he wondered if she had understood him. When he had finished she gave a little gasp and whispered indistinctly: Too awkward, so inconvenient. Disappointing.' And her mottled hands clutched at the sheet.

'Don't worry,' Alleyn said, 'don't worry about anything. We'll look after you.'

Like a sick animal, she gave him a heart-rending look of gratitude and shut her eyes. For a moment Troy and Alleyn watched her being slightly but inexorably jolted by the train and then stole uneasily from the compartment. They found their son dithering with agitation in the corridor and the attendant bringing out the last of their luggage.

Troy said hurriedly: 'This is frightful. We can't take the responsibility. Or must we?'

'I'm afraid we must. There's no time to do anything else. I've got a card of sorts up my sleeve in Roqueville. If it's no good we'll get her back to St Christophe.'

'What's your card? *Not,*' Troy ejaculated, 'Mr Garbel?'

'No, no, it's – hi – look! We're there.'

The little town of Roqueville, wan in the first thin wash of dawn-light, slid past the windows and the train drew into the station.

Fortified by a further tip from Troy and in evident relief at the prospect of losing Miss Truebody, the attendant enthusiastically piled the Alleyns' luggage on the platform while the guard plunged into earnest conversation with Alleyn and the Roqueville station-master. The doctor reappeared fully clad and gave Miss Truebody a shot of morphine. He and Troy, in incredible association, got her into a magenta dressing-gown in which she looked like death itself. Troy hurriedly packed Miss Truebody's possessions, uttered a few words of encouragement, and with Ricky and the doctor joined Alleyn on the platform.

Ricky, his parents once deposited on firm ground and fully accessible, forgot his terrors and contemplated the train with the hard-boiled air of an experienced traveller.

The station-master with the guard and three attendants in support was saying to the doctor: 'One is perfectly conscious Monsieur le Docteur, of the extraordinary circumstances. Nevertheless, the schedule of the Chemin de Fer des Alpes Maritimes cannot be indefinitely protracted.'

The doctor said: 'One may, however, in the few moments that are being squandered in this unproductive conversation, M. le Chef de Gare, consult the telephone directory and ascertain if there is a doctor in Roqueville.'

'One may do so undoubtedly, but I can assure M. le Docteur that such a search will be fruitless. Our only doctor is at a conference in St Christophe. Therefore, since the train is already delayed one minute and forty seconds . . . '

He glanced superbly at the guard who began to survey the train like a sergeant-major. A whistle was produced. The attendants walked towards their several cars.

'Rory!' Troy cried out. 'We can't . . . '

Alleyn said: 'All right,' and spoke to the station-master. 'Perhaps,' he said, M. le Chef de Gare, you are aware of the presence of a surgeon – I believe his name is Dr Baradi – among the guests of M. Oberon some twenty kilometres back at the Château de la Chèvre d'Argent. He is an Egyptian gentleman. I understand he arrived two weeks ago.'

'Alors, M. l'Inspecteur-en-Chef . . . ' the doctor began but the station-master, after a sharp glance at Alleyn, became alert and neatly deferential. He remembered the arrival of the Egyptian gentleman for whom he had caused a taxi to be produced. If the gentleman should be – he bowed – as M. l'Inspecteur-en-Chef evidently was informed, a surgeon, all their problems were solved, were they not? He began to order the sleeping-car attendants about and was briskly supported by the guard. Troy, to the renewed agitation of her son, and with the assistance of their attendant, returned to the sleeping-car and supported Miss Truebody out of it, down to the platform and into the waiting-room, where she was laid out, horribly corpse-like, on a bench. Her luggage followed. Troy, on an afterthought, darted back and retrieved from a tumbler in the washing cabinet, Miss Truebody's false teeth, dropping them with a shudder into a tartan sponge-bag. On the platform the doctor held a private conversation with Alleyn. He wrote in his notebook, tore out the page and gave it to Alleyn with his card. Alleyn, in the interests of Franco-British relationships, insisted on paying the doctor's fee and the train finally drew out of Roqueville in an atmosphere of the liveliest cordiality. On the strangely quiet platform Alleyn and Troy looked at each other.

'This,' Alleyn said, 'is not your holiday as I had planned it.'

'What do we do now?'

'Ring up the Chèvre d'Argent and ask for Dr Baradi, who, I have reason to suppose, is an admirable surgeon and an unmitigated blackguard.'

They could hear the dawn cocks crowing in the hills above Roqueville.

III

In the waiting-room Ricky fell fast asleep on his mother's lap. Troy was glad of this as Miss Truebody had begun to look quite dreadful. She too had drifted into a kind of sleep. She breathed unevenly, puffing out her unsupported lips, and made unearthly noises in her throat. Troy could hear her husband and the station-master talking in the office next door and then Alleyn's voice only, speaking on the telephone and in French! There were longish pauses during which Alleyn said: *'Allô! Allô!'* and *'Ne coupez pas, je vous en prie, Mademoiselle,'* which Troy felt rather proud of understanding. A grey light filtered into the waiting-room; Ricky made a touching little sound, rearranged his lips, sighed, and turned his face against her breast in an abandonment of relaxation. Alleyn began to speak at length, first in French, and then in English. Troy heard fragments of sentences.

' . . . I wouldn't have roused you up like this if it hadn't been so urgent . . . Dr Claudel said definitely that it was really a matter of the most extreme urgency . . . He will telephone from St Celeste. I am merely a fellow passenger . . . yes: yes, I have a car here . . . Good . . . Very well . . . Yes, I understand. Thank you.' A bell tinkled.

There was a further conversation and then Alleyn came into the waiting-room. Troy, with her chin on the top of Ricky's silken head, gave him a nod and an intimate familiar look: her comment on Ricky's sleep. He said: 'It's not fair.'

'What?'

'Your talent for turning my heart over.'

'I thought,' Troy said, 'you meant about our holiday. What's happened?'

'Baradi says he'll operate if it's necessary.' Alleyn looked at Miss Truebody. 'Asleep?'

'Yes. So, what are we do do?'

'We've got a car. The Sûreté rang up the local Commissioner yesterday and told him I was on the way. He's actually one of their experts who's been sent down here on a special job, superseding the local chap for the time being. He's turned on an elderly Mercedes and a driver. Damn' civil of him. I've just been talking to him. Full of apologies for not coming down himself but he thought, very wisely, that we'd better not be seen together. He says our chauffeur is a reliable chap with an admirable record. He and the car are on tap outside the station now and our luggage will be collected by the hotel wagon. Baradi suggests I take Miss Truebody straight to the Chèvre d'Argent. While we're on the way he will make what preparations he can. Luckily he's got his instruments and Claudel has given me some pipkins of anaesthetic. Baradi asked if I could give the anaesthetic.'

'Can you?'

'I did once, in a ship. As long as nothing goes very wrong, it's fairly simple. If Baradi thinks it is safe to wait he'll try to get an anaesthetist from Douceville or somewhere. But it seems there's some sort of doctors' jamboree on today at St Christophe and they've all cleared off to it. It's only ten kilometres from here to the Chèvre d'Argent by the inland road. I'll drop you and Ricky at the hotel here, darling, and take Miss Truebody on.'

'Are there any women in the house?'

'I don't know.' Alleyn stopped short and then said: 'Yes. Yes I do. There are women.'

Troy watched him for a moment and then said: 'All right. Let's get her aboard. You take Ricky.'

Alleyn lifted him from her lap and she went to Miss Truebody. 'She's tiny,' Troy said under her breath. 'Could she be carried?'

'I think so. Wait a moment.'

He took Ricky out and was back in a few seconds with the stationmaster and a man wearing a chauffeur's cap over a mop of glossy curls.

He was a handsome little fellow with an air of readiness. He saluted Troy gallantly, taking off his peaked cap and smiling at her. Then he saw Miss Truebody and made a clucking sound. Troy had put a travelling rug on the bench and they made a sort of stretcher of it and carried Miss Truebody out to a large car in the station yard. Ricky was curled up on the front seat. They managed to fit Miss Truebody into the back one. The driver pulled down a tip-up seat and Troy sat on that. Miss Truebody had opened her eyes. She said in a quite clear voice: 'Too kind,' and Troy took her hand. Alleyn, in the front, held Ricky on his lap and they started off up a steep little street through Roqueville. The thin dawnlight gave promise of a glaring day. It was already very warm.

'To the Hôtel Royal, Monsieur?' asked the driver.

'No,' said Troy with Miss Truebody's little claw clutching at her fingers. 'No, please, Rory. I'll come with her. Ricky won't wake for hours. We can wait in the car or he can drive us back. I might be of some use.'

'To the Château de la Chèvre d'Argent,' Alleyn said, 'and gently.'

'Perfectly, Monsieur,' said the driver. 'Always, always gently.'

Roqueville was a very small town. It climbed briefly up the hill and petered out in a string of bleached villas. The road mounted between groves of olive trees and the air was like a benison, soft and clean. The sea extended itself beneath them and enriched itself with a blueness of incredible intensity.

Alleyn turned to look at Troy. They were quite close to each other and spoke over their shoulders like people in a Victorian 'Conversation' chair. It was clear that Miss Truebody, even if she could hear them, was not able to concentrate or indeed to listen. 'Dr Claudel,' Alleyn said, 'thought it was the least risky thing to do. I half expected Baradi would refuse but he was surprisingly co-operative. He's supposed to be a good man at his job.' He made a movement of his head to indicate the driver. 'This chap doesn't speak English,' he said. 'And, by the way, darling, no more chat about my being a policeman.'

Troy said: 'Have I been a nuisance?'

'It's all right. I asked Claudel to forget it and I don't suppose Miss Truebody will say anything or that anybody will pay much attention if she does. It's just that I don't want to brandish my job at the

Chèvre d'Argent.' He turned and looked into her troubled face. 'Never mind, my darling. We'll buy false beards and hammers in Roqueville and let on we're archaeologists. Or load ourselves down with your painting-gear.' He paused for a moment. 'That, by the way, is not a bad idea at all. Distinguished painter visits Côte d'Azur with obscure husband and child. We'll keep it in reserve.'

'But honestly, Rory. How's this debacle going to affect your job at the Chèvre d'Argent?'

'In a way it's a useful entrée. The Sûreté suggested that I called there representing myself either to be an antiquarian captivated by the place itself . . . it's an old Saracen stronghold . . . or else I was to be a seeker after esoteric knowledge and offer myself as a disciple. If both failed I could use my own judgment about being a heroin addict in search of fuel. Thanks to Miss Truebody, however, I shall turn up as a reluctant Good Samaritan. All the same,' Alleyn said, rubbing his nose, 'I wish Dr Claudel could have risked taking her on to St Céleste or else waiting for the evening train back to St Christophe. I don't much like this party, and that's a fact. This'll larn the Alleyn family to try combining business with pleasure, won't it?'

'Ah, well' said Troy, looking compassionately at Miss Truebody, 'we're doing our blasted best and no fool can do more.'

They were silent for some time. The driver sang to himself in a light tenor voice. The road climbed the Maritime Alps into early sunlight. They traversed a tilted landscape compounded of earth and heat, of opaque clay colours – ochres and pinks – splashed with magenta, tempered with olive-grey and severed horizontally at its base by the ultramarine blade of the Mediterranean. They turned inland. Villages emerged as logical growths out of rock and earth. A monastery safely folded among protective hills spoke of some tranquil adjustment of man's spirit to the quiet rhythm of soil and sky.

'It's impossible,' Troy said, 'to think that anything could go very much amiss in these hills.'

A distant valley came into view. Far up it, a strange anachronism in that landscape, was a long modern building with glittering roofs and a great display of plate glass.

'The factory,' the driver told them, 'of the Compagnie Chimique des Alpes Maritimes.'

Alleyn made a little affirmative sound as if he saw something that he had expected and for as long as it remained in sight he looked at the glittering building.

They drove on in silence. Miss Truebody turned her head from side to side and Troy bent over her. 'Hot,' she whispered, 'such an oppressive climate. Oh, dear!'

'One approaches the objective,' the driver announced and changed gears. The road tipped downwards and turned the flank of a hill. They had crossed the headland and were high above the sea again. Immediately below them the railroad emerged from a tunnel. On their right was a cliff that mounted into a stone face pierced irregularly with windows. This in turn broke against the skyline into fabulous turrets and parapets. Troy gave a sharp ejaculation, 'Oh, *no!*' she said. 'It's not that! No, 'It's too much!'

'Well, darling,' Alleyn said, 'I'm afraid that's what it is.'

'La Chèvre d'Argent,' said the driver and turned up a steep and exceedingly narrow way that ended in a walled platform from which one looked down at the railway and beyond it sheer down again to the sea. 'Here one stops, Monsieur,' said the driver. 'This is the entrance.'

He pointed to a dark passage between two masses of rock from which walls emerged as if by some process of evolution. He got out and opened the doors of the car. 'It appears,' he said, 'that Mademoiselle is unable to walk.'

'Yes,' Alleyn said. 'I shall go and fetch the doctor. Madame will remain with Mademoiselle and the little boy.' He settled the sleeping Ricky into the front seat and got out. 'You stay here, Troy,' he said. 'I shan't be long.'

'Rory, we shouldn't have brought her to this place.'

'There was no alternative that we could honestly take.'

'Look!' said Troy.

A man in white was coming through the passage. He wore a Panama hat. His hands and face were so much the colour of the shadows that he looked like a white suit walking of its own accord towards them. He moved out into the sunlight and they saw that he was olive-coloured with a large nose, full lips and a black moustache. He wore dark glasses. The white suit was made of sharkskin and beautifully cut. His sandals were white suède. His shirt was pink and his tie green. When he saw Troy he took off his hat and the corrugations of his oiled hair shone in the sunlight.

'Dr Baradi?' Alleyn said.

Dr Baradi smiled brilliantly and held out a long dark hand. 'So you bring my patient?' he said. 'Mr Allen, is it not?' He turned to Troy. 'My wife,' Alleyn said and saw Troy's hand lifted to the full lips. 'Here is your patient,' he added. 'Miss Truebody.'

'Ah, yes,' Dr Baradi went to the car and bent over Miss Truebody. Troy, rather pink in the face, moved to the other side. 'Miss Truebody,' she said, 'here is the doctor.'

Miss Truebody opened her eyes, looked into the dark face and cried out: 'Oh! No. No!'

Dr Baradi smiled at her. 'You must not trouble yourself about anything,' they heard him say. He had a padded voice. 'We are going to make everything much more comfortable for you, isn't it? You must not be frightened of my dark face, I assure you I am quite a good doctor.'

Miss Truebody said: 'Please excuse me. Not at all. Thank you.'

'Now, without moving you, if I may just – that will do very nicely. You must tell me if I hurt you.' A pause. Cicadas had broken out in a chittering so high-pitched that it shrilled almost above the limit of human hearing. The driver moved away tactfully. Miss Truebody moaned a little. Dr Baradi straightened up, walked to the edge of the platform and waited there for Troy and Alleyn. 'It is a perforated appendix undoubtedly,' he said. 'She is very ill. I should tell you that I am the guest of Mr Oberon, who places a room at our disposal. We have an improvised stretcher in readiness.' He turned towards the passage-way: 'And here it comes!' he said looking at Troy with an air of joyousness which she felt to be entirely out of place.

Two men walked out of the shadowed way on to the platform carrying between them a gaily striped object, evidently part of a garden seat. Both the men wore aprons. 'The gardener,' Dr Baradi explained, 'and one of the indoor servants, strong fellows both and accustomed to the exigencies of our entrance. She has been given morphine, I think.'

'Yes,' Alleyn said. 'Dr Claudel gave it. He has sent you an adequate amount of something called, I think, pentothal. He was taking a supply of it to a brother-medico, an anaesthetist, in St Céleste and said that you would probably need some and that the local chemist would not be likely to have it.'

'I am obliged to him. I have already telephoned to the pharmacist in Roqueville who can supply ether. Fortunately he lives above his establishment. He is sending it up here by car. It is fortunate also that I have my instruments with me.' He beamed and glittered at Troy. 'And now, I think . . . '

He spoke in French to the two men, directing them to stand near the car. For the first time apparently he noticed the sleeping Ricky and leant over the door to look at him.

'Enchanting,' he murmured and his teeth flashed at Troy. 'Our household is also still asleep,' he said, 'but I have Mr Oberon's warmest invitation that you, Madame, and the small one join us for *petit-déjeuner*. As you know, your husband is to assist me. There will be a little delay before we are ready and coffee is prepared.'

He stood over Troy. He was really extremely large: his size and his padded voice and his smell, which was compounded of hair-lotion, scent and something that reminded her of the impure land-breeze from an eastern port, all flowed over her.

She moved back and said quickly: 'It's very nice of you but I think Ricky and I must find our hotel.'

Alleyn said: Thank you so much, Dr Baradi. It's extremely kind of Mr Oberon and I hope I shall have a chance to thank him for all of us. What with one thing and another, we've had an exhausting journey and I think my wife and Ricky are in rather desperate need of a bath and a rest. The man will drive them down to the hotel and come back for me.'

Dr Baradi bowed, took off his hat and would have possibly kissed Troy's hand again if Alleyn had not somehow been in the way.

'In that case,' Dr Baradi said, 'we must not insist.'

He opened the door of the car. 'And now, dear lady,' he said to Miss Truebody, 'we make a little journey, isn't it? Don't move. There is no need.'

With great dexterity and no apparent expenditure of energy he lifted her from the car and laid her on the improvised stretcher. The sun beat down on her glistening face. Her eyes were open, her lips drawn back a little from her gums. She said: 'But where is . . . You're not taking me away from . . . ? I don't know her name.'

Troy went to her. 'Here I am, Miss Truebody,' she said. 'I'll come and see you quite soon. I promise.'

'But I don't know where I'm going. It's so unsuitable . . . Unseemly really . . . Somehow with another lady . . . English . . . I don't know what they'll do to me . . . I'm afraid I'm nervous . . . I had hoped . . . '

Her jaw trembled. She made a thin shrill sound, shocking in its nakedness. 'No,' she stammered, 'no . . . no . . . no.' Her arm shot out and her hand closed on Troy's skirt. The two bearers staggered a little and looked agitatedly at Dr Baradi.

'She should not be upset,' he murmured to Troy. 'It is most undesirable. Perhaps, for a little while, you'll be kind . . . '

'But of course,' Troy said, and in answer to a look from her husband. 'Of course, Rory, I must.'

And she bent over Miss Truebody and told her she wouldn't go away. She felt as though she herself was trapped in the kind of dream that, without being a positive nightmare, threatens to become one. Baradi released Miss Truebody's hand and as he did so, his own brushed against Troy's skirt.

'You're so kind,' he said. 'Perhaps Mr Allen will bring the little boy. It is not well for such tender ones to sleep overlong in the sun on the Côte d'Azur.'

Without a word Alleyn lifted Ricky out of the car. Ricky made a small questioning sound, stirred and slept again.

The men walked off with the stretcher. Dr Baradi followed them. Troy, Alleyn and Ricky brought up the rear.

In this order the odd little procession moved out of the glare into the shadowed passage that was the entrance to the Château de la Chèvre d'Argent.

The driver watched them go, his lips pursed in a soundless whistle and an expression of concern darkening his eyes. Then he drove the car into the shade of the hill and composed himself for a long wait.

CHAPTER 2

Operation Truebody

At first their eyes were sun-dazzled so that they could scarcely see their way. Dr Baradi paused to guide them. Alleyn, encumbered with Ricky and groping up a number of wide, shallow and irregular steps, was aware of Baradi's hand piloting Troy by the elbow. The blotches of nonexistent light that danced across their vision faded and they saw that they were in a sort of hewn passageway between walls that were incorporated in rock, separated by outcrops of stone and pierced by stairways, windows and occasional doors. At intervals they went through double archways supporting buildings that straddled the passage and darkened it. They passed an open doorway and saw into a cave-like room where an old woman sat among shelves filled with small gaily-painted figures. As Troy passed, the woman smiled at her and gestured invitingly, holding up a little clay goat.

Dr Baradi was telling them about the Chèvre d'Argent.

'It is a fortress built originally by the Saracens. One might almost say it was sculptured out of the mountain, isn't it? The Normans stormed it on several occasions. There are legends of atrocities and so on. The fortress is, in effect, a village since the many caves beneath and around it have been shaped into dwellings and house a number of peasants, some dependent on the château and some, like the woman you have noticed, upon their own industry. The château itself is most interesting, indeed unique. But not inconvenient. Mr Oberon has, with perfect tact, introduced the amenities. We are civilized, as you shall see.

They arrived at a double gate of wrought iron let into the wall on their left. An iron bell hung beside it. A butler appeared beyond the doors and opened them. They passed through a courtyard into a wide hall with deep-set windows through which a cool ineffectual light was admitted.

Without, at first, taking in any details of this shadowed interior, Troy received an impression of that particular kind of suavity that is associated with costliness. The rug under her feet, the texture and colour of the curtains, the shape of cabinets and chairs and, above all, a smell which she thought must arise from the burning of sweet-scented oils, all united to give this immediate reaction. 'Mr Oberon,' she thought, 'must be immensely rich.' Almost at the same time, she saw above the great fireplace a famous Breughel which, she remembered, had been sold privately some years ago. It was called: 'Consultation of Sorceresses.' An open door showed a stone stairway built inside the thickness of the wall.

'The stairs,' Mr Baradi said, 'are a little difficult. Therefore we have prepared rooms on this floor.'

He pulled back a leather curtain. The men carried Miss Truebody into a heavily carpeted stone passage hung at intervals with rugs and lit with electric lights fitted into ancient hanging lamps, witnesses, Troy supposed, of Mr Oberon's tact in modernization. She heard Miss Truebody raise her piping cry of distress.

Dr Baradi said: 'Perhaps you would be so kind as to assist her into bed?'

Troy hurried after the stretcher and followed it into a small bed-room charmingly furnished and provided, she noticed, with an adjoining bathroom. The two bearers waited with an obliging air for further instructions. As Baradi had not accompanied them, Troy supposed that she herself was for the moment in command. She got Miss Truebody off the stretcher and on to the bed. The bearers hovered solicitously. She thanked them in her schoolgirl French and managed to get them out of the room, but not before they had persuaded her into the passage, opened a further door, and exhibited with evident pride a bare freshly-scrubbed room with a bare freshly-scrubbed table near its window. A woman rose from her knees as the door opened, a scrubbing brush in her hand and a pail beside her. The room reeked of disinfectant. The indoor servant said something about it being 'convenable' and the gardener said something about somebody, she thought himself, being 'bien fatigué', 'infiniment fatigué'. It dawned upon her that they wanted a tip. Poor Troy scuffled in her bag, produced a 500 fr. note and gave it to the indoor servant, indicating that they were to share it. They thanked her and, effulgent with smiles, went back to get the luggage. She hurried to Miss Truebody and found her crying feverishly.

Remembering what she could of hospital routine, Troy washed the patient, found a clean nightdress (Miss Truebody wore white locknit nightdresses, sprigged with posies, and got her into bed. It was difficult to make out how much she understood of her situation. Troy wondered if it was the injection of morphine or her condition or her normal habit of mind or all three, that made her so confused and vague. When she was settled in bed she began to talk with hectic fluency about herself. It was difficult to understand her as she had frantically waved away the offer of her false teeth. Her father, it seemed, had been a doctor, a widower, living in the Bermudas. She was his only child and had spent her life with him until, a year ago, he had died leaving her, as she put it, quite comfortably though not well off. She had decided that she could just afford a trip to England and the Continent. Her father, she muttered distractedly, had 'not kept up,' had 'lost touch.' There had been an unhappy break in the past, she believed, and their relations were never mentioned. Of course there were friends in the Bermudas but not, it appeared, very many or very intimate friends. She rambled on for a little while, continually losing the thread of her narrative and frowning incomprehensibly at nothing. The pupils of her eyes were contracted and her vision seemed to be confused. Presently her voice died away and she dozed uneasily.

Troy stole out and returned to the hall. Alleyn, Ricky and Baradi had gone but the butler was waiting for her and showed her up the steep flight of stairs in the wall. It seemed to turn about a tower and they passed two landings with doors leading off them. Finally the man opened a larger and heavier door and Troy was out in the glare of full morning on a canopied roof-garden hung, as it seemed, in blue space where sky and sea met in a wide crescent. Not till she had advanced some way towards the balustrade did Cap St Gilles appear, a sliver of earth pointing south.

Alleyn and Baradi rose from a breakfast-table near the balustrade. Ricky lay, fast asleep, on a suspended seat under a gay canopy. The smell of freshly ground coffee and of *brioches* and *croissants* reminded Troy that she was hungry.

They sat at the table. It was long, spread with a white cloth and set for a number of places. Troy was foolishly reminded of the Mad Hatter's Tea-party. She looked over the parapet and saw the railroad about eighty feet below her and perhaps a hundred feet from the base of the Chèvre d'Argent. The walls, buttressed and pierced with windows, fell away beneath her in a sickening perspective. Troy had a hatred of heights and drew back quickly. 'Last night,' she thought, 'I looked into one of those windows.'

Dr Baradi was assiduous in his attentions and plied her with coffee. He gazed upon her remorselessly and she sensed Alleyn's annoyance rising with her own embarrassment. For a moment she felt weakly inclined to giggle.

Alleyn said: 'See here, darling, Dr Baradi thinks that Miss Truebody is extremely ill, dangerously so. He thinks we should let her people know at once.'

'She has no people. She's only got acquaintances in the Bermudas; I asked. There seems to be nobody at all.'

Baradi said: in that case . . . ' and moved his head from side to side. He turned to Troy and parodied helplessness with his hands. 'So, in that direction, we can do nothing.'

'The next thing,' Alleyn said, speaking directly to his wife, 'is the business of giving an anaesthetic. We could telephone to a hospital in St Christophe and try to get someone but there's this medical jamboree and in any case it'll mean a delay of some hours. Or Dr Baradi can try to get his own anaesthetist to fly from Paris to the nearest airport. More delay and considerable expense. The other way is for me to have a shot at it. Should we take the risk?'

'What,' Troy asked, making herself look at him, 'do you think, Dr Baradi?'

He sat near and a little behind her on the balustrade. His thighs bulged in their sharkskin trousers. 'I think it will be less risky if your husband, who is not unfamiliar with the procedure, gives the anaesthetic. Her condition is not good.'

His voice flowed over her shoulder. It was really extraordinary, she thought, how he could invest information about peritonitis and ruptured abscesses with such a gross suggestion of flattery. He might have been paying her the most objectionable compliments imaginable.

'Very well,' Alleyn said, 'that's decided, then. But you'll need other help, won't you?'

'If possible, two persons. And here we encounter a difficulty.' He moved round behind Troy but spoke to Alleyn. His manner was now authoritative. 'I doubt,' he said, 'if there is anyone in the house-party who could assist me. It is not every layman who enjoys a visit to an operating theatre. Surgery is not everybody's cup of tea.' The colloquialism came oddly from him. 'I have spoken to our host, of course. He is not yet stirring. He offers every possible assistance and all the amenities of the château with the reservation that he himself shall not be asked to perform an active part. He is,' said Dr Baradi, putting on his sunglasses, 'allergic to blood.'

'Indeed,' said Alleyn politely.

'The rest of our household – we are seven – ' Dr Baradi explained playfully to Troy, 'is not yet awake. Mr Oberon gave a party here last night. Some friends with a yacht in port. We were immeasurably gay and kept going till five o'clock. Mr Oberon has a genius for parties and a passion for charades. They were quite wonderful, our cha-rades.' Troy gave a little ejaculation which she immediately checked. He beamed at her. 'I was cast for one of King Solomon's concubines. And we had the Queen of Sheba, you know. She stabbed Solomon's favourite wife. It was all a little strenuous. I don't think any of my friends will be in good enough form to help us. Indeed, I doubt if any of them even at the top of his or her form, would care to offer for the role. I don't know if you have met any of them. Grizel Locke, perhaps? The Hon. Grizel Locke?'

The Alleyns said they did not know Miss Locke.

'What about the servants?' Alleyn suggested. Troy was all too eas-ily envisaging Dr Baradi as one of King Solomon's concubines.

'One of the men is a possibility. He is my personal attendant and valet and is not quite unfamiliar with surgical routine. He will not lose his head. Any of the others would almost certainly be worse than useless. So we need one other, you see.'

A silence fell upon them, broken at last by Troy.

'I know,' she said, 'what Dr Baradi is going to suggest.'

Alleyn looked fixedly at her and raised his left eyebrow.

'It's quite out of the question. You well know that you're punctually sick at the sight of blood, my darling.'

Troy, who was nothing of the sort said: 'In that case I've no suggestions. Unless you like to appeal to cousin Garbel.'

There was a moment of silence.

'Too whom?' said Baradi softly.

'I'm afraid I was being facetious,' Troy mumbled.

Alleyn said: 'What about our driver? He seems a hardy, intelligent sort of chap. What would he have to do?'

'Fetch and carry,' Dr Baradi said. He was looking thoughtfully at Troy. 'Count sponges. Hand instruments. Clean up. Possibly, in an emergency, play a minor role as unqualified assistant.'

'I'll speak to him. If he seems at all possible I'll bring him in to see you. Would you like to stroll back to the car with me, darling?'

'Please don't disturb yourselves,' Dr Baradi begged them. 'One of the servants will fetch your man.'

Troy knew that her husband was in two minds about this suggestion and also about leaving her to cope with Dr Baradi. She said: 'You go, Rory, will you? I'm longing for my sun-glasses and they're locked away in my dressing-case.'

She gave him her keys and a ferocious smile. 'I think, perhaps, I'll have a look at Miss Truebody,' she added.

He grimaced at her and walked out quickly.

Troy went to Ricky. She touched his forehead and found it moist. His sleep was profound and when she opened the front of his shirt he did not stir. She stayed, lightly swinging the seat, and watched him, and she thought with tenderness that he was her defence in a stupid situation which fatigue and a confusion of spirit, brought about by many untoward events, had perhaps created in her imagination. It was ridiculous, she thought, to feel anything but amused by her embarrassment. She knew that Baradi watched her and she turned and faced him.

'If there is anything I can do before I go,' she said and kept her voice down because of Ricky, 'I hope you'll tell me.'

It was a mistake to speak softly. He at once moved towards her and with an assumption of intimacy, lowered his own voice. 'But how helpful!' he said, 'so we shall have you with us for a little longer? That is good; though it should not be to perform these unlovely tasks.'

'I hope I'm equal to them.' She moved away from Ricky and raised her voice. 'What are they?'

'She must be prepared for the operation.'

He told her what should be done and explained that she would find everything she needed for her purpose in Miss Truebody's bathroom. In giving these specifically clinical instructions, he reverted to his professional manner, but with an air of amusement that she found distasteful. When he had finished she said: 'Then I'll get her fixed up now, shall I?'

'Yes,' he agreed, more to himself than to her. 'Yes, certainly, we shouldn't delay too long.' And seeing a look of preoccupation and responsibility on his face, she left him, disliking him less in that one moment than at any time since they had met. As she went down the stone stairway she thought: 'Thank heaven, at least, for the Queen of Sheba.'

II

Alleyn found their driver in his vest and trousers on the running-board of the car. A medallion of St Christopher dangled from a steel chain above the mat of hair on his chest. He was exchanging improper jokes with a young woman and two small boys who, when he rose to salute his employer, drifted away without embarrassment. He gave Alleyn a look that implied a common understanding of women, and opened the car door.

Alleyn said: 'We're not going yet. What is your name?'

'Raoul, Monsieur. Raoul Milano.'

'You've been a soldier, perhaps?'

'Yes, Monsieur. I am thirty-three and therefore I have seen some service.'

'So your stomach is not easily outraged; then; by a show of blood, for instance? By a formidable wound, shall we say?'

'I was a medical orderly, Monsieur. My stomach also, is an old campaigner.'

'Excellent! I have a job for you, Raoul. It is to assist Dr Baradi, the gentleman you have already seen. He is about to remove Mademoiselle's appendix and since we cannot find a second doctor, we must provide unqualified assistants. If you will help us there may be a little reward and certainly there will be much grace in performing this service. What do you say?'

Raoul looked down at his blunt hands and then up at Alleyn:

'I say yes, M'sieur. As you suggest, it is an act of grace and in any case one may as well do something.'

'Good. Come along then.' Alleyn had found Troy's sunglasses. He and Raoul turned towards the passage, Raoul slinging his coat across his shoulders with the grace of a ballet-dancer.

'So you live in Roqueville?' Alleyn asked.

'In Roqueville, M'sieur. My parents have a little café, not at all smart, but the food is good and I also hire myself out in my car, as you see.'

'You've been up to the château before, of course?'

'Certainly. For little expeditions and also to drive guests and sometimes tourists. As a rule Mr Oberon sends a car for his guests.' He waved a hand at a row of garage-doors, incongruously set in a rocky face at the back of the platform. 'His cars are magnificent.'

Alleyn said: 'The Commissaire at the Préfecture sent you to meet us, I think?'

'That is so, M'sieur.'

'Did he give you my name?'

'Yes, M'sieur L'Inspecteur-en-Chef. It is Ahrr-lin. But he said that M'sieur L'Inspecteur-en-Chef would prefer, perhaps, that I did not use his rank.'

'I would greatly prefer it, Raoul.'

'It is already forgotten, M'sieur.'

'Again, good.'

They passed the cave-like room, where the woman sat among her figurines. Raoul hailed her in a cheerful manner and she returned his greeting. 'You must bring your gentleman in to see my statues,' she shouted. He called back over his shoulder: 'All in good time, Marie,' and added, 'she is an artist, that one. Her saints are pretty and of assistance in one's devotions; but then she overcharges ridiculously, which is not so amusing.'

He sang a stylish little cadence and titled up his head. They were walking beneath a part of the Château de la Chèvre d'Argent that straddled the passageway. 'It goes everywhere, this house,' he remarked. 'One would need a map to find one's way from the kitchen to the best bedroom. Anything might happen.'

When they reached the entrance he stood aside and took off his chauffeur's cap. They found Dr Baradi in the hall. Alleyn told him that Raoul had been a medical orderly and Baradi at once described the duties he would be expected to perform. His manner was cold and uncompromising. Raoul gave him his full attention. He stood easily, his thumbs crooked in his belt. He retained at once his courtesy, his natural grace of posture and his air of independence.

'Well,' Baradi said sharply when he had finished: 'Are you capable of this work?'

'I believe so, M'sieur le Docteur.'

'If you prove to be satisfactory, you will be given 500 francs. That is extremely generous payment for unskilled work.'

'As to payment M'sieur le Docteur,' Raoul said, 'I am already employed by this gentleman and consider myself entirely at his disposal. It is at his request that I engaged myself in this task.'

Baradi raised his eyebrows and looked at Alleyn. 'Evidently an original,' he said in English. 'He seems tolerably intelligent but one never knows. Let us hope that he is at least not too stupid. My man will give him suitable clothes and see that he is clean'

He went to the fireplace and pulled a tapestry bell-rope. 'Mrs Allen;' he said, 'is most kindly preparing our patient. There is a room at your disposal and I venture to lend you one of my gowns. It will, I'm afraid, be terribly voluminous but perhaps some adjustment can be made. We are involved in compromise, isn't it?'

A man wearing the dress of an Egyptian house-servant came in. Baradi spoke to him in his own language, and then to Raoul in French: 'Go with Mahomet and prepare yourself in accordance with his instructions. He speaks French.' Raoul acknowledged this direction with something between a bow and a nod. He said to Alleyn: 'Monsieur will perhaps excuse me?' and followed the servant, looking about the room with interest as he left it.

Baradi said: 'Italian blood there, I think. One comes across these hybrids along the coast. May I show you to my room?'

It was in the same passage as Miss Truebody's but a little farther along it. In Alleyn the trick of quick observation was a professional habit. He saw not only the general sumptuousness of the room but the details also: the Chinese wallpaper, a Wu Tao-tzu scroll, a Ming vase.

'This,' Dr Baradi needlessly explained, 'is known as the Chinese room but, as you will observe, Mr Oberon does not hesitate to introduce modulation. The bureau is by Vernis-Martin.'

'A modulation, as you say, but an enchanting one. The cabinet there is a bolder departure. It looks like a Mussonier.'

'One of his pupils, I understand. You have a discerning eye. Mr Oberon will be delighted.'

A gown was laid out on the bed. Baradi took it up. 'Will you try this? There is an unoccupied room next door with access to a bathroom. You have time for a bath and will, no doubt, be glad to take one. Since morphine has been given there is no immediate urgency but I should prefer all the same to operate as soon as possible. When you are ready, my own preparations will be complete and we can discuss final arrangements.'

Alleyn said: 'Dr Baradi, we haven't said anything about your fee for the operation: indeed, it is neither my business nor my wife's, but I do feel some concern about it. I imagine Miss Truebody will at least be able . . . '

Baradi held up his hand. 'Let us not discuss it,' he said. 'Let us assume that it is of no great moment.'

'If you prefer to do so.' Alleyn hesitated and then added: 'This is an extraordinary situation. You will, I'm sure, realize that we are reluctant to take such a grave responsibility. Miss Truebody is a complete stranger to us. You yourself must feel it would be much more satisfactory if there was a relation or friend from whom we could get some kind of authority. Especially as her illness is so serious.'

'I agree. However, she would undoubtedly die if the operation was not performed and, in my opinion, would be in the gravest danger if it was unduly postponed. As it is, I'm afraid there is a risk, a great risk, that she will not recover. We can,' Baradi added with what Alleyn felt was a genuine, if controlled, anxiety, 'only do our best and hope that all may be well.'

And on this note Alleyn turned to go. As he was in the doorway Baradi, with a complete change of manner, said: 'Your enchanting wife is with her. Third door on the left. Quite enchanting. Delicious, if you will permit me.'

Alleyn looked at him and found what he saw offensive.

'Under these unfortunate circumstances,' he said politely, 'I can't do anything else.'

Evidently Dr Baradi chose to regard this observation as a pleasantry. He laughed richly. 'Delicious!' he repeated, but whether in reference to Alleyn's comment or as a reiterated observation upon Troy it was impossible to determine. Alleyn, who had every reason and no inclination for keeping his temper, walked into the next room.

III

Troy had carried out her instructions and Miss Truebody had slipped again into sleep. The sound of her breathing cut the silence into irregular intervals. Her eyes were not quite closed. Segments of the eyeballs appeared under the pathetic insufficiency of her lashes. Troy was at once unwilling to leave her and anxious to return to Ricky. She heard Alleyn and Dr Baradi in the passage. Their voices were broken off by a door slam and again there was only Miss Truebody's breathing. Troy waited, hoping that Alleyn knew where she was and would come to her. After what seemed an interminable interval there was a tap at the door. She opened it and he was there in a white gown looking tall, elegant and angry. Troy shut the door behind her and they whispered together in the passage.

'Rum go,' he said, 'isn't it?'

'Not 'alf. When do you begin?'

'Soon. He's trying to make himself aseptic. A losing battle, I should think.'

'Frightful, isn't he?'

The bottom. I'm so sorry, darling, you have to suffer his atrocious gallantries.'

'Well, I dare say they're just elaborate oriental courtesy, or something.'

'Elaborate bloody impertinence.'

'Never mind, Rory. I'll skip out of his way.'

'I shouldn't have brought you to this damn' place.'

'Fiddle! In any case he's going to be too busy.'

'Is she asleep?'

'Sort of. I don't like to leave her but suppose Ricky should wake?'

'Go up to him. I'll stay with her. Baradi's going to give her an injection before I get going with the ether. And, Troy –'

'Yes?'

'It's important these people don't get a line on who I am.'

'I know.'

'I haven't told you anything about them but I think I'll have to come moderately clean when there's a chance. It's a rum set up. I'll get you out of it as soon as possible.'

'I'm not worrying now we know about the charades. Funny! You said there might be an explanation but we never thought of charades, did we?'

'No,' Alleyn said, 'we didn't, did we?' and suddenly kissed her. 'Now, I suppose I'll have to wash again,' he added.

Raoul came down the passage with Baradi's servant. They were carrying the improvised stretcher and were dressed in white overalls.

Raoul said: 'Madame!' to Troy and to Alleyn, 'it appears, Monsieur, that M. le Docteur orders Mademoiselle to be taken to the operating room. Is that convenient for Monsieur?'

'Of course. We are under Dr Baradi's orders.'

'Authority,' Raoul observed, 'comes to roost on strange perches, Monsieur.'

'That,' Alleyn said, 'will do.'

Raoul grinned and opened the door. They took the stretcher in and laid it on the floor by the bed. When they lifted her down to it, Miss Truebody opened her eyes and said distinctly: 'But I would prefer to stay in bed.' Raoul deftly tucked blankets under her. She began to wail dismally.

Troy said: 'It's all right, dear. You'll be all right,' and thought: 'But I never call people dear!'

They carried Miss Truebody into the room across the passage and put her on the table by the window. Troy went with them, holding her hand. The window coverings had been removed and a

hard glare beat down on the table. The room still reeked of disinfectant. There was a second table on which a number of objects
were now laid out. Troy, after one glance, did not look at them
again. She held Miss Truebody's hand and stood between her and
the instrument table. A door in the wall facing her opened and
Baradi appeared against a background of bathroom. He wore his
gown and a white cap. Their austerity of design emphasized the
opulence of his nose and eyes and teeth. He had a hypodermic
syringe in his left hand.

'So, after all, you are to assist me?' he murmured to Troy. But it
was obvious that he didn't entertain any such notion.

Still holding the flaccid hand, she said: 'I thought perhaps I should
stay with her until . . . '

'But of course! Please remain a little longer.' He began to give
instructions to Alleyn and the two men. He spoke in French presumably, Troy thought, to spare Miss Truebody's feelings. 'I am left-
handed,' he said. 'If I should ask for anything to be handed to me
you will please remember that. Now, Mr Allen, we will show you
your equipment, isn't it? Milano!' Raoul brought a china dish from
the instrument table. It had a bottle and a hand towel on it. Alleyn
looked at it and nodded. '*Parfaitement*,' he said.

Baradi took Miss Truebody's other hand and pushed up the long
sleeve of her nightgown. She stared at him and her mouth worked
soundlessly.

Troy saw the needle slide in. The hand she held flickered momentarily and relaxed.

'It is fortunate,' Baradi said as he withdrew the needle, 'that this
little Dr Claudel had pentothal. A happy coincidence.'

He raised Miss Truebody's eyelid. The pupil was out of sight.
'Admirable,' he said. 'Now, Mr Allen, we will, in a moment or two,
induce a more profound anaesthesia which you will continue. I shall
scrub up and in a few minutes more we begin operations.' He smiled
at Troy who was already on the way to the door. 'One of our party
will join you presently on the roof-garden. Miss Locke; the
Honourable Grizel Locke. I believe she has a vogue in England.
Quite mad but utterly charming.'

Troy's last impression of the room, a vivid one, was of Baradi,
enormous in his white gown and cap, of Alleyn standing near the

table and smiling at her, of Raoul and the Egyptian servant waiting near the instruments and of Miss Truebody's wide-open mouth and of the sound of her breathing. Then the door shut off the picture as abruptly as the tunnel had shut off her earlier glimpse into a room in the Chèvre d'Argent.

'Only *that* time,' Troy told herself, as she made her way back to the roof-garden, 'it was only a charade.'

CHAPTER 3

Morning with Mr Oberon

The sun shone full on the roof-garden now, but Ricky was shielded from it by the canopy of his swinging couch. He was, as he himself might have said, lavishly asleep. Troy knew he would stay so for a long time.

The breakfast-table had been cleared and moved to one side and several more seats like Ricky's had been set out. Troy took the one nearest to his. When she lifted her feet it swayed gently. Her head sank back into a heap of cushions. She had slept very little in the train.

It was quiet on the roof-garden. A few cicadas chittered far below and once, somewhere a long way away, a car hooted. The sky, as she looked into it, intensified itself in blueness and bemused her drowsy senses. Her eyes closed and she felt again the movement of the train. The sound of the cicadas became a dismal chattering from Miss Truebody and soared up into nothingness. Presently, she too, was fast asleep.

When she awoke, it was to see a strange lady perched, like some fantastic fowl, on the balustrade near Ricky's seat. Her legs, clad in scarlet pedal-pushers, were drawn up to her chin which was sunk between her knees. Her hands, jewelled and claw-like, with vermilion talons, clasped her shins, and her toes protruded from her sandals like branched corals. A scarf was wound around her skull and her eyes were hidden by sun-glasses in an enormous frame below which a formidable nose jutted over a mouth whose natural shape could only be conjectured. When she saw Troy was awake and on her feet she unfolded herself, dropped to the floor and advanced with a hand extended. She was six feet tall and about forty-five to fifty years old.

'How do you do?' she whispered. 'I'm Grizel Locke. I like to be called Sati, though. The Queen of Heaven, you will remember. Please call me Sati. Had a good nap, I hope? I've been looking at your son and wondering if I'd like to have one for myself.'

'How do you do?' Troy said without whispering and greatly taken aback. 'Do you think you would?'

'Won't he wake? I've got *such* a voice as you can hear when I speak up.' Her voice was indeed deep and uncertain like an adolescent boy's. 'It's hard to say,' she went on. 'One might go all possessive and peculiar and, on the other hand, one might get bored and off-load him on repressed governesses. I was off-loaded as a child which, I am told, accounts for almost everything. Do lie down again. You must feel like a boiled owl. So do I. Would you like a drink?'

'No, thank you,' Troy said, running her fingers through her short hair.

'Nor would I. What a poor way to begin your holiday. Do you know anyone here?'

'Not really. I've got a distant relation somewhere in the offing but we've never met.'

'Perhaps we know them. What name?'

'Garbel. Something to do with a rather rarified kind of chemistry. I don't suppose you – ?'

'I'm afraid not,' she said quickly. 'Has Baradi started on your friend?'

'She's not a friend or even an acquaintance. She's a fellow-traveller.'

'How sickening for you,' said the lady earnestly.

'I mean, literally,' Troy explained. She was indeed feeling like a boiled owl and longed for nothing so much as a bath and solitude.

'Lie down,' the lady urged. 'Put your boots up. Go to sleep again if you like. I was just going to push ahead with my tanning, only your son distracted my attention.'

Troy sat down and as her companion was so insistent she did put her feet up.

'That's right,' the lady observed. 'I'll blow up my Li-lo. The servants, alas, have lost the puffer.'

She dragged forward a flat rubber mattress. Sitting on the floor she applied her painted mouth to the valve and began to blow. 'Uphill work,' she gasped a little later, 'still, it's an exercise in itself and I daresay will count as such.'

When the Li-lo was inflated she lay face down upon it and untied the painted scarf that was her sole upper garment. It fell away from a back so thin that it presented, Troy thought, an anatomical subject of considerable interest. The margins of the scapulae shone like ploughshares and the spinal vertebrae looked like those of a flayed snake.

'I've given up oil,' the submerged voice explained, 'since I became a Child of the Sun. Is there any particular bit that seems underdone, do you consider?'

Troy, looking down upon a uniformly dun-coloured expanse, could make no suggestions and said so.

'I'll give it ten minutes for luck and then toss over the bod.,' said the voice. 'I must say I feel ghastly.'

'You had a late night, Dr Baradi tells us,' said Troy, who was making a desperate effort to pull herself together.

'Did we?' the voice became more indistinct and added something like: 'I forget.'

'Charades and everything, he said.'

'Did he? Oh. Was I in them?'

'He didn't say particularly,' Troy answered.

'I passed,' the voice muttered, 'utterly and definitely out.' Troy had just thought how unattractive such statements always were when she noticed with astonishment that the shoulder blades were quivering as if their owner was convulsed. 'I suppose you might call it charades,' the lady was heard to say.

Troy was conscious of a rising sense of uneasiness.

'How do you mean?' she asked.

Her companion rolled over. She had taken off her sunglasses. Her eyes were green with pale irises and small pupils. They were singularly blank in expression. Clad only in her scarlet pedal-pushers and head-scarf, she was an uncomfortable spectacle.

'The whole thing is,' she said rapidly, 'I wasn't at the party. I began one of my headaches after luncheon which was a party in itself and I passed, as I mentioned a moment ago, out. That must have been at about four o'clock, I should think, which is why I am up so early, you know.' She yawned suddenly and with gross exaggeration as if her jaws would crack.

'Oh, God,' she said, 'here I go again!'

Troy's jaws quivered in imitation. 'I hope your headache is better,' she said.

'Sweet of you. In point of fact it's hideous.'

'I'm so sorry.'

'I'll have to find Baradi if it goes on. And it will, of course. How long will he be over your fellow-traveller's appendix? Have you seen Ra?'

'I don't think so. I've only seen Dr Baradi.'

'Yes, yes,' she said restlessly and added, 'you wouldn't know, of course. I mean Oberon, our Teacher, your know. That's our name for him – Ra. Are you interested in The Truth?'

Troy was too addled with unseasonable sleep and a surfeit of anxiety to hear the capital letters. 'I really don't know,' she stammered. 'In the truth – ?'

'Poor sweet, I'm muddling you.' She sat up. Troy had a painter's attitude towards the nude but the aspect of this lady, so wildly and so unpleasingly displayed, was distressing, and doubly so because Troy couldn't escape the impression that the lady herself was far from unselfconscious. Indeed she kept making tentative clutches at her scarf and looking at Troy as if she felt she ought to apologize for herself. In her embarrassment Troy turned away and looked vaguely at the tower wall which rose above the roof-garden not far from where she sat. It was pierced at ascending intervals by narrow slits. Troy's eyes, glazed with fatigue, stared in aimless fixation at the third slit from the floor level. She listened to a strange exposition on The Truth as understood and venerated by the guests of Mr Oberon.

' . . . just a tiny group of Seekers . . . Children of the Sun in the Outer . . . Evil exists only in the minds of the earth-bound . . . goodness is oneness . . . the great Dark co-exists with the great Light . . . ' The phrases disjointed and eked out by ineloquent and unco-ordinated gestures, tripped each other up by the heels. Clichés and aphorisms were tumbled together from the most unlikely sources. One must live dangerously, it appeared, in order to attain merit. Only by encompassing the gamut of earthly experience could one return to the oneness of universal good. One ascended through countless ages by something which the disciple, corkscrewing an unsteady finger in illustration, called the mystic navel spiral. It all sounded the most dreadful nonsense to poor Troy but she listened politely and, because her companion so clearly expected them, tried to ask one or two intelligent questions. This was a mistake. The lady, squinting earnestly up at her, said abruptly: 'You're fey, of course. But you know that, don't you?'

'Indeed, I don't.'

'Yes, yes,' she persisted, nodding like a mandarin. 'Unawakened perhaps, but it's there, oh! so richly. Fey as fey can be.'

She yawned again with the same unnatural exaggeration and twisted round to look at the door into the tower.

'He won't be long appearing,' she whispered. 'It isn't as if he ever touched anything and he's always up for the rites of Ushas. What's the time?'

'Just after ten,' said Troy, astonished that it was no later. Ricky, she thought, would sleep for at least another hour, perhaps for two hours. She tried to remember if she had ever heard how long an appendicectomy took to perform. She tried to console herself with the thought that there must be a limit to this vigil, that she would not have to listen forever to Grizel Locke's esoteric small-talk, that somewhere down at the Hôtel Royal in Roqueville there was a tiled bathroom and a cool bed, that perhaps Miss Locke would go in search of whoever it was she seemed to await with such impatience and finally that she herself might, if left alone, sleep away the remainder of this muddled and distressing interlude.

It was at this juncture that something moved behind the slit in the tower wall. Something that tweaked at her attention. She had an impression of hair or fur and thought at first that it was an animal, perhaps a cat. It moved again and was gone but not before she recognized a human head. She came to the disagreeable conclusion that someone had stood at the slit and listened to their conversation. At that moment she heard steps inside the tower. The door moved.

'Someone's coming!' she cried out in warning. Her companion gave an ejaculation of relief but made no attempt to resume her garment. 'Miss Locke! Do look out!'

'What? Oh! Oh, all right. Only, do call me Sati.' She picked up the square of printed silk. Perhaps, Troy thought, there was something in her own face that awakened in Miss Locke a dormant regard for the conventions. She blushed and began clumsily to knot the scarf behind her.

But Troy's gaze was upon the man who had come through the tower door on to the roof-garden and was walking towards them. The confusion of spirit that had irked her throughout the morning clarified into one recognizable emotion.

She was frightened.

II

Troy would have been unable to say at that moment why she was afraid of Mr Oberon. There was nothing in his appearance, one would have thought, to inspire fear. Rather, he had, at first sight, a look of mildness.

Beards, in general, are not rare nowadays though beards like his are perhaps unusual. It was blond, sparse and silky and divided at the chin, which was almost bare. The moustache was a mere shadow at the corners of his mouth which was fresh in colour. The nose was straight and delicate and the light eyes abnormally large. His hair was parted in the middle and so long that it overhung the collar of his gown. This, and a sort of fragility in the general structure of his head, gave him an air of effeminacy. What was startling and to Troy quite shocking, was the resemblance to Roman Catholic devotional prints such as the 'Sacred Heart.' She was to learn that this resemblance was deliberately cultivated. He wore a white dressing-gown to which his extraordinary appearance gave the air of a ceremonial robe.

It seemed incredible that such a being could make normal conversation. Troy would not have been surprised if he had acknowledged the introduction in Sanskrit. However, be gave her his hand, which was small and well-formed, and a conventional greeting. He had a singularly musical voice, and spoke without any marked accent though Troy fancied she heard a faint American inflection. She said something about his kindness in offering harbourage to Miss Truebody. He smiled gently, sank on to an Algerian leather seat, drew his feet up under his gown and placed them, apparently, against his thighs. His hands fell softly to his lap.

'You have brought,' he said, 'a gift of great price. We are grateful.'

From the time they had confronted each other he had looked fully into Troy's eyes and he continued to do so. It was not the half-unseeing attention of ordinary courtesy but an unswerving fixed regard. He seemed to blink less than most people.

His disciple said: 'Dearest Ra, I've got the most monstrous headache.'

'It will pass,' he said, still looking at Troy. 'You know what you should do, dear Sati.'

'Yes, I do, don't I! But it's so hard sometimes to feel the light. One gropes and gropes.'

'Patience, dear Sati. It will come.'

She sat up on her Li-lo, seized her ankles and with a grunt of discomfort adjusted the soles of her feet to the inside surface of her thighs. 'Om,' she said discontentedly.

Mr Oberon said to Troy: 'We speak of things that are a little strange to you. Or perhaps they are not altogether strange.'

'Just what I thought.' The lady began eagerly. 'Isn't she fey?'

He disregarded her.

'Should I explain that we – my guests here and I – follow what we believe to be the true Way of Life? Perhaps, up here, in this ancient house, we have created an atmosphere that to a visitor is a little overwhelming. Do you feel it so?'

Troy said: 'I'm afraid I'm just rather addled with a long journey, not much sleep and an anxious time with Miss Truebody.'

'I have been helping her. And, I hope, our friend Baradi.'

'Have you?' Troy exclaimed in great surprise. 'I thought . . . but how kind of you . . . is . . . is the operation going well?'

He smiled, showing perfect teeth. 'Again, I do not make myself clear. I have been with them, not in the body but in the spirit.'

'Oh,' mumbled Troy. 'I'm sorry.'

'Particularly with your friend. This was easy because when by the will, or, as with her, by the agency of an anaesthetic, the soul is set free of the body, it may be greatly helped. Hers is a pure soul. She should be called Miss Truesoul instead of Miss Truebody.' He laughed, a light breathy sound, and showed the pink interior of his mouth. 'But we must not despise the body,' he said, apparently as an afterthought.

His disciple whispered: 'Oh no! No, indeed! No,' and started to breathe deeply, stopping one nostril with a finger and expelling her breath with a hissing sound. Troy began to wonder if she was, perhaps, a little mad.

Oberon had shifted his gaze from Troy. His eyes were still very wide open and quite without expression. He had seen the sleeping Ricky.

It was with the greatest difficulty that Troy gave her movement towards Ricky a semblance of casualness. Her instinct, she afterwards told Alleyn, was entirely that of a mother-cat. She leant over her small son and made a pretence of adjusting the cushion behind him. She heard Oberon say: 'A beautiful child,' and thought that no matter how odd it might look, she would stand between Ricky and his eyes until something else diverted their gaze. But Ricky himself stirred a little, flinging out his arm. She moved him over with his face away from Oberon. He murmured: 'Mummy?' and she answered: 'Yes,' and kept her hand on him until he had fallen back to sleep.

She turned and looked past the ridiculous back of the deep-breathing disciple to the figure in the glare of the sun, and, being a painter, she recognized, in the midst of her alarm a remarkable object. At the same time it seemed to her that Oberon and she acknowledged each other as enemies.

This engagement, if it was one, was broken off by the appearance of two more of Mr Oberon's guests: a tall girl and a lame young man who were introduced as Ginny Taylor and Robin Herrington. Both their names were familiar to Troy, the girl's as that of a regular sacrifice on the altars of the glossy weeklies and the man's as that of the reputably wildish son of a famous brewer who was also an indefatigable patron of the fine arts. To Troy their comparative normality was as a freshening breeze and she was ready to overlook the shadows under their eyes and their air of unease. They greeted her politely, lowered their voices when they saw Ricky and sat together on one seat, screening him from Mr Oberon. Troy returned to her former place.

Mr Oberon was talking. It seemed that he had bought a book in Paris, a newly-discovered manuscript, one of those assembled by Roger de Gaignières. Troy knew that he must have paid a fabulous sum for it and, in spite of herself, listened eagerly to a description of the illuminations. He went on to speak of other works; of the calendar of Charles d'Angoulême, of Indian art, and finally of the moderns – Rouault, Picasso and André Derain. 'But, of course, André is not a modern. He derives quite blatantly from Rubens. Ask Carbury, when he comes, if I am not right.'

Troy's nerves jumped. Could he mean Carbury Glande, a painter whom she knew perfectly well who would certainly, if he appeared, greet her with feverish effusiveness? Mr Oberon no longer looked at her or at anyone in particular, yet she had the feeling that he talked at her and he was talking very well. Yes, here was a description of one of Glande's works. 'He painted it yesterday from the Saracens' Watchtower: the favourite interplay of lemon and lacquer-red with a single note of magenta, and everything arranged about a central point. The esoteric significance was eloquent and the whole thing quite beautiful.' It was undoubtedly Carbury Glande. Surely, surely, the operation must be over and if so, why didn't Alleyn come and take them away? She tried to remember if Carbury Glande knew she was married to a policeman.

Ginny Taylor said: 'I wish I knew about Carbury. I can't get anything from his works. I can only say awful philistinish things such as they look as if they were too easy to do.' She glanced in a friendly manner at Troy. 'Do *you* know about modern art?' she asked.

'I'm always ready to learn,' Troy hedged with a dexterity born of fright.

'I shall never learn however much I try,' sighed Ginny Taylor and suddenly yawned.

The jaws of everyone except Mr Oberon quivered responsively.

'Lord, I'm sorry,' said Ginny and for some unaccountable reason looked frightened. Robin Herrington touched her hand with the tip of his fingers. 'I wonder why they're so infectious,' he said. 'Sneezes, coughs and yawns. Yawns worst of all. To read about them's enough to set one going.'

'Perhaps,' Mr Oberon suggested, 'it's another piece of evidence, if a homely one, that separateness is an illusion. Our bodies as well as our souls have reflex actions.' And while Troy was still wondering what on earth this might mean his Sati gave a little yelp of agreement.

'True! True!' she cried. She dived, stretched out with her right arm and grasped her toes. At the same time she wound her left arm behind her head and seized her right ear. Having achieved this unlikely posture, she gazed devotedly upon Mr Oberon. 'Is it all right, dearest Ra,' she asked, 'for me to press quietly on with my Prana and Pranayama?'

'It is well at all times, dear Sati, if the spirit also is attuned.'

Troy couldn't resist stealing a glance at Ginny Taylor and Robin Herrington. Was it possible that they found nothing to marvel at in these antics? Ginny was looking doubtfully at Sati and young Herrington was looking at Ginny as if, Troy thought with relief, he invited her to be amused with him.

'Ginny?' Mr Oberon said quietly.

The beginning of a smile died on Ginny's lips. 'I'm sorry,' she said quickly. 'Yes, Ra?'

'Have you formed a design for today?'

'No. At least . . . this afternoon . . . '

'I thought, if it suited general arrangements,' Robin Herrington said, 'that I might ask Ginny to come into Douceville this afternoon. I want her to tell me what colour I should have for new awnings on the afterdeck.'

But Ginny had got up and walked past Troy to Mr Oberon. She stood before him white-faced with the dark marks showing under her eyes.

'Are you going, then, to Douceville?' he asked. 'You look a little pale, my child. We were so late with our gaities last night. Should you rest this afternoon?'

He was looking at her as he had looked at Troy.

'I think perhaps I should,' she said in a flat voice.

'I, too. The colour of the awnings can wait until the colour of the cheeks is restored. Perhaps Annabella would enjoy a drive to Douceville. Annabella Wells,' he explained to Troy, 'is with us. Her latest picture is completed and she is to make a film for *Durant Frères* in the spring.'

Troy was not much interested in the presence of a notoriously erratic, if brilliant actress. She had been watching young Herrington, whose brows were drawn together in a scowl. He got up and stood behind Ginny looking at Oberon over the top of her head. His hands closed and he thrust them into his pockets.

'I thought a drive might be a good idea for Ginny,' he said.

But Ginny had sunk down on the end of the Li-lo at Mr Oberon's feet. She settled herself there quietly, with an air of obedience. Mr Oberon said to Troy: 'Robin has a most wonderful yacht. You must ask him to show it to you.' He put his hand on Ginny's head.

'I should be delighted,' said Robin and sounded furious. He had turned aside and now added in a loud voice: 'Why not this afternoon? I still think Ginny should come to Douceville.'

Troy knew that something had happened that was unusual between Mr Oberon and his guests and that Robin Herrington was frightened as well as angry. She wanted to give him courage. Her heart thumped against her ribs.

In the dead silence they all heard someone come quickly up the stone stairway. When Alleyn opened the door their heads were already turned towards him.

III

He waited for a moment to accustom his eyes to the glare and during that moment he and the five people whose faces were turned towards him were motionless.

One grows scarcely to see one's lifelong companions and it is more difficult to call up the face of one's beloved than that of a mere acquaintance. Troy had never been able to make a memory-drawing of her husband. Yet, at that moment, it was as if a veil of familiarity was withdrawn and she looked at him with fresh perception.

She thought: 'I've never been gladder to see him.'

'This is my husband,' she said.

Mr Oberon had risen and came forward. He was five inches shorter than Alleyn. For the first time Troy thought him ridiculous as well as disgusting.

He held out his hand. 'We're so glad to meet you at last. The news is good?'

'Dr Baradi will be able to tell you better than I,' Alleyn said. 'Her condition was pretty bad. He says she will be very ill.'

'We shall all help her,' Mr Oberon said, indicating the antic Sati, the bemused Ginny Taylor and the angry-looking Robin Herrington. 'We can do so much.'

He put his hand on Alleyn's arm and led him forward. The reek of ether accompanied them. Alleyn was introduced to the guests and offered a seat but he said: 'If we may, I think perhaps I should see my wife and Ricky on their way back to Roqueville. Our driver is free now and can take them. He will come back for me. We're expecting a rather urgent telephone call at our hotel.'

Troy, who dreaded the appearance of Carbury Glande, knew Alleyn had said 'my wife,' because he didn't want Oberon to learn her name. He had an air of authority that was in itself, she thought, almost a betrayal. She got up quickly and went to Ricky.

'Perhaps,' Alleyn said, 'I should stay a little longer in case there's any change in her condition. Baradi is going to telephone to St Christophe for a nurse and, in the meantime, two of your maids will take turns sitting in the room. I'm sure, sir, that if she were able, Miss Truebody would tell you how grateful she is for your hospitality.'

'There is no need. She is with us in a very special sense. She is in safe hands. We must send a car for the nurse. There is no train until the evening.'

'I'll go,' Robin Herrington said. 'I'll be there in an hour.'

'Robin,' Oberon explained lightly, 'has driven in the Monte Carlo rally. We must hope that the nurse has iron nerves.'

Alleyn said to Robin: 'It sounds an admirable idea. Will you suggest it to Dr Baradi?'

He went to Ricky and lifted him in his arms. Troy gave her hand to Mr Oberon. His own wrapped itself round hers, tightened, and was suddenly withdrawn. 'You must visit us again,' he said. 'If you are a voyager of the spirit, and I think you are, it might interest you to come to one of our meditations.'

'Yes, do come,' urged his Sati, who had abandoned her exercises on Alleyn's entrance. 'It's madly wonderful. You must. Where are you staying?'

'At the Royal.'

'Couldn't be easier. No need to hire a car. The Douceville bus leaves from the corner. Every half-hour. You'll find it perfectly convenient.'

Troy was reminded vividly of Mr Garbel's letters. She murmured something non-committal, said goodbye and went to the door.

'I'll see you out,' Robin Herrington offered and took up his heavy walking-stick.

As she groped down the darkened stairway she heard their voices rumbling above her. They came slowly; Alleyn because of Ricky and Herrington because of his stiff leg. The sensation of nightmare that threatened without declaring itself, mounted in intensity. The stairs seemed endless yet when she reached the door into the hall she was half-scared of opening it because Carbury Glande might be on the other side. But the hall was untenanted. She hurried through it and out to the courtyard. The iron gates had an elaborate fastening. Troy fumbled with it, dazzled by the glare of sunlight beyond. She pulled at the heavy latch, bruising her fingers. A voice behind her and at her feet said: 'Do let me help you.'

Carbury Glande must have come up the stairs from beneath the courtyard. His face, on a level with her knees, peered through the interstices of the wrought-iron banister. Recognition dawned on it.

'Can it be Troy?' he ejaculated hoarsely. 'But it *is*!' Dear heart, how magical and how peculiar. Where *have* you sprung from? And why are you scrabbling away at doors? Has Oberon alarmed you? I may say he petrifies me. What are you up to?'

He had arrived at her level, a short gnarled man whose hair and beard were red and whose face, at the moment, was a dreadful grey. He blinked up at Troy as if he couldn't get her into focus. He was wearing a pair of floral shorts and a magenta shirt.

'I'm not up to anything,' said Troy. 'In fact, I'm scarcely here at all. We've brought your host a middle-aged spinster with a perforated appendix and now we're on our way.'

'Ah, yes. I heard about the spinster. Ali Baradi woke me at cockcrow, full of professional zeal, and asked me if I'd like to thread needles and count sponges. How he dared! Are you going?'

'I must,' Troy said. 'Do open this damned door for me.'

She could hear Alleyn's and Herrington's voices in the hall and the thump of Herrington's stick.

Glande reached for the latch. His hand, stained round the nails with paint, was tremulous. 'I am, as you can see, a wreck,' he said. 'A Homeric party and only four hours' sottish insensitivity in which to recover. Imagine it! There you are.'

He opened the doors and winced at the glare outside. 'Oberon will be thrilled you're here,' he said. 'Did you know he bought a thing of yours at the Rond-Point show? It's in the library. 'Boy with a Kite.' He adores it.'

'Look here,' Troy said hurriedly, 'be a good chap and don't tell him I'm me. I've come here for a holiday and I'd so much rather . . . '

'Well, if you like. Yes, of course. Yes, I understand. And on mature consideration I fancy this *ménage* is not entirely your cup of tea. You're almost pathologically normal, aren't you? Forgive me if I bolt back to my burrow, the glare is really *more* than I can endure. God, somebody's coming!'

He stumbled away from the door. Alleyn with Ricky in his arms, came out of the hall followed by Robin Herrington. Glande ejaculated: 'Oh, sorry!' and bolted down the stairs. Herrington scowled after him and said: 'That's our tame genius. I'll come to the car, if I may.'

As they walked in single file down the steps and past the maker of figurines, Troy had the feeling that Robin wanted to say something to them and didn't know how to begin. They had reached the open platform where Raoul waited by the car before he blurted out:

'I do hope you will let me drive you down, to see the yacht. Both of you, I mean. I mean . . . ' he stopped short.

Alleyn said: 'That's very nice of you. I hadn't heard about a yacht.'

'She's quite fun.' He stood there, still with an air of hesitancy. Alleyn shifted Ricky and looked at Troy, who held out her hand to Robin.

'Don't come any farther,' she said. 'Goodbye and thank you.'

'Goodbye. If we may, Ginny and I will call at the hotel. It's the Royal, I suppose. I mean, it might amuse you to come for a drive. I mean, if you don't know anybody here . . . '

'It'd be lovely,' Troy temporized, wondering if Alleyn wanted her to accept.

'As a matter of fact,' Alleyn said, 'we *have* got someone we ought to look up in Roqueville. Do you know anybody about here with the unlikely name of Garbel?'

Robin's jaw dropped. He stared at them with an expression of extraordinary consternation. 'I . . . no. No. We haven't really met any of the local people. No. Well I mustn't keep you standing in the sun. Goodbye.'

And with a precipitancy as marked as his former hesitation, he turned and limped off down the passageway.

'Now what,' Troy asked her husband, 'in a crazy world, is the significance of that particular bit of lunacy?'

'I've not the beginning of a notion,' he said. 'But I suggest that when we've got time to think, we call on Mr Garbel.'

CHAPTER 4

The Elusiveness of Mr Garbel

Ricky woke up before they could get him to the car and was bewildered to find himself transported. He was hot, hungry, thirsty and uncomfortable and he required immediate attention.

While Troy and Alleyn looked helplessly about the open platform Raoul advanced from the car, his face brilliant with understanding. He squatted on his heels beside the flushed and urgent Ricky and addressed him in very simple French which he appeared to understand and to which he readily responded. Marie, of the figurines, Raoul explained to the parents, would offer suitable hospitality and he and Ricky went off together, Ricky glancing up at him with admiration.

'It appears,' Alleyn said, 'that a French nanny and those bi-weekly conversational tramps with Mademoiselle to the Round Pond have not been unproductive. Our child has the rudiments of the language.'

'Mademoiselle,' Troy rejoined, 'says he's prodigiously quick for his age. An amazing child, she thinks.' And she added hotly; 'Well, all right, I don't say so to anyone else, do I?'

'My darling, you do not and you shall never say so too often to me. But for the moment let us take our infant phenomenon for granted and look at the situation Chèvre d'Argent. Tell me as quickly as you can, what happened before I cropped up among those cups-of-tea on the rooftop.'

They sat together on the running-board of the car and Troy did her best. 'Admirable,' he said when she had finished. 'I fell in love with you in the first instance because you made such beautiful state-ments. Now, what do you suppose goes on in that house?'

'Something quite beastly,' she said vigorously. 'I'm sure of it. Oberon's obviously dishing out to his chums some fantastic hodge-podge of mysticism-cum-religion-cum, I'm very much afraid, eroti-cism. Grizel Locke attempted a sort of résumé. You never heard such a rigmarole . . . yoga, Nietzsche, black magic. Voodoo, I wouldn't be surprised. With Lord knows what fancy touches of their own thrown in. It ought to be merely silly but it's not, it's frightening. Grizel Locke, I should say, is potty, but the two young ones in any other setting would have struck me as being pleasant children. The boy's obviously in a state about the girl who seems to be completely in Oberon's toils. It's so fantastic, it isn't true.'

'Have you ever heard of the case of Horus and the Swami Vivi Ananda?'

'No.'

'They appeared before Curtis Bennett with Edward Carson pros-ecuting and got swinging sentences for their pains. There's no time to tell you about them now but you've more or less described their set-up, and I assure you there's nothing so very unusual about the religio-erotic racket. Oberon's name, by the way, is Albert George Clarkson. He's a millionaire and undoubtedly one of the drug barons. The cult of the Children of the Sun in the Outer is merely a useful sideline and a means, I suspect, of gratifying a particularly nasty personal taste. They suggested as much at the Sûreté though they don't know exactly what goes on among the Sun's Babies. The Sûreté is interested solely in the narcotics side of the show and the Yard's watching it from our end.'

'And you?'

'I'm supposed to be the perishing link or something. What about the red-headed gentleman with painty hands and a carryover who was letting you out?'

'He might be serious, Rory. He's Carbury Glande. He paints those post-surrealist things . . . witches' sabbaths and mystic unions. You must remember. Rather pretty colour and good design but a bit nasty in feeling. The thing is, he knows me and although I asked him not to, he'll probably talk.'

'Does he know about us?'

'I can't tell. He might.'

'Damn!'

'I shouldn't have come, should I? If Glande knows who you are, he won't be able to resist telling them and bang goes your job.'

'They didn't give me Glande's name at the Sûreté. He must be a later arrival. Never mind, we'll gamble on his not knowing you made a mésalliance with a policeman. Now, listen, my darling, I don't know how long I'll be up here. It may be an hour and it may be twenty-four. Will you settle yourself and Ricky at the Royal and forget about the Chèvre d'Argent? If there's any goat on the premises it will probably be your devoted husband. I'll make what hay I can while the sun shines in the Outer and I'll turn up as soon as maybe. One thing more. Will you try, when you've come to your poor senses, to ring up Mr Garbel? He may not be on the telephone, of course, but if he is . . . '

'Lord, yes! Mr Garbel! Now why, for pity's sake, did Robin Herrington run like a rabbit at the mention of P.E.Garbel? Can cousin Garbel be a drug baron? Or an addict, if it comes to that? It might account for his quaint literary style.'

'Have you by any chance, brought his letters?'

'Only the last, for the sake of his address.'

'Hang on to it, I implore you. If he is on the telephone and answers, ask him to luncheon tomorrow and I'll be there. If, by any chance, he turns up before then, find out if he knows any of Oberon's chums and is prepared to talk about them. Here comes Raoul and Ricky. Forget about this blasted business, my own true love, and enjoy yourself if you can.'

'What about Miss Truebody?'

'Baradi is pretty worried, he says. I'm quite certain he's doing all that can be done for her. He's a kingpin at his job, you know, however much he may stink to high heaven as a chap.'

'Shouldn't I wait with her?'

'*No.* Any more of that and I'll begin to think you like having your hand kissed by luscious Oriental gentlemen. Hallo, Rick, ready for your drive?'

Ricky advanced with his hands behind his back and with strides designed to match those of his companion. 'Is Raoul driving us?' he asked.

'He is. You and Mummy.'

'Good. Daddy, look! Look, Mummy!'

He produced from behind his back a little goat, painted silver grey, with one foot upraised and mounted on a base that roughly traced the outlines of the Château de la Chèvre d'Argent. 'The old lady made it and Raoul gave it to me,' Ricky said. 'It's a silver goat and when it's night-time it makes itself shine. Doesn't it Raoul? *N'est ce pas, Raoul?*'

'*Oui, oui. Une chèvre d'argent qui s'illumine.*'

'Daddy, isn't Raoul kind?'

Alleyn, a little embarrassed, told Raoul how kind he was and Troy, haltingly, attempted to say that he shouldn't.

Raoul said: 'But it is nothing, Madame. If it pleases this young gallant and does not offend Madame, all is well. What are my orders, Monsieur?'

'Will you drive Madame and Ricky to their hotel? Then go to M. le Commissaire at the Préfecture and give him this letter. Tell him that I will call on him as soon as possible. Tell him also about the operation and of course reply to any questions he may ask. Then return here. There is no immediate hurry and you will have time for *déjeuner*. Do not report at the château but wait here for me. If I haven't turned up by 3.30 you may ask for me at the château. You will remember that?'

Raoul repeated his instructions. Alleyn looked steadily at him. 'Should you be told that I am not there, drive to the nearest telephone, ring up the Préfecture and tell M. le Commissaire precisely what has happened. Understood?'

'Well understood, Monsieur.'

'Good. One thing more, Raoul. Do you know anyone in Roqueville called Garbel?'

'Garr-bel? No, Monsieur. It will be an English person for whom Monsieur inquires?'

'Yes. The address is 16 Rue des Violettes.'

Raoul repeated the address. 'It is an apartment house, that one. It is true one finds a few English there, for the most part ladies no longer young and with small incomes who do not often engage taxis.'

'Ah, well,' Alleyn said. 'No matter.'

He took off his hat and kissed his wife. 'Have a nice holiday,' he said, 'and give my love to Mr Garbel.'

'What were you telling Raoul?'

'Wouldn't you like to know! Goodbye, Rick. Take care of your Mama, she's a good kind creature and means well.'

Ricky grinned. He was quick, when he didn't understand his father's remarks, to catch their intention from the colour of his voice. '*Entendu*,' he said, imitating Raoul, and climbed into the car beside him.

'I suppose I may sit here?' he said airily.

'He *is* a precocious little perisher and no mistake,' Alleyn muttered. 'Do you suppose it'll all peter out and he'll be a dullard by the time he's eight.'

'A lot of it's purely imitative. It sounds classier than it is. Move up, Ricky, I'm coming in front, too.'

Alleyn watched the car drive down the steep lane to the main road. Then he turned back to the Château de la Chèvre d'Argent.

II

On the way back to Roqueville Raoul talked nursery French to Ricky and his mother, pointing out the places of interest: the Alpine monastery where, in the cloisters, one might see many lively pictures executed by the persons of the district whose relations had been saved from abrupt destruction by the intervention of Our Lady of Paysdoux; villages that looked as if they had been thrown against the rocks and had stuck to them; distant prospects of little towns. On a lonely stretch of road, Troy offered him a cigarette and while he lit it he allowed Ricky to steer the scarcely moving car. Ricky's dotage on Raoul intensified with every kilometre they travelled together and Troy's understanding of French improved with astonishing rapidity. Altogether they enjoyed each other's company immensely and the journey seemed a short one. They could scarcely believe that the cluster of yellow and pink buildings that presently appeared beneath them was Roqueville.

Raoul turned aside from the steeply descending road and drove down a narrow side-street past an open market where bunches of dyed immortelles hung shrilly above the stalls and the smell of tuberoses was mingled with the pungency of fruit and vegetables. All the world, Raoul said, was abroad at this hour in the market and he flung loud unembarrassed greetings to many persons of his acquaintance. Troy felt her spirits rising and Ricky dropped into the stillness that with him was a sign of extreme pleasure. He sighed deeply and laid one hand on Raoul's knee and one, clasping his silver goat, on Troy's.

They were in a shadowed street where the houses were washed over with faint candy-pink, lemon and powder-blue. Strings of washing hung from one iron balcony to another.

'Rue des Violettes,' Raoul said, pointing to the street-sign and presently halted. '*Numero seize*.'

Troy gathered that he offered her an opportunity to call on Mr Garbel or, if she was not so inclined, to note the whereabouts of his lodgings. She could see through the open door into a dim and undistinguished interior. A number of raffish children clustered about the car. They chattered in an incomprehensible patois and stared with an air of hardihood at Ricky, who instantly became stony.

Troy thought Raoul was offering to accompany her into the house, but sensing panic in the breast of her son, she managed to say that she would go in by herself. 'I can't leave a note,' she thought and said to Ricky: 'I won't be a moment. You stay with Raoul, darling.'

'OK,' he agreed, still fully occupied with disregarding the children. He was like a dog who, when addressed by his master, wags his tail but does not lower his hackles. Raoul shouted at the children and made a shooing noise driving them from the car. They retreated a little, skittishly twitting him. He got out and opened the door for Troy, removing his cap as if she were a minor royalty. Impressed by this evidence of prestige, most of the children fell back, though two of the hardier raised a beggar's plaint and were silenced by Raoul.

The door of No. 16 was ajar. Troy pushed it open and crossed a dingy tessellated floor to a lift-well beside which hung a slotted board holding cards, some with printed and some with written names on them. She had begun hunting up and down the board when a voice behind her said: 'Madame?'

Troy turned as if she'd been struck. The door of a sort of cubby-hole opposite the lift was held partly open by a grimy and heavily ringed hand. Beyond the hand Troy could see folds of a black satin dress, an iridescence of bead-work and three-quarters of a heavy face and piled-up coiffure.

She felt as if she'd been caught doing something shady. Her nursery French deserted her.

'*Pardon*,' she stammered. '*Je désire – je cherche – Monsieur Garbel – le nom de Garbel*.'

The woman said something incomprehensible to Troy who replied, '*Je ne parle pas Français. Malheureusement*,' she added on an afterthought. The woman made a resigned noise and waddled out of her cubby-hole. She was enormously fat and used a walking-stick. Her eyes were like black currants sunk in uncooked dough. She prodded with her stick at the top of the board and, strangely familiar in that alien place, a spidery signature in faded ink was exhibited: 'P.E.Garbel.'

'*Ah, merci*,' Troy cried out but the fat woman shook her head contemptuously and appeared to repeat her former remark. This time Troy caught something like . . . '*Pas chez elle . . . il y a vingt-quatre heures*.'

'Not at home?' shouted Troy in English. The woman shrugged heavily and began to walk away. 'May I leave a note?' Troy called to her enormous back. '*Puis-je vous donner un billet pour Monsieur?*'

The woman stared at her as if she were mad. Troy scrabbled in her bag and produced a notebook and the stub of a BB pencil. Sketches she had made of Ricky in the train fell to the floor. The woman glanced at them with some appearance of interest. Troy wrote: 'Called at 11.15. Sorry to have missed you. Hope you can lunch with us at the Royal tomorrow.' She signed the note, folded it over and wrote: 'M. P.E.Garbel' on the flap. She gave it to the woman (was she a concierge?) and stooped to recover her sketches, aware as she did so, of a dusty skirt, dubious petticoats and broken shoes. When she straightened up it was to find her note displayed with a grey-rimmed sunken finger-nail jabbing at the inscription. 'She can't read my writing,' Troy thought and pointed first to the card and then to the note, nodding like a mandarin and smiling constrainedly. 'Garbel,' said Troy, 'Gar-r-bel.' She remembered about tipping and pressed a 200 franc note into the padded hand. This had an instantaneous effect. The woman coruscated with black unlovely smiles.

'Mademoiselle,' she said, gaily waving the note. 'Madame,' Troy responded. *'Non, non, non, non, Mademoiselle.'* insisted the woman with an ingratiating leer.

Troy supposed this to be a compliment. She tried to look deprecating, made an ungraphic gesture and beat a retreat.

Ricky and Raoul were in close conversation in the car when she rejoined them. Three of the hardboiled children were seated on the running board while the others played leap-frog in an exhibitionist manner up and down the street.

'Darling,' Troy said as they drove away, 'you speak French much better than I do.'

Ricky slewed his eyes round to her. They were a brilliant blue and his lashes, like his hair, were black. *'Naturellement!'* he said.

'Don't be a prig, Ricky,' said his mother crossly. 'You're much too uppity. I think I must be bringing you up very badly.'

'Why?'

'Now then!' Troy warned him.

'Did you see Mr Garbel, Mummy?'

'No, I left a note.'

'Is he coming to see us?'

'I hope so,' said Troy and after a moment's thought added: 'If he's true.'

'If he writes letters to you he must be true,' Ricky pointed out. *'Naturellement!'*

Raoul drove them into a little square and pulled up in front of the hotel.

At that moment the concierge at 16 Rue des Violettes, after having sat for ten minutes in morose cogitation, dialled the telephone number of the Chèvre d'Argent.

III

Alleyn and Baradi stood on either side of the bed. The maid, an elderly pinched-looking woman, had withdrawn to the window. The beads of her rosary clicked discreetly through her fingers.

Miss Truebody's face, still without its teeth, seemed to have collapsed about her nose and forehead and to be less than human-sized.

Her mouth was a round hole with puckered edges. She was snoring. Each expulsion of her breath blew the margin of the hole outwards and each intake sucked it in so that in a dreadful way her face was busy. Her eyes were incompletely closed and her almost hairless brows drawn together in a meaningless scowl.

'She will be like this for some hours,' Baradi said. He drew Miss Truebody's wrist from under the sheet: 'I expect no change. She is very ill, but I expect no change for some hours.'

'Which sounds,' Alleyn said absently, 'like a rough sketch for a villanelle.'

'You are a poet?'

Alleyn waved a hand: 'Shall we say, an undistinguished amateur.'

'You underrate yourself, I feel sure,' Baradi said still holding the flaccid wrist. 'You publish?'

Alleyn was suddenly tempted to say: 'The odd slim vol.,' but he controlled himself and made a slight modest gesture that was entirely noncommittal. Dr Baradi followed this up with his now familiar comment. 'Mr Oberon,' he said, 'will be delighted,' and added: 'He is already greatly moved by your personality and that of your enchanting wife.'

'For my part,' Alleyn said, 'I was enormously impressed with his.'

He looked with an air of ardent expectancy into that fleshy mask and could find in it no line or fold that was either stupid or credulous. What was Baradi? Part Egyptian, part French? Wholly Egyptian? Wholly Arab? 'Which is the king-pin?' Alleyn speculated, 'Baradi or Oberon?' Baradi, taking out his watch, looked impassively into Alleyn's face. Then he snapped open his watch and a minute went past, clicked out by the servant's beads.

'Ah, well,' Baradi muttered, putting up his watch, 'it is as one would expect. Nothing can be done for the time being. This woman will report any change. She is capable and, in the village, has had some experience of sick bed attendance. My man will be able to relieve her. We may have difficulty in securing a trained nurse for tonight but we shall manage.'

He nodded at the woman who came forward and listened passively to his instructions. They left her, nun-like and watchful, seated by the bed.

'It is eleven o'clock, the hour of meditation,' Baradi said as they walked down the passage, 'so we must not disturb. There will be something to drink in my room. Will you join me? Your car has not yet returned.'

He led the way into the Chinese room where his servant waited behind a table set with Venetian goblets, dishes of olives and sandwiches and something that looked like Turkish delight. There was also champagne in a silver ice-bucket. Alleyn was almost impervious to irregular hours but the last twenty-four had been exciting, the heat was excessive, and the reek of ether had made him feel squeamish. Lager was his normal choice but champagne would have done very nicely indeed. It was an arid concession to his job that obliged him to say with what he hoped was the right degree of complacency: 'Will you forgive me if I have water? You see, I've lately become rather interested in a way of life that excludes alcohol.'

'But how remarkable. Mr Oberon will be most interested. Mr Oberon,' Baradi said, signing to the servant that the champagne was to be opened, 'is perhaps the greatest living authority on such matters. His design for living transcends many of the ancient cults, drawing from each its purest essence. A remarkable synthesis. But while he himself achieves a perfect balance between austerity and, shall we say, selective enjoyment, he teaches that there is no merit in abstention for the sake of abstention. His disciples are encouraged to experience many pleasures, to choose them with the most exquisite discrimination: 'arrange' them, indeed, as a painter arranges his pictures or a composer traces out the design for a fugue. Only thus, he tells us, may the Ultimate Goal be reached. Only thus may one experience Life to the Full. Believe me, Mr Allen, he would smile at your rejection of this admirable vintage, thinking it as gross an error, if you will forgive me, as overindulgence. Let me persuade you to change your mind. Besides, you have had a trying experience. You are a little nauseated, I think, by the fumes of ether. Let me, as a doctor,' he ended playfully, 'insist on a glass of champagne.'

Alleyn had taken up a ruby goblet and was looking into it with admiration. 'I must say,' he said, 'this is all most awfully interesting; what you've been saying about Mr Oberon's teaching, I mean. You make my own fumbling ideas seem pitifully naive.' He smiled. 'I should adore some champagne from this quite lovely goblet.'

He held it out and watched the champagne mount and cream. Baradi was looking at him across the rim of his own glass. One could scarcely, Alleyn thought, imagine a more opulent picture: the corrugations of hair glistened, the eyes were lustrous, the nose overhung a bubbling field of amber stained with ruby, one could guess at the wide expectant lips.

'To the fullness of life,' said Dr Baradi.

'Yes, indeed.' Alleyn rejoined and they drank.

The champagne was, in fact, admirable.

Alleyn's head was as strong as the next man's but he had had a light breakfast and therefore helped himself freely to the sandwiches which were delicious. Baradi, always prepared, Alleyn supposed, to experience life to the full, gobbled up the sweetmeats, popping them one after another into his red mouth and abominably washing them down with champagne.

The atmosphere took on a spurious air of unbuttoning which Alleyn was careful to encourage. So far, he felt tolerably certain, Baradi knew nothing about him, but was nevertheless concerned to place him accurately. The situation was a delicate one. If Alleyn could establish himself as an eager neophyte to the synthetic mysteries preached by Mr Oberon, he would have taken a useful step towards the performance of his job. At least he would be able to give an inside report on the domestic set-up in the Château de la Chèvre d'Argent. Officers on loan to the Special Branch preserve a strict anonymity and it was unlikely that his name would be known in the drug-racket as an MI5 investigator. It might be recognized, however, as that of a detective-officer of the CID Carbury Glande might respect Troy's request but if he didn't, it was more than likely that he or one of the others would remember she had married a policeman. Alleyn himself remembered the exuberance of the gossip columnists at the time of their marriage and later, when Troy had held one-man shows or when he had appeared for the police in some much-publicized case. It looked as if he should indeed make what hay he could while the sun shone on the Chèvre d'Argent.

'If Miss Truebody and I get through this party,' he thought, 'blow me down if I don't take her out and we'll break a bottle of fizz on our own account.'

Greatly cheered by this thought, be began to talk about poetry and esoteric writing, speaking of Rabindranath Tagore and the Indian 'Tantras,' of the 'Amanga Ranga' and parts of the Kabbala.

Baradi listened with every appearance of delight but Alleyn felt a little as if he were prodding at a particularly resilient mattress. There seemed to be no vulnerable spot and, what was worse, his companion began to exhibit signs of controlled restlessness. It was clear that the champagne was intended for a stirrup cup and that he waited for Alleyn to take his departure. Yet somewhere, there must be a point of penetration. And remembering with extreme distaste Dr Baradi's attentions to Troy, Alleyn drivelled hopefully onward, speaking of the secret rites of Eleusis and the cult of Osiris. Something less impersonal at last appeared in Baradi as he listened to these confidences. The folds of flesh running from the corners of his nostrils to those of his mouth became more apparent and he began to look like an Eastern and more fleshy version of Charles II. He went to the bureau by Vernis-Martin, unlocked it and presently laid before Alleyn a book bound in grey silk on which a design had been painted in violet, green and repellent pink.

'A rare and early edition,' he said. 'Carbury Glande designed and executed the cover. Do admire it!'

Alleyn opened the book at the title page. It was copy of *The Memoirs of Donatien Alphonse François, Marquis de Sade*.

'A present,' said Baradi, 'from Mr Oberon.'

It was unnecessary, Alleyn decided, to look any further for the chink in Dr Baradi's armour.

From this moment, when he set down his empty goblet on the table in Dr Baradi's room, his visit to the Chèvre d'Argent developed into a covert battle between himself and the doctor. The matter under dispute was Alleyn's departure. He was determined to stay for as long as the semblance of ordinary manners could be preserved. Baradi obviously wanted to get rid of him, but for reasons about which Alleyn could only conjecture, avoided any suggestion of precipitancy. Alleyn felt that his safest line was to continue in the manner of a would-be disciple to the cult of the Children of the Sun. Only thus, he thought, could he avoid planting in Baradi a rising suspicion of his own motives. He must be a bore, a persistent bore, but no more than a bore. And he went gassing on, racking his memory for remnants of esoteric gossip. Baradi spoke of a telephone call. Alleyn talked of telepathic communication. Baradi said that Troy would doubtless be anxious to hear about Miss Truebody; Alleyn

asked if Miss Truebody would not be greatly helped by the banish-
ment of anxiety from everybody's mind. Baradi mentioned luncheon. Alleyn prattled of the lotus posture. Baradi said he must not
waste any more of Alleyn's time; Alleyn took his stand on the pos-
tulate that time, in the commonly accepted sense of the word, did
not exist. A final skirmish during which an offer to inquire for
Alleyn's car was countered by Rosicrucianism and the fiery cross of
the Gnostics, ended with Baradi saying that he would have another
look at Miss Truebody and must then report to Mr Oberon. He said
he would be some time and begged Alleyn not to feel he must wait
for his return. At this point Baradi's servant reappeared to say a telephone call had come through for him. Baradi at once remarked that
no doubt Alleyn's car would arrive before he returned. He regretted
that Mr Oberon's meditation class would still be in progress and
must not be interrupted and he suggested that Alleyn might care to
wait for his car in the hall or in the library. Alleyn said that he would
very much like to stay where he was and to examine the de Sade.
With a flush of exasperation mounting on his heavy cheeks, Baradi
consented, and went out, followed by his man.

They had turned to the right and gone down the passage to the
hall. The rings on an embossed leather curtain in the entrance
clashed as they went through.

Alleyn was already squatting at the Vernis-Martin bureau.

He had the reputation in his department of uncanny accuracy when
a quick search was in question. It's doubtful if he ever acted more swiftly
than now. Baradi had left the bottom drawer of the bureau open.

It contained half a dozen books, each less notorious if more infamous than the de Sade and all on the proscribed list at Scotland
Yard. He lifted them one by one and replaced them.

The next drawer was locked but yielded to the application of a
skeleton-key Alleyn had gleaned from a housebreaker of virtuosity.
It contained three office ledgers and two notebooks. The entries in
the first ledger were written in a script that Alleyn took to be
Egyptian but occasionally there appeared proper names in English
characters. Enormous sums of money were shown in several curren-
cies: piastres, francs, pounds and lire, neatly flanked each other in
separate columns. He turned the pages rapidly, his hearing fixed on
the passage outside, his mind behind his eyes.

Between the first ledger and the second lay a thin quarto volume in violet leather, heavily embossed. The design was tortuous, but Alleyn recognized a pentagram, a triskelion, winged serpents, bulls and a broken cross. Super-imposed over the whole was a double-edged sword with formalized flames rising from it in the shape of a raised hand. The covers were mounted with a hasp and lock which he had very little trouble in opening.

Between the covers was a single page of vellum, elaborately illuminated and embellished with a further number of symbolic ornaments. Baradi had been gone three minutes when Alleyn began to read the text.

'Here is the names of Ra and the Sons of Ra and the Daughters of Ra who are also, in the Mystery of the Sun, the Sacred Spouses of Ra, I, about to enter into the Secret Fellowship of Ra, swear before Horus and Osiris, before Annum and Apsis, before the Good and the Evil that are One God, who is both Good and Evil, that I will set a seal upon my lips and eyes and keep forever secret the mysteries of the Sacred Rites of Ra.

'I swear that all that passes in this place shall be as if it had never been. If I break this oath in the least degree may my lips be burnt away with the fire that is now set before them. May my eyes be put out with the knife that is now set before them. May my ears be stopped with molten lead. May my entrails rot and my body perish with the disease of the crab. May I desire death before I die and suffer torment for evermore. If I break silence may these things be unto me. I swear by the fire of Ra and the Blade of Ra. So be it.'

Alleyn uttered a single violent expletive, relocked the covers and opened the second ledger.

It was inscribed: '*Compagnie Chimique des Alpes Maritimes.*' and contained names, dates and figures in what appeared to be a balance of expenditure and income. Alleyn's attention sharpened. The company seemed to be showing astronomical profits. His fingers, nervous and delicate, leafed through the pages, moving rhythmically.

Then abruptly they were still. Near the bottom of the page, starting out of the unintelligible script and written in a small, rather elaborate handwriting, was a name – P.E.Garbel.

The curtain rings clashed in the passage. He had locked the drawer and with every appearance of avid attention was hanging over the de Sade, when Baradi returned.

IV

Baradi had brought Carbury Glande with him and Alleyn thought he knew why. Glande was introduced and after giving Alleyn a damp runaway handshake, retired into the darker part of the room fingering his beard, and eyed him with an air, half curious, half defensive. Baradi said smoothly that Alleyn had greatly admired the de Sade book-wrapper and would no doubt be delighted to meet the distinguished artist. Alleyn responded with an enthusiasm which he was careful to keep on an amateurish level. He said he wished so much he knew more about the technique of painting. This would do nicely, he thought, if Glande, knowing he was Troy's husband was still unaware of his job. If, on the other hand, Glande knew he was a detective, Alleyn would have said nothing to suggest that he tried to conceal his occupation. He thought it extremely unlikely that Glande had respected Troy's request for anonymity. No. Almost certainly he had reported that their visitor was Agatha Troy, the distinguished painter of Mr Oberon's 'Boy with a Kite.' And then? Either Glande had also told them that her husband was a CID officer in which case they would be anxious to find out if his visit was pure coincidence; or else Glande had been able to give little or no information about Alleyn and they merely wondered if he was as ready a subject for skulduggery as he had tried to suggest. A third possibility and one that he couldn't see at all clearly, involved the now highly debatable integrity of P.E.Garbel.

Baradi said that Alleyn's car had not arrived and with no hint of his former impatience suggested that they show him the library.

It was on the far side of the courtyard. On entering it he was confronted with Troy's 'Boy with a Kite.' Its vigour and cleanliness struck like a sword-thrust across the airlessness of Mr Oberon's library. For a second the Boy looked with Ricky's eyes at Alleyn.

A sumptuous company of books lined the walls with the emphasis, as was to be expected, upon mysticism, the occult and orientalism. Alleyn recognized a number of works that a bookseller's catalogue would have described as rare, curious, and collector's items. Of far greater interest to Alleyn, however, was a large framed drawing that hung in a dark corner of that dark room. It was, he saw, a representation, probably medieval, of the Château de la Chèvre d'Argent and it was part elevation and part plan. After one desirous glance he avoided it. He professed himself fascinated with the books and took them down with ejaculations of interest and delight. Baradi and Glande watched him and listened.

'You are a collector, perhaps, Mr Allen?' Baradi conjectured.

'Only in a humble way. I'm afraid my job doesn't provide for the more expensive hobbies.'

There was a moment's pause. 'Indeed?' Baradi said. 'One cannot, alas, choose one's profession. I hope yours is at least congenial.'

Alleyn thought: 'He's fishing. He doesn't know or he isn't sure.' And he said absently as he turned the pages of a superb *Book of the Dead*, 'I suppose everyone becomes a little bored with his job at times. What a wonderful thing this is, this book. Tell me, Dr Baradi, as a scientific man –'

Baradi answered his question. Glande glowered and shuffled impatiently. Alleyn reflected that by this time it was possible that Baradi and Robin Herrington had told Oberon of the Alleyn's inquiries for Mr Garbel. Did this account for the change in Baradi's attitude? Alleyn was now unable to bore Dr Baradi.

'It would be interesting,' Carbury Glande said in his harsh voice, 'to hear what Mr Alleyn's profession might be. I am passionately interested in the employment of other people.'

'Ah, yes,' Baradi agreed. 'Do you ever play the game of guessing at the occupation of strangers and then proving yourself right or wrong by getting to know them? Come!' he cried with a great show of frankness. 'Let us confess, Carbury, we are filled with unseemly curiosity about Mr Allen. Will he allow us to play our game? Indulge us, my dear Allen. Carbury, what is your guess?'

Glande muttered. 'Oh, I plump for one of the colder branches of learning. Philosophy.'

'Do you think so? A don, perhaps? And yet there is something that to me suggests that Mr Allen was born under Mars. A soldier. Or, no. I take that back. A diplomat.'

'How very perceptive of you,' Alleyn ejaculated, looking at him over the *Book of the Dead*.

'Then I am right?'

'In part, at least. I started in the Diplomatic,' said Alleyn truthfully, 'but left it at the file-and-corridor stage.'

'Really? Then, perhaps, I am allowed another guess. No!' he cried after a pause. 'I give up. Carbury, what do you say?'

'I? God knows! Perhaps he left the Diplomatic Service under a cloud and went big game hunting.'

'I begin to think that you are all psychic in this house,' Alleyn said delightedly. 'How on earth do you do it?'

'A mighty hunter!' Baradi ejaculated, clapping his hands softly.

'Not at all mighty. I'm afraid, only pathetically persevering.'

'Wonderful,' Carbury Glande said, drawing his hand across his eyes and suppressing a yawn. 'You live in South Kensington, I feel sure, in some magnificently dark apartment from the walls of which glower the glass eyes of monstrous beasts. Horns, snouts, tusks. Coarse hair. Lolling tongues made of suitable plastic. Quite wonderful.'

'But Mr Allen is a poet and a hunter of rare books as well as of rare beasts. Perhaps,' Baradi speculated, 'it was during your travels that you became interested in the esoteric?'

Alleyn suppressed a certain weariness of spirit and renewed his raptures. 'You saw some rum things,' he said with an air of simple credulity, 'in native countries.' He had been told and told on good authority – He rambled on, saying that he greatly desired to learn more about the primitive beliefs of ancient races.

'Does your wife accompany you on safari?' Glande asked. 'I should have thought – 'he stopped short. Alleyn saw a flash of exasperation in Baradi's eyes.

'My wife,' Alleyn said lightly, 'couldn't approve less of blood sports. She is a painter.'

'I am released,' Glande cried, 'from bondage!' He pointed to the 'Boy with a Kite.' *'Ecco!'*

'No!' Really, Alleyn thought, Baradi was a considerable actor. Delight and astonishment were admirably suggested.

'Not . . . ? Not Agatha Troy? But, my dear Mr Allen, this is quite remarkable. Mr Oberon will be enchanted.'

'I can't wait,' Carbury Glande said, 'to tell him.' He showed his teeth through his moustache. 'I'm afraid you're in for a scolding, Alleyn. Troy swore me to secrecy. I may say,' he added, 'that I knew in a vague way, that she was a wedded woman but she has kept the Mighty Hunter from us.' His tongue touched his upper lip. 'Understandably, perhaps,' he added.

Alleyn thought that nothing would give him more pleasure than to seize Dr Baradi and Mr Carbury Glande by the scruffs of their respective necks and crash their heads together.

He said apologetically: 'Well, you see, we're on holiday.'

'Quite,' said Baradi and the conversation languished.

'I think you told us,' Baradi said casually, 'that you have friends in Roqueville and asked if we knew them. I'm afraid that I've forgotten the name.'

'Only one. Garbel.'

Baradi's smile looked as if it had been left on his face by an oversight. The red hairs of Glande's beard quivered very slightly as if his jaw was clenched.

'A retired chemist of sorts,' Alleyn said.

'Ah, yes! Possibly attached to the monstrous establishment which defaces our lovely olive groves. Monstrous,' Baradi added, 'aesthetically speaking.'

'Quite abominable!' said Glande. His voice cracked and he wetted his lips.

'No doubt admirable from a utilitarian point of view. I believe they produce artificial manure in great quantities.'

'The place,' Glande said, 'undoubtedly stinks,' and he laughed unevenly.

'Aesthetically?' Alleyn asked.

'Always, aesthetically,' said Baradi.

'I noticed the factory on our way up. Perhaps we'd better ask there for our friend.'

There was a dead silence.

'I can't think what has become of that man of mine,' Alleyn said lightly.

Baradi was suddenly effusive. 'But how inconsiderate we are! You, of course, are longing to rejoin your wife. And who can blame you? No woman has the right to be at once so talented and so beautiful. But your car? No doubt, a puncture or perhaps merely our Mediterranean *dolce far niente*. You must allow us to send you down. Robin would, I am sure, be enchanted. Or, if he is engaged in meditation, Mr Oberon would be delighted to provide a car. How thoughtless we have been!'

This, Alleyn realized, was final. 'I wouldn't dream of it,' he said. 'But I do apologize for being such a pestilent visitor. I've let my

ruling passion run away with me and kept you hovering inter-
minably. The car will arrive any moment now, I feel sure, and I particularly want to see the man. If I might just wait here among these
superb books I shan't feel I'm making a nuisance of myself.'

It was a toss-up whether this would work. They wanted, he supposed, to consult together. After a fractional hesitation, Baradi said
something about their arrangements for the afternoon. Perhaps, if
Mr Allen would excuse them, they should have a word with Mr
Oberon. There was the business of the nurse – Glande, less adroit,
muttered unintelligibly and they went out together.

Alleyn was in front of the plan two seconds after the door had
shut behind them.

It was embellished with typical medieval ornaments – a coat of
arms, a stylized goat and a great deal of scrollwork. The drawing
itself was in two main parts, an elevation, treated as if the entire face
of the building had been removed and a multiple plan of great intri-
cacy. It would have taken an hour to follow out the plan in detail.
With a refinement of concentration that Mr Oberon himself might
have envied, Alleyn fastened his attention upon the main outlines of
the structural design. The great rooms and principal bedrooms were
all, more or less, on the library level. Above this level the château
rose irregularly in a system of connected turrets to the battlements.
Below it, the main stairway led down by stages through a maze of
rooms that grew progressively smaller until, at a level which must
have been below that of the railway, they were no bigger than prison
cells and had probably served as such for hundreds of years. A vast
incoherent maze that had followed, rather than overcome the contour of the mountain: an architectural compromise, Alleyn murmured, and sharpened his attention upon one room and its relation
to the rest.

It was below the library and next to a room that had no outside
windows. He marked its position and cast back in his mind to the silhouette of the château as he had seen it, moonlit, in the early hours
of that morning. He noticed that it had a window much longer than
it was high and he remembered the shape of the window they had
seen.

If it was true that Mr Oberon and his guests were now occupied,
as Baradi had represented, with some kind of esoteric keep-fit exer-

cises on the roof-garden, it might be worth taking a risk. He thought of two or three plausible excuses, took a final look at the plan, slipped out of the library and ran lightly down a continuation of the winding stair that, in its upper reaches, led to the roof garden.

He passed a landing, a closed door and three narrow windows. The stairs corkscrewed down to a wider landing from which a thickly carpeted passage ran off to the right. Opposite the stairway was a door and, a few steps away, another – the door he sought.

He went up to it and knocked.

There was no answer. He turned the handle delicately. The door opened inwards until there was a wide enough gap for him to look through. He found himself squinting along a wall hung with silk rugs and garnished about midway along, with a big prayer wheel. At the far end there was an alcove occupied by an extremely exotic-looking divan. He opened the door fully and walked into the room.

From inside the door his view of Mr Oberon's room was in part blocked by the back of an enormous looking-glass screwed to the floor at an angle of about 45 degrees to the outside wall. For the moment he didn't move beyond this barrier, but from where he stood, looked at the left-hand end of the room. It was occupied by a sort of altar hung with a stiffly embroidered cloth and garnished with a number of objects: a pentacle in silver, a triskelion in bronze and a large crystal affair resembling a sunburst. Beside the altar was a door, leading, he decided, into the windowless room he had noted on the plan.

He moved forward with the intention of walking round the looking-glass into the far part of the room.

'Bring me the prayer-wheel,' said a voice beyond the glass.

It fetched Alleyn up with the jolt of a punch over the heart. He looked at the door. If the glass had hidden him on his entrance it would mask his exit. He moved towards the door.

'I am at the Third Portal of the Outer and must not uncover my eyes. Do not speak. Bring me the Prayer Wheel. Put it before me.'

Alleyn walked forward.

There, on the other side of the looking-glass facing it and seated on the floor, was Mr Oberon, stark naked, with the palms of his hands pressed to his eyes. Beyond him was a long window masked by a dyed silk blind, almost transparent, with the design of the sun upon it.

Alleyn took the prayer-wheel from the wall. It was an elaborate affair, heavily carved, with many cylinders. He set it before Oberon.

He turned and had reached the door when somebody knocked peremptorily on it. Alleyn stepped back as it was flung open. It actually struck his shoulder. He heard someone go swiftly past and into the room.

Baradi's voice said: 'Where are you? Oh. Oh, there you are! See here, I've got to talk to you.'

He must be behind the glass. Alleyn slipped round the door and darted out. As he ran lightly up the stairs he heard Baradi shut the door.

There was nobody on the top landing. He walked back into the library, having been away from it for five and a half minutes.

He took out his notebook and made a very rough sketch of Mr Oberon's room, taking particular pains to mark the position of the prayer-wheel on the wall. Then he set about memorizing as much of its detail as he had been able to take in. He was still at this employment when the latch turned in the door.

Alleyn pulled out from the nearest shelf a copy of Mr Montague Summers' major work on witchcraft. He was apparently absorbed in it when a woman came into the library.

He looked up from the book and knew that as far as preserving his anonymity was concerned, he was irrevocably sunk.

'If it's not Roderick Alleyn!' said Annabella Wells.

CHAPTER 5

Ricky in Roqueville

It was some years ago, in a transatlantic steamer, that Alleyn had met Annabella Wells: the focal point of ship-board gossip to which she had seemed to be perfectly indifferent. She had watched him with undisguised concentration for four hours and had then sent her secretary with an invitation for drinks. She herself drank pretty heavily and, he thought, was probably a drug addict. He had found her an embarrassment and was glad when she suddenly dropped him. Since then she had turned up from time to time as an onlooker at criminal trials where he appeared for the police. She was, she told him, passionately interested in criminology.

In the English theatre her brilliance had been dimmed by her outrageous eccentricities, but in Paris, particularly in the motion picture studios, she was still one of the great ones. She retained a ravaged sort of beauty and an individuality, which would be arresting when the last of her good looks had been rasped away. A formidable woman, and an enchantress still.

She gave him her hand and the inverted and agonized smile for which she was famous. 'They said you were a big-game hunter,' she said. 'I couldn't wait.'

'It was nice of them to give that impression.'

'An accurate one, after all. Are you on the prowl down here? After some master-felon?'

'I'm on holiday with my wife and small boy.'

'Ah, yes! The beautiful woman who paints famous pictures. I am told by Baradi and Glande that she is beautiful. There is no need to look angry, is there?'

'Did I look angry?'

'You looked as if you were trying not to show a certain uxorious irritation.'

'Did I, indeed?' said Alleyn.

'Baradi *is* a bit lush. I will allow and admit that he's a bit lush. Have you seen Oberon?'

'For a few moments.'

'What did you think of *him*?'

'Isn't he your host?'

'Honestly,' she said, 'you're not true. Much more fabulous, in your way, than Oberon.'

'I'm interested in what I have been told of his philosophy.'

'So they said. What sort of interest?'

'Personal and academic'

'My interest is personal and unacademic' She opened her cigarette case. Alleyn glanced at the contents. 'I see,' he said, 'that it would be useless to offer you a Capstan.'

'Will you have one of these? They're Egyptian. The red won't come off on your lips.'

'Thank you. They would be wasted on me.' He lit her cigarette. 'I wonder,' he said, 'if I could persuade you to say nothing about my job.'

'Darling,' she rejoined (she called everyone 'darling'), 'you could persuade me to do anything. My trouble was, you wouldn't try. Why do you look at me like that?'

'I was wondering if any dependence could be placed on a heroin addict. Is it heroin?'

'It is. I get it,' said Miss Wells, 'from America.'

'How very tragic'

'Tragic?'

'You weren't taking heroin when you played Hedda Gabler at the Unicorn in '42. Could you give a performance like that now?'

'*Yes,*' she said vehemently.

'But what a pity you don't!'

'My last film is the best thing I've ever done. Everyone says so.' She looked at him with hatred. 'I can still do it,' she said.

'On your good days, perhaps. The studio is less exacting than the theatre. Will the cameras wait when the gallery would boo? I couldn't know less about it.'

She walked up to him and struck him across the face with the back of her hand.

'You have deteriorated,' said Alleyn.

'Are you mad? What are you up to? Why are you here?'

'I brought a woman who may be dying to your Dr Baradi. All I want is to go away as I came in – a complete nonentity.'

'And you think that by insulting me you'll persuade me to oblige you.'

'I think you've already talked to your friends about me and that they've sent you here to find out if you were right.'

'You're a very conceited man. Why should I talk about you?'

'Because,' Alleyn said, 'you're afraid.'

'Of you?'

'Specifically. Of me.'

'You idiot,' she said. 'Coming here with a dying spinster and an arty-crafty wife and a dreary little boy! For God's sake, get out and get on with your holiday.'

'I should like it above all things.'

'Why don't you want them to know who you are?'

'It would quite spoil my holiday.'

'Which might mean anything.'

'It might.'

'Why do you say I'm afraid?'

'You're shaking. That may be a carry-over from alcohol or heroin, or both, but I don't think it is. You're behaving like a frightened woman. You were in a blue funk when you hit me.'

'You're saying detestable, unforgivable things to me.'

'Have I said anything that is untrue?'

'My life's my own. I've a right to do what I like with it.'

'What's happened to your intelligence? You should know perfectly well that this sort of responsibility doesn't end with yourself. What about those two young creatures? The girl?'

'I didn't bring them here.'

'No, really,' Alleyn said, going to the door, 'you're saying such very stupid things. I'll go down to the front and see if my car's come. Goodbye to you.'

She followed him and put her hand on her arm. 'Look!' she said. 'Look at me. I'm terrifying, aren't I? A wreck? But I've still got more than my share of what it takes. Haven't I?'

'For Baradi and his friends?'

'Baradi!' she said contemptuously.

'I really didn't want to insult you with Oberon.'

'What do you know about Oberon?'

'I've seen him.'

She left her hand on him but with an air of forgetfulness. A tremor communicated itself to his arm. 'You don't know,' she said. 'You don't know what he's like. It's no good thinking about him in the way you think about other men. There are *hommes fatals*, too, you know. He's terrifying and he's marvellous. You can't understand that, can you?'

'No. To me, if he wasn't disgusting, he'd be ludicrous. A slug of a man.'

'Do you believe in hypnotism?'

'Certainly. If the subject is willing.'

'Oh,' she said hopelessly, 'I'm willing enough. Not that it's as simple as hypnotism.' She hung her head, looking, with that gesture, like the travesty of a shamed girl. He couldn't hear all she said but caught one phrase: ' . . . wonderful degradation . . . '

'For God's sake,' Alleyn said, 'what nonsense is this?'

She frowned and looked at him out of her disastrous eyes. 'Could you help me?' she said.

'I have no idea. Probably not.'

'I'm in a bad way.'

'Yes.'

'If I were to keep faith? I don't know what you're up to, but if I were to keep faith and not tell them who you are? Even if it ruined me? Would you think you could help me then?'

'Are you asking me if I could help you to cure yourself of drugging? I couldn't. Only an expert could do that. If you've still got enough character and sense of purpose to keep faith, as you put it, perhaps you should have enough guts to go through with a cure. I don't know.'

'I suppose you think I'm trying to bribe you?'

'In a sense – yes.'

'Do you know,' she said discontentedly, 'you're the only man I've ever met – ' She stopped and seemed to hesitate. 'I can't get this right,' she said. 'With you it's not an act, is it?'

Alleyn smiled for the first time. 'I'm not attempting the well-known gambits of rudeness introduced with a view to amorous occasions,' he said. 'Is that what you mean?'

'I suppose it is.'

'You should stick to classical drama. Shakespeare's women don't fall for the insult-and-angry-seduction stuff. Sorry. I'm forgetting Richard III.'

'Beatrice and Benedick? Petruchio and Katherine?'

'I was excluding comedy.'

'How right you are. There's nothing very funny about my situation.'

'No, it seems appalling.'

'What can I do? Tell me, what I can do?'

'Leave the Chèvre d'Argent today. Now, if you like. I've got a car outside. Go to a doctor in Paris and offer yourself for a cure. Recognize your responsibility and, before further harm can come of this place, tell me or the local commissary or anyone else in a position of authority, everything you know about the people here.'

'Betray my friends?'

'A meaningless phrase. In protecting them you betray decency itself. Can you think of that child Ginny Taylor and still question what you should do?'

She stepped back from him as if he was a physical menace.

'You're not here by accident,' she said. 'You've planned this visit.'

'I could hardly plan a perforated appendix in an unknown maiden lady. The place and all of you speak for yourselves. Yawning your heads off because you want your heroin. Pin-point pupils and leathery faces.'

She caught her breath in what sounded like a sigh of relief. 'Is that all,' she said.

'I really must go. Goodbye.'

'I can't do it. I can't do what you ask.'

'I'm sorry.'

He opened the door. She said: 'I won't tell them what you are. But don't come back. Don't come back here. I'm warning you. Don't come back.'

'Goodbye,' Alleyn said and without encountering anyone walked out of the house and down the passageway to the open platform.

Raoul was waiting there with the car.

II

When she returned to the roof-garden, Annabella Wells found the men of the houseparty waiting for her. Dr Baradi closed his hand softly round her arm, leading her forward.

'Don't,' she said, 'you smell of hospitals.'

Carbury Glande said: 'Annabella, who is he? I mean we all know he's Agatha Troy's husband, but for God's sake, *who* is he?'

'You know as much as I do.'

'But you said you'd crossed the Atlantic with him. You said it was a shipboard affair and one knows they don't leave many stones unturned, especially in your hands, my angel.'

'He was one of my rare failures. He talked of nothing but his wife. He spread her over the Atlantic like a overflow from the Gulf Stream. I gave him up as a bad job. A dull chap, I decided,'

'I rather liked him,' young Herrington said defiantly.

Mr Oberon spoke for the first time. 'A dangerous man,' he said. 'Whoever he is and whatever he may be. Under the circumstances, a dangerous man.'

Baradi said: 'I agree. The inquiry for Garbel is inexplicable.'

'Unless they are initiates,' Glande said, 'and have been given the name.'

'They are not initiates,' Oberon said.

'No,' Baradi agreed.

Young Herrington said explosively: 'My God, is there no other way out?'

'Ask yourself,' said Glande.

Mr Oberon rose. 'There is no other way,' he said tranquilly. 'And they must not return. That at least is clear. They must not return.'

III

As they drove back to Roqueville, Alleyn said: 'You did your job well this morning, Raoul. You are, evidently, a man upon whom one may depend.'

'It pleases Monsieur to say so,' said Raoul cheerfully. 'The Egyptian gentleman is also, it appears, good at his job. In wartime a medical orderly learns to recognize talent, Monsieur. Very often one saw the patients zipped up like a placket-hole. *Paf!* and he's open. *Pan!* and he's shut. But this was different.'

'Dr Baradi is afraid that she may not recover.'

'She had not the look of death upon her.'

'Can you recognize it?'

'I fancy that I can, Monsieur.'

'Did Madame and the small one get safely to their hotel?'

'Safely, Monsieur. On the way we stopped in the Rue des Violettes. Madame inquired for Mr Garbel.'

Alleyn said sharply: 'Did she see him?'

'I understand he was not at home, Monsieur.'

'Did she leave a message?'

'I believe so, Monsieur. I saw Madame give a note to the concierge.'

'I see.'

'She is a type, that one.' Raoul said thoughtfully.

'The concierge? Do you know her?'

'Yes, Monsieur. In Roqueville all the world knows all the world. She's an original, is old Blanche.'

'In what way?'

'*Un article défrâichi.* One imagines she has other interests beside the door-keeping. To be fat is not always to be idle. But the apartments,' Raoul added politely, 'are perfectly correct.' Evidently he felt it would be in bad taste to disparage the address of any friend of the Alleyns.

Alleyn said, choosing his French very carefully: 'I am minded to place a great deal of confidence in you, Raoul.'

'If Monsieur pleases.'

'I think you were more impressed with Dr Baradi's skill than with his personality.'

'That is a fact, Monsieur.'

'I also. Have you seen Mr Oberon?'

'On several occasions.'

'What do you think about him?'

'I have no absolute knowledge of his skill, Monsieur, but I think even less of his personality than of the Egyptian's.'

'Do you know how he entertains his guests?'

'One hears a little gossip from time to time. Not much, Monsieur. The servants at the Château are for the most part imported and extremely reticent. But there is an under-chambermaid from the Paysdoux, who is not unapproachable. A blonde, which is unusual in the Paysdoux.'

'What has the unusual blonde to say about it?'

Raoul did not answer at once and Alleyn turned his head to look at him. He was scowling magnificently.

'I do not approve of what Teresa has to say. Her name, Monsieur, is Teresa. I find what she has to say immensely unpleasing. You see, it's like this, Monsieur. The time has come when I should marry and for one reason or another – one cannot rationalize about these things – my preference is for Teresa. She has got what it takes.' Raoul said, using a phrase – *elle a du fond* – which reminded Alleyn of Annabella Well's desperate claim. 'But in a wife,' Raoul continued, 'one expects certain reticences where other men are in question. I dislike what Teresa tells me of her employer, Monsieur. I particularly disklike her account of a certain incident.'

'Am I to hear it?'

'I shall be glad to recount it. It appears, Monsieur, that Teresa's duties are confined to the sweeping of carpets and polishing of floors and that it is not required of her to take *petit déjeuner* to guests or to perform any personal services for them. She is young and inexperienced. And so, one morning, this Egyptian surgeon witnesses Teresa from the rear when she is on her knees polishing. Teresa is as good from behind as she is from in front, Monsieur. And the doctor passes her and pauses to look. Presently he returns with Mr Oberon and they pause and speak to each other in a foreign language. Next, the *femme de charge* sends for Teresa and she is instructed that she is to serve *petit déjeuner* to this animal Oberon, if Monsieur will overlook the description, in his bedroom and that her wage is to be raised. So Teresa performs this service. On the first morning there is no conversation. On the second he inquires her name. On the third this *vilain coco* asks her if she is not a fine strong girl. On the fourth he talks a lot of *blague* about the spirituality of the body and the non-existence of evil and on the fifth, when Teresa enters, he is displayed, immodestly clad, before a full-length glass in his *salon*. I must tell you, Monsieur, that to reach the bedroom, Teresa must first pass through the *salon*. She is obliged to approach this unseemly animal. He looks at her fixedly and speaks to her in a manner that is irreligious and blasphemous and anathema. Monsieur, Teresa is a good girl. She is frightened, not so much of this animal, she tells me, as of herself because she feels herself to be like a bird when it is held in terror by a snake. I have told her she must leave but she says that the wages are good and they are a large family with sickness and much in debt. Monsieur, I repeat, she is a good girl and it is true she needs the money but I cannot escape the thought that she is in a kind of bondage from which she cannot summon enough character to escape. And some mornings, when she goes in, there is nothing to which one could object but on others he talks and talks and stares and stares at Teresa. So that when I last saw her we quarrelled and I have told her that unless she leaves her job before she is no longer respectable she may look elsewhere for a husband. So she wept and I was discomfited. She is not unique but, there it is, I have a preference for Teresa.'

Alleyn thought: 'This is the first bit of luck I've had since we got here.' He looked up the valley at the glittering works of the Maritime Alps Chemical Company and said: 'I think it is well to tell you that I am interested professionally in the *ménage* at the Chèvre d'Argent. If it had not been for the accident of Mademoiselle's illness I should have tried to gain admittance there. M. le Commissaire is also interested. We are colleagues in this affair. You and I agreed to forget my rank, Raoul, but for the purpose of this discussion perhaps we should recall it.'

'Good, M. l'Inspecteur-en-Chef.'

'There's no reason on earth why you should put yourself out for an English policeman in an affair which, however much it may concern the French police, hasn't very much to do with you. Apart from Teresa, for whom you have a preference.'

'There is always Teresa.'

'Are you a discreet man?'

'I don't chatter like a one-eyed magpie, Monsieur.'

'I believe you. It is known to the police here and in London that the Chèvre d'Argent is used as a place of distribution in a particularly ugly trade.'

'Women, Monsieur?'

'Drugs. Women, it seems, are a purely personal interest. A side-line. I believe neither Dr Baradi nor Mr Oberon is a drug addict. They are engaged in the traffic from a business point of view. I think that they have cultivated the habit of drug-taking among their guests and are probably using at least one of them as a distributor. Mr Oberon has also established a cult.

'A cult, Monsieur?'

'A synthetic religion concocted from scraps of mysticism, witch-craft, mythology, Hinduism, Egyptology, what-have-you, with, I very much suspect, a number of particularly revolting fancy touches invented by Mr Oberon.'

'Anathema,' Raoul said, 'all this is anathema. What do they do?' he added with undisguised interest.

'I don't know exactly but I must, I'm afraid, find out. There have been other cases of this sort. No doubt there are rites. No doubt the women are willing to be drugged.'

Raoul said: 'It appears that I must be firm with Teresa.'

'I should be very firm, Raoul.'

'This morning she is in Roqueville at the market, I am to meet her at my parents' restaurant where I shall introduce a firm note. I am disturbed for her. All this, Monsieur, that you have related is borne out by Teresa. On Thursday nights the local servants and some of the other permanent staff are dismissed. It is on Thursday, therefore, that I escort Teresa to her home up in the Paysdoux where she sleeps the night. She has heard a little gossip, not much, because the servants are discreet, but a little. It appears that there is a ceremony in a room which is kept locked at other times. And on Fridays nobody appears until late in the afternoon and then with an air of having a formidable *gueule de bois*. The ladies are strangely behaved on Fridays. It is as if they are half-asleep, Teresa says. And last Friday a young English lady, who has recently arrived, seemed as if she was completely *bouleversée;* dazed, Monsieur,' Raoul said, making a graphic gesture with one hand. 'In a trance. And also as if she had wept.'

'Isn't Teresa frightened by what she sees on Fridays?'

'That is what I find strange, Monsieur. Yes; she says she is frightened but it is clear to me that she is also excited. That is what troubles me in Teresa.'

'Did she tell you where the room is? The room that is unlocked on Thursday nights?'

'It is in the lower part of the château Monsieur. Beneath the library, Teresa thinks. Two flights beneath.'

'And today is Wednesday.'

'Well, Monsieur?'

'I am in need of an assistant.'

'Yes, Monsieur?'

'If I asked at the Préfecture they would give me the local gendarme who is doubtless well-known. Or they would send me a clever man from Paris who as a stranger would be conspicuous. But a man of Roqueville who is well-known and yet is accepted as the friend of one of the maids at the Chèvre d'Argent is not conspicuous if he calls. Do you in fact call often to see Teresa?'

'Often, Monsieur.'

'Well, Raoul?'

'Well, Monsieur?'

'Do you care, with M. le Commissaire's permission, to come adventuring with me on Thursday night?'

'Enchanted,' said Raoul, gracefully.

'It may not be uneventful, you know. They are a formidable lot, up there.'

'That is understood, Monsieur. Again, it will be an act of grace.'

'Good. Here is Roqueville. Drive to the hotel if you please. I shall see Madame and have some luncheon and at three o'clock I shall call on M. le Commissaire. You will be free until then but leave me a telephone number and your address.'

'My parents' restaurant is in the street above that of the hotel. L'Escargot Bienvenue, 20 Rue des Sarrasins. Here is a card, Monsieur, with the telephone number.'

'Right.'

'My father is a good cook. He has not a great repertoire but his judgment is sound. Such dishes as he makes he makes well. His *filets mignons* are a speciality of the house, Monsieur, and his sauces are inspired.'

'You interest me profoundly. In the days when there was steak in England, one used to dream of *filet mignon* but even then one came to France to eat it.'

'Perhaps if Monsieur and Madame find themselves a little weary of the *table d'hôte* at the Royal they may care to eat cheaply but with satisfaction at the Escargot Bienvenu.'

'An admirable suggestion.'

'Of course, we are not at all smart. But good breeding,' Raoul said simply, 'creates its own background and Monsieur and Madame would not feel out of place. Here is your hotel, Monsieur, and – ' His voice changed. 'Here is Madame.'

Alleyn was out of the car before it stopped. Troy stood in the hotel courtyard with her clasped hands at her lips and a look on her face that he had never seen there before. When he took her arms in his hands he felt her whole body trembling. She tried to speak to him but at first was unable to find her voice. He saw her mouth frame the word 'Ricky.'

'What is it, darling?' he said. 'What's the matter with him?'

'He's gone,' she said. 'They've taken him. They've taken Ricky.'

IV

For the rest of their lives they would remember too vividly the seconds in which they stood on the tessellated courtyard of the hotel, plastered by the midday sun. Raoul on the footpath watched them and the blank street glared behind him. The air smelt of petrol. There was a smear of magenta Bougainvillaea on the opposite wall and in the centre of the street a neat pile of horse-droppings. It was already siesta time and so quiet that they might have been the only people awake in Roqueville.

'I'll keep my head and be sensible,' Troy whispered. 'Won't I, Rory?'

'Of course. We'll go indoors and you'll tell me about it.'

'I want to get into the car and look somewhere for him but I know that won't do.'

'I'll ask Raoul to wait.'

He did so. Raoul listened, motionless. When Alleyn had spoken Raoul said, 'Tell Madame it will be all right, Monsieur. Things will come right.' As they turned away he called his reassurance after them and the sound of his words followed them: '*Les affaires s'arrangeront. Tout ira bien, Madame.*'

Inside the hotel it seemed very dark. A porter sat behind a reception desk and an elegantly dressed man stood in the hall wringing his hands.

Troy said: 'This is my husband. This is the manager, Rory. He speaks English. I'm sorry, Monsieur, I don't know your name.'

'Malaquin, Madame. Mr Alleyn, I am sure there is some simple explanation – There have been other cases –'

'I'll come and see you, if I may, when I've heard what has happened.'

'But of course *Garçon* –'

The porter, looking ineffably compassionate, took them up in the lift. The stifling journey was interminable.

Troy faced her husband in a large bedroom made less impersonal by the slight but characteristic litter that accompanied her wherever she went. Beyond her was an iron-railed balcony and beyond that the arrogant laundry-blue of the Mediterranean. He pushed a chair up and she took it obediently. He sat on his heels before her and put his hands on the arms of the chair.

'Now, tell me darling,' he said. 'I can't do anything until you've told me.'

'You were such a lifetime coming.'

'I'm here now. Tell me.'

'Yes.'

She did tell him. She made a great effort to be lucid, frowning when she hesitated or when her voice shook and always keeping her gaze on him. He had said she was a good witness and now she stuck to the bare bones of her story but every word was shadowed by a multitude of unspoken terrors.

She said that when they arrived at the hotel Ricky was fretful and white after his interrupted sleep and the excitement of the drive. The manager was attentive and suggested that Ricky could have a tray in their rooms. Troy gave him a bath and put him into pyjamas and dressing-gown and he had his luncheon, falling asleep almost before it was finished. She put him to bed in a dressing-room opening off her own bedroom. She darkened the windows and seeing him comfortably asleep with his silver goat clutched in his hand, had her bath, changed and lunched in the dining-room of the hotel. When she returned to their rooms Ricky had gone.

At first she thought that he must have wakened and gone in
search of a lavatory or that perhaps he had had one of his panics and
was looking for her. It was only after a search of their bathroom and
passages, stairs and such rooms as were open that with mounting
anxiety she rang for the chambermaid and then, as the woman didn't
understand English, spoke on the telephone to the manager. M.
Malaquin was helpful and expeditious. He said that he would at
once speak to the servants on duty and report to her. As she put
down the receiver Troy looked at the chair across which she had laid
Ricky's day clothes ready for his awakening – a yellow shirt and
brown linen shorts – and she saw that they were gone.

From that moment she had fought against a surge of terror so
imperative that it was accompanied by a physical pain. She ran
downstairs and told the manager. The porter and two of the waiters
and Troy herself had gone out into the deserted and sweltering
streets, Troy running uphill and breathlessly calling Ricky's name.
She stopped the few people she met, asking them for a *'petit garçon,
mon fils.'* The men shrugged, one woman said something that sounded sympathetic. They all shook their heads or made negative gestures with their fingers. Troy found herself in a maze of back streets
and stone stairways. She thought she was lost, but looking down a
steep alleyway, saw one of the waiters walk across at the lower end
and she ran down after him. When she reached the cross-alley she
was just in time to see his coat-tails disappear round a farther corner. Finally she caught him up. They were back in the little square,
and there was the hotel. Her heart rammed against her ribs and she
suffered a disgusting sense of constriction in her throat. Sweat
poured between her shoulder-blades and ran down her forehead
into her eyes. She was in a nightmare.

The waiter grimaced. He was idiotically polite and deprecating
and he couldn't understand a word that she said. He pursed his lips,
bowed and went indoors. She remembered the Commissary of
Police and was about to ask the manager to telephone the Préfecture
when she heard Raoul's car turn into the street.

Alleyn said: 'Right. I'll talk to the Préfecture. But before I do, my
dearest dear, will you believe one thing?'

'All right. I'll try.'

'Ricky isn't in danger. I'm sure of it.'

'But it's true. He's been – it's those people up there – they've kidnapped him, haven't they?'

'It's possible that they've taken a hand. If they have it's because they want to keep me busy. It's also possible, isn't it, that something entered into his head and he got himself up and trotted out.'

'He'd never do it, Rory. Never. You know he wouldn't.'

'All right. Now, I'll ring the Préfecture. Come on.'

He sat beside her on the bed and kept his arm about her. While he waited for the number he said: 'Did you lock the door?'

'No. I didn't like the idea of locking him in. The manager's spoken to the servants. They didn't see anybody. Nobody asked for our room numbers.'

'The heavy trunk is still in the hall downstairs and the room number's chalked on it. What colour are his clothes?'

'Pale yellow shirt and brown shorts.'

'Right. We may as well – Allô Allô! . . . '

He began to talk into the telephone, keeping his free hand on her shoulder. Troy turned her cheek to it for a moment and then freed herself and went out on the balcony.

The little square – it was called the *Place de Sarrasins* – was at the top of a hilly street and the greater part of Roqueville lay between it and the sea. The maze of alleys where Troy had lost herself was out of sight behind and above the hotel. As if from a high tower she looked down into the streets and prayed incoherently that in one of them she would see a tiny figure: Ricky, in his lemon-coloured shirt and brown linen shorts. But all Troy could see was a pattern of stucco and stone, a distant row of carriages whose drivers and horses were snoozing, no doubt, in the shadows, a system of tiled roofs and the paintlike blue of the sea. She looked nearer at hand and there, beneath her was Raoul Milano's car, seeming like a toy, and Raoul himself, rolling a cigarette. The hotel porter, at that moment, came out and she heard the sound of his voice. Raoul got up and they disappeared beneath her, into the hotel.

The tone of Alleyn's voice suggested that he was near the end of his telephone call. She had turned away from her fruitless search of the map-like town and was about to go indoors when out of the tail of her eye she caught a flicker of colour.

It was a flicker of lemon-yellow and brown.

The hot iron of the balcony rail scorched the palms of her hands. She leant far out and stared at a tall building on a higher level than herself, a building that was just in view round the corner of the hotel. It was perhaps a quarter of a mile away and from behind a huddle of intervening roofs, rose up in a series of balconies. It was on the highest of these behind a blur of iron railings, that she saw her two specks of colour.

'Rory,' she cried. 'Rory!'

It took several seconds that seemed like many minutes for Alleyn to find the balcony. 'It's Ricky,' she said, 'isn't it? It must be Ricky.' And she ran back into the room, snatched the thin cover from her bed and waved it frantically from the balcony.

'Wait a moment,' Alleyn said.

His police case had been brought up to their room and contained a pair of very powerful field-glasses. While he focused them on the distant balcony he said: 'Don't be too certain, darling, there may be other small boys in yellow and – no – no, it's Ricky. He's all right. Look.'

Troy's eyes were masked with tears of relief. Her hands shook and her fingers were too precipitant with the focusing governors. 'I can't do it – I can't see.'

'Steady. Wipe your eyes. Here, I will. He's still there. He may have spotted us. Try this way. Kneel down and rest the glasses on the rail. Get each eye right in turn. Quietly does it.'

Circles of blurred colour mingled and danced in the two fields of vision. They swam together and clarified. The glasses were in focus now but were trained on some strange blue door, startling in its closeness. She moved them and an ornate gilded steeple was before her with a cross and a clock telling a quarter to two. 'I don't know where I am. It's a church. I can't find him.'

'You're nearly there. Keep at that level and come round gently.'

And suddenly Ricky looked through iron rails with vague, not quite frightened eyes whose gaze, while it was directed at her, yet passed beyond her.'

'Wave,' she said. 'Go on waving.'

Ricky's strangely impersonal and puzzled face moved a little so that an iron standard partly hid it. His right arm was raised and his hand moved to and fro above the railing.

'He's seen!' she said. 'He's waving back.'

The glasses slipped a little. The wall of their hotel, out-of-focus and stupid, blotted out her vision. Someone was tapping on the bedroom door behind them.

'*Entrez!*' Alleyn called and then sharply. 'Hallo! Who's that?'

'What? I've lost him.'

'A woman came out and led him away. They've gone indoors.'

'A woman?'

'Fat and dressed in black.'

'Please let's go quickly.'

Raoul had come through the bedroom and stood behind them. Alleyn said in French, 'Do you see that tall building, just to the left of our wall and to the right of the church? It's pinkish with blue shutters and there's something red on one of the balconies?'

'I see it, Monsieur.'

'Do you know what building it is?'

'I think so, Monsieur. It will be No. 16 the Rue des Violettes where Madame inquired this morning.'

'Troy,' Alleyn said. 'The lord knows why, but Ricky's gone to call on Mr Garbel.'

Troy stopped short on her way to the door. 'Do you mean . . . ?'

'Raoul says that's the house.'

'But – No.' Troy said vigorously. 'No, I don't believe it. He wouldn't just get up and go there. Not of his own accord. Not like that. He wouldn't. Come on, Rory.'

They were following her when Alleyn said: 'When did these flowers come?'

'What flowers? Oh, that. I hadn't noticed it. I don't know. Dr Baradi, I should think. Please don't let's wait.'

An enormous florist's box garnished with a great bow of ribbon lay on the top of a pile of suitcases.

Watched in an agony of impatience by his wife, Alleyn slid a card from under the ribbon and looked at it.

'So sorry,' he read, 'that I shall be away during your visit. Welcome to Roqueville. P.E.Garbel.'

CHAPTER 6

Consultation

Troy wouldn't wait for the lift. She ran downstairs with Alleyn and Raoul at her heels. Only the porter was there, sitting at the desk in the hall.

Alleyn said: 'This will take thirty seconds, darling. I'm in as much of a hurry as you. Please believe it's important. You can get into the car. Raoul can start the engine.' And to the porter he said: 'Please telephone this number and give the message I have written on the paper to the person who answers. It is the number of the Préfecture and the message is urgent. It is expected. Were you on duty here when flowers came for Madame?'

'I was on duty when the flowers arrived, Monsieur. It was about an hour ago. I did not know they were for Madame. The woman went straight upstairs without inquiry, as one who knows the way.'

'And returned?'

The porter lifted his shoulders. 'I did not see her return, Monsieur. No doubt she used the service stairs.'

'No doubt,' Alleyn said and ran out to the car.

On the way to the Rue des Violettes he said: 'I'm going to stop the car a little way from the house, Troy, and I'm going to ask you to wait in it while I go indoors.'

'Are you? But why? Ricky's there, isn't he? We saw him.'

'Yes, we saw him. But I'm not too keen for other people to see us. Cousin Garbel seems to be known, up at the Chèvre d'Argent.'

'But Robin Herrington said he didn't know him, and anyway, according to the card on the flowers, Cousin Garbel's gone away.

That must be what the concierge was trying to tell me. She said he was '*pas chez elk.*'

'*Pas chez soi,*' surely?'

'All right. Yes, of course. I couldn't really understand her. I don't understand anything.' Troy said desperately. 'I just want to get Ricky.'

'I know, darling. Not more than I do.'

'He didn't look as if he was in one of his panics. Did he?'

'No.'

'I expect we'll have a reaction and be furiously snappish with him for frightening us, don't you?'

'We must learn to master our ugly tempers,' he said, smiling at her.

'Rory, he will be there still? He won't have gone?'

'It's only ten minutes ago that we saw him on the sixth floor balcony.'

'Was she a fat shiny woman who led him in?'

'I hadn't got the glasses. I couldn't spot the shine with the naked eye.'

'I didn't like the concierge. Ricky would hate her.'

'That is the street, Monsieur,' said Raoul. 'At the intersection.'

'Good. Draw up here by the kerb. I don't want to frighten Madame but I think all may not be well with the small one whom we have see on the balcony at No. 16. If anyone were to leave by the back or side of the house, Raoul, would they have to come this way from that narrow side-street and pass this way to get out of Roqueville?'

'This way, Monsieur, either to go east or west out of Roqueville. For the rest there are only other alleyways with flights of steps that lead nowhere.'

'Then if a car should emerge from behind No. 16 perhaps it may come about that you start your car and your engine stalls and you block the way. In apologizing you would no doubt go up to the other car and look inside. And if the small one were in the car you would not be able to start your own though you would make a great disturbance by leaning on your horn. And by that time, Raoul, it is possible that M. le Commissaire will have arrived back in his car. Or that I have come out of No. 16.'

'Aren't you going, Rory?'

'At once, darling. All right, Raoul?'

'Perfectly, Monsieur.'

Alleyn got out of the car, crossed the intersection, turned right and entered No. 16.

The hall was dark and deserted. He went at once to the lift-well, glanced at the index of names and pressed the call-button.

'Monsieur?' said the concierge, partly opening the door of her cubby-hole.

Alleyn looked beyond the ringed and grimy hand at one beady eye, the flange of a flattened nose and half a grape-coloured mouth.

'Madame,' he said politely and turned back to the lift.

'Monsieur desires?'

'The lift, Madame.'

'To ascend where, Monsieur?'

'To the sixth floor, Madame.'

'To which apartment on the sixth floor?'

'To the principal apartment. With a balcony.'

The lift was wheezing its way down.

'Unfortunately,' said the concierge, 'the tenant is absent on vacation. Monsieur would care to leave a message?'

'It is the small boy for whom I have called. The small boy whom Madame has been kind enough to admit to the apartment.'

'Monsieur is mistaken. I have admitted no children. The apartment is locked.'

'Can Nature have been so munificent as to lavish upon us a twin sister of Madame? If so she has undoubtedly admitted a small boy to the principal apartment on the sixth floor.'

The lift came into sight and stopped. Alleyn opened the door.

'One moment,' said the concierge. He paused. Her hand was withdrawn from the cubby-hole door. She came out, waddling like a duck and bringing a bunch of keys.

'It is not amusing,' she said, 'to take a fool's trip. However, Monsieur shall see for himself.'

They went up in the lift. The concierge quivered slightly and gave out the combined odours of uncleanliness, frangipane, garlic and hot satin. On the sixth floor she opened a door opposite the lift, waddled through it and sat down panting and massively triumphant on a high chair in the middle of a neat and ordered room whose french windows gave on to a balcony.

Alleyn completely disregarded the concierge. He stopped short in the entrance to the room and looked swiftly round it; at the dressing-table, the shelf above the wash-basin, the gown hanging on the bed-rail and at the three pairs of shoes set out against the wall. He moved to the wardrobe and pulled open the door. Inside it were three sober dresses and a couple of modestly trimmed straw hats. An envelope was lying on the floor of the wardrobe. He stooped down to look at it. It was a business envelope and bore the legend 'Compagnio Chimique des Alpes Maritimes.' He read the superscription:

A Mlle Penelope E. Garbel,
16 Rue des Violettes,
Roqueville-de-Sud,
Côte d'Azur.

He straightened up, shut the wardrobe door with extreme deliberation and contemplated the concierge, still seated like some obscene goddess, in the middle of the room.

'You disgusting old bag of tripe,' Alleyn said thoughtfully in English, 'you little know what a fool I've been making of myself.'

And he went out to the balcony.

II

He stood where so short a time ago he had seen Ricky stand and looked across the intervening rooftops to one that bore a large sign: 'Hôtel Royal.' Troy had left the bedcover hanging over the rail of their balcony.

'A few minutes ago,' Alleyn said, returning to the immovable concierge, 'from the Hôtel Royal over there I saw my son who was here, Madame, on this balcony.'

'It would require the eyes of a hawk to recognize a little boy at that distance. Monsieur is mistaken.'

'It required the aid of binoculars and those I had.'

'Possibly the son of the laundress who was on the premises and has now gone.'

'I saw you, Madame, take the hand of my son, who like yourself, was clearly recognizable, and lead him indoors.'

'Monsieur is mistaken. I have not left my office since this morning. Monsieur will be good enough to take his departure. I do not insist,' the concierge said magnificently 'upon an apology.'

'Perhaps,' Alleyn said, taking a mille franc note from his pocket book, 'you will accept this instead.'

He stood well away from her, holding it out. The eyes glistened and the painted lips moved but she did not rise. For perhaps four seconds they confronted each other. Then she said, if Monsieur will wait downstairs I shall be pleased to join him. I have another room to visit.'

Alleyn bowed, stooped and pounced. His hand shot along the floor and under the hem of the heavy skirt. She made a short angry noise and tried to trample on the hand. One of her heels caught his wrist.

'Calm yourself, Madame. My intentions are entirely honourable.'

He stepped back neatly and extended his arm, keeping the hand closed.

'A strange egg, Madame Blanche,' Alleyn said, 'for a respectable hen to lay.'

He opened his hand. Across the palm lay a little clay goat, painted silver.

III

From that moment the proceedings in No. 16 Rue des Violettes were remarkable for their unorthodoxy.

Alleyn said: 'You have one chance. Where is the boy?'

She closed her eyes and hitched her colossal shoulders up to her earrings.

'Very good,' Alleyn said and walked out of the room. She had left the key in the lock. He turned it and withdrew the bunch.

It did not take long to go through the rest of the building. For the rooms that were unoccupied he found a master-key. As he crossed each threshold he called once: 'Ricky?' and then made a rapid search. In the occupied rooms his visits bore the character of a series of disconnected shots on a cinema screen. He exposed in rapid succession persons of different ages taking their siestas in varying degrees of *déshabillé*. On being told that there was no small boy within, he uttered a word of apology and under the dumfounded gaze of spinsters, elderly gentlemen, married or romantic couples and, in one instance, an outraged negress of uncertain years, walked in, opened cupboards, looked under and into beds and, with a further apology, walked out again.

The concierge had begun to thump on the door of the principal apartment of the sixth floor.

On the ground floor he found a crisp bright-eyed man with a neat moustache, powerful shoulders and an impressive uniform.

'M. l'Inspecteur-en-Chef Alleyn? Allow me to introduce myself. Dupont of the Sûreté, at present acting as Commissary at the Préfecture, Roqueville.' He spoke fluent English with a marked accent. 'So we are already in trouble,' he said as they shook hands. 'I have spoken to Madame Alleyn and to Milano. And the boy is not yet found?'

Alleyn quickly related what had happened.

'And the woman Blanche? Where is she, my dear Inspecteur-en-Chef?'

'She is locked in the apartment of Miss.P.E.Garbel on the sixth floor. The distant thumping which perhaps you can hear is produced by the woman Blanche.'

The Commissary smiled all over his face. 'And we are reminded how correct is the department of Scotland Yard. Let us leave her to her activities and complete the search. As we do so will you perhaps be good enough to continue your report.'

Alleyn complied and they embarked on an exploration of the unsavoury private apartments of Madame Blanche. Alleyn checked a list of telephone numbers and pointed to the third. 'The Château Chèvre d'Argent,' he said.

'Indeed? Very suggestive,' said M. Dupont and with a startling and incredible echo from Baker Street added, 'Pray continue your most interesting narrative while we explore the basement.'

But Ricky was not in any room on the ground floor nor in the cellars under the house. 'Undoubtedly they have removed him,' said

Dupont, 'when they saw you wave from your balcony. I shall at once warn my confrères in the surrounding districts. There are not many roads out of Roqueville and all cars can be checked. We then proceed with a tactful but thorough investigation of the town. This affair is not without precedent. Have no fear for your small son. He will come to no harm. Excuse me. I shall telephone from the office of the woman Blanche. Will you remain or would you prefer to rejoin Madame?'

'Thank you. I will have a word with her if I may.'

'Implore her,' M. Dupont said briskly, 'to remain calm. The affair will arrange itself. The small one is in no danger.' He bowed and went into the cubby-hole. As he went out Alleyn heard the click of a telephone dial.

A police-car was drawn up by the kerb outside No. 16. Alleyn crossed the road to Raoul's car.

There was no need to calm Troy: she was very quiet indeed, and perfectly collected. She looked ill with anxiety but she smiled at him and said: 'Bad luck, darling. No sign?'

'Some signs,' he said, resting his arms on the door beside her. 'Dupont agrees with me that it's an attempt to keep me occupied. He's sure Ricky's all right.'

'He *was* there, wasn't he? We did see him?'

Alleyn said: 'We did see him,' and after a moment's hesitation he took the little silver goat from his pocket. 'He left it behind him.'

Raoul ejaculated: '*La petite chèvre d'argent.*'

Troy's lips quivered. She took the goat in her hands and folded it between them. 'What do we do now?'

'Dupont is stopping all cars driving out of Roqueville and will order a house-to-house search in the town. He's a good man.'

'I'm sure he is,' Troy said politely. She looked terrified. 'You're not going back to the Chèvre d'Argent, are you? You're not going to call their bluff?'

'We're going to take stock.' Alleyn closed his hand over hers. 'I know one wants to drive off madly in all directions, yelling for Ricky, but honestly, darling, that's not the form for this kind of thing. We've *got* to take stock. So far we've scarcely had time to think, much less reason.'

'It's just – when he knows he's lost – it's his nightmare – mislaying us.'

Two gendarmes, smart in their uniforms and sun-helmets, rode past on bicycles, turned into the Rue des Violettes, dismounted and went into No. 16.

'Dupont's chaps,' said Alleyn. 'Now we shan't be long. And I have got one bit of news for you. Cousin Garbel is a spinster.'

'What on earth do you mean?'

'His name is Penelope and he wears a straw hat trimmed with parma violets.'

Troy said: 'Don't muddle me, darling. I'm so desperately addled already.'

'I'm terribly sorry. It's true. Your correspondent is a woman who has some connection with the chemical works we saw this morning. For reasons I can only guess at, she's let you address her letters as if to a man. How *did* you address them?'

'To M. P.E.Garbel.'

'Perhaps she thought you imagined 'M.' to be the correct abbreviation of Mademoiselle?'

Troy shook her head: 'It doesn't seem to matter much now, but it's quite incredible. Look: something's beginning to happen.'

The little town was waking up. Shop doors opened and proprietors came out in their shirt sleeves scratching their elbows. At the far end of the Rue des Violettes there was an eruption of children's voices and a clatter of shoes on stone. The driver of the police-car outside No. 16 started up his engine and the Commissary came briskly down the steps. He made a crisp signal to the driver, who turned his car, crossed the intersection and finally pulled up in front of Raoul. M. Dupont walked across, saluted Troy and addressed himself to Alleyn.

'We commence our search of houses in Roqueville, my dear Inspecteur-en-Chef. The road patrols are installed and a general warning is being issued to my colleagues in the surrounding territory. Between 2.15 by the church clock when you saw your son until the moment when you arrived at these apartments, there was an interval of about ten minutes. If he was removed in an auto it was during those minutes. The patrols were instructed at five minutes to three. Again if he was removed in an auto it has had half an hour's advance and can in that time have gone at the most no farther on our roads than fifty kilometres. Outside every town beyond that radius we have posted a patrol and if they have nothing to report we shall search exhaustively within the radius. Madame, it is most unfortunate that you saw the small one from your hotel. Thus have you hurled a screwdriver in the factory.'

The distracted Troy puzzled over the Commissary's free use of English idiom but Alleyn gave a sharp ejaculation. '*The factory!*' he said. 'By the lord, I wonder.'

'Monsieur?'

'My dear Dupont, you have acted with the greatest expedition and judgment. What do you suggest we do now?'

'I am entirely at your disposal, M. l'Inspecteur-en-Chef. May I suggest that perhaps a fuller understanding of the situation –'

'Yes, indeed. Shall we go to our hotel?'

'Enchanted, Monsieur.'

'I think,' Alleyn said, 'that our driver here is very willing to take an active part. He's been extremely helpful already.'

'He is a good fellow, this Milano,' said Dupont and addressed Raoul in his own language: 'See here, my lad, we are making inquiries for the missing boy in Roqueville. If he is anywhere in the town it will be at the house of some associate of the woman Blanche at No. 16. Are you prepared to take a hand?'

Raoul, it appeared, was prepared. 'If he is in the town, M. le Commissaire, I shall know it inside an hour.'

'Oh, là-là!' M. Dupont remarked, 'what a song our cock sings.'

He scowled playfully at Raoul and opened the doors of the car. Troy and Alleyn were ushered ceremoniously into the police-car and the driver took them back to the hotel.

In their bedroom, which had begun to take on a look of half-real familiarity, Troy and Alleyn filled in the details of their adventures from the time of the first incident in the train until Ricky's disappearance. M. Dupont listened with an air of deference tempered by professional detachment. When they had finished he clapped his knees lightly and made a neat gesture with his thumb and forefinger pressed together.

'Admirable!' he said. 'So we are in possession of our facts and now we act in concert, but first I must tell you one little fact that I have in my sleeve. There has been, four weeks ago, a case of child-stealing in the Paysdoux. It was the familiar story. A wealthy family from Lyons. A small one. A flightish nurse. During the afternoon promenade a young man draws the attention of this sexy nurse. The small one gambols in the gardens by our casino. The nurse and the young man are *tête à tête* upon a seat. Automobiles pass to and fro, sometimes stopping. In one are the confederates of the young man. Presently the nurse remembers her duty. The small one is vanished and remains so. Also vanished is the young man. A message is thrown through the hotel window. The small one is to be recovered with five thousand mille francs at a certain time and at a place outside. St Céleste. There are the customary threats in the matter of informing the police. Monsieur Papa, under pressure from Madame Maman obeys. He is driven to within a short distance of the place. He continues on foot. A car appears. Stops. A man with a handkerchief over his face and a weapon in his hand gets out. Monsieur Papa, again following instructions, places the money under a stone by the road and retires with his hands above his head. The man collects and examines the money and returns to the car. The small one gets out. The car drives away. The small one,' said M. Dupont opening his eyes very wide at Troy, 'is not pleased. He wishes to remain with his new acquaintances.'

'Oh, *no!*' Troy cried out.

'But yes. He has found them enchanting. Nevertheless he rejoins his family. And now having facilitated the escape of the cat Monsieur Papa attempts to close the bag. He informs the police.' M. Dupont spread his hands in the classic gesture and waited for his audience-reaction.

'The usual story,' Alleyn said.

'M. Dupont,' Troy said, 'do you think the same men have taken Ricky?'

'No, Madame. I think we are intended to believe it is the same men.'

'But why? Why should it not be these people?'

'Because,' M. Dupont rejoined, touching his small moustache, 'this morning at 7.30 these people were apprehended and are now locked up in the *poste de police* at St Céleste. Monsieur Papa had the forethought to mark the notes. It was tactfully done. A slight addition to the dècor. And the small one gave useful information. The news of the arrest would have appeared in the evening papers but I have forbidden it. The affair was already greatly publicized.'

'So our friends,' Alleyn suggested, 'unaware of the arrest, imitate the performance and hope our reactions will be those of Monsieur Papa and Madame Maman and that you will turn our attention to St Céleste.'

'But can you be so sure – ' Troy began desperately.

M. Dupont bent at the waist and gazed respectfully at her. 'Ah, Madame,' he said, 'consider. Consider the facts. At the Château de la Chèvre d'Argent there is a group of persons very highly involved in the drug 'raquette.' By a strange accident your husband, already officially interested in these persons, is precipitated into their midst. One, perhaps two of the guests, know who he is. The actress Wells, who is an addict, is sent to make sure. She returns and tells them: 'We entertain, let me inform you, the most distinguished and talented officer of The Scotland Yard. If we do not take some quick steps he will return to inquire for his invalid. It is possible he already suspects.' And it is agreed he must not return. How can he be prevented from doing so? By the apparent kidnapping of his son. This is effected very adroitly. The woman with the bouquet tells the small Ricketts that his mother awaits him at the house she visited this morning. In the meantime a car is on its way from the château to take them to St Céleste. He is to be kept in the apartment of Garbel until it comes. The old Blanche takes him there. She omits to lock the doors on to the balcony. He goes out. You see him. He sees you. Blanche observes. He is removed and before you can reach him there the car arrives and he is removed still farther.'

'Where?'

'If, following the precedent, they go to St Céleste, they will be halted by our patrols, but I think perhaps they will have thought of that and changed their plans and if so it will not be to St Céleste.'

'I agree,' Alleyn said.

'We shall be wiser when their message arrives as arrive it assuredly will. There is also the matter of this Mademoiselle Garbel whose name is in the books and who has some communication with the *Compagnie Chimique des Alpes Maritimes* which may very well be better named the *Compagnie pour l'Elaboration de Diactylmorphine.* She is of the 'raquette,' no doubt, and you have inquired for her.'

'For him. We thought: 'him'.'

'Darling,' Alleyn said, 'can you remember the letters pretty clearly?'

'No,' said poor Troy, 'how should I? I only know they were full of dreary information about buses and roads and houses.'

'Have you ever checked the relationship?'

'No. He – she – talked about distant cousins who I knew had existed but were nearly all dead.'

'Did she ever write about my job?'

'I don't think so, directly. I don't think she ever wrote things like 'how awful' or 'how lovely' to be married to a chief detective-inspector. She said things about my showing her letters to my distinguished husband who would no doubt be interested in their contents.'

'And, unmitigated clod that I am, I wasn't. My dear Dupont,' Alleyn said, 'I've been remarkably stupid. I think this lady has been trying to warn me about the activities of the drug racket in the Paysdoux.'

'But I thought,' Troy said, 'I thought it was beginning to look as if it was she who had taken Ricky. Weren't the flowers a means of getting into our rooms while I was at luncheon? Wasn't the message about being away a blind? Doesn't it look as if she's one of the gang? She knew we were coming here. If she wanted to tell you about the drug racket why did she go away?'

'Why indeed? We don't know why she went away.'

'Rory, I don't want to be a horror, but – No,' said Troy, 'I won't say it.'

'I'll say it for you. Why in Heaven's name can't we do something about Ricky instead of sitting here gossiping about Miss Garbel?'

'But, dear Madame,' cried M. Dupont, 'we *are* doing things about Ricketts. Only,' M. Dupont continued, fortunately mistaking for an agonized sob the snort of hysteria that had escaped Troy, 'only by an assemblage of the known facts can we arrive at a rational solution. Moreover, if the former case is to be imitated we shall certainly receive a message and it is important that we are here when it arrives. In the meantime all precautions have been taken. But all!'

'I know,' Troy said, 'I'm terribly sorry. I know.'

'You brought Miss Garbel's last letter, darling. Let's have a look at it.'

'I'll get it.'

Troy was not very good at keeping things tidy. She had a complicated rummage in her travelling case and handbag before she unearthed the final Garbel letter which she handed with an anxious look to Alleyn. It was in a crumpled condition and he spread it out on the arm of his chair.

'Here it is,' he said, and read aloud:

'My DEAR AGATHA TROY,

    'I wrote to you on December 17th of last year and hope that you received my letter and that I may have the pleasure of hearing from you in the not *too* distant future! I pursue my usual round of activities. Most of my jaunts take me into the district lying *west* of Roqueville, a district known as the Paysdoux (Paysdoux, literally translated, but allowing for the reversed position of the adjective, means Sweet Country) though a close acquaintance with some of the inhabitants might suggest that Pays *Dopes* would be a better title!!! (Forgive the parenthesis and the indifferent and slangy *pun*. I have never been able to resist an opportunity to play on words.)'

'Hell's boots!' Alleyn said, 'under our very noses! *Pays Dopes* indeed, District of Dopes and Dope Pays.' He read on:

    'As the acquaintances I visit most frequently live some thirty kilometres (about seventeen miles) away on the western reaches of the Route Maritime I make use of the omnibus, No. 16, leaving the Place des Sarrasins at five minutes past the hour. The fare at the present rate of exchange is about ls. English, single, and ls.9d. return. I enclose a ticket which will no doubt be of interest. It is a pleasant drive and commands a pretty prospect of the Mediterranean on one's left and on one's right a number of ancient buildings as well as some evidence of progress, if progress it can be called, in the presence of a large *chemical* works, in which, owing to my chosen profession, I have come to take some interest.'

'Oh lord!' Alleyn lamented, 'why didn't I read this before we left. We have been so bloody superior over this undoubtedly admirable spinster.'

'Please?' said M. Dupont.

'Listen to this, Dupont. Suppose this lady, who is a qualified chemist, was in the hands of the drug racket. Suppose she worked for them. Suppose she wanted to let someone in authority in England know what goes on inside the racket. Now. Do you imagine that there is any reason why she shouldn't write what she knows to this person and put the letter in the post?'

'There is a good reason to suppose she might fear to do so, Mr Chief,' rejoined Dupont who no doubt considered that the time had come for a more familiar mode of address. 'As an Englishwoman she is perhaps not quite trusted in the 'raquette.' Her correspondence may be watched. Someone who can read English at the *bureau-de-postes* may be bribed. Perhaps she merely suspects that this may be so. They are thorough, these blackguards. Their net is fine in the mesh.'

'So she writes her boring letters and every time she writes, she drops a veiled hint, hoping I may see the letter. The Chèvre d'Argent is about thirty kilometres west on the Route Maritime. She tells us by means of tedious phrases, ferocious puns, and used bus tickets that she is a visitor there. How did she address her letters, Troy?'

'To 'Agatha Troy.' She said in her first letter that she understood that I would prefer to be addressed by my professional name. Like an actress, she added, though not in other respects. With the usual row of ejaculation marks. I don't think she ever used your name. You were always my brilliant and distinguished husband!'

'And is my face red!' said Alleyn. M. Dupont's was puzzled. Alleyn continued reading the letter.

'If ever you and your distinguished husband should visit 'these parts'! you may care to take this drive which is full of interesting topographic features that often escape the notice of the *ordinary Tourist*. I fear my own humble account of our local background is somewhat *Garbelled* (! ! ! !) version and suggest that first-hand observation would be much more rewarding! With kindest regards, etc.'

'Really,' Alleyn said, handing the letter back to Troy, 'short of cabling: 'Drug barons at work come and catch them,' she could scarcely have put it more clearly.'

'You didn't read the letters. I only told you about bits of them. I ought to have guessed.'

'Well, it's no good blackguarding ourselves. Look here, both of you. Suppose we're on the right track about Miss Garbel. Suppose, for some reason, she's in the racket yet wants to put me wise about it and has hoped to lure me over here. Why, when Troy writes and tells her we're coming, does she go away without explanation?'

'And why,' Troy interjected, 'does she send flowers by someone who used them as a means of kidnapping Ricky and taking him to her flat?'

'The card on the flowers isn't in her writing.'

'She might have telephoned the florist.'

'Which can be checked,' said M. Dupont, 'of course. Will you allow me? This, I assume is the bouquet.'

He inspected the box of tuberoses. 'Ah, yes. *Le Pot des Fleurs*. May I telephone Madame?'

While he did so, Troy went out to the balcony and Alleyn, seeing her there, her fingers against her lips in the classic gesture of the anxious woman, joined her and put his arm about her shoulders.

'I'm looking at that other balcony,' she said. 'It's silly, isn't it? Suppose he came out again. It's like one of those dreams of frustration.'

He touched her cheek and she said: 'You mustn't be too nice to me.'

'Little perisher,' Alleyn muttered, 'you may depend upon it he's airing his French and saying 'why' with every second breath he draws. Did you know W.S. Gilbert was pinched by bandits when he was a kid?'

'I think I did. Might they have taken him to the Chèvre d'Argent? As a sort of double bluff?'

'I don't think so, my darling. My bet is he's somewhere nearer than that.'

'Nearer to Roqueville? Where, Rory, where?'

'It's a guess and an unblushing guess, but –'

M. Dupont came bustling out to the balcony.

'*Alors!*' he began and checked himself. 'My dear Monsieur and Madame, we progress a little. The *Pot des Fleurs* tells me the flowers were bought and removed by a woman of the servant class, not of the district, who copied the writing on the card from a piece of paper. They do not remember seeing the woman before. We may find she is a maid at the château, may we not?'

'May we?' said Troy a little desperately.

'But there are better news than these, Madame. The good Raoul Milano has reported to the hotel. It appears that an acquaintance of his, an idle fellow living in the western suburb, has seen a car, a light blue Citroën, at 2.30 p.m. driving out of Roqueville by the western route. In the car were the driver, a young woman and a small boy dressed in yellow and brown. The man wears a red beret and the woman is bare-headed. The car was impeded for a moment by an omnibus and the acquaintance of Milano heard the small one talking. He spoke in French but childishly and with a little difficulty, using foreign words. He appeared to be making an inquiry. The acquaintance heard him say '*pourquoi*' several times.'

'Conclusive,' Alleyn said, watching Troy. She cried out: 'Did he seem frightened?'

'Madame, no. It appears that Milano made the same inquiry. The acquaintance said the small one seemed exigent. The actual phrase,' M. Dupont said, turning to Alleyn, 'was: "*Il semblait être impatient de comprendre quelquechose*"!'.

'He was impatient to understand something,' Troy ejaculated, 'is that it?'

'*Mais oui, Madame,*' said Dupont and added a playful compliment in French to the effect that Troy evidently spoke the language as if she were born to it. Troy failed to understand a word of this and gazed anxiously at him. He continued in English: 'Now, between Roqueville and the point where our nearest patrol on the western route is posted there are three deviations: all turning inland. Two are merely rural lanes. The third is a road that leads to a monastery and also – ' here M. Dupont raised his forefinger and looked roguish.

'And also,' Alleyn said, 'to the Factory of the Maritime Alps Chemical Company.'

'Parfaitement!' said M. Dupont.

IV

'And you think he's there!' Troy cried out. 'But why? Why take him there?'

Alleyn said: 'As I see it, and I don't pretend, lord knows, to see at all clearly, this might be the story. Oberon & Co. have a strong interest in the factory but they don't realize we know it. Baradi and your painting chum Glande were at great pains to deplore the factory: to repudiate the factory as an excrescence in the landscape. But we suspect it probably houses the most impudent manufactory of hyoscine in Europe and we know Oberon's concerned in the traffic. All right. They realize we've seen Ricky on the balcony of No. 16 and have called in the police. If Blanche has succeeded in getting herself out of durance vile she's told them all about it. They've lost their start. They daren't risk taking Ricky to St Céleste, as they originally planned. What are they to do with him? It would be easy and safe to house him in one of the offices at the factory and have him looked after. You must remember that nobody up at the château knows that he understands a certain amount of French.'

'The people who've got him will have found that out by now.'

'And also that his French doesn't go beyond the nursery stage. They may have told him that we've gone back to look after Miss Truebody and have arranged for him to be minded until we are free. I think they may have meant to keep him at No. 16 while we went haring off to St Céleste. *La Belle Blanche* (damn her eyes) probably rang up and said we'd spotted him on the balcony and they thought up the factory in a hurry.'

'Could they depend on our going to St Céleste? Just on the strength of our probably getting to hear about the other kidnapping?'

'No,' said Alleyn and Dupont together.

'Then – I don't understand.'

'Madame,' said Dupont, 'there is no doubt that you shall be directed, if not to a place near St Céleste, at least to some other place along the eastern route. To some place as far as possible from the true whereabouts of Ricketts.'

'Directed?'

'There will be a little note or a little telephone message. Always remember they fashion themselves on the pattern of the former affair, being in ignorance of this morning's arrest.'

'It all sounds so terribly like guesswork,' Troy said after a moment. 'Please, what do we do?'

Alleyn looked at Dupont whose eyebrows rose portentously. 'It is a little difficult,' he said. 'From the point of view of my department, it is a delicate situation. We are not yet ready to bring an accusation against the organization behind the factory. When we are ready, Madame, it will be a very big matter, a matter not only for the department but for the police forces of several nations, for the International Police and for the United Nations Organization itself.'

Troy suddenly had a nightmarish vision of Ricky in his lemon shirt and brown shorts abandoned to a labyrinth of departmental corridors.

Watching her, Alleyn said: 'So that we mustn't suggest, you see, that we are interested in anything but Ricky.'

'Which, God knows, I'm not,' said Troy.

'Ah,Madame,' Dupont ejaculated, 'I, too, am a parent.' And to Troy's intense embarrassment he kissed her hand.

'It seems to me,' Alleyn said, 'that the best way would be for your department, my dear Dupont, to make a great show of watching the eastern route and the country round St Céleste and for us to make an equally great show of driving in a panic-stricken manner about the countryside. Indeed, it occurs to me that I might very well help matters by ringing up the château and *registering* panic. What do you think?'

Dupont made a tight purse of his mouth, drew his brows together, looked pretty sharply at Alleyn and then lightly clapped his hands together.

'In effect,' he said, 'why not?'

Alleyn went to the telephone. 'Baradi, I fancy,' he said thoughtfully, and after a moment's consideration: 'Yes, I think it had better be Baradi.'

He dialled the hotel office and gave the number. While he waited he grimaced at Troy: 'Celebrated imitation about to begin. You will notice that I have nothing in my mouth.'

They could hear the bell ringing, up at the Chèvre d'Argent.

'*Allô, allô!*' Alleyn began in a high voice and broke into a spate of indifferent French. Was that the Chèvre d'Argent? Could he speak to Dr Baradi? It was extremely urgent. He gave his name. They heard the telephone quack: '*Un moment, Monsieur*'. He grinned at Troy and covered the receiver with his hand. 'Let's hope they have to wake him up,' he said. 'Give me a cigarette, darling.'

But before he could light it Baradi had come to the telephone. Alleyn's deep voice was pitched six tones above its normal range and sounded as if it was only just under control. He began speaking in French, corrected himself, apologized and started again in English. 'Do forgive me,' he said, 'for bothering you again. The truth is, we are in trouble here. I know it sounds ridiculous but *has* my small boy by any chance turned up at the château? Yes. Yes, we've lost him. We thought there might be a chance – there are buses, they say – and we're at our wit's end. No, I was afraid not. It's just that my wife is quite frantic. Yes. Yes, I know. Yes, so we've been told. Yes, I've seen the police but you know what they're like.' Alleyn turned towards M. Dupont who immediately put on a heroic look. 'They're the same wherever you go, red tape and inactivity. Most unsatisfactory.' M. Dupont bowed. 'Yes, if it's the same blackguards we shall be told what we have to do. No, no, I refuse to take any risks of that sort. Somehow or another I'll raise the money but it won't be easy with the restrictions.' Alleyn pressed his lips together. His long fingers blanched as they tightened round the receiver. 'Would you really?' he said and the colour of his voice, its diffidence and its hesitancy, so much at variance with the look in his eyes, gave him the uncanny air of a ventriloquist. 'Would you really? I say, that's *most* awfully kind of you both. I'll tell my wife. It'll be a great relief to her to know – yes, well I ought to have said something about that, only I'm so damnably worried – I'm afraid we shan't be able to do anything about Miss Truebody until we've found Ricky. I am taking my wife to St Céleste, if that's where – yes, probably this afternoon if – I don't think we'll feel very like coming back after what's happened, but of course – Is she? O, dear! I'm very sorry. That's very good of him. I *am* sorry. Well, if you really don't mind. I'm afraid I'm not much use. Thank you. Yes. Well, goodbye.'

He hung up the receiver. His face was white.

'He offers every possible help,' he said, 'financial and otherwise, and is sure Mr Oberon will be immeasurably distressed. He has now, no doubt, gone away to enjoy a belly laugh at our expense. It is going to be difficult to keep one's self-control over Messrs. Oberon and Baradi.'

'I believe you,' said M. Dupont.

'Rory, you're certain now, in your own mind, aren't you?'

'Yes. He didn't utter a word that was inconsistent with genuine concern and helpfulness, but I'm certain in my own mind.'

'Why?'

'One gets a sixth sense about that sort of bluff. And I think he made a slip. He said: 'Of course you can do nothing definite until these scoundrels ring you up.' '

M. Dupont cried: 'Ahah!'

'But you said to him,' Troy objected, 'that we would be told what to do.'

' "Would be *told* what to do"! Exactly. In the other case the kidnappers' instructions came by letter. Why should Baradi think that this time they would telephone?'

As if in answer, the bedroom telephone buzzed twice.

'This will be it,' said Alleyn and took up the receiver.

CHAPTER 7

Sound of Ricky

Alleyn was used to anonymous calls on the telephone. There was a quality of voice that he had learnt to recognize as common to them all. Though this new voice spoke in French it held the familiar tang of artifice. He nodded to Dupont who at once darted out of the room.

The voice said: 'M. Allen?'

'*C'est Allen qui parle.*'

'*Bien. Ecoutez. A sept heures demain soir, presentez-vous à pied et tout seul, vis-à-vis du pavillon de chasse en ruines, il y a sept kilomètres vers le midi du village St Céleste-des-Alpes. Apportez avec vouc cent mille francs en billets de cent. N'avertissez-pas la police, ou le petit apprendra bien les consequences. Compris?*'

Alleyn repeated it in stumbling French, as slowly as possible and with as many mistakes as he dared to introduce. He wanted to give Dupont time. The voice grew impatient in correction. Alleyn, however, repeated his instructions for the third time and began to expostulate in English. '*Plus rien à dire,*' said the voice and rang off.

Alleyn turned to Troy. 'Did you understand?' he asked.

'I don't know. I think so.'

'Well, it's all right, my dearest. It's as we thought. Tomorrow evening outside the village called St Céleste-des-Alpes with a hundred quid in my hand. The village, no doubt, will be somewhere above St Céleste.'

'You didn't recognize the voice?'

'It wasn't Baradi or Oberon. It wasn't young Herrington. I wouldn't swear it wasn't Carbury Glande who was croaking with hangover this morning and might have recovered by now. And I would by no means swear that it wasn't Baradi's servant whom I've only heard utter about six phrases in Egyptian but who certainly understands French. There was a bit of an accent and I didn't think it sounded local.'

Dupont tapped and entered. 'Any luck?' Alleyn said.

'Of a kind. I rang the *centrale* and was answered by an imbecile but the call has been traced. And to where do you suppose?'

'No. 16 Rue des Violettes?'

'Precisely!'

'Fair enough,' Alleyn said. 'It must be their town office.'

'I also rang the *Préfecture*. No reports have come in from the patrols. What was the exact telephone message, if you please?'

Alleyn told him in French, wrapping up the threats to Ricky in words that were outside Troy's vocabulary.

'The same formula,' Dupont said, 'as in the reported version of the former affair. My dear Mr Chief and Madame, it seems that we should now pursue our hunch.'

'To the chemical works?'

'Certainly.'

'Thank God!' Troy ejaculated.

'All the same,' Alleyn said, 'it's tricky. As soon as we get there the gaff is blown. The château, having been informed that the telephone message went through, will wait for us to go to St Céleste. When we turn up at the factory, the factory will ring the château. Tricky! How far away is St Céleste?'

'About seventy kilometres.'

'Is it possible to start off on the eastern route and come round to the factory by a detour? Behind Roqueville?'

M. Dupont frowned. 'There are some mountain lanes,' he said. 'Little more than passages for goats and cattle but of a width that is possible.'

'Possible for Raoul who is, I have noticed, a good driver.'

'He will tell us, at least. He is beneath.'

'Good.' Alleyn turned to his wife. 'See here, darling. Will you go down and ask Raoul to fill up his tank – *faire plein d'essence* will be all right – and ask him to come back as soon as he's done it. Will you then ask for the manager and tell him we're going to St Céleste but would like to leave our heavy luggage here and keep our rooms. Perhaps you should offer to pay a week in advance. Here's some money. I'll bring down a couple of suitcases and join you in the hall. All right?'

'All right. *Voulez-vous,*' Troy said anxiously, *'faire plein d'essence et revenez ici.* OK?'

'OK.'

When she had gone Alleyn said: 'Dupont, I wanted a word with you. You can see what a hellish business this is for me, can't you? I know damn' well how important it is not to let our investigations go off like a damp squib. I realize, nobody better, that a premature inquiry at the factory might prejudice a very big coup. I'm here on a job and my job is with the police of your country and my own. In a way it's the most critical assignment I've ever had.'

'And for me, also.'

'But the boy's my boy and his mother's my wife. It looked perfectly safe to bring them here and they gave me admirable cover but as things have turned put, I shouldn't have brought them. But for the unfortunate Miss Truebody, of course, it *would* have been all right.'

'And she, too, provided admirable cover. An unquestioned entrée.'

'Not for long, however. What I'm trying to say is this: I've fogged out a scheme of approach. I realize that in suggesting it I'm influenced by an almost overwhelming anxiety about Ricky. I'll be glad if you tell me at once if you think it impracticable and, from the police angle, unwise.'

Dupont said: 'M. l'Inspecteur-en-Chef, I understand the difficulty and respect, very much, your delicacy. I shall be honoured to advise.'

'Thank you. Here goes, then. It's essential that we arouse no suspicion of our professional interest in the factory. It's highly probable that the key men up there have already been informed from the château of my real identity. There's a chance, I suppose, that Annabella Wells has kept her promise but it's a poor chance. After all, if these people don't know who I am why should they kidnap Ricky? All right. We make a show of leaving this hotel and taking the eastern route for St Céleste. That will satisfy anybody who may be watching us at this end. We take to the hills and double back to the factory. By this time, you, with a suitable complement of officers, are on your way there. I go in and ask for Ricky. I am excitable and agitated. They say he's not there. I insist that I've unimpeachable evidence that he is there. I demand to see the manager. I produce Raoul who says he took his girl for a drive and saw a car with Ricky in it, turn in at the factory gates. They stick to their guns. I make a hell of a row. I tell them I've applied to you. You arrive with a carload of men. You take the manager aside and tell him I am a VIP on holiday.'

'*Comment?* VIP?'

'A very important person. You see it's extremely awkward. That you think the boy's been kidnapped and that it's just possible one of their workmen has been bribed to hide him. You'll say I'll make things very hot for you at the Sûreté if you don't put on a show of searching for Ricky. You produce a *mandat de perquisition.* You are terribly apologetic and very bored with me but you say that unfortunately you have no alternative. As a matter of form you must search the factory. Now, what does the manager do?'

Dupont's sharp eyebrows were raised to the limit. Beneath them his round eyes stared with glazed impartiality at nothing in particular. His arms were folded. Alleyn waited.

'In effect,' Dupont said at last, 'he sends his secretary to investigate. The secretary returns with Ricketts and there are a great many apologies. The manager assures me that there will be an exhaustive inquiry and appropriate dismissals.'

'What do you say to this?'

'Ah,' said Dupont suddenly lowering his eyebrows and unfolding his arms. 'That is more difficult.'

'Do I perhaps intervene? Having clasped my son to my bosom and taken him out with his mother to the car, thus giving the manager an opportunity to attempt bribery at a high level, do I not return and take it as a matter of course that you consider this an admirable opportunity to pursue your search for the kidnappers?'

Dupont's smile irradiated his face. 'It is possible,' he said. 'It is conceivable.'

'Finally, my dear Dupont, can we act along these lines or any other that suggest themselves without arousing the smallest suspicion that we are interested in anything but the recovery of the child?'

'The word of operation is indeed 'act.' From your performance on
the telephone, Mr Chief, I can have no misgivings about your own
performance. And for myself,' here Dupont tapped his chest,
touched his moustache and gave Alleyn an indescribably roguish
glance, 'I believe I shall do well enough.'

They stood up. Alleyn put his police bag inside a large suitcase.
After looking at the chaos within Troy's partly unpacked luggage, he
decided on two cases. He also collected their overcoats and Ricky's.

'Shall we about it?' he asked.

'*En avant, alors!*' said Dupont.

II

Mr Oberon looked down at the figure on the bed. 'Quite peaceful,'
he said. 'Isn't it strange?'

'The teeth,' Baradi pointed out, 'make a great difference.'

'There is a certain amount of discoloration.'

'Hypostatic staining. The climate.'

'Then there is every reason,' Mr Oberon observed with satisfaction, 'for an immediate funeral.'

'Certainly.'

'If they have in fact gone off to St Céleste they cannot return
until the day after tomorrow.'

'If, on the other hand, this new man at the Préfecture is intelligent,
which Alleyn says is not the case, they may pick up some information.'

'Let us,' Mr Oberon suggested as he absent-mindedly re-arranged
the sprigged locknit nightgown which was pinned down by crossed
hands to the rigid bosom, 'let us suppose the worst. They recover the
child,' he raised his hand. 'Yes, yes, it is unlikely, but suppose it happens. They call to inquire. They ask to see her.'

The two men were silent for a time. 'Very well,' Baradi said. 'So
they see her. She will not be a pretty sight, but they see her.'

Mr Oberon was suddenly inspired. 'There must be flowers,' he
ejaculated. 'Masses and masses of flowers. A nest. A coverlet all of
flowers, smelling like incense. Tuberoses,' he cried softly, clapping
his hands together. 'They will be entirely appropriate. I shall order
them. Tuberoses! And orchids.'

III

The eastern route followed the seaboard for three miles out of Roqueville and then turned slightly inland. At this point a country road branched off it to the left. Raoul took the road which mounted into the hills by a series of hairpin bends. They climbed out of soft coastal air and entered a region of mountain freshness. A light breeze passed like a hand through the olive groves and sent spirals of ruddy dust across the road. The seaboard with its fringe of meretricious architecture had dwindled into an incident while the sea and sky and warm earth widely enlarged themselves.

The road turning about the contour of the hills was littered with rock and scarred by wheel tracks. Sometimes it became a ledge traversing the face of sheer cliffs and in normal times Troy, who disliked heights, would have feared these passages. Now she dreaded them merely because they had to be taken slowly.

'How long,' she asked, 'will it be, do you suppose?'

'Roqueville's down there a little ahead of us. We'll pass above it in a few minutes. I gather we now cast back into the mountains for about the same distance as we've travelled already and then work round to a junction with the main road to the factory. Sorry about these corners, darling,' Alleyn said as they edged round a bend that looked like a take-off into space. 'Are you minding it very much?'

'Only because it's slow. Raoul's a good driver, isn't he?'

'Very good indeed. Could you bear it if I told you about this job? I think perhaps I ought to but it'll be a bit dreary.'

'Yes,' Troy said. 'I'd like that. The drearier the better because I'll have to concentrate.'

'Well, you know it's to do with the illicit drug trade but I don't suppose you know much about the trade itself. By and large it's probably the worst thing apart from war that's happened to human beings in modern times. Before the 1914 war the nations most troubled by the opium racket had begun to do something about it. There was a Shanghai Conference and a Hague Convention. Both were cautious tentative shows. None of the nations came to them with a clean record and all the delegates were embarrassed by murky backgrounds in which production, manufacture and distribution involved the revenue both of states and of highly placed individuals. Dost thou attend me?'

'Sir,' said Troy, 'most heedfully.'

They exchanged the complacent glances of persons who recognize each other's quotations.

'At the Hague Convention they did get round to making one or two conservative decisions but before they were ratified the war came along and the whole thing lapsed. After the peace the traffic was stepped up most murderously. It's really impossible to exaggerate the scandal of those years. At the top end were nations getting a fat revenue out of the sale of opium and its derivatives. An investigator said at one stage that half Europe was being poisoned to bolster up the domestic policy of Bulgaria. The goings-on were fantastic. Chargés d'Affaires smuggled heroin in their diplomatic baggage. Drug barons built works all over Europe. Diacetylmorphine, which is heroin to you, was brewed on the *Champs-Élysées*. Highly qualified chemists were offered princely salaries to work in drug factories and a great number of them fell for it. Many of the smartest and most fashionable people in European society lived on the trade: murderers, if the word has any meaning. At the other end of the stick were the street pedlars, at the foot of Nurse Cavell's statue among other places, and the addicts. The addicts were killing themselves in studies, studios, dressing-rooms, brothels, boudoirs and garrets; young intellectuals and young misfits were ruining themselves by the score. Girls were kept going by their *souteneurs* with shots of the stuff. And so on. Thou attendest not.'

'O, good Sir, I do.'

'I pray thee, mark me. At the Peace Conference this revolting baby was handed over to the League of Nations who appointed an Advisory Committee who began the first determined assault on the thing. The International Police came in, various bodies were set up and a bit of real progress was made. Only a bit. Factories pulled down in Turkey were rebuilt in Bulgaria. Big centralized industries were bust only to reappear like crops of small ulcers in other places. But something was attempted and a certain amount was achieved by 1919.'

'O, dear! History at it again?'

'More or less. The difference lies in the fact that this time the preliminary work had been done and the machinery for investigation partly set up. But the second world war did its stuff and everything lapsed. U.N.O. doesn't start from scratch in the way that the League did. But it faces the old situation and it's still up against the Big Boys. The police still catch the sprats at the Customs counter and miss the mackerels in high places. The factories have again moved: from Bulgaria into post-war Italy and from post-war Italy, it appears, into the Paysdoux of Southern France. And the Big Boys have moved with them. Particularly Dr Baradi and Mr Oberon.'

'Are they really big?'

'Not among the tops, perhaps. There we climb into very rarefied altitudes and by as hazardous a road as this one. But Oberon and Baradi are certainly in the mackerel class. Oberon I regret to tell you, is a British subject at the moment although he began in the Middle East, where he ran a quack religion of a dubious sort and got six months for his pains. He came to us by way of Portugal and Egypt. In Portugal he practised the same game during the war and made his first connection with the dope trade. In Egypt he was stepped up in the racket and made the acquaintance of his chum Baradi. By that time he'd acquired large sums of money. Two fortunes fell into his lap from rich disciples in Lisbon – middle-aged women, who became Daughters of the Sun or something, re-made their wills and died shortly afterwards.'

'O, lord!'

'You may well say so. Baradi's a different story. Baradi was a really brilliant medical student who trained in Paris and has become one of the leading surgeons of his time. At one time he had some sort of entrée to court circles in Cairo and, thanks to his skill and charms, any number of useful connections in France. *You* may not think him very delicious but it appears that a great many women do. He got in with the Boys in Paris and Egypt and is known to be a trafficker in a big way. It's his money and Oberon's that's behind the Chemical Company of the Maritime Alps. That's as much as the combined efforts of the International Police, the Sûreté and the Yard have gleaned about Baradi and Oberon and it's on that information I'm meant to act.'

'And is Ricky a spanner in the works?'

'He may be a spanner in the works, my pretty. He gives us an excuse for getting into the factory. They may have played into our hands when they took Ricky into the factory.'

'*If* they took him there,' Troy said under her breath.

'If they drove beyond the turn-off to the factory the patrols would have got them. Of course he may be maddening the monks in the monastery farther up.'

'Mightn't the car have pushed on and come round by this appalling route?'

'The patrols on the eastern route will get it if it did and there are no fresh tyre tracks.'

'It's so strange,' Troy said, 'to hear you doing your stuff.'

Raoul humoured the car down a steep incline and past a pink-washed hovel overhanging the cliff. A peasant stood in the doorway. At Alleyn's suggestion Raoul called to him.

'*Hé* friend! Any other driver comes this way today?'

'*Pas un de si bête!*'

'That was: 'no such fool' wasn't it?' Troy asked.

'It was.'

'I couldn't agree more.'

They bumped and sidled on for some time without further conversation. Raoul sang. The sky was a deeper blue and the Mediterranean, now almost purple, made unexpected gestures between the tops of hills. Troy and Alleyn each thought privately how much, in spite of the road, they would have enjoyed themselves if Ricky had been with them.

Presently Raoul, speaking slowly out of politeness to Troy, pointed to a valley they were about to enter.

'The monastery road, M'sieur – Madame. We descend.'

They did so, precipitately. The roofs of the Monastery of Our Lady of Paysdoux appeared, tranquil and modest, folded in a confluence of olive groves. As they came into the lower valley they looked down on an open place where a few cars were parked and where visitors to the cloisters moved in and out of long shadows. The car dived down behind the monastery, turned and ran out into the head of a good sealed road. 'The factory,' Raoul said, 'is round the next bend. Beyond, Monsieur can see the main road and away to the right is the headland with the tunnel that comes out by the Château de la Chèvre d'Argent.'

'Is there a place lower down and out of sight of the factory where we can watch the main road on the Roqueville side?'

'Yes, Monsieur. As one approaches the bend.'

'Let us stop there for a moment.'

'Good, Monsieur.'

Raoul's point of observation turned out to be a pleasant one over-looking the sea and commanding a full view of the main road as it came through the hills from Roqueville. He ran the car to the outer margin of their road and stopped. Alleyn looked at his watch. 'A quarter-past four. The works shut down at five. I hope Dupont's punctual. We'll have a final check. Raoul first, darling, if you don't mind. See how much you can follow and keep your eye on the main road for the police car. *Alors, Raoul.*'

Raoul turned to listen. He had taken off his chauffeur's cap and his head, seen in profile against the homeric blue of the Mediterranean, took on a classic air. Its colour was a modulation of the tawny earth. Grapelike curls clustered behind his small ear, his mouth was fresh, reflected light bloomed on his cheekbones and his eyes held a look of untroubled acceptance. It was a beautiful head and Troy thought: 'When we're out of this nightmare I shall want to paint it.'

Alleyn was saying: ' . . . so you will remain at first in the car. After a time I may fetch or send for you. If I do you will come into the offices and tell a fairy story. It will be to this effect . . . '

Raoul listened impassively, his eyes on the distant road. When Alleyn had done, Raoul made a squaring movement with his shoulders, blew out his cheeks into a mock-truculent grimace and intimated that he was ready for anything.

'Now, darling,' Alleyn said, 'do you think you can come in with me and keep all thought of our inside information out of your mind? You know only this: Ricky has been kidnapped and Raoul has seen him being driven into the factory. I'm going to have a shot at the general manager who is called Callard. We don't know much about him. He's a Parisian who worked in the States for a firm that was probably implicated in the racket and he speaks English. Any of the others we may run into may also speak English. We'll assume, what-ever we find, that they understand it. So don't say anything to me that they shouldn't hear. On the other hand, you can with advan-tage keep up an agitated chorus. I shall speak bad French. We don't know what may develop so we'll have to keep our heads and ride the skids as we meet them. How do you feel about it?'

'Should I be a brave little woman biting on the bullet or should I go in, boots and all, and rave?'

'Rave if you feel like it, my treasure. They'll probably expect it.'

'I daresay a spartan mother would seem more British in their eyes or is that a contradiction in terms? O, Rory!' Troy said in a low voice. 'It's so grotesque. Here we are half-crazy with anxiety and we have to put on a sort of anxiety-act. It's – it's a cruel thing, isn't it?'

'It'll be all right,' Alleyn said. 'It *is* cruel but it'll be all right. I promise. You'll be as right as a bank whatever you do. Hallo, there's Dupont.'

A car had appeared on the main road from Roqueville.

'M. le Commissaire,' said Roul and flicked his headlamps on and off. The police car, tiny in the distance, winked briefly in response.

'We're off,' said Alleyn.

IV

The entrance hall of the factory was impressive. The décor was carried out in obscured glass, chromium and plastic and was beautifully lit. In the centre was a sculptured figure, modern in treatment, suggestive of some beneficent though pin-headed being, who drew strength from the earth itself. Two flights of curved stairs led airily to remote galleries. There was an imposing office on the left. Double doors at the centre back and a series of single doors in the right wall all bore legends in chromium letters. The front wall was plate-glass and commanded a fine view of the valley and the sea.

Beyond a curved counter in the outer office a girl sat over a ledger. When she saw Alleyn and Troy she rose and stationed herself behind a chromium notice on the counter:

'*Renseignements.*'

'Monsieur?' asked the girl. 'Madame?'

Alleyn, without checking his stride, said: 'Don't disarrange yourself, Mademoiselle,' and made for the central doors.

The girl raised her voice: 'One moment, Monsieur, whom does Monsieur wish to see?'

'*M. Callard, le Controller.*'

The girl pushed a bell on her desk. Before Alleyn could reach the double doors they opened and a commissionaire came through. Alleyn turned to the desk.

'Monsieur has an appointment?' asked the girl.

'No,' Alleyn said, 'but it is a matter of extreme urgency. I must see M. Callard, Mademoiselle.'

The girl was afraid that M. Callard saw nobody without an appointment. Troy observed that her husband was making his usual impression on the girl, who touched her hair, settled her shoulders and gave him a look.

Troy said in a high voice: 'Darling, what's she saying? Has she seen him?'

The girl just glanced at Troy and then opened her eyes at Alleyn. 'Perhaps I can be of assistance to Monsieur?' she suggested.

Alleyn leant over the counter and haltingly asked her if by any chance she had seen a little boy in brown shorts and a yellow shirt. The question seemed to astonish her. She made an incredulous sound and repeated it to the commissionaire who merely hitched up his shoulders. They had not seen any little boys, she said. Little boys were not permitted on the premises.

Alleyn stumbled about with his French and asked the girl if she spoke English. She said that unfortunately she did not.

'Mademoiselle,' Alleyn said to Troy, 'doesn't speak English. I think she says M. Callard won't see us. And she says she doesn't know anything about Ricky.'

Troy said: 'But we know he's here. We must see the manager. Tell her we must.'

This time the girl didn't so much as glance at Troy. With a petunia-tipped finger and thumb she removed a particle of mascara from her lashes and discreetly rearranged her figure for Alleyn to admire. She said it was too bad that she couldn't do anything for him. She thought he had better understand this and said that at any other time she might do a lot. She reacted with a facial expression which corresponded, Troy thought, with the 'haughty little moue' so much admired by Edwardian novelists.

He said: 'Mademoiselle, will you have the kindness of an angel? Will you take a little message to M. Callard?' She hesitated and he added in English: 'And do you know that there is a large and I believe poisonous spider on your neck?'

She flashed a smile: 'Monsieur makes a *grivoiserie* at my expense. He says naughty things in English, I believe, "to pull a carrot at me." '

'Doesn't speak English,' Alleyn said to Troy without moving his eyes from the girl. He took out his pocketbook, wrote a brief message and slid it across the counter with a 500 franc note underneath. He playfully lifted the girl's hand and closed it over both.

'Well, I must say!' said Troy, and she thought how strange it was that she could be civilized and amused and perhaps a little annoyed at this incident.

With an air that contrived to suggest that Alleyn as well as being a shameless flirt was also a gentleman, the girl moved back from the counter, glanced through the plate-glass windows of the main office where a number of typists and two clerks looked on with undisguised curiosity, seemed to change her mind, and came out by way of a gate at the top of the counter and walked with short steps to the double doors. The commissionaire opened them for her. They looked impassively at each other. She passed through and he followed her.

Alleyn said: 'She's taking my note to the boss. It ought to surprise him. By all the rules he should have been rung up and told we're on the road to St Céleste.'

'Will he see us?'

'I don't see how he can refuse.'

While they waited, Troy looked at the spidery stairs, the blind doors and the distant galleries. 'If he should appear!' she thought. 'If there could be another flash of yellow and brown.' She began to imagine how it would be when they found Ricky. Would his face be white with smudges under the eyes? Would he cry in the stifled inarticulate fashion that always gripped her heart in a stricture? Would he shout and run to her? Or, by a merciful chance, would he behave like the other boy and want to stay with his terrible new friends? She thought: 'It's unlucky to anticipate. He may not be here at all. If we don't find him before tonight I think I shall crack up.'

She knew Alleyn's mind followed hers as closely as one mind can follow another and she knew that as far as one human being can find solace in another she found solace in him, but she suffered, nevertheless, a great loneliness of spirit. She turned to him and saw compassion and anger in his eyes.

'If anything could make me want more to get these gentlemen,' he said, 'it would be this. We'll get them, Troy.'

'Oh, yes,' she said. 'I expect you will.'

'Ricky's here. I know it in my bones. I promise you.'

The girl came back through the double doors. She was very formal. 'Monsieur Callard will see Monsieur and Madame,' she said. The commissionaire waited on the far side, holding one door open. As Alleyn stood aside for Troy to go through, the girl moved nearer to him. Her back was turned to the commissionaire. Her eyes made a sign of assent.

He murmured: 'And I may understand – what, Mademoiselle?'

'What Monsieur pleases,' she said and minced back to the desk.

Alleyn caught Troy up and took her arm in his hand. The commissionaire was several paces ahead. 'Either that girl's given me the tip that Ricky's here,' Alleyn muttered, 'or she's the smartest job off the skids in the Maritime Alps.'

'What did she say?'

'Nothing. Just gave the go-ahead signal.'

'Good lord! Or did it mean Ricky?'

'It'd better mean Ricky,' Alleyn said grimly.

They were in an inner hall, heavily carpeted and furnished with modern wall-tables and chairs. They passed two doors and were led to a third in the end wall. The commissionaire opened it and went in. They heard a murmur of voices. He returned and asked them to enter.

A woman with blue hair and magnificent poise rose from a typewriter. '*Bon jour, Monsieur et Madame,*' she said. '*Entrez s'il vous plaît.*' She opened another door. '*Monsieur et Madame Allen,*' she announced.

'Come right in!' invited a voice in hearty American. 'C'm on! Come right in.'

V

M. Callard was a fat man with black eyebrows and bluish chops. He was not a particularly evil-looking man: rather one would have said that there was something meretricious about him. His mouth looked as if it had been disciplined by meaningless smiles and his eyes seemed to assume rather than possess an air of concentration. He was handsomely dressed and smelt of expensive cigars. His English was fluent and falsely Americanized with occasional phrases and inflections that made it clear he wasn't speaking his native tongue.

'Well, well, well,' he said, pulling himself up from his chair and extending his hand. The other held Alleyn's note. 'Very pleased to meet you, Mr – I just can't quite get the signature.'

'Alleyn.'

'Mr Allen.'

'This is my wife.'

'Mrs Allen,' said M. Callard bowing. 'Now, let's sit down, isn't it, and get acquainted. What's all this I hear about Junior?'

Alleyn said: 'I wouldn't have bothered you if we hadn't by chance heard that our small boy who went missing early this afternoon, had, Heavens knows how, turned up at your works. In your office they didn't seem to know anything about him and our French doesn't go very far. It's a great help that your English is so good. Isn't it darling?' he said to Troy.

'Indeed, yes. M. Callard, I can't tell you how anxious we are. He just disappeared from our hotel. He's only six and it's so dreadful – '

To her horror Troy heard her voice tremble. She was silent.

'Now, that's just too bad,' M. Callard said. 'And what makes you think he's turned up in this part of the world?'

'By an extraordinary chance,' Alleyn said, 'the man we've engaged to drive us took his car up this road earlier this afternoon and he saw Ricky in another car with a man and woman. They turned in at the entrance to your works. We don't pretend to understand all this, but you can imagine how relieved we are to know he's all right.'

M. Callard sat with a half smile on his mouth, looking at Alleyn's left ear. 'Well,' he said, 'I don't pretend to understand it either. Nobody's told me anything. But we'll soon find out.'

He bore down with a pale thumb on his desk bell. The blue-haired secretary came in and he spoke to her in French.

'It appears,' he said, 'that Monsieur and Madame have been given information by their chauffeur that their little boy who has disappeared was seen in an auto somewhere on our premises. Please make full inquiries, Mademoiselle in all departments.'

'At once, Monsieur le Directeur,' said the secretary and went out.

M. Callard offered Troy a cigarette and Alleyn a cigar both of which were refused. He seemed mysteriously to expand. 'Maybe,' he said, 'you folks are not aware there's a gang of kidnappers at work along this territory. Child-kidnappers.'

Alleyn at once broke into a not too coherent and angry dissertation on child-kidnappers and the inefficiency of the police. M. Callard listened with an air of indulgence. He had taken a cigar and he rolled it continuously between his thumb and fingers, which were flattish and backed with an unusual amount of hair. This movement was curiously disturbing. But he listened with perfect courtesy to Alleyn and every now and then made sympathetic noises. There was, however, a certain quality in his stillness which Alleyn recognized. M. Callard was listening to him with only part of his attention. With far closer concentration he listened for something outside the room: and for this, Alleyn thought, he listened so far in vain.

The secretary came back alone.

She told M. Callard that in no department of the works nor among the gardens outside had anyone seen a small boy. Troy only understood the tenor of this speech. Alleyn, who had perfectly understood the whole of it, asked to have it translated. M. Callard obliged, the secretary withdrew and the temper of the interview hardened. Alleyn got up and moved to the desk. His hand rested on top of a sound system apparatus. Troy found herself looking at the row of switches and the loud-speaker and at the good hand above them.

Alleyn said he was not satisfied with the secretary's report. M. Callard said he was sorry, but evidently there had been some mistake. Alleyn said he was certain there was no mistake. Troy, taking her cue from him, let something of her anxiety and anger escape. M. Callard received her outburst with odious compassion and said it was quite understandable that she was not just one hundred per cent reasonable. He rose but before his thumb could reach the bell-push Alleyn said that he must ask him to listen to the account given by their chauffeur.

'I'm sure that when you hear the man you will understand why we are so insistent,' Alleyn said. And before Callard could do anything to stop him he went out, leaving Troy to hold, as it were, the gate open for his return.

Callard made a fat, wholly Latin gesture, and flopped back into his chair. 'My dear lady,' he said, 'this good man of yours is just a lit- tle difficult. Certainly I'll listen to your chauffeur who is, no doubt, one of the local peasants. I know how they are around here. They say what they figure you want them to say and they don't worry about facts: it's not conscious lying, it's just that they come that way. They're just naturally obliging. Now, your husband's French isn't so hot and my guess is, he's got this guy a little bit wrong. We'll soon find out if I'm correct. Pardon me if I make a call. This is a busy time with us and right now I'm snowed under.'

Having done his best to make Troy thoroughly uncomfortable he put through a call on his telephone, speaking such rapid French that she scarcely understood a word of what he said. He had just hung up the receiver when something clicked. This sound was followed by a sense of movement and space beyond the office. M. Callard glanced at the switchboard on his desk and said: '*Ah?*' A disembodied voice spoke in mid-air.

'*Monsieur le Directeur? Le service de transport avise qu'il est incapable d'expédier la marchandise.*'

'*Qu'est ce qu'il se passe?*'

'*Rue barrée!*'

'*Bien. Prenez garde. Remettez la marchandise à sa place.*'

'*Bien, Monsieur,*' said the voice. The box clicked and the outside world was shut off.

'My, oh my,' sighed M. Callard, 'the troubles I have!' He opened a ledger on his desk and ran his flattened forefinger down the page.

Troy thought distractedly that perhaps he was right about Raoul and then, catching herself up, remembered that Raoul had in fact never seen the car drive in at the factory gates with Ricky and a man and woman in it, that they were bluffing and that perhaps all Alleyn's and Dupont's theories were awry. Perhaps this inhuman building had never contained her little son. Perhaps it was idle to torture herself by thinking of him: near at hand yet hopelessly with- held.

M. Callard looked at a platinum mounted wristwatch and then at Troy, and sighed again. 'He's trying to shame me out of this office,' she thought and she said boldly: 'Please don't let me interrupt your work.' He glanced at her with a smile from which he seemed to make no effort to exclude the venom.

'My work requires the closest concentration, Madame,' said M. Callard.

'Sickening for you,' said Troy.

Alleyn came back with Raoul at his heels. Through the door Troy caught a glimpse of the blue-haired secretary, half-risen from her desk, expostulation frozen on her face. Raoul shut the door.

'This is Milano, M. Callard,' Alleyn said. 'He will tell you what he saw. If I have misunderstood him you will be able to correct me. He doesn't speak English.'

Raoul stood before the desk and looked about him with the same air of interest and ease that had irritated Dr Baradi. His gaze fell for a moment on the sound system apparatus and then moved to M. Callard's face.

'Well, my friend,' said M. Callard in rapid French. 'What's the tarradiddle Monsieur thinks you've told him?'

'I think Monsieur understood what I told him,' Raoul said cheerfully and even more rapidly. 'I spoke slowly and what I said, with all respect, was no tarradiddle. With Monsieur's permission I will repeat it. Early this afternoon, I do not know the exact time, I drove my young lady along the road to the factory. I parked my car and we climbed a little way up the hillside opposite the gates. From here we observed a car come up from the main road. In it were a man and a woman and the small son of Madame and Monsieur who is called Riki. This little Monsieur Riki was removed from the car and taken into the factory. That is all, Monsieur le Directeur.'

M. Callard's eyelids were half-closed. His cigar rolled to and fro between his fingers and thumb.

'So. You see a little boy and a man and a woman. Let me tell you that early this afternoon a friend of my works superintendent visited the factory with his wife and boy and that undoubtedly it was this boy whom you saw.'

'With respect, what is the make of the car of the friend of Monsieur's works superintendent?'

'I do not concern myself with the cars of my employees' acquaintances.'

'Or with the age and appearance of their children, Monsieur?'

'Precisely.'

'This was a light blue Citroën, 1946, Monsieur, and the boy was Riki, the son of Monsieur and Madame, a young gentleman whom I know well. He was not two hundred yards away and was speaking his bizarre French, the French of an English child. His face was as unmistakable,' said Raoul, looking full into M. Callard's face, 'as Monsieur's own. It was Riki.'

M. Callard turned to Alleyn: 'How much of all that did you get?' he asked.

Alleyn said: 'Not a great deal. When he talks to us he talks slowly. But I'm sure – '

'Pardon me,' M. Callard said and turned smilingly to Raoul.

'My friend,' he said, 'you are undoubtedly a conscientious man. But I assure you that you are making a mistake. Mistakes can cost a lot of money. On the other hand, they sometimes yield a profit. As much, for the sake of argument, as five thousand francs. Do you follow me?'

'No, Monsieur.'

'Are you sure? Perhaps,' suggested M. Callard, thrusting his unoccupied hand casually into his breast pocket, 'when we are alone I may have an opportunity to make my meaning plainer and more acceptable.'

'I regret. I shall still be unable to follow it,' Raoul said.

M. Callard drew a large handkerchief from his breast pocket and dabbed his lips with it. '*Sacré nigaud,*' he said pleasantly and shot a venomous glance at Raoul before turning to Troy and Alleyn.

'My dear good people,' he said expansively, 'I'm afraid this boy has kidded you along quite a bit. He admits that he did not get a good look at the child. He was up on the hillside with a dame and his attention was – well, now,' said M. Callard smirking at Troy, 'shall we say kind of semi-detached. It's what I thought. He's told you what he figures you'd like to be told and if you ask him again he'll roll out the same tale all over.'

'I'm afraid I don't believe that,' said Alleyn.

'I'm afraid you don't have an alternative,' said M. Callard. He turned on Raoul. '*Fichez-moi le camp,*' he said roughly.

'What's that?' Alleyn demanded.

'I've told him to get out.'

'*Vous permettez, Madame, Monsieur?*' Raoul asked and placed himself between the two men with his back to M. Callard.

'What?' Alleyn said. He winked at Raoul. Raoul responded with an ineffable grimace. 'What? Oh, all right. *All right. Oui. Allez.*'

With a bow to Troy and another that was rather less respectful than a nod to M. Callard, Raoul went out. Alleyn walked up to the desk and took up his former position.

'I'm not satisfied,' he said.

'That's too bad.'

'I must ask you to let me search this building.'

'You!' said M. Callard and laughed. 'Pardon my mirth but I guess there'd be two of you gone missing if you tried that one. This is quite a building, Mr' – he glanced again at Alleyn's note – 'Mr Allen.'

'If it's as big as all that your secretary's inquiries were too brief to be effective. I don't believe any inquiries have been made.'

'*Look!*' M. Callard said and smacked the top of his desk with a flat palm. 'This sound system operates throughout these works. I can speak to every department or all departments together. We don't have to go round on a hiking trip when we make general inquiries. Now!'

'Thank you,' Alleyn said and his hand darted over the switchboard. There was a click. '*Ricky!*' he shouted and Troy cried out: '*Ricky! Are you there! Ricky!*'

And as if they had conjured it from the outer reaches of space a small voice said excitedly: 'They've come! *Mummy!*'

A protesting outcry was cut off as M. Callard struck at Alleyn's hand with a heavy paper knife. At the same moment M. Dupont walked into the room.

CHAPTER 8

Ricky Regained

Troy could scarcely endure the scene that followed and very nearly lost control of herself. She couldn't understand a word of what was said. Alleyn held her by the arm and kept saying: 'In a minute, darling. He'll be here in a minute. He's all right. Hold on. He's all right.'

Dupont and Callard were behaving like Frenchmen in English farces. Callard, especially, kept giving shrugs that began in his middle and surged up to his ears. His synthetic Americanisms fell away and when he threw a sentence in English at Troy or at Alleyn he spoke it like a Frenchman. He shouted to Alleyn: 'If I lose my temper it is natural. I apologize. I knew nothing. It was the fault of my staff. There will be extensive dismissals. I am the victim of circumstances. I regret that I struck you.'

He pounded his desk bell and shouted orders into the sound system. Voices from the other places said in midair: *'Immédiatement, M le Directeur.' 'Tout de suite, Monsieur.' 'Parfaitement, M. le Directeur.'* The secretary ran in at a high-heeled double and set up a gabble of protest which was cut short by Dupont. She teetered out again and could be heard yelping down her own sound system.

With one part of her mind Troy thought of the door and how it must soon open for Ricky, and with another part she thought it was unlucky to anticipate this event and that the door would open for the secretary or a stranger and, so complicated were her thoughts, she also wondered if, when she saw Ricky, he would have a blank look of panic in his eyes, or if he would cry or be casually pleased or if these speculations too were unlucky and he wouldn't come at all.

Stifled and terrified, she turned on Dupont and Callard and cried out: 'Please speak English. You both can. Where is he? Why doesn't he come?'

'Madame,' said Dupont gently, 'he is here.'

He had come in as she turned away from the door.

The secretary was behind him. She gave his shoulder a little push and he made a fastidious movement away from her and into the room. Troy knew that if she spoke her voice would shake. She held out her hand.

'Hallo, Rick,' Alleyn said. 'Sorry we've muddled you about.'

'You have, rather,' Ricky said. He saw Dupont and Callard. 'How do you do,' he said. He looked at Troy and his lip trembled. He ran savagely into her arms and fastened himself upon her. His fierce hard little body was rammed against hers, his arms gripped her neck and his face burrowed into it. His heart thumped piston-like at her breast.

'We'll take him out to the car,' Alleyn said.

Troy rose, holding Ricky with his legs locked about her waist. Alleyn steadied her and they went out through the secretary's room and the lobby and the entrance hall to where Raoul waited in the sunshine.

II

When they approached the car Ricky released his hold on his mother as abruptly as he had imposed it. She put him down and he walked a little distance from her. He acknowledged Raoul's greeting with an uncertain nod and stood with his back turned to them apparently looking at M. Dupont's car, which was occupied by three policemen.

Alleyn murmured; 'He'll get over it all right. Don't worry.'

'He thinks we've let him down. He's lost his sense of security.'

'We can do something about that. He's puzzled. Give him a moment and then I'll try.'

He went over to the police car.

'I suppose,' Ricky said to nobody in particular, 'Daddy's not going away again.'

Troy moved close to him. 'No, darling, I don't think so. Not far anyway. He's on a job, though, helping the French police.'

'Are those French policemen?'

'Yes. And the man you saw in that place is a French detective.'

'As good as Daddy?'

'I don't expect quite as good but good all the same. He helped us find you.'

Ricky said: 'Why did you let me be got lost?'

'Because,' Troy explained with a dryness in her throat, 'Daddy didn't know about it. As soon as he knew, it was all right, and you weren't lost any more. We came straight up here and got you.'

The three policemen were out of the car and listening ceremoniously to Alleyn. Ricky watched them. Raoul, standing by his own car, whistled a lively air and rolled a cigarette.

'Let's go and sit with Raoul, shall we?' Troy suggested, 'until Daddy's ready to come home with us.'

Ricky looked miserably at Raoul and away again. 'He might be cross with me,' he muttered.

'*Raoul* cross with you, darling? *No.* Why?'

'Because – because – I – lost – I lost – '

'No, you didn't!' Troy cried. 'We found it. Wait a moment.' She rootled in her bag. 'Look.'

She held out the little silver goat. Ricky's face was transfused with a flush of relief. He took the goat carefully into his square hands. 'He's the nicest thing I've ever had,' he said. 'He shines in the night. *Il s'illume.* Raoul and lady said he does.'

'Has he got a name?'

'His name's Goat,' Ricky said.

He walked over to the car. Raoul opened the door and he got into the front seat casually displaying the goat.

'*C'est ça,*' Raoul said comfortably. He glanced down at Ricky, nodded three times with an air of sagacity and lit his cigarette. Ricky shoved one hand in the pocket of his shorts and leant back. 'Coming, Mum?' he asked.

Troy got in beside him. Alleyn called Raoul who swept off his chauffeur's cap to Troy and excused himself.

'What's going to happen?' Ricky asked.

'I think Daddy's got a job for them. He'll come and tell us in a minute.'

'Could we keep Raoul?'

'While we are here I think we can.'

'I daresay he wouldn't like to live with us always.'

'Well, his family lives here. I expect he likes being with them.'

'I do think he's nice, however. Do you?'

'Very,' Troy said warmly. 'Look, there he goes with the policemen.'

M. Dupont had appeared in the factory entrance. He made a crisp signal. Raoul and the three policemen walked across and followed him into the factory. Alleyn came to the car and leant over the door. He pulled Ricky's forelock and said: 'How's the new policeman?'

Ricky blinked at him. 'Why?' he asked.

'I think you've helped us to catch up with some bad lots.'

'Why?'

'Well, because they thought we'd be so busy looking for you we wouldn't have time for them. But sucks to them, we didn't lose you and do you know why?'

'Why?'

'Because you waved from the balcony and dropped your silver goat and that was a clue and because you called out to us and we knew you were there. Pretty good.'

Ricky was silent.

Troy said: 'Jolly good, helping Daddy like that.'

Ricky was turned away from her. She could see the charming back of his neck and the curve of his cheek. He hunched his shoulders and tucked in his chin.

'Was the fat, black smelly lady a bad lot?' he asked in a casual tone.

'Not much good,' Alleyn said.

'Where is she?'

'Oh, I shut her up. She's a silly old thing, really. Better shut up.'

'Was the other one a bad lot?'

'Which one?'

'The Nanny.'

Alleyn and Troy looked at each other over his head.

'The one who fetched you from the hotel?' Alleyn asked.

'Yes, the new Nanny.'

'Oh, *that* one. Hadn't she got a red hat or something?'

'She hadn't got a hat. She'd got a moustache.'

'Really? Was her dress red perhaps?'

'No. Black with kind of whitey blobs.'

'Did you like her?'

'Not extra much. Quite, though. She wasn't bad. I didn't think I had to have a Nan over here.'

'Well, you needn't. She was a mistake. We won't have her.'

'Anyway, she shouldn't have left me there with the fat lady, should she, Daddy?'

'No,' Alleyn reached over the door and took the goat. He held it up admiring it. 'Nice, isn't it?' he said. 'Did she speak English, that Nanny?'

'Not properly. A bit. The man didn't.'

'The driver?'

''M.'

Was he a chauffeur like Raoul?'

'No. He had funny teeth. Sort of black. Funny sort of driver for a person to have. He didn't have a cap like Raoul or anything. Just a red beret and no coat and he wasn't very clean either. He's Mr Garbel's driver, only Mr Garbel's a *Mademoiselle* and not a Mr.'

'*Is* he? How d'you know?'

'May I have Goat again, please? Because the Nanny said you were waiting for me in Mademoiselle Garbel's room. Only you weren't. And because Mademoiselle Garbel rang up. The lady in the goat shop has got other people that light themselves at night too. Saints and shepherds and angels and Jesus. Pretty decent.'

'I'll have a look next time I'm there. When did Miss Garbel ring up, Rick?'

'When I was in her room. The fat lady told the Nanny. They didn't know about me understanding, which was sucks to them.'

'What did the fat lady say?'

'"*Mademoiselle Garbel a téléphoné.*" Easy!'

'What did she telephone about, do you know?'

'Me. She said they were to take me away and they told me you would be here. Only – '

Ricky stopped short and looked wooden. He had turned rather white.

'Only – ?' Alleyn said and then after a moment: 'Never mind. I think I know. They went away to talk on the telephone and you went out on the balcony. And you saw Mummy and me waving on our balcony and you didn't quite know what was up with everybody. Was it like that?'

'A bit.'

'Muddly?'

'A bit,' Ricky said tremulously.

'I know. We were muddled too. Then that fat old thing came out and took you away, didn't she?'

Ricky leant back against his mother. Troy slipped her arm round him and her hand protected his two hands and the silver goat. He looked at his father and his lip trembled.

'It was beastly,' he said. 'She was beastly.' And then in a most desolate voice: 'They took me away. I was all by myself for ages in there. They said you'd be up here and you weren't. You weren't here at all.' And he burst into a passion of sobs, his tear-drenched face turned in bewilderment to Alleyn. His precocity fell away from him: he was a child who had not long ago been a baby.

'It's all right, old boy,' Alleyn said, 'it was only a sort of have. They're silly bad lots and we're going to stop their nonsense. We wouldn't have been able to if you hadn't helped.'

Troy said: 'Daddy *did* come, darling. He'll always come. We both will.'

'Well, anyway,' Ricky sobbed, 'another time you'd jolly well better be a bit quicker.'

A whistle at the back of the factory gave three short shrieks. Ricky shuddered, covered his ears and flung himself at Troy.

'I'll have to go in,' Alleyn said. He closed his hand on Ricky's shoulder and held it for a moment. 'You're safe, Rick,' he said, 'you're safe as houses.'

'OK,' Ricky said in a stifled voice. He slewed his head round and looked at his father out of the corner of his eyes.

'Do you think in a minute or two you could help us again? Do you think you could come in with me to the hall in there and tell me if you can see that old Nanny and Mr Garbel's driver?'

'Oh, *no*, Rory,' Troy murmured. 'Not now!'

'Well, of course, Rick needn't if he'd hate it but it'd be helping the police quite a lot.'

Ricky had stopped crying. A dry sob shook him but he said: 'Would you be there? And Mummy?'

'We'll be there.'

Alleyn reached over, picked up Troy's gloves from the floor of the car and put them in his pocket.

'Hi!' Troy said, 'what's that for?'

'"To be worn in my beaver and borne in the van,"' he quoted, 'or something like that. If Raoul or Dupont or I come out and wave will you and Ricky come in? There'll be a lot of people there, Rick, and I just want you to look at 'em and tell me if you can see that Nanny and the driver. OK?'

'OK,' Ricky said in a small voice.

'Good for you, old boy.'

He saw the anxious tenderness in Troy's eyes and added: 'Be kind enough, both of you, to look upon me as a tower of dubious strength.'

Troy managed a grin at him. 'We have every confidence,' she said, 'in our wonderful police.'

'Like hell!' Alleyn said and went back to the factory.

III

He found a sort of comic opera scene in full swing in the central hall. Employees of all conditions were swarming down the curved stairs and through the doors: men in working overalls, in the white coat of the laboratory, in the black jacket of bureaucracy; women equally varied in attire and age: all of them looking in veiled annoyance at their watches. A loud-speaker bellowed continually:

'*Allô, Allô, Messieurs et Dames, faites attention, s'il vous plaît. Tous les employés, ayez la bonté de vous rendre immédiatement au grand vestibule. Allô, allô.*'

M. Dupont stood in a commanding position on the base of the statue and M. Callard, looking sulky, stood at a little distance below him. A few paces distant, Raoul, composed and godlike in his simplicity, surveyed the milling chorus. The gendarmes were nowhere to be seen.

Alleyn made his way to Dupont who was obviously in high fettle and, as actors say, well inside the skin of his part. He addressed Alleyn in English with exactly the right mixture of deference and veiled irritability. Callard listened moodily.

'Ah, Monsieur! You see we make great efforts to clear up this little affair. The entire staff is summoned by Monsieur le Directeur. We question everybody. This fellow of yours is invited to examine the persons. You are invited to bring the little boy, also to examine. Monsieur le Directeur is most anxious to assist. He is immeasurably distressed, is it not, Monsieur le Directeur?'

'That's right,' said M. Callard without enthusiasm.

Alleyn said with a show of huffiness that he was glad to hear that they recognized their responsibilities. M. Dupont bent down as if to soothe him and he murmured: 'Keep going as long as you can. Spin it out.'

'To the last thread.'

Alleyn made his way to Raoul and was able to mutter: 'Ricky describes the driver as a man with black teeth, a red beret, as your friend observed, and no jacket. The woman has a moustache, is bareheaded and wears a black dress with a whitish pattern. If you see a man and woman answering to that description you may announce that they resemble the persons in the car.'

Raoul was silent. Alleyn was surprised to see that his face, usually a ready mirror of his emotions, had gone blank. The loud-speaker kept up its persistent demands. The hall was filling rapidly.

'Well, Raoul?'

'Would Monsieur describe again the young woman and the man?'

Alleyn did so. 'If there are any such persons present you may pretend to recognize them but not with positive determination. The general appearance, you may say, is similar. Then we may be obliged to bring Ricky in to see if he identifies them.'

Raoul made a singular little noise in his throat. His lips moved. Alleyn saw rather than heard the response.

'*Bien, Monsieur,*' he said.

'M. Dupont will address the staff when they are assembled. He will speak at some length. I shall not be present. He will continue proceedings until I return. Your *soi-disant* identification will then take place. *Au'voir, Raoul.*'

'*'Voir, Monsieur.*'

Alleyn edged through the crowd and round the wall of the room to the double doors. The commissionaire stood near them and eyed him dubiously. Alleyn looked across the sea of heads and caught the notice of M. Dupont who at once held up his hand. '*Attention!*' he shouted. '*Approchez-vous d'avantage, je vous en prie.*' The crowd closed in on him and Alleyn, left on the margin, slipped through the doors.

He had at the most fifteen minutes in which to work. The secretary's office was open but the door into M. Callard's room was, as he had anticipated, locked. It responded to his manipulation and he relocked it behind him. He went to the desk and turned on the general intercommunication switch in the sound-system releasing the vague rumour of a not quite silent crowd and the voice of M. Dupont embarked on an elaborate exposé of child-kidnapping on the Mediterranean coast.

Perhaps, Alleyn thought, at this rate he would have a little longer than he had hoped. If he could find a single piece of evidence, enough to ensure the success of a surprise investigation by the French police, he would be satisfied. He looked at the filing cabinet against the walls. The drawers had independent key-holes but the first fifteen were unlocked. He tried them and shoved them back without looking inside. The sixteenth, marked with the letter P, was locked. He got it open. Inside he found a number of the usual folders each headed with its appropriate legend: '*Produits chimiques en commande*,' '*Peron et Cie,*': '*Plastiques,*' and so on. He went through the first of these, memorizing one or two names of drugs he had been told to look out for. *Peron et Cie* was on the suspect list at the Sûreté and a glance at the correspondence showed a close business relationship between the two firms. He flipped over the next six folders and came to the last which was headed: '*Particulier à M. Callard. Secret et confidential.*'

It contained rough notes, memoranda and a number of letters and Alleyn would have given years of routine plodding for the right to put the least of them in his pocket. He found letters from distributors in New York, Cairo, London, Paris and Istanbul, letters that set out modes of conveyance, suggested suitable contacts, gave details of the methods used by other illicit traders and warnings of leakage. He found a list of the guests at the Chèvre d'Argent with Robin Herrington's name scored under and a query beside it.

'*Cette pratique abominable,*' boomed the voice of M. Dupont, warming to its subject, '*cette tache indéracinable sur l'honneur de notre communauté –* '

'Boy,' Alleyn muttered in the manner of M. Callard, 'you said it.'

He laid on the desk a letter from a wholesale firm dealing in cosmetics in Chicago. It suggested quite blandly that '*Crème Veloutée*' in tubes might be a suitable mode of conveyance for diacetylmorphine and complained that the last consignment of calamine lotion had been tampered with in transit and had proved on opening to contain nothing but lotion. It suggested that a certain Customs official had set up in business on his own account and had better be dealt with pretty smartly.

Alleyn unzipped from his breast-pocket a minute and immensely expensive camera. Groaning to himself he switched on M. Callard's fluorescent lights.

' – et, Messieurs, Dames,' thundered the voice of M. Dupont, '*parmi vous, ici, ici, dans cette usine, ce crime dégoûtant a élevé sa tête hideuse.*'

Alleyn took four photographs of the letter, replaced it in the folder and the folder in its file, relocked the drawer and stowed away his lilliputian camera. Then, with an ear to M. Dupont, who had evidently arrived at the point where he could not prolong the cackle but must come to the 'osses, Alleyn made notes, lest he should forget them, of points from the other documents. He returned his notebook to his pocket, switched off the loud-speaker and turned to the door.

He found himself face to face with M. Callard.

'And what the hell,' M. Callard asked rawly, 'do you think you are doing?'.

Alleyn took Troy's gloves from his pocket. 'My wife left these in your office. I hope you don't mind.'

'She did not and I do. I locked this office.'

'If you did someone obviously unlocked it. Perhaps your secretary came back for something.'

'She did not,' said M. Callard punctually. He advanced a step. 'Who the hell are you?'

'You know very well who I am. My boy was kidnapped and brought into your premises. You denied it until you were forced to give him up. Your behaviour is extremely suspicious, M. Callard, and I shall take the matter up with the appropriate authorities in Paris. I have never,' continued Alleyn who had decided to lose his temper, 'heard such damned impudence in my life! I was prepared to give you the benefit of the doubt but in view of your extraordinary behaviour I am forced to suspect that you are implicated personally in this business. And in the former affair of child-stealing. Undoubtedly in the former affair.'

M. Callard began to shout in French, but Alleyn shouted him down. 'You are a child-kidnapper, M. Callard. You speak English like an American. No doubt you have been to America where child-kidnapping is a common racket.'

'*Sacré nom d'un chien –* '

'It's no use talking jargon to me, I don't understand a bloody word of it. Stand aside and let me out.'

M. Callard's face was not an expressive one, but Alleyn thought he read incredulity and perhaps relief in it.

'You broke into my office,' M. Callard insisted.

'I did nothing of the sort. Why the hell should I? And pray what have you got in your office,' Alleyn asked as if on a sudden inspiration, 'to make you so damned touchy about it? Ransom money?'

'*Imbécile! Sale cochon!*'

'Oh, get to hell!' Alley said and advanced upon him. He stood, irresolute, and Alleyn with an expert movement neatly shouldered him aside and went back to the hall.

IV

Dupont saw him come in. Dupont, Alleyn considered, was magnificent. He must have had an appalling job spinning out a short announcement into a fifteen minute harangue but he wore the air of an orator in the first flush of his eloquence.

His gaze swept over Alleyn and round his audience.

'*Eh bien, Messieurs, Dames, chacun à sa tâche. Defilez, s'il vous plaît, devant cette statue . . . Rappelez-vous de mes instructions. Milano!*'

He signalled magnificently to Raoul who stationed himself below him, at the base of the statue. Raoul was pale and stood rigid like a man who faces an ordeal. M. Callard appeared through the double doors and watched with a leaden face.

The gendarmes, who had also reappeared, set about the crowd in a business-like manner, herding it to one side and then sending it across in single file in front of Raoul. Alleyn adopted a consequential air and bustled over to Dupont.

'What's all this, Monsieur?' he asked querulously. 'Is it an identification parade? Why haven't I been informed of the procedure?'

Dupont bent over in a placatory manner towards him and Alleyn muttered: 'Enough to justify a search,' and then shouted: 'I have a right to know what steps are being taken in this affair.'

Dupont spread his blunt hands over Alleyn as if he were blessing him.

'Calm yourself, Monsieur. Everything arranges itself,' he said magnificently and added in French for the benefit of the crowd: 'The gentleman is naturally overwrought. Proceed, if you please.'

Black-coated senior executive officers and white-coated chemists advanced, turned and straggled past with deadpan faces. They were followed by clerks, assistant chemists, stenographers and laboratory assistants. One or two looked at Raoul, but by far the greater number kept on without turning their heads. When they had gone past, the gendarmes directed them to the top of the hall where they were formed up into lines.

Alleyn watched the thinning ranks of those who were yet to come. At the back, sticking together, were a number of what he supposed to be the lesser fry: cleaners, van-drivers, workers from the canteen and porters. In a group of women he caught sight of one a little taller than the rest. She stood with her back towards the statue and at first he could see only a mass of bronze hair with straggling tendrils against the opulent curve of a full neck. Presently her neighbour gave her a nudge and for a moment she turned. Alleyn saw the satin skin and liquid eyes of a Murillo peasant. She had a brilliant mouth and had caught her under-lip between her teeth. Above her upper lip was a pencilling of hair.

Her face flashed into sight and was at once turned away again with a movement that thrust up her shoulder. It was clad in a black material spattered with a whitish-grey pattern.

Behind the girls was a group of four or five men in labourer's clothes: boiler-men, perhaps, or outside hands. As the girls hung back, the gendarme in charge of this group sent the men forward.

They edged self-consciously past the girls and slouched towards Raoul. The third was a thick-set fellow wearing a tight-fitting short-sleeved vest and carrying a red beret. He walked hard on the heels of the men in front of him and kept his eyes to the ground. He had two long red scratches on the cheek nearest to Raoul. As he passed by, Alleyn looked at Raoul who swallowed painfully and muttered: '*Voici le type.*'

Dupont raised an eyebrow. The gendarme at the top of the room moved out quietly and stationed himself near the men. The girls came forward one by one and Alleyn still watched Raoul. The girl in the black dress with the whitish-grey pattern advanced, turned and went past with averted head. Raoul was silent.

Alleyn moved close to Dupont. 'Keep your eye on that girl, Dupont. I think she's our bird.'

'Indeed? Milano has not identified her.'

'I think Ricky will.'

Watched by the completely silent crowd, Alleyn went out of the hall and, standing in the sunshine, waved to Troy. She and Ricky got out of the car and, hand-in-hand, came towards him.

'Come on, Ricky,' he said, 'let's see if you can find the driver and the Nanny. If you do we'll go and call on the goat-shop lady again. What do you say?'

He hoisted his little son across his shoulders and, holding his ankles in either hand, turned him towards the steps.

'Coming, Mum?' Ricky asked.

'Rather! Try and stop me.'

'Strike up the band,' Alleyn said. 'Here comes the Alleyn family on parade.'

He heard his son give a doubtful chuckle. A small hand was laid against his cheek. 'Good old horse,' Ricky said courageously and in an uncertain falsetto: 'How many miles to Babylon?'

'Five score and ten,' Alleyn and Troy chanted and she linked her arm through his.

They marched up the steps and into the hall.

The crowd was still herded at one end of the great room and had broken into a subdued chattering. One of the gendarmes stood near the man Raoul had identified. Another had moved round behind the crowd to a group of girls. Alleyn saw the back of that startlingly bronze head of hair and the curve of the opulent neck. M. Callard had not moved. M. Dupont had come down from his eminence and Raoul stood by himself behind the statue, looking at his own feet.

'A-ha!' cried M. Dupont, advancing with an air of camaraderie, 'so here is Ricketts.'

He reached up his hand, Ricky stooped uncertainly from his father's shoulders and put his own in it.

'This is Ricky,' Alleyn said, 'M. Dupont, Ricky, Superintendent of Police in Roqueville. M. Dupont speaks English.'

'How do you do, sir,' said Ricky in his company voice.

M. Dupont threw a complimentary glance at Troy.

'So we have an assistant,' he said. 'This is splendid. I leave the formalities to you, M. Alleyn.'

'Just have a look at all these people, Rick,' Alleyn said, 'and tell us if you can find the driver and the Nanny who brought you up here.'

Troy and Dupont looked at Ricky. Raoul, behind the statue, continued to look at his boots. Ricky, wearing the blank expression he reserved for strangers, surveyed the crowd. His attention came to a halt on the thick-set fellow in the short-sleeved jersey. Dupont and Troy watched him.

'Mum?' said Ricky.

'Hallo?'

Ricky whispered something inaudible and nodded violently.

'Tell Daddy.'

Ricky stooped his head and breathed noisily into his father's ear.

'OK,' Alleyn said. 'Sure?'

''M.'

'Tell M. Dupont.'

'*Monsieur, voici le chauffeur.*'

'*Montrez avec le doigt, mon brave,*' *said M. Dupont.*

'Point him out, Rick,' said Alleyn.

Ricky had been instructed by his French Nanny that it was rude to point. He turned pink in the face and made a rapid gesture, shooting out his finger at the man. The man drew back his upper lip and bared a row of blackened teeth. The first gendarme shoved in beside him. The crowd stirred and shifted.

'Bravo,' said M. Dupont.

'Now the Nanny,' Alleyn said. 'Can you see her?'

There was a long pause. Ricky, looking at the group of girls at the back, said: 'There's someone that hasn't turned round.'

M. Dupont shouted: *'Présentez-vous de face, tout le monde!'*

The second gendarme pushed through the group of girls. They melted away to either side as if an invisible wedge had been driven through them. The impulse communicated itself to their neighbours: the gap widened and stretched, opening out as Alleyn carried Ricky towards it. Finally Ricky, on his father's shoulders, looked up an exaggerated perspective to where the girl stood with her back to them, her hands clasped across the nape of her neck as if to protect it from a blow. The gendarme took her by the arm, turned her and held down the hands that now struggled to reach her face. She and Ricky looked at each other.

'Hallo, Teresa,' said Ricky.

V

Two cars drove down the Roqueville road. In the first was M. Callard and two policemen and in the second, a blue Citroën, were its owner and a third policeman. The staff of the factory had gone. M. Dupont was busy in M. Callard's office and a fourth gendarme stood, lonely and important, in the empty hall. Troy had taken Ricky, who had begun to be very pleased with himself, to Raoul's car. Alleyn, Raoul and Teresa sat on an ornamental garden seat in the factory grounds. Teresa wept and Raoul gave her cause to do so.

'Infamous girl,' Raoul said, 'to what sink of depravity have you retired? I think of your perfidy,' he went on, 'and I spit.'

He rose, retired a few paces, spat and returned. 'I compare your behaviour,' he continued, 'to its disadvantage with that of Herod, the Jewish Anti-Christ who slit the throats of first-born innocents. Ricky is an innocent and also, Monsieur will correct me if I speak in error, a first-born. He is, moreover, the son of Monsieur, my employer, who, as you observe, can find no words to express his loathing of the fallen woman with whom he finds himself in occupation of this contaminated piece of garden furniture.'

'Spare me,' Teresa sobbed. 'I can explain myself.'

Raoul bent down in order to place his exquisite but distorted face close to hers. 'Female ravisher of infants,' he apostrophized. 'Trafficker in unmentionable vices. Associate of perverts.'

'You insult me,' Teresa sobbed. She rallied slightly. 'You also lie like a brigand. The Holy Virgin is my witness.'

'She blushes to hear you. Answer me,' Raoul shouted and made a complicated gesture a few inches from her eyes. 'Did you not steal the child? Answer!'

'Where there is no intention, there is no sin,' Teresa bawled, taking her stand on dogma. 'I am as pure as the child himself. If anything, purer. They told me his papa wished me to call for him.'

'Who told you?'

'Monsieur,' said Teresa, changing colour.

'Monsieur Goat! Monsieur Filth! In a word, Monsieur Oberon.'

'It is a lie,' Teresa repeated but rather vaguely. She turned her sumptuous and tear-blubbered face to Alleyn. 'I appeal to Monsieur who is an English nobleman and will not spit upon the good name of a virtuous girl. I throw myself at his feet and implore him to hear me.'

Raoul also turned to Alleyn and spread his hands out in a gesture of ineffable poignancy.

'If Monsieur pleases,' he said, making Alleyn a present of the whole situation.

'Yes,' Alleyn said. 'Yes. Well now – '

He looked from one grand-opera countenance to the other. Teresa gazed at him with nerveless compliance, Raoul with grandeur and a sort of gloomy sympathy. Alleyn got up and stood over the girl.

'Now, see here, Teresa,' began. Raoul took a respectful step backwards. 'It appears that you have behaved very foolishly for a long time and you are a fortunate girl to have come out of it without involving yourself in disaster.'

'Undoubtedly,' Teresa said with a hint of complacency. 'I am under the protection of Our Lady of Paysdoux for whom I have a special devotion.'

'Which you atrociously abuse,' Raoul remarked to the landscape.

'Be that as it may,' Alleyn hurriedly intervened. 'It's time you pulled yourself together and tried to make amends for all the harm you have done. I think you must know very well that your employer at the château is a bad man. In your heart you know it, don't you, Teresa?'

Teresa placed her hand on her classic bosom. 'In my heart, Monsieur, I am troubled to suffocation in his presence. It is in my soul that I find him impure.'

'Well, wherever it is, you are perfectly correct. He is a criminal who is wanted by the police of several countries. He has made fools of many silly girls before you. You're lucky not to be in gaol, Teresa. M. le Commissaire would undoubtedly have locked you up if I had not asked him to give you a chance to redeem yourself.'

Teresa opened her mouth and let out an appropriate wail.

'To such deplorable depths have you reduced yourself,' said Raoul who had apparently assumed the maddening role of chorus. 'And me!' he pointed out.

'However,' Alleyn went on, 'we have decided to give you this chance. On condition, Teresa, that you answer truthfully any questions I ask you.'

'The Holy Virgin is my witness – ' Teresa began.

'There are also other less distinguished witnesses,' said Raoul. 'In effect, there is the child-thief Georges Martel with whom you conspired and who is probably your paramour.'

'It is a lie.'

'How,' Alleyn asked, 'did it come about that you took Ricky from the hotel?'

'I was in Roqueville. I go to the market for the *femme de charge*. At one o'clock, following my custom I visited the restaurant of the parents of Raoul who is killing me with cruelty,' Teresa explained, throwing a poignant glance at her fiancé. 'There is a message for me to telephone the château. I do so. I am told to wait as Monsieur wishes to speak to me. I do so. My heart churns in my bosom because that unfortunately is the effect Monsieur has upon it: it is not a pleasurable sensation.'

'Tell that one in another place,' Raoul advised.

'I swear it. Monsieur instructs me: there is a little boy at the Hôtel Royal who is the son of his dear friends, Monsieur and Madame All*aine*. He plans with Monsieur All*aine* a little trick upon Madame, a drollery, a *blague*. They have *nounou* for the child and while they are here I am to be presented by Monsieur as a *nounou* and I am to receive extra salary.'

'More atrocity,' said Raoul. 'How much?'

'Monsieur did not specify. He said an increase. And he instructs me to go to *Le pot de Fleurs* and purchase tuberoses. He tells me, spelling it out, the message I am to write. I have learned a little English from the servants of English guests at the château so I understand. The flowers are from Mademoiselle Garbel who is at present at the château.'

'Is she, by Heaven!' Alleyn ejaculated. 'Have you seen her?'

'Often, Monsieur. She is often there.'

'What does she look like?'

'Like an Englishwoman. All Englishwomen with the exception, no doubt, of Madame, the wife of Monsieur, have teeth like mares and no *poitrine*. So, also, Mademoiselle Garbel.'

'Go on, Teresa.'

'In order that the drollery shall succeed, I am to go to the hôtel while Madame is at *déjeuner*. I shall have the tuberoses and if without inquiry I can ascertain the apartments of Monsieur and Madame I am to go there. If I am questioned I am to say I am the new *nounou* and go up to the *appartements*. I am to remove the little one by the service stairs. Outside Georges Martel, who is nothing to me, waits in his auto. And, from that point Georges will command the proceedings!'

'And that's what you did? No doubt you saw the number of the *appartement* on the luggage in the hall.'

'Yes, Monsieur.'

'And then?'

'Georges drives us to 16 Rue des Violettes where the concierge tells me she will take the little boy to the *appartement* of Mademoiselle Garbel where his father awaits him. I am to stay in the auto in the back streets with Georges. Presently the concierge returns with the little boy. She says to Georges that the affair is in the water as the parents have seen the boy. She says that the orders are to drive at once to the factory. Georges protests: is it not to St Céleste? She says, 'No, at once, quickly to the factory.' The little boy is angry and perhaps frightened and he shouts in French and in English that his papa and mama are not in a factory but in their hotel. But Georges uses blasphemous language, and drives quickly away. And Monsieur will, I entreat, believe me when I tell him

I regretted then very much everything that had happened. I was afraid. Georges would tell me nothing except to keep my mouth sewn up. So I see that I am involved in wickedness and I say several decades of the rosary and try to make amusements for the little boy who is angry and frightened and weeps for the loss of a statue bought from Marie of the Chèvre d'Argent. I think also of Raoul,' said Teresa.

'It's easy to see,' Raoul observed, 'that in the matter of intelligence you have not invented the explosive.' But be was visibly affected, nevertheless. 'You should have known at once that it was a lot of *blague* about the *nounou*.'

'And when you got to the factory?' Alleyn asked.

'Georges took the little boy inside. He then returned alone and we drove round to the garages at the back. I tried to run away and when he grasped my arms I inflicted some formidable scratches on his face. But he threw me a smack on the ear and told me Monsieur Oberon would put me under a malediction.'

'When he emerges from gaol,' Raoul said thoughtfully, 'I shall make a meat *pâté* of Georges. He is already fried.'

'And then, Teresa?'

'I was frightened again, Monsieur, not of Georges but of what Monsieur Oberon might do to me. And presently the whistle blew and a loud-speaker summoned everybody to the hall. And Georges said we should clear out. He walked a little way and peeped round the corner and came back saying there were gendarmes at the gates and we must conceal ourselves. But one of the gendarmes came into the garage and said we must go into the hall. And when we arrived Georges left me saying: get out, don't hang round my heels. So I went to some of the girls I knew and when I heard the announcement of Monsieur le Commissaire and saw Raoul and they said Raoul had seen me: Oh, Monsieur, judge of my feelings! Because, say what you will, Raoul is the friend of my heart and if he no longer loves me I am desolate.'

'You are silly as a fool,' said Raoul, greatly moved, 'but it is true that I love you.'

'Ah!' said Teresa simply, '*Quelle extase!*'

'And upon that note,' said Alleyn, 'we may return to Roqueville and make our plans.'

CHAPTER 9

Dinner in Roqueville

On the return journey Alleyn and Troy sat in the back seat with Ricky between them. Teresa, who was to be given a lift to the nearest bus stop, sat in the front by Raoul. She leant against him in a luxury of reconciliation, every now and then twisting herself sideways in order to gaze into his face. Ricky, who suffered from an emotional hangover and was, therefore, inclined to be querulous and in any case considered Raoul his especial property, looked at these manifestations with distaste.

'Why does she do that?' he asked fretfully. 'Isn't she silly? Does Raoul like her?'

'Yes,' said Troy, hugging him.

'I bet he doesn't really.'

'They are engaged to be married,' said Troy, 'I think.'

'You and Mummy are married, aren't you, Daddy?'

'Yes.'

'Well, Mummy doesn't do it.'

'True,' said Alleyn who was in good spirits, 'but I should like it if she did.'

'Oo, Daddy, you would *not*.'

Teresa wound her arm round Raoul's neck.

'*Je t'adore!*' she crooned.

'Oh, gosh!' said Ricky and shut his eyes.

'All the same,' Alleyn said, 'we'll have to call a halt to her raptures.' He leant forward. 'Raoul, shall we stop for a moment. If Teresa misses her bus you may drive her back from Roqueville.'

'Monsieur, may I suggest that we drive direct to Roqueville where, if Monsieur and Madame please, my parents will be enchanted to invite them to an *apéritif*, or, if preferred, a glass of good wine, and perhaps an early but well-considered dinner. The afternoon has been fatiguing. Monsieur has not eaten, I think, since morning and Madame and Monsieur Ricky may be glad to dine early. Teresa is, no doubt, not expected at the house of infamy, being, as they will suppose, engaged in the abduction of Ricky and in any case I do not permit her to return.'

Teresa made a complicated noise, partly protesting but mostly acquiescent. She essayed to tuck one of Raoul's curls under his cap.

Ricky, with his eyes still shut, said: 'Is Raoul asking us to tea, Daddy? May we go? Just as however,' he added pointedly.

'We shall all go,' Alleyn said, 'including Teresa. Unless, Troy darling, you'd rather take Ricky straight to the hotel.'

Ricky opened his eyes. 'Please not, Mummy. Please let's go with Raoul.'

'All right, my mammet. How kind of Raoul.'

So Alleyn thanked Raoul and accepted his invitation and as they had arrived at the only stretch of straight road on their journey Raoul passed his right arm round Teresa and broke into song.

They drove on through an evening drenched in a sunset that dyed their faces and hands crimson and closely resembled the coloured postcards that are sold on the Mediterranean coast. Two police cars passed them with a great sounding of horns and Alleyn told Troy that M. Dupont had sent for extra men to effect a search of the factory. 'It was too good an opening to miss,' he said. 'He'll certainly find enough evidence to throw a spanner through the plate-glass and thanks for the greater part, let's face it, to young Rick.'

'What have I done, Daddy?'

'Well, you mustn't buck too much about it, but by being a good boy and not making a fuss when you were a bit frightened you've helped us to shut up that factory back there and stop everybody's nonsense.'

'Lavish!' said Ricky.

'Not bad. And now you can pipe down for a bit while I talk to Mummy.'

Ricky looked thoughtfully at his father, got down from his seat and placed himself between Alleyn's knees. He then aimed a blow with his fist at Alleyn's chest and followed it up with a tackle. Alleyn picked him up. 'Pipe down, now,' he said and Ricky, suddenly quiescent, lay against his father and tried to hide his goat from the light in the hope that it would illuminate itself.

'The next thing,' Alleyn said to Troy, 'is to tackle our acquaintances of this morning. And from this point onwards, my girl, you fade graciously but inexorably *out*. You succour your young, reside in your classy pub and if your music grows exigent you go out with Raoul and your young and paint pretty peeps of the bay, glimpsed between sprays of bougainvillaea.'

'And do we get any pretty peeps of you?'

'I expect to be busyish. Would you rather move on to St Céleste or back to St Christophe? Does this place stink for you, after today?'

'I don't think so. We know the real kidnappers are in jug, don't we? And I imagine the last thing Oberon and Co. will try on is another shot at the same game.'

'The very last. After tomorrow night,' Alleyn said, 'I hope they will have no chance of trying anything on except the fruitless contemplation of their past infamies and whatever garments they are allowed to wear in the local lock-up.'

'Really? A coup in the offing?'

'With any luck. But see here, Troy, if you're going to feel at all jumpy we'll pack you both off to – well, home, if necessary.'

'I don't want to go home,' Ricky said from inside Alleyn's jacket. 'I think Goat's beginning to illumine himself, Daddy.'

'Good. What about it, Troy?'

'I'd rather stay, Rory. Indeed, if it wasn't for the young, and yet I suppose because of him, I'd rather muck in on the job. I'm getting a first-hand look at the criminal classes and it's surprising how uncivilized it makes one feel.'

Alleyn glanced at the now hazardously entwined couple in the front seat. He adjusted Ricky and flung an arm round Troy.

'A fat lot they know about it,' he muttered.

As the car slipped down the familiar entry into Roqueville he said: 'And how would you muck in, may I ask?'

'I might say I wanted to do a portrait of Oberon in the lotus bud position and thus by easy degrees become a Daughter of the Sun.'

'Like hell, you might.'

'Anyway, let's stay if only to meet Cousin Garbel.'

She felt Alleyn's arm harden. Like Teresa, she turned to look at her man.

'Rory,' she said, 'did you believe Baradi's story about the charades?'

'Did you?'

'I thought I did. I wanted to. Now, I don't think I do.'

'Nor do I,' Alleyn said.

'*On arrive*,' said Raoul turning into a narrow street, '*Voici L'Escargot Bienvenue*.'

II

It was, as Raoul had said, an unpretentious restaurant. They entered through a *portière* of wooden beads into a whitewashed room with fresh window curtains and nine tables. A serving counter ran along one side and on it stood baskets of fresh fruit, of bread and of *langoustes* bedded in watercress. Bottles of wine and polished glasses filled the shelves behind the counter and an open door led into an inner room where a voice was announcing the weather forecast in French. There were no customers in the restaurant, and Raoul having drawn out three chairs and seated his guests, placed his arm about Teresa's waist and led her into the inner room.

'Maman! Papa!' he shouted.

An excited babble broke out in the background.

'Come to think of it,' Alleyn said, 'I'm damned hungry. Raoul told me his papa was particularly good with steak. *Filet mignon?* What do you think?'

'Are we going to be allowed to pay?'

'No. Which means that good or bad we'll have to come back for more. But my bet is, it'll be good.'

The hubbub in the background came closer and Raoul reappeared, accompanied by a magnificent Italian father and a plump French mother, both of whom he introduced with ceremony. Everybody was very polite, Ricky was made much of and a bottle of extremely good sherry was opened. Ricky was given grenadine.

Healths were drunk, Teresa giggled modestly in the background. M. Milano made a short but succinct speech in which he said he understood that Monsieur and Madame Ah-laine had been instrumental in saving Teresa from a fate that was worse than death and had thus preserved the honour of both families and made possible an alliance that was the dearest wish of their hearts. It was also, other things being equal, a desirable match from the practical point of view. Teresa and Raoul listened without embarrassment and with the detachment of connoisseurs. M. Milano then begged that he and Madame might be excused as they believed they were to have the great pleasure of serving an early dinner and must therefore make a little preparation with which Teresa would no doubt be pleased to assist. They withdrew. Teresa embraced Raoul with passionate enthusiasm and followed them.

Alleyn said: 'Bring a chair, Raoul. We have much to say to each other.'

'Monsieur,' Raoul said without moving, 'no mention has been made of my neglect of duty this afternoon. I mean, Monsieur, my failure, which was deliberate, to identify Teresa.'

'I have decided to overlook it. The circumstances were extraordinary.'

'That is true, Monsieur. Nevertheless, the incident had the effect of incensing me against Teresa who, foolish as she is, has yet got something which caused me to betray my duty. That is why I spoke a little sharply to Teresa. With results,' he added, 'that are, as Monsieur may have noticed, not undesirable.'

'I have noticed. Sit down, Raoul.'

Raoul bowed and sat down. Madame Milano, beaming and business-like returned with a book in her hands. It was a large shabby book with a carefully mended binding. She laid it on the table in front of Ricky.

'When my son was no larger than this little Monsieur,' she said, 'it afforded him much amusement.'

'*Merci, Madame,*' Ricky said, eyeing it.

Troy and Alleyn also thanked her. She made a deprecating face and bustled away. Ricky opened the book. It was a tale of heroic and fabulous adventures enchantingly illustrated with coloured lithographs. Ricky honoured it with the silence he reserved for special occasions. He removed himself and the book to another table. 'Coming, Mum?' he said and Troy joined him. Alleyn looked at the two dark heads bent together over the book and for a moment or two he was lost in abstraction. He heard Raoul catch his breath in a vocal sigh, a sound partly affirmative, partly envious. Alleyn looked at him.

'Monsieur is fortunate,' Raoul said simply.

'I believe you,' Alleyn muttered. 'And now, Raoul, we make a plan. Earlier today, and I must say it feels more like last week, you said you were willing to join in an enterprise that may be a little hazardous: an enterprise that involves an unsolicited visit to the Chévre d'Argent on Thursday night.'

'I remember, Monsieur.'

'Are you still of the same mind?'

'If possible, I feel an increase of enthusiasm.'

'Good, now, listen. It is evident that there is a close liaison between the persons at the château and those at the factory. To-night the commissary will conduct an official search of the factory and he will find documentary evidence of the collaboration. It is also probable that he will find quantities of illicitly manufactured heroin. It is not certain whether he will find direct and conclusive evidence of sufficient weight to warrant an arrest of M. Oberon and Dr Baradi and their associates. Therefore, it would be of great assistance if they could be arrested for some other offence and could be held while further investigations were made.'

'There is no doubt, Monsieur, that their sins are not confined to contraband.'

'I agree.'

'They are capable of all.'

'Not only capable but culpable! I think,' Alleyn said, 'that one of them is a murderer.'

Raoul narrowed his eyes. His stained mechanic's hands lying on the table, fixed and then stretched.

'Monsieur speaks with confidence,' he said.

'I ought to,' Alleyn said dryly, 'considering that I saw the crime.'

'You – ?'

'Through a train window.' And Alleyn described the circumstances.

'Bizarre,' Raoul commented summing up the incident. 'And the criminal, Monsieur?'

'Impossible to say. I had the impression of a man or woman in a white gown with a cowl or hood. The right arm was raised and held a weapon. The face was undistinguishable although there was a strong light thrown from the side. The weapon was a knife of some sort.'

'The animal,' said Raoul who had settled upon this form of reference to M. Oberon, 'displays himself in a white robe.'

'Yes.'

'And the victim was a woman, Monsieur?'

'A woman. Also, I should say, wearing some loose-fitting garment. One saw only a shape against a window blind and then for a second, against the window itself. The man, if it was a man, had already struck and had withdrawn the weapon which he held aloft. The impression was melodramatic,' he added, almost to himself. 'Over-dramatic. One might have believed it was a charade.'

'A charade, Monsieur?'

'Dr Baradi offered the information that there were charades last night. It appears that someone played the part of the Queen of Sheba stabbing King Solomon's principal wife. He himself enacted a concubine.'

'Obviously he is not merely a satyr but also a perverted being – a distortion of nature. Only such a being could invent such a disgusting lie.'

While he grinned at Raoul's scandalized sophistry Alleyn wondered at the ease with which they talked to each other. And, being a modest man, he found himself ashamed. Why, in Heaven's name, he thought, should he not find it good to talk to Raoul who had an admirable mind and a simple approach? He thought: 'We understand so little of our fellow creatures. Somewhere in Raoul there is a limitation but when it comes to the Oberons and Baradis he, probably by virtue of his limitation, is likely to be a much more useful judge than . . .'

'The Queen of Sheba,' Raoul fumed, 'is a Biblical personage. She was the *chère amie* of the Lord's Anointed. To murder he adds a blasphemy which has not even the merit of being true. Unfortunately, he is left-handed,' he added in a tone of acute disappointment.

'Exactly! Moreover, he offered this information,' Alleyn pointed out. 'One must remember the circumstances. The scene, real or simulated, reached its climax as the train drew up and stopped. The blind was released as the woman fell against it. And the man, not necessarily Oberon or Baradi, you know, saw other windows – those of the train.'

'So knowing Monsieur must have been in the train and awake, since he was to alight at Roqueville, this blasphemer produces his lies.'

'It might well be so. M. Dupont and I both incline to think so. Now, you see, don't you, that if murder *was* done in that room in the early hours of this morning, we have great cause to revisit the château. Not only to arrest a killer but to discover why he killed. Not only to arrest a purveyor of drugs who has caused many deaths but to discover his associates. And not only for these reasons, but also to learn if we can what happens in the locked rooms on Thursday nights. For all these reasons, Raoul, it seems imperative that we visit the château.'

'Well, Monsieur.'

'Two courses suggest themselves. I may return openly to inquire after the health of Mademoiselle Truebody. If I do this I shall have to admit that Ricky has been found.'

'They will have learnt as much from the man Callard, Monsieur.'

'I am not so sure. This afternoon M. Dupont ordered that all outward calls from the factory should be blocked at central and that the château should be cut off. At the château they will be extremely anxious to avoid any sign that they are in touch with the factory. They will, of course, question Teresa to whom we must give instructions. If I pursue our first course I shall tell the story of the finding of Ricky to M. Oberon and his guests and I shall utter many maledictions against Callard as a child-kidnapper. And, having seen Miss Truebody, I must appear to go away and somehow or another remain. I've no idea how this can be done. Perhaps, if one had a colleague within the place one might manage it. The alternative is for me, and you, Raoul, to go secretly to the château. To do this we would again need a colleague who would admit and conceal us.'

Raoul put his head on one side and with the air of a collector examining a doubtful treasure. 'Monsieur refers, of course to Teresa.' he said.

'I do.'

'Teresa,' Raoul continued anxiously, 'has not displayed herself to advantage this afternoon. She was *bouleversée* and therefore behaved foolishly. Nevertheless, she is normally a girl of spirit. She is also at the present time desirous of re-establishing herself in my heart. Possibly I have been too lenient with her but one inclines to leniency where one's affections are engaged. I have, as Monsieur knows, forbidden her return to this temple of shame. Nevertheless, where the cause is just and with the protection of Our Lady of Paysdoux (about whose patronage Teresa is so unbecomingly cocksure) there can be no sin.'

'I take it,' Alleyn said, 'that you withdraw your objection?'

'Yes, Monsieur. Not without misgivings, because Teresa is dear to me and, say what you like, it is no place for one's girl.'

'Judging by the lacerations on Georges Martel's face, Teresa is able to defend herself on occasion.'

'True;' Raoul agreed, cheering up. 'She has enterprise.'

'Suppose we talk to her about it?'

'I will produce her.'

Raoul went out to the kitchen.

'Hallo, you two,' Alleyn said.

'Hallo, yourself,' Troy said.

'Daddy, this is a lavish book. I can read it better than Mummy.'

'Don't buck,' Alleyn said automatically.

'Have you sent Raoul to get that nanny person? Teresa?'

'Yes.'

'Why?'

'We've got a job for her.'

'*Not* minding me?'

'No, no. Nothing to do with you, old boy.'

'Well, good, anyway,' said Ricky returning to his book. Raoul came back with Teresa who now wore an apron and seemed to be in remarkably high spirits. On Alleyn's invitation she sat down, using, however, the very edge of her chair. Alleyn told her briefly what he wanted her to do. Raoul folded his arms and scowled thoughtfully at the tablecloth.

'You see, Teresa,' Alleyn said, 'these are bad men and also unfortunately extremely clever men. They think they've made a fool of you as they have of a great many other silly girls. The thing is – are you ready to help Raoul and me and the police of your own country to put a stop to their wickedness?'

'Ah, yes, Monsieur,' said Teresa cheerfully. 'I now perceive my duty and with the help of Raoul and the holy saints, dedicate myself to the cause.'

'Good. Do you think you can keep your head and behave sensibly and with address if an emergency should arise?'

Teresa gazed at him and said that she thought she could.

'Very well. Now, tell me: were you on duty last evening?'

'Yes, Monsieur. During the dinner I helped the housemaids go round the bedrooms and then I worked in the kitchen.'

'Was there a party?'

'A party? Well, Monsieur, there was the new guest, Mlle Wells, who is an actress. And after dinner there was a gathering of all the guests in the private apartments of Monsieur Oberon. I know this because I heard the butler say that Monsieur wished it made ready for a special welcome for Mlle Wells. And this morning,' said Teresa looking prim, 'Jeanne Barre who is an underhousemaid said that Mlle Lock, the English noblewoman, must have taken too much wine because her door was locked with a notice not to disturb and this is always a sign she has been indiscreet.'

'I see. Tell me, Teresa: have you ever seen into the room that is only opened on Thursday night?'

'Yes, Monsieur. On Thursday morning I dust this room and on Fridays it is my duty to clean it.'

'Where is it exactly?'

'It is down the stairs, three flights, from the vestibule, and beneath the library. It is next to the private apartments of M. Oberon.'

'Has it many windows?'

'It has no windows, Monsieur. It is in a very old part of the château.'

'And M. Oberon's rooms?'

'Oh, yes, Monsieur. The *salon* has a window which is covered always by a white blind with a painting of the sun because Monsieur dislikes a brilliant light. So it is always closed. But Monsieur has nevertheless a great lamp fashioned like the sun and many strange ornaments and a strange wheel which Monsieur treasures and a magnificent bed and in the *salon* a rich divan,' said Teresa warming to her subject, 'and an enormous mirror where – 'there she stopped short and blushed.

'Continue,' Raoul ordered, with a face of thunder.

'Where once when I took in *petit déjeuner* I saw Monsieur contemplating himself in a state of nature.'

Alleyn, with an eye on Raoul, said hurriedly, 'Will you describe the room that you clean?'

Raoul reached across the table and moved his forefinger to and fro in front of his beloved's nose. 'Choose your words, my treasure,' he urged. 'Invent nothing. Accuracy is all.'

'Yes, indeed it is,' said Alleyn heartily.

Thus warned, Teresa looked self-consciously at her folded hands and with a slightly sanctimonious air began her recital.

'If you please, Monsieur, it is a large room and at first I thought perhaps it was a chapel.'

'*A chapel?*' Alleyn exclaimed. Raoul made a composite noise suggestive of angry incredulity.

'Yes, Monsieur. I thought perhaps it was reserved for the private devotions of Monsieur Oberon and his friends. Because at one side is a raised place with a table like the holy altar, covered in a cloth which is woven in a rich pattern with gold and silver and jewels. But although one saw the holy cross, there were other things in the pattern that one does not see in altar cloths.'

'The hoof prints of Anathema!' Raoul ejaculated.

'Go on, Teresa,' said Alleyn.

'And on the table there was something that was also covered with an embroidered cloth.'

'What was that, do you suppose?'

Teresa's white eyelids were raised. She gave Alleyn the glance of a cunning child.

'Monsieur must not think badly of me if I tell him I raised the cloth and looked. Because I wanted to see if it was a holy relic.'

'And was it?'

'No, Monsieur. At first I thought it was a big monstrance made of glass. Only it was not a monstrance although in shape it resembled a great sun and inside the sun a holy cross broken and a figure like this.'

With a sort of disgusted incredulity Alleyn watched her trace with her finger on the table, a pentagram. Raoul groaned heavily.

'And it was, as I saw when I looked more closely, Monsieur, a great lamp because there were many, many electric bulbs behind it and behind the sun at the back was a bigger electric bulb than I have ever seen before. So I dropped the heavy cloth over it and wondered.'

'What else did you see?'

'There was nothing else in the room, Monsieur. No chairs or any furniture or anything. The walls were covered with black velvet and there were no pictures.'

'Any doors, other than the one leading from Mr Oberon's room?'

'Yes, Monsieur. There was a door in the wall opposite the table. I didn't notice it the first time I cleaned the room because it is covered like the walls and had no handle. But the second time it was open and I was told to clean the little room beyond.'

'What was it like, this room?'

'On the floor there were many black velvet cushions and one large one like the mattress for a divan. And the walls here also were covered in black velvet and there was a black velvet curtain behind which were hanging a great number of white robes such as the robe Monsieur wears and one black velvet robe. And on the table there were many candles in black candlesticks which I had to clean. There was also a door from the passage into this little room.'

'Nastier and nastier,' Alleyn muttered in English.

'I beg Monsieur's pardon?'

'Nothing. And this was the only door into the big room?'

'No, Monsieur, there was another, very small like a trapdoor behind the table, painted with signs like the signs on the sun-lamp and on the floor.'

'There were signs on the floor?'

'Yes, Monsieur. I had been told to clean the floor, Monsieur. It is a beautiful floor with a pattern made of many pieces of stone and the pattern is the same as the other.' Her finger traced the pentagram again. 'And when I came to clean it, Monsieur; I knew the room was not a chapel.'

'Why?'

'Because the floor in front of the table was as dirty as a farmyard,' said Teresa. 'It was like our yard at my home in the Paysdoux. There had been an animal in the room.'

'An animal!' Raoul ejaculated. 'I believe you! And what sort of animal?'

'That was easy to see,' Teresa said simply. 'It was a goat.'

III

Alleyn decided finally that the following evening he and Raoul would call at the Chèvre d'Argent. He would arrive after the hour of six when, according to Teresa, the entire household would have retired for something known as a private meditation but which was supposed by Teresa to be a sound sleep. It was unusual at this time for anyone to appear and indeed, again according to Teresa, a rule of silence and solitude was imposed from six until nine by Mr Oberon. On Thursdays there was no dinner, but Teresa understood that there was a very late supper at which the guests were served by the Egyptian servant only. Teresa herself was dismissed with the other servants as soon as their late afternoon and early evening tasks were executed. If they didn't encounter any member of the household on their way through the tunnel Alleyn and Raoul were to go past the main entrance and down a flight of steps to a little-used door through which Teresa would admit them. No attention would be paid to Raoul if he was seen by any other servants who might still be about and if Alleyn kept in the background it might be possible to suggest that he was a relative from Marseilles. 'A distinguished relative,' Raoul amended, 'seeing that in appearance and in speech Monsieur is clearly of a superior class.'

Teresa would then conceal Alleyn and Raoul in her own room, where with any luck she would have already secreted two of the white robes. She was pretty certain there were many more in the little ante-room than would be needed by M. Oberon's guests. It would be tolerably easy when she cleaned this room to remove them under cover of the laundry it was her duty to collect from the bedroom.

'Is it not as I have said, Monsieur?' Raoul remarked, indicating his fiancée, 'she is not without enterprise, is Teresa.' Teresa looked modestly at Alleyn and passionately at Raoul.

If all went well, up to this point, Teresa would have done as much as could be expected of her. She would take her departure as usual and could either wait in Raoul's car or catch the evening bus to her home in Paysdoux. It should be possible for Alleyn and Raoul to pass through the house without attracting attention. The cowls of their robes would be drawn over their heads and it might be supposed if they were seen that they were belated guests or even early arrivals for the ceremony: Teresa had heard that occasionally there were extra people on Thursday nights, people staying in Roqueville or in St Chrisophe.

And then? 'Then,' Alleyn said, 'it will be up to us, Raoul.'

The alternative to this plan was tricky. If he was spotted on his way into the Chévre d'Argent, Alleyn would put a bold face on it and say that he had come to see Miss Truebody. No doubt Baradi would be summoned from his private meditation and Alleyn would have to act upon the situations as they arose. Raoul would still call on Teresa and hide in her room.

'All right,' Alleyn said. 'That's as far as we need go. Now Teresa, this evening you will return to the château and M. Oberon will no doubt question you about today's proceedings. You will tell him exactly what happened at the factory, up to and after the identification parade. I will tell him that Ricky identified you. Then, you will say, the police made you come back to Roqueville and asked you many questions, accusing you of complicity in the former kidnapping affair and asking who were your colleagues in that business. You will say that you told the police you know nothing: that Georges Martel offered you a little money to fetch the boy and beyond that you know nothing at all. This is important, Teresa. Repeat it, please.'

Teresa folded her hands and repeated it, prompted without necessity by Raoul.

'Excellent,' Alleyn said. 'And you will, of course, have had no conversation with me. Perhaps it will be well to say if you are asked, that you returned to Roqueville in Raoul's car. You may have been seen doing so. But you will say that Madame and I were so overjoyed on recovering our son that we had nothing to say except that no doubt the police would deal with you.'

'Yes, Monsieur.'

'Have courage, my little one,' Raoul admonished her, 'lie no more than is necessary, you understand, but when you do lie, lie like a brigand. It is in the cause of the angels.'

'Upon whose protection and of that of Our Lady of Paysdoux,' Teresa neatly interpolated, 'I hurl myself.'

'Do so.'

Teresa rose and made a convent-child's bob. Raoul also asked to be excused. As they went together to the door, Alleyn said: 'By the way, did you hear tomorrow's weather forecast for the district?'

'Yes, Monsieur. It is for thunderstorms. There are electrical disturbances.'

'Indeed? How very apropos. Thank you, Raoul.'

'Monsieur,' said Raoul obligingly and withdrew his beloved into the inner room.

Alleyn rejoined his family. 'Did you get much of that?' he asked.

'I've reached exhaustion point for French,' Troy said. 'I can't even try to listen. And Ricky, as you see, is otherwise engaged.'

Ricky looked up from a brilliant picture of two knights engaged in single combat. 'I bet there'll be a wallop when they crash,' he said. 'Whang! I daresay I'd be able to read this pretty soon if we stayed here. I can read a bit, can't I, Mummy?'

'English, you can.'

'I know. So don't you dare say I could French, Daddy?'

'I wouldn't put it past you. Did you know what we were talking about, just now?'

'I wasn't listening much,' Ricky lowered his voice to a polite whisper. 'If it isn't a rude question!' he said, 'when's dinner?'

'Soon. Pipe down, now. I want to talk to Mummy.'

'OK. What are you going to do in Teresa's bedroom tomorrow night, Daddy?'

'I must say I should like to be associated with that inquiry,' said Troy warmly.

'I am changing there for a party.'

'Who's having a party?' Ricky demanded.

'A silver goat. I rather think he lights himself up.'

The door opened. Teresa came in with a tray.

IV

The dinner was superb, the *filets mignons* particularly, being inspired. When it was finished the Alleyns invited the Milanos to join them for *fines* and M. Milano produced a bottle of distinguished cognac. The atmosphere was gay and *comme il faut*. Presently the regular *clientèle* of the house began to come in: quiet middle-class people who greeted Madame Milano and took down their own table-napkins from hooks above their special places. A game of draughts was begun at the corner table. Troy, who had enjoyed herself enormously but was in a trance of fatigue, said she thought that they should go. Elaborate leave-takings were begun. Ricky, full of vegetables and rich gravy and sticky with grenadine, yawned happily and bestowed a smile of enchanting sweetness upon Madame Milano.

'*Mille remerciements, chère Madame,*' he said, stumbling a little over the long word, '*de mon beau repas,*' and held out his hand. Madame made a complicated, motherly, bustling movement and ejaculated, '*Ah, mon Dieu, quel amour d'enfant!*' There followed a great shaking of hands and interchange of compliments and the Alleyns took their departure on the crest of the wave.

Raoul drove them back to their hotel where, regrettably, a great fuss was again made over Ricky, who began to show infantile signs of vainglory and struck an attitude before M. Malaquin, the proprietor, shouting: 'Kidnappers! Huh! Easy!' and was applauded by the hall porter.

Alleyn said: 'That's more than enough from you, my friend,' picked his son up and bore him into the lift. Troy followed wearily, saying: 'Don't be an ass, Ricky darling.' When they got upstairs Ricky, who had been making tentative sounds of defiance, became quiet. When he was ready for bed he turned white and said he wouldn't sleep in 'that room.' His parents exchanged the look that recognizes a dilemma. Troy muttered: 'It *is* trying him a bit high, isn't it?' Alleyn locked the outer door of Ricky's room and took him into the passage to show him that it couldn't be opened. They returned leaving the door between the two rooms open. Ricky hung back. He had shadows under his eyes and looked exhausted and miserable.

'Why can't Daddy go in there?' he asked angrily.

Alleyn thought for a moment and then said: 'I can of course, and you can be with Mummy.'

'Please,' Ricky said. 'Please.'

'Well, I must say that's a bit more civil. Look here, old boy, will you lend me your goat to keep me company? I want to see if it really does light itself up.'

'Yes, of course he will,' said Troy with an attempt at maternal prompting, 'which,' she thought, 'I should find perfectly maddening if I were Ricky.'

Ricky said: 'I want to be in here with Mummy and I want Goat to be here too. Please.' he added.

'All right,' Alleyn said. 'You won't see him light himself up, of course, because Mummy will want her lamp on for some time, won't you darling?'

'For ages and ages,' Troy agreed who desired nothing less.

Ricky said: 'Please take him in there and tell me if he illumines.' He fished his silver goat out of the bosom of his yellow shirt. Alleyn took it into the next room, put it on the bedside table, shut the door and turned out the lights.

He sat on the bed staring into the dark and thinking of the events of the long day and of Troy and Ricky and presently a familiar experience revisited him. He seemed to see himself for the first time, a stranger, a being divorced from experience, a chrysalis from which his spirit had escaped and which it now looked upon, he thought, with astonishment as a soul might look after death at its late housing. He thought: 'I suppose Oberon imagines he's got all this sort of thing taped. Raoul and Teresa too, after *their* fashion and belief. But I have never found an answer.' The illusion, if it was an illusion and he was never certain about this, could be dismissed, but he held to it still and in a little while he found he was looking at a fluorescence, a glimmering of something, no more than a bat-light. It grew into a shape. It was Ricky's little figurine faithfully illuminating itself in the dark. And Ricky's voice still rather fretful, brought Alleyn back to himself.

'Daddy!' he was shouting, 'is he doing it? DADdy!'

'Yes,' Alleyn called, rousing himself, 'he's doing it. Come and see. But shut the door after you or you'll spoil it.'

There was a pause. A blade of light appeared and widened. He saw Ricky come in, a tiny figure in pyjamas. 'Shut the door, Ricky,' Alleyn repeated, 'and wait a moment. If you come to me, you'll see.'

The room was dark again.

'If you'd go on talking, however,' Ricky's voice said, very small and polite, 'I'd find you.'

Alleyn went on talking and Ricky found him. He stood between his father's knees and watched the goat shining. 'He honestly is silver,' he said. 'It's all true.' He leant back against his father, smelling of soap, and laid his relaxed hand on Alleyn's. Alleyn lifted him on to his knee. 'I'm fizzily and motionly zausted,' Ricky said in a drawling voice.

'What in the world does that mean?'

'It's what Mademoiselle says I am when I'm overtired.' He yawned cosily. 'I'll look at Goat a bit more and then I daresay . . . ' His voice trailed into silence.

Alleyn could hear Troy moving about quietly in the next room. He waited until Ricky was breathing deeply and then put him to bed. The door opened and Troy stood there listening. Alleyn joined her. 'He's off,' he said and watched while she went to see for herself. They left the door open.

'I don't know whether that was sound child-psychiatry or a barefaced cheat,' Alleyn said, 'but it's settled his troubles. I don't think he'll be frightened of his bedroom now.'

'Suppose he wakes and gets a panic, poor sweet.'

'He won't. He'll see his precious goat and go to sleep again. What about you?'

'I'm practically snoring on my feet.'

'Fizzily and motionly zausted?'

'Did he say that?'

'Queer little bloke that he is, he did. Shall I stay with you, too, until you go to sleep?'

'But – what about you?'

'I'm going up to the factory. Dupont's still there and Raoul's hiring me his car.'

'Rory, you can't. You must be dead.'

'Not a bit of it. The night's young and it'll be tactful to show up. Besides, I've got to make arrangements for tomorrow.'

'I don't know how you do it?'

'Of course you don't, my darling. You're not a cop.'

She tried to protest but was so bemused with sleepiness that her voice trailed away as Ricky's had done. By the time Alleyn had washed and found himself an overcoat, Troy, too, was in bed and fast asleep. He turned off the lights and slipped out of the room.

Left to itself the little silver goat glowed steadfastly through the night.

CHAPTER 10

Thunder in the Air

Alleyn left word at the office that he might be late coming in and said that unless he himself rang up no telephone calls were to be put through to Troy. Anybody who rang was to be asked to leave a message. It was nine o'clock.

The porter opened the doors and Alleyn ran down the steps to Raoul's car. There was another car drawn up beside it, a long and stylish racing model with a G.B. plate. The driver leant out and said cautiously: 'Hallo, sir.'

It was Robin Herrington.

'Hallo,' Alleyn said.

'I'm on my way back, actually from Douceville. As a matter of fact, I was just coming in on the chance of having a word with you,' Herrington said rapidly and in a muted voice. 'I'm sorry you're going out. I mean, I don't suppose you could give me five minutes. Sorry not to get out but as a matter of fact, I sort of thought – It wouldn't take long. Perhaps I could drive you to wherever you're going and then I wouldn't waste your time. Sort of.'

'Thank you. I've got a car but I'll give you five minutes with pleasure. Shall I join you?'

'Frightfully nice of you sir. Yes, please do.'

'Alleyn walked round and climbed in.

'It won't take five minutes,' Herrington said nervously and was then silent.

'How,' Alleyn asked after waiting for some moments, 'is Miss Truebody?'

Robin shuffled his feet. 'Pretty bad,' he said. 'She was when I left. Pretty bad, actually.'

Alleyn waited again and was suddenly offered a drink. His companion opened a door and a miniature cocktail cabinet lit itself up.

'No, thank you,' Alleyn said. 'What's up?'

'I will, if you don't mind. A very small one.' He gave himself a tot of neat brandy and swallowed half of it. 'It's about Ginny,' he said.

'Oh!'

'As a matter of fact, I'm rather worried about her, which may sound a bit funny.'

'Not very.'

'Oh. Well, you see, she's so terrifyingly young, Ginny. She's only nineteen. And, as a matter of fact, I don't think this is a madly appropriate setting for her.' Alleyn was silent and after a further pause Robin went on,' I don't know if you've any idea what sort of background Ginny's got. Her people were killed when she was a kid. In the blitz. She was trapped with them and hauled out somehow, which rocked her a good deal at the time and actually hasn't exactly worn off even now. She's rather been nobody's baby. Her guardian's a pretty odd old number. More interested in marmosets and miniatures than children, really. He's her great-uncle.'

'You don't mean Mr Penderby Locke?' Alleyn said, recognizing this unusual combination of hobbies.

'Yes, that's right. He's quite famous on his own pitch, I understand, but he couldn't have been less interested in Ginny.'

'Then – Miss Taylor is related to Miss Grizel Locke who, I think, is Mr Penderby Locke's sister, isn't she?'

'Is she? I don't know. Yes, I think she must be,' Robin said, shooting out the words quickly and hurrying on. 'The thing is, Ginny just sort of grew up rather much under her own steam. She was sent to a French family and they weren't much cop, I gather, and then she came back to England and somebody brought her out and she got in with a pretty vivid set and had a miserable love affair with a poor type of chap and felt life wasn't as gay as it's cracked up to be. And this affair bust up when they were staying with some of his chums at Cannes and Ginny felt what was the good of anything anyway, and I must say I know what that's like.'

'She arrived at this philosophy in Cannes?'

'Yes. And she met Baradi and Oberon there. And I was there too, as it happened,' said Robin with a change of voice. 'So we were both asked to come on here. About a fortnight ago.'

'I see. And then?'

'Well, it's a dimmish sort of thing to talk about one's hosts, but I don't think it was a particularly good thing, her coming. I mean it's all right for oneself.'

'Is it?'

'Well, I don't know. Just to do once and – and perhaps not do again. Quite amusing, really,' said Robin miserably. 'I mean, I'm not madly zealous about being a Child of the Sun. I just thought it might be fun. Of a sort. I mean, one knows one's way about.'

'One would, I should think, need to.'

'Ginny doesn't,' Robin said.

'No?'

'She thinks she does, poor sweet, but actually she hasn't a clue when it comes to – well, to this sort of party, you know.'

'What sort of party?'

Robin pushed his glass back and shut the cupboard with a bang. 'You saw, didn't you, sir?'

'I believe Dr Baradi is a very good surgeon. I only met the others for a few moments, you know.'

'Yes, but – well, you know Annabella Wells, don't you? She said so.'

'We crossed the Atlantic in the same ship. There were some five hundred other passengers.'

'I'd have thought she'd have shown up if there'd been five million,' Robin said with feeling. Alleyn glanced at his watch.

'I'm sorry, I'm not exactly pressing ahead with this,' Robin said.

'Don't you think you'd better tell me what you want me to do?'

'It sounds odd. MrsAllen will think it such cheek.'

'Troy? How can it concern her?'

'I – well, I was wondering if MrsAllen would ask Ginny to dinner tomorrow night.'

'Why tomorrow night, particularly?'

Robin muttered: 'There's going to be a sort of party up there. I'd rather Ginny was out of it.'

'Would she rather be out of it?'

'Hell!' Robin shouted. 'She would if she were herself. My God, she would!'

'And what exactly,' Alleyn asked, 'do you mean by that?'

Robin hit the wheel of his car with his clenched fist and said almost inaudibly: 'He's got hold of her. Oberon. She thinks he's the bottom when he's not – it's just one of those bloody things.'

'Well,' Alleyn said, 'we'd be delighted if Miss Taylor would dine with us but don't you think she'll find the invitation rather odd? After all, we've scarcely met her. She'll probably refuse.'

'I'd thought of that,' Robin said eagerly. 'I know. But I thought if I could get her to come for a run in the car, I'd suggest we called on MrsAllen. Ginny liked MrsAllen awfully. And you, sir, if I may say so. Ginny's interested in art and all that and she was quite thrilled when she knew MrsAllen was Agatha Troy. So I thought if we might we could call about cocktail time and I'd say I'd got to go somewhere to see about something for the yacht or something and then I could ring up from somewhere and say I'd broken down.'

'She would then take a taxi back to the Chèvre d'Argent.'

Robin gulped. 'Yes, I know,' he said. 'But – well, I thought perhaps by that time Mrs Allen might have sort of talked to her and got her to see. Sort of.'

'But why doesn't Miss Locke talk to her? Surely, as her aunt – What's the matter?'

Robin had made a violent ejaculation. He mumbled incoherently: 'Not that sort. I've told you. They didn't care about Ginny.'

Alleyn was silent for a moment.

'I know it's a hell of a lot to ask,' Robin said desperately.

'I think it is,' Alleyn said, 'when you are so obviously leaving most of the facts out of your story.'

'I don't know what you mean.'

'You are asking us to behave in a difficult and extremely odd manner. You want us, in effect, to kidnap Miss Taylor. We have had,' Alleyn said, 'our bellyful of kidnapping this afternoon. I suppose you heard about Ricky.'

Robin made an inarticulate noise that sounded rather like a groan. 'I know. Yes. We did hear. I'm awfully sorry. It must be terribly worrying.'

'And how,' Alleyn asked, 'did you hear about it?' and would have given a good deal to have had a clear view of Robin's face.

'Well, I – well, we rang up the hotel this afternoon.'

'I thought you said you had been to Douceville all the afternoon.'

'Hell!'

'I think you must have known much earlier that Ricky was kidnapped, didn't you?'

'Look here, sir, I don't know what to say.'

'I'll tell you. If you want me to help you with this child, Ginny, and I believe you do, you will answer, fully and truthfully, specific questions that I shall put to you. If you don't want to answer, we'll say goodnight and forget we had this conversation. But don't lie. I shall know,' Alleyn said mildly, 'if you lie.'

Robin waited for a moment and then said: 'Please go ahead.'

'Right. What precisely do you expect to happen at this party?'

A car came down the square. Its headlights shone momentarily on Robin's face. It looked very young and frightened, like the face of a sixth form boy in serious trouble with his tutor. The car turned and they were in the dark again.

Robin said: 'It's a regular thing. They have it on Thursday nights. It's a sort of cult. They call it The Rites of the Children of the Sun in the Outer, and Oberon's the sort of high priest. You have to swear not to talk about it. I've sworn. I can't talk. But it ends pretty hectically. And tomorrow Ginny – I've heard them – Ginny's cast for the leading part.'

'And beforehand?'

'Well – it's different from ordinary nights. There's no dinner. We go to our rooms until the Rites begin at eleven. We're meant not to speak to each other or anything.'

'Do you not eat or drink?'

'Oh, there are drinks. And so on.'

'What does "so on" mean?' Robin was silent. 'Do you take drugs? Reefers? Snow?'

'What makes you think that?'

'Come on. Which is it?'

Reefers mostly. There's food when we smoke. There has to be. I don't know if they are the usual kind. Oberon doesn't smoke. I don't think Baradi does.'

'Are they traffickers?'

'I don't know much about them.'

'Do you know that much?'

'I should think they might be.'

'Have they asked you to take a hand?'

'Look,' Robin said, 'I'm sorry, but I've got to say it. I don't know much about you either, sir. I mean, I don't know that you won't –' He had turned his head and Alleyn knew he was peering at him.

'Inform the police?' Alleyn suggested.

'Well – you might.'

'Come: you don't, as you say, know me. Yet you've elected to ask me to rescue this wretched child from the clutches of your friends. You can't have it both ways.'

'You don't know,' Robin said. 'You don't know how tricky it all is. If they thought I'd talked to you!'

'What would they do?'

'Nothing!' Robin cried in a hurry. 'Nothing! Only I've accepted, as one says, their hospitality.'

'You *have* got your values muddled, haven't you?'

'Have I? I daresay I have.'

'Tell me this. Has anything happened recently – I mean within the last twenty-four hours – to precipitate the situation?'

Robin said: 'Who are you?'

'My dear chap, I don't need to be a thought-reader to see there's a certain urgency behind all this preamble.'

'I suppose not. I'm sorry. I'm afraid I can't answer any more questions. Only – only, for God's sake, sir, will you do something about Ginny?'

'I'll make a bargain with you. I gather that you want to remove the child without giving a previous warning to the house-party.'

'That's it, sir. Yes.'

'All right. *Can* you persuade her, in fact, to drive into Roqueville at six o'clock?'

'I don't know. I was gambling on it. If *he's* not about. I might. She – I think she is quite fond of me,' Robin said humbly, 'when he's not there to bitch it all up.'

'Failing a drive, could you get her to walk down to the car park?'

'I might do that. She wants to buy one of old Marie's silver goats.'

'Would it help to tell her we had rung up and asked if she would choose a set of the figures for Ricky? Aren't there groups of them for Christmas? Cribs?'

'That might work. She'd like to do that.'

'All right. Have your car waiting and get her to walk on to the park. Suggest you drive down to our hotel with the figures.'

'You know, sir, I believe that'd do it.'

'Good. Having got her in the car it's up to you to keep her away from the château. Take her to see Troy by all means. But I doubt if you'll get her to stay to dinner. You may have to stage a break-down on a lonely road. I don't know. Use your initiative. Block up the air vent in your petrol cap. One thing more. Baradi, or some-one, said something about a uniform of sorts that you all wear on occasion.'

'That's right. It's called the mantle of the sun. We wear them about the house and – and always on Thursday nights.'

'It it the white thing Oberon had on this morning?'

'Yes. A sort of glorified monk's affair with a hood.'

'Could you bring two of them with you?'

Robin turned his head and peered at Alleyn in astonishment. 'I suppose I could.'

'Put them in your car during the day.'

'I don't see – '

'I'm sure you don't. Two of your own will do, if you have two. You needn't worry about bringing Miss Taylor's gown specifically.'

'Hers!' Robin cried out. 'Bring hers! But that's the whole thing! Tomorrow night they'll make Ginny wear the Black Robe.'

'Then you must bring a black robe,' Alleyn said.

II

On Thursday evening the Côte d'Azur, inclined always to the theatrical, became melodramatic and, true to the weather report, staged a thunderstorm.

'It's going to rain,' a voice croaked from the balustrade of the Chèvre d'Argent. 'Listen! Thunder!'

Far to southward the heavens muttered an affirmative.

Carbury Glande looked at the brilliantly-clad figure perched, knees to chin, on the balustrade. It mingled with a hanging swag of bougainvillaea. 'One sees a voice rather than a person. You look like some fabulous bird, dear Sati,' he said. 'If I didn't feel so ghastly I'd like to paint you.'

'Rumble, mumble, jumble and clatter,' said the other, absorbed in delighted anticipation. 'And then the rains. That's the way it goes.' She pursed her lips out and, drawing in air with the smoke, took a long puff at an attenuated cigarette.

Baradi walked over to her and removed the cigarette. 'Against the rules,' he said. 'Everything in its appointed time. You're over-excited.' He threw the cigarette away and returned to his chair.

A whiteness flickered above the horizon and was followed after a pause by a tinny rattle.

'We do this sort of thing much better at the Comédie Française,' Annabella Wells paraphrased, twisting her mouth in self-contempt.

Baradi leant forward until his nose was placed in surrealistic association with her ear. Beneath the nose his moustache shifted as if it had a life of its own and beneath the moustache his lips pouted and writhed in almost soundless articulation. Annabella Wells's expression did not change. She nodded slightly. His face hung for a moment above her neck and then he leant back in his chair.

Above the blacked Mediterranean the sky splintered with forked lightning.

'One. Two. Three. Four,' the hoarse voice counted to an accompaniment of clapping hands. The other guests ejaculated under a canopy of thunder.

'You always have to count,' the voice explained when it could be heard again.

'The thing I really hate,' Ginny Taylor said rapidly, 'is not the thunder or lightning but the pauses between bouts. Like this one.'

'Come indoors,' Robin Herrington said. 'You don't have to stay out here.'

'It's a kind of dare I have with myself.'

'Learning to be brave?' Annabella Wells asked with a curious inflexion in her voice.

'Ginny will have the courage of a lioness,' said Baradi, 'and the fire of a phoenix.'

Annabella got up with an abrupt expert movement and walked over to the balustrade. Baradi followed her. Ginny pushed her hair back from her forehead and looked quickly at Robin and away again. He moved nearer to her. She turned away to the far end of the roof-garden. Robin hovered uncertainly. The other four guests had drawn closer together. Carbury Glande half-closed his eyes and peered at the cloud-blocked sky and dismal sea. 'Gloriously ominous,' he said, 'and quite unpaintable. Which is such a good thing.'

The pause was not really one of silence. It was dramatized by minor noises, themselves uncannily portentous. Mr Oberon's canary, for instance, hopped scratchily from cage floor to perch and back again. A cicada had forgotten to stop chirruping in the motion-less cactus slopes that Mr Oberon called his *jardin exotique.* Down in the servants' quarters a woman laughed and many kilometres away towards Douceville a train shrieked effeminately. Still, beside the threat of thunder, these desultory sounds added up to silence.

Glande, with an eye on Ginny, muttered: 'I damned well think we need something. After all –' He swallowed. 'After everything. It's nervy work waiting.' His voice shot up into falsetto. 'I don't pretend to be phlegmatic. I'm a bloody artist, I am.'

Baradi said: 'Keep your voice down. You certainly have a flair for the appropriate adjective,' and laughed softly.

Glande fingered his lips and stared at Baradi. 'How you can!' he whispered.

Annabella, looking out to sea, said: 'Keep your hand to the plough, Carbury dear. You've put it there. No looking back.'

'*I'm* on your side,' announced the voice from the balustrade. 'Look what I am doing for you all.'

From her remote station Ginny said: 'I can't stand this.'

'Well, don't,' Robin said quietly. 'Old Marie asked me to tell you there's only one of the big silver goats left. Why not dodge down before the rain and get it? In the passage you won't see if there's lightning. Come on.'

Ginny looked at Baradi. He caught her glance and walked across to her. 'What is it?' he said.

'I thought I might go to old Marie's shop,' Ginny said. 'It's away from the storm.'

'Why not?' he said. 'What a good idea.'

'I thought I might,' Ginny repeated doubtfully.

For a split second lightning wrote itself across the sky in livid calligraphy. The voice on the balustrade had counted two when the heavens crashed together in a monstrous report. Ginny's mouth was wide open. She ran into the tower and Robin followed her.

The initial clap was succeeded by a prolonged rattle and an ambiguous omnipotent muttering. Above this rumpus Glande could be heard saying: 'What I mean to say: do we know we can trust them? After all, they're comparative strangers and I must say I don't like the boy's manner.'

Baradi, who was watching Annabella Wells, said: 'There's no need to disturb yourself on their account. Robin is much too heavily involved and as for Ginny, can we not leave her safely to Ra? In any case, she knows nothing.'

'The boy does. He might blurt out something to those other two – Troy and her bloody high-hat husband.'

'If Mr and MrsAllen should arrive there need be no meeting.'

'How do you know they don't suspect something already?'

'I have told you. The girl Teresa reports that having recovered the boy, they have retired to their hotel in high glee.'

'There was a bungle over the kid. There might be another bungle. Suppose Allen hangs about like he did last time asking damn'-fool esoteric questions?'

'They were not as silly as you may think, my dear Carbury. The man is an intelligent man. He behaved intelligently during the operation. He would make a good anaesthetist.'

'Well – there you are!'

'Please don't panic. He is both intelligent and inquisitive. That is why we thought it better to remove him, if possible, to St Celeste until the Truebody has been disposed of.' Baradi's teeth gleamed under his moustache.

'I can see no cause for amusement.'

'Can you not? You must cultivate a taste for irony. Annabella,' Baradi continued, looking at her motionless figure against the steel-dark sky. 'Annabella tells us that Mr Allen, as far as she knows, is the person he appears to be: a dilettante with a taste for mysticism, curious literature and big-game hunting. The latter, I may add, in the generally accepted sense of the expression.'

'Oh, for God's sake!' Glande cried out. The voice from the balustrade broke into undisciplined laughter. 'Shut up!' he shouted. 'Shut up, Sati! You of all people to laugh. It's so damned undignified. Remember who you are!'

'Yes, Grizel dear,' Annabella Wells said, 'pray do remember that.'

It had grown so dark that the lightning darted white on their faces. They saw one another momentarily as if by a flash-lamp, each wearing a look of fixity. The thunderclap followed at once. One might have imagined the heavens had burst outward like a gas-filled cylinder.

Mr Oberon, wearing his hooded gown, stepped out of the tower door and contemplated his followers.

'*Cher maître*,' shouted Baradi, waving his hand, 'you come most carefully upon your hour. What an entrance! Superb!'

The volley rolled away into silence. Mr Oberon moved forward and, really as if he had induced it, rain struck down in an abrupt deluge.

'You will get wet, dear Sati,' said Mr Oberon.

Glande said: 'What's happened?'

They all drew near to Mr Oberon. The rain made a frightful din, pelting like bullets on water and earth and stone and on the canvas awning above their heads. Landscape and seascape were alive with its noise. The four guests, with the anxious air of people who are hard of hearing, inclined their heads towards their host.

'What's happened?' Glande repeated but with a subdued and more deferential manner.

'All is well. It is arranged for tomorrow afternoon. An Anglican ceremony,' said Oberon, smiling slightly. 'I have spoken to the – should I call him priest? I was obliged to call on him. The telephone is still out of order. He is a dull man but very obliging. A private funeral, of course.'

'But the other business - the permit or whatever it is?'

'I've already explained,' Baradi cut in irritably, 'that my authority as a medical man is perfectly adequate. The appropriate official will be happy to receive me tomorrow when the necessary formalities will be completed.'

'Poor old Truebody,' said Annabella Wells.

'The name is, by the way, to be Halebory. Pronounced Harber. So English.'

'They'll want to see the passport,' Glande said instantly.

'They shall see it. It has received expert attention.'

'Sati,' said Oberon gently, 'you have been smoking, I think.'

'Dearest Ra, only the least puff.'

'Yet, there is our rule. Not until tonight.'

'I was upset. It's so difficult. Please forgive me. Please.'

Mr Oberon looked blankly at her. 'You will go to your room and make an exercise. The exercise of the Name. You will light your candle and looking at the flame without blinking you will repeat one hundred times: "I am Sati who am Grizel Locke!" Then you will remain without moving until it is time for the Rites. So.'

She touched her forehead and lips and chest with a jerky movement of her hand and went at once.

'Where is Ginny?' Mr Oberon asked.

'She was nervous,' said Baradi. 'The storm upset her. She went down to the shop where one buys those rather vulgar figurines.'

'And Robin?'

'He went with her,' said Annabella loudly.

Mr Oberon's mouth parted to show his teeth. 'She must rest,' he said. 'You are, of course, all very careful to say nothing of an agitating nature in front of her. She knows the lady has died as the result of a perforated appendix. Unfortunately it was unavoidable that she should be told so much. There must be no further disturbance. When she returns send her to her room. It is the time of meditation. She is to remain in her room until it is time for the Rites. There she will find the gift of enlightenment.'

He moved to the tower door. The rain drummed on the awning above their heads but they heard him repeat: 'She must rest,' before he went indoors.

III

Old Marie's shop was a cave sunk in the face of the hill and protected at its open end by the Chévre d'Argent which at this point straddled the passage. Ginny and Robin were thus hidden from the lightning and even the thunder sounded less formidable in there. The walls of the cave had been hewn out in shelves and on those stood

Marie's figurines. She herself sat at a table over an oil lamp and wheezed out praises for her wares.

'She's got lots of goats,' Ginny pointed out, speaking English.

'Cunning old cup-of-tea,' Robin said. 'Thought you needed gingering up, I suppose. By the way,' he added, 'Miss Troy or Mrs Allen or whatever she should be called, wanted a set of nativity figures – don't you call it a crib? – for the little boy. Marie wasn't here when I left yesterday. I promised I'd get one and take it down this afternoon. How awful! I entirely forgot.'

'Robin! How could you! And they'll want it more than ever after losing him like that.'

'She thought perhaps you wouldn't mind choosing one.'

'Of course I will,' Ginny said and began to inspect the groups of naïve little figures. Old Marie shouted: 'Look, Mademoiselle, the Holy Child illuminates himself. And the beasts! One would say the she-ass almost burst herself with good milk. And the lamb is infinitely touching. And the ridiculous price! I cannot bring myself to charge more. It is an act of piety on my part.'

Robin bought a large silver goat and Ginny bought the grandest of the cribs. 'Let's take it down now,' he said. 'The storm's nearly over, I'm sure, and the car's out. It'd save my conscience. Do come, Ginny.'

She raised her troubled face and looked at him. 'I don't know,' she said, 'I suppose – I don't know.'

'We shan't be half an hour. Come on.'

He took her by the arm and hurried her into the passageway. They ran into a world of rain, Ginny protesting and Robin shouting encouragement. With the help of his stick be broke into quite a lively sort of canter. 'Do be careful!' Ginny cried. 'Your dot-and-go-one leg!'

'Dot-and-go-run, you mean. Come on.'

Their faces streamed with cool water and they laughed without cause.

'It's better out here,' Robin said. 'Isn't it, Ginny?'

The car stood out on the platform like a rock in a waterfall. He bundled her into it. 'You look like – you look as you're meant to look,' he said. 'It's better outside. Say it's better, Ginny.'

'I don't know what's come over you,' Ginny said, pressing her hands to her rain-blinded face.

'I've got out. We've both got out.' He scrambled in beside her and peered into the trough behind the driver's seat. 'What are you doing?' Ginny asked hysterically. 'What's happened? We've gone mad. What are you looking for?'

'Nothing. A parcel for my tailor. It's gone. Who cares! Away we go.'

He started up his engine. Water splashed up like wings on either side and cascaded across the windscreen. They roared down the steep incline and turned left above the tunnel and over the high headland, on the road to Roqueville.

IV

High up in the hills on their vantage point in the factory road, Alleyn and Raoul waited in Raoul's car.

'In five minutes,' Alleyn said, 'it will be dark.'

'I shall still know the car, Monsieur.'

'And I. The rain's lifting a little.'

'It will stop before the light goes, I think.'

'How tall are you, Raoul?'

'One metre, seventy, Monsieur.'

'About five foot eight,' Alleyn muttered, 'and the girl's tall. It ought to be all right. Where was the car exactly?'

'Standing out on the platform, Monsieur. The parcel was in the trough behind the driver's seat.'

'He's stuck to his word so far, at least. Where did you put the note?'

'On the driver's seat, Monsieur. He could not fail to see it.'

But Robin, driving in a state of strange exhilaration towards Roqueville, sat on the disregarded note and wondered if it was by accident or intention that Ginny leant a little towards him.

'It will be fine on the other side of the hill,' he shouted. 'What do you bet?'

'It couldn't be.'

'You'll see. You'll see. You'll jolly well see.'

'Robin, what *has* come over you?'

'I'll tell you when we get to Roqueville. There you are! What did I say?'

They drove down the mountain-side into a translucent dusk, rain-washed and fragrant.

'There they go,' Alleyn said and turned his field-glasses on the tiny car. 'She's with him. He's brought it off. So far.'

'And now, Monsieur?'

Alleyn watched the car diminish. Just before it turned the point of a distant headland, Robin switched on his lamps. Alleyn lowered his glasses. 'It is almost lighting-up time, Raoul. We wait a little longer.' They turned as if by a shared consent and looked to the west where, above and beyond the tunnelled hill, the turrets of the Chèvre d'Argent stood black against a darkling sky.

Presently, out on Cap St Gilles pricks of yellow began to appear. The window of a cottage in the valley showed red. Behind them the factory presented a dark front to the dusk but higher up in its folded hills the Monastery of Our Lady of Paysdoux was alive with glowing lights.

'They are late with their lamps at the Chèvre d'Argent,' said Raoul.

'Which is not surprising,' Alleyn rejoined. 'Seeing that Monsieur le Commissaire has arranged that their electrical service is disconnected. The thunderstorm will have lent a happy note of credibility to the occurrence. The telephone also is still disconnected.' He used his field-glasses. 'Yes,' he said, 'they are lighting candles. Start up your engine, Raoul. It is time to be off.

V

'You disturb yourself without cause,' Baradi said, 'she is buying herself a silver goat. Why not? It is a good omen.'

'Already she's been away half an hour.'

'She has gone for a walk, no doubt.'

'With him.'

'Again, why not? The infatuation is entirely on one side. Let it alone.'

'I am unusually interested and therefore nervous,' said Mr Oberon. 'It means more to me, this time, than ever before and besides the whole circumstances are extraordinary. The mystic association. The blood sacrifice and then, while the victim is still here, the other, the living sacrifice. It is unique.'

Baradi looked at him with curiosity. 'Tell me,' he said, 'how much of all this' – he made a comprehensive gesture – 'means anything to you? I mean I can understand the, what shall I call it, the factual pleasure. That is a great deal. I envy you your flair. But the esoteric window-dressing – is it possible that for you – ?' He paused. Mr Oberon's face was as empty as a mask. He touched his lips with the tip of his tongue.

He said: 'Wherein, if not in my belief, do you suppose the secret of my flair is to be found? I am what I am and I go back to beyond the dawn. I was the King of the Wood.'

Baradi examined his own shapely hands. 'Ah, yes?' he said politely. 'A fascinating theory.'

'You think me a *poseur?*'

'No, no. On the contrary. It is only as a practical man I am concerned with the hazards of the situation. You, I gather, though you have every cause, are not at all anxious on that account? The Truebody situation, I mean?'

'I find it immeasurably stimulating.'

'Indeed,' said Baradi dryly.

'Only the absence of the girl disturbs me. It is almost dark. Turn on the light.'

Baradi reached out his hand to the switch. There was a click.

'No lights, it seems,' he said and opened the door. 'No lights anywhere. There must be a fuse.'

'How can she be walking in the dark? And with a cripple like Robin? It is preposterous.'

'The British do these things.'

'I am British. I have my passport. Telephone the bureau in Roqueville.'

'The telephone is still out of order.'

'We must have light.'

'It may be a fault in the house. The servants will attend to it. One moment.'

He lifted the receiver from Mr Oberon's telephone. A voice answered.

'What is the matter with the lights?' Baradi asked.

'We cannot make out, Monsieur. There is no fault here. Perhaps the storm has brought down the lines.'

'Nothing but trouble. And the telephone? Can one telephone yet to Roqueville?'

'No, Monsieur. The *centrale* sent up a man. The fault is not in the château. They are investigating. They will ring through when the line is clear.'

'Since yesterday afternoon we have been without the telephone. Unparalleled incompetence!' Baradi ejaculated. 'Have Mr Herrington and Mlle Taylor returned?'

'I will inquire, Monsieur.'

'Do so, and ring Mr Oberon's apartments if they are in.'

He clapped down the receiver. 'I am uneasy,' he said. 'It has happened at a most tiresome moment. We have only the girl Teresa's account of the affair at the factory. No doubt she is speaking the truth. Having found the boy they are satisfied. All the same it is not too amusing, having had the police in the factory.'

'Callard will have handled them with discretion.'

'No doubt. The driver, Georges Martel, however, will be examined by the police.'

'Can he be trusted?'

'He has too much at stake to be anything but dependable. We pay him very highly. Also he has his story. He was rung up by an unknown client purporting to be the boy's father. He took the job in good faith and merely asked the girl Teresa to accompany him. They know nothing. The police will at once suspect the former kidnappers. Nevertheless, I wish we had not attempted the affair with the boy.'

'One wanted to rid oneself of the parents.'

'Exactly. Of the father. If circumstances were different,' Baradi said softly, 'I should not be nearly so interested in ridding myself of Mama. Women!' he ejaculated sententiously.

'Women!' Mr Oberon echoed with an inexplicable laugh and added immediately: 'All the same I am getting abominably anxious. I don't trust him. And then, the light! Suppose it doesn't come on again before the Rites. How shall we manage?'

'Something can be done with car batteries, I think, and a soldering iron. Mahomet is ingenious in such matters. I shall speak to him in a moment.'

Baradi walked over to the window and pulled back the silk blind. 'It is quite dark.' The blind shot up with a whirr and click.

'It really is much too quick on the trigger,' he observed.

Mr Oberon said loudly: 'Don't do that! You exacerbate my nerves. Pull it down. Tie it down.'

And while Baradi busied himself with the blind he added: 'I shall send out. My temper is rising and that is dangerous. I must not become angry. If his car has gone I shall send after it.'

'I strongly suggest you do nothing of the sort. It would be an unnecessary and foolish move. She will return. Surely you have not lost your flair.'

Mr Oberon, in the darkness, said: 'You are right. She will return. She must.'

'As for your rising temper,' said Baradi, 'you had better subdue it. It is dangerous.'

CHAPTER 11

P.E. Garbel

Raoul slowed down at a point above the entrance to the tunnel.

'Where should we leave the car, Monsieur?'

'There's a recess off the road, on the far side, near the tunnel and well under the lee of the hill. Pull in there.'

The silhouette of the Chèvre d'Argent showed black above the hills against a clearing but still stormy sky. A wind had risen and cloud-rack scurried across a brilliant display of stars.

'Gothic in spirit,' Alleyn muttered, 'if not in design.'

The road turned the headland. Raoul dropped to a crawl and switched off his lights. Alleyn used a pocket torch. When they came down to the level of the tunnel exit he got out and guided Raoul into a recess hard by the stone facing.

Raoul dragged out a marketing basket from which the intermingled smells of cabbage, garlic and flowers rose incongruously on the rain-sweetened air.

'Have you hidden the cloaks underneath?' Alleyn asked him.

'Yes, Monsieur. It was an excellent notion. It is not unusual for me to present myself with such gear. The aunt of Teresa is a market-gardener.'

'Good. We'll smell like two helpings of a particularly exotic soup.'

'Monsieur?'

'No matter. Now, Raoul, to make certain we understand each other will you repeat the instructions?'

'Very well, Monsieur. We go together to the servants' entrance. If, by mischance we encounter anybody on the way who recognizes

398

Monsieur, Monsieur will at once say he has come to inquire for the
sick Mademoiselle. I will continue on and will wait for Monsieur at
the servants' entrance. If Monsieur, on arriving there, is recognized
by one of the servants who may not yet have left, he will say he has
been waiting for me and is angry. He will say he wishes to speak to
Teresa about the stealing of Riki. If, on the other hand, all goes well
and we reach the servants' quarters together and unchallenged, we
go at once to Teresa's room. Monsieur is seen but not recognized, he
is introduced as the intellectual cousin of Teresa who has been to
England, working in a bank and has greatly improved his social status and again we retire quickly to Teresa's room before the Egyptian
valet or the butler can encounter Monsieur. In either case, Teresa is
to give a message saying it has come by a peasant on a bicycle. It is
to say that Mr Herrington's car has broken down but that Miss Taylor
and he will arrive in time for the party. Finally, if Monsieur does not
come at all, I wait for an hour then go to seek for him.'

'And if something we have not in the least anticipated turns up?'

Raoul laughed softly in the dark: 'One must then use one's wits,
Monsieur.'

'Good, shall we start?'

They walked together up the steep incline to the platform.

A goods train came puffing up from Douceville. The glow from the
engine slid across the lower walls and bastions of the Chèvre d'Argent.
Behind the silk blind a dim light burned: a much fainter light than the
one they had seen from the window of their train. Higher up, at odd
intervals in that vast façade, other windows glowed or flickered where
candles had been placed or were carried from one room to another.

The train tooted and clanked into the tunnel.

It was quite cold on the platform. A mountain breeze cut across it
and lent credibility to the turned-up collar of Alleyn's raincoat and
the scarf across his mouth. The passage was almost pitch dark but
they thought it better not to use a torch. They slipped and stumbled
on wet and uneven steps. The glow from old Marie's door was a
guide. As they passed by she shouted from behind the oil-lamp:
'Hola, there! Is it still raining?'

Raoul said quietly: 'The stars are out. Goodnight, Marie,' and they
hurried into the shadows. They heard her shouting jovially after
them: 'Give her something to keep out the cold.'

'She speaks of Teresa,' Raoul whispered primly. 'There is a hint of vulgarity in Marie.'

Alleyn stifled a laugh. They groped their way round a bend in the passage, brushing their hands against damp stone. Presently an elegant design of interlaced rosettes appeared against a background of reflected warmth. It was the wrought-iron gate of the Chèvre d'Argent.

'As quick as we dare,' Alleyn whispered.

The passage glinted wet before the doorway. The soles of his shoes were like glass. He poised himself and moved lightly forward. As he entered the patch of light he heard a slither and an oath. Raoul hurtled against him, throwing him off his balance. He clung to the gate while Raoul, in a wild attempt to recover himself, clutched at the nearest object.

It was the iron bell-pull.

The bell gave tongue with a violence that was refracted intolerably by the stone walls.

Three cabbages rolled down the steps. Raoul by some desperate effort still clung to the basket with one hand and to the bell-pull with the other.

'Monsieur! Monsieur!' he stammered.

'Go on,' Alleyn said, '*Go on!*'

Raoul let go the bell-pull and a single note fell inconsequently across the still-echoing clangour. He plunged forward and was lost in shadow.

Alleyn turned to face the door.

'Why, if it's not Mr Alleyn!' said Mr Oberon.

II

He stood on the far side of the door with his back to a lighted candelabrum that had been set down on a chest in the entry. Little could be seen of him but his shape, enveloped in his white gown with the hood drawn over his head. He moved towards the door and his hands emerged and grasped two of the iron bars.

Alleyn said: 'I'm afraid we made an appalling din. My chauffeur slipped and grabbed your bell-pull.'

'Your chauffeur?'

'He's taken himself off. I fancy he knows one of your maids. He had some message for her, it seems.'

Mr Oberon said, as if to explain his presence at the door: 'I am waiting for someone. Have you seen –' He paused and shifted his hands on the bars. His voice sounded out of focus. 'Perhaps you met Ginny. Ginny Taylor? And Robin Herrington? We are a little anxious about them.'

'No,' Alleyn said. 'I didn't see them. I came to ask about Miss Truebody.'

Mr Oberon didn't move. Alleyn peered at him. 'How is she?' he asked.

Mr Oberon said abruptly: 'Our telephone has been out of order since yesterday afternoon. Do forgive me. I am a little anxious, you know.'

'How is Miss Truebody?'

'Alas, she is dead,' said Mr Oberon.

They faced each other like actors in some medieval prison scene. The shadow of twisted iron was thrown across Alleyn's face and chest.

'Perhaps,' Alleyn said, 'I may come in for a moment.'

'But, of course. How dreadful of me! We are all so distressed. Mahomet!'

Evidently the Egyptian servant had been waiting in the main hall. He unlocked the door, opened it and stood aside. When Alleyn had come in he relocked the door.

With the air of having arrived at a decision, Mr Oberon led the way into the great hall. Mahomet came behind them bringing the candelabrum which he set down on a distant table. In that vast interior it served rather to emphasize the dark than relieve it.

'Monsieur,' said Mahomet in French, 'may I speak?'

'Well?'

'There is a message brought by a peasant from Mr Herrington. He has had trouble with his auto. He is getting a taxi. He and Mlle Taylor will arrive in time for the ceremony.'

'Ah!' It was a long drawn-out sigh. 'Who took the message?'

'The girl Teresa, who was on her way to catch the omnibus. The peasant would not wait so the girl returned with the message. Miss

Taylor also sent a message. It was that Monsieur must not trouble himself. She will not fail the ceremony. She will go immediately to her room.'

'Is all prepared?'

'All is prepared, Monsieur.'

Mr Oberon raised his hand in dismissal. Mahomet moved away into the shadows. Alleyn listened for the rattle of curtain rings but there was no other sound than that of Mr Oberon's uneven breathing. 'Forgive me again,' he said, coming closer to Alleyn. 'As you heard from him it was news of our young people.'

'I'm afraid my French is too rudimentary for anything but the most childish phrases.'

'Indeed? It appears they have had a breakdown but all is now well.'

Alleyn said: 'When did Miss Truebody die?'

'Ah, yes. We are so sorry. Yesterday afternoon. We tried to get you at the hotel, of course, but were told that you had gone to St Céleste for a few days.'

'We changed our plans,' Alleyn said. 'May I speak to Dr Baradi?'

'To Ali? I am not sure – I will inquire – Mahomet!'

'Monsieur!' said a voice in the shadows.

'Tell your master that the English visitor is here. Tell him the visitor knows that his compatriot has left us.'

'Monsieur.'

The curtain rings jangled together.

'He will see if our friend is at home.'

'I feel,' Alleyn said, 'that I should do everything that can be done. In a way she is our responsibility.'

'That is quite wonderful of you, Mr Alleyn,' said Mr Oberon who seemed to have made a return to his normal form. 'But I already sensed in you a rare and beautiful spirit. Still, you need not distress yourself. We felt it our privilege to speed this soul to its new life. The interment is tomorrow at three o'clock. Anglican. I shall, however, conduct a little valedictory ceremony here.'

The curtain rings clashed again. Alleyn saw a large whiteness move towards him.

'Mr Allen?' said Baradi, looming up on the far side of the candelabrum. He wore a white robe and his face was a blackness within the hood. 'I am so glad you've come. We were puzzled what to do when we heard you had gone to St Céleste.'

'Fortunately there was no occasion. We ran Ricky to earth, I'm glad to say.'

They both made enthusiastic noises. They rejoiced. An atrocious affair. Where had he been found?

'In the chemical factory, of all places,' Alleyn said. 'The police think the kidnappers must have got cold feet and dumped him there.' He allowed their ejaculations a decent margin and then said: 'About poor Miss Truebody – '

'Yes, about her,' Baradi began crisply. 'I'm sorry it happened as it did. I can assure you that it would have made no difference if there had been a hospital with an entire corps of trained nurses and surgeons. And certainly, may I add, she could not have had a more efficient anaesthetist. But, as you know, peritonitis was greatly advanced. Her condition steadily deteriorated. The heart, by the way, was not in good trim. Valvular trouble. She died at 4.28 yesterday afternoon without recovering consciousness. We found her address in her passport. I have made a report which I shall send to the suitable authorities in the Bermudas. Her effects, of course, will be returned to her home there. I understand there are no near relatives. I have completed the necessary formalities here. I should have preferred, under the circumstances to have asked a brother medico to look at her but it appears they are all in conclave at St Christophe.'

'I expect I should write to – well, to somebody.'

'By all means. Enclose a letter with my report. The authorities in the Bermudas will see that it reaches the lawyer or whoever is in charge of her affairs.'

'I think perhaps – one has a feeling of responsibility – I think perhaps I should see her.'

There was an infinitesimal pause.

'Of course,' Baradi said. 'If you wish, of course, I must warn you that the climatic conditions and those of her illness and death have considerably accelerated the usual postmortem changes.'

'We have done what we could,' Mr Oberon said. 'Tuberoses and orchids.'

'How very kind. If it's not troubling you too much.'

There was a further slight pause. Baradi said: 'Of course,' again and clapped his hands. 'No electricity,' he explained. 'So provoking.' The servant reappeared, carrying a single candle. Baradi spoke to him in their own language and took the candle from him. 'I'll go with you,' he said. 'We have moved her into a room outside the main part of the château. It is quite suitable and cooler.'

With this grisly little announcement he led Alleyn down the now familiar corridor past the operating room and into a much narrower side-passage that ended in a flight of descending steps and a door. This, in turn, opened on a further reach of the outside passageway. The night air smelt freshly after the incense-tainted house. They turned left and walked a short distance down the uneven steps. Alleyn thought that they could not be far from the servants' entrance.

Baradi stopped at a deeply recessed doorway and asked Alleyn to hold the candle. Alleyn produced his torch and switched it on. It shone into Baradi's face.

'Ah!' he said blinking, 'that will be better. Thank you.' He set down the candle. It flickered and guttered in the draught. He thrust his hand under his gown and produced a heavily furnished key-ring that might have hung from the girdle of a medieval gaoler. Alleyn turned his light on it and Baradi selected a great key with a wrought-iron loop. He stooped to fit it in a key-hole placed low in the door. His wide sleeves drooped from his arms, his hood fell over his face and his shadow, grotesque and distorted, sprawled down the steps beyond him.

'If you would lend me your torch,' he said. 'It is a little awkward, this lock.'

Alleyn gave him his torch. The shadow darted across the passage and reared itself up the opposite wall. After some fumbling, the key was engaged and noisily turned. Baradi shoved at the door and with a grind of its hinges it opened suddenly inwards and he fell forward with it, dropping the torch, nose first, in the stone threshold. There was a tinkle of glass and they were left with the guttering candle.

'*Ah, sacré nom d'un chien!*' Baradi ejaculated. 'My dear Mr Allen, what have I done!'

Alleyn said: 'Be careful of the broken glass.'

'I am wearing sandals. But how careless! I am so sorry.'

'Never mind. The passage seems to be unlucky for us this evening. Let's hope there's not a third mishap. Don't give it another thought. Shall we go in?' Alleyn laid down his walking-stick and took up the candle and the broken torch. They went in, Baradi shutting the door with a heave and a weighty slam.

It seemed to be a small room with white-washed stone walls and a shuttered window. Candlelight wavered over a bank of flowers. A coffin stood in the middle of trestles. The mingled odours of death and tuberoses were horrible.

'I hope you are not over-sensitive,' Baradi said. 'We have done our best. Mr Oberon was most particular, but – well – as you see – '

Alleyn saw. The lid of the coffin had been left far enough withdrawn to expose the head of its inhabitant which was literally bedded in orchids. A white veil of coarse net lay over the face but it did little to soften the inexorable indignities of death.

'The teeth,' said Baradi, 'make a difference, don't they?'

Looking at them Alleyn was reminded of Teresa's generality to the effect that all English spinsters have teeth like mares. This lonely spinster's dentist had evidently subscribed to Teresa's opinion and Alleyn saw the other stigmata of her kind: the small mole, the lines and pouches, the pathetic tufts of grey hair from which the skin had receded.

He backed away. 'I thought it better to see her,' he said, and his voice was constrained and thin. 'In case there should be any questions of identification.'

'Much better. Are you all right? For the layman it is not a pleasant experience.'

Alleyn said: 'I find it quite appalling. Shall we go? I'm afraid I –' His voice faded. He turned away with a violent movement and at the same time jerked his handkerchief. It flapped across the candle flame and extinguished it.

In the malodorous dark Baradi cursed unintelligibly. Alleyn gabbled: 'The door, for God's sake, where is the door? I'm going to be sick.' He lurched against Baradi and sent him staggering to the far end of the room. He drop-kicked the candlestick in the opposite direction. His hands were on the coffin. His left hand discovered the edge of the lid, slid under it, explored a soft material, a tight band and the surface beneath. His fingers, inquisitive and thrusting, found what they sought.

'I can't stand this!' he choked out. 'The door!'

Baradi was now swearing in French. '*Idiot!*' he was saying. '*Maladroit, imbécile!*'

Alleyn made retching noises. He found his way unerringly to the door and dragged it open. A pale lessening of the dark was admitted. He staggered out into the passageway and leant against the stone wall. Baradi came after him and dragged the door shut. Alleyn heard him turn the key in the lock.

'That was not an amusing interlude,' Baradi said. 'I warned you it would not be pleasant.'

Alleyn had his handkerchief pressed to his mouth. He said indistinctly: 'I'm sorry. I didn't realize – I'll be all right.'

'Of course you will,' Baradi snapped at him. 'So shall I when my bruises wear off.'

'Please don't let me keep you. Fresh air. I'll go back to the car. Thank you: I'm sorry.'

Apparently Baradi had regained his temper. He said: 'It is undoubtedly the best thing you can do. I recommend a hot bath, a stiff drink, two aspirins and bed. If you're sure you're all right and can find your way back – '

'Yes, yes. It's passing off.'

'Then if you will excuse me. I am already late. Goodnight, Mr Allen.'

Alleyn, over his handkerchief, watched Baradi return up the steps, open the side door and disappear into the house. He waited for some minutes, accustoming his eyes to the night.

'Somehow,' he thought, 'I must get a wash,' and he wiped his left hand vigorously on his handkerchief which he then threw into the shadows.

But he did not wipe away the memory of a not very large cavity under the left breast of a sprigged locknit nightgown.

III

He had been right about the nearness of the servants' entrance. The stone passageway dipped, turned and came to an end by a sort of open penthouse. Alleyn had to grope his way down steps but the non-darkness that is starlight had filtered into the purlieus of the Chèvre d'Argent and glistened faintly on ledges and wet stone. He paused for a moment and looked back and upwards. The great mass of stone and rock made a black hole in the spangled heavens. The passageway had emerged from beneath a bridge-like extension of the house. This linked the seaward portion with what he imagined must be the original fortress, deep inside the cliff-face. Alleyn moved into an inky-dark recess. A light had appeared on the bridge.

It was carried by the Egyptian servant, who appeared to have something else, possibly a tray, in his hand. He was followed by Baradi. Unmistakably it was Baradi. The servant turned and his torchlight flickered across the dark face. The doctor no longer wore his robe. Something that looked like a smooth cord hung round his neck. They moved on and were lost inside the house. Alleyn gave a little grunt of satisfaction and continued on his way.

A lantern with a stub of candle in it hung by a half-open door and threw a yellow pool on the flat surface beneath.

'Monsieur?' a voice whispered.

'Raoul?'

'*Oui, Monsieur. Tout va bien. Allons.*'

Raoul slid out of the penthouse. Alleyn's wrist was grasped. He moved into the pool of light. Raoul pushed the door open with his foot. They entered a stone corridor, passed two closed doors and turned right. Raoul tapped with his finger-tips on a third door. Teresa opened it and admitted them.

It was a small neat bedroom, smelling a little fusty. One of old Marie's Madonnas, neatly inscribed: 'Notre Dame de Paysdoux' stood on a corner shelf with a stool before it. Dusty paper flowers, candles and a photograph of Teresa in her confirmation dress, with folded hands and upturned eyes, completed the décor. A sacred print, looking dreadfully like Mr Oberon, hung nearby. Across the bed were disposed two white gowns. A washstand with a jug and basin stood in a farther corner.

Teresa, looking both nervous and complacent, pushed forward her only chair.

Alleyn said: 'Is is possible to wash one's hands, Teresa? A little water and some soap?'

'I will slip out for some warm water, Monsieur. It is quite safe to do so. Monsieur will forgive me. I had forgotten. The English always wish to wash themselves.'

Alleyn did not correct this aphorism. When she had gone he said: 'Well, Raoul?'

'The servants have gone out, Monsieur, with the exception of the Egyptian who is occupied downstairs. The guests are in their rooms. It is unlikely that they will emerge before the ceremony.' He extended his hands, palms upwards. 'Monsieur, how much mischief have I made by my imbecility?'

Alleyn said: 'Well, Raoul, you certainly rang the bell,' and then seeing his companion's bewilderment and distress, added: 'It was not so bad after all. It worked out rather well. Dr Baradi and I have visited the body of a murdered woman.'

'Indeed, Monsieur?'

'It lies among orchids in a handsome coffin in a room across the passage of entrance. The coffin, as M. le Commissaire had already ascertained, arrived this morning from an undertaker in Roqueville.'

'But Monsieur – '

'There is a wound, covered by a surgical dressing, under the left breast.'

'Teresa has told me that the English lady died.'

'Here *is* Teresa,' Alleyn said and held up his hand.

While he washed he questioned Teresa about Miss Truebody.

'Teresa, in what room of the house did the English lady die? Was it where we put her after the operation?'

'No, Monsieur. She was moved at once from there. The Egyptian and the porter carried her to a room upstairs in the Saracen's watch-tower. It is not often used. She was taken there because it would be quieter, Monsieur.'

'I'll be bound she was,' Alleyn muttered. He dried his hands and began to outline a further plan of action. 'Last night,' he said, 'I learnt from Mr Herrington a little more than Teresa perhaps may know, of the normal procedure on Thursday nights. At eleven o'clock a bell is rung. The guests then emerge from their rooms wearing their robes which have been laid out for them. They go in silence to the ceremony known as the Rites of the Children of the Sun. First they enter the small ante-room where each takes up a lighted candle. They then go into the main room and stay there until after midnight. Supper is served in Mr Oberon's *salon*. The whole affair may go on, after a fashion, until five o'clock in the morning.'

Teresa drew in her breath with an excited hiss.

'Now it is my intention to witness this affair. To that end I propose that you, Raoul, and I replace Miss Taylor and Mr Herrington who will not be there. Electricity will not be restored in the château to-night and by candlelight we have at least a chance of remaining unrecognized.'

Teresa made a little gesture. 'If Monsieur pleases,' she said.

'Well, Teresa?'

'The Egyptian has brought in iron boxes from Mr Oberon's auto and a great deal of electrical cord and a soldering iron, he has arranged that the sun lamp in the room of ceremonies shall be lighted.'

'Indeed? How very ingenious of him.'

'Monsieur,' Raoul said, eyeing the gowns on the bed, 'is it your intention that I make myself pass for a lady?'

Teresa cackled and clapped her hand over her mouth.

'Exactly so,' said Alleyn. 'You are about the same height as Miss Taylor. In the black gown with the hood drawn over your face and your hands (by the way, you too must wash your hands) hidden in the sleeves, you should, with luck, pass muster. You have small feet. Perhaps you may be able to wear Miss Taylor's slippers.'

'*Ah, mon Dieu, quelle blague!*'

'Comport yourself with propriety, Teresa, Monsieur is speaking.'

'If you cannot manage this I have bought a pair of black slippers which will have to do instead.'

'And my costume, Monsieur?' Raoul asked, indicating with an expressive gesture his stained singlet, his greenish black trousers and his mackintosh hitched over his shoulders.

'I understand that, apart from the gown and slippers there is no costume at all.'

'*Ah, mon Dieu, en voilà une affaire!*'

'*Teresa! Attention!*'

'However, the gown is voluminous. For propriety's sake, Raoul, you may retain your vest and underpants. In any case you must be careful to conceal your legs which, no doubt, are unmistakably masculine.'

'They are superb,' said Teresa. 'But undoubtedly masculine.'

'It seems to me,' continued Alleyn, who had become quite used to the peculiarities of conversation with Raoul and Teresa, 'that our first difficulty is the problem of getting from here to the respective rooms of Mr Herrington and Miss Taylor. Teresa, I see, has brought two white gowns. Mr Herrington has provided us with a white and a black one. Miss Taylor would have appeared in black tonight. Therefore, you must put on the black, Raoul, and I shall wear the longest of the white. Teresa must tell us where these rooms are. If the Egyptian or any of the guests should see us on our way to them we must hope they will observe the rule of silence which is enforced before the ceremony and pay no attention. It will be best if we can find our way without candles. Once inside our rooms we remain there until we hear the bell. How close, Teresa, are these rooms to the room where the ceremony is held? The room you described to me yesterday.'

'The young lady's is nearby, Monsieur. It is therefore close to the apartment of Mr Oberon.'

'In that case, Raoul, when you hear the bell, go at once to the ante-room. Take a candle and, by the communicating door, go into the ceremonial room. There will be five or six black cushions on the floor and a large black divan. If there are six cushions, yours will be apart from the others. If there are five, your position will be on the divan. I am only guessing at this. One thing I do know – the rule of silence will be observed until the actual ceremony begins. If you are in the wrong position it will be attributed, with luck, to stage-fright and somebody will put you right. Where is Mr Herrington's room, Teresa?'

'It is off the landing, Monsieur, going down to the lower storey where the ceremonies are held.'

'And the other guests?'

'They are in the higher parts of the château, Monsieur. Across the outside passage and beyond it.'

'Do you know the room of Miss Grizel Locke?'

'Yes, Monsieur.'

'Have you seen her today?'

'Not since two days ago, Monsieur, but that is not unusual. As I have informed Monsieur, it is the lady's habit to keep to her room and leave a notice that she must not be disturbed.'

'I see. Now, if I leave Mr Herrington's room on the first stroke of the bell, I should arrive hard on your heels, Raoul, and in advance of the others. I may even go in a little earlier.' He looked at his watch. 'It is half-past seven. Let us put on our gowns. Then, Teresa, you must go out and, if possible, discover the whereabouts of the Egyptian.'

'Monsieur, he was summoned by M. Baradi before you came in. I heard him speaking on the house telephone.'

'Let us hope the doctor keeps his man with him for some time. Now then, Raoul. On with the motley!'

The gowns proved to be amply made, wrapping across under their girdles. The hoods would come well forward and, when the head was bent, completely exclude any normal lighting from the face. 'But it will be a different story if one holds a lighted candle,' Alleyn said. 'We must not be seen with our candles in our hands.'

He had bought for Raoul a pair of feminine sandals, black and elegant with highish heels. Raoul said he thought they would fit admirably. With a grimace of humorous resignation he washed his small, beautiful and very dirty feet and then fitted them into the sandals. '*Oh, là là!*' he said, 'one must be an acrobat, it appears.' And for the diversion of Teresa he minced to and fro, wagging his hips and making unseemly gestures. Teresa crammed her fists in her mouth and was consumed with merriment. '*Ah, mon Dieu,*' she gasped punctually, '*quel drôle de type!*'

Alleyn wondered rather desperately if he was dealing with children or merely with the celebrated latin *joie de vivre*. He called them to order and they were at once as solemn as owls.

'Teresa,' he said, 'you will go a little ahead of us with your candle. Go straight through the house and down the stairs to the landing beneath the library. If you see anybody, blow your nose loudly.'

'Have you a handkerchief, my jewel?'

'No.'

'Accept mine,' said Raoul, offering her a dubious rag.

'If anybody speaks to you and, perhaps, asks you why you are still on the premises, say that you missed your bus because of the message about Miss Taylor. If it is necessary, you must say you are going to her room to do some little act of service that you had forgotten and that then you will leave to catch the later bus. If it is possible, in

this event, Raoul and I will conceal ourselves until the coast is clear.
If this is not possible, we will behave as Mr Herrington and Miss
Taylor would behave under the rule of silence. You will continue to
Miss Taylor's room, open the door for Raoul and go in for a moment,
but only for a moment. Then, Teresa, I have another task for you,'
continued Alleyn, feeling for the second time in two days that he
had become as big a bore as Prospero. Teresa, however, was a complacent Ariel and merely gazed submissively upon him.

'You will find Mr Oberon and will tell him that Miss Taylor has
returned and asks to be allowed her private meditation alone in her
room until the ceremony. That is very important.'

'Ah, Monsieur, if he were not so troubling to my soul!'

'If you value my esteem, Teresa – ' Raoul began.

'Yes, yes, Monsieur,' said Teresa in a hurry, 'I am resolved! I will
face it.'

'Good. Having given this message, come and report to me. After
that your tasks for the night are finished. You will catch the late bus
for your home in the Paysdoux. Heaven will reward you and I shall
not forget you. Is all that clear, Teresa?'

Teresa repeated it all.

'Good. Now, Raoul, we may not have a chance to speak to each
other again. Do as I have said. You are enacting the role of a frightened yet fascinated girl who is under the rule of silence. What will
happen during the ceremony I cannot tell you. Mr Herrington could
not be persuaded to confide more than you already know. You can
only try to behave as the others do. If there is a crisis I shall deal with
it. You will probably see and hear much that will shock and anger
you. However beastly the behaviour of these people, you must control yourself. Have you ever heard of the Augean Stables?'

'No, Monsieur.'

'They were filthy and were cleansed. It was a heroic task. Now,
when you get to Miss Taylor's room you will find a robe, like the
one you are wearing, laid out for her. If there is no difference you
need not change. I don't think you need try to wear her shoes but
if there is anything else set out for her – gloves perhaps – you must
wear whatever it may be. One thing more. There may be cigarettes
in Miss Taylor's room. Don't smoke them. If cigarettes are given to
us during the ceremony we must pretend to smoke. Like this.'

Alleyn pouted his lips as if to whistle, held a cigarette in the gap between them and drew in audibly. 'They will be drugged cigarettes. Air and smoke will be inhaled together. Keep your thumb over the end like this and you will be safe. That's all. A great deal depends upon us, Raoul. There have been many girls before Miss Taylor who have become the guests of Mr Oberon. I think perhaps of all evil-doers, his kind are the worst. Monsieur le Commissaire and I are asking much of you.'

Raoul, perched on his high heels and peering out of the black hood, said: 'Monsieur l'Inspecteur-en-Chef, in the army one learns to recognize authority. I recognize it in you, Monsieur, and I shall serve it to the best of my ability.'

Alleyn was acutely embarrassed and more than a little touched by this speech. He said: 'Thank you. Then we must all do our best. Shall we set about it? Now, Teresa, as quietly as you can unless you meet anybody, and then – boldly. Off you go.'

'Courage, my beloved. Courage and good sense.'

Teresa bestowed a melting glance upon Raoul, opened the door and, after a preliminary look down the passage, took up her candle and went out. Alleyn followed with his walking-stick in his hand and Raoul, clicking his high heels and taking small steps, brought up the rear.

V

Down in Roqueville Troy absentmindedly arranged little figures round a crib and pondered on the failure of her session with Ginny and Robin. She heard again Ginny's desperate protest: 'I don't want to, I don't want to but I must. I've taken the oath. Dreadful things will happen if I don't go back.'

'You don't really believe that,' Robin had said and she had cried out: '*You've* sworn and *you* won't tell. If we don't believe why don't we tell?'

Suddenly, with something of Ricky's abandon, she had flung her arms round Troy, 'If you could help,' she had stammered, 'but you can't; you can't!' And she had run out of the room like a frightened animal. Robin, limping after her, had turned at the door.

'It's all right,' he had said. 'MrsAllen, it's all right. She won't go back.'

There was a tidily arranged pile of illustrated papers in the private sitting-room where they had had their drinks. Troy found herself idly turning the pages of the top one. Photographs of sun-bathers and race-goers flipped over under her abstracted gaze. Dresses by Dior and dresses by Path, Prince Aly Khan leading in his father's horse, the new ballet at the Marigny – *'Les invités reunis pour quelques jours au Château de la Chèvre d'Argent. De gauche à droite: L'Hôte, M. Oberon; Mlle Imogen Taylor, M. Carbury Glande, Dr Baradi, M. Robin Herrington et la Hon. Grizel Locke.'* Troy's attention was arrested and then transfixed. It was a clear photograph taken on the roof-garden. There they were, perfectly recognizable, all except Grizel Locke.

The photograph of Grizel Locke was that of a short, lean woman with the face of a complete stranger.

V

Robin was driving up a rough lane into the hills with Ginny beside him saying feverishly: 'You're sure this is a shorter way? It's a quarter to eight, Robin! Robin, you're sure?'

He thought: 'The tank was three-quarter full. How long before the petrol stopped flowing?'

'There's tons of time,' he said, 'and I'm quite sure.' As he turned the next corner the engine missed and then stopped. Robin crammed on his brakes.

Looking at Ginny's blank face he thought: 'Now, we're for it. It's tonight or nevermore for Ginny and me.'

Dupont, waiting under the stars on the platform outside the Chèvre d'Argent looked at his watch. It was a quarter to eight. He sighed and settled himself inside his coat. He expected a long vigil.

VI

Teresa's candle bobbed ahead. Sometimes it vanished round corners, sometimes dipped or ascended as she arrived at steps and sometimes it was stationary for a moment as she stopped and listened. Presently they were on familiar ground. Forward, on their left, was the operating room: opposite this, the room where Miss Truebody had waited. Nearer, on their right, a thin blade of light across the carpet indicated the door into Baradi's room. Teresa's hand, dramatized by candlelight, shielded the flame. Beyond her, the curtain at the end of the passage was faintly defined against some further diffusion of light.

She passed Baradi's door. Alleyn and Raoul approached it. Alleyn held up a warning hand. He halted and then crept forward. His ear was at the door. Beyond it, like erring souls, Baradi and his servant were talking together in their own language.

Alleyn and Raoul moved on. Teresa had come to the curtain. They saw her lift it and a triangle of warmth appeared. Her candle sank to the floor. The foot of the curtain was raised and the candle, followed by the doubled-up shape of Teresa disappeared beneath it.

'Good girl,' Alleyn thought, 'she's remembered the rings.'

He followed quickly. He was tall enough to reach the rings and hold the top of the curtain to the rail while he raised the skirt for Raoul to pass through.

Now Raoul was in the great hall where the candelabrum still burned on the central table. Teresa had already passed into the entrance lobby. Alleyn still held the curtain in his hand when Teresa blew her nose.

He slipped back behind the curtain, leaving a peephole for himself. He saw Raoul hesitate and then move forward until his back was to the light and he saw a white-robed figure that might have been himself come in from the lobby. Looking beyond the six burning candles he watched the two figures confront each other. The white hood was thrust back and Carbury Glande's red beard jutted out. Alleyn heard him mutter.

'Well, thank God for you, anyway. You *have* put him in a tizzy! What happened?'

The black cowl moved slightly from side to side. The head was bent.

'Oh, *all* right!' Glande said pettishly. 'What a stickler you are, to be sure!'

The white figure crossed the end of the hall and disappeared up the stairway.

Raoul moved on into the lobby and Alleyn came out of cover and followed him. When he entered the lobby, Alleyn went to the carved chest that stood against the back wall. It was there that the Egyptian servant had put the key of the wrought-iron door. Alleyn found the key and through the grill tossed it out of reach into the outside passageway.

From the lobby, the staircase wound downwards. Teresa's candle, out of sight and sinking, threw up her own travelling shadow and that of Raoul. Alleyn followed them, but they moved faster than he and he was left to grope his way down in a kind of twilight. He had completed three descending spirals when he arrived at the landing. The door he had noticed on his previous visit was now open and beyond it was a bedroom with a light burning before a looking-glass. This, evidently, was Robin Herrington's room. Alleyn went in. On the outside doorhandle hung a notice: 'Heure de Méditation. Ne érangez pas.' He hung it outside and shut the door.

The room had the smell and sensation of luxury that were characteristic of the Chèvre d'Argent. A white robe, like his own, was laid out together with silk shorts and shirt and a pair of white sandals. Alleyn changed quickly. On a table near the bed was a silver box, an ashtray, an elaborate lighter and, incongruously, a large covered dish which, on examination, proved to contain a sumptuous assortment of hors d'oeuvres and savouries. In the box were three cigarettes; long, thin and straw-coloured. He took one up, smelt it, broke it across and put the two halves in his case. He held a second to the candle, kept it going by returning it continuously to the flame and, as it was consumed, broke the ash into the tray.

'Three of those,' he thought, 'and young Herrington's values would be as cockeyed as one of Carbury Glande's abstracts.'

There was the lightest of taps on the door. It opened slightly, 'Monsieur?' whispered Teresa.

He let her in.

'Monsieur, it is to tell you that I have executed your order. I have spoken to M. Oberon. Tonight he was not as formerly he has been. He was not interested in me but all the same he was excited. One would have thought he was intoxicated, Monsieur, but he does not take wine.'

'You gave the message?'

'Yes, Monsieur. He listened eagerly and questioned me, saying: 'Have you seen her?' and I thought best, with the permission of the Saints, to say 'yes.'

'Quite so, Teresa.'

'He then asked me if Mademoiselle Taylor was quite well and I said she was and then if she seemed happy and I said 'yes, she seemed pleased and excited' because that is how one is, Monsieur, when one keeps an appointment. And I repeated that Mademoiselle had asked to be alone and he said: 'Of course, of course. It is essential,' as if to himself. And he was staring in a strange manner as if I was not there and so I left him. And although I was frightened, Monsieur, I was not troubled as formerly by M. Oberon because Raoul is the friend of my bosom and to him I will be constant.'

'I should certainly stick to that, if I were you. You are a good girl, Teresa, and now you must catch your bus. Tomorrow you shall choose a fine present against your wedding day.'

'Ah, Monsieur!' Teresa exclaimed and neatly sketching ineffable astonishment and delight, she slipped out of the room.

It was now eight o'clock. Alleyn settled down to his vigil. He thought of poor Miss Truebody and of the four remaining guests and Mr Oberon, each in his or her room, and each, he believed, oppressed by an almost intolerable sense of approaching climax. He wondered if Robin Herrington had followed his advice about blocking the vent in the cap on his petrol tank and he wondered if Troy had had any success in breaking down Ginny's enthralment.

He turned over in his mind all he had read of that curious expression of human credulity called magic. As it happened he had been obliged on a former case to dig up evidence of esoteric ritual and had become fascinated by its witness to man's industry in the pursuit of a chimera. Hundreds and hundreds of otherwise intelligent men, he found, had subjected themselves throughout the centuries to the boredom of memorizing and reciting senseless formulae, to the indignity of unspeakable practices and to the threat of the most ghastly reprisals. Through age after age men and woman had starved, frightened and exhausted themselves, had got themselves racked, broken and burnt, had delivered themselves up to what they believed to be the threat of eternal damnation and all without any first hand evidence of the smallest success. Age after age the Oberons and Baradis had battened on this unquenchable credulity, had traced their pentagrams, muttered their interminable spells, performed their gruelling ceremonies and taken their toll. And at the same time, he reflected, the Oberons (never the Baradis) had ended by falling into their own traps. The hysteria they induced was refracted upon themselves. Beyond the reek of ceremonial smoke they too began to look for the terrifying reward.

He wondered to what class of adept Oberon belonged. There was a definite hierarchy. There had always been practitioners who, however misguided, could not be accused of charlatanism. To this day, he believed, such beings existed, continuing their barren search for a talisman, for a philosopher's stone, for power and for easy money.

Magical rituals from the dawn of time had taken on the imprint of their several ages. From the scope and dignity of the Atkadian Inscriptions to the magnificence of the Graeco-Egyptian Papyri, from the pious Jewish mysteries to the squalors, brutalities and sheer silliness of the German pseudo-Faustian cults. From the Necromancer of the Coliseum to the surprisingly fresh folklorishness of the English genre: each had its peculiar character and its own formula of frustration. And alongside the direct line like a bastard brother ran the cult of Satanism, the imbecile horrors of the Black Mass, the Amatory Mass and the Mortuary Mass.

If Oberon had read all the books in his own library he had a pretty sound knowledge of these rituals together with a generous helping of Hinduism, Voodoo and Polynesian mythology: a wide field from which to concoct a ceremony for the downfall of Ginny Taylor and her predecessors. Alleyn fancied that the orthodox forms would not be followed. The oath of silence he had read in Baradi's room was certainly original. 'If it's the Amatory Mass as practised by Madame de Montespan,' he thought, 'poor old Raoul's sunk from the word go.' And he began to wonder what he should do if this particular crisis arose.

He spent the rest of his vigil eating the savouries that had no doubt been provided to satisfy the hunger of the reefer addict and smoking his own cigarettes. He checked over the possibilities of disaster and found them many and formidable. 'All the same,' he thought, 'it's worth it. And if the worst comes to the worst we can always – '

Somebody was scratching at his door.

He ground out his cigarette, extinguished his candle and seated himself on the floor with his back to the door and his legs folded Oberon-wise under his gown. He was facing the dressing-table with its large tilted looking-glass. The scratching persisted and turned into a feather-light tattoo of fingertips. He kept his gaze on that part of the darkness where he knew the looking-glass must be. He heard a fumbling and a slight rap and guessed that the notice had been moved from the door-handle. A vertical sliver of light appeared. He watched the reflection of the opening door and of the white-robed candle-bearer. He caught a glimpse, under the hood, of a long face with a beaked nose. Robed like that she seemed incredibly tall: no longer the figure of fantasy that she had presented yesterday in pedal-pushers and scarf and yet, unmistakably, the same woman. The door was shut. He bent his head and looked from under his brows at the reflection of the woman who advanced so close that he could hear her breathing behind him.

'I know it's against the Rule,' she whispered, 'I've got to speak to you.'

He made no sign.

'I don't know what they'll do to me if they find out but I'm actually past caring!' In the glass he saw her put the candle on the table. 'Have you smoked?' she said. 'If you have I suppose it's no good. I haven't.' He heard her sit heavily in the chair. 'Well,' she whispered almost cosily, 'it's about Ginny. You've never seen an initiation, have you? I mean of that sort. You might at least nod or shake your head.'

Alleyn shook his head.

'I thought not. You've got to stop her doing it. She's fond of you, you may depend upon it. If it was not for *him* she'd be in love like any other nice girl, with you. And you're fond of her. I know. I've watched. Well, you've got to stop it. She's a thoroughly nice girl,' the prim whisper insisted, 'and you're still a splendid young fellow. Tell her she mustn't.'

Alleyn's shoulders rose in an exaggerated shrug.

'Oh, *don't*!' The whisper broke into a vocal protest, 'If you only knew how I've been watching you both. If you only knew what I'm risking. Why, if you tell on me I don't know what they won't do. Murder me, as likely as not. It wouldn't be the first time unless you believe she killed herself, and I certainly don't.'

The voice stopped. Alleyn waited.

'One way or another,' the voice said quite loudly, 'you've got to give me a sign.'

He raised his hand and made the Italian negative sign with his finger.

'You won't! You mean you'll let it happen. To Ginny? In front of everybody. Oh, dear me!' the voice sighed out most lamentably, 'Oh, dear, dear me, it's enough to break one's heart!' There was a further silence. Alleyn thought: 'The time's going by: we haven't much longer. If she'd just say one thing!'.

The voice said strongly, as if its owner had taken fresh courage: 'Very well. I shall speak to her. It won't do any good. I look at you and I ask myself what sort of creature you are. I look – '

She broke off. She had moved her candle so that its reflection in the glass was thrown back upon Alleyn. He sat frozen.

'*Who are you?*' the voice demanded strongly. 'You're not Robin Herrington.'

She was behind him. She jerked the hood back from his head and they stared at each other in the looking-glass.

'And you're not Grizel Locke,' Alleyn said. He got up, faced her and held out his hand. 'Miss P.E. Garbel, I presume,' he said gently.

CHAPTER 12

Eclipse of the Sun

'Then you guessed!' said Miss Garbel, clinging to his hand and shaking it up and down as if it was a sort of talisman. 'How did you guess? How did you get here? What's happening?'

Alleyn said: 'We've got twenty-five minutes before that damn' bell goes. Don't let's squander them. I wasn't sure. Yesterday morning, when you talked like one of your letters, I wondered.'

'I couldn't let either of you know who I was. Oberon was watching. They all were. I thought the remark about the bus might catch your attention.'

'I didn't dare ask outright, of course. Now, tell me. Grizel Locke's dead, isn't she?'

'Yes; small hours of yesterday morning. We were told an overdose of self-administered heroin. *I* think – murdered.'

'Why was she murdered?'

'*I* think, because she protested about Ginny. Ginny's her niece. *I* think she may have threatened them with exposure.'

'Who killed her?'

'I haven't an idea. Oh, not a notion!'

'What exactly were you told?'

'That if it was found out we'd all be in trouble. That the whole thing would be discovered – the trade in diacetylmorphine, the connection with the factory – have you discovered about the factory? – everything, they said, would come out and we'd all be arrested and the British subjects would be extradited and tried and imprisoned. Then, it appears, you rang up about Miss Truebody. Baradi saw it as a chance to dispose of poor Grizel Locke. She would be buried, you see, and you would be told it was Miss Truebody. Then later on, when you were out of the way and Miss Truebody was well, a made-up name would be put over the grave. Baradi said that if anybody could save Miss Truebody's life, he could. I'm guessing at how much you know. Stop me if I'm not clear. And then you or your wife asked about 'Cousin Garbel.' You can imagine how that shocked them! I was there, you see. I'm their liaison with the factory. I work at the factory. I'll tell you why and how if we've time. Of course I guessed who you were but I told them I hadn't a notion. I said I supposed you must be some unknown people with an introduction or something. They were terribly suspicious. They said I must see you both and find out what you were doing, and why you'd asked about me. Then Baradi said it would be better if I didn't present myself as me. And then they said I must pretend to be Grizel Locke so that if there was ever an inquiry or trouble, you and Cousin Aggie – '

'*Who!*' Alleyn ejaculated.

'Your wife, you know. She was called Agatha after my second-cousin, once – '

'Yes, yes. Sorry. I call her Troy.'

'Really? Quaint! I've formed the habit of thinking of her as Cousin Aggie. Well, the plan was that I'd be introduced to you as Grizel Locke and I should tell them afterwards if I recognized you or knew anything about you. They made me wear Grizel's clothes and paint my face, in face you'd heard about her or would be asked about her afterwards. And then, tomorrow, after the funeral we are meant to meet again and I've to say I'm leaving for a trip to Budapest. If possible, you are to see me go. So that if a hue-and-cry goes out for Grizel Locke, you will support the story that she's left for Hungary. I'm to go as far as Marseilles and stay there until you're both out of the way. The factory has extensive connections in Marseilles. At the same time we're to give out that I, as myself, you know, have gone on holiday. How much longer have we got?'

'Twenty-one minutes.'

'I've time, at least, to tell you quickly that whatever you're planning you mustn't depend too much on me. You see, I'm one of them.'

'You mean,' Alleyn said, 'you've formed the habit –?'

'I'm fifty. Sixteen years ago I was a good analytical chemist but terribly poor. They offered me a job on a wonderful salary. Research. They started me off in New York and after the war they brought me over here. At first I thought it was all right and then gradually I discovered what was happening. They handled me on orthodox lines. A man, very attractive, and parties. I was always plain and he was experienced and charming. He started me on marihuana – reefers, you know – and I've never been able to break off. They see to it I get just enough to keep me going. They get me up here and make me nervous and then give me cigarettes. I'm very useful to them. When I smoke I get very silly. I hear myself saying things that fill me with bitter shame. But when I've got the craving to smoke and when *he's* given me cigarettes, I – well, you've seen. It wasn't all play acting when I pretended to be Grizel Locke. We all get like that with Oberon. He has a genius for defilement.'

'Why did you write as you did to Troy? I must tell you that we didn't realize what you were up to until yesterday.'

'I was afraid you wouldn't. But I daren't be explicit. Their surveillance is terribly thorough and my letters might have been opened. They weren't, as it turned out, otherwise you would have been recognized as my correspondent. I wrote – '

The voice, half vocal, half whispering, faltered. She pushed back her hood and tilted her tragi-comic face towards his. 'I began to write because of the girls like Ginny. You've seen me and you've seen Annabella Wells – frightful, aren't we? Grizel Locke was the same. Drug-soaked old horrors. We're what happens to the Ginnys. And there are lots and lots of Ginnys: bomb-children I call 'em. No moral stamina and no nervous reserve. Parents killed within the child's memory and experience. Sense of insecurity and impending disaster. The poor ones with jobs have the best chance. But the others – the rich Ginnys – if they run into our sort of set – whoof! And once they're made Daughters of the Sun it's the end of them. Too ashamed to look back or up or anywhere but at him. So when I saw in the English papers that my clever kinswoman had married *you*, I thought: 'I'll do it. I haven't the nerve or self-control to fight on my own but I'll try and hint.' So I did. I was a little surprised when Cousin Aggie replied as if to a man but I did not correct her. Her mistake gave me a foolish sense of security. How long, now?'

'Just over seventeen minutes. Listen! Herrington and Ginny won't come back tonight. My chauffeur and I are replacing them. Can we get away with it? What happens in the ceremony?'

She had been talking eagerly and quickly, watching him with a bird-like attentiveness. Now it was as if his question touched her with acid. She actually threw up her hands in a self-protective movement and shrank away from him.

'I can't tell you. I've taken an oath of silence.'

'All that dagger and fire and molten lead nonsense?'

'You can't know! How do you know? Who's broken faith?'

'Nobody. I hoped you might.'

'Never!'

'A silly gimcrack rigmarole. Based on infamy.'

'It's no good. I told you. I'm no good.'

'My man's about Ginny's height and he's wearing the black robe. Has he a chance of getting by?'

'Not to the end. Of course not.' She caught her breath in something that might have been a sob or a wretched giggle. 'How can you dream of it?'

'Will anybody be asked to take this oath – alone?'

'No – I can tell you nothing – but – he – no. Why are you doing this?'

'We think the ceremony may give us an opportunity for an arrest on a minor charge. Not only that – ' Alleyn hesitated, 'I feel as you do,' he said hurriedly, 'about this wretched child. For one thing she's English and there's a double sense of responsibility. At the same time I'm not here to do rescue work, particularly if it prejudices the success of my job. What's more, if Oberon and Baradi suspect that this child and young Herrington have done a bolt, they'll also suspect a betrayal. They'll have the machinery for meeting such a crisis. All evidence of their interest in the racket will be destroyed and they'll shoot the moon. Whereas, if, by good luck, we can diddle them into thinking Ginny Taylor and Robin Herrington have returned to their unspeakable fold we may learn enough, here, tonight to warrant an arrest. We can then hold the principals, question the smaller fry and search the whole place.'

'I'm small fry. How do you know I won't warn them?'

'I've heard you plead for Ginny.'

'You've told me she's safe,' whimpered Miss Garbel. She bit her fingertips and looked at them out of the corner of her pale eyes. 'That's all I wanted. You ask me to bring ruin on myself. I've warned you. I'm no good. I've no integrity left. In a minute I must smoke and then I'll be hopeless. You ask too much.'

Alleyn said: 'You're a braver woman that you admit. You've tried for months to get me here, knowing that if I succeed your job will be gone and you will have to break yourself of your drug. You risked trying to tip me off yesterday morning and you risked coming to plead with young Herrington here tonight. You're a woman of science with judgment and curiosity and a proper scepticism. You know, positively, that this silly oath of silence was taken under the influence of your drug, that the threats it carries are meaningless, that it's your clear duty to abandon it. I think you will believe me when I say that if you keep faith with us tonight you will have our full protection afterwards.'

'You can't protect me,' she said, 'from myself.'

'We can try. Come! Having gone so far, why not all the way?'

'I'm so frightened,' said Miss Garbel. 'You can't think. So dreadfully frightened.'

She clasped her claw-like hands together. Alleyn covered them with his own. 'All right,' he said. 'Never mind. You've done a lot. I won't ask you to tell me about the rites. Don't go to the ceremony. Can you send a message?'

'I must go. There must be seven.'

'One for each point of the pentagram, with Oberon and the Black Robe in the middle?'

'Did *they* tell you? Ginny and Robin? They wouldn't dare.'

'Call it a guess. Before we separate I'm going to ask you to make one promise tonight. Shall we say for Grizel Locke's sake? Don't smoke so much marihuana that you may lose control of yourself and perhaps betray us.'

'I shan't betray you. I *can* promise that. I don't promise not to smoke and I implore you to depend on me for nothing more than this. I won't give you away.'

'Thank you a thousand times, my dear cousin-by-marriage. Before the night is over I shall ask if I may call you Penelope.'

'Naturally you may. In my bad moments,' said poor Miss Garbel, 'I have often cheered myself up by thinking of you both as Cousins Roddy and Aggie.'

'Have you really?' Alleyn murmured and was saved from the necessity of further comment by the sound of a cascade of bells.

Miss Garbel was thrown into a great state of perturbation by the bells which, to Alleyn, were reminiscent of the dinner chimes that tinkle through the corridors of ocean liners.

'There!' she ejaculated with a sort of wretched triumph. 'The Temple bells! And here we are in somebody else's room and goodness *knows* what will become of us.'

'I'll see if the coast's clear.' Alleyn said. He took up his stick and then opened the door. The smell of incense hung thick on the air. Evidently candles had been lit on the lower landing. The stairwell sank into reflected light through which there rose whorls and spirals of scented smoke. As he watched, a shadow came up from below and the sound of bells grew louder. It was the Egyptian servant. Alleyn watched the distorted image of his tarboosh travel up the curved wall followed by that of his body and of his hands bearing the chime of bells. Alleyn stood firm, leaning on his stick with his hood over his face. The Egyptian followed his own shadow upstairs, ringing his little carillon. He crossed the landing, made a salutation as he passed Alleyn and continued on his way upstairs.

Alleyn looked back into the room. Miss Garbel stood there, biting her knuckles. He went to her.

'It's all right,' he said. 'You can go down. If you feel *very* brave and venturesome keep as close as you dare to the Black Robe and if he looks like making a mistake try and stop him. He only speaks French. Now, you'd better go.'

She shook her head two or three times. Then, with an incredible suggestion of conventional leave-taking she began to settle herself inside her robe. She actually held out her hand.

'Goodbye. I'm sorry I'm not a braver woman,' she said.

'You've been very brave for a long time and I'm exceedingly grateful,' Alleyn said.

He watched her go and after giving her about thirty seconds blew out the candle and followed her.

II

The stairs turned three times about the tower before he came limping to the bottom landing. Here a lighted candelabrum stood near a door: the door he had noticed yesterday morning. Now it was open. The air was dense with the reek of incense so that each candle flame blossomed in a nimbus. His feet sank into the deep carpet and dimly he could make out the door into Oberon's room and the vista of wall-tapestries, receding into a passage.

Through the open door he saw four separate candlesticks, each with a lighted black candle. This, then, was the anteroom. Alleyn went in. The black velvet walls absorbed light and an incense-burner hanging from the ceiling further obscured it. He could make out a partly-opened curtain and hehind this a rack of hanging robes. He could not be sure he was alone. Limping carefully he made for the candles and took one up.

Remembering what Teresa had told him, he turned to the right and with his free hand explored the wall. The velvet surface was disagreeable to his touch. He moved along still pressing it and in a moment it yielded. He had found the swing door into the temple.

There was an unwholesomeness about the silent obedience of the velvet door. It was as if everyday objects had begun to change their values. He followed his hand and walked, as it seemed, through the retreating wall into the temple.

At first he was aware only of two candle flames below the level of his knees and some distance ahead, six glowing braziers. Then he saw a white robe, squatting not far from a candle and then a black robe, near a second flame. He felt the tessellated floor under his feet and, using his stick, tapped his way across. 'All the same,' he thought, 'young Herrington's stick is rubber-shod.'

By the light of his own candle he made out the shape of the giant pentagram in the mosaic of the floor. It had been let into the pavement and was traced in some substance that acted as a reflector. The five-pointed star was enclosed in a double circle and he saw that at each of the points there was a smaller circle and in this a black cushion and a brazier filled with glowing embers. It was on one of these cushions that the white robe squatted. He drew close to it. A recognizable hand crept out from under the sleeve. It was Miss Garbel's.

He turned to the centre of the pentagram. Raoul was holding his candle under his own face. His hands and arms were gloved in black. He was seated cross-legged on a black divan and in front of him was a brazier.

Alleyn murmured: 'The lady behind you and to your right is not unfriendly. She knows who you are.'

Raoul signalled an assent.

'Depend on me for nothing – nothing,' admonished a ghost-whisper in French and then added in a sort of frenzy: 'Not there! Not in the middle. Not yet. Like me. *There!*'

Raoul darted into the point of the pentagram in front of Miss Garbel's. He put down his candle on the floor and pulled forward his hood.

Alleyn moved to the encircled point opposite Miss Garbel's. He had seated himself on the cushion before his brazier and had laid down his stick and candle when a light danced across the facets of the pentagram. He sensed, rather than heard, the entrance of a new figure. It passed so close that he recognized Annabella Well's scent. She moved into the encircled point on his right and seated herself facing outwards as he did. At the same time there was a new glint of candlelight and the sound of a subsidence behind and to the left of Alleyn. In a moment or two a figure, unmistakably Baradi's, swept round the pentagram and entered it between Annabella and Raoul. Alleyn guessed he had taken up his position at the centre. At the same time the bells cascaded close at hand. 'Here we go,' he thought

The five candles and six braziers furnished light enough for him to get a fitful impression of the preposterous scene. By turning his head slightly and slewing his eyes, he could see the neighbouring points of the great pentagonal star, each protected by its circle and each containing its solitary figure, seated before a brazier and facing outward. Outside the pentagram and facing the points occupied by Annabella and Raoul was the altar. Alleyn could see the glint of metal in the embroidered cloth, and quite distinctly could make out the shape of the great crystal sun-burst standing in the middle.

The sound of bells came close and then stopped. A door opened in the wall beside the altar and the Egyptian servant walked through. He wore only a loin cloth and the squarish head-dress of antiquity. Before each of the initiates he set down a little box. 'More reefers,' thought Alleyn, keeping his head down. 'Damned awkward if he wants to light them for us.'

But the Egyptian made no attempt to do so. He moved away and out of the tail of his eye, Alley saw Annabella Wells reach out to her brazier, take a pair of tongs and light her cigarette with a piece of charcoal. Alleyn found that his brazier, too, was provided with tongs.

Because of the form of the pentagram the occupants of the five points all had their backs turned to Baradi and their shoulders to each other. If Baradi was on his feet he would have a sort of aerial survey of their backs. If he was seated on the divan he would have a still less rewarding view. Alleyn reached out for a cigarette, hid it inside his robe and produced one of his own. This he lit with a coal from the brazier. He wondered if it had occurred to Raoul to employ the same ruse.

Little spires of smoke began to rise from the five points of the star. The Egyptian had retired to a dark corner beyond the altar and presently began to strike a drum and play a meandering air on some reed instrument. To Alleyn the scene was preposterous and phony. He remembered Troy's comment on the incident of the train window: hadn't she compared it to bad cinematography? Even the ritual, for what it was worth, was bogus: a vamped up synthesis, he thought, of several magic formulae. The reedy phrase trickled on like a tourist-class advertisement for Cairo, the drum throbbed and presently he sensed an air of excitement among the initiates. The Egyptian began to chant and to increase the pace and volume of his drumming. Drum and voice achieved a sort of crescendo at the peak of which a second voice entered with a long vibrant call, startling in its unexpectedness. It was Baradi's.

From that moment it was impossible altogether to dismiss the Rites of the Sun as cheap or ridiculous. No doubt they were both but they were also alarming.

Alleyn supposed that Baradi spoke Egyptian and that his chant was one of the set invocations of ritual magic. He thought he recognized the characteristic repetition of names: 'O Oualbpaga! O Kammara! O Kamalo! O Karjenmou! O Amagaa! O Thouth! O Anubis!' The drum thumped imperatively. Small feral noises came from the points of the pentagram. Behind Alleyn, Carbury Glande began to beat with his palm on the floor. The other initiates followed, Alleyn with them. The Egyptian left his drum and running about the pentagram, threw incense on the braziers. Columns of heavily scented smoke arose amid sharp cries from the initiates. A gong crashed and there was immediate silence.

It was startling, after the long exhortations in an incomprehensible tongue to hear Baradi cry in a loud voice: 'Children of the Sun in the Outer, turn inward, now turn in. Silence, silence, silence, symbol of the imperishable god protect us, silence. Turn inward now, turn in.'

This injunction was taken literally by the initiates who reversed their positions on the cushions and thus faced Baradi and the centre of the pentagram. Looking across, diagonally, to the Black Robe, Alleyn saw that Raoul had not moved. The exhortations, being in English, had meant nothing to him. Alleyn dared not look up at Baradi. He could see his feet and his white robe, up to his knees. Between drifts of incense he caught sight of the other initiates, all waiting. It seemed as if an age went by before the Black Robe rose, turned and reseated itself. He saw Baradi's feet shift and his robe swing as he faced the altar.

Baradi intoned in a loud voice: 'Here is the Names of Ra and the sons of Ra – '

It was the oath Alleyn had read. Baradi gave it out phrase by phrase and the initiates repeated it after him. Alleyn spoke on the top register of his deep voice. Raoul, of course, said nothing. Miss Garbel's thin pipe was unmistakable. Annabella's trained and vibrant voice rang out loudly. Carbury Glande's sounded unco-ordinated and hysterical.

'If I break this oath in the least degree,' Baradi dictated and was echoed, 'may my lips be burnt with the fire that is now set before them.' He gestured over his brazier. A tongue of flame darted up from it.

'May my eyes be put out by the knife that is now set before them.'

With a suddenness that was extraordinarily unnerving, five daggers dropped from the ceiling and checked with a jerk before the five initiates' faces. A sixth, bigger, fell in front of Baradi who seized and flourished it. The others hung glittering in the flame-light of the brazier. The women gave little whimpering febrile cries.

The oath of silence was taken through to its abominable conclusion. The flame subsided, the smaller daggers were drawn up to the ceiling, presumably by the Egyptian. The initiates turned outward again and Baradi settled down to a further exhortation, this time in English.

It was the blackest possible kind of affair, quite short and entirely infamous. Baradi demanded darkness and the initiates put out their candles. Alleyn dared not look at Raoul but knew by the delayed flicker of light that he was a little slow with his. Then Baradi urged first of all the necessity of experiencing something called 'The caress of the left hand of perfection' and went on to particularize in terms that would have appalled anyone who was not an alienist or a member of Mr Oberon's chosen circle. The Egyptian had returned to his reed and drum and the merciless repetition of a single phrase had its own effect. Baradi began to pour out a stream of names: Greek, Jewish, Egyptian: – Pan, Enlil, Elohim, Ra, Anubis, Seti, Adonis, Ra, Silenus, Ereschigal, Tetragramatom, Ra. The recurrent 'Ra' was presently taken up by the initiates who began to bark it out with an enthusiasm; Alleyn thought, only to be equalled by the organized cheers of an American ball game.

'There are two signs,' Baradi intoned. 'There is the Sign of the Sun, Ra' ('Ra,' barked the initiates), 'and there is the sign of the Goat, Pan. And between the Sun and the Goat runs the endless cycle of the senses. Ra!'

'Ra!'

'We demand a sign.'

'We demand a sign.'

'What shall the sign be?'

'The sign of the goat which is also the sign of the Sun which is also the sign of Ra.'

'Let the goat come forth which is the Sun which is Ra.'

'Ra!'

The drumming was increased to a frenzy. The initiates beat on the floor and clapped. Baradi must have thrown more incense on the brazier: the air was thick with billowing fumes. Alleyn could scarcely make out the shape of the altar. Now Baradi must be striking cymbals together.

The din was intolerable. The initiates, antic figures, half masked by whorls of smoke, seemed to have gone down on all-fours and to

be flinging their hands high as they slapped the floor and cried out.
Baradi broke into a chant, possibly in his own language, interspersed
with further strings of names – Pan, Hylaesos, Lupercus, Silenos,
Faunus – names that were caught up and shouted in fury of abandon by the other voices. Alleyn, shouting with the rest, edged round
on his knees, until he could look across the pentagram to Raoul. In
the glow of the braziers he could just make out the black crouching
figure and the black gloved hands rising and falling like drumsticks.

'A Sign, a Sign, let there be a Sign!'

'*It comes.*'

'It comes.'

'*It is here.*'

Again the well-staged crescendo that ended, this time, in a deafening crash of cymbals followed by a dead silence.

And across that silence: pathetic, ridiculous and disturbing, broke
the unmistakable bleat of a billy-goat.

The smoke eddied and swirled, and there, on the altar for all the
world like one of old Marie's statuettes, it appeared, horned and
shining, a silver goat whose hide glittered through the smoke. It
opened its mouth sideways and superciliously bleated. Its pale eyes
stared and it stamped and tossed its head.

'It's been shoved up there from the back,' Alleyn thought.
'They've treated it with fluorescent paint. *Ça s'illumine.*'

Baradi was speaking again.

'Prepare, prepare,' he chanted. 'The Sign is the Shadow of the
Substance. The Goat-god is the precursor of the Man-god. The Man-
god is the Bridegroom. He is the Spouse. He is Life. He is the Sun. Ra!'

There was a blare of light, for perhaps a second literally blinding
in its intensity. 'Flash-powder,' thought Alleyn. 'The Egyptian must
be remarkably busy.' When his eyes had adjusted themselves, the
goat had disappeared and in its place the sun-burst blazed on
the altar. 'Car batteries,' thought Alleyn, 'perhaps. Flex soldered at
the terminals. Well done, Mahomet or somebody.'

'Ra! Ra! Ra!' the initiates ejaculated, with Baradi as their cheer-
leader.

The door to the left of the altar had opened. It admitted a naked man.

He advanced through wreaths of incense and stood before the
blazing sun-burst. It was, of course, Mr Oberon.

III

Of the remainder of the ceremony, as far as he witnessed it, Alleyn afterwards prepared an official report. Neither this, nor a manual called *The Book of Ra*, which contained the text of the ritual, has ever been made public. Indeed, they have been stowed away in the archives of Scotland Yard where they occupy a place of infamy rivalling that of the *Book of Horus and the Swami Viva Ananda*. There are duplicates at the Sûretè. In the trial they were not put in as primary evidence and the judge, after a distasteful glance, said that he saw no reason why the jury should be troubled to look at them.

For purpose of this narrative it need only be said that with the appearance of Oberon, naked, in the role of Ra or Horus, or both, the Rites took on the character of unbridled phallicism. He stood on some raised place before the blazing sun-burst, holding a dagger in both hands. More incense burners were set reeking at his feet, and there he was, the nearest approach, Alleyn afterwards maintained, that he had ever seen, to a purely evil being.

His entry stung the initiates into their last pitch of frenzy. Incredible phrases were chanted, indescribable gestures were performed. The final crescendo of that scandalous affair rocketed up to its point of climax. For the last time the Egyptian's drum rolled and Baradi clashed his cymbals. For the last time pandemonium gave place to silence.

Oberon came down from his eminence and walked towards the encircled pentagram. His feet slapped the tessellated pavement. His hair, lit from behind, was a nimbus about his head. He entered the pentagram and the initiates turned inwards, crouching beastily at the points. Oberon placed himself at the centre. Baradi spoke.

'Horus who is Savitar who is Baldur who is Ra. The Light, The Beginning and The End, The Life, The Source and The Fulfilment. Choose, now, Lord, O choose.'

Oberon extended his arm and pointed his dagger at Raoul.

Baradi went to Raoul. He held out his hand. In the capricious glare from he sunburst Alleyn could see Raoul on his knees, his shadow thrown before him towards Oberon's feet. His face was deeply hidden in his hood. Alleyn saw the gloved hand and arm reach out. Baradi took the hand. He passed Raoul across him with a dancer's gesture.

Raoul now faced Oberon.

Somewhere in the shadows the Egyptian servant cried out shrilly.

Baradi's dark hands, themselves seeming gloved, closed on the shoulders of Raoul's robe. Suddenly, with a flourish, and to a roll of the drum, he swept it free of its wearer. 'Behold!' he shouted: 'The Bride!'

And then, in the glare from the sun-burst, where, like an illustration from *La Vie Parisienne*, Mr Oberon's victim should have been discovered – there stood Raoul in his underpants, black slippers and Ginny Taylor's gloves.

A complete surprise is often something of an anti-climax and so, for a moment or two, was this. It is possible that Annabella Wells and Carbury Glande were too fuddled with marihuana to get an immediate reaction. Miss Garbel, of course, had been prepared. As for Oberon and Baradi, they faced each other across the preposterous Thing they had unveiled and their respective jaws dropped like those of a pair of simultaneous comedians. Raoul himself merely cast a scandalized glance at Oberon and uttered in a loud apocalyptic voice the single word: *'Anathema!'*

It was then that Miss Garbel erupted in a single hoot of hysteria. It escaped from her and was at once cut off by her own hand clapped across her mouth. She squatted, heaving, in the corner of the pentacle, her terrified eyes staring over her knuckles at Baradi.

Baradi, in an unrecognizable voice and an unconscious quotation, said: 'Which of you has done this?'

Oberon gave a bubbling cry: 'I am betrayed!'

Raoul, hearing his voice, repeated: 'Anathema!' and made the sign of the cross.

Oberon dragged Miss Garbel to her feet. He held her with his right hand; in his left was the dagger. She chattered in his face: 'You can't! You can't! I'm protected. You can't!'

Alleyn advanced until he was quite close to them. Glande and Annabella Wells were on their feet.

'Is this your doing?' Oberon demanded, lowering his face to Miss Garbel's.

'Not mine!' she chattered. 'Not this time. Not mine!'

He flung her off. Baradi turned to Raoul.

'Well!' Baradi said in French, 'so I know you, now. Where's your master?'

'Occupy yourself with your own affairs, Monsieur.'

'We are lost!' Oberon cried out in English.

His hand moved. The knife glinted.

'*Alors, Raoul!*' said Alleyn.

Raoul stooped and ran. He ran out of the pentacle and across the floor. The Egyptian darted out and was knocked sideways. His head struck the corner of the altar and he lay still. Raoul sped through the open door into Oberon's room. Oberon followed him. Alleyn followed Oberon and caught him up on the far side of the great looking-glass. He seized his right hand as it was raised. 'Not this time,' Alleyn grunted and jerked his arm. The dagger flew from Oberon's hand and splintered the great glass. At the same moment Raoul kicked. Oberon gave a scream of pain, staggered across the room and lurched against the window. With a whirr and a clatter the blind flew up and Oberon sank on the floor moaning. Alleyn turned to find Baradi facing him with the knife in his hand.

'You,' Baradi said, 'I might have guessed. *You!*'

IV

From the moment that the affair began, as it were, to wind itself up in Oberon's room, it became a straightout conflict between Alleyn and Baradi. Alleyn had guessed that it would be so. Even while he sweated to remember his police training in unarmed combat he found time to consider that Oberon, naked and despicable, had at last become a negligible element. Alleyn was even aware of Carbury Glande and Annabella Wells teetering uncertainly in the doorway, and of Miss Garbel who hovered like a spinsterly half-back on the edge of the scrimmage.

But chiefly he was aware of Baradi's dark infuriated body, smelling of sandalwood. and sweat, and of the knowledge that he himself was the fitter man. They struggled together ridiculously and ominously, looking in their white robes, like a couple of frenzied monks. There was, for Alleyn, a sort of pleasure in this fight. 'I needn't worry. For once, I needn't worry,' he thought. 'For once the final arbitrament is as simple as this. I'm fitter than he is.'

And when Raoul, absurd in his underpants and long gloves, suddenly hurled himself at Baradi and brought him down with a crash, Alleyn was conscious of a sort of irritation. He looked across the floor and saw that Raoul's foot, in its ridiculous sandal, had pinned down Baradi's left wrist. He saw Baradi's fingers uncurl from the knife-handle. He shoved free, landed a short-arm jab on the point of Baradi's jaw and felt him go soft. They had brought down the prayer-wheel in their struggle. Alleyn reached for it and flung it at the window. It crashed through and he heard it fall with the broken glass on the railway line below. Oberon screamed out an oath. Alleyn fetched his breath and blew with all the wind he had on M. Dupont's police whistle. It trilled shrilly, like a toy, and was answered and echoed and answered again outside.

'The house is surrounded,' Alleyn said, looking at Glande and Oberon. 'I have a police authority. Anyone trying violence or flight will be dealt with out-of-hand. Stay where you are, all of you.'

The glare from the sun-burst streamed through the doorway on clouds of incense. Alleyn bound Baradi's arms behind his back with the cord of his gown. Raoul tied his ankles together with the long gloves. Baradi's head lolled drunkenly and he made uncouth noises.

'I want to make a statement,' Oberon said shrilly. 'I am a British subject. I have my passport. I offer myself for Queen's evidence. I have my passport.'

Annabella Wells, standing in the doorway, began to laugh. Carbury Glande said: 'Shut up, for God's sake. This is IT.'

Abruptly the room was lit. Wall-lamps, a bedside lamp and a standard lamp all came to life. By normal standards it was not a brilliant illumination but it had the effect of reducing that unlikely interior to an embarrassing state of anti-climax. Glande, Annabella Wells and poor Miss Garbel, huddled in their robes, looked dishevelled and ineffectual. Baradi had a trickle of blood running from his nose into his moustache. The Egyptian servant staggered into the doorway holding his head in his hands and wearing the foolish expression of a punch-happy pugilist. Oberon, standing before the cracked looking-glass as no doubt he had often done before: Oberon, naked, untactfully lit, was so repellent a sight that Alleyn threw the cover of the divan at him.

'You unspeakable monstrosity,' he said, 'get behind that.'

'I offer a full statement. I am the victim of Dr Baradi. I claim protection.'

Baradi opened his eyes and shook the blood from his moustache.

'I challenge your authority,' he said, blinking at Alleyn.

'Alleyn, Chief Detective-Inspector, CID, New Scotland Yard. On loan to the Sûreté. My card and my authority are in my coat-pocket and my coat's in young Herrington's room.'

Baradi twisted his head to look at Annabella. 'Did you know this?' he demanded.

'Yes, darling,' she said.

'You little – '

'Is that Gyppo for what, darling?'

'In a moment,' Alleyn said, 'the Commissioner of Police will be here and you will be formally arrested and charged. I don't know that I'm obliged to give you the customary warning, but the habit's irresistible. Anything you say – '

Baradi and Annabella entirely disregarded him.

'*Why* didn't you tell me who he was?' Baradi said. '*Why?*'

'He asked me not to. He's got something. I didn't know he was here tonight. I didn't know he'd come back.'

'Liar!'

'As you choose, my sweet.'

' – May be used in evidence.'

'You can't charge *me* with anything,' Carbury Glande said, 'I am an artist. I've formed the habit of smoking and I come to France to do it. I'm not mixed up in anything. If I hadn't had my smokes tonight I'd bloody well fight you.'

'Nonsense,' said Alleyn.

'I desire to make a statement,' said Oberon, who was now wrapped in crimson satin and sitting on the divan.

'I wish to speak to you alone, Mr Alleyn,' said Baradi.

'All in good time.'

'Garbel!' Baradi ejaculated.

'Shall I answer him, Roddy dear?'

'If you want to, Cousin Penelope.'

'*Cousin!*' Mr Oberon shouted.

'Only by marriage. I informed you,' Miss Garbel reminded him, 'of the relationship. And I think it only right to tell you that if it hadn't been for all the Ginnys – '

'My God,' Carbury Glande shouted, 'where are Ginny and Robin?'

'Ginny!' Oberon cried out, 'where is Ginny?'

'I hope,' rejoined Miss Garbel, 'in no place so unsanctified where such as thou mayst find her.' The quotation, cousin, is from Macbeth.'

'And couldn't be more appropriate,' murmured Alleyn, bowing to her. He sat down at Mr Oberon's desk and drew a sheet of paper towards him.

'This woman,' Baradi said to Alleyn, 'is not in her right mind. I tell you this professionally. She has been under my observation for some time. In my considered opinion she is unable to distinguish between fact and fantasy. If you base your preposterous behaviour on any statement of hers – '

'Which I don't, you know.'

'I am an Egyptian subject. I claim privilege. And I warn you, that if you hold me, you'll precipitate a political incident.'

'My dear M. l'Inspecteur-en-chef,' said M. Dupont coming in from the passage, 'do forgive me if I am a little unpunctual.'

'On the contrary, my dear M. le Commisssaire, you come most punctually upon your cue.'

M. Dupont shook hands with Alleyn. He was in tremendous form, shining with leather and wax and metal: gloved, holstered and batoned. Three lesser officers appeared inside the door.

'And these,' said M. Dupont touching his moustache and glancing round the room, 'are the personages. You charge them?'

'For the moment, with conspiracy.'

'I am a naturalized British subject. I offer myself as Queen's Evidence. I charge Dr Ali Baradi with murder.'

Baradi turned his head and in his own language shot a stream of raw-sounding phrases at his late partner.

'All these matters,' said Dupont, 'will be dealt with in an appropriate manner. In the meantime, Messieurs et Dames, it is required that you accompany my officers to the *Commissariat de Police* in Roqueville where an accusation will be formally laid.' He nodded to his men who advanced with a play of handcuffs.

Annabella Wells held her robe about her with one practised hand and swept back her hair with the other. She addressed herself in French to Dupont.

'M. le Commissaire, do you recognize me?'

'Perfectly, Madame. Madame is the actress Annabella Wells.'

'Monsieur, you are a man of the world. You will understand that I find myself in a predicament.'

'It is not necessary to be a man of the world to discover your predicament, Madame. It is enough to be a policeman. If Madame would care to make such adjustment to her toilette – a walking costume perhaps – I shall be delighted to arrange the facilities. There is a *femme-agent de police* in attendance.'

She looked at him for a moment, seemed to hesitate, and then turned to Alleyn.

'What are you going to do with me?' she said. 'You've trapped me finely, haven't you? What a fool I was! Yesterday morning I might have guessed. And I kept faith! I didn't tell them what you were. God, *what* a fool!'

'It's probably the only really sensible thing you've done since you came here. Don't regret it.'

'Is it wishful thinking or do I seem to catch the suggestion that I may be given a chance?'

'Give yourself a chance, why not?'

'Ah,' she said, shaking her head. 'That'll be the day, won't it?'

She grinned at him and moved over to the door where Raoul waited. Raoul stared at her with a kind of incredulity. He had kicked off his sandals and wore only his pants and his St Christopher medal and, thus arrayed, contrived to look godlike.

'What a charmer!' she said in English. 'Aren't you?'

'*Madame?*'

'*Quel charmeur vous êtes!*'

'Madame!'

She asked him how old he was and if he had seen many of her films. He said he believed he had seen them all. Was he a cinephile, then? '*Madame,*' said Raoul, '*Je suis un fervent – de vous!*'

'When they let me out of gaol,' Annabella promised, 'I shall send you a photograph.'

The wreckage of her beauty spoke through the ruin of her make-up. She made a good exit.

'Ah, Monsieur,' said Raoul. 'What a tragedy! And yet it is the art that counts and she is still an artist.'

This observation went unregarded. They could hear Annabella in conversation with the *femme-agent* in the passage outside.

'My dear Dupont,' Alleyn murmured, 'may I suggest that in respect of this woman we make no arrest. I feel certain that she will be of much greater value as a free informant. Keep her under observation, of course, but for the moment, at least – '

'But, of course, my dear Alleyn,' M. Dupont rejoined, taking the final plunge into intimacy, 'I understand, perfectly, but perfectly.'

Alleyn was not quite sure what Dupont understood so perfectly but thought it better merely to thank him. He said: 'There is a great deal to be explained. May we get rid of the men first?'

Dupont's policemen had taken charge of the four men. Oberon, still wrapped in crimson satin, was huddled on his bed. His floss-like hair hung in strands over his face. Above the silky divided beard the naked mouth was partly open. The eyes stared, apparently without curiosity, at Alleyn.

Dupont's men had lifted Baradi from the floor, seated him on the divan and pulled his white robe about him. His legs had been unbound, but he was now handcuffed. He, too, watched Alleyn, but sombrely, with attentiveness and speculation.

Carbury Glande stood nearby, biting his nails. The Egyptian servant flashed winning smiles at anybody who happened to look at him. Miss Garbel sat at the desk with an air of readiness, like an eccentrically uniformed secretary.

Dupont glanced at the men. 'You will proceed under detention to the *Commissariat de Police* at Roqueville. M. l'Inspecteur-en-Chef and I will later conduct an interrogation. The matter of your nationalities and the possibility of extradition will be considered. And now – forward.'

Oberon said: 'A robe. I demand a robe.'

'Look here, Alleyn,' Glande said, 'what's going to be done about me? I'm harmless, I tell you. For God's sake tell him to let me get some clothes on.'

'Your clothes'll be sent after you and you'll get no more and no less than was coming to you,' Alleyn said. 'In the interest of decency, my dear Dupont, Mr Oberon, should, perhaps, be given a garment of some sort.'

Dupont spoke to one of his men who opened a cupboard door and brought out a white robe.

'If,' Miss Garbel said delicately, 'I might be excused. Of course, I don't know – ?' she looked inquiringly from Alleyn to Dupont.

'This is Miss Garbel, Dupont, of whom I have told you.'

'Truly? Not, as I supposed the Honourable Locke?'

'Miss Locke has been murdered. She was stabbed through the heart at five thirty-eight yesterday morning in this room. Her body is in a coffin in a room on the other side of the passage-of-entry. Dr Baradi was good enough to show it to me.'

Baradi clasped his manacled hands together and brought them down savagely on his knees. The steel must have cut and bruised him but he gave no sign.

Glande cried out: 'Murdered! My God, they told us she'd given herself an overdose.'

'Then the – pardon me, Mademoiselle, if I express it a little crudely – the third English spinster, my dear Inspecteur-en-Chef? The Miss Truebody?'

'Is to the best of my belief recovering from her operation in a room beyond a bridge across the passage-of-entry.'

Baradi got clumsily to his feet. He faced the great cheval-glass. He said something in his own language. As he spoke, through the broken window, came the effeminate shriek of a train whistle followed by the labouring-up-hill clank of the train itself. Alleyn held up his hand and they were all still and looked through the broken window. Alleyn himself stood beside Baradi, facing the looking-glass which was at an angle to the window. Baradi made to move but Alleyn put his hand on him and he stood still, as if transfixed. In the great glass they both saw the reflection of the engine pass by and then the carriages, some of them lit and some in darkness. The train dragged to a standstill. In the last carriage a lighted window, which was opposite to their own window, was unshuttered. They could see two men playing cards. The men looked up. Their faces were startled.

Alleyn said: 'Look, Baradi. Look in the glass. The angle of inci-
dence is always equal to the angle of refraction, isn't it? We see their
reflection and they see ours. They see you in your white robes. They
see your handcuffs. Look, Baradi!'

He had taken a paperknife from the desk. He raised it in his left
hand as if to stab Baradi.

The men in the carriage were agitated. Their images in the glass
talked excitedly and gestured. Then, suddenly, they were jerked
sideways and in the glass was only the reflection of the wall and the
broken window and the night outside.

'Yesterday morning, at five thirty-eight, I was in a railway carriage out there,' Alleyn said, 'I saw Grizel Locke fall against the blind
and when the blind shot up I saw a man with a dark face and a knife
in his right hand. He stood in such a position that the prayer-wheel
showed over his shoulder and I now know that I saw, not a man, but
his reflection in that glass and I know he stood where you stand and
that he was a left-handed man. I know that he was you, Baradi.'

'And really, my dear Dupont,' Alleyn said a little later, when the
police car had removed the four men and the two ladies had gone
away to change, 'really, this is all one has to say about the case.
When I saw the room yesterday morning I realized what had happened. There was this enormous cheval-glass screwed into the floor
at an angle of about forty-five degrees to the window. To anybody
looking in from outside it must completely exclude the right-hand
section of the room. And yet, I saw a man, apparently *in* this right-
hand section of the room. He must, therefore, have been an image
in the glass of a man in the left-hand section of the room. To clinch
it, I saw part of the prayer wheel near the right shoulder of the
image. Now, if you sit in a railway carriage outside that window, you
will, I think, see part of the prayer-wheel, or rather, since I chucked
the prayer-wheel through the window, you will see part of its trace
on the faded wall, just to your left of the glass. The stabber, it was
clear, must be a left-handed man and Baradi is the only left-handed
man we have. I was puzzled that his face was more shadowed than
the direction of the light seemed to warrant. It is, of course, a dark
face.'

'It is perfectly clear,' Dupont said, 'though the verdict is not to be
decided in advance. The motive was fear, of course.'

'Fear of exposure. Miss Garbel believes that Grizel Locke was horrified when her young niece turned up at the Chèvre d'Argent. It became obvious that Ginny Taylor was destined to play the major role, opposite Oberon, in these unspeakable Rites. The day before yesterday it was announced that she would wear the Black Robe tonight. My guess is that Grizel Locke, herself the victim of the extremes of mood that agonize all drug-addicts, brooded on the affair, and became frantic with – with what emotion? Remorse? Anxiety? Shame?'

'But jealousy? She is, after all, about to become the supplanted mistress, is she not? Always an unpopular assignment.'

'Perhaps she was moved by all of these emotions. Perhaps, after a sleepless night or – God knows – a night of pleading, she threatened to expose the drug racket if Oberon persisted with Ginny Taylor. Oberon, finding her intractable, summoned Baradi. She threatened both of them. The scene rose to a climax. Perhaps – is it too wild a guess? – she hears the train coming and threatens to scream out their infamy from the window. Baradi reverts to type and uses a knife, probably one of the symbolic knives with which they frighten the initiates. She falls against the blind and it flies up. There, outside, is a train with a dimly lighted compartment opposite their window. And, between the light and the window of the compartment is the shape of a man – myself.'

Dupont lightly struck his hands together. 'A pretty situation, in effect!'

'He no sooner takes it in that it is over. The train enters the tunnel and Baradi and Oberon are left with Grizel Locke's body on their hands. And within an hour I ring up about Miss Truebody. And by the way, I suggest we visit Miss Truebody. Here comes Miss Garbel, who, I dare say, will show us to her room.'

Miss Garbel appeared, scarcely recognizable, wearing an unsmart coat and skirt and no make-up. It was impossible to believe that this was the woman who, an hour ago, had lent herself to the Rites of the Children of the Sun and who, yesterday morning, had appeared in pedal-pushers and a scarf on the roof-garden. Dupont looked at her with astonishment. She was very tremulous and obviously distressed. She went to the point, however, with the odd directness that Alleyn was learning to expect from her.

'You are yourself again, I see.' he said.

'Alas, yes! Or not, of course altogether, alas. It is nice not having to pretend to be poor Grizel any more but, as you noticed, I found it only too easy, at certain times, to let myself go. I sometimes think it is a peculiar property of marihuana to reduce all its victims to a common denominator. When we are 'high' as poor Grizel used to call it, we all behave rather in her manner. I am badly in need of a smoke now, after all the upset, which is why I'm so shaky, you know.'

'I expect you'd like to go back to your room in the Rue des Violettes. We'll take you there.'

'I would like it of all things, but I think I should stay to look after our patient. I've been doing quite a bit of the nursing – Mahomet and I took it in turns with one of the maids. Under the doctor's instructions, of course. Would you like to see her?'

'Indeed, we should. It's going to be difficult to cope with Miss Truebody. Of course, they never sent for a nurse?'

'No, no! Too dangerous, by far. But I assure you every care has been taken of the poor thing.'

'I'll bet it has. They didn't want two bodies on their hands. M. le Commissaire has arranged for a doctor and a nurse to come up by the night train from St Christophe. In the meantime, shall we visit her?'

Miss Garbel led the way up to the front landing. M. Dupont indicated the wrought-iron door. 'We discovered the key, my dear Alleyn,' he said gaily. 'An excellent move!' They climbed to the roof-garden and thence through a labyrinth of rooms to one of the bridge-like extensions that straddled the outside passageway.

They were half-way across this bridge when their attention was caught by the sound of voices and of boots on the cobblestones below.

From the balustrade they looked down into a scene that might have been devised by a film director. The sides of the house fell away from moon-patched shadow into a deep blackness. At one point a pool of light from an open door lay across the passageway. Into this light moved an incongruous company of foreshortened figures: the Egyptian servant, Baradi and Oberon in their white robes, Carbury Glande bareheaded and in shorts, and six gendarmes in uniform. They shifted in and out of the light, a curious pattern of heads and shoulders.

'*Alors,*' said Dupont, looking down at them: '*Bon débarras!*'

His voice echoed stonily in the passage. One of the white hoods was tilted backwards. The face inside it was thus exposed to the light but, being itself dark, seemed still to be in shadow. Alleyn and Baradi looked at each other. With a peck of his head Baradi spat into the night.

'*Pas de ça!*' said one of the gendarmes and turned Baradi about. It was then seen that he was handcuffed to his companion.

'Mr Oberon,' Alleyn said, 'will be delighted.'

The procession moved off with a hollow clatter down the passage. Raoul appeared in the doorway, rolling a cigarette, and watched them go.

Miss Garbel made a curious and desolate sound but immediately afterwards said brightly: 'Shall we – ?' and led them indoors.

'Here we are!' she said and tapped. A door was opened by the woman Alleyn had already seen at Miss Truebody's bedside.

'These are the friends of Mademoiselle,' said Miss Garbel. 'Is she awake?'

'She is awake but M. le Docteur left orders, Mademoiselle, that no one – ' She saw Dupont's uniform and her voice faded.

'M. le Docteur,' said Miss Garbel, 'has reconsidered his order.'

The woman stood aside and they went into the room. Dupont stayed by the door but Alleyn walked over to the bed. There, on the pillow, was the smooth blunt and singularly hairless face he had remembered. She looked at him and smiled and this time she was wearing her teeth. They made a great difference.

'Why, it's Mr Alleyn,' she murmured in a threadlike voice. 'How kind!'

'You're getting along splendidly,' Alleyn said, 'I won't tire you now but if there is anything you want you'll let us know.'

'Nothing. Much better. The doctor – too kind.'

'There will be another doctor tomorrow and a new nurse to help these ones.'

'Not – ? But – Dr Baradi – ?'

'He has been obliged to go away,' Alleyn said, 'on a case of some urgency.'

'Oh,' she closed her eyes.

Alleyn and Dupont went outside. Miss Garbel came to the door.

'If you don't want me,' she said, 'I'll stay and take my turn. I'm all right, you know. Quite reliable until morning.'

'And always,' he rejoined warmly.

'Ah,' she said, shaking her head. 'That's another story.'

She showed them where a staircase ran down to ground level and she peered after them, smiling and nodding over the bannister.

'We must pay one more visit,' Alleyn said.

'The third English spinster,' Dupont agreed. He seemed to have a sort of relish for this phrase.

But when they stood in the white-washed room and the raw light from an unshaded lamp now shone dreadfully on what was left of Grizel Locke, he looked thoughtful and said: 'All three, each after her own fashion, may be said to have served the cause of justice.'

'This one,' Alleyn said dryly, 'may be said to have died for it.'

V

It was a quarter-past two when Grizel Locke was carried in her coffin down to a mortuary van that shone glossily in the moonlight. Two hours later Alleyn and Dupont walked out of the Château de la Chèvre d'Argent. They left two men on guard and with Raoul went down the passageway to the open platform. It was flooded in moonlight. The Mediterranean glittered down below and the hills reared themselves up fabulously against the stars. Robin Herrington's rakish car was parked at the edge of the platform.

Alleyn said: 'These are our chickens come home to roost.'

'Ah!' said M. Dupont cosily, 'it is a night for love.'

'Nevertheless, if you will excuse me – '

'But, of course!'

Alleyn, whistling tunelessly and tactfully, went over to the car. Robin was in the driver's seat with Ginny beside him. Her head was on his shoulder. He showed no particular surprise at seeing Alleyn.

'Good morning,' Alleyn said. 'So you had a breakdown.'

'We did, sir, but we think we're under our own steam again.'

'I'm glad to hear it. You will find the Chèvre d'Argent rather empty. Here's my card. The gendarme at the door will let you in. If you'd rather collect your possessions and come back to Roqueville, I expect we could get rooms for you both at the Royal.'

He waited for an answer but it was perfectly clear to him that although they smiled and nodded brightly they had not taken in a word of his little speech.

Robin said: 'Ginny's going to marry me.'

'I hope you will both be *very* happy.'

'We think of beginning again in one of the Dominions.'

'The Dominions are, on the whole, both tolerant and helpful.'

Ginny, speaking for the first time, said: 'Will you please thank Mrs Alleyn? She sort of did the trick.'

'I shall. She'll be delighted to hear it.' He looked at them for a moment and they beamed back at him. 'You'll be all right,' he said. 'Get a tough job and forget you've had bad dreams. I'm sure it will work out.'

They smiled and nodded.

'I'll have to ask you to come and see me later in the morning. At the Préfecture at eleven?'

'Thank you,' they said vaguely. Ginny said: 'You can't think how happy we are, all of a sudden. And just imagine, I was furious when the car broke down! And yet, if it hadn't, we might never have found out.'

'Strange coincidence,' said Alleyn, looking at Robin. And seeing that they were incapable of coming out of the moonlight he said: 'Good morning and good luck to you both,' and left them to themselves.

On the way down to Roqueville he and Dupont discussed the probable development of the case. 'Oberon,' Alleyn said, 'has gone to pieces, as you see. He will try and buy his way out with information.'

'Callard also is prepared to upset the peas. But thanks to your admirable handling of the case we shall be able to dispense with such aids and Oberon, I trust, will be tried with Baradi.'

'Of the pair, Oberon is undoubtedly the more revolting,' Alleyn said thoughtfully, 'I wonder how many deaths could be laid at the door of those two. I don't know how you feel about it, Dupont, but I put their sort at the top of the criminal list. If they hadn't directly killed poor Grizel Locke, by God, they'd still be mass murderers.'

'Undoubtedly,' said Dupont, stifling a yawn, 'I imagine we take statements from the painter, the actress Wells and the two young ones and let it go at that. They may be more useful running free. Particularly if they return to the habit.'

'The young ones won't. I'm sure of that. As for the others: there are cures.'

In the front seat, Raoul, influenced no doubt by the moonlight and by his glimpse of Ginny and Robin, began to sing:

'*La nuit est faite pour l'amour.*'

'Raoul,' Alleyn said in French for his benefit, 'did a good job of work tonight, didn't he?'

'Not so bad, not so bad. We shall have you in the service yet, my friend,' said Dupont. He leant forward and struck Raoul lightly on the shoulder.

'No, M. le Commissaire, that is not my *métier*. I am about to settle with Teresa. And yet, if M. l'Inspecteur-en-Chef Alleyn should come back one day, who knows?'

They drove through the sleeping town to the little Square des Sarracins and put Alleyn down at the hotel.

Troy was fast asleep, with Ricky curled in beside her. The little silver goat illuminated himself on the bedside table. The french windows were wide open and Alleyn went out for a moment on the balcony. To the east the stars had turned pale and the first dawn cock was crowing in the hills above Roqueville.

Scales of Justice

For Stella

My most grateful thanks to Michael Godby M.A. (Oxon) for his learned advice in the matter of scales, to Eileen Mackay, to Eskdale Moloney and, as ever, to Vladimir and Anita Muling without whom . . .

Contents

NUNSPARDON

MR. DANBERRY-PHINN'S FISHING

THE VALLEY OF THE CHYNE

RIVER CHYNE

BRIDGE

RIVER PAT

UPLANDS

JACOB'S COTTAGE

HAMMER

WATT'S LANE

WATT'S HILL

COL. CARTAR

TE'S FISHING

BOY & DONKEY

WILLOW GROVE

WATT'S LANE

SWEVENINGS

Cast of Characters

Nurse Kettle

Mr Octavius Danberry-Phinn   *Of Jacob's Cottage*

Commander Syce

Colonel Cartarette   *Of Hammer Farm*

Rose Cartarette   *His daughter*

Kitty Cartarette   *His wife*

Sir Harold Lacklander Bt.   *Of Nunspardon*

Lady Lacklander   *His wife*

George Lacklander   *Their son*

Dr Mark Lacklander   *George's son*

Chief Detective-Inspector Alleyn

Detective-Inspector Fox   *Of the CID*

Detective-Sergeants Bailey and   *New Scotland Yard*
    Thompson

Dr Curtis   *Pathologist*

Sergeant Oliphant   *Of the Chyning*

PC Gripper   *Constabulary*

Sir James Punston   *Chief Constable of Barfordshire*

CHAPTER 1

Swevenings

Nurse Kettle pushed her bicycle to the top of Watt's Hill and there paused. Sweating lightly, she looked down on the village of Swevenings. Smoke rose in cosy plumes from one or two chimneys; roofs cuddled into surrounding greenery. The Chyne, a trout stream, meandered through meadow and coppice and slid blamelessly under two bridges. It was a circumspect landscape. Not a *faux-pas*, architectural or horticultural, marred the seemliness of the prospect.

'Really,' Nurse Kettle thought with satisfaction, 'it is as pretty as a picture.' And she remembered all the pretty pictures Lady Lacklander had made in irresolute watercolour, some from this very spot. She was reminded, too, of those illustrated maps that one finds in the Underground, with houses, trees and occupational figures amusingly dotted about them. Seen from above, like this, Swevenings resembled such a map. Nurse Kettle looked down at the orderly pattern of field, hedge, stream, and land, and fancifully imposed upon it the curling labels and carefully naïve figures that are proper to picture-maps.

From Watt's Hill, Watt's Lane ran steeply and obliquely into the valley. Between the lane and the Chyne was contained a hillside divided into three strips, each garnished with trees, gardens and a house of considerable age. These properties belonged to three of the principal householders of Swevenings: Mr Danberry-Phinn, Commander Syce and Colonel Cartarette.

Nurse Kettle's map, she reflected, would have a little picture of Mr Danberry-Phinn at Jacob's Cottage surrounded by his cats, and one of

Commander Syce at Uplands, shooting off his bow-and-arrow. Next door at Hammer Farm (only it wasn't a farm now but had been much converted) it would show Mrs Cartarette in a garden chair with a cocktail shaker, and Rose Cartarette, her stepdaughter, gracefully weeding. Her attention sharpened. There, in point of fact, deep down in the actual landscape, *was* Colonel Cartarette himself, a lilliputian figure, moving along his rented stretch of the Chyne, east of Bottom Bridge, and followed at a respectful distance by his spaniel Skip. His creel was slung over his shoulder and his rod was in his hand.

'The evening rise,' Nurse Kettle reflected, 'he's after the Old 'Un.' And she added to her imaginary map the picture of an enormous trout lurking near Bottom Bridge with a curly label above it bearing a legend: 'The Old 'Un.'

On the far side of the valley on the private golf course at Nunspardon Manor there would be Mr George Lacklander, doing a solitary round with a glance (thought the gossip-loving Nurse Kettle) across the valley at Mrs Cartarette. Lacklander's son, Dr Mark, would be shown with his black bag in his hand and a stork, perhaps, quaintly flying overhead. And to complete, as it were, the gentry, there would be old Lady Lacklander big-bottomed on a sketching stool and her husband, Sir Harold, on a bed of sickness, alas, in his great room, the roof of which, after the manner of pictorial maps, had been removed to display him.

In the map it would be demonstrated how Watt's Lane, wandering to the right and bending back again, neatly divided the gentry from what Nurse Kettle called the 'ordinary folk.' To the west lay the Danberry-Phinn, the Syce, the Cartarette and above all the Lacklander demesnes. Neatly disposed along the east margin of Watt's Lane were five conscientiously preserved thatched cottages, the village shop and, across Monk's Bridge, the church and rectory and the Boy and Donkey.

And that was all. No Pulls-In for Carmen, no Olde Bunne Shoppes (which Nurse Kettle had learned to despise), no spurious half-timbering, marred the perfection of Swevenings. Nurse Kettle, bringing her panting friends up to the top of Watt's Hill, would point with her little finger at the valley and observe triumphantly: 'Where every prospect pleases,' without completing the quotation, because in Swevenings not even Man was Vile.

With a look of pleasure on her shining and kindly face she mounted her bicycle and began to coast down Watt's Lane. Hedges and trees flew by. The road surface improved and on her left appeared the quickset hedge of Jacob's Cottage. From the far side came the voice of Mr Octavius Danberry-Phinn.

'Adorable!' Mr Danberry-Phinn was saying. 'Queen of Delight! Fish!' He was answered by the trill of feline voices.

Nurse Kettle turned to the footpath, dexterously backpedalled, wobbled uncouthly and brought herself to anchor at Mr Danberry-Phinn's gate.

'Good evening,' she said, clinging to the gate and retaining her seat. She looked through the entrance cut in the deep hedge. There was Mr Danberry-Phinn in his Elizabethan garden giving supper to his cats. In Swevenings, Mr Phinn (he allowed his nearer acquaintances to neglect the hyphen) was generally considered to be more than a little eccentric, but Nurse Kettle was used to him and didn't find him at all disconcerting. He wore a smoking-cap, tasselled, embroidered with beads; and falling to pieces. On top of this was perched a pair of ready-made reading-glasses which he now removed and gaily waved at her.

'You appear,' he said, 'like some exotic deity mounted on an engine quaintly devised by Inigo Jones. Good evening to *you*, Nurse Kettle. Pray, what has become of your automobile?'

'She's having a spot of beauty treatment and a minor op'.' Mr Phinn flinched at this relentless breeziness, but Nurse Kettle, unaware of his reaction, carried heartily on, 'And how's the world treating you? Feeding your kitties, I see.'

'The Persons of the House,' Mr Phinn acquiesced, 'now, as you observe, sup. Fatima,' he cried squatting on his plump haunches, '*Femme fatale*. Miss Paddy-Paws! A morsel more of haddock? Eat up, my heavenly felines.' Eight cats of varying kinds responded but slightly to these overtures, being occupied with eight dishes of haddock. The ninth, a mother cat, had completed her meal and was at her toilet. She blinked once at Mr Phinn and with a tender and gentle expression stretched herself out for the accommodation of her three fat kittens.

'The celestial milk-bar is now open,' Mr Phinn pointed out with a wave of his hand.

Nurse Kettle chuckled obligingly. 'No nonsense about *her*, at least,' she said. 'Pity some human mums I could name haven't got the same idea,' she added, with an air of professional candour. 'Clever Pussy!'

'The name,' Mr Phinn corrected tartly, 'is Thomasina Twitchett, Thomasina modulating from Thomas and arising out of the usual mistake and Twitchett. . . . ' He bared his crazy-looking head. '*Hommage à la Divine Potter*. The boy children are Ptolemy and Alexis. The girl-child who suffers from a marked mother-fixation is Edie.'

'Edie?' Nurse Kettle repeated doubtfully.

'Edie Puss, of course,' Mr Phinn rejoined and looked fixedly at her.

Nurse Kettle, who knew that one must cry out against puns, ejaculated: 'How you *dare*! *Honestly!*'

Mr Phinn gave a short cackle of laughter and changed the subject.

'What errand of therapeutic mercy,' he asked, 'has set you darkling in the saddle? What pain and anguish wring which brow?'

'Well, I've one or two calls,' said Nurse Kettle, 'but the long and the short of me is that I'm on my way to spend the night at the big house. Relieving with the old gentleman, you know.'

She looked across the valley to Nunspardon Manor.

'Ah, yes,' said Mr Phinn softly. 'Dear me! May one inquire . . . ? Is Sir Harold – ?'

'He's seventy-five,' said Nurse Kettle briskly, 'and he's very tired. Still, you never know with cardiacs. He may perk up again.'

'Indeed?'

'Oh, yes. We've got a day-nurse for him but there's no night-nurse to be had anywhere so I'm stop-gapping. To help Dr Mark out, really.'

'Dr Mark Lacklander is attending his grandfather?'

'Yes. He had a second opinion but more for his own satisfaction than anything else. But there! Talking out of school! I'm ashamed of you, Kettle.'

'I'm very discreet,' said Mr Phinn.

'So'm I, really. Well, I suppose I had better go on me way rejoicing.'

Nurse Kettle did a tentative back-pedal and started to wriggle her foot out of one of the interstices in Mr Phinn's garden gate. He disengaged a sated kitten from its mother and rubbed it against his ill-shaven cheek.

'Is he conscious?' he asked.

'Off and on. Bit confused. There now! Gossiping again! Talking of gossip,' said Nurse Kettle, with a twinkle, 'I see the Colonel's out for the evening rise.'

An extraordinary change at once took place in Mr Phinn. His face became suffused with purple, his eyes glittered and he bared his teeth in a canine grin.

'A hideous curse upon his sport,' he said. 'Where is he?'

'Just below the bridge.'

'Let him venture a handspan above it and I'll report him to the authorities. What fly has he mounted? Has he caught anything?'

'I couldn't see,' said Nurse Kettle, already regretting her part in the conversation, 'from the top of Watt's Hill.'

Mr Phinn replaced the kitten.

'It is a dreadful thing to say about a fellow-creature,' he said, 'a shocking thing. But I do say advisedly and deliberately that I suspect Colonel Cartarette of having recourse to improper practices.'

It was Nurse Kettle's turn to blush.

'I am sure I don't know to what you refer,' she said.

'Bread! Worms!' said Mr Phinn, spreading his arms. 'Anything! Tickling, even! I'd put it as low as that.'

'I'm sure you're mistaken.'

'It is not my habit, Miss Kettle, to mistake the wanton extravagances of infatuated humankind. Look, if you will, at Cartarette's associates. Look, if your stomach is strong enough to sustain the experience, at Commander Syce.'

'Good gracious me, what has the poor Commander done!'

'That man,' Mr Phinn said, turning pale and pointing with one hand to the mother-cat and with the other in the direction of the valley; 'that intemperate filibuster, who divides his leisure between alcohol and the idiotic pursuit of archery, that wardroom cupid, my God, murdered the mother of Thomasina Twitchett.'

'Not deliberately, I'm sure.'

'How can you be sure?'

Mr Phinn leant over his garden gate and grasped the handlebars of Nurse Kettle's bicycle. The tassel of his smoking-cap fell over his face and he blew it impatiently aside. His voice began to trace the pattern of a much-repeated, highly relished narrative.

'In the cool of the evening Madame Thorns, for such was her name, was wont to promenade in the bottom meadow. Being great with kit she presented a considerable target. Syce, flushed no doubt with wine, and flattering himself he cut the devil of a figure, is to be pictured upon his archery lawn. The instrument of destruction, a bow with the drawing power, I am told, of sixty pounds, is in his grip and the lust of blood in his heart. He shot an arrow in the air,' Mr Phinn concluded, 'and if you tell me that it fell to earth he knew not where I shall flatly refuse to believe you. His target, his deliberate mark, I am persuaded, was my exquisite cat. Thomasina, my fur of furs, I am speaking of your mamma.'

The mother-cat blinked at Mr Phinn and so did Nurse Kettle.

'I must *say*,' she thought, 'he really *is* a little off.' And since she had a kind heart she was filled with a vague pity for him.

'Living alone,' she thought, 'with only those cats. It's not to be wondered at, really.'

She gave him her brightest professional smile and one of her standard valedictions.

'Ah, well,' said Nurse Kettle, letting go her anchorage on the gate, 'be good, and if you can't be good be careful.'

'Care,' Mr Danberry-Phinn countered with a look of real intemperance in his eye, 'killed the Cat. I am not likely to forget it. Good evening to you, Nurse Kettle.'

II

Mr Phinn was a widower but Commander Syce was a bachelor. He lived next to Mr Phinn, in a Georgian house called Uplands, small and yet too big for Commander Syce, who had inherited it from an uncle. He was looked after by an ex-naval rating and his wife. The greater part of the grounds had been allowed to run to seed, but the kitchen garden was kept up by the married couple and the archery lawn by Commander Syce himself. It overlooked the valley of the Chyne and was, apparently, his only interest. At one end in fine weather stood a target on an easel and at the other on summer evenings from as far away as Nunspardon, Commander Syce could be observed, in the classic pose, shooting a round from his sixty-pound bow. He was reputed to be a fine marksman and it was noticed that however much his gait might waver, his stance, once he had opened his chest and stretched his bow, was that of a rock. He lived a solitary and aimless life. People would have inclined to be sorry for him if he had made any sign that he would welcome their sympathy. He did not do so and indeed at the smallest attempt at friendliness would sheer off, go about and make away as fast as possible. Although never seen in the bar, Commander Syce was a heroic supporter of the pub. Indeed, as Nurse Kettle pedalled up his overgrown drive, she encountered the lad from the Boy and Donkey pedalling down it with his bottle-carrier empty before him.

'There's the Boy,' thought Nurse Kettle, rather pleased with herself for putting it that way, 'and I'm very much afraid he's just paid a visit to the Donkey.'

She, herself, had a bottle for Commander Syce, but it came from the chemist at Chyning. As she approached the house she heard the sound of steps on the gravel and saw him limping away round the far end, his bow in his hand and his quiver girt about his waist. Nurse Kettle pedalled after him.

'Hi!' she called out brightly. 'Good evening, Commander!'

Her bicycle wobbled and she dismounted.

Syce turned, hesitated for a moment and then came towards her.

He was a fairish, sunburned man who had run to seed. He still reeked of the Navy and, as Nurse Kettle noticed when he drew nearer, of whisky. His eyes, blue and bewildered, stared into hers.

'Sorry,' he said rapidly. 'Good evening. I beg your pardon.'

'Dr Mark,' she said, 'asked me to drop in while I was passing and leave your prescription for you. There we are. The mixture as before.'

He took it from her with a darting movement of his hand. 'Most awfully kind,' he said. 'Frightfully sorry. Nothing urgent.'

'No bother at all,' Nurse Kettle rejoined, noticing the tremor of his hand. 'I see you're going to have a shoot.'

'Oh, yes. Yes,' he said loudly, and backed away from her. 'Well, thank you, thank you, thank you.'

'I'm calling in at Hammer. Perhaps you won't mind my trespassing. There's a footpath down to the right-of-way, isn't there?'

'Of course. Please do. Allow me.'

He thrust his medicine into a pocket of his coat, took hold of her bicycle and laid his bow along the saddle and handlebars.

'Now *I'm* being a nuisance,' said Nurse Kettle cheerfully. 'Shall I carry your bow?'

He shied away from her and began to wheel the bicycle round the end of the house. She followed him, carrying the bow and talking in the comfortable voice she used for nervous patients. They came out on the archery lawn and upon a surprising and lovely view over the little valley of the Chyne. The trout stream shone like pewter in the evening light, meadows lay as rich as velvet on either side, the trees looked like pincushions, and a sort of heraldic glow turned the whole landscape into the semblance of an illuminated illustration to some forgotten romance. There was Major Cartarette winding in his line below Bottom Bridge and there up the hill on the Nunspardon golf course were old Lady Lacklander and her elderly son George, taking a post-prandial stroll.

'*What* a clear evening,' Nurse Kettle exclaimed with pleasure. 'And *how* close everything looks. Do tell me, Commander,' she went on, noticing that he seemed to flinch at this form of address, 'with this bow of yours could you shoot an arrow into Lady Lacklander?'

Syce darted a look at the almost square figure across the little valley. He muttered something about a clout at two hundred and forty yards and limped on. Nurse Kettle, chagrined by his manner, thought: 'What you need, my dear, is a bit of gingering up.'

He pushed her bicycle down an untidy path through an overgrown shrubbery and she stumped after him.

'I have been told,' she said, 'that once upon a time you hit a mark you didn't bargain for, down there.'

Syce stopped dead. She saw that beads of sweat had formed on the back of his neck. 'Alcoholic,' she thought. 'Flabby. Shame. He must have been a fine man when he looked after himself.'

'Great grief!' Syce cried out, thumping his fist on the seat of her bicycle, 'you mean the bloody cat!'

'Well!'

'Great grief, it was an accident. I've told the old perisher! An accident! I *like* cats.'

He swung round and faced her. His eyes were misted and his lips trembled. 'I *like* cats,' he repeated.

'We all make mistakes,' said Nurse Kettle, comfortably.

He held his hand out for the bow and pointed to a little gate at the end of the path.

'There's the gate into Hammer,' he said, and added with exquisite awkwardness, 'I beg your pardon, I'm very poor company as you see. Thank you for bringing the stuff. Thank you, thank you.'

She gave him the bow and took charge of her bicycle. 'Dr Mark Lacklander may be very young,' she said bluffly, 'but he's as capable a GP as I've come across in thirty years' nursing. If I were you, Commander, I'd have a good down-to-earth chinwag with him. Much obliged for the assistance. Good evening to you.'

She pushed her bicycle through the gate into the well-tended coppice belonging to Hammer Farm and along a path that ran between herbaceous borders. As she made her way towards the house she heard behind her at Uplands, the twang of a bow string and the 'tock' of an arrow in a target.

'Poor chap,' Nurse Kettle muttered, partly in a huff and partly compassionate. 'Poor chap! Nothing to keep him out of mischief.' And with a sense of vague uneasiness, she wheeled her bicycle in the direction of the Cartarettes' rose garden where she could hear the snip of garden secateurs and a woman's voice quietly singing.

'That'll be either *Mrs*,' thought Nurse Kettle, 'or the stepdaughter. Pretty tune.'

A man's voice joined in, making a second part.

> '*Come away, come away Death*
> *And in sad cypress let me be laid.*'

The words, thought Nurse Kettle, were a trifle morbid but the general effect was nice. The rose garden was enclosed behind quickset hedges and hidden from her, but the path she had taken led into it, and she must continue if she was to reach the house. Her rubber-shod feet made little sound on the flagstones and the bicycle discreetly clicked along beside her. She had an odd feeling that she was about to break in on a scene of exquisite intimacy. She approached a green archway and as she did so the woman's voice broke off from its song, and said: 'That's my favourite of all.'

'Strange,' said a man's voice that fetched Nurse Kettle up with a jolt, 'strange, isn't it, in a comedy, to make the love songs so sad! Don't you think so, Rose? Rose . . . Darling . . .'

Nurse Kettle tinkled her bicycle bell, passed through the green archway and looked to her right. She discovered Miss Rose Cartarette and Dr Mark Lacklander gazing into each other's eyes with unmistakable significance.

III

Miss Cartarette had been cutting roses and laying them in the basket held by Dr Lacklander. Dr Lacklander blushed to the roots of his hair and said, 'Good God! Good heavens! Good evening,' and Miss Cartarette said, 'Oh, hallo, Nurse. Good evening.' She, too, blushed, but more delicately than Dr Lacklander.

Nurse Kettle said: 'Good evening, Miss Rose. Good evening, Doctor. Hope it's all right my taking the short cut.' She glanced with decorum at Dr Lacklander. 'The child with the abscess,' she said, in explanation of her own appearance.

'Ah, yes,' Dr Lacklander said. 'I've had a look at her. It's your gardener's little girl, Rose.'

They both began to talk to Nurse Kettle who listened with an expression of good humour. She was a romantic woman and took pleasure in the look of excitement on Dr Lacklander's face and of shyness on Rose's.

'Nurse Kettle,' Dr Lacklander said rapidly, 'like a perfect angel, is going to look after my grandfather tonight. I don't know what we should have done without her.'

'*And* by that same token,' Nurse Kettle added, 'I'd better go on me way rejoicing or I shall be late on duty.'

They smiled and nodded at her. She squared her shoulders, glanced in a jocular manner at her bicycle and stumped off with it through the rose garden.

'Well,' she thought, 'if that's not a case, I've never seen young love before. Blow me down flat, but I never guessed! Fancy!'

As much refreshed by this incident as she would have been by a good strong cup of tea, she made her way to the gardener's cottage, her last port of call before going up to Nunspardon.

When her figure, stoutly clad in her District Nurse's uniform, had bobbed its way out of the enclosed garden, Rose Cartarette and Mark Lacklander looked at each other and laughed nervously.

Lacklander said: 'She's a fantastically good sort, old Kettle, but at that particular moment I could have done without her. I mustn't stay, I suppose.'

'Don't you want to see my papa?'

'Yes. But I shouldn't wait. Not that one can do anything much for the grandparent, but they like me to be there.'

'I'll tell Daddy as soon as he comes in. He'll go up at once, of course.'

'We'd be very grateful. Grandfather sets great store by his coming.'

Mark Lacklander looked at Rose over the basket he carried and said unsteadily: 'Darling.'

'Don't,' she said. 'Honestly; don't.'

'No? Are you warning me off, Rose? Is it all a dead loss?'

She made a small ineloquent gesture, tried to speak and said nothing.

'Well,' Lacklander said, 'I may as well tell you that I was going to ask if you'd marry me. I love you very dearly and I thought we seemed to sort of suit. Was I wrong about that?'

'No,' Rose said.

'Well, I know I wasn't. Obviously, we suit. So for pity's sake what's up? Don't tell me you love me like a brother, because I can't believe it.'

'You needn't try to.'

'Well, then?'

'I can't think of getting engaged, much less married.'

'Ah!' Lacklander ejaculated. 'Now we're coming to it! This is going to be what I suspected. Oh, for God's sake let me get rid of this bloody basket! Here. Come over to the bench. I'm not going till I've cleared this up.'

She followed him and they sat down together on a garden seat with the basket of roses at their feet. He took her by the wrist and stripped the heavy glove off her hand. 'Now, tell me,' he demanded. 'Do you love me?'

'You needn't bellow it at me like that. Yes, I do.'

'Rose, darling! I was so panicked you'd say you didn't.'

'Please listen, Mark. You're not going to agree with a syllable of this, but please listen.'

'All right. I know what it's going to be but . . . all right.'

'You can see what it's like here. I mean the domestic set-up. You must have seen for yourself how much difference it makes to Daddy my being on tap.'

'You are so funny when you use colloquialisms . . . a little girl shutting her eyes and firing off a popgun. All right; your father likes to have you about. So he well might and so he still would if we married. We'd probably live half our time at Nunspardon.'

'It's much more than that.' Rose hesitated. She had drawn away from him and sat with her hands pressed together between her knees. She wore a long house-dress, her hair was drawn back into a knot at the base of her neck but a single fine strand had escaped and shone on her forehead. She used very little make-up and could afford this economy for she was a beautiful girl.

She said: 'It's simply that his second marriage hasn't been a success. If I left him now he'd really and truly have nothing to live for. Really.'

'Nonsense,' Mark said uneasily.

'He's never been able to do without me. Even when I was little. Nanny and I and my governess all following the drum. So many countries and journeys. And then after the war when he was given all those special jobs: Vienna and Rome and Paris. I never went to school because he hated the idea of separation.'

'All wrong, of course. Only half a life.'

'No, no, no, that's not true, honestly. It was a wonderfully rich life. I saw and heard and learnt all sorts of splendid things other girls miss.'

'All the same . . . '

'No, honestly, it was grand.'

'You should have been allowed to get under your own steam.'

'It wasn't a case of being allowed. I was allowed almost anything I wanted. And when I did get under my own steam just see what happened! He was sent with that mission to Singapore and I stayed in Grenoble and took a course at the University. He was delayed and delayed . . . and I found out afterwards that he was wretchedly at a loose end. And then . . . it was while he was there . . . he met Kitty.'

Lacklander closed his well-kept doctor's hand over the lower half of his face and behind it made an indeterminate sound.

'Well,' Rose said, 'it turned out as badly as it possibly could, and it goes on getting worse, and if I'd been there I don't think it would have happened.'

'Why not? He'd have been just as likely to meet her. And even if he hadn't, my heavenly and darling Rose, you cannot be allowed to think of yourself as a twister of the tail of fate.'

'If I'd been there . . . '

'Now *look* here!' said Lacklander. 'Look at it like this. If you removed yourself to Nunspardon as my wife, he and your stepmother might get together in a quick comeback.'

'Oh, no,' Rose said. 'No, Mark. There's not a chance of that.'

'How do you know? Listen. We're in love. I love you so desperately much it's almost more than I can endure. I know I shall never meet anybody else who could make me so happy and, incredible though it may seem, I don't believe you will either. I won't be put off, Rose. You shall marry me and if your father's life here is too unsatisfactory, well, we'll find some way of improving it. Perhaps if they part company he could come to us.'

'Never! Don't you see? He couldn't bear it. He'd feel sort of extraneous.'

'I'm going to talk to him. I shall tell him I want to marry you.'

'No, Mark, darling! No . . . please . . . '

His hand closed momentarily over hers. Then he was on his feet and had taken up the basket of roses. 'Good evening, Mrs Cartarette,' he said. 'We're robbing your garden for my grandmother. You're very much ahead of us at Hammer with your roses.'

Kitty Cartarette had turned in by the green archway and was looking thoughtfully at them.

IV

The second Mrs Cartarette did not match her Edwardian name. She did not look like a Kitty. She was so fair that without her make-up she would have seemed bleached. Her figure was well-disciplined and her face had been skilfully drawn up into a beautifully cared-for mask. Her greatest asset was her acquired inscrutability. This, of itself, made a *femme fatale* of Kitty Cartarette. She had, as it were, been manipulated into a menace. She was dressed with some elaboration and, presumably because she was in the garden, she wore gloves.

'How nice to see you, Mark,' she said. 'I thought I heard your voices. Is this a professional call?'

Mark said: 'Partly so at least. I ran down with a message for Colonel Cartarette, and I had a look at your gardener's small girl.'

'How too kind,' she said, glancing from Mark to her stepdaughter. She moved up to him and with her gloved hand took a dark rose from the basket and held it against her mouth.

'What a smell!' she said. 'Almost improper, it's so strong. Maurice is not in, but he won't be long. Shall we go up?'

She led the way to the house. Exotic wafts of something that was not roses drifted in her wake. She kept her torso rigid as she walked and slightly swayed her hips. 'Very expensive,' Mark Lacklander thought; 'but not entirely exclusive. Why on earth did he marry her?'

Mrs Cartarette's pin heels tapped along the flagstone path to a group of garden furniture heaped with cushions. A tray with a decanter and brandy glasses was set out on a white iron table. She let herself down on a swinging seat, put up her feet, and arranged herself for Mark to look at.

'Poorest Rose,' she said, glancing at her stepdaughter, 'you're wearing such suitable gloves. Do cope with your scratchy namesakes for Mark. A box perhaps.'

'Please don't bother,' Mark said. 'I'll take them as they are.'

'We can't allow that,' Mrs Cartarette murmured. 'You doctors mustn't scratch your lovely hands, you know.'

Rose took the basket from him. He watched her go into the house and turned abruptly at the sound of Mrs Cartarette's voice.

'Let's have a little drink, shall we?' she said. 'That's Maurice's pet brandy and meant to be too wonderful. Give me an infinitesimal drop and yourself a nice big one. I really prefer *crème de menthe*, but Maurice and Rose think it a common taste so I have to restrain my carnal appetite.'

Mark gave her the brandy. 'I won't, if you don't mind,' he said. 'I'm by way of being on duty.'

'Really? Who are you going to hover over, apart from the gardener's child?'

'My grandfather,' Mark said.

'How awful of me not to realize,' she rejoined with the utmost composure. 'How is Sir Harold?'

'Not so well this evening, I'm afraid. In fact, I must get back. If I go by the river path perhaps I'll meet the Colonel.'

'Almost sure to, I should think,' she agreed indifferently, 'unless he's poaching for that fabled fish on Mr Phinn's preserves which, of course, he's much too county to think of doing, whatever the old boy may say to the contrary.'

Mark said formally: 'I'll go that way, then, and hope to see him.'

She waved her rose at him in dismissal and held out her left hand in a gesture that he found distressingly second rate. He took it with his own left and shook it crisply.

'Will you give your father a message from me?' she said. 'I know how worried he must be about your grandfather. Do tell him I wish so much one could help.'

The hand inside the glove gave his a sharp little squeeze and was withdrawn. 'Don't forget,' she said.

Rose came back with the flowers in a box. Mark thought: 'I can't leave her like this, half-way through a proposal, damn it.' He said coolly: 'Come and meet your father. You don't take enough exercise.'

'I live in a state of almost perpetual motion,' she rejoined, 'and I'm not suitably shod or dressed for the river path.'

Mrs Cartarette gave a little laugh. 'Poor Mark!' she murmured. 'But in any case, Rose, here *comes* your father.'

Colonel Cartarette had emerged from a spinney halfway down the hill and was climbing up through the rough grass below the lawn. He was followed by his spaniel, Skip, an old, obedient dog. The evening light had faded to a bleached greyness. Silvered grass, trees, lawns, flowers and the mildly curving thread of the shadowed trout stream joined in an announcement of oncoming night. Through this setting Colonel Cartarette moved as if he were an expression both of its substance and its spirit. It was as if from the remote past, through a quiet progression of dusks, his figure had come up from the valley of the Chyne.

When he saw the group by the lawn he lifted his hand in greeting. Mark went down to meet him. Rose, aware of her stepmother's heightened curiosity, watched him with profound misgiving.

Colonel Cartarette was a native of Swevenings. His instincts were those of a countryman and he had never quite lost his air of belonging to the soil. His tastes, however, were for the arts and his talents for the conduct of government services in foreign places. This odd assortment of elements had set no particular mark upon their host. It was not until he spoke that something of his personality appeared.

'Good evening, Mark,' he called as soon as they were within comfortable earshot of each other. 'My dear chap, what do you think? I've damned near bagged the Old 'Un.'

'No!' Mark shouted with appropriate enthusiasm.

'I assure you! The Old 'Un! Below the bridge in his usual lurk, you know. I could see him . . . '

And as he panted up the hill the Colonel completed his classic tale of a magnificent strike, a homeric struggle and a broken cast. Mark, in spite of his own preoccupations, listened with interest. The Old 'Un was famous in Swevenings: a trout of magnitude and cunning, the despair and desire of every rod in the district.

' . . . so I lost him,' the Colonel ended, opening his eyes very wide and at the same time grinning for sympathy at Mark. 'What a thing! By jove, if I'd got him I really believe old Phinn would have murdered me.'

'Are you still at war, sir?'

'Afraid so. The chap's impossible, you know Good God, he's accused me in so many words of poaching. Mad! How's your grandfather?'

Mark said: 'He's failing pretty rapidly, I'm afraid. There's nothing we can do. It's on his account I'm here, sir.' And he delivered his message.

'I'll come at once,' the Colonel said. 'Better drive round. Just give me a minute or two to clean up. Come with me, won't you?'

But Mark felt suddenly that he could not face another encounter with Rose and said he would go home at once by the river path and would prepare his grandfather for the Colonel's arrival.

He stood for a moment looking back through the dusk towards the house. He saw Rose gather up the full skirt of her housecoat and run across the lawn, and he saw her father set down his creel and rod, take off his hat and wait for her, his bald head gleaming. She joined her hands behind his neck and kissed him. They went on towards the house arm-in-arm. Mrs Cartarette's hammock had begun to swing to and fro.

Mark turned away and walked quickly down into the valley and across Bottom Bridge.

The Old 'Un, with Colonel Cartarette's cast in his jaw, lurked tranquilly under the bridge.

CHAPTER 2

Nunspardon

Sir Harold Lacklander watched Nurse Kettle as she moved about his room. Mark had given him something that had reduced his nightmare of discomfort and for the moment he seemed to enjoy the tragic self-importance that is the prerogative of the very ill. He preferred Nurse Kettle to the day-nurse. She was after all a native of the neighbouring village of Chyning and this gave him the same satisfaction as the knowledge that the flowers on his table came out of the Nunspardon conservatories.

He knew now that he was dying. His grandson had not told him in so many words but he had read the fact of death in the boy's face and in the behaviour of his own wife and son. Seven years ago he had been furious when Mark wished to become a doctor; a Lacklander and the only grandson. He had made it as difficult as he could for Mark. But he was glad now to have the Lacklander nose bending over him and the Lacklander hands doing the things doctors seemed to think necessary. He would have taken a sort of pleasure in the eminence to which approaching death had raised him if he had not been tormented by the most grievous of all ills. He had a sense of guilt upon him.

'Long time,' he said. He used as few words as possible because with every one he uttered it was as if he squandered a measure of his dwindling capital. Nurse Kettle placed herself where he could see and hear her easily, and said: 'Doctor Mark says the Colonel will be here quite soon. He's been fishing.'

'Luck?'

472

'I don't know. He'll tell you.'

'Old'n.'

'Ah,' said Nurse Kettle comfortably, 'they won't catch *him* in a hurry.'

The wraith of a chuckle drifted up from the bed and was followed by an anxious sigh. She looked closely at the face that seemed during that day to have receded from its own bones.

'All right?' she asked.

The lacklustre eyes searched hers. 'Papers?' the voice asked.

'I found them just where you said. They're on the table over there.'

'Here.'

'If it makes you feel more comfortable.' She moved into the shadows at the far end of the great room and returned carrying a package, tied and sealed, which she put on his bedside table.

'Memoirs,' he whispered.

'Fancy,' said Nurse Kettle. 'There must be a deal of work in them. I think it's lovely to be an author. And now I'm going to leave you to have a little rest.'

She bent down and looked at him. He stared back anxiously. She nodded and smiled, and then moved away and took up an illustrated paper. For a time there were no sounds in the great bedroom but the breathing of the patient and the rustle of a turned page.

The door opened. Nurse Kettle stood up and put her hands behind her back as Mark Lacklander came into the room. He was followed by Colonel Cartarette.

'All right, Nurse?' Mark asked quietly.

'Pretty much,' she murmured. 'Fretting. He'll be glad to see the Colonel.'

'I'll just have a word with him first.'

He walked down the room to the enormous bed. His grandfather stared anxiously up at him and Mark, taking the restless old hand in his, said at once: 'Here's the Colonel, Grandfather. You're quite ready for him, aren't you?'

'Yes. Now.'

'Right.' Mark kept his fingers on his grandfather's wrist. Colonel Cartarette straightened his shoulders and joined him.

'Hallo, Cartarette,' said Sir Harold so loudly and clearly that Nurse Kettle made a little exclamation. 'Nice of you to come.'

'Hallo, sir,' said the Colonel who was by twenty-five years the younger. 'Sorry you're feeling so cheap. Mark says you want to see me.'

'Yes.' The eyes turned towards the bedside table. 'Those things,' he said. 'Take them, will you? Now.'

'They're the memoirs,' Mark said.

'Do you want me to read them?' Cartarette asked, stooping over the bed.

'If you will.' There was a pause. Mark put the package into Colonel Cartarette's hands. The old man's eyes watched in what seemed to be an agony of interest.

'I think,' Mark said, 'that Grandfather hopes you will edit the memoirs, sir.'

'I'll . . . Of course,' the Colonel said after an infinitesimal pause. 'I'll be delighted; if you think you can trust me.'

'Trust you. Implicitly. Implicitly. One other thing. Do you mind, Mark?'

'Of course not, Grandfather. Nurse, shall we have a word?'

Nurse Kettle followed Mark out of the room. They stood together on a dark landing at the head of a wide stairway.

'I don't think,' Mark said, 'that it will be much longer.'

'Wonderful, though, how he's perked up for the Colonel.'

'He'd set his will on it. I think,' Mark said, 'that he will now relinquish his life.'

Nurse Kettle agreed: 'Funny how they can hang on and funny how they will give up.'

In the hall below a door opened and light flooded up the stairs. Mark looked over the banister and saw the enormously broad figure of his grandmother. Her hand flashed as it closed on the stair rail. She began heavily to ascend. He could hear her laboured breathing.

'Steady does it, Gar,' he said.

Lady Lacklander paused and looked up. 'Ha!' she said, 'it's the Doctor, is it?' Mark grinned at the sardonic overtone.

She arrived on the landing. The train of her old velvet dinner-dress followed her and the diamonds which every evening she

absentmindedly stuck about her enormous bosom burned and
winked as it rose and fell.

'Good evening, Kettle,' she panted. 'Good of you to come and
help my poor old boy. How is he, Mark? Has, Maurice Cartarette
arrived? Why are you both closeted together out here?'

'The Colonel's here, Gar. Grandfather wanted to have a word
privately with him, so Nurse and I left them together.'

'Something about those damned memoirs,' said Lady Lacklander
vexedly. 'I suppose, in that case, I'd better not go in.'

'I don't think they'll be long.'

There was a large Jacobean chair on the landing. He pulled it forward. She let herself down into it, shuffled her astonishingly small
feet out of a pair of old slippers and looked critically at them.

'Your father,' she said, 'has gone to sleep in the drawing-room
muttering that he would like to see Maurice.' She shifted her great
bulk towards Nurse Kettle. 'Now, before you settle to your watch,
you kind soul,' she said, 'you won't mind saving my mammoth legs
a journey. Jog down to the drawing-room, rouse my lethargic son,
tell him the Colonel's here and make him give you a drink and a
sandwich. Um?'

'Yes, of course, Lady Lacklander,' said Nurse Kettle, and descended
briskly. 'Wanted to get rid of me, she thought, 'but it was tactfully
done.'

'Nice woman, Kettle,' Lady Lacklander grunted. 'She knows I
wanted to be rid of her. Mark, what is it that's making your grandfather unhappy?'

'Is he unhappy, Gar?'

'Don't hedge. He's worried to death. . . .' She stopped short. Her
jewelled hands twitched in her lap. 'He's troubled in his mind,' she
said, 'and for the second occasion in our married life I'm at a loss to
know why. Is it something to do with Maurice and the memoirs?'

'Apparently. He wants the Colonel to edit them.'

'The first occasion,' Lady Lacklander muttered, 'was twenty years
ago and it made me perfectly miserable. And now, when the time has
come for us to part company . . . and it has come, child, hasn't it?'

'Yes, darling, I think so. He's very tired.'

'I know. And I'm not, I'm seventy-five and grotesquely fat, but I
have a zest for life. There are still,' Lady Lacklander said with a

change in her rather wheezy voice, 'there are still things to be tidied up. George, for example.'

'What's my poor papa doing that needs a tidying hand?' Mark asked gently.

'Your poor papa,' she said, 'is fifty and a widower and a Lacklander. Three ominous circumstances.'

'Which can't be altered, even by you.'

'They can, however be . . . Maurice! What is it?'

Colonel Cartarette had opened the door and stood on the threshold with the packages still under his arm.

'Can you come, Mark? Quickly.'

Mark went past him into the bedroom. Lady Lacklander had risen and followed with more celerity than he would have thought possible. Colonel Cartarette stopped her in the doorway.

'My dear,' he said, 'wait a moment.'

'Not a second,' she said strongly. 'Let me in, Maurice.'

A bell rang persistently in the hall below. Nurse Kettle, followed by a tall man in evening clothes, came hurrying up the stairs. Colonel Cartarette stood on the landing and watched them go in.

Lady Lacklander was already at her husband's bedside. Mark supported him with his right arm and with his left hand kept his thumb on a bell-push that lay on the bed. Sir Harold's mouth was open and he was fetching his breath in a series of half-yawns. There was a movement under the bedclothes that seemed to be made by a continuous flexion and extension of his leg. Lady Lacklander stood massively beside him and took both his hands between hers.

I'm here, Hal,' she said.

Nurse Kettle had appeared with a glass in her hand.

'Brandy,' she said. 'Old-fashioned but good.'

Mark held it to his grandfather's open mouth. 'Try,' he said. 'It'll help. Try.'

The mouth closed over the rim.

'He's got a little,' Mark said. 'I'll give an injection.'

Nurse Kettle took his place. Mark turned away and found himself face-to-face with his father.

'Can I do anything?' George Lacklander asked.

'Only wait here, if you will, Father.'

'Here's George, Hal,' Lady Lacklander said. 'We're all here with you, my dear.'

From behind the mask against Nurse Kettle's shoulder came a stutter. 'Vic – Vic . . . Vic,' as if the pulse that was soon to run down had become semi-articulate like a clock. They looked at each other in dismay.

'What is it?' Lady Lacklander asked. 'What is it, Hal?'

'Somebody called Vic?' Nurse Kettle suggested brightly.

'There is nobody called Vic,' said George Lacklander, and sounded impatient. 'For God's sake, Mark, can't you help him?'

'In a moment,' Mark said from the far end of the room.

'Vic . . . '

'The Vicar?' Lady Lacklander asked, pressing his hand and bending over him. 'Do you want the Vicar to come, Hal?'

His eyes stared up into hers. Something like a smile twitched at the corners of the gaping mouth. The head moved slightly.

Mark came back with a syringe and gave the injection. After a moment Nurse Kettle turned away. There was something in her manner that gave definition to the scene. Lady Lacklander and her son and grandson drew closer to the bed. She had taken her husband's hands again.

'What is it, Hal? What is it, my dearest?' she asked. 'Is it the Vicar?'

With a distinctness that astonished them, he whispered: 'After all, you never know.' And with his gaze still fixed on his wife he then died.

II

On the late afternoon three days after his father's funeral, Sir George Lacklander sat in the study at Nunspardon going through the contents of the files and the desk. He was a handsome man with a look of conventional distinction. He had been dark but was now grizzled in the most becoming way possible with grey wings at his temples and a plume above his forehead. Inevitably, his mouth was firm and the nose above it appropriately hooked. He was, in short, rather like an illustration of an English gentleman in an American magazine.

He had arrived at the dangerous age for such men, being now fifty years old and remarkably vigorous.

Sir Harold had left everything in apple-pie order and his son anticipated little trouble. As he turned over the pages of his father's diaries it occurred to him that as a family they richly deserved their too-much-publicized nickname of 'Lucky Lacklanders.' How lucky, for instance, that the eighth baronet, an immensely wealthy man, had developed a passion for precious stones and invested in them to such an extent that they constituted a vast realizable fortune in themselves. How lucky that their famous racing stables were so phe-nomenally successful. How uniquely and fantastically lucky they had been in that no fewer than three times in the past century a Lacklander had won the most famous of all sweepstakes. It was true, of course, that he himself might be said to have had a piece of ill-for-tune when his wife had died in giving birth to Mark but as he remembered her, and he had to confess he no longer remembered her at all distinctly, she had been a disappointingly dull woman. Nothing like . . . But here he checked himself smartly and swept up his moustache with his thumb and forefinger. He was disconcerted when at this precise moment the butler came in to say that Colonel Cartarette had called and would like to see him. In a vague way the visit suggested a judgment. He took up a firm position on the hearthrug.

'Hallo, Maurice,' he said when the Colonel came in. 'Glad to see you.' He looked self-consciously into the Colonel's face and with a changed voice said: 'Anything wrong?'

'Well, yes,' the Colonel said. 'A hell of a lot actually. I'm sorry to bother you, George, so soon after your trouble and all that but the truth is I'm so damned worried that I feel I've got to share my responsibility with you.'

'Me!' Sir George ejaculated, apparently with relief and a kind of astonishment. The Colonel took two envelopes from his pocket and laid them on the desk. Sir George saw that they were addressed in his father's writing.

'Read the letter first,' the Colonel said, indicating the smaller of the two envelopes. George gave him a wondering look. He screwed in his eyeglass, drew a single sheet of paper from the envelope, and began to read. As he did so, his mouth fell gently open and his expression grew increasingly blank. Once he looked up at the troubled Colonel as if to ask a question but seemed to change his mind and fell again to reading.

At last the paper dropped from his fingers and his monocle from his eye to his waistcoat.

'I don't,' he said, 'understand a word of it.'

'You will,' the Colonel said, 'when you have looked at this.' He drew a thin sheaf of manuscript out of the larger envelope and placed it before George Lacklander. 'It will take you ten minutes to read. If you don't mind, I'll wait.'

'My dear fellow! Do sit down. What am I thinking of. A cigar! A drink.'

'No, thank you, George. I'll smoke a cigarette. No, don't move. I've got one.'

George gave him a wondering look, replaced his eyeglass and began to read again. As he did so his face went through as many changes of expression as those depicted in strip-advertisements. He was a rubicund man but the fresh colour drained out of his face. His mouth lost its firmness and his eyes their assurance. When he raised a sheet of manuscript it quivered in his grasp.

Once, before he had read to the end, he did speak. 'But it's not true,' he said. 'We've always known what happened. It was well known.' He touched his lips with his fingers and read on to the end. When the last page had fallen on the others Colonel Cartarette gathered them up and put them into their envelope.

'I'm damned sorry, George,' he said. 'God knows I didn't want to land you with all this.'

'I can't see now, why you've done it. Why bring it to me? Why do anything but throw it at the back of the fire?'

Cartarette said sombrely: 'I see you haven't listened to me. I told you. I've thought it over very carefully. He's left the decision with me and I've decided I must publish' – he held up the long envelope – 'this. I must, George. Any other course would be impossible.'

'But have you thought what it will do to us? Have you thought? It – it's *un*thinkable. You're an old friend, Maurice. My father trusted you with this business because he thought of you as a friend. In a way,' George added, struggling with an idea that was a little too big for him, 'in a way he's bequeathed you our destiny.'

'A most unwelcome legacy if it were so but of course it's not. You're putting it altogether too high. I know, believe me, George, I know, how painful and distressing this will be to you all, but I think the public will take a more charitable view than you might suppose.'

'And since when,' George demanded with a greater command of rhetoric than might have been expected of him, 'since when have the Lacklanders stood cap in hand, waiting upon the charity of the public?'

Colonel Cartarette's response to this was a helpless gesture. 'I'm terribly sorry,' he said; 'but I'm afraid that that sentiment has the advantage of sounding well and meaning nothing.'

'Don't be so bloody supercilious.'

'All right, George, all right.'

'The more I think of this the worse it gets. Look here, Maurice, if for no other reason, in common decency . . . '

'I've tried to take common decency as my criterion.'

'It'll kill my mother.'

'It will distress her very deeply, I know. I've thought of her, too.'

'And Mark? Ruin! A young man! My son! Starting on his career.'

'There was another young man, an only son, who was starting on his career.'

'He's dead!' George cried out. 'He can't suffer. He's dead.'

'And *his* name? And *his* father?'

'I can't chop logic with you. I'm a simple sort of bloke with, I dare say, very unfashionable standards. I believe in the loyalty of friends and in the old families sticking together.'

'At whatever the cost to other friends and other old families? Come off it, George,' said the Colonel.

The colour flooded back into George's face until it was em-purpled. He said in an unrecognizable voice: 'Give me my father's manuscript. Give me that envelope. I demand it.'

'I can't, old boy. Good God, do you suppose that if I could chuck it away or burn it with anything like a clear conscience I wouldn't do it? I tell you I hate this job.'

He returned the envelope to the breast pocket of his coat. 'You're free, of course,' he said, 'to talk this over with Lady Lacklander and Mark. Your father made no reservations about that. By the way, I've brought a copy of his letter in case you decide to tell them about it. Here it is.' The Colonel produced a third envelope, laid it on the desk and moved towards the door. 'And George,' he said, 'I beg you to believe I am sorry. I'm deeply sorry. If I could see any other way I'd thankfully take it. What?'

George Lacklander had made an inarticulate noise. He now pointed a heavy finger at the Colonel.

'After this,' he said, 'I needn't tell you that any question of an understanding between your girl and my boy is at an end.'

The Colonel was so quiet for so long that both men became aware of the ticking of a clock on the chimney breast.

'I didn't know,' he said at last, 'that there was any question of an understanding. I think you must be mistaken.'

'I assure you that I am not. However, we needn't discuss it. Mark . . . and Rose, I am sure . . . will both see that it is quite out of the question. No doubt you are as ready to ruin her chances as you are to destroy our happiness.' For a moment he watched the Colonel's blank face. 'She's head over heels in love with him,' he added, 'you can take my word for it.'

'If Mark has told you this – '

'Who says Mark told me? . . . I – I . . . '

The full, rather florid voice faltered and petered out.

'Indeed,' the Colonel said, 'then may I ask where you got your information?'

They stared at each other and, curiously, the look of startled conjecture which had appeared on George Lacklander's face was reflected on the Colonel's. 'It couldn't matter less, in any case,' the Colonel said. 'Your informant, I am sure, is entirely mistaken. There's no point in my staying. Goodbye.'

He went out. George, transfixed, saw him walk past the window. A sort of panic came over him. He dragged the telephone across his desk and with an unsteady hand dialled Colonel Cartarette's number. A woman's voice answered.

'Kitty!' he said. 'Kitty, is that you?'

III

Colonel Cartarette went home by the right-of-way known as the River Path. It ran through Nunspardon from the top end of Watt's

Lane skirting the Lacklanders' private golf course. It wound down to
Bottom Bridge and up the opposite side to the Cartarettes' spinney.
From thence it crossed the lower portion of Commander Syce's and
Mr Phinn's demesnes and rejoined Watt's Lane just below the crest
of Watt's Hill.

The Colonel was feeling miserable. He was weighed down by his
responsibility and upset by his falling out with George Lacklander
who, pompous old ass though the Colonel thought him, was a life-
time friend. Worst of all he was wretchedly disturbed by the suggestion that Rose had fallen in love with Mark and by the inference,
which he couldn't help drawing, that George Lacklander had collected
this information from the Colonel's wife.

As he walked down the hillside he looked across the little valley
into the gardens of Jacob's Cottage, Uplands and Hammer Farm.
There was Mr Phinn dodging about with a cat on his shoulder. 'Like
a blasted old warlock,' thought the Colonel, who had fallen out with
Mr Phinn over the trout stream, and there was poor Syce blazing
away with his bow-and-arrow at his padded target. And there, at
Hammer, was Kitty. With a characteristic movement of her hips she
had emerged from the house in skintight velvet trousers and a flame-
coloured top. Her long cigarette-holder was in her hand. She seemed
to look across the valley at Nunspardon. The Colonel felt a sickening
jolt under his diaphragm. 'How I could!' he thought (though subcon-
sciously). 'How I could!' Rose was at her evening employment cutting off the deadheads in the garden. He sighed and looked up to the
crest of the hill and there, plodding homewards, pushing her bicycle
up Watt's Lane, her uniform and hat appearing in gaps and vanishing
behind hedges, was Nurse Kettle. 'In Swevenings,' thought the
Colonel, 'she crops up like a recurring decimal.'

He came to the foot of the hill and to Bottom Bridge. The bridge
divided his fishing from Mr Danberry-Phinn's; he had the lower
reaches and Mr Phinn the upper. It was about the waters exactly
under Bottom Bridge that they had fallen out. The Colonel crossed
from Mr Phinn's side to his own, folded his arms on the stone parapet and gazed into the sliding green world beneath. At first he stared
absently but after a moment his attention sharpened. In the left bank
of the Chyne near a broken-down boat shed where an old punt was
moored, there was a hole. In its depths eddied and lurked a shadow

among shadows; the Old 'Un. 'Perhaps,' the Colonel thought, 'perhaps it would ease my mind a bit if I came down before dinner. He may stay on my side.' He withdrew his gaze from the Old 'Un to find when he looked up at Jacob's Cottage, that Mr Phinn, motionless, with his cat still on his shoulder, was looking at him through a pair of field-glasses.

'Ah, hell!' muttered the Colonel. He crossed the bridge and passed out of sight of Jacob's Cottage and continued on his way home.

The path crossed a narrow meadow and climbed the lower reach of Watt's Hill. His own coppice and Commander Syce's spinney concealed from the Colonel the upper portions of the three demesnes. Someone was coming down the path at a heavy jog-trot. He actually heard the wheezing and puffing of this person and recognized the form of locomotion practised by Mr Phinn before the latter appeared wearing an old Norfolk jacket and tweed hat which, in addition to being stuck about with trout-fishing flies, had Mr Phinn's reading spectacles thrust through the band like an Irishman's pipe. He was carrying his elaborate collection of fishing impediments. He had the air of having got himself together in a hurry and was attended by Mrs Thomasina Twitchett, who, after the manner of her kind, suggested that their association was purely coincidental.

The path was narrow. It was essential that someone should give way and the Colonel, sick of rows with his neighbours, stood on one side. Mr Phinn jogged glassily down upon him. The cat suddenly cantered ahead.

'Hallo, old girl,' said the Colonel. He stooped down and snapped a finger and thumb at her. She stared briefly and passed him with a preoccupied air, twitching the tip of her tail.

The Colonel straightened up and found himself face to face with Mr Phinn.

'Good evening,' said the Colonel.

'Sir,' said Mr Phinn. He touched his dreadful hat with one finger, blew out his cheeks and advanced. 'Thomasina,' he added, 'hold your body more seemly.'

For Thomasina, waywardly taken with the Colonel, had returned and rolled on her back at his feet.

'Nice cat,' said the Colonel, and added: 'Good fishing to you. The Old 'Un lies below the bridge on my side, by the way.'

'Indeed?'

'As no doubt you guessed,' the Colonel added against his better judgement, 'when you watched me through your field-glasses.'

If Mr Phinn had contemplated a conciliatory position he at once abandoned it. He made a belligerent gesture with his net. 'The landscape, so far as I am aware,' he said, 'is not under some optical interdict. It may be viewed, I believe. To the best of my knowledge, there are no squatter's rights over the distant prospect of the Chyne.'

'None whatever. You can stare,' said the Colonel, 'at the Chyne, or me or anything else you fancy till you are black in the face for all I care. But if you realized . . . If you . . .' He scratched his head, a gesture that with the Colonel denoted profound emotional disturbance. 'My dear Phinn . . .' he began again, 'if you only knew. . . . God bless my soul what *does* it matter! Good evening to you.'

He encircled Mr Phinn and hurried up the path. 'And for that grotesque,' he thought resentfully, 'for that impossible, that almost certifiable buffoon I have saddled myself with a responsibility that may well make me wretchedly uncomfortable for the rest of my life.'

He mended his pace and followed the path into the Hammer coppice. Whether summoned by maternal obligations or because she had taken an inscrutable cat's fancy to the Colonel, Thomasina Twitchett accompanied him, trilling occasionally and looking about for an evening bird. They came within view of the lawn and there was Commander Syce, bow in hand, quiver at thigh and slightly unsteady on his feet, hunting about in the underbrush.

'Hallo, Cartarette,' he said. 'Lost a damned arrow. What a thing! Missed the damned target and away she went.'

'Missed it by a dangerously wide margin, didn't you?' the Colonel rejoined rather testily. After all, people did use the path, he reflected and he began to help in the search. Thomasina Twitchett, amused by the rustle of leaves, pretended to join in the hunt.

'I know,' Commander Syce agreed, 'rotten bad show, but I saw old Phinn and it put me off. Did you hear what happened about me and his cat? Damnedest thing you ever knew! Purest accident, but the old whatnot wouldn't have it. Great grief, I told him, I *like* cats.'

He thrust his hand into a heap of dead leaves. Thomasina Twitchett leapt merrily upon it and fleshed her claws in his wrist. 'Perishing little bastard,' said Commander Syce. He freed himself and aimed a spank at her which she easily avoided and being tired of their company, made for her home and kittens. The Colonel excused himself and turned up through the spinney into the open field below his own lawn.

His wife was in her hammock dangling a tightly-encased black velvet leg, a flame-coloured sleeve and a pair of enormous earrings. The cocktail tray was ready on her iron table.

'How late you are,' she said idly. 'Dinner in half an hour. What have you been up to at Nunspardon?'

'I had to see George.'

'What about?'

'Some business his father asked me to do.'

'How illuminating.'

'It was very private, my dear.'

'How *is* George?'

The Colonel remembered George's empurpled face and said: 'Still rather upset.'

'We must ask him to dinner. I'm learning to play golf with him tomorrow, by the way. He's giving me some clubs. Nice, isn't it?'

'When did you arrange that?'

'Just now. About twenty minutes ago,' she said, watching him.

'Kitty, I'd rather you didn't.'

'You don't by any chance suspect me of playing you false with George, do you?'

'Well,' said the Colonel after a long pause, 'are you?'

'No.'

'I still think it might be better not to play golf with him tomorrow.'

'Why on earth?'

'Kitty, what have you said to George about Mark and Rose?'

'Nothing you couldn't have seen for yourself, darling. Rose is obviously head over heels in love with Mark.'

'I don't believe you.'

'My good Maurice, you don't suppose the girl is going to spend the rest of her existence doting on Daddy, do you?'

'I wouldn't have it for the world. Not for the world.'

'Well, then.'

'But I . . . I didn't know. . . . I still don't believe . . . '

'He turned up here five minutes ago looking all churned up and they're closeted together in the drawing-room. Go and see. I'll excuse your changing, if you like.'

'Thank you, my dear,' the Colonel said miserably and went indoors.

If he hadn't been so rattled and worried he would no doubt have given some sort of warning of his approach. As it was he crossed the heavy carpet of the hall, opened the drawing-room door and discovered his daughter locked in Mark Lacklander's arms from which embrace she was making but ineffectual attempts to escape.

CHAPTER 3

The Valley of the Chyne

Rose and Mark behaved in the classic manner of surprised lovers. They released each other, Rose turned white and Mark red, and neither of them uttered a word.

The Colonel said: I'm sorry, my dear. Forgive me,' and made his daughter a little bow.

Rose, with a sort of agitated spontaneity, ran to him, linked her hands behind his head, and cried: 'It had to happen some time, darling, didn't it?'

Mark said: 'Sir, I want her to marry me.'

'But I won't,' Rose said. 'I won't unless you can be happy about it. I've told him.'

The Colonel, with great gentleness, freed himself and then put an arm round his daughter.

'Where have you come from, Mark?' he asked.

'From Chyning. It's my day at the hospital.'

'Yes, I see.' The Colonel looked from his daughter to her lover and thought how ardent and vulnerable they seemed. 'Sit down, both of you,' he said. 'I've got to think what I'm going to say to you. Sit down.'

They obeyed him with an air of bewilderment.

'When you go back to Nunspardon, Mark,' he said, 'you will find your father very much upset. That is because of a talk I've just had with him. I'm at liberty to repeat the substance of that talk to you, but I feel some hesitation in doing so. I think he should be allowed to break it to you himself.'

'*Break* it to me?'

'It is not good news. You will find him entirely opposed to any thought of your marriage with Rose.'

'I can't believe it,' Mark said.

'You will, however. You may even find that you yourself (forgive me, Rose, my love, but it may be so), feel quite differently about' – the Colonel smiled faintly – 'about contracting an alliance with a Cartarette.'

'But, my poorest Daddy,' Rose ejaculated, clinging to a note of irony. 'What have you been up to?'

'The very devil and all, I'm afraid, my poppet,' her father rejoined.

'Well, whatever it may be,' Mark said, and stood up, 'I can assure you that blue murder wouldn't make me change my mind about Rose.'

'Oh,' the Colonel rejoined mildly, 'this is not blue murder.'

'Good.' Mark turned to Rose. 'Don't be fussed, darling,' he said. 'I'll go home and sort it out.'

'By all means go home,' the Colonel agreed, 'and try.'

He took Mark by the arm and led him to the door.

'You won't feel very friendly towards me tomorrow, Mark,' he said. 'Will you try to believe that the action I've been compelled to take is one that I detest taking?'

'Compelled?' Mark repeated. 'Yes – well . . . yes, of course.' He stuck out the Lacklander jaw and knitted the Lacklander brows. 'Look here, sir,' he said, 'if my father welcomes our engagement – and I can't conceive of his doing anything else – will you have any objection? I'd better tell you now that no objection on either side will make the smallest difference.'

'In that case,' the Colonel said, 'your question is academic. And now I'll leave you to have a word with Rose before you go home.' He held out his hand. 'Goodbye, Mark.'

When the Colonel had gone, Mark turned to Rose and took her hands in his. 'But how ridiculous,' he said. 'How in the wide world could these old boys cook up anything that would upset us?'

'I don't know. I don't know how they could but it's serious. He's terribly worried, poor darling.'

'Well,' Mark said, 'it's no good attempting a diagnosis before we've heard the history. I'll go home, see what's happened and ring you up in about fifteen minutes. The all-important, utterly bewildering and heaven-sent joy is that you love me, Rose. Nothing,' Mark continued with an air of coining a brand-new phrase, 'nothing can alter that. *Au revoir*, darling.'

He kissed Rose in a business-like manner and was gone.

She sat still for a time hugging to herself the knowledge of their feeling for each other. What had happened to all her scruples about leaving her father? She didn't even feel properly upset by her father's extraordinary behaviour and when she realized this circumstance she realized the extent of her enthralment. She stood in the french window of the drawing-room and looked across the valley to Nunspardon. It was impossible to be anxious . . . her whole being ached with happiness. It was now and for the first time, that Rose understood the completeness of love.

Time went by without her taking thought for it. The gong sounded for dinner and at the same moment the telephone rang. She flew to it.

'Rose,' Mark said. 'Say at once that you love me. At once.'

'I love you.'

'And on your most sacred word of honour that you'll marry me. Say it, Rose. Promise it. Solemnly promise.'

'I solemnly promise.'

'Good,' said Mark. 'I'll come back at nine.'

'Do you know what's wrong?'

'Yes. It's damn' ticklish. Bless you, darling. Till nine.'

'Till nine,' Rose said, and in a state of enthralment went in to dinner.

II

By eight o'clock the evening depression had begun to settle over Commander Syce. At about five o'clock when the sun was over the yard arm he had a brandy and soda. This raised his spirits. With its successors, up to the third or fourth, they rose still farther. During this period he saw himself taking a job and making a howling success of it. From that emotional eminence he fell away with each succeeding dram and it was during his decline that he usually took to archery. It had been in such a state of almost suicidal depression that he had suddenly shot an arrow over his coppice into Mr Danberry-Phinn's bottom meadow and slain the mother of Thomasina Twitchett.

Tonight the onset of depression was more than usually severe. Perhaps his encounter with the Colonel, whom he liked, gave point to his own loneliness. Moreover, his married couple were on their annual holiday and he had not been bothered to do anything about an evening meal. He found his arrow and limped back to the archery lawn. He no longer wanted to shoot. His gammy leg ached but he thought he'd take a turn up the drive.

When he arrived at the top it was to discover Nurse Kettle seated by the roadside in gloomy contemplation of her bicycle which stood upside down on its saddle and handlebars.

'Hallo, Commander,' said Nurse Kettle, 'I've got a puncture.'

'Evening. Really? Bore for you,' Syce shot out at her.

'I can't make up me great mind to push her the three miles to Chyning so I'm going to have a shot at running repairs. Pumping's no good,' said Nurse Kettle.

She had opened a tool kit and was looking dubiously at its contents. Syce hung off and on, and watched her make a pass with a lever at her tyre.

'Not like that,' he shouted when he could no longer endure it. 'Great grief, you'll get nowhere that fashion.'

'I believe you.'

'And in any case, you'll want a bucket of water to find the puncture.' She looked helplessly at him. 'Here!' he mumbled. 'Give it here.'

He righted the bicycle and with a further, completely inaudible remark began to wheel it down his drive. Nurse Kettle gathered up her tool kit and followed. A look strangely compounded of compassion and amusement had settled on her face.

Commander Syce wheeled the bicycle into a gardener's shed and without the slightest attempt at any further conversation set about the removal of the tyre. Nurse Kettle hitched herself up on a bench and watched him. Presently she began to talk.

'I *am* obliged to you. I've had a bit of a day. Epidemic in the village, odd cases all over the place and then this happens. There! Aren't you neat-fingered. I looked in at Nunspardon this evening,' she continued. 'Lady Lacklander's got a Toe and Dr Mark arranged for me to do the fomentations.'

Commander Syce made an inarticulate noise.

'If you ask *me* the new baronet's feeling his responsibilities. Came in just as I was leaving. Very bad colour and jumpy,' Nurse Kettle gossiped cosily. She swung her short legs and interrupted herself from time to time to admire Syce's handiwork. 'Pity!' she thought. 'Shaky hands. Alcoholic skin. Nice chap, too. Pity!'

He repaired the puncture and replaced the tube and tyre. When he had finished and made as if to stand up, he gave a sharp cry of pain, clapped his hands to the small of his back and sank down again on his knees.

'Hal-lo!' Nurse Kettle ejaculated. 'What's all this? 'Bago?'

Commander Syce swore under his breath. Between clenched teeth he implored her to go away. 'Most frightfully sorry,' he groaned. 'Ask you to excuse me. Ach!'

It was now that Nurse Kettle showed the quality that caused people to prefer her to grander and more up-to-date nurses. She exuded dependability, resourcefulness and authority. Even the common and pitilessly breezy flavour of her remarks was comfortable. To Commander Syce's conjurations to leave him alone followed in the extremity of his pain by furious oaths, she paid no attention. She went down on all-fours beside him, enticed and aided him towards the bench, encouraged him to use it and her own person as aids to rising and finally had him, though almost bent double, on his feet. She helped him into his house and lowered him down on a sofa in a dismal drawing-room.

'Down-a-bumps,' she said. Sweating and gasping, he reclined there and glared at her. 'Now, what are we going to do about *you*, I wonder? Did I or did I not see a rug in the hall? Wait a bit.'

She went out and came back with a rug. She called him 'dear' and, taking his pain seriously, covered him up, went out again and returned with a glass of water. 'Making myself at home, I suppose you're thinking. Here's a couple of aspirins to go on with,' said Nurse Kettle.

He took them without looking at her. 'Please don't trouble,' he groaned. 'Thank you. Under my own steam.' She gave him a look and went out again.

In her absence, he attempted to get up but was galvanized with a monstrous jab of lumbago and subsided in agony. He began to think she had gone for good and to wonder how he was to support life while the attack lasted, when he heard her moving about in some remote part of the house. In a moment she came in with two hot-water bags.

'At this stage,' she said, 'heat's the ticket.'

'Where did you get those things?'

'Borrowed 'em from the Cartarettes.'

'My God!'

She laid them against his back.

'Dr Mark's coming to look at you,' she said.

'My God!'

'He was at the Cartarettes and if you ask me there's going to be some news from that quarter before any of us are much older. At least,' Nurse Kettle added rather vexedly, 'I *would* have said so, if it hadn't been for them all looking a bit put out.' To his horror she began to take off his shoes.

'With a yo-heave-ho,' said Nurse Kettle out of compliment to the navy. 'Aspirin doing its stuff?'

'I – I think so. I *do beg* – '

'I suppose your bedroom's upstairs?'

'I do BEG – '

'We'll see what the doctor says, but I'd suggest you doss down in the housekeeper's room to save the stairs. I mean to say,' Nurse Kettle added with a hearty laugh, 'always provided there's no house-keeper.'

She looked into his face so good-humouredly and with such an air of believing him to be glad of her help that he found himself accepting it.

'Like a cup of tea?' She asked.

'No, thank you.'

'Well, it won't be anything stronger unless the doctor says so.'

He reddened, caught her eye and grinned.

'Come,' she said, 'that's better.'

'I'm really ashamed to trouble you so much.'

'I might have said the same about my bike, mightn't I? There's the doctor.'

She bustled out again and came back with Mark Lacklander.

Mark, who was a good deal paler than his patient, took a crisp line with Syce's expostulations.

'All right,' he said. 'I dare say I'm entirely extraneous. This isn't a professional visit if you'd rather not.'

'Great grief, my dear chap, I don't mean that. Only too grateful but . . . I mean . . . busy man . . . right itself . . . '

'Well, suppose I take a look-see,' Mark suggested. 'We won't move you.'

The examination was brief. 'If the lumbago doesn't clear up we can do something a bit more drastic,' Mark said, 'but in the meantime Nurse Kettle'll get you to bed. . . . '

'Good God!'

' . . . and look in again tomorrow morning. So will I. you'll need one or two things. I'll ring up the hospital and get them sent out at once. All right?'

'Thank you. Thank you. You don't,' said Syce to his own surprise, 'look terribly fit yourself. Sorry to have dragged you in.'

'That's all right. We'll bring your bed in here and put it near the telephone. Ring up if you're in difficulties. By the way, Mrs Cartarette offered – '

'No!' shouted Commander Syce, and turned purple.

' . . . to send in meals,' Mark added. 'But of course you may be up and about again tomorrow. In the meantime I think we can safely leave you to Nurse Kettle. Goodnight.'

When he had gone Nurse Kettle said cheerfully: 'You'll have to put up with me, it seems, if you don't want lovely ladies all round you. Now we'll get you washed up and settled for the night.'

Half an hour later when he was propped up in bed with a cup of hot milk and a plate of bread-and-butter, and a lamp within easy reach, Nurse Kettle looked down at him with her quizzical air.

'Well,' she said, 'I shall now, as they say, love you and leave you. Be good and if you can't be good be careful.'

'Thank you,' gabbled Commander Syce, nervously. 'Thank you, thank you, thank you.'

She had plodded over to the door before his voice arrested her.
'I – ah . . . I don't suppose,' he said, 'that you are familiar with
Aubrey's *Brief Lives*, are you?'

'No,' she said. 'Who was *he* when he was at home?'

'He wrote a *Brief Life* of a man called Sir Jonas Moore. It begins:
"Sciatica he cured it, by boyling his buttocks." I'm glad, at least, you
don't propose to try that remedy.'

'Well!' cried Nurse Kettle delightedly. 'You *are* coming out of your
shell to be sure. Nighty-bye.'

III

During the next three days Nurse Kettle, pedalling about her duties,
had occasion to notice, and she was sharp in such matters, that
something untoward was going on in the district. Wherever she
went, whether it was to attend upon Lady Lacklander's toe, or upon
the abscess of the gardener's child at Hammer, or upon Commander
Syce's strangely persistent lumbago, she felt a kind of heightened
tension in the behaviour of her patients and also in the behaviour of
young Dr Mark Lacklander. Rose Cartarette, when she encountered
her in the garden, was white and jumpy, the Colonel looked strained
and Mrs Cartarette singularly excited.

'Kettle,' Lady Lacklander said, on Wednesday, wincing a little as
she endured the approach of a fomentation to her toe, 'have you got
the cure for a bad conscience?'

Nurse Kettle did not resent being addressed in this restoration-
comedy fashion by Lady Lacklander who had known her for some
twenty years and used the form with an intimate and even an affec-
tionate air much prized by Nurse Kettle.

'Ah,' said the latter, 'there's no mixture-as-before for *that* sort of
trouble.'

'No. How long,' Lady Lacklander went on, 'have you been looking after us in Swevenings, Kettle?'

'Thirty years if you count five in the hospital at Chyning.'

'Twenty-five years of fomentations, enemas, slappings and
thumpings,' mused Lady Lacklander. 'And I suppose you've learnt
quite a lot about us in that time. There's nothing like illness to reveal

character and there's nothing like a love affair,' she added unexpectedly, 'to disguise it. This is agony,' she ended mildly, referring to the fomentation.

'Stick it if you can, dear,' Nurse Kettle advised, and Lady Lacklander for her part did not object to being addressed as 'dear' by Nurse Kettle, who continued: 'How do you mean I wonder about love disguising character?'

'When people are in love,' Lady Lacklander said, with a little scream as a new fomentation was applied, 'they instinctively present themselves to each other in their most favourable light. They assume pleasing characteristics as unconsciously as a cock pheasant puts on his spring plumage. They display such virtues as magnanimity, charitableness and modesty and wait for them to be admired. They develop a positive genius for suppressing their least attractive points. They can't help it, you know, Kettle. It's just the behaviourism of courtship.'

'Fancy.'

'Now don't pretend you don't know what I'm talking about because you most certainly do. You think straight and that's more than anybody else seems to be capable of doing in Swevenings. You're a gossip, of course,' Lady Lacklander added, 'but I don't think you're a malicious gossip, are you?'

'Certainly not. The idea!'

'No. Tell me, now, without any frills, what do you think of us.'

'Meaning, I take it,' Nurse Kettle returned, 'the aristocracy?'

'Meaning exactly that. Do you,' asked Lady Lacklander with relish, 'find us effete, ineffectual, vicious, obsolete and altogether extraneous?'

'No,' said Nurse Kettle stoutly, 'I don't.'

'Some of us are, you know.'

Nurse Kettle squatted back on her haunches, retaining a firm grip on Lady Lacklander's little heel. 'It's not the people so much as the idea,' she said.

'Ah,' said Lady Lacklander, 'you're an Elizabethan, Kettle. You *believe* in degree. You're a female Ulysses, old girl. But degree is now dependent upon behaviour, I'd have you know.'

Nurse Kettle gave a jolly laugh and said she didn't know what that meant. Lady Lacklander rejoined that, among other things, it meant that if people fall below something called a certain standard they are asking for trouble. 'I mean,' Lady Lacklander went on, scowling with physical pain and mental concentration, 'I mean we'd better behave ourselves in the admittedly few jobs that by right of heritage used to be ours. I mean, finally, that whether they think we're rubbish or whether they think we're not, people still expect that in certain situations we will give certain reactions. Don't they, Kettle?'

Nurse Kettle said she supposed they did.

'Not,' Lady Lacklander said, 'that I give a damn what they think. But still.'

She remained wrapped in moody contemplation while Nurse Kettle completed the treatment and bandaged the toe.

'In short,' her formidable patient at last declaimed, 'we can allow ourselves to be almost anything but shabbily behaved. That we'd better avoid. I'm extremely worried, Kettle.' Nurse Kettle looked up inquiringly. Tell me, is there any gossip in the village about my grandson? Romantic gossip?'

'A bit,' Nurse Kettle said, and after a pause added: 'It'd be lovely, wouldn't it? She's a sweet girl. *And* an heiress into the bargain.'

'Umph.'

'Which is not to be sneezed at nowadays, I suppose. They tell me everything goes to the daughter.'

'Entailed.' Lady Lacklander said: 'Mark, of course, gets nothing until he succeeds. But it's not that that bothers me.'

'Whatever it is, if I were you I should consult Dr Mark, Lady Lacklander. An old head on young shoulders if ever I saw one.'

'My dear soul, my grandson is, as you have observed, in love. He is therefore, as I have tried to point out, extremely likely to take up a high-falutin attitude. Besides, he's involved. No, I must take matters into my own hands, Kettle. Into my own hands. You go past Hammer on your way home, don't you?'

Nurse Kettle said she did.

'I've written a note to Colonel Cartarette. Drop it there like a good creature, will you?'

Nurse Kettle said she would and fetched it from Lady Lacklander's writing-desk.

'It's a pity,' Lady Lacklander muttered, as Nurse Kettle was about to leave her. 'It's a pity poor George is such an ass.'

IV

She considered that George gave only too clear a demonstration of being an ass when she caught a glimpse of him on the following evening. He was playing a round of golf with Mrs Cartarette. George, having attained the tricky age for Lacklanders, had fallen into a muddled, excited dotage upon Kitty Cartarette. She made him feel dangerous and this sensation enchanted him. She told him repeatedly how chivalrous he was and so cast a glow of knight-errantry over impulses that are not usually seen in that light. She allowed him only the most meagre rewards, doling out the lesser stimulants of courtship in positively homeopathic doses. Thus on the Nunspardon golf course, he was allowed to watch, criticize and correct her swing. If his interest in this exercise was far from being purely athletic, Mrs Cartarette gave only the slightest hint that she was aware of the fact and industriously swung and swung again while he fell back to observe, and advanced to adjust, her technique.

Lady Lacklander, tramping down River Path in the cool of the evening with a footman in attendance to carry her sketching impedimenta and her shooting-stick, observed her son and his pupil as it were in pantomime on the second tee. She noticed how George rocked on his feet, with his head on one side while Mrs Cartarette swung, as Lady Lacklander angrily noticed, everything that a woman could swing. Lady Lacklander looked at the two figures with distaste tempered by speculation. 'Can George,' she wondered, 'have some notion of employing the strategy of indirect attack upon Maurice? But no, poor boy, he hasn't got the brains.'

The two figures disappeared over the crest of the hill and Lady Lacklander plodded heavily on in great distress of mind. Because of her ulcerated toe she wore a pair of her late husband's shooting-boots. On her head was a battered solar topee of immense antiquity which she found convenient as an eye-shade. For the rest, her vast person was clad in baggy tweeds and a tent-like blouse. Her hands, as always, were encrusted with diamonds.

She and the footman reached Bottom Bridge, turned left and came to a halt before a group of alders and the prospect of a bend in the stream. The footman, under Lady Lacklander's direction, set up her easel, filled her water-jar at the stream, placed her camp stool and put her shooting-stick beside it. When she fell back from her work in order to observe it as a whole, Lady Lacklander was in the habit of supporting her bulk upon the shooting-stick.

The footman left her. She would reappear in her own time at Nunspardon and change for dinner at nine o'clock. The footman would return and collect her impedimenta. She fixed her spectacles on her nose, directed at her subject the sort of glance Nurse Kettle often bestowed on a recalcitrant patient, and set to work, massive and purposeful before her easel.

It was at six-thirty that she established herself there, in the meadow on the left bank of the Chyne not far below Bottom Bridge.

At seven, Mr Danberry-Phinn, having assembled his paraphernalia for fishing, set off down Watt's Hill. He did not continue to Bottom Bridge but turned left, and made for the upper reaches of the Chyne.

At seven, Mark Lacklander, having looked in on a patient in the village, set off on foot along Watt's Lane. He carried his case of instruments, as he wished to lance the abscess of the gardener's child at Hammer, and his racket and shoes as he proposed to play tennis with Rose Cartarette. He also hoped to have an extremely serious talk with her father.

At seven, Nurse Kettle, having delivered Lady Lacklander's note at Hammer, turned in at Commander Syce's drive and free-wheeled to his front door.

At seven, Sir George Lacklander, finding himself favourably situated in a sheltered position behind a group of trees, embraced Mrs Cartarette with determination, fervour and an ulterior motive.

It was at this hour that the hopes, passions and fears that had slowly mounted in intensity since the death of Sir Harold Lacklander began to gather an emotional momentum and slide towards each other like so many downhill streams, influenced in their courses by accidents and detail, but destined for a common and profound agitation.

At Hammer, Rose and her father sat in his study and gazed at each other in dismay.

'When did Mark tell you?' Colonel Cartarette asked.

'On that same night . . . after you came in and – and found us. He went to Nunspardon and his father told him and then he came back here and told me. Of course,' Rose said, looking at her father with eyes as blue as periwinkles behind their black lashes, 'of course it wouldn't have been any good for Mark to pretend nothing had happened. It's quite extraordinary how each of us seems to know exactly what the other one's thinking.'

The Colonel leant his head on his hand and half-smiled at this expression of what he regarded as one of the major fallacies of love. 'My poor darling,' he murmured.

'Daddy, you do understand, don't you, that theoretically Mark is absolutely on your side? Because – well, because the facts of any case always should be demonstrated. I mean that's the scientific point of view.'

The Colonel's half-smile twisted, but he said nothing.

'And I agree too, absolutely,' Rose said, 'other things being equal.'

'Ah!' said the Colonel.

'But they're not, darling,' Rose cried out, 'they're nothing like equal. In terms of human happiness, they're all cock-eyed. Mark says his grandmother's so desperately worried that with all this coming on top of Sir Harold's death and everything she may crack up altogether.'

The Colonel's study commanded a view of his own spinney and of that part of the valley that the spinney did not mask; Bottom Bridge and a small area below it on the right bank of the Chyne. Rose went to the window and looked down. 'She's down there somewhere,' she said, 'sketching in Bottom Meadow on the far side. She only sketches when she's fussed.'

'She's sent me a chit. She wants me to go down and talk to her at eight o'clock when I suppose she'll have done a sketch and hopes to feel less fussed. Damned inconvenient hour, but there you are. I'll cut dinner, darling, and try the evening rise. Ask them to leave supper for me, will you, and apologize to Kitty?'

'OK,' Rose said with forced airiness. 'And, of course,' she added, 'there's the further difficulty of Mark's papa.'

'George.'

'Yes, indeed, George. Well, we know he's not exactly as bright as sixpence, don't we? But, all the same, he *is* Mark's papa and he's cutting up most awfully rough and . . . '

Rose caught back her breath, her lips trembled and her eyes filled with tears. She launched herself into her father's arms and burst into a flood of tears. 'What's the use,' poor Rose sobbed, 'of being a brave little woman? I'm not in the least brave. When Mark asked me to marry him I said I wouldn't because of you and there I was: so miserable that when he asked me again I said I would. And now, when we're so desperately in love, this happens. We have to do them this really frightful injury. Mark says: of course they must take it and it won't make any difference to us, but of course it *will*. And how can I bear to be married to Mark and know how his people feel about you when next to Mark, my darling, darling Daddy, I love you best in the world? And *his* father' – Rose wept – '*his* father says that if Mark marries me he'll never forgive him and that they'll do a sort of Montague and Capulet thing at us and, darling, it wouldn't be much fun for Mark and me, would it, to be star-crossed lovers?'

'My poor baby,' murmured the agitated and sentimental Colonel; 'my poor baby!' And he administered a number of unintentionally hard thumps between his daughter's shoulder blades.

'It's so many people's happiness,' Rose sobbed. 'It's all of us.'

Her father dabbed at her eyes with his own handkerchief, kissed her and put her aside. In his turn he went over to the window and looked down at Bottom Bridge, and up at the roofs of Nunspardon. There were no figures in view on the golf course.

'You know, Rose,' the Colonel said in a changed voice, 'I don't carry the whole responsibility. There is a final decision to be made and mine must rest upon it. Don't hold out too many hopes, my darling, but I suppose there is a chance. I've time to get it over before I talk to Lady Lacklander and indeed I suppose I should. There's nothing to be gained by any further delay. I'll go now.'

He went to his desk, unlocked a drawer and took out an envelope.

Rose said: 'Does Kitty?'

'Oh, yes,' the Colonel said. 'She knows.'

'Did you tell her, Daddy?'

The Colonel had already gone to the door. Without turning his head and with an air too casual to be convincing he said: 'Oh, no. No. She arranged to play a round of golf with George and I imagine he elected to tell her. He's a fearful old gas-bag is George.'

'She's playing now, isn't she?'

'Is she? Yes,' said the Colonel; 'I believe she is. He came to fetch her, I think. It's good for her to get out.'

'Yes, rather,' Rose agreed.

Her father went out to call on Mr Octavius Danberry-Phinn. He took his fishing gear with him as he intended to go straight on to his meeting with Lady Lacklander and to ease his troubled mind afterwards with the evening rise. He also took his spaniel Skip who was trained to good behaviour when he accompanied his master to the trout stream.

V

Lady Lacklander consulted the diamond-encrusted watch which was pinned to her tremendous bosom and discovered that it was now seven o'clock. She had been painting for half an hour and an all-too-familiar phenomenon had emerged from her efforts.

'It's a curious thing,' she meditated, 'that a woman of my character and determination should produce such a puny affair. However, it's got me in better trim for Maurice Cartarette and that's a damn' good thing. An hour to go if he's punctual and he's sure to be that.'

She tilted her sketch and ran a faint green wash over the foreground. When it was partly dry she rose from her stool, tramped some distance away to the crest of a hillock, seated herself on her shooting-stick and contemplated her work through a lorgnette tricked out with diamonds. The shooting-stick sank beneath her in the soft meadowland so that the disc which was designed to check its descent was itself imbedded to the depth of several inches. When Lady Lacklander returned to her easel she merely abandoned her shooting-stick which remained in a vertical position and from a distance looked a little like a giant fungoid growth. Sticking up above intervening hillocks and rushes it was observed over the top of his glasses by the long-sighted Mr Phinn when, accompanied by Thomasina Twitchett, he came nearer to Bottom Bridge. Keeping on the right bank, he began to cast his fly in a somewhat mannered but adroit fashion over the waters most often frequented by the Old 'Un. Lady Lacklander, whose ears were as sharp as his, heard the whirr of his reel and, remaining invisible, was perfectly able to deduce the identity and movements of the angler. At the same time, far above them on Watt's Hill, Colonel Cartarette, finding nobody but seven

cats at home at Jacob's Cottage, walked round the house and looking down into the little valley, at once spotted both Lady Lacklander
and Mr Phinn, like figures in Nurse Kettle's imaginary map, the one
squatting on her camp stool, the other in slow motion near Bottom
Bridge.

'I've time to speak to him before I see her,' thought the Colonel.
'But I'll leave it here in case we don't meet.' He posted his long envelope in Mr Phinn's front door and then greatly troubled in spirit he
made for the River Path and went down into the valley, the old
spaniel, Skip, walking at his heels.

Nurse Kettle, looking through the drawing-room window at
Uplands, caught sight of the Colonel before he disappeared beyond
Commander Syce's spinney. She administered a final tattoo with the
edges of her muscular hands on Commander Syce's lumbar muscles,
and said: 'There goes the Colonel for the evening rise. You wouldn't
have stood *that* amount of punishment two days ago, would you?'

'No,' a submerged voice said, 'I suppose not.'

'Well! So that's all I get for my trouble.'

'No, no! Look here, look here!' he gabbled, twisting his head in
an attempt to see her. 'Good heavens! What are you saying?'

'All right. I know. I was only pulling your leg. There!' she said.
'That's all for today and I fancy it won't be long now before I wash
my hands of you altogether.'

'Of course I can't expect to impose on your kindness any longer.'

Nurse Kettle was clearing up. She appeared not to hear this
remark and presently bustled away to wash her hands. When she
returned Syce was sitting on the edge of his improvised bed. He wore
slacks, a shirt, a scarf and a dressing-gown.

'Jolly D.,' said Nurse Kettle. 'Done it all yourself.'

'I hope you will give me the pleasure of joining me for a drink
before you go.'

'On duty?'

'Isn't it off duty, now?'

'Well,' said Nurse Kettle, 'I'll have a drink with you but I hope it
won't mean that when I've gone on me way rejoicing you're going
to have half a dozen more with yourself.'

Commander Syce turned red and muttered something about a
fellah having nothing better to do.

'Get along,' said Nurse Kettle, 'find something better. The idea!'

They had their drinks, looking at each other with an air of comradeship. Commander Syce, using a walking-stick and holding himself at an unusual angle, got out an album of photographs taken when he was on the active list in the navy. Nurse Kettle adored photographs and was genuinely interested in a long sequence of naval vessels, odd groups of officers and views of seaports. Presently she turned a page and discovered quite a dashing watercolour of a corvette and then an illustrated menu with lively little caricatures in the margin. These she greatly admired and observing a terrified and defiant expression on the face of her host, ejaculated: 'You never did these yourself! You *did*! Well, aren't you the clever one!'

Without answering he produced a small portfolio which he silently thrust at her. It contained many more sketches. Although Nurse Kettle knew nothing about pictures, she did, she maintained, know what she liked. And she liked these very much indeed. They were direct statements of facts and she awarded them direct statements of approval and was about to shut the portfolio when a sketch that had faced the wrong way round caught her attention. She turned it over. It was of a woman lying on a *chaise-longue* smoking a cigarette in a jade holder. A bougainvillaea flowered in the background.

'Why,' Nurse Kettle ejaculated. 'Why, that's Mrs Cartarette!'

If Syce had made some kind of movement to snatch the sketch from her he checked himself before it was completed. He said very rapidly: 'Party. Met her Far East. Shore leave. Forgotten all about it.'

'That would be before they were married, wouldn't it?' Nurse Kettle remarked with perfect simplicity. She shut the portfolio, said: 'You know, I believe *you* could make my picture-map of Swevenings.' And told him of her great desire for one. When she got up and collected her belongings he, too, rose, but with an ejaculation of distress.

'I see I haven't made a job of you yet,' she remarked. 'Same time tomorrow suit you?'

'Admirably,' he said. 'Thank you, thank you, thank you.' He gave her one of his rare painful smiles and watched her as she walked down the path towards his spinney. It was now a quarter to nine.

VI

Nurse Kettle had left her bicycle in the village where she was spending the evening with the Women's Institute. She therefore took the River Path. Dusk had fallen over the valley of the Chyne and as she descended into it her own footfall sounded unnaturally loud on the firm turf. Thump, thump, thump she went, down the hillside. Once, she stopped dead, tilted her head and listened. From behind her at Uplands, came the not-unfamiliar sound of a twang followed by a sharp penetrating blow. She smiled to herself and walked on. Only desultory rural sounds disturbed the quiet of nightfall. She could actually hear the cool voice of the stream.

She did not cross Bottom Bridge but followed a rough path along the right bank of the Chyne, past a group of alders and another of willows. This second group, extending in a sickle-shaped mass from the water's edge into Bottom Meadow rose up vapourishly in the dusk. She could smell willow-leaves and wet soil. As sometimes happens when we are solitary, she had the sensation of being observed but she was not a fanciful woman and soon dismissed this feeling.

'It's turned much cooler,' she thought.

A cry of mourning, intolerably loud, rose from beyond the willows and hung on the night air. A thrush whirred out of the thicket close to her face and the cry broke and wavered again. It was the howl of a dog.

She pushed through the thicket into an opening by the river and found the body of Colonel Cartarette with his spaniel Skip beside it, mourning him.

CHAPTER 4

Bottom Meadow

Nurse Kettle was acquainted with death. She did not need Skip's lament to tell her that the curled figure resting its head on a turf of river grass was dead. She knelt beside it and pushed her hand under the tweed jacket and silk shirt. 'Cooling,' she thought. A tweed hat with fisherman's flies in the band lay over the face. Someone, she thought, might almost have dropped it there. She lifted it and remained quite still with it suspended in her hand. The Colonel's temple had been broken as if his head had come under a waxworker's hammer. The spaniel threw back his head and howled again.

'Oh, do be quiet!' Nurse Kettle ejaculated. She replaced the hat and stood up, knocking her head against a branch. The birds that spent the night in the willows stirred again and some of them flew out with a sharp whirring sound. The Chyne gurgled and plopped and somewhere up in Nunspardon woods an owl hooted. 'He has been murdered,' thought Nurse Kettle.

Through her mind hurtled all the axioms of police procedure as laid down in her chosen form of escape-literature. One must, she recollected, not touch the body, and she had touched it. One must send at once for the police but she had nobody to send. She thought there was also something about not leaving the body, yet to telephone or to fetch Mr Oliphant, the police-sergeant at Chyning, she would have to leave the body and while she was away the spaniel, she supposed, would sit beside it and howl. It was now quite dark-ish and the moon not yet up. She could see, however, not far from the Colonel's hands the glint of a trout's scales in the grass and of a knife blade nearby. His rod was laid out on the lip of the bank, less than a pace from where he lay. None of these things, of course, must be disturbed. Suddenly Nurse Kettle thought of Commander Syce whose Christian name she had discovered was Geoffrey and wished with all her heart that he was at hand to advise her. The discovery in herself of this impulse, astonished her and, in a sort of flurry, she swapped Geoffrey Syce for Mark Lacklander. 'I'll find the Doctor,' she thought.

She patted Skip. He whimpered and scraped at her knees with his paws. 'Don't howl, doggy,' she said in a trembling voice. 'Good boy! Don't howl.' She took up her bag and turned away.

As she made her way out of the willow grove she wondered for the first time about the identity of the being who had reduced Colonel Cartarette to the status of a broken waxwork. A twig snapped. 'Suppose,' she thought, 'he's still about! Help, what a notion!' And as she hurried back along the path to Bottom Bridge she tried not to think of the dense shadows and dark hollows that lay about her. Up on Watt's Hill the three houses – Jacob's Cottage, Uplands and Hammer – all had lighted windows and drawn blinds. They looked very far off to Nurse Kettle.

She crossed Bottom Bridge and climbed the zigzag path that skirted the golf course coming finally to the Nunspardon home spinney. Only now did she remember that her flashlamp was in her bag. She got it out and found that she was breathless. Too quick up the hill,' she thought. 'Keep your shirt on, Kettle.' River Path proper ran past the spinney to the main road but a by-path led up through the trees into the grounds of Nunspardon. This she took and presently came out into the open gardens with the impressive Georgian façade straight ahead of her.

The footman who answered the front-door bell was well enough known to her. 'Yes, it's me again, William,' she said. 'Is the Doctor at home?'

'He came in about an hour ago, miss.'

'I want to see him. It's urgent.'

'The family's in the library, miss. I'll ascertain . . . '

'Don't bother,' said Nurse Kettle. 'Or, yes. Ascertain if you like, but I'll be hard on your heels. Ask him if he'll come out here and speak to me.'

He looked dubiously at her, but something in her face must have impressed him. He crossed the great hall and opened the library door. He left it open and Nurse Kettle heard him say: 'Miss Kettle, to see Dr Lacklander, my lady.'

'Me?' said Mark's voice. 'Oh Lord! All right, I'll come.'

'Bring her in here,' Lady Lacklander's voice commanded. 'Talk to her in here, Mark, I want to see Kettle.' Hearing this, Nurse Kettle, without waiting to be summoned, walked quickly into the library. The three Lack-landers had turned in their chairs. George and Mark got up. Mark looked sharply at her and came quickly towards her. Lady Lacklander said: 'Kettle! What's happened to *you!*'

Nurse Kettle said: 'Good evening, Lady Lacklander. Good evening, Sir George.' She put her hands behind her back and looked full at Mark. 'May I speak to you, sir?' she said. 'There's been an accident.'

'All right, Nurse,' Mark said. 'To whom?'

'To Colonel Cartarette, sir.'

The expression of inquiry seemed to freeze on their faces. It was as if they retired behind newly-assumed masks.

'What sort of accident?' Mark said.

He stood between Nurse Kettle and his grandmother and father. She shaped the word 'killed' with her lips and tongue.

'Come out here,' he muttered, and took her by the arm.

'Not at all,' his grandmother said. She heaved herself out of her chair and bore down upon them. 'Not at all, Mark. What has happened to Maurice Cartarette? Don't keep things from me, I am probably in better trim to meet an emergency than anyone else in this house. What has happened to Maurice?'

Mark, still holding Nurse Kettle by the arm, said: 'Very well, Gar. Nurse Kettle will tell us what has happened!'

'Let's have it, then. And in case it's as bad as you look, Kettle, I suggest we all sit down. What did you say, George?'

Her son had made an indeterminate noise. He now said galvanically: 'Yes, of course, Mama, by all means.'

Mark pushed a chair forward for Nurse Kettle and she took it thankfully. Her knees, she discovered, were wobbling.

'Now, then, out with it,' said Lady Lacklander. 'He's dead, isn't he, Kettle?'

'Yes, Lady Lacklander.'

'Where?' Sir George demanded. Nurse Kettle told him.

'When,' Lady Lacklander said, 'did you discover him?'

'I've come straight up here, Lady Lacklander.'

'But why here, Kettle? Why not to Uplands?'

'I must break it to Kitty,' said Sir George.

'I must go to Rose,' said Mark simultaneously.

'Kettle,' said Lady Lacklander, 'you used the word accident. What accident?'

'He has been murdered, Lady Lacklander,' said Nurse Kettle.

The thought that crossed her mind after she had made this announcement was that the three Lacklanders were, in their several generations, superficially very much alike but that, whereas in Lady Lacklander and Mark the distance between the eyes and the width of mouth suggested a certain generosity, in Sir George they seemed merely to denote the naïve. Sir George's jaw had dropped and handsome though he undoubtedly was, he gaped unhandsomely. As none of them spoke, she added: 'So I thought I'd better report to you, sir.'

'Do you mean,' Sir George said loudly, 'that he's lying there in my bottom meadow, murdered?'

'Yes, Sir George,' Nurse Kettle said. 'I do.'

'How?' Mark said.

'Injuries to the head.'

'You made quite sure, of course?'

'Quite sure.'

Mark looked at his father. 'We must ring the Chief Constable,' he said. 'Would you do that, Father? I'll go down with Nurse Kettle. One of us had better stay there till the police come. If you can't get the C.C. would you ring Sergeant Oliphant at Chyning?'

Sir George's hand went to his moustache. 'I think,' he said, 'you may take it, Mark, that I understand my responsibilities.'

Lady Lacklander said: 'Don't be an ass, George. The boy's quite right.' And her son, scarlet in the face, went off to the telephone. 'Now,' Lady Lacklander continued, 'what are we going to do about Rose and that wife of his?'

'Gar . . .' Mark began, but his grandmother raised a fat glittering hand.

'Yes, yes,' she said. 'No doubt you want to break it to Rose, Mark, but in my opinion you will do better to let me see both of them first. I shall stay there until you appear. Order the car.'

Mark rang the bell. 'And you needn't wait,' she added. 'Take Miss Kettle with you.' It was characteristic of Lady Lacklander that she restricted her use of the more peremptory form of address to the second person. She now used it. 'Kettle,' she said, 'we're grateful to you and mustn't impose. Would you rather come with me or go back with my grandson? Which is best, do you think?'

'I'll go with the Doctor, thank you, Lady Lacklander. I suppose,' Nurse Kettle added composedly, 'that as I found the body I'll be required to make a statement.'

She had moved with Mark to the door when Lady Lacklander's voice checked her.

'And I suppose,' the elderly voice said, 'that as I may have been the last person to speak to him, I shall be required to make one too.'

II

In the drawing-room at Hammer there was an incongruous company assembled. Kitty Cartarette, Mark Lacklander and Nurse Kettle waited there while Lady Lacklander sat with Rose in the Colonel's study. She had arrived first at Hammer, having been driven round in her great car while Mark and Nurse Kettle waited in the valley and George rang up the police station at Chyning. George had remembered he was a Justice of the Peace and was believed to be in telephonic conference with his brethren of the bench.

So it had fallen to Lady Lacklander to break the news to Kitty whom she had found, wearing her black velvet tights and flame-coloured top, in the drawing-room. Lady Lacklander in the course of a long life spent in many embassies had encountered every kind of eccentricity in female attire and was pretty well informed as to the predatory tactics of women whom, in the Far East, she had been wont to describe as 'light cruisers.' She had made up her mind about Kitty Cartarette, but had seemed to be prepared to concede her certain qualities if she showed any signs of possessing them.

She had said: 'My dear; I'm the bearer of bad tidings.' And noticing that Kitty at once looked very frightened, had remarked to herself: 'She thinks I mean to tackle her about George.'

'Are you?' Kitty had said. 'What sort of tidings, please?'

'About Maurice.' Lady Lacklander, who had waited for a moment, added: 'I'm afraid it's the worst kind of news,' and had then told her. Kitty stared at her. 'Dead?' she said. 'Maurice dead? I don't believe you. How can he be dead? He's been fishing down below there and I dare say he's looked in at the pub.' Her hands with their long painted nails began to tremble. 'How can he be dead?' she repeated.

Lady Lacklander became more specific and presently Kitty broke into a harsh strangulated sobbing, twisting her fingers together and turning her head aside. She walked about the room, still, Lady Lacklander noticed, swaying her hips. Presently she fetched up by a grog tray on a small table and shakily poured herself a drink.

'That's a sensible idea,' Lady Lacklander said as the neck of the decanter chattered against the glass. Kitty awkwardly offered her a drink which she declined with perfect equanimity. 'Her manner,' she thought to herself, 'is really too dreadful. What shall I do if George marries her?'

It was at this juncture that Nurse Kettle and Mark had appeared outside the french windows. Lady Lacklander signalled to them. 'Here is my grandson and Nurse Kettle,' she said to Kitty. 'Shall they come in? I think it would be a good idea, don't you?'

Kitty said shakily: 'Yes, please. Yes, if you like.' Lady Lacklander heaved her bulk out of her chair and let them in.

'Sergeant Oliphant's there,' Mark murmured. 'They're going to ring Scotland Yard. Does Rose – ?'

'Not yet. She's out in the garden, somewhere.'

Mark went across to Kitty and spoke to her with a quiet authority that his grandmother instantly approved. She noticed how Kitty steadied under it, how Mark, without fussing, got her into a chair. Nurse Kettle as a matter of course came forward and took the glass when Kitty had emptied it. A light and charming voice sang in the hall.

'Come away, come away death . . . '

And Mark turned sharply.

'I'll go,' his grandmother said, 'and I'll fetch you when she asks for you.'

With a swifter movement than either her size or her age would have seemed to allow she had gone into the hall. The little song of death stopped and the door shut behind Lady Lacklander.

Kitty Cartarette was quieter but still caught her breath now and again in a harsh sob.

'Sorry,' she said, looking from Nurse Kettle to Mark. 'Thanks. It's just the shock.'

'Yes, of course, dear,' Nurse Kettle said.

'I sort of can't believe it. You know?'

'Yes, of course,' Mark said.

'It seems so queer . . . Maurice!' She looked at Mark. 'What was that,' she said, 'about somebody doing it? Is it true?'

'I'm afraid it looks very much like it.'

'I'd forgotten,' she muttered vaguely, 'you've seen him, haven't you, and you're a doctor, of course?' Her mouth trembled. She wiped the back of her hand over it. A trail of red was dragged across her cheek. It was a sufficient indication of her state of mind that she seemed to be unaware of it. She said: 'No, it's no good, I can't believe it. We saw him down there, fishing.' And then she suddenly demanded: 'Where's George?'

Nurse Kettle saw Mark's back stiffen. 'My father?' he asked.

'Oh, yes, of course, I'd forgotten,' she said again, shaking her head. 'He's your father. Silly of me.'

'He's looking after one or two things that must be done. You see the police have had to be told at once.'

'Is George getting the police?'

'He's rung them up. He will, I think, come here as soon as he can.'

'Yes,' she said. 'I expect he will.'

Nurse Kettle saw George's son compress his lips. At that moment George himself walked in and the party became even less happily assorted.

Nurse Kettle had acquired a talent for retiring into whatever background presented itself and this talent she now exercised. She moved through the open french window on to the terrace, shut the door after her and sat on a garden seat within view of the drawing-room but facing across the now completely dark valley. Mark, who would perhaps have liked to follow her, stood his ground. His father looking extraordinarily handsome and not a little self-conscious went straight to Kitty. She used the gesture that Mark had found embarrassing and extended her left hand to Sir George who kissed it with an air nicely compounded of embarrassment, deference, distress and devotion.

'My dear Kitty,' said Sir George in a special voice. I'm so terribly, terribly sorry. What can one say? What can one do?'

He apparently had already said and done more than any of the others to assuage Kitty's distress, for it began perceptibly to take on a more becoming guise. She looked into his eyes, and said: 'How terribly good of you to come.' He sat down beside her, began to pat her hand, noticed his son, and said: 'I'll have a word with you in a moment, old boy.'

Mark was about to retire to the terrace when the door opened and his grandmother looked in. 'Mark?' she said. He went quickly into the hall. 'In the study,' Lady Lacklander said and in a moment he was there with Rose sobbing bitterly in his arms.

'You need pay no attention to me,' Lady Lacklander said. 'I am about to telephone New Scotland Yard. Your father tells me they have been called in, and I propose to send for Helena Alleyn's boy.'

Mark, who was kissing Rose's hair, left off abruptly to say: 'Can you mean Chief Inspector Alleyn, Gar?'

'I don't know what his rank is, but he used to be a nice boy twenty-five years ago before he left the Service to become a constable. Central? This is Hermione, Lady Lacklander. . . . I want New Scotland Yard, London. The call is extremely urgent as it is concerned with murder. . . . Yes, murder. You will oblige me by putting it through at once. . . . Thank you.' She glanced at Mark. 'In the circumstances,' she said, 'I prefer to deal with a gent.'

Mark had drawn Rose to a chair and was kneeling beside her, gently wiping away her tears.

'Hallo!' Lady Lacklander said after an extremely short delay. 'New Scotland Yard? This is Hermione, Lady Lacklander speaking. I wish to speak to Mr Roderick Alleyn. If he is not on your premises you will no doubt know where he is to be found. . . . I don't know his rank . . . '

Her voice, aristocratic, cool, sure of itself, went steadily on. Mark dabbed at Rose's eyes. His father, alone with Kitty in the drawing-room, muttered agitatedly:' . . . I'm sorry it's hit you so hard, Kit.'

Kitty looked wanly at him. 'I suppose it's the shock,' she said, and added without rancour: 'I'm not as tough as you all think.' He protested chaotically. 'Oh,' she said quite gently, 'I know what they'll say about me. Not you, p'r'aps, but the others. They'll say it's cupboard-sorrow. 'That's what's upsetting the widow,' they'll say. I'm the outsider, George.'

'Don't, Kit. Kit, listen . . .' He began to plead with her. 'There's something I must ask you – if you'd just have a look for – you know – that thing – I mean – if it was found . . .'

She listened to him distractedly. 'It's awful,' George said. 'I know it's awful to talk like this now, Kitty, but all the same – all the same – with so much at stake. I know you'll understand.'

Kitty said: 'Yes. All right. . . . Yes. But let me *think*.'

Nurse Kettle out on the terrace was disturbed by the spatter of a few giant raindrops.

'There's going to be a storm,' she said to herself. 'A summer storm.'

And since she would have been out of place in the drawing-room and in the study she took shelter in the hall. She had no sooner done so than the storm broke in a downpour over the valley of the Chyne.

III

Alleyn and Fox had worked late, tidying up the last phase of a tedious case of embezzlement. At twelve minutes to ten they had finished. Alleyn shut the file with a slap of his hand.

'Dreary fellow,' he said. 'I hope they give him the maximum. Damn' good riddance. Come back with me and have a drink, Brer Fox. I'm a grass-widower and hating it. Troy and Ricky are in the country. What do you say?'

Fox drew his hand across the lower part of his face. 'Well, now, Mr Alleyn, that sounds very pleasant,' he said. 'I say yes and thank you.'

'Good.' Alleyn looked round the familiar walls of the Chief Inspector's room at New Scotland Yard. 'There are occasions,' he said, 'when one suddenly sees one's natural habitat as if for the first time. It is a terrifying sensation. Come on. Let's go while the going's good.'

They were half-way to the door when the telephone rang. Fox said: 'Ah, hell!' without any particular animosity and went back to answer it.

'Chief Inspector's room,' he said heavily. 'Well, yes, he's here. Just.' He listened for a moment gazing blandly at his superior. 'Say I'm dead,' Alleyn suggested moodily. Fox laid his great palm over the receiver. 'They make out it's a Lady Lacklander on call from somewhere called Swevenings,' he said.

'Lady *Lacklander?* Good lord! That's old Sir Harold Lacklander's widow,' Alleyn ejaculated. 'What's up with her, I wonder.'

'Chief Inspector Alleyn will take the call,' Fox said, and held out the receiver.

Alleyn sat on his desk and put the receiver to his ear. An incisive elderly voice was saying: ' . . . I don't know his rank and I don't know whether he's on your premises or not, but you'll be good enough, if you please, to find Mr Roderick Alleyn for me. It is Hermione, Lady Lacklander speaking. Is that New Scotland Yard and have you heard me? . . . I wish to speak to . . . '

Alleyn announced himself cautiously into the receiver. 'Indeed!' the voice rejoined. 'Why on earth couldn't you say so in the first instance? . . . Hermione Lacklander speaking. I won't waste time reminding you about myself. You're Helena Alleyn's boy and I want an assurance from you. A friend of mine has just been murdered,' the voice continued, 'and I hear the local police are calling in your people. I would greatly prefer you, personally, to take charge of the whole thing. That can be arranged, I imagine?'

Alleyn, controlling his astonishment, said: 'I'm afraid only if the Assistant Commissioner happens to give me the job.'

'Who's he?'

Alleyn told her.

'Put me through to him,' the voice commanded.

A second telephone began to ring. Fox answered it and in a moment held up a warning hand.

'Will you wait one second, Lady Lacklander?' Alleyn asked. Her voice, however, went incisively on and he stifled it against his chest. 'What the hell is it, Fox?' he asked irritably.

'Central office, sir. Orders for Swevenings. Homicide.'

'Blistering apes! Us?'

'Us,' said Fox stolidly.

Alleyn spoke into his own receiver. 'Lady Lacklander? I *am* taking this case, it appears.'

'Glad to hear it,' said Lady Lacklander. 'I suggest you look pretty sharp about it. *Au revoir,*' she added with unexpected modishness, and rang off.

Fox, in the meantime, had noted down instructions. 'I'll inform Mr Alleyn,' he was saying. 'Yes, very good, I'll inform him. Thank you.' He hung up his receiver. 'It's a Colonel Cartarette,' he said. 'We go to a place called Chyning in Barfordshire, where the local sergeant will meet us. Matter of two hours. Everything's laid on down below.'

Alleyn had already collected his hat, coat and professional case. Fox followed his example. They went out together through the never-sleeping corridors.

It was a still hot night. Sheet-lightning played fretfully over the East End. The air smelt of petrol and dust. 'Why don't we join the River Police?' Alleyn grumbled. 'One long water carnival.'

A car waited for them with Detective-Sergeants Bailey and Thompson and their gear already on board. As they drove out of the Yard, Big Ben struck ten.

'That's a remarkable woman, Fox,' Alleyn said. 'She's got a brain like a turbine and a body like a tun. My mother, who has her share of guts, was always terrified of Hermione Lacklander.'

'Is that so, Mr Alleyn? Her husband died only the other day, didn't he?'

'That's right. A quarter of a century ago, he was one of my great white chiefs in the Foreign Service. Solemn chap . . . . Just missed being brilliant. She was a force to be reckoned with even then. What's she doing in this party? What's the story, by the way?'

'A Colonel Maurice Cartarette found dead with head injuries by a fishing stream. The C.C. down there says they're all tied up with the Royal Visit at Siminster and are understaffed anyway so they've called us in.'

'Who found him?'

'A district nurse. About an hour ago.'

'Fancy,' said Alleyn mildly, and after a pause. 'I wonder just why that old lady has come plunging in after me.'

'I dare say,' Fox said with great simplicity, 'she has a fancy for someone of her own class.'

Alleyn replied absently: 'Do you, now?' And it said something for their friendship that neither of them felt the smallest embarrassment. Alleyn continued to ruminate on the Lacklanders. 'Before the war,' he said, 'the old boy was Chargé d'Affaires at Zlomce. The Special Branch got involved for a time, I remember. There was a very nasty bit of leakage: a decoded message followed by the suicide of the chap concerned. He was said to have been in cahoots with known agents. I was with the Special Branch at that time and had quite a bit to do with it. Perhaps the Dowager wishes to revive old memories or something. Or perhaps she merely runs the village of Swevenings, murdered colonels and all, with the same virtuosity she brought to her husband's public life. Do you know Swevenings, Brer Fox?'

'Can't say I do, sir.'

'I do. Troy did a week's painting there a summer or two ago. It's superficially pretty and fundamentally beautiful,' Alleyn said. 'Quaint as hell but take a walk after dusk and you wouldn't be surprised at anything you met. It's one of the oldest in England. 'Swevenings,' meaning Dreams. There was some near-prehistoric set-to in the valley, I forget what, and another during Bolingbroke's rebellion and yet another in the Civil Wars. This Colonel's blood is not the first soldier's by a long chalk to be spilt at Swevenings.'

'They *will* do it,' Fox said cryptically and with resignation. For a long time they drove on in a silence broken at long intervals by the desultory conversation of old friends.

'We're running into a summer storm,' Alleyn said presently. Giant drops appeared on the windscreen and were followed in seconds by a blinding downpour.

'Nice set-up for fieldwork,' Fox grumbled.

'It may be local. Although . . . no, by gum, we're nearly there. This is Chyning. Chyning; meaning I fancy, a yawn or yawning.'

'Yawns and dreams,' Fox said. 'Funny sort of district! What language would that be, Mr Alleyn?'

'Chaucerian English, only don't depend on me. The whole district is called the Vale of Traunce or brown-study. It all sounds hellishly quaint, but that's how it goes. There's the blue lamp.'

The air smelt fresher when they got out. Rain drummed on roofs and flagstones and cascaded down the sides of houses. Alleyn led the way into a typical county police station and was greeted by a tall sandy-haired sergeant.

'Chief Inspector Alleyn, sir? Sergeant Oliphant. Very glad to see you, sir.'

'Inspector Fox,' Alleyn said, introducing him. There followed a solemn shaking of hands and a lament that has become increasingly common of late years in the police force. 'We're that short of chaps in the country,' Sergeant Oliphant said. 'We don't know which way to turn if anything of this nature crops up. The Chief Constable said to me, 'Can we do it, Oliphant? Suppose we call on Siminster can we do it?' And, look, Mr Alleyn, I had to say no, we can't.'

Fox said: 'T'ch.'

'Well, exactly, Mr Fox,' Oliphant said. 'If you haven't got the chaps it's no good blundering in, is it? I've left my one PC in charge of the body and that reduces my staff to me. Shall we move off, Mr Alleyn? You'll find it wettish.'

Alleyn and Fox accompanied the sergeant in his car while Bailey, Thompson and the Yard driver followed their lead. On the way Sergeant Oliphant gave a businesslike report. Sir George Lacklander had rung up Sir James Punston, the Chief Constable, who in turn had rung Oliphant at about nine o'clock. Oliphant and his constable had then gone to Bottom Meadow and had found Dr Mark Lacklander, Nurse Kettle and the body of Colonel Cartarette. They had taken a brief statement from Nurse Kettle and asked her to remain handy. Dr Lacklander who, in Oliphant's presence, made a very brief examination of the body, had then gone to break the news to the relatives of the deceased, taking Nurse Kettle with him. The sergeant had returned to Chyning and reported to the Chief Constable who decided to call in the Yard. The constable had remained on guard by the body with Colonel Cartarette's spaniel, the latter having strenuously resisted all attempts to remove him.

'Did you form any opinion at all, Oliphant?' Alleyn asked. This is the most tactful remark a CID man can make to a county officer and Oliphant coruscated under its influence.

'Not to say opinion, sir,' he said. 'Not to say that. One thing I did make sure of was not to disturb anything. He's lying on a patch of shingle screened in by a half-circle of willows and cut off on the open side by the stream. He's lying on his right side, kind of curled up as if he'd been bowled over from a kneeling position, like. His hat was over his face. Nurse Kettle moved it when she found him and Dr Lacklander moved it again when he examined the wound which is in the left temple. A dirty great puncture,' the sergeant continued, easing off his official manner a point or two, 'with what the doctor calls extensive fractures all round it. Quite turned my chap's stomach, drunks-in-charge and disorderly behaviour being the full extent of his experience.'

Alleyn and Fox having chuckled in the right place, the sergeant continued: 'No sign of the weapon so far as we could make out, flashing our torches round. I was particular not to go hoofing over the ground.'

'Admirable,' said Alleyn.

'Well,' said Sergeant Oliphant, 'it's what we're told, sir, isn't it?'

'Notice anything at all out of the way?' Alleyn asked. The question was inspired more by kindliness than curiosity and the sergeant's reaction surprised him. Oliphant brought his two freckled hams of hands down on the driving-wheel and made a complicated snorting noise. 'Out of the way!' he shouted. 'Ah, my God, I'll say we did. Out of the way! Tell me, now, sir, are you a fly-fisherman?'

'Only fair to middling to worse. I do when I get the chance. Why?'

'Now listen,' Sergeant Oliphant said, quite abandoning his official position. 'There's a dirty great fish in this Chyne here would turn your guts over for you. Pounds if he's an ounce, he is. Old in cunning, he is; wary and sullen and that lordly in his lurkings and slinkings he'd break your heart. Sometimes he'll rise like a monster,' said Sergeant Oliphant, urging his car up Watt's Hill, 'and snap, he's took it, though that's only three times. Once being the deceased's doing a matter of a fortnight ago, which he left his cast in his jaws he being a mighty fighter. And once the late squire, Sir Harold Lacklander, he lost him through being, as the man himself frankly admitted, overzealous in the playing of him. Now,' the sergeant shouted, 'NOW, for the last and final cast, hooked, played and landed by the poor Colonel, sir, and lying there by his dead body, or I can't tell a five-pound trout from a stickleback. Well, if he had to die, he couldn't have had a more glorious end. The Colonel, I mean, Mr Alleyn, not the Old 'Un,' said Sergeant Oliphant.

They had followed Watt's Lane down into the valley and up the slope through blinding rain to the village. Oliphant pulled up at a spot opposite the Boy and Donkey. A figure in a mackintosh and tweed hat stood in the lighted doorway.

'The Chief Constable, sir,' said Oliphant. 'Sir James Punston. He said he'd drive over and meet you.'

'I'll have a word with him, before we go in. Wait a moment.'

Alleyn crossed the road and introduced himself. The Chief Constable was a weather-beaten tough-looking man who had been a chief commissioner of police in India.

'Thought I'd better come over,' Sir James said, 'and take a look at this show. Damn' bad show it is. Damn' nice fellow, Cartarette. Can't imagine who'd want to set about him, but no doubt you'll be able to tell us. I'll come down with you. Filthy night, isn't it?'

The Yard car had drawn up behind Oliphant's. Bailey, Thompson and the driver got out and unloaded their gear with the economic movements of long usage and a stubborn disregard of the rain. The two parties joined up and led by the Chief Constable climbed a stile and followed a rough path down a drenched hillside. Their torches flashed on rods of rain and dripping furze bushes.

'They call this River Path,' the Chief Constable said. 'It's a right-of-way through the Nunspardon estate and comes out at Bottom Bridge which we have to cross. I hear the Dowager rang you up.'

'She did indeed,' Alleyn said.

'Lucky they decided it was your pigeon, anyway. She'd have raised hell if they hadn't.'

'I don't see where she fits in.'

'She doesn't in any ordinary sense of the phrase. She's merely taken it upon herself ever since she came to Nunspardon to run Chyning and Swevenings. For some reason they seem to like it. Survival of the feudal instinct you might think. It does survive, you know, in isolated pockets. Swevenings is an isolated pocket and Hermione, Lady Lacklander, has got it pretty well where she wants it.' Sir James continued in this local strain as they slid and squelched down the muddy hillside. He gave Alleyn an account of the Cartarette family and their neighbours with a particularly racy profile of Lady Lacklander herself.

'There's the local gossip for you,' he said. 'Everybody knows everybody and has done so for centuries. There have been no stockbroking overflows into Swevenings. The Lacklanders, the Phinns, the Syces and the Cartarettes have lived in their respective houses for a great many generations. They're all on terms of intimacy except that of late years there's been, I fancy, a little coolness between the Lacklanders and old Occy Phinn. And now I come to think of it, I fancy Maurice Cartarette fell out with Phinn over fishing or something. But then old Occy is really a bit mad. Rows with everybody. Cartarette, on the other hand, was a very pleasant nice chap. Oddly formal and devilishly polite, though, especially with people he didn't like or had fallen out with. Not that he was a quarrelsome chap. Far from it. I have heard, by the way,' Sir James gossiped, 'that there's been some sort of coldness between Cartarette and that ass George Lacklander. However! And after all that, here's the bridge.'

As they crossed it they could hear the sound of rain beating on the surface of the stream. On the far side their feet sank into mud. They turned left on the rough path. Alleyn's shoes filled with water and water poured off the brim of his hat.

'Hell of a thing to happen, this bloody rain,' said the Chief Constable. 'Ruin the terrain.'

A wet branch of willow slapped Alleyn's face. On the hill to their right they could see the lighted windows of three houses. As they walked on, however, distant groups of trees intervened and the windows were shut off.

'Can the people up there see into the actual area?' Alleyn asked.

Sergeant Oliphant said: 'No, sir. Their own trees as well as this belt of willows screen it. They can see the stretch on the far side above the bridge, and a wee way below it.'

'That's Mr Danberry-Phinn's preserve, isn't it?' asked the Chief Constable, 'above the bridge?'

'Mr *Danberry*-Phinn?' Alleyn said sharply.

'Mr Octavius Danberry-Phinn to give you the complete works. The 'Danberry' isn't insisted upon. He's the local eccentric I told you about. He lives in the top house up there. We don't have a village idiot in Swevenings; we have a bloody-minded old gentleman. It's more classy,' said Sir James acidly.

'Danberry-Phinn,' Alleyn repeated. 'Isn't there some connection there with the Lacklanders?'

Sir James said shortly: 'Both Swevenings men, of course.' His voice faded uncertainly as he floundered into a patch of reeds. Somewhere close at hand a dog howled dismally and a deep voice apostrophized it. 'Ah, stow it, will you.' A light bobbed up ahead of them.

'Here we are,' Sir James said. 'That you, Gripper?'

'Yes, sir,' said the deep voice. The mackintosh cape of a uniformed constable shone in the torchlight.

'Dog still at it seemingly,' said the sergeant.

'That's right, Mr Oliphant. I've got him tethered here.' A torch flashed on Skip, tied by a handkerchief to a willow branch.

'Hallo, old fellow,' Alleyn said.

They all waited for him to go through the thicket. The constable shoved back a dripping willow branch for him.

'You'll need to stoop a little, sir.'

Alleyn pushed through the thicket. His torchlight darted about in the rain and settled almost at once on a glistening mound.

'We got some groundsheets down and covered him,' the sergeant said. 'When it looked like rain.'

'Good.'

' . . . and we've covered up the area round the corpse as best we could. Bricks and one or two planks from the old boat shed yonder. But I dare say the water's got under just the same.'

Alleyn said: 'Fair enough. We couldn't ask for better. I think before we go any nearer we'll get photographs. Come through, Bailey. Do the best you can. As it stands and then uncovered, with all the detail you can get in case it washes out before morning. By jove, though, I believe it's lifting.'

They all listened. The thicket was loud with the sound of dripping foliage, but the heavy drumming of rain had stopped and by the time Bailey had set up his camera a waxing moon had ridden out over the valley.

When Bailey had taken his last flash-photograph of the area and the covered body, he took away the groundsheet and photographed the body again from many angles, first with the tweed hat over the face and then without it. He put his camera close to Colonel Cartarette's face and it flashed out in the night with raised eyebrows and pursed lips. Only when all this had been done did Alleyn, walking delicately, go closer, stoop over the head and shine his torch full on the wound.

'Sharp instrument?' said Fox.

'Yes,' Alleyn said. 'Yes, a great puncture, certainly. But could a sharp instrument do all that, Brer Fox? No use speculating till we know what it was.' His torchlight moved away from the face and found a silver glint on a patch of grass near Colonel Cartarette's hands and almost on the brink of the stream. 'And this is the Old 'Un?' he murmured.

The Chief Constable and Sergeant Oliphant both broke into excited sounds of confirmation. The light moved to the hands, lying close together. One of them was clenched about a wisp of green.

'Cut grass,' Alleyn said. 'He was going to wrap his trout in it. There's his knife, and there's the creel beside him.'

'What we reckoned, sir,' said the sergeant in agreement.

'Woundy great fish, isn't it?' said the Chief Constable, and there was an involuntary note of envy in his voice.

Alleyn said: 'What was the surface like before it rained?'

'Well, sir,' the sergeant volunteered, 'as you see, it's partly gravel. There was nothing to see in the willows where the ground was dry as a chip. There was what we reckoned were the deceased's foot-prints on the bank where it was soft and where he'd been fishing and one or two on the earthy bits near where he fell, but I couldn't make out anything else and we didn't try for fear of messing up what little there was.'

'Quite right. Will it rain again before morning?'

The three local men moved back into the meadow and looked up at the sky.

'All over, I reckon, sir,' said the sergeant.

'Set fine,' said the deep-voiced constable.

'Clearing,' said Sir James Punston.

'Cover everything up again, Sergeant, and set a watch till morning. Have we any tips of any sort about times? Anybody known to have come this way?'

'Nurse Kettle, sir, who found him. Young Dr Lacklander came back with her to look at him and *he* says he came through the valley and over the bridge earlier in the evening. We haven't spoken to anyone else, sir.'

'How deep,' Alleyn asked, 'is the stream just here?'

'About five foot,' said Sergeant Oliphant.

'Really? And he lies on his right side roughly parallel with the stream and facing it. Not more than two feet from the brink. Head pointing downstream, feet towards the bridge. The fish lies right on the brink by the strand of grass he was cutting to wrap it in. And the wound's in the left temple. I take it he was squatting on his heels within two feet of the brink and just about to bed his catch down in the grass. Now, if, as the heelmarks near his feet seem to indicate, he keeled straight over into the position the body still holds, one or two things must have happened, wouldn't you say, Brer Fox?'

'Either,' Fox said stolidly, 'he was coshed by a left-handed person standing behind him or by a right-handed person standing in front of him and at least three feet away.'

'Which would place the assailant,' said Alleyn, 'about twelve inches out on the surface of the stream. Which is not as absurd as it sounds when you put it that way. All right. Let's move on. What comes next?'

The Chief Constable who had listened to all this in silence now said: 'I gather there's a cry of possible witnesses waiting for you at Hammer. That's Cartarette's house up here on Watt's Hill. If you'll forgive me, Alleyn, I won't go up with you. Serve no useful purpose. If you want me I'm five miles away at Tourets. Anything I can do, delighted, but sure you'd rather be left in peace. I would in my day. By the way, I've told them at the Boy and Donkey that you'll probably want beds for what's left of the night. You'll find a room at the head of the stairs. They'll give you an early breakfast if you leave a note. Goodnight.'

He was gone before Alleyn could thank him.

With the sergeant as guide, Alleyn and Fox prepared to set out for Hammer. Alleyn had succeeded in persuading the spaniel Skip to accept them and after one or two false starts and whimperings, he followed at their heels. They used torches in order to make their way with as little blundering as possible through the grove. Oliphant, who was in the lead, suddenly uttered a violent oath.

'What is it?' Alleyn asked, startled.

'*Gawd!*' Oliphant said. 'I thought someone was looking at me. *Gawd, d'you see that!*'

His wavering torchlight flickered on wet willow leaves. A pair of luminous discs stared out at them from the level of a short man's eyes.

'Touches of surrealism,' Alleyn muttered. 'In Bottom Meadow.' He advanced his own torch and they saw a pair of spectacles caught up in a broken twig.

'We'll pluck this fruit with grateful care,' he said, and gathered the spectacles into his handkerchief.

The moon now shone on Bottom Meadow, turning the bridge and the inky shadow it cast over the broken-down boat shed and punt into a subject for a wood engraving. A group of tall reeds showed up romantically in its light and the Chyne took on an air of enchantment.

They climbed the River Path up Watt's Hill. Skip began to whine and to wag his tail. In a moment the cause of his excitement came into view, a large tabby cat sitting on the path in the bright moonlight washing her whiskers. Skip dropped on his haunches and made a ridiculous sound in his throat. Thomasina Twitchett, for it was she, threw him an inimical glance, rolled on her back at Alleyn's feet and trilled beguilement. Alleyn liked cats. He stooped down and found that she was in the mood to be carried. He picked her up. She kneaded his chest and advanced her nose towards his.

'My good woman,' Alleyn said, 'you've been eating fish.'

Though he was unaware of it at the time, this was an immensely significant discovery.

CHAPTER 5

Hammer Farm

When they approached Hammer Farm Alleyn saw that the three demesnes on Watt's Hill ended in spinneys that separated them from the lower slopes and, as the sergeant had observed, screened them from the reaches of the Chyne below Bottom Bridge. The River Path ran upwards through the trees and was met by three private paths serving the three houses. The sergeant led the way up the first of these. Thomasina Twitchett leapt from Alleyn's embrace and with an ambiguous remark darted into the shadows.

'That'll be one of Mr Phinn's creatures, no doubt,' said Sergeant Oliphant. 'He's crackers on cats, is Mr Phinn.'

'Indeed,' Alleyn said, sniffing at his fingers.

They emerged in full view of Hammer Farm house with its row of french windows lit behind their curtains.

'Not,' said the sergeant, 'that it's been a farm or anything like it, for I don't know how long. The present lady's had it done up considerable.'

Skip gave a short bark and darted ahead. One of the curtains was pulled open and Mark Lacklander came through to the terrace, followed by Rose.

'Skip?' Rose said. 'Skip?'

He whined and flung himself at her. She sank to her knees crying and holding him in her arms. 'Don't, darling,' Mark said; 'don't. He's wet and muddy. Don't.'

Alleyn, Fox and Sergeant Oliphant had halted. Mark and Rose looked across the lawn and saw them standing in the moonlight with their wet clothes shining and their faces shadowed by their hat-brims. For a moment neither group moved or spoke and then Alleyn crossed the lawn and came towards them, bareheaded. Rose stood up. The skirts of her linen housecoat were bedabbled with muddy pawmarks.

'Miss Cartarette?' Alleyn said. 'We are from the CID. My name is Alleyn.'

Rose was a well-mannered girl with more than her share of natural dignity. She shook hands with him and introduced him to Mark. Fox was summoned and Sergeant Oliphant eased up the path in an anonymous manner and waited at the end of the terrace.

'Will you come in?' Rose said, and Mark added:

'My grandmother is here, Mr Alleyn, and my father who informed the local police.'

'And Nurse Kettle, I hope?'

'And Nurse Kettle.'

'Splendid. Shall we go in, Miss Cartarette?'

Alleyn and Fox took off their wet mackintoshes and hats and left them on a garden seat.

Rose led the way through the french window into the drawing-room where Alleyn found an out-of-drawing conversation piece established. Lady Lacklander, a vast black bulk, completely filled an armchair. Alleyn noticed that upon one of her remarkably small feet she wore a buckled velvet shoe and upon the other, a man's bath slipper. Kitty Cartarette was extended on a sofa with one black velvet leg dangling, a cigarette in her holder, a glass in her hand and an ashtray loaded with butts at her elbow. It was obvious that she had wept but repairs had been effected in her make-up, and though her hands were still shaky she was tolerably composed. Between the two oddly assorted women; poised on the hearthrug with a whisky and soda, looking exquisitely uncomfortable and good-looking, was Sir George Lacklander. And at a remove in a small chair perfectly at her ease, sat Nurse Kettle, reclaimed from her isolation in the hall.

'Hallo,' said Lady Lacklander, picking her lorgnette off her bosom and flicking it open. 'Good evening to you. You're Roderick Alleyn, aren't you? We haven't met since you left the Foreign Service and that's not yesterday nor the day before that. How many years is it? And how's your mama?'

'More than I care to remind you of and very well considering,' Alleyn said, taking a hand like a pincushion in his.

'Considering what? Her age? She's five years my junior and there's nothing but fat amiss with me. Kitty, this is Roderick Alleyn: Mrs Cartarette. My son George.'

'Hah-yoo?' George intervened coldly.

' . . . and over there is Miss Kettle, our district nurse. . . . Good evening,' Lady Lacklander continued looking at Fox.

'Good evening, my lady,' said Fox placidly.

'Inspector Fox,' Alleyn said.

'Now; what do you propose to do with us all? Take your time,' she added kindly.

Alleyn thought to himself: 'Not only must I take my time, but I must also take control. This old lady is up to something.'

He turned to Kitty Cartarette. 'I'm sorry,' he said, 'to come so hard on the heels of what must have been an appalling shock. I'm afraid that in these cases, police inquiries are not the easiest ordeals to put up with. If I may, Mrs Cartarette, I'll begin by asking you' – he glanced briefly round the room – 'indeed, all of you, if you've formed any opinion at all about this affair.'

There was a pause. He looked at Kitty Cartarette and then steadily for a moment at Rose who was standing at the far end of the room with Mark.

Kitty said: 'Somehow, I can't sort of get it. It seems so – so *unlikely*.'

'And you, Miss Cartarette?'

'No,' Rose said. 'No. It's unthinkable that anyone who knew him should want to hurt him.'

George Lacklander cleared his throat. Alleyn glanced at him. 'I . . . ah . . .' George said, 'I . . . ah . . . personally believe it must have been some tramp or other. Trespassing or something. There's nobody in the district, I mean. I mean, it's quite incredible.'

'I see,' Alleyn said. 'The next point is: do we know of anybody who was near Colonel Cartarette within, let us say, two hours of the time . . . I believe it was five minutes to nine . . . when you, Miss Kettle, found him?'

'Exactly what,' Lady Lacklander said, 'do you mean by 'near"?'

'Let us say within sight or hearing of him.'

'I was,' said Lady Lacklander. 'I made an appointment with him for eight which he kept twenty minutes early. Our meeting took place on the river bank opposite the willow grove where I understand he was found.'

Fox, unobtrusively stationed by the piano, had begun to take notes. Although her back was turned towards him, Lady Lacklander appeared to sense this activity. She shifted massively in her chair and looked at him without comment.

'Come,' Alleyn said, 'that's a starting point, at least. We'll return to it later if we may. Does anyone know anything about Colonel Cartarette's movements after this meeting which lasted . . . How long do you think, Lady Lacklander?'

'About ten minutes. I remember looking at my watch after Maurice Cartarette left me. He recrossed Bottom Bridge, turned left and disappeared behind the willow grove. It was then nine minutes to eight. I packed up my things and left them to be collected and went home. I'd been sketching.'

'About nine minutes to eight?' Alleyn repeated.

Kitty said: 'I didn't see him, but . . . I must have been somewhere near him, I suppose, when I came back from the golf course. I got home at five past eight, I remember.'

'The golf course?'

'At Nunspardon,' George Lacklander said. 'Mrs Cartarette and I played a round of golf there this evening.'

'Ah, yes. The course is above the stream, isn't it, and on the opposite side of the valley from where we are now?'

'Yes, but the greater part is over the crest of the hill.'

'The second tee,' Mark said, 'overlooks the valley.'

'I see. You came home by the Bottom Bridge, Mrs Cartarette?'

'Yes. The River Path.'

'On the far side wouldn't you overlook the willow grove?'

Kitty pressed the palms of her hands against her head.

'Yes, I suppose you would. I don't think he could have been there. I'm sure I'd have seen him if he had been there. As a matter of fact,' Kitty said, 'I wasn't looking much in that direction. I was looking, actually, at the upper reaches to see . . .' She glanced at George Lacklander. 'Well, to see if I could spot Mr Phinn,' she said.

In the silence that followed, Alleyn was quite certain that the Lacklander wariness had been screwed up to its highest tension. All three had made slight movements that were instantly checked.

'Mr Danberry-Phinn?' Alleyn said. 'And did you see him?'

'Not then. No. He must have either gone home or moved beyond the upper bend.'

'Fishing?'

'Yes.'

'Poaching!' George Lacklander ejaculated. 'Yes, by God, poaching!'

There were subdued ejaculations from Mark and his grandmother.

'Indeed?' Alleyn asked. 'What makes you think so?'

'We saw him. No, Mama, I insist on saying so. We saw him from the second tee. He rents the upper reaches above the bridge from me, by God, and Maurice Cartarette rents – I'm sorry, Kitty – rented the lower. And there – damnedest thing you ever saw – there he was on his own ground on the right bank above the bridge, casting above the bridge and letting the stream carry his cast under the bridge and below it into Cartarette's waters.'

Lady Lacklander gave a short bark of laughter. George cast an incredulous and scandalized glance at her. Mark said, 'Honestly! How he dared!'

'Most blackguardly thing I ever saw,' George continued. 'Deliberate. And the cast, damme, was carried over that hole above the punt where the Old 'Un lurks. I saw it with my own eyes! Didn't I, Kitty? Fellow like that deserves no consideration at all. *None*,' he repeated with a violence that made Alleyn prick up his ears and seemed to rebound (to his embarrassment) upon George himself.

'When did this nefarious bit of trickery occur?' Alleyn asked.

'I don't know when.'

'When did you begin your round?'

'At six-thirty. No!' shouted George in a hurry and turning purple. 'No! Later. About seven.'

'It wouldn't be later than seven-fifteen then, when you reached the second tee?'

'About then, I dare say.'

'Would you say so, Mrs Cartarette?'

Kitty said: 'I should think, about then.'

'Did Mr Phinn see you?'

'Not he. Too damned taken up with his poaching,' said George.

'Why didn't you tackle him?' Lady Lacklander inquired.

'I would have for tuppence, Mama, but Kitty thought better not. We walked away,' George said virtuously, 'in disgust.'

'I saw you walking away,' said Lady Lacklander, 'but from where I was you didn't look particularly disgusted, George.'

Kitty opened her mouth and shut it again and George remained empurpled.

'Of course,' Alleyn said, 'you were sketching, Lady Lacklander, weren't you? Whereabouts?'

'In a hollow about the length of this room below the bridge on the left bank.'

'Near a clump of alders?'

'You're a sharpish observant fellow, it appears. Exactly there. I saw my son and Mrs Cartarette in peeps,' Lady Lacklander said rather grimly, 'through the alders.'

'But you couldn't see Mr Phinn poaching?'

'I couldn't,' Lady Lacklander said, 'but somebody else could and did.'

'Who was that, I wonder?'

'None other,' said Lady Lacklander, 'than poor Maurice Cartarette himself. He saw it and the devil of a row they had over it I may tell you.'

If the Lacklanders had been a different sort of people, Alleyn thought, they would have more clearly betrayed the emotion that he suspected had visited them all. It was, he felt sure, from one or two slight manifestations, one of relief rather than surprise on Mark's part and of both elements on his father's. Rose looked troubled and Kitty merely stared. It was, surprisingly, Nurse Kettle who made the first comment.

'That old fish,' she said. 'Such a lot of fuss!'

Alleyn looked at her and liked what he saw. 'I'll talk to her first,' he thought, 'when I get round to solo interviews.'

He said: 'How do you know, Lady Lacklander, that they had this row?'

'A. because I heard 'em and B. because Maurice came straight to me when they parted company. That's how, my dear man.'

'What happened, exactly?'

'I gathered that Maurice Cartarette came down intending to try the evening rise when I'd done with him. He came out of his own spinney and saw Occy Phinn up to no good down by the bridge. Maurice crept up behind him. He caught Occy redhanded, having just landed the Old 'Un. They didn't see *me*,' Lady Lacklander went on, 'because I was down in my hollow on the other bank. Upon my soul, I doubt if they'd have bridled their tongues if they had. They sounded as if they'd come to blows. I heard them tramping about on the bridge. I was debating whether I should rise up like some rather over-sized deity and settle them when Occy bawled out that Maurice could have his so-and-so fish and Maurice said he wouldn't be seen dead with it.' A look of absolute horror appeared for one second in Lady Lacklander's eyes. It was as if they had all shouted at her: 'But he *was* seen dead with it, you know.' She made a sharp movement with her hands and hurried on. 'There was a thump, as if someone had thrown something wet and heavy on the ground. Maurice said he'd make a county business of it and Occy said if he did he, Occy, would have Maurice's dog empounded for chasing his, Occy's, cats. On that note they parted. Maurice came fuming over the hillock and saw me. Occy, as far as I know, stormed back up the hill to Jacob's Cottage.'

'Had Colonel Cartarette got the fish in his hands, then?'

'Not he. I told you, he refused to touch it. He left it there, on the bridge. I saw it when I went home. For all I know it's still lying there on the bridge.'

'It's lying by Colonel Cartarette,' Alleyn said, 'and the question seems to be, doesn't it, who put it there?'

II

This time the silence was long and completely blank.

'He must have come back and taken it, after all,' Mark said dubiously.

'No,' Rose said strongly. They all turned to her. Rose's face was dimmed with tears and her voice uncertain. Since Alleyn's arrival she had scarcely spoken and he wondered if she was so much shocked that she did not even try to listen to them.

'No?' he said gently.

'He wouldn't have done that,' she said. 'It's not at all the sort of thing he'd do.'

'That's right,' Kitty agreed. 'He wasn't like that.' And she caught her breath in a sob.

'I'm sorry,' Mark said at once. 'Stupid of me. Of course, you're right. The Colonel wasn't like that.'

Rose gave him a look that told Alleyn as much as he wanted to know about their relationship. 'So they're in love,' he thought. 'And unless I'm growing purblind, his father's got more than half an eye on her stepmother. What a very compact little party, to be sure.'

He said to Lady Lacklander: 'Did you stay there long after he left you?'

'No. We talked for about ten minutes and then Maurice recrossed the bridge, as I told you, and disappeared behind the willows on the right bank.'

'Which way did you go home?'

'Up through the Home Spinney to Nunspardon.'

'Could you see into the willow grove at all?'

'Certainly. When I was half-way up I stopped to pant and I looked down and there he was, casting into the willow grove reach.'

'That would be about eight.'

'About eight, yes.'

'I think you said you left your painting gear to be collected, didn't you?'

'I did.'

'Who collected it, please?'

'One of the servants. William, the footman probably.'

'No,' Mark said. 'No, Gar. I did.'

'You?' his grandmother said. 'What were you doing . . .' And stopped short.

Mark said rapidly that after making a professional call in the village he had gone in to play tennis at Hammer and had stayed there until about ten minutes past eight. He had returned home by the River Path and as he approached Bottom Bridge had seen his grandmother's shooting-stick, stool and painting gear in a deserted group on a hillock. He carried them back to Nunspardon and was just in time to prevent the footman from going down to collect them. Alleyn asked him if he had noticed a large trout lying on Bottom Bridge. Mark said that he hadn't done so, but at the same moment his grandmother gave one of her short ejaculations.

'You must have seen it, Mark,' she said. 'Great gaping thing lying there where Octavius Phinn must have chucked it down. On the bridge, my dear boy. You must have practically stepped over it.'

'It wasn't there,' Mark said. 'Sorry, Gar, but it wasn't, when I went home.'

'Mrs Cartarette,' Alleyn said, 'you must have crossed Bottom Bridge a few minutes after Lady Lacklander had gone home, mustn't you?'

'That's right,' Kitty said. 'We saw her going into the Nunspardon Home Spinney as we came over the hill by the second tee.'

'And Sir George, then, in his turn, went home through the Home Spinney and you came down the hill by the River Path?'

'That's right,' she said drearily.

'Did you see the fabulous trout lying on Bottom Bridge?'

'Not a sign of it, I'm afraid.'

'So that between about ten to eight and ten past eight the trout was removed by somebody and subsequently left in the willow grove. Are you all of the opinion that Colonel Cartarette would have been unlikely to change his mind and go back for it?' Alleyn asked.

George looked huffy and said he didn't know he was sure and Lady Lacklander said that judging by what Colonel Cartarette had said to her she was persuaded that wild horses wouldn't have induced him to touch the trout. Alleyn thought to himself: 'If he was disinclined to touch it, still less would he feel like wrapping it up in grass in order to stow it away in his creel which apparently was what he had been doing when he died.'

'I suppose there's no doubt about this fish being the classic Old 'Un?' Alleyn asked.

'None,' Mark said. There's not such another in the Chyne. No question.'

'By the way, did you look down at the willow grove as you climbed up the hill to the Home Spinney?'

'I don't remember doing so. I was hung about with my grand-mother's sketching gear, and I didn't . . . '

It was at this moment that Kitty Cartarette screamed.

She did not scream very loudly; the sound was checked almost as soon as it was born, but she had half-risen from her sofa and was staring at something beyond and behind Alleyn. She had clapped her hands over her mouth. Her eyes were wide open beneath their raised brows. He noticed that they were inclined to be prominent.

They all turned to discover what it was that Kitty stared at but found only an uncovered french window reflecting the lighted room and the ghosts of their own startled faces.

'There's someone out there!' Kitty whispered. 'A man looked in at the window, George!'

'My dear girl,' Lady Lacklander said, 'you saw George's reflection. There's nobody there.'

'There is.'

'It's probably Sergeant Oliphant,' Alleyn said. 'We left him outside. Fox?'

Fox was already on his way, but before he reached the french window the figure of a man appeared beyond its reflected images. The figure moved uncertainly, coming in from the side and halting when it was some way from the glass. Kitty made a slight retching sound. Fox's hand was on the knob of the french window when beyond it the beam of Sergeant Oliphant's torchlight shot across the dark and the man's face was illuminated. It was crowned by a tasselled smoking-cap and was deadly pale.

Fox opened the french window.

'Pray forgive an unwarrantable intrusion,' said Mr Danberry-Phinn. 'I am in quest of a fish.'

III

Mr Phinn's behaviour was singular. The light from the room seemed to dazzle him. He screwed up his eyes and nose and this gave him a supercilious look greatly at variance with his extreme pallor and unsteady hands. He squinted at Fox and then beyond him at the company in the drawing-room.

'I fear I have called at an inconvenient moment,' he said. 'I had no idea . . . I had hoped to see . . . ' His Adam's apple bobbed furiously. '. . . to see,' he repeated, 'in point of fact, Colonel Cartarette.' He disclosed his teeth, clamped together in the oddest kind of smile.

Kitty made an indeterminate sound and Lady Lacklander began: 'My dear Octavius . . . ' But before either of them could get any further, Alleyn moved in front of Mr Phinn.

'Did you say, sir,' Alleyn asked, 'that you are looking for a fish?'

Mr Phinn said: 'Forgive me, I don't *think* I have the pleasure . . .' and peered up into Alleyn's face. '*Have* I the pleasure?' he asked. He blinked away from Alleyn towards Fox. Fox was one of those, nowadays rather rare, detectives who look very much like their job. He was a large, grizzled man with extremely bright eyes.

'And in this case,' Mr Phinn continued with a breathless little laugh, 'I indubitably have *not* the pleasure.'

'We are police officers,' Alleyn said. 'Colonel Cartarette has been murdered, Mr Phinn. You are Mr Octavius Danberry-Phinn, I think, aren't you?'

'But how perfectly terrible!' said Mr Phinn. 'My dear Mrs Cartarette! My dear Miss Rose! I am appalled. APPALLED!' Mr Phinn repeated opening his eyes as wide as they could go.

'You'd better come in, Occy,' Lady Lacklander said. 'They'll want to talk to you.'

'To *me*!' he ejaculated. He came in and Fox shut the french window behind him.

Alleyn said: 'I shall want to have a word with you, sir. In fact, I think it is time that we saw some of you individually rather than together, but before we do that, I should like Mr Phinn to tell us about the fish he is looking for.' He raised his hand. If any of his audience had felt like interjecting they now thought better of the impulse. 'If you please, Mr Phinn?' Alleyn said.

'I'm so confused, indeed so horrified at what you have told me . . .'

'Dreadful,' Alleyn said, 'isn't it? About the fish?'

'The fish? The fish, my dear sir, is or was a magnificent trout. The fish is a fish of great fame. It is the trout to end all trout. A piscine emperor. And I, let me tell you, I caught him.'

'Where?' Lady Lacklander demanded.

Mr Phinn blinked twice. 'Above Bottom Bridge, my dear Lady L.,' he said. 'Above Bottom Bridge.'

'You *are* an old humbug, Occy,' she said.

George suddenly roared out: 'That's a bloody lie, Octavius. You poached him. You were fishing under the bridge. We saw you from the second tee.'

'Dear me, George,' said Mr Phinn, going white to the lips. 'What a noise you do make to be sure.'

Fox had stepped unobtrusively aside and was busy with his notebook.

'To talk like that!' Mr Phinn continued with two half-bows in the direction of Kitty and Rose, 'in a house of mourning! Really, George, I must say!'

'By God – !' George began, but Alleyn intervened.

'What,' he asked Mr Phinn, 'happened to your catch?'

Mr Phinn sucked in a deep breath and began to speak very quickly indeed. 'Flushed,' he said in a voice that was not quite steady, 'with triumph, I resolved to try the upper reaches of the Chyne. I therefore laid my captive to rest on the very field of his defeat, *id est* the upper, repeat upper, approach to Bottom Bridge. When I returned, much later, I cannot tell you *how* much later for I did not carry a watch, but much, *much* later, I went to the exact spot where my Prince of Piscines should have rested and . . . ' He made a wide gesture during the execution of which it was apparent that his hands were tremulous. ' . . . Gone! Vanished! Not a sign! Lost!' he said.

'Now, look here, Occy . . .' Lady Lacklander in her turn began and in her turn was checked by Alleyn.

'Please, Lady Lacklander,' Alleyn interjected. She glared at him. 'Do you mind?' he said.

She clasped her plump hands together and rested the entire system of her chins upon them. 'Well,' she said, 'I called you in, after all. Go on.'

'What did you do,' Alleyn asked Mr Phinn, 'when you discovered your loss?'

Mr Phinn looked very fixedly at him. 'Do?' he repeated. 'What should I do? It was growing dark. I looked about in the precincts of the bridge but to no avail. The trout was gone. I returned home, a bitterly chagrined man.'

'And there you remained, it seems, for about four hours. It's now five minutes past one in the morning. Why, at such an hour, are you paying this visit, Mr Phinn?'

Looking at Mr Phinn, Alleyn thought: 'He was ready for that one.'

'Why?' Mr Phinn exclaimed, spreading his unsteady hands. 'My dear sir, I will tell you why. Rendered almost suicidal by the loss of this homeric catch I was unable to contemplate my couch with any prospect of repose. Misery and frustration would have been my bed-fellows I assure you had I sought it. I attempted to read, to commune with the persons of my house (I refer to my cats, sir), to listen to an indescribably tedious piece of buffoonery upon the wireless. All, I regret to say, was of no avail: my mind was wholly occupied by The Great Fish. Some three-quarters of an hour or so ago, I sought the relief of fresh air and took a turn down the River Path. On emerging from the ruffian Syce's spinney I observed lights behind these windows. I heard voices. Knowing,' he said with a singular gulp, 'knowing that poor Cartarette's interest as a fellow angler would be aroused I . . . My dear Lady L., why *are* you looking at me in this most disconcerting fashion?'

'Occy!' Lady Lacklander said. 'Yard or no Yard, I can't contain my information for another second. I was within a stone's throw of you when you had your row with Maurice Cartarette. What's more, a few minutes earlier his wife and George both saw you poaching under the bridge. I heard you or Maurice throw down the trout on the bridge and I heard you part company in a high rage. What's more Maurice came hotfoot to where I was painting and I had the whole story all over again from him. Now, my dear Roderick Alleyn, you may be as cross with me as you please, but I really could not allow this nonsensical tarradiddle to meander on for another second.'

Mr Phinn blinked and peered and fumbled with his lips. 'It used to be quite a little joke between my dear wife and me,' he said at last, 'that one must never contradict a Lacklander.'

Only Alleyn and Fox looked at him.

'Mr Phinn,' Alleyn said, 'you normally wear spectacles, I think, don't you?'

Mr Phinn made a strange little gesture with his thumb and forefinger as if he actually adjusted his glasses. Thus, momentarily, he hid the red groove across the top of his nose and the flush that had begun to spread across his face. 'Not all the time,' he said. 'Only for reading.'

Lady Lacklander suddenly clapped the palms of her hands down on the arms of her chair. 'So there we are,' she said. 'And having said my say, George, I should like you, if you please, to take me home.'

She put out her right arm and as George was a little slow in coming, Alleyn took her hand, braced himself and hauled.

'Up she rises,' Lady Lacklander quoted self-derisively and up she rose. She stared for a moment at Mr Phinn, who gaped back at her and mouthed something indistinguishable. She looked straight into Alleyn's eyes 'Do you, after all,' she said, 'propose to let me go home?'

Alleyn raised an eyebrow. 'I shall feel a good deal safer,' he said, 'with you there than here, Lady Lacklander.'

'Take me to my car. I have to shuffle a bit because of my damn' toe. It's no better, Kettle. George, you may join me in five minutes. I want to have a word with Roderick Alleyn.'

She said goodbye to Rose, holding her for a moment in her arms. Rose clung to her and gave a shuddering sob. Lady Lacklander said: 'My poor child, my poor little Rose; you must come to us as soon as possible. Get Mark to give you something to make you sleep.'

Kitty had risen. 'It was awfully kind of you to come,' she said, and held out her hand. Lady Lacklander took it and after a scarcely perceptible pause let it be known that Kitty was expected to kiss her. This Kitty did with caution.

'Come and see me tomorrow, Kettle,' said Lady Lacklander, 'unless they lock you up.'

'Let 'em try,' said Nurse Kettle, who had been entirely silent ever since Mr Phinn's arrival. Lady Lacklander gave a short laugh. She paid no attention to Mr Phinn but nodded to Alleyn. He hastened to open the door and followed her through a large and charmingly shaped hall to the main entrance. Outside this a vast elderly car waited.

'I'll sit in the back,' she said. 'George will drive. I find him an irritating companion in time of trouble.'

Alleyn opened the door and switched on a light in the car.

'Now, tell me,' she said, after she had heaved herself in, 'tell me, not as a policeman to an octogenarian dowager but as a man of discretion to one of your mother's oldest friends, what did you think of Occy Phinn's behaviour just now?'

Alleyn said: 'Octogenarian dowagers even if they are my mother's oldest friend shouldn't lure me out of doors at night and make improper suggestions.'

'Ah,' she said, 'so you're not going to respond.'

'Tell me, did Mr Phinn have a son called Ludovic? Ludovic Danberry-Phinn?'

In the not very bright light he watched her face harden as if, behind its mask of fat, she had set her jaw. 'Yes,' she said. 'Why?'

'It could hardly not be, could it, with those names?'

'I wouldn't mention the boy if I were you. He was in the Foreign Service and blotted his copybook as I dare say you know. It was quite a tragedy. It's never mentioned.'

'Is it not? What sort of a man was Colonel Cartarette?'

'Pig-headed, quixotic fellow. Obstinate as a mule. One of those pathetically conscientious people who aim so high they get a permanent crick in their conscience.'

'Are you thinking of any particular incident?'

'No,' Lady Lacklander said firmly, 'I am not.'

'Do you mind telling me what you and Colonel Cartarette talked about?'

'We talked,' Lady Lacklander said coolly, 'about Occy poaching and about a domestic matter that is for the moment private and can have no bearing whatever on Maurice's death. Goodnight to you, Roderick. I suppose I call you Roderick, don't I?'

'When we're alone together.'

'Impudent fellow!' she said, and aimed a sort of dab at him. 'Go back and bully those poor things in there. And tell George to hurry.'

'Can you remember exactly what Mr Phinn and Colonel Cartarette said to each other when they had their row?'

She looked hard at him, folded her jewelled hands together, and said: 'Not word for word. They had a row over the fish. Occy rows with everybody.'

'Did they talk about anything else?'

Lady Lacklander continued to look at him, and said: 'No,' very coolly indeed.

Alleyn made her a little bow. 'Goodnight,' he said. 'If you remember specifically anything that they said to each other, would you be terribly kind and write it down?'

'Roderick,' Lady Lacklander said, 'Occy Phinn is no murderer.'

'Is he not?' Alleyn said. 'Well, that's something to know, isn't it? Goodnight.'

He shut the door. The light in the car went out.

IV

As he turned back to the house Alleyn met George Lacklander. It struck him that George was remarkably ill at ease in his company and would greatly have preferred to deal exclusively with Fox.

'Oh . . . ah, hallo,' George said. 'I . . . ah . . . I wonder may I have a word with you? I don't suppose you remember, by the way, but we have met a thousand years ago, ha, ha, when I think you were one of my father's bright young men, weren't you?'

Alleyn's twenty-five-year-old recollection of George rested solely on the late Sir Harold Lacklander's scorching comments on his son's limitations. 'No damn' use expecting anything of George,' Sir Harold had once confided. 'Let him strike attitudes at Nunspardon and in the ripeness of time become a J.P. That is George's form.' It occurred to Alleyn that this prophecy had probably been fulfilled.

He answered George's opening question and blandly disregarded its sequel. 'Please do,' he said.

'Fact is,' George said, 'I'm wondering just what the drill is. I am, by the way and not that it makes any real difference, a Beak. So I suppose I may be said to fill my humble pigeonhole in the maintenance of the Queen's peace, what?'

'And why not?' Alleyn infuriatingly replied.

'Yes,' George continued, goggling at him in the dark. 'Yes. Well, now, I wanted to ask you what exactly will be the drill about poor Maurice Cartarette's – ah – about the – ah – the body. I mean, one is concerned for Kitty's sake. For their sake, I mean. His wife and daughter. One can perhaps help with the arrangements for the funeral and all that. What?'

'Yes, of course,' Alleyn agreed. 'Colonel Cartarette's body will remain where it is under guard until tomorrow morning. It will then be taken to the nearest mortuary and a police surgeon will make an examination and possibly an extensive autopsy. We will, of course, let Mrs Cartarette know as soon as possible when the funeral may be held. I think we shall probably be ready to hand over in three days, but it doesn't do to be positive about these things.'

'Oh, quite!' George said. 'Quite. Quite. Quite.'

Alleyn said: 'Simply for the record: I shall have to put this sort of question to everybody who was in Colonel Cartarette's landscape last evening – you and Mrs Cartarette began your round of golf, I think you said, at seven?'

'I didn't notice the exact time,' George said in a hurry.

'Perhaps Mrs Cartarette will remember. Did she meet you on the course?'

'Ah – no. No, I – ah – I called for her in the car. On my way back from Chyning.'

'But you didn't drive her back?'

'No. Shorter to walk, we thought. From where we were.'

'Yes, I see. . . . And Mrs Cartarette says she arrived here at about five past eight. Perhaps you played golf, roughly for an hour. How many holes?'

'We didn't go round the course. Mrs Cartarette is learning. It was her first – ah – attempt. She asked me to give her a little coaching. We – ah – we only played a couple of holes. We spent the rest of the time practising some of her shots,' George said haughtily.

'Ah, yes. And you parted company at about ten to eight. Where?'

'At the top of the River Path,' he said, and added: 'As far as I remember.'

'From there would you see Lady Lacklander coming up towards you? She began her ascent at ten to eight.'

'I didn't look down. I didn't notice.'

'Then you won't have noticed Colonel Cartarette either. Lady Lacklander says he was fishing in the willow grove at the time and that the willow grove is visible from the River Path.'

'I didn't look down. I – ah – I merely saw Mrs Cartarette to the River Path and went on through the Home Spinney to Nunspardon. My mother arrived a few minutes later. And now,' George said, 'if you'll excuse me, I really must drive my mama home. By the way, I do hope you'll make use of us. I mean you may need a headquarters and so on. Anything one can do.'

'How very kind,' Alleyn rejoined. 'Yes, I think we may let you go now. Afraid I shall have to ask you to stay in Swevenings for the time being.' He saw George's jaw drop.

'Of course,' he added, 'if you have important business elsewhere it will be quite in order to come and tell me about it, and we'll see what can be done. I shall be at the Boy and Donkey.'

'Good God, my dear Alleyn'

'Damn' nuisance I know,' Alleyn said; 'but there you are. If they *will* turn on homicide in your bottom meadow. Goodnight to you.'

He circumnavigated George and returned to the drawing-room where he found Rose, Mark and Kitty uneasily silent, Mr Phinn biting his fingers and Inspector Fox in brisk conversation with Nurse Kettle on the subject of learning French conversation by means of gramophone records. 'I don't,' Mr Fox was saying, 'make the headway I'd like to.'

'I picked up more on a cycling tour in Brittany when I *had* to than I ever got out of *my* records.'

'That's what they all tell me, but in our line what chance do you get?'

'You must get a holiday some time, for heaven's sake.'

True,' Fox said, sighing. 'That's a fact. You do. But somehow I've never got round to spending it anywhere but Birchington. Excuse me, Miss Kettle, here's the Chief.'

Alleyn gave Fox a look that both of them understood very well and the latter rose blandly to his feet. Alleyn addressed himself to Kitty Cartarette.

'If I may,' he said, 'I should like to have a very short talk with Miss Kettle. Is there perhaps another room we may use? I saw one, I think, as I came across the hall. A study perhaps.'

He had a feeling that Mrs Cartarette was not overanxious for him to use the study. She hesitated but Rose said: 'Yes, of course. I'll show you.'

Fox had gone to the french window and had made a majestical signal to the sergeant who now came into the drawing-room.

'You all know Sergeant Oliphant, of course,' Alleyn said. 'He will be in charge of the local arrangements, Mrs Cartarette, and I thought perhaps you would like to have a word with him. I would be grateful if you would give him the names of your husband's solicitor and bank, and also of any relations who should be informed. Mr Phinn, I will ask you to repeat the substance of your account to Sergeant Oliphant who will take it down and get you to sign it if it is correct.'

Mr Phinn blinked at him. 'I cannot,' he said, with a show of spirit, 'of course be compelled.'

'Of course not. But I'm afraid we shall have to trouble all of you to give us signed statements, if you are willing to do so – if you do yours first it will leave you free to go home. I hope,' Alleyn concluded, 'that you will not find it too difficult without your glasses. And now, Miss Cartarette, may we indeed use the study?'

Rose led the way across the hall into the room where eight hours ago she had talked to her father about her love for Mark. Alleyn and Fox followed her. She waited for a moment and stared, as it seemed to Alleyn, with a kind of wonder at the familiar chairs and desk. Perhaps she saw a look of compassion in his face. She said: 'He seems to be here, you know. The room can't go on without him, one would think. This was his place more than anywhere else.' She faltered for a moment, and then said: 'Mr Alleyn, he was such a darling, my father. He was as much like my child as my father, he depended on me so completely. I don't know why I'm saying this to you.'

'It's sometimes a good idea to say things like that to strangers. They make uncomplicated confidants.'

'Yes,' she said and her voice was surprised, 'that's quite true. I'm glad I told you.'

Alleyn saw that she suffered from the kind of nervous ricochet that often follows a severe shock. Under its impetus the guard that people normally set over their lightest remarks is lowered and they speak spontaneously of the most surprising matters: as now when Rose suddenly added: 'Mark says he couldn't have felt anything. I'm sure he's not just saying that to comfort me because being a doctor he wouldn't. So I suppose in a way it's what people call a release. From everything.'

Alleyn asked quietly: 'Was he worried about anything in particular?'

'Yes,' Rose said sombrely, 'he was indeed. But I can't tell you about that. It's private; and even if it wasn't it couldn't possibly be of any use.'

'You never know,' he said lightly.

'You do in this case.'

'When did you see him last?'

'This evening. I mean last evening, don't I? He went out soon after seven. I think it was about ten past seven.'

'Where did he go?'

She hesitated, and then said: 'I believe to call on Mr Phinn. He took his rod and told me he would go on down to the Chyne for the evening rise. He said he wouldn't come in for dinner and I asked for something to be left out for him.'

'Do you know why he called on Mr Phinn?'

Rose waited for a long time and then said: 'I think it had something to do with – with the publishing business.'

'The *publishing* business?'

She pushed a strand of hair back and pressed the heels of her hands against her eyes. '*I* don't know who could do such a thing to him,' she said. Her voice was drained of all its colour. 'She's exhausted,' Alleyn thought and against his inclination, decided to keep her a little longer.

'Can you tell me, very briefly, what sort of pattern his life has taken over the last twenty years?'

Rose sat on the arm of her father's chair. Her right arm was hooked over its back and she smoothed and resmoothed the place where his bald head had rested. She was quite calm and told Alleyn in a flat voice of the Colonel's appointments as military attaché at various embassies, of his job at Whitehall during the war, of his appointment as military secretary to a post-war commission that had been set up in Hong Kong and finally, after his second marriage, of his retirement and absorption in a history he had planned to write of his own regiment. He was a great reader it seemed, particularly of the Elizabethan dramatists, an interest that his daughter had ardently shared. His only recreation apart from his books had been fishing. Rose's eyes, fatigued by tears, looked for a moment at a table against the wall where a tray of threads, scraps of feathers and a number of casts was set out.

'I always tied the flies. We made up a fly he nearly always fished with. I tied one this afternoon.'

Her voice trembled and trailed away and she yawned suddenly like a child.

The door opened and Mark Lacklander came in looking angry.

'Ah, there you are!' he said. He walked straight over to her and put his fingers on her wrist. 'You're going to bed at once,' he said. 'I've asked Nurse Kettle to make a hot drink for you. She's waiting for you now. I'll come and see you later and give you a nembutal. I'll have to run into Chyning for it. You don't want me again, I imagine?' he said to Alleyn.

'I do for a few minutes, I'm afraid.'

'Oh!' Mark said, and after a pause. 'Well, yes, of course, I suppose you do. Stupid of me.'

'I don't want any dope, Mark, honestly,' Rose said.

'We'll see about that when you're tucked up. Go to bed now.' He glared at Alleyn. 'Miss Cartarette is my patient,' he said, 'and those are my instructions.'

'They sound altogether admirable,' Alleyn rejoined.

'Goodnight, Miss Cartarette. We'll try to worry you as little as possible.'

'You don't worry me at all,' Rose said politely, and gave him her hand.

'I wonder,' Alleyn said to Mark, 'if we may see Nurse Kettle as soon as she is free. And you, a little later if you please, Doctor Lacklander.'

'Certainly, sir,' Mark said stiffly, and taking Rose's arm led her out of the room.

'And I also wonder, Brer Fox,' Alleyn said, 'apart from bloody murder, what it is that's biting all these people.'

'I've got a funny sort of notion,' Fox said, 'and mind, it's only a notion so far, that the whole thing will turn out to hang on that fish.'

'And I've got a funny sort of notion you're right.'

CHAPTER 6

The Willow Grove

Nurse Kettle sat tidily on an armless chair with her feet crossed at the ankles and her hands at the wrists. Her apron was turned up in the regulation manner under her uniform coat and her regulation hat was on her head. She had just given Alleyn a neat account of her finding of Colonel Cartarette's body and Fox, who had taken the notes, was gazing at her with an expression of the liveliest approval.

'That's all, really,' she said, 'except that I had a jolly strong feeling I was being watched. There now!'

Her statement hitherto had been so positively one of fact that they both stared at her in surprise. 'And now,' she said, 'you'll think I'm a silly hysterical female because although I thought once that I heard a twig snap and fancied that when a bird flew out of the thicket it was not me who'd disturbed it, I didn't *see* anything at all. Not a thing. And yet I thought I was watched. You get it on night duty in a ward. A patient lying awake and staring at you. You always know before you look. Now laugh that away if you like.'

'Who's laughing?' Alleyn rejoined. 'We're not, are we, Fox?'

'On no account,' Fox said. 'I've had the same sensation many a time on night beat in the old days and it always turned out there was a party in a dark doorway having a look at you.'

'Well, fancy!' said the gratified Nurse Kettle.

'I suppose,' Alleyn said, 'you know all these people pretty well, don't you, Miss Kettle? I always think in country districts the Queen's Nurses are rather like liaison officers.'

Nurse Kettle looked pleased. 'Well, now,' she said, 'we do get to know people. Of course our duties take us mostly to the ordinary folk although with the present shortage we find ourselves doing quite a lot for the other sort. They pay the full fee and that helps the Association, so, as long as it's not depriving the ones who can't afford it, we take the odd upper-class case. Like me and Lady Lacklander's toe, for instance.'

'Ah, yes,' Alleyn said, 'there's the toe.' He observed with surprise the expression of enraptured interest in his colleague's elderly face.

'Septic,' Nurse Kettle said cosily.

''T, 't, 't,' said Fox.

'And then again, for example,' Nurse Kettle went on, 'I night-nursed the old gentleman. With him when he died actually. Well, so was the family. And the Colonel, too, as it happens.'

'Colonel Cartarette?' Alleyn asked without laying much stress on it.

'That's right. Or wait a moment. I'm telling stories. The Colonel didn't come back into the room. He stayed on the landing with the papers.'

'The papers?'

'The old gentleman's memoirs they were. The Colonel was to see about publishing them, I fancy, but I don't really know. The old gentleman was very troubled about them. He couldn't be content to say good-bye and give up until he'd seen the Colonel. Mind you, Sir Harold was a great man in his day and his memoirs'll be very impor-tant affairs, no doubt.'

'No doubt. He was a distinguished ambassador.'

'That's right. Not many of that sort left I always say. Everything kept up. Quite feudal.'

'Well,' Alleyn said, 'there aren't many families left who can afford to be feudal. Don't they call them the Lucky Lacklanders?'

'That's right. Mind, there are some who think the old gentleman overdid it.'

'Indeed?' Alleyn said, keeping his mental fingers crossed. 'How?'

'Well, not leaving the grandson anything. Because of him taking up medicine instead of going into the army. Of course, it'll all come to him in the end, but in the meantime, he has to make do with what he earns, though of course – but listen to me gossiping. Where was I now. Oh, the old gentleman and the memoirs. Well, no sooner had he handed them over than he took much worse and the Colonel gave the alarm. We all went in. I gave brandy. Dr Mark gave an injection but it was all over in a minute. '"Vic,"' he said, '"Vic, Vic,"' and that was all.' Alleyn repeated '"Vic?"' and then was silent for so long that Nurse Kettle had begun to say: 'Well, if that's all I can do . . . ' when he interrupted her.

'I was going to ask you,' he said, 'who lives in the house between this one and Mr Phinn's?'

Nurse Kettle smiled all over her good-humoured face. 'At Uplands?' she said. 'Commander Syce, to be sure. He's another of my victims,' she added, and unaccountably turned rather pink. 'Down with a bad go of 'bago, poor chap.'

'Out of the picture, then, from our point of view?'

'Yes, if you're looking for . . . oh, my gracious,' Nurse Kettle suddenly ejaculated, 'here we are at goodness knows what hour of the morning talking away as pleasant as you please and all the time you're wondering where you're going to find a murderer. Isn't that frightful!'

'Don't let it worry you,' Fox begged her.

Alleyn stared at him.

'Well, of course I'm worried. Even suppose it turns out to have been a tramp. Tramps are people just like other people,' Nurse Kettle said vigorously.

'Is Mr Phinn one of your patients?' Alleyn asked.

'Not to say patient. I nursed a carbuncle for him years ago. I wouldn't go getting ideas about him if I were you.'

'In our job,' Alleyn rejoined, 'we have to get ideas about everybody.'

'Not about *me*, I hope and trust.'

Fox made a complicated soothing and scandalized noise in his throat.

Alleyn said: 'Miss Kettle, you liked Colonel Cartarette, didn't you? It was clear from your manner, I thought, that you liked him very much indeed.'

'Well, I did,' she said emphatically. 'He was one of the nicest and gentlest souls: a gentle man if ever I saw one. Devoted father. Never said an unkind word about anybody.'

'Not even about Mr Phinn?'

'Now *look* here,' she began, then caught herself up. 'Listen,' she said; 'Mr Phinn's eccentric. No use my pretending otherwise for you've seen him for yourselves and you'll hear what others say about him. But there's no malice. No, perhaps I wouldn't say there's no *malice* exactly, but there's no real harm in him. Not a scrap. He's had this tragedy in his life, poor man, and in my opinion he's never been the same since it happened. Before the war, it was. His only son did away with himself. Shocking thing.'

'Wasn't the son in the Foreign Service?'

'That's right. Ludovic was his name, poor chap. Ludovic! I ask you! Nice boy and very clever. He was in some foreign place when it happened. Broke his mother's heart they always say, but she was a cardiac anyway, poor thing. Mr Phinn never really got over it. You never know, do you?'

'Never. I remember hearing about it,' Alleyn said vaguely. 'Wasn't he one of Sir Harold Lacklander's young men?'

'That's right. The old gentleman was a real squire. You know: the old Swevenings families and all that. I think he asked for young Phinn to be sent out to him, and I know he was very cut up when it happened. I dare say he felt responsible.'

'You never know,' Alleyn repeated. 'So the Swevenings families,' he added, 'tend to gravitate towards foreign parts?'

Nurse Kettle said that they certainly seemed to do so. Apart from young Viccy Danberry-Phinn getting a job in Sir Harold's embassy there was Commander Syce whose ship had been based on Singapore and the Colonel himself who had been attached to a number of missions in the Far East, including one at Singapore. Nurse Kettle added, after a pause, that she believed he had met his second wife there.

'Really?' Alleyn said, with no display of interest. 'At the time when Syce was out there, do you mean?' It was the merest shot in the dark, but it found its mark. Nurse Kettle became pink in the face and said with excessive brightness that she believed that 'the Commander and the second Mrs C.' had known each other out in the East. She added, with an air of cramming herself over some emotional hurdle, that she had seen a very pretty drawing that the Commander had made of Mrs Cartarette. 'You'd pick it out for her at once,' she said. 'Speaking likeness, really, with tropical flowers behind and all.'

'Did you know the first Mrs Cartarette?'

'Well, not to say *know*. They were only married eighteen months when she died giving birth to Miss Rose. She was an heiress, you know. The whole fortune goes to Miss Rose. It's well known. The Colonel was quite hard up but he's never touched a penny of his first wife's money. It's well known,' Nurse Kettle repeated, 'so I'm not talking gossip.'

Alleyn skated dexterously on towards Mark Lacklander and it was obvious that Nurse Kettle was delighted to sing Mark's praises. Fox respectfully staring at her, said there was a bit of romance going on there, seemingly, and she at once replied that *that* was as plain as the noses on all their faces and a splendid thing, too. A real Swevenings romance, she added.

Alleyn said: 'You *do* like to keep yourselves to yourselves in this district, don't you?'

'Well,' Nurse Kettle chuckled, 'I dare say we do. As I was saying to a gentleman patient of mine, we're rather like one of those picture-maps. Little world of our own if you know what I mean. I was suggesting . . . ' Nurse Kettle turned bright pink and primmed up her lips. 'Personally,' she added rather obscurely, 'I'm all for the old families and the old ways of looking at things.'

'Now, it strikes me,' Fox said, raising his brows in bland surprise, 'and mind, I may be wrong: very likely I am: but it strikes *me* that the present Mrs Cartarette belongs to quite a different world. Much more *mondaine* if you'll overlook the faulty accent, Miss Kettle.'

Miss Kettle muttered something that sounded like 'demi-mondaine,' and hurried on. 'Well, I dare say we're a bit stodgy in our ways in the Vale,' she said, 'and she's been used to lots of gaiety and there you are.' She stood up. 'If there's nothing more,' she said, 'I'll just have a word with the Doctor and see if there's anything I can do for Miss Rose or her stepmother before they settle down.'

'There's nothing more here. We'll ask you to sign a statement about finding the body and of course you'll be called at the inquest.'

'I suppose so.' She got up and the two men also rose. Alleyn opened the door. She looked from one to the other.

'It won't be a Vale man,' she said. 'We're not a murderous lot in the Vale. You may depend upon it.'

II

Alleyn and Fox contemplated each other with the absentminded habit of long association.

'Before we see Doctor Lacklander,' Alleyn said, 'let's take stock, Brer Fox. What are you thinking about?' he added.

'I was thinking,' Fox said with his customary simplicity, 'about Miss Kettle. A very nice woman.'

Alleyn stared at him. 'You are not by any chance transfixed by Dan Cupid's dart?'

'Ah,' Fox said complacently, 'that would be the day, wouldn't it, Mr Alleyn? I like a nice compact woman,' he added.

'Drag your fancy away from thoughts of Nurse Kettle's contours, compact or centrifugal, and consider. Colonel Cartarette left this house about ten past seven to call on Octavius Danberry-Phinn. Presumably there was no one at home because the next we hear of him he's having a violent row with Phinn down by the Bottom Bridge. That's at about seven-thirty. At twenty to eight he and Phinn part company. The Colonel crosses the bridge and at twenty minutes to eight is having an interview with Lady Lacklander who is sketching in a hollow on the left bank almost opposite the willow grove on the right bank. Apparently this *al fresco* meeting was by arrangement. It lasted about ten minutes. At ten to eight Cartarette left Lady Lacklander, recrossed the bridge, turned left and evidently went straight into the willow grove because she saw him there as she herself panted up the hill to Nunspardon. Soon after eight Mrs Cartarette said goodbye to that prize ass George Lacklander and came down the hill. At about a quarter past seven she and he had seen old Phinn poaching and as she tripped down the path she looked along his fishing to see if she could spot him anywhere. She must have just missed Lady Lacklander who, one supposes, had by that time plunged into this Nunspardon Home Spinney they talk so much about. Kitty . . . '

Fox said: 'Who?'

'Her name's Kitty, Kitty Cartarette. She came hipping and thighing down the hill with her eyes on the upper reaches of the Chyne where she expected to see Mr Phinn. She didn't notice her husband in the willow grove, but that tells us nothing until we get a look at the landscape, and, anyway, her attention, she says, was elsewhere. She continued across the bridge and so home. She saw nothing unusual on the bridge. Now Lady Lacklander saw a woundy great trout lying on the bridge where, according to Lady L., Mr Phinn had furiously chucked it when he had his row, thirty-five minutes earlier, with Colonel Cartarette. The next thing that happens is that Mark Lacklander (who had been engaged in tennis and one supposes, rather solemn dalliance with that charming girl Rose Cartarette) leaves this house round about the time Mrs Cartarette returns to it and goes down to the Bottom Bridge where he does *not* find a woundy great trout and is certain that there was no trout to find. He does, however, find his grandmother's sketching gear on the left bank of the Chyne and like a kind young bloke carries it back to Nunspardon, thus saving the footman a trip. He disappears into the spinney and as far as we know this darkling valley is left to itself until a quarter to nine when Nurse Kettle, who has been slapping Commander Syce's lumbago next door, descends into Bottom Meadow, turns off to the right, hears the dog howling and discovers the body. Those are the facts, if they are facts, arising out of information received up to date. What emerges?'

Fox dragged his palm across his jaw. 'For a secluded district,' he said, 'there seems to have been quite a bit of traffic in the valley of the Chyne.'

'Doesn't there? Down this hill. Over the bridge. Up the other hill and t'other way round. None of them meeting except the murdered man and old Phinn at half past seven and the murdered man and Lady Lacklander ten minutes later. Otherwise, it seems to have been a series of near misses on all hands. I can't remember the layout of the valley with any accuracy but it appears that from the houses on this side only the upper reaches of the Chyne and a few yards below the bridge on the right bank are visible. We'll have to do an elaborate check as soon as it's light, which is hellish soon, by the way. Unless we find signs of angry locals hiding in the underbrush or of mysterious coloured gentlemen from the East lurking in the village, it's going to look a bit like a small field of suspects.'

'Meaning this lot,' Fox said, with a wag of his head in the direction of the drawing-room.

'There's not a damn' one among them except the Nurse who isn't holding something back; I'll swear there isn't. Let's have a word with young Lacklander, shall we? Fetch him in, Foxkin, and while you're there see how Mr Phinn's getting on with his statement to the sergeant. I wanted an ear left in that room, the sergeant's was the only one available and the statement seemed the best excuse for planting him there. We'll have to go for dabs on those spectacles we picked up and I swear they'll be Mr Phinn's. If he's got off his chest as much as he's decided to tell us, let him go home. Ask him to remain on tap, though, until further notice. Away you go.'

While Fox was away Alleyn looked more closely at Colonel Cartarette's study. He thought he found in it a number of interesting divergences from the accepted convention. True there were leather saddle-back chairs, a pipe-rack and a regimental photograph, but instead of sporting prints the Colonel had chosen half a dozen Chinese drawings and the books that lined two of his walls, although they included army lists and military biographies, were for the greater part well-worn copies of Elizabethan and Jacobean dramatists and poets with one or two very rare items on angling. With these Alleyn was interested to find a sizeable book with the title *The Scaly Breed* by Maurice Cartarette. It was a work on the habits and characteristics of freshwater trout. On his desk was a photograph of Rose, looking shy and misty, and one of Kitty looking like an imitation of something it would be difficult to define.

Alleyn's gaze travelled over the surface of the desk and down the front. He tried the drawers. The top pair were unlocked and contained only writing-paper and envelopes and a few notes written in a distinguished hand, evidently by the Colonel himself. The centre pairs on each side were locked. The bottom left-hand drawer pulled out. It was empty. His attention sharpened. He had stooped down to look more closely at it when he heard Fox's voice in the hall. He pushed the drawer to and stood away from the desk.

Mark Lacklander came in with Fox.

Alleyn said: 'I shan't keep you long: indeed, I have only asked you to come in to clear up one small point and to help us with another: not so small. The first question is this: When you went home at a quarter past eight last evening, did you hear a dog howling in Bottom Meadow?'

'No,' Mark said. 'No, I'm sure I didn't.'

'Did Skip really stick close to the Colonel?'

'Not when he was fishing,' Mark said at once. 'The Colonel had trained him to keep a respectful distance away.'

'But you didn't see Skip?'

'I didn't see or hear a dog, but I remember meeting a tabby cat. One of Occy Phinn's menagerie, I imagine, on an evening stroll.'

'Where was she?'

'This side of the bridge,' said Mark, looking bored.

'Right. Now, you'd been playing tennis here, hadn't you, with Miss Cartarette and you returned to Nunspardon by the Bottom Bridge and River Path. You collected your grandmother's sketching gear on the way, didn't you?'

'I did.'

'Were you carrying anything else?'

'Only my tennis things. Why?'

'I'm only trying to get a picture. Collecting these things must have taken a few moments. Did you hear or see anything at all out of the ordinary?'

'Nothing. I don't think I looked across the river at all.'

'Right. And now will you tell us, as a medical man, what you make of the injuries to the head?'

Mark said very readily: 'Yes, of course, for what my opinion's worth on a superficial examination.'

'I gather,' Alleyn said, 'that you went down with Miss Kettle after she gave the alarm and that with exemplary economy you lifted up the tweed hat, looked at the injury, satisfied yourself that he was dead, replaced the hat and waited for the arrival of the police. That it?'

'Yes. I had a torch and I made as fair an examination as I could without touching him. As a matter of fact, I was able to look pretty closely at the injuries.'

'Injuries,' Alleyn repeated, stressing the plural. 'Then you would agree that he was hit more than once?'

'I'd like to look again before giving an opinion. It seemed to me he had been hit on the temple with one instrument before he was stabbed through it with another. Although – I don't know – a sharp object striking the temple could of itself produce very complex results. It's useless to speculate. Your man will no doubt make a complete examination and what he finds may explain the appearances that to me are rather puzzling.'

'But on what you saw your first reaction was to wonder if he'd been stunned before he was stabbed? Is that right?'

'Yes,' Mark said readily. 'That's right.'

'As I saw it,' Alleyn said; 'there seemed to be an irregular bruised area roughly about three by two inches and inside that a circular welt that might have been made by a very big hammer with a concave striking surface if such a thing exists. And inside that again is the actual puncture, a hole that, it seemed to me, must have been made by a sharply pointed instrument.'

'Yes,' Mark said, 'that's an accurate description of the superficial appearance. But, of course, the queerest appearances can follow cranial injuries.'

'The autopsy may clear up the ambiguities,' Alleyn said. He glanced at Mark's intelligent and strikingly handsome face. He decided to take a risk.

'Look here,' he said, 'it's no good us trying to look as if we're uninterested in Mr Danberry-Phinn. He and Colonel Cartarette had a flaming row less than an hour, probably, before Cartarette was murdered. What do you feel about that? I don't have to tell you this is entirely off the record. What sort of a chap *is* Mr Phinn? You must know him pretty well.'

Mark thrust his hands into his pockets and scowled at the floor. 'I don't know him as well as all that,' he said. 'I mean I've known him all my life, of course, but he's old enough to be my father and not likely to be much interested in a medical student or a young practitioner.'

'Your father would know him better, I suppose.'

'As a Swevenings man and my father's elder contemporary, yes, but they haven't much in common.'

'You knew his son, Ludovic, of course?'

'Oh, yes,' Mark said composedly. 'Not well,' he added. 'He was at Eton and I'm a Wykehamist. He trained for the Diplomatic and I left Oxford for the outer darkness of the dissecting rooms at Thomas's. Completely *déclassé*. I dare say,' Mark added, with a grin, 'that my grandfather thought much the same about you, sir. Didn't you desert him and the Diplomatic for Lord Trenchard and the lonely beat?'

'If you like to put it that way, which is a good deal more flattering to me than it is to either of my great white chiefs. Young Phinn, by the way, was at your grandfather's Embassy in Zlomce, wasn't he?'

'He was,' Mark said, and as if he realized that his reply sounded uncomfortably short, he added: 'My grandfather was a terrific "Vale Man" as we say in these parts. He liked to go all feudal and surround himself with local people. When Viccy Phinn went into the Service I fancy grandfather asked if he could have him with the idea of making one corner of a Zlomce field for ever Swevenings. My God,' Mark added, 'I didn't mean to put it like that. I mean . . . '

'You've remembered, perhaps, that young Phinn blew out his brains in one corner of a Zlomce field.'

'You knew about that?'

'It must have been a great shock to your grandfather.'

Mark compressed his lips and turned away. 'Naturally,' he said. He pulled out a case and still with his back to Alleyn, lit himself a cigarette. The match scraped and Fox cleared his throat.

'I believe,' Alleyn said, 'that Sir Harold's autobiography is to be published.'

Mark said: 'Did Phinn tell you that?'

'Now, why in the wide world,' Alleyn asked, 'should Mr Octavius Phinn tell me?'

There was a long silence broken by Mark.

'I'm sorry, sir,' Mark said. 'I must decline absolutely to answer any more questions.'

'You are perfectly within your rights. It's not so certain that you are wise to do so.'

'After all,' Mark said, 'I must judge of that for myself. Is there any objection now to my driving to the dispensary?'

Alleyn hesitated for the fraction of a second. 'No objection in the world,' he said. 'Good morning to you, Dr Lacklander.'

Mark repeated: 'I'm sorry.' And with a troubled look at both of them went out of the room.

'Brer Fox,' Alleyn said, 'we shall snatch a couple of hours' sleep at the Boy and Donkey, but before we do so will you drag your fancy away from thoughts of District Nurses and bend it upon the bottom drawer on the left-hand side of Colonel Cartarette's desk?'

Fox raised his eyebrows, stationed himself before the desk, bent his knees, placed his spectacles across his nose and did as he was bidden.

'Forced,' he said. 'Recent. Chipped.'

'Quite so. The chip's on the floor. The paper knife on the desk is also chipped and the missing bit is in the otherwise empty drawer. The job's been done unhandly by an amateur in a hurry. We'll seal this room and tomorrow we'll put in the camera and dabs boys. Miss Kettle's, Mr Phinn's and Dr Lacklander's prints'll be on their statements. Lacklander's and Mrs Cartarette's grog glasses had better be rescued and locked up in here. If we want dabs from the others we'll pick them up in the morning.' He took a folded handkerchief from his pocket, put it on the desk and opened it up. A pair of cheap spectacles was revealed. 'And before we go to bed,' he said, 'we'll discover if Mr Danberry-Phinn has left his dabs on his reach-me-down specs. And in the morning, Foxkin, if you are a good boy, you shall be told the sad and cautionary story of Master Ludovic Phinn.'

III

Kitty Cartarette lay in a great Jacobean bed. She had asked, when she was first married, to have it done over in quilted and buttoned peach velvet, but had seen at once that this would be considered an error in taste. Anxious at that time to establish her position, she had given up this idea but the dressing-table and chairs and lamp had all been her own choice. She stared miserably at them now and a fanciful observer might have found something valedictory in her glance. By shifting across the bed, she was able to see herself in her long glass. The pink silk sheet billowed up round her puffed and tear-stained face. 'I do look a sight,' she muttered. She may have then remembered that she lay in her husband's place and if a coldness came over her at this recollection, nobody in Swevenings would have suggested that it was because she had ever really loved him. Lady Lacklander had remarked, indeed, that Kitty was one of those rare women who seem to get through life without forming a deep attachment to anybody, and Lady Lacklander would have found it difficult to say why Kitty had been weeping. It would not have occurred to her to suppose that Kitty was lonelier than she had ever been before, but merely that she suffered from shock, which of course was true.

There was a tap on the door and this startled Kitty. Maurice, with his queer old-fashioned delicacy, had always tapped.

'Hallo?' she said.

The door opened and Rose came in. In her muslin dressing-gown and with her hair drawn into a plait she looked like a schoolgirl. Her eyelids, like Kitty's, were swollen and pink, but even this disfigurement, Kitty noticed with vague resentment, didn't altogether blot out Rose's charm. Kitty supposed she ought to have done a bit more about Rose. 'But I can't think of everything,' she told herself distractedly.

Rose said: 'Kitty, I hope you don't mind my coming in. I couldn't get to sleep and I came out and saw the light under your door. Mark's fetching me some sleeping things from Chyning and I wondered if you'd like one.'

'I've got some things of my own, thanks all the same. Has everybody gone?'

'Lady Lacklander and George have and, I think, Occy Phinn. Would you like Mark to look in?'

'What for?'

'You might find him sort of helpful,' Rose said in a shaky voice. 'I do.'

'I dare say,' Kitty rejoined dryly. She saw Rose blush faintly. 'It was nice of you to think of it, but I'm all right. What about the police? Are they still making themselves at home in your father's study?' Kitty asked.

'I think they must have gone. They're behaving awfully well, really, Kitty. I mean it *is* a help, Mr Alleyn being a gent.'

'I dare say,' Kitty said again. 'OK, Rose,' she added. 'Don't worry. I know.'

Her manner was good-naturedly dismissive, but Rose still hesitated. After a pause she said: 'Kitty, while I've been waiting – for Mark to come back, you know – I've been thinking. About the future.'

'The *future*?' Kitty repeated and stared at her. 'I should have thought the present was enough!'

'I can't think about that,' Rose said quickly. 'Not yet. Not about Daddy. But it came into my mind that it was going to be hard for you. Perhaps you don't realize – I don't know if he told you but – well –'

'Oh, yes,' Kitty said wearily, 'I know. He did tell me. He was awfully scrupulous about anything to do with money, wasn't he?' She looked up at Rose. 'OK, Rose,' she said. 'Not to fuss. I'll make out; I wasn't expecting anything. My sort,' she added obscurely, 'don't.'

'But I wanted to tell you: you needn't worry. Not from any financial point of view. I mean – it's hard to say and perhaps I should wait till we're more used to what's happened but I *want* to help,' Rose stammered. She began to speak rapidly. It was almost as if she had reached that point of emotional exhaustion that is akin to drunkenness. Her native restraint seemed to have forsaken her and to have been replaced by an urge to pour out some kind of sentiment upon somebody. She appeared scarcely to notice her stepmother as an individual. 'You see,' she was saying, weaving her fingers together, 'I might as well tell you. I shan't need Hammer for very long. Mark and I are going to be engaged.'

Kitty looked up at her, hesitated, and then said: 'Well, that's fine, isn't it? I do hope you'll be awfully happy. Of course, I'm not exactly surprised.'

'No,' Rose agreed. 'I expect we've been terribly transparent,' Her voice trembled and her eyes filled with reiterant tears. 'Daddy knew,' she said.

'Yes,' Kitty agreed, with a half-smile. 'I told him.'

'*You* did?'

It was as if Rose was for the first time positively aware of her stepmother.

'You needn't mind,' Kitty said. 'It was natural enough. I couldn't help noticing.'

'We told him ourselves,' Rose muttered.

'Was he pleased? Look, Rose,' Kitty said, still in that half-exhausted, half-good-natured manner, 'don't let's bother to hedge. I know about the business over old man Lacklander's memoirs.'

Rose made a slight distasteful movement. 'I hadn't thought of it,' she said. 'It doesn't make any difference.'

'No,' Kitty agreed, 'in a way, I suppose it doesn't – now. What's the matter?'

Rose's chin had gone up. 'I think I hear Mark,' she said.

She went to the door.

'Rose,' Kitty said strongly, and Rose stopped short. 'I know it's none of my business but – you're all over the place now. We all are. I wouldn't rush anything! "Don't rush your fences," that's what your father would have said, isn't it?'

Rose looked at Kitty with an air of dawning astonishment. 'I don't know what you mean,' she said. 'What fences?'

She had opened the door. A well-kept hand came round it and closed over hers.

'Hallo?' Mark's voice said. 'May I come in?'

Rose looked at Kitty, who again hesitated. 'Why, yes,' she said. 'Of course. Come in, Mark.'

He was really a *very* handsome young man: tall, dark and with enough emphasis in his mouth and jaw to give him the masterful air that is supposed to be so irresistible to women. He stood looking down at Kitty with Rose's hand drawn through his arm. They made what used to be known as a striking couple.

'I heard your voices,' he said, 'and thought I'd look in. Is there anything I can do at all? I've brought some things for Rose to help her get to sleep; if you'd like to take one it might be quite an idea.'

'I'll see,' she said. 'I've got something actually somewhere.'

'Shall we leave one in case?' Mark suggested. He shook a couple of capsules from a packet on to her bedside table and fetched a glass of water. 'One is enough,' he said.

He was standing above Kitty and between her and Rose, who had not moved from the door at the far end of the room. Kitty looked up into his face and said loudly: 'You were the first there, weren't you?'

Mark made a slight admonitory gesture and turned towards Rose. 'Not actually the first,' he said quietly. 'Miss Kettle – '

'Oh, old Kettle,' Kitty said irritably, dismissing her. 'What I want to know – after all, I am his wife – what *happened*?'

'Rose,' Mark said. 'You run along to bed.'

'No, Mark, darling,' Rose said, turning deadly white. 'I want to know, too. Please. It's worse not to.'

'Yes, much worse,' Kitty agreed. 'Always.'

Mark waited for an appreciable time and then said quickly: 'Well, first of all – there's no disfigurement to his face.'

Kitty made a sharp grimace and Rose put her hands to her eyes.

' – and I don't think he felt anything at all,' Mark said. He lifted a finger. 'All right. It was a blow. Here. On the temple.'

'That?' Rose said. 'Just that?'

'It's a very vulnerable part, darling.'

'Then – might it be some sort of accident?'

'Well – no, I'm afraid not.'

'Oh, Mark, why not?'

'It's out of the question, Rose, darling.'

'But why?'

'The nature of the injuries.'

'More than one?' she said. He went quickly to her and took her hands in his.

'Well – yes.'

'But you said –' Rose began.

'You see, there are several injuries all in that one small area. It wouldn't do any good if I let you think they might have been caused accidentally because the – the pathologist will certainly find that they were not.'

Kitty, unnoticed, said: 'I see.' And added abruptly: 'I'm sorry, but I don't think I can take any more tonight. D'you mind?'

Mark looked at her with sharpened interest. 'You should try to settle down.' He lifted her wrist professionally.

'No, no,' she said, and drew it away. 'That's unnecessary, thanks all the same. But I do think Rose ought to go to bed before she drops in her tracks.'

'I quite agree,' Mark said again, rather coldly, and opened the door. Rose said: 'Yes, I'm going. I hope you do manage to sleep, Kitty.' And went out. Mark followed her to her own door.

'Mark, darling, goodnight,' Rose said. She freed herself gently.

'Tomorrow,' he said, 'I'm going to carry you off to Nunspardon.'

'Oh,' she said, 'no – I don't think we can quite do that, do you? Why Nunspardon?'

'Because I want to look after you and because, making all due allowances, I don't think your stepmother's particularly sympathetic or congenial company for you,' Mark Lacklander said, frowning.

'It's all right,' Rose said. 'It doesn't matter. I've learned not to notice.'

IV

Fox was duly acquainted with the story of Ludovic Phinn over a breakfast of ham and eggs in the parlour of the Boy and Donkey shortly after dawn. Bailey and Thompson, who had also spent the tag-end of the night at the pub, were already afoot in Bottom Meadow with the tools of their trade, and the Home Office pathologist was expected from London. The day promised to be fine and warm.

'I know about young Phinn,' Alleyn said, 'because his debacle occurred when I was doing a spell in the Special Branch in 1937. At that time the late Sir Harold Lacklander was our Ambassador at Zlomce and Master Danberry-Phinn was his personal secretary. It was known that the German Government was embarked on a leisurely and elaborate party with the local government over railway concessions. We picked up information to the effect that the German boys were prepared to sign an important and, to us, disastrous undertaking in the fairly distant future. Lacklander was instructed to throw a spanner in the works. He was empowered to offer the Zlomce boys certain delectable concessions and it was fully expected that they would play. The Germans, however, learnt of his little plot and immediately pressed on their own negotiations to a successful and greatly accelerated conclusion. Our government wanted to know why. Lacklander realized that there had been a leakage of information and, since there was nobody else in a position to let the leakage occur, he tackled young Phinn who at once broke down and admitted that it was his doing. It seems that he had not been able to assimilate his Zlomce oats too well. It's an old and regrettable story. He arrived with his alma mater's milk wet on his lips, full of sophisticated backchat and unsophisticated thinking. He made some very dubious Zlomce chums, among whom was a young gent whom we afterwards found to be a German agent of a particularly persuasive sort. He was said to have fastened on young Phinn who became completely sold on the Nazi formula and agreed to act for the Germans. As usual, our sources of information were in themselves dubious: Phinn was judged on results and undoubtedly he behaved like a traitor. On the night after a crucial cable had come through for his chief, he went off to the gypsies or somewhere with his Nazi friend. The decoding of the cable had been entrusted to him. It developed that he presented his Zlomce chums with the whole story. It was said afterwards that he'd taken bribes. Lacklander gave him bottled hell and he went away and blew his brains out. We were told that he'd had a kind of hero-fixation on Lacklander, and we always thought it odd that he should have behaved as he did. But he was, I believe, a brilliant but unbalanced boy, an only child whose father, the Octavius we saw last night, expected him to retrieve the fortunes of their old and rather reduced family. His mother died a few months afterwards, I believe.'

'Sad,' said Mr Fox.

'It was indeed.'

'Would you say, Mr Alleyn, now, that this Mr Phinn senior, was slightly round the bend?'

'Dotty?'

'Well . . . Eccentric.'

'His behaviour in the watches of last night was certainly oddish. He was a frightened man, Fox, if ever I saw one. What do you think?'

'The *opportunity* was there,' Fox said, going straight to the first principle of police investigation.

'It was. And, by the way, Bailey's done his dab-drill. The spectacles *are* Mr Danberry-Phinn's.'

'There now!' Fox ejaculated with the utmost satisfaction.

'It's not conclusive, you know. He might have lost them down there earlier in the day. He'd still be very chary of owning to them.'

'Well . . . ' Fox said sceptically.

'I quite agree. I've got my own idea about when and how they got there which is this.'

He propounded his idea. Fox listened with raised brows. 'And as for opportunity, Fox,' Alleyn went on, 'as far as we've got, it was also there for his wife, all three Lacklanders and, for a matter of that, Nurse Kettle herself.'

Fox opened his mouth, caught a derisive glint in his senior's eye and shut it again.

'Of course,' Alleyn said, 'we can't exclude the tramps or even the dark-skinned stranger from the Far East. But there's one item that emerged last night which I don't think we can afford to disregard, Fox. It seems that Colonel Cartarette was entrusted by Sir Harold Lacklander, then on his death-bed, with the Lacklander memoirs. He was to supervise their publication.'

'Well, now,' Fox began, 'I can't say . . . '

'This item may be of no significance whatever,' Alleyn rejoined. 'On the other hand, isn't it just possible that it may be a link between the Lacklanders on the one hand and Mr Octavius Phinn on the other, that link being provided by Colonel Cartarette with the memoirs in his hands.'

'I take it,' Fox said in his deliberate way, 'that you're wondering if there's a full account of young Phinn's offence in the memoirs and if his father's got to know of it, and made up his mind to stop publication.'

'It sounds hellish thin when you put it like that, doesn't it? Where does such a theory land us? Cartarette goes down the hill at twenty-past seven, sees Phinn poaching, and, overheard by Lady Lacklander, has a flaming row with him. They part company. Cartarette moves on to talk to Lady Lacklander, stays with her for ten minutes and then goes to the willow grove to fish. Lady L. returns home and Phinn comes back and murders Cartarette because Cartarette is going to publish old Lacklander's memoirs to the discredit of young Phinn's name. But Lady L. doesn't say a word about this to me. She doesn't say she heard them quarrel *about the memoirs* although, if they did there's no reason that I can see why she shouldn't. She merely says they had a row about poaching and that Cartarette talked about this to her. She adds that he and she also discussed a private and domestic business which had nothing to do with Cartarette's death. This, of course, is as it may be. Could the private and domestic business by any chance be anything to do with the publication of the memoirs? If so, why should she refuse to discuss it with me?'

'Have we any reason to think it might be about these memoirs, though?'

'No. I'm doing what I always say you shouldn't do: I'm speculating. But it was clear, wasn't it, that young Lacklander didn't like the memoirs being mentioned. He shut up like a trap over them. They crop up, Brer Fox. They occur. They link the Cartarettes with the Lacklanders and they may well link Mr Phinn with both. They provide, so far, the only connecting theme in this group of apparently very conventional people.'

'I wouldn't call her ladyship conventional,' Fox observed.

'She's unconventional along orthodox lines, believe me. There's a car pulling up. It'll be Dr Curtis. Let's return to the Bottom Field and to the question of opportunity and evidence.'

But before he led the way out he stood rubbing his nose and staring at his colleague.

'Don't forget,' he said, 'that old Lacklander died with what sounds like an uneasy conscience and the word "Vic" on his lips.'

'Ah. Vic.'

'Yes. And Mark Lacklander referred to young Phinn as Viccy! Makes you fink, don't it? Come on.'

V

By midsummer morning light, Colonel Cartarette looked incongruous in the willow grove. His coverings had been taken away and there, close to the river's brink he was; curled up, empty of thought and motion, wearing the badge of violence upon his temple . . . a much photographed corpse. Bailey and Thompson had repeated the work of the previous night but without, Alleyn thought, a great deal of success. Water had flooded under duck boards, seeped up through earthy places and washed over gravel. In spite of the groundsheet it had soaked into Colonel Cartarette's Harris tweeds and had collected in a pool in the palm of his right hand.

Dr Curtis completed a superficial examination and stood up.

'That's all I want here, Alleyn,' he said. 'I've given Oliphant the contents of the pockets. A bundle of keys, tobacco, pipe, lighter. Fly case. Handkerchief. Pocket-book with a few notes and a photograph of his daughter. That's all. As for general appearances; rigor is well established and is, I think, about to go off. I understand you've found out that he was alive up to eight-fifteen and that he was found dead at nine. I won't get any closer in time than that.'

'The injuries?'

'I'd say tentatively, two weapons or possibly one weapon used in two ways. There's a clean puncture with deep penetration, there's circular indentation with the puncture as its centre and there's been a heavy blow over the same area that has apparently caused extensive fracturing and a lot of extravasation. It might have been made by one of those stone-breaker's hammers or even by a flat oval-shaped stone itself. I think it was the first injury he got. It would almost certainly have knocked him right out. Might have killed him; in any case, it would have left him wide open to the second attack.'

Alleyn had moved round the body to the edge of the stream.

'And no prints?' he said, looking at Bailey.

'There's prints from the people that found him,' Bailey said, 'clear enough. Man and woman. Overlapping and straightforward . . . walk towards, squat down, stand, walk away. And there's his own heel marks, Mr Alleyn, as you noticed last night. Half-filled with surface drainage they were then, but you can see how he was, clear enough.'

'Yes,' Alleyn said. 'Squatting on a bit of soft ground. Facing the stream. He'd cut several handfuls of grass with his knife and was about to wrap up that trout. There's the knife, there's the grass in his hands and there's the trout! A whopper if ever there was one. Sergeant Oliphant says the Colonel himself hooked and lost him some days ago.'

He stooped and slipped an exploratory finger into the trout's maw. 'Ah, yes,' he said, 'it's still there. We'd better have a look at it.'

His long fingers were busy for a minute. Presently they emerged from the jaws of the Old 'Un with a broken cast. 'That's not a standard commercial fly,' he said. 'It's a beautiful home-made one. Scraps of red feather and gold cloth bound with bronze hair, and I think I've seen its mates in the Colonel's study. Rose Cartarette tied the flies for her father and I fancy this is the one he lost when he hooked the Old 'Un on the afternoon before Sir Harold Lacklander's death.'

Alleyn looked at the Colonel's broken head and blankly acquiescent face. 'But you didn't hook him this time,' he said, 'and why in the world should you shout, at half-past seven, that you wouldn't be seen dead with him, and be found dead with him at nine?'

He turned towards the stream. The willow grove sheltered a sort of miniature harbour with its curved bank going sheer down to the depth of about five feet at the top end of the little bay and running out in a stony shelf at the lower end. The stream poured into this bay with a swirling movement, turning back upon its course.

Alleyn pointed to the margin of the lower bank of the bay. It carried an indented scar running horizontally below the lip.

'Look here, Fox,' Alleyn said, 'and here, above it.' He nodded at a group of tall daisies, strung along the edge of the bank upstream from where the Colonel lay and perhaps a yard from his feet. They were in flower. Alleyn pointed to three leggy stems, taller than their fellows, from which the blooms had been cut away.

'You can move him,' he said. 'But don't tramp over the ground more than you can help. We *may* want another peer at it. And, by the way, Fox, have you noticed that inside the willow grove, near the point of entry, there's a flattened patch of grass and several broken and bent twigs. Remember that Nurse Kettle thought she was observed. Go ahead, Oliphant.'

Sergeant Oliphant and PC Gripper came forward with a stretcher. They put it down some distance from the body which they now raised. As they did so a daisy-head, crumpled and sodden, dropped from the coat.

'Pick it up, tenderly,' Alleyn said as he did so, 'and treat it with care. We must find the other two if we can. This murderer said it with flowers.' He put it away in his case. Oliphant and Gripper laid the body on the stretcher and waited.

Alleyn found a second daisy on the bank below the point where Colonel Cartarette's head had lain. 'The third,' he said, 'may have gone downstream, but we'll see.'

He now looked at Colonel Cartarette's rod, squatting beside it where it rested on the bank, its point overhanging the stream.

Alleyn lifted the cast, letting it dangle from his long fingers. 'The fellow of the one that the Old 'Un broke for him,' he said.

He looked more closely at the cast and sniffed at it.

'He hooked a fish yesterday,' he said, 'there's a flake of flesh on the barb. Where, then, is this trout he caught? Too small? Did he chuck it back? Or what? Damn this ruined ground.' He separated the cast from the line and put it away in his case. He sniffed into the dead curved hands. 'Yes,' he said, 'he's handled a fish. We'll go over the hands, fingernails, and clothes for any more traces. Keep that tuft of grass that's in his hand. Where's the rest of it?'

He turned back to the riverbank and gathered up every blade of grass that was scattered where the Colonel had cut it. He examined the Colonel's pocket-knife and found that, in addition to having traces of grass, it smelt of fish. Then he very cautiously lifted the Old 'Un and examined the patch of stones where the great fish had lain all night.

'Traces there, all right,' he said. 'Are they all off this one fish, however? Look, there's a sharp flinty bit of stone with a flap of fish skin on it. Now let's see.'

He turned the great trout over and searched its clamminess for a sign of a missing piece of skin and could find none. 'This looks more like business,' he muttered, and took out his pocket lens. His subordinates coughed and shifted their feet. Fox watched him with calm approval.

'Well,' Alleyn said at last, 'we'll have to get an expert's opinion and it may be crucial. But it's pretty clear that he made a catch of his own, that it lay on this patch, that a bit of its skin was torn off on this stone, that the fish itself was subsequently removed and the Old 'Un put in its place. It doesn't look as if it was chucked back in the stream, does it? In that case, he would have taken it off his hook and thrown it back at once. He wouldn't have laid it down on the bank. And why was a flap of its skin scraped off on the stone? And why was the Old 'Un laid over the trace of the other fish? And by whom? And when?'

Fox said: 'As for when: before the rain at all events. The ground shows that.'

'That doesn't help since he was killed before the rain and found before the rain. But consider, Brer Fox, he was killed with a tuft of cut grass in his hand. Isn't it at least possible that he was cutting his grass to wrap up his own catch? He had refused to touch the Old 'Un and had left it lying on the bridge. The people who knew him best all agree he'd stick to his word. All right. Somebody kills him. Is it that 'somebody" who takes the Colonel's fish and replaces it with the Old 'Un?'

'You'd think so, Mr Alleyn, wouldn't you?'

'And why did he do it?'

'Gawd knows!' said Oliphant in disgust. Sergeants Bailey and Thompson and PC Gripper made sympathetic noises. Dr Curtis, squatting by the stretcher, grinned to himself.

'What was the actual position of the killer at the time of the blow or blows?' Alleyn continued. 'As I read it, and you'll correct me here, Curtis, Colonel Cartarette was squatting on his heels facing the stream with the cut grass in his hands. The heel marks and subsequent position suggest that when he was struck on the left temple he keeled over, away from the blow, and fell in the position in which Nurse Kettle found him. Now, he was either belted from behind by a left-hander or rammed by a sort of crouching charge from his left side or struck from the front by a swinging right-handed swipe. . . . Yes, Oliphant?'

Sergeant Oliphant said: 'Well, pardon me, sir, I was only going to remark would it be, for example, something like the sort of blow a quarryman gives a wedge that is sticking out from a rock-face at the level of his knee?'

'Ah!' said PC Gripper appreciatively. 'Or an underhand serve, like tennis.'

'That kind of thing,' Alleyn said, exchanging a look with Fox. 'Now there wasn't enough room between the Colonel and the brink for such a blow to be delivered: which is why I suggested his assailant would have had to be three feet out on the surface of the stream. Now, take a look upstream towards the bridge, Brer Fox. Go roundabout, because we'll still keep the immediate vicinity unmucked up, and then come out here.'

Fox joined Alleyn on the lower bank of the little bay at the point where it jutted farthest out into the stream. They looked up the Chyne past the willow grove, which hid the near end of the bridge, to the far end which was just visible about forty feet away with the old punt moored in the hole beneath it.

Alleyn said: 'Charming, isn't it? Like a lead pencil vignette in a Victorian album. I wonder if Lady Lacklander ever sketches from this point. Have you read *The Rape of Lucrece*, Brer Fox?'

'I can't say I have unless it's on the police list which it sounds as if it might be. Or would it be Shakespeare?'

'The latter. There's a bit about the eccentricities of river currents. The poem really refers to the Avon and Clopton Bridge, but it might have been written about the Chyne at this very point. Something about the stream that, coming through an arch, "yet in the eddy boundeth in his pride back to the strait that forced him on." Look at that twig sailing towards us now. It's got into just such a current, do you see, and instead of passing down the main stream is coming into this bay. Here it comes. Round it swirls in the eddy and back it goes towards the bridge. It's a strong and quite considerable sort of counter-current. Stay where you are, Fox, for a moment, will you? Get down on your sinful old hunkers and bow your head over an imaginary fish. Imitate the action of the angler. Don't look up and don't move till I tell you.'

'Ah, what's all this, I do wonder,' Mr Fox speculated, and squatted calmly at the water's edge with his great hands between his feet.

Alleyn skirted round the crucial area and disappeared into the willow grove.

'What's he up to?' Curtis asked of no one in particular and added a rude professional joke about Mr Fox's posture. Sergeant Oliphant and PC Gripper exchanged scandalized glances. Bailey and Thompson grinned. They all heard Alleyn walk briskly across Bottom Bridge though only Fox, who faithfully kept his gaze on the ground, was in a position to see him. The others waited, expecting him for some reason of his own to appear on the opposite bank.

It was quite a shock to Dr Curtis, Bailey, Thompson, Oliphant and Gripper when round the upstream point of the willow grove bay the old punt came sliding with Alleyn standing in it, a wilted daisy-head in his hand.

The punt was carried transversely by the current away from the far bank and across the main stream into the little willow-grove harbour. It glided silently to rest, its square prow fitting neatly into the scar Alleyn had pointed out in the downstream bank. At the same time its bottom grated on the gravel spit and it became motionless.

'I suppose,' Alleyn said, 'you heard that, didn't you?'

Fox looked up.

'I heard it,' he said. 'But I saw and heard nothing until then.'

'Cartarette must have heard it too,' Alleyn said. 'Which accounts, I fancy, for the daisies. Brer Fox; do we think we know whodunit?'

Fox said: 'If I take your meaning, Mr Alleyn, I think you think *you* do.'

CHAPTER 7

Watt's Hill

'Things to be borne in mind,' Alleyn said, still speaking from the punt. 'Point one: I found the daisy-head in the prow. That is to say on the same line with the other two heads but a bit farther from the point of impact. Point two: this old crock has got a spare mooring line about thirty feet long. It's still made fast at the other end and I've only got to haul myself back. I imagine the arrangement is for the convenience of Lady Lacklander who, judging by splashes of old watercolour and a squashed tube, occasionally paints from the punt. It's a sobering thought. I should like to see her, resembling one of the more obese female deities, seated in the prow of the punt, hauling herself back to harbourage. There is also, by the way, a pale-yellow giant hairpin in close association with two or three cigarette butts, some with lipstick and some not. Been there for some considerable time, I should say, so that's another story.'

'Sir G.,' Fox ruminated, 'and the girlfriend?'

'Trust you,' Alleyn said, 'for clamping down on the sex-story. To return. Point three: remember that the punt-journey would be hidden from the dwellers on Watt's Hill. Only this end of the bridge and the small area between it and the willow grove is visible to them. You can take him away now, Gripper.'

Dr Curtis covered the body with the groundsheet. PC Gripper and the constable-driver of the Yard car, assisted by Bailey and Thompson, carried Colonel Cartarette out of the willow grove and along the banks of his private fishing to Watt's Lane where the Swevenings hospital van awaited him.

'He was a very pleasant gentleman,' said Sergeant Oliphant. 'I hope we get this chap, sir.'

'Oh, we'll *get* him,' Fox remarked, and looked composedly at his principal.

'I suggest,' Alleyn said, 'that the killer saw Cartarette from the other bank, squatting over his catch. I suggest that the killer, familiar with the punt, slipped into it, let go the painter and was carried by what I'd like to call Shakespeare's current across the stream and into this bay where the punt grounded and left the scar of its prow in the bank there. I suggest that this person was well enough acquainted with the Colonel for him merely to look up when he heard the punt grate on the gravel and not rise. You can see the punt's quite firmly grounded. Now if I stand about here, rather aft of amidships, I'm opposite the place where Cartarette squatted over his task and within striking distance of him if the blow was of the kind I think it was.'

'If,' said Fox.

'Yes, I know "if." If you know of a better damn' theory, you can damn' well go to it,' Alleyn said cheerfully.

'OK,' Fox said. 'I don't, sir. So far.'

'What may at first look tiresome,' Alleyn went on 'is the position of the three decapitated daisy stalks and their heads. It's true that one swipe of a suitable instrument might have beheaded all three and landed one daisy on the Colonel, a second on the bank and a third in the punt. Fair enough. But the same swipe couldn't have reached the Colonel himself.'

Oliphant stared pointedly at the pole lying in the punt.

'No, Oliphant,' Alleyn said. 'You try standing in this punt, whirling that thing round your head, swishing it through the daisies and catching a squatting man neatly on the temple with the end. What do you think our killer is – a caber-tosser from Braemar?'

'Do you reckon then,' Fox said, 'that the daisies were beheaded by a second blow or earlier in the day? Or something?'

Sergeant Oliphant suddenly remarked: 'Pardon me, but did the daisies necessairily have anything to do with the crime?'

'I think there's probably a connection,' Alleyn rejoined, giving the sergeant his full attention. 'The three heads are fresh enough to suggest it. One was in the Colonel's coat and one was in the punt.'

'Well, pardon me, sir,' the emboldened sergeant continued with a slight modulation of his theme; 'but did the punt necessairily have any bearing on the crime?'

'Unless we find a left-handed suspect I think we must accept the punt as a working hypothesis. Have a look at the area between the punt and the place where the body lay, and the patch of stones between the tuft from which the grass was cut and the place where the fish lay. It would be possible to step from the punt on to that patch of stones and you would then be standing close to the position of Colonel Cartarette's head. You would leave little or no trace of your presence. Now, on the willow grove side of the body, the ground is soft and earthy. The Colonel himself, Nurse Kettle and Dr Lacklander have all left recognizable prints there. But there are no traces of a fourth visitor. Accept for the moment the theory that, after the Colonel had been knocked out, our assailant did step ashore on to the stony patch to deliver the final injury or perhaps merely to make sure the victim was already dead. How would such a theory fit in with the missing trout, the punt and the daisies?'

Alleyn looked from Oliphant to Fox. The former had assumed that air of portentousness that so often waits upon utter bewilderment. The latter merely looked mildly astonished. This expression indicated that Mr Fox had caught on.

Alleyn elaborated his theory of the trout, the punt and the daisies, building up a complete and detailed picture of one way in which Colonel Cartarette might have been murdered. 'I realize,' he said, 'that it's all as full of "ifs" as a passport to paradise. Produce any other theory that fits the facts and I'll embrace it with fervour.'

Fox said dubiously: 'Funny business if it works out that way. About the punt, now . . . '

'About the punt, yes. There are several pieces of cut grass in the bottom of the punt and they smell of fish.'

'Do they, now?' said Fox appreciatively, and added: 'So what we're meant to believe in is a murderer who sails up to his victim in a punt and lays him out. Not satisfied in his own mind that the man's dead, he steps ashore and has another go with another instrument. Then for reasons you've made out to sound OK, Mr Alleyn, though there's not much solid evidence, he swaps the Colonel's fish for the Old 'Un. To do this he has to tootle back in the punt and fetch it. And by way of a change at some time or another he swipes the heads off daisies. Where he gets his weapons and what he does with the first fish is a great big secret. Is that the story, Mr Alleyn?'

'It is and I'm sticking to it. Moreover, I'm leaving orders, Oliphant, for a number one search for the missing fish. And meet me,' Alleyn said to Fox, 'on the other bank. I've something to show you.'

He gathered up the long tow rope, pulled himself easily into the contra-current and so back across the stretch of water to the boat shed. When Fox, having come round by the bridge, joined him there, he was shaking his head.

'Oliphant and his boys have been over the ground like a herd of rhinos,' he said. 'Getting their planks last night. Pity. Still . . . have a look here, Fox.'

He led the way into a deep hollow on the left bank. Here the rain had not obliterated the characteristic scars left by Lady Lacklander's sketching stool and easel. Alleyn pointed to them. 'But the really interesting exhibit is up here on the hillock. Come and see.'

Fox followed him over grass that carried faint signs of having been trampled. In a moment they stood looking down at a scarcely perceptible hole in the turf. It still held water. The grass nearby showed traces of pressure.

'If you examine that hole closely,' Alleyn said, 'you'll see it's sur-rounded by a circular indentation.'

'Yes,' Fox said after a long pause, 'yes, by God, so it is. Same as the injury, by God.'

'It's the mark of the second weapon,' Alleyn said. 'It's the mark of a shooting-stick, Brer Fox.'

II

'Attractive house,' Alleyn said as they emerged from the Home Coppice into full view of Nunspardon. 'Attractive house, Fox, isn't it?'

'Very fine residence,' Fox said. 'Georgian, would it be?'

'It would. Built on the site of the former house which was a nun-nery. Hence Nunspardon. Presented (as usual, by Henry VIII) to the

Lacklanders. We'll have to go cautiously here, Brer Fox, by gum, we shall. They'll have just about finished their breakfast. I wonder if Lady Lacklander has it downstairs or in her room. She has it downstairs,' he added as Lady Lacklander herself came out of the house with half a dozen dogs at her heels.

'She's wearing men's boots!' Fox observed.

'That may be because of her ulcerated toe.'

'Ah, to be sure. Lord love us!' Fox ejaculated. 'She's *got* a shooting-stick on her arm.'

'So she has. It may not be the one. And then again,' Alleyn muttered as he removed his hat and gaily lifted it on high to the distant figure, 'it may.'

'Here she comes. No, she doesn't.'

'Hell's boots, she's going to sit on it.'

Lady Lacklander had, in fact, begun to tramp towards them but had evidently changed her mind. She answered Alleyn's salute by waving a heavy gardening glove at him. Then she halted, opened her shooting-stick and, with alarming empiricism, let herself down on it.

'With her weight,' Alleyn said crossly, 'she'll bloody well bury it. Come on.'

As soon as they were within hailing distance Lady Lacklander shouted: 'Good morning to you.' She then remained perfectly still and stared at them as they approached. Alleyn thought: 'Old basilisk! She's being deliberately embarrassing, damn her.' And he returned the stare with inoffensive interest, smiling vaguely.

'Have you been up all night?' she asked when they were at an appropriate distance. 'Not that you look like it, I must say.'

Alleyn said: 'We're sorry to begin plaguing you so early, but we're in a bit of a jam.'

'Baffled?'

'Jolly nearly. Do you mind,' Alleyn went on with what his wife would have called sheer rude charm; 'do you mind having your brains picked at nine o'clock in the morning?'

'What do *you* want with other people's brains, I should like to know,' she said. Her eyes, screwed in between swags of flesh, glittered at him.

Alleyn embarked on a careful tarradiddle. 'We begin to wonder,' he said, 'if Cartarette's murderer may have been lying doggo in the vicinity for some time before the assault.'

'Do you?'

'Yes.'

'*I* didn't see him.'

'I mean really doggo. And as far as we know, which is not as far as we'd like, there's no telling exactly where the hiding place could have been. We think it might have been somewhere that commanded, at any rate, a partial view of the bridge and the willow grove. We also think that it may have overlooked your sketching hollow.'

'You've discovered where that is, have you?'

'Simplicity itself, I promise you. You used an easel and a sketching stool.'

'And with my weight to sustain,' she said, rocking, to his dismay, backwards and forwards on the shooting-stick, 'the latter, no doubt, left its mark.'

'The thing is,' Alleyn said, 'we think this person in hiding may have waited until he saw you go before coming out of cover. Did you stay down in your hollow all the time?'

'No, I had a look at my sketch several times from a distance. Anaemic beast it turned out, in the end.'

'Where exactly did you stand when you looked at it?'

'On the rise between the hollow and the bridge. You can't have gone over your ground properly or you'd have found that out for yourself.'

'Should I? Why?' Alleyn asked, and mentally touched wood.

'Because, my good Roderick, I used this shooting-stick and drove it so far into the ground that I was able to walk away and leave it, which I did repeatedly.'

'Did you leave it there when you went home?'

'Certainly. As a landmark for the boy when he came to collect my things. I dumped them beside it.'

'Lady Lacklander,' Alleyn said, 'I want to reconstruct the crucial bit of the landscape as it was after you left it. Will you lend us your shooting-stick and your sketching gear for an hour or so? We'll take the greatest care of them.'

'I don't know what you're up to,' she said, 'and I suppose I may as well make up my mind that I won't find out. Here you are.'

She heaved herself up and, sure enough, the disc and spike of her shooting-stick had been rammed down so hard into the path that both were embedded and the shooting-stick stood up of its own accord.

Alleyn desired above all things to release it with the most delicate care, perhaps dig it up, turf and all, and let the soil dry and fall away. But there was no chance of that; Lady Lacklander turned and with a single powerful wrench tore the shooting-stick from its bondage.

'There you are,' she said indifferently, and gave it to him. 'The sketching gear is up at the house. Come and get it?'

Alleyn thanked her and said that they would. He carried the shooting-stick by its middle and they all three went up to the house. George Lacklander was in the hall. His manner had changed overnight and he now spoke with the muted solemnity with which men of his type approach a sickroom or a church service. He made a further reference to his activities as a Justice of the Peace, but otherwise was huffily reserved.

'Well, George,' his mother said, and bestowed a peculiar smirk upon him. 'I don't suppose they'll let me out on bail, but no doubt you'll be allowed to visit me.'

'Really, Mama!'

'Roderick is demanding my sketching gear on what appears to me to be a sadly trumped-up excuse. He has not yet, however, administered what I understand to be the Usual Warning.'

'Really, Mama!' George repeated with a miserable titter.

'Come along, Rory,' Lady Lacklander continued and led Alleyn out of the hall into a cloakroom where umbrellas, an assortment of goloshes, boots and shoes and a variety of rackets and clubs were assembled. 'I keep them here to be handy,' she said, 'for garden peeps. I'm better at herbaceous borders than anything else, which just about places my prowess as a watercolourist, as, no doubt, your wife would tell you.'

'She's not an aesthetic snob,' Alleyn said mildly.

'She's a damn' good painter, however,' Lady Lacklander continued. 'There you are. Help yourself.'

He lifted a canvas haversack to which were strapped an easel and an artist's umbrella. 'Did you use the umbrella?' he asked.

'William, the boy, put it up. I didn't want it, the sun was gone from the valley. I left it, standing but shut, when I came home.'

'We'll see if it showed above the hollow.'

'Roderick,' said Lady Lacklander suddenly, 'what exactly *were* the injuries?'

'Hasn't your grandson told you?'

'If he had I wouldn't ask you.'

'They were cranial.'

'You needn't be in a hurry to return the things. I'm not in the mood.'

'It's very kind of you to lend them.'

'Kettle will tell me,' said Lady Lacklander, 'all about it!'

'Of course she will,' he agreed cheerfully, 'much better than I can.'

'What persuaded you to leave the Service for this unlovely trade?'

'It's a long time ago,' Alleyn said; 'but I seem to remember that it had something to do with a liking for facts – '

'Which should never be confused with the truth.'

'I still think they are the raw material of the truth. I mustn't keep you any longer. Thank you so much for helping us,' Alleyn said, and stood aside to let her pass.

He and Fox were aware of her great bulk, motionless on the steps, as they made their way back to the Home Coppice. Alleyn carried the shooting-stick by its middle and Fox the sketching gear. 'And I don't mind betting,' Alleyn said, 'that from the rear we look as self-conscious as a brace of snowballs in hell.'

When they were out of sight in the trees they examined their booty.

Alleyn laid the shooting-stick on a bank and squatted beside it.

'The disc,' he said, 'screws on above the ferrule, leaving a two-inch spike. Soft earth all over it and forced up under the collar of the disc which obviously hasn't been disengaged for weeks! All to the good. If it's the weapon, it may have been washed in the Chyne and wiped, and it has of course been subsequently rammed down in soft earth, but it hasn't been taken apart. There's a good chance of a blood-trace under the collar. We must let Curtis have this at once. Now let's have a look at her kit.'

'Which we didn't really want, did we?'

'You never know. It's a radial easel with spiked legs and it's a jointed gamp with a spiked foot. Lots of spikes available, but the shooting-stick fits the picture best. Now for the interior. Here we are,' Alleyn said, unbuckling the straps and peering inside. 'Large watercolour box. Several mounted boards of not-surface paper. Case of brushes. Pencils. Bunjy. Water jar. Sponge. Paint rag. Paint rag,' he repeated softly, and bent over the kit sniffing. He drew a length of stained cotton rag out of the kit. It was blotched with patches of watery colour and with one dark brownish-reddish stain that was broken by a number of folds as if the rag had been twisted about some object.

Alleyn looked up at his colleague.

'Smell, Fox,' he said.

Fox squatted behind him and sniffed stertorously.

'Fish,' he said.

III

Before returning they visited the second tee and looked down on the valley from the Nunspardon side. They commanded a view of the far end of the bridge and the reaches of the Chyne above it. As from the other side of the valley, the willow grove, the lower reaches and the Nunspardon end of the bridge were hidden by intervening trees through which they could see part of the hollow where Lady Lacklander had worked at her sketch.

'So you see,' Alleyn pointed out, 'it was from here that Mrs Cartarette and that ass George Lacklander saw Mr Phinn poaching under the bridge and it was from down there in the hollow that Lady Lacklander glanced up and saw them.' He turned and looked back at a clump of trees on the golf course. 'And I don't mind betting,' he added, 'that all this chat about teaching her to play golf is the cover-story for a pompous slap-and-tickle.'

'Do you reckon, Mr Alleyn?'

'Well, I wouldn't be surprised. There's Oliphant at the bridge,' Alleyn said, waving his hand. 'We'll get him to take this stuff straight to Curtis who'll be in Chyning by now. He's starting his PM at eleven. Dr Lacklander's arranged for him to use the hospital mortuary. I want a report as soon as we can get it, on the rag and the shooting-stick.'

'Will the young doctor attend the autopsy, do you think?'

'I wouldn't be surprised. I think our next move had better be a routine check up on Commander Syce.'

'That's the chap Miss Kettle mentioned, with lumbago, who lives in the middle house,' Fox observed. 'I wonder would he have seen anything.'

'Depends on the position of his bed.'

'It's a nasty thing, lumbago,' Fox mused.

They handed over Lady Lacklander's property to Sergeant Oliphant with an explanatory note for Dr Curtis and instructions to search the valley for the whole or part of the missing trout. They then climbed the River Path to Uplands.

They passed through the Hammer Farm spinney and entered that of Commander Syce. Here they encountered a small notice nailed to a tree. It was freshly painted and bore in neatly executed letters the legend: 'Beware of Archery.'

'Look at that!' Fox said. 'And we've forgotten our green tights.'

'It may be a warning to Nurse Kettle,' Alleyn said.

'I don't get you, sir?'

'Not to flirt with the Commander when she beats up his lumbago.'

'Very far-fetched,' Fox said stiffly.

As they emerged from Commander Syce's spinney into his garden they heard a twang followed by a peculiar whining sound and the 'tuck' of a penetrating blow.

'What the hell's that!' Fox ejaculated. 'It sounded like the flight of an arrow.'

'Which is not surprising,' Alleyn rejoined, 'as that is what it was.'

He nodded at a tree not far from where they stood and there, astonishing and incongruous, was embedded an arrow prettily flighted in red, and implanted in the centre of a neatly and freshly carved heart. It still quivered very slightly. 'We can't say we weren't warned,' Alleyn pointed out.

'Very careless!' Fox said crossly.

Alleyn pulled out the arrow and looked closely at it. 'Deadly if they hit the right spot. I hope you've noticed the heart. It would appear that Commander Syce has recovered from his lumbago and fallen into love's sickness. Come on.'

They emerged from the spinney to discover Commander Syce himself some fifty yards away, bow in hand, quiver at thigh, scarlet-faced and irresolute.

'Look here!' he shouted. 'Damn' sorry and all that, but great grief, how was I to know and, damn it all, what about the notice?'

'Yes, yes,' Alleyn rejoined. 'We're here at our own risk.'

He and Fox approached Syce who, unlike Lady Lacklander, evidently found the interval between the first hail and, as it were, boarding distance, extremely embarrassing. As they plodded up the hill he looked anywhere but at them and when, finally, Alleyn introduced himself and Fox, he shied away from them like an unbroken colt.

'We are,' Alleyn explained, 'police officers.'

'Good lord!'

'I suppose you've heard of last night's tragedy?'

'What tragedy?'

'Colonel Cartarette.'

'Cartarette?'

'He has been murdered.'

'Great grief!'

'We're calling on his neighbours in case . . . '

'What time?'

'About nine o'clock, we think.'

'How d'you know it's murder?'

'By the nature of the injuries, which are particularly savage ones, to the head.'

'Who found him?'

'The District Nurse. Nurse Kettle.'

Commander Syce turned scarlet. 'Why didn't she get me?' he said.

'Would you expect her to?'

'No.'

'Well, then . . . '

'I say, come in, won't you? No good nattering out here, what!' shouted Commander Syce.

They followed him into his desolate drawing-room and noted the improvized bed, now tidily made up and a table set out with an orderly array of drawing-materials and watercolours. A large picture-map in the early stages of composition was pinned to a drawing-board. Alleyn saw that its subject was Swevenings and that a number of lively figures had already been sketched in.

'That's very pleasant,' Alleyn said, looking at it.

Commander Syce made a complicated and terrified noise and interposed himself between the picture-map and their gaze. He muttered something about doing it for a friend.

'Isn't she lucky?' Alleyn remarked lightly. Commander Syce turned, if anything, deeper scarlet and Inspector Fox looked depressed.

Alleyn said he was sure Commander Syce would understand that as a matter of routine the police were calling upon Cartarette's neighbours. 'Simply,' he said, 'to try and get a background. When one is casting about in a case like this . . . '

'Haven't you got the fellah?'

'No. But we hope that by talking to those of the Colonel's neighbours who were anywhere near . . . '

'I wasn't. Nowhere near.'

Alleyn said with a scarcely perceptible modulation of tone: 'Then you know where he was found?'

''Course I do. You say nine o'clock. Miss . . . ah . . . the . . . ah . . . the lady who you tell me found him, left here at five to nine, and I saw her go down into the valley. If she found him at nine he must have been in the perishing valley, mustn't he? I watched her go down.'

'From where?'

'From up here. The window. She told me she was going down the valley.'

'You were on your feet, then? Not completely prostrate with lumbago?'

Commander Syce began to look wretchedly uncomfortable. 'I struggled up, don't you know,' he said.

'And this morning you've quite recovered?'

'It comes and goes.'

'Very tricky,' said Alleyn. He still had the arrow in his hand and now held it up. 'Do you often loose these things off into your spinney?' he asked.

Commander Syce muttered something about a change from target shooting.

'I've often thought I'd like to have a shot at archery,' Alleyn lied amiably. 'One of the more blameless sports. Tell me, what weight of bow do you use?'

'A sixty-pound pull.'

'Really! What's the longest – is clout the word? – that can be shot with a sixty pounder?'

'Two hundred and forty yards.'

'Is that twelve score? "A" would have clapped i' the clout at twelve score?" '

'That's right,' Commander Syce agreed, and shot what might have been an appreciative glance at Alleyn.

'Quite a length. However, I mustn't keep you gossiping about archery. What I really want to ask you is this. I understand that you've known Colonel Cartarette a great many years?'

'Off and on. Neighbours. Damn' nice fellah.'

'Exactly. And I believe that when Cartarette was in the Far East, you ran up against him. At Hong Kong, was it?' Alleyn improvised hopefully.

'Singapore.'

'Oh, yes. The reason why I'm asking you is this. From the character of the crime and the apparently complete absence of motive, *here*, we are wondering if it can possibly be a back kick from his work out in the East.'

'Wouldn't know.'

'Look here, can you tell us anything at all about his life in the East? I mean, anything that might start us off. When actually did you see him out there?'

'Last time would be four years ago. I was still on the active list. My ship was based on Singapore and he looked me up when we were in port. I was axed six months later.'

'Did you see much of them out there?'

'Them?'

'The Cartarettes.'

Commander Syce glared at Alleyn. 'He wasn't married,' he said, 'then.'

'So you didn't meet the second Mrs Cartarette until you came back here, I suppose?'

Commander Syce thrust his hands into his pockets and walked over to the window. 'I had met her, yes,' he mumbled. 'Out there.'

'Before they married?'

'Yes.'

'Did you bring them together?' Alleyn asked lightly, and he saw the muscles in the back of Syce's neck stiffen under the reddened skin.

'I introduced them, as it happens,' Syce said loudly without turning his head.

'That's always rather amusing. Or I find it so, being,' Alleyn said, looking fixedly at Fox, 'an incorrigible matchmaker.'

'Good God, nothing like that!' Syce shouted. 'Last thing I intended. Good God, no!'

He spoke with extraordinary vehemence and seemed to be moved equally by astonishment, shame and indignation. Alleyn wondered why on earth he himself didn't get the snub he had certainly invited and decided it was because Syce was too embarrassed to administer one. He tried to get something more about Syce's encounters with Cartarette in Singapore but was unsuccessful. He noticed the unsteady hands, moist skin and patchy colour, and the bewildered unhappy look in the very blue eyes. 'Alcoholic, poor devil,' he thought.

'It's no good asking me anything,' Syce abruptly announced. 'Nobody tells me anything. I don't go anywhere. I'm no good to anybody.'

'We're only looking for a background, and I hoped you might be able to provide a piece of it. Miss Kettle was saying last night how close the Swevenings people are to each other; it all sounded quite feudal. Even Sir Harold Lacklander had young Phinn as his secretary. What did you say?'

'Nothing. Young perisher. Doesn't matter.'

' . . . and as soon as your ship comes in, Cartarette naturally looks you up. You bring about his first meeting with Miss . . . I don't know Mrs Cartarette's maiden name.'

Commander Syce mumbled unhappily.

'Perhaps you can give it to me,' Alleyn said apologetically. 'We have to get these details for the files. Save me bothering her.'

He gazed mildly at Syce who threw one agonized glance at him, swallowed with difficulty, and said in a strangulated voice: 'de Vere.'

There was a marked silence. Fox cleared his throat.

'Ah, yes,' Alleyn said.

IV

'Would you have thought,' Fox asked as he and Alleyn made their way through Mr Phinn's coppice to Jacob's Cottage, 'that the present Mrs Cartarette was born into the purple, Mr Alleyn?'

'I wouldn't have said so, Brer Fox. No.'

'De Vere, though?'

'My foot.'

'Perhaps,' Fox speculated, reverting to the language in which he so ardently desired to become proficient, 'perhaps she's – er – déclassée.'

'I think, on the contrary, she's on her way up.'

'Ah. The baronet, now,' Fox went on, 'he's sweet on her as anyone could see. Would you think it was a strong enough attraction to incite either of them to violence?'

'I should think he was going through the silly season most men of his type experience. I must say I can't see him raising an amatory passion to the power of homicide in any woman. You never know of course. I should think she must find life in Swevenings pretty dim. What did you collect from Syce's general behaviour, Fox?'

'Well, now, he *did* get me wondering what exactly are his feelings about this lady? I mean, they seem to be old acquaintances, don't they? Miss Kettle said he made a picture of Mrs Cartarette before she was married. And then he didn't seem to have fancied the marriage much, did he? Practically smoked when it was mentioned, he got so hot. My idea is there was something between him and her, and the magnolia bush wherever East meets West.'

'You dirty old man,' Alleyn said absently. 'We'll have to find out, you know.'

'*Crime passionel?*'

'Again you never know. We'll ring the Yard and ask them to look him up in the Navy List. They can find out when he was in Singapore and get a confidential report.'

'Say,' Fox speculated, 'that he was sweet on her. Say they were engaged when he introduced her to the Colonel. Say he went off in his ship and then was retired from the Navy, and came home and found Kitty de Vere changed into the second Mrs Cartarette. So he takes to the bottle and gets,' said Mr Fox, 'an *idée fixe.*'

'So will you, if you go on speculating with such insatiable virtuosity. And what about his lumbago? Personally, I think he's having a dim fling with Nurse Kettle.'

Fox looked put out.

'Very unsuitable,' he said.

'Here is Mr Phinn's spinney and here, I think, is our girlfriend of last night.'

Mrs Thomasina Twitchett was, in fact, taking a stroll. When she saw them she wafted her tail, blinked and sat down.

'Good morning, my dear,' said Alleyn.

He sat on his heels and extended his hand. Mrs Twitchett did not advance upon it, but she broke into an extremely loud purring.

'You know,' Alleyn continued severely, 'if you could do a little better than purrs and mews, I rather fancy you could give us exactly the information we need. You were in the Bottom Meadow last night, my dear, and I'll be bound you were all eyes and ears.'

Mrs Twitchett half-closed her eyes, sniffed at his extended forefinger, and began to lick it.

'Thinks you're a kitten,' Fox said sardonically.

Alleyn in his turn sniffed at his finger, and then lowered his face almost to the level of the cat's. She saluted him with a brief dab of her nose.

'What a girl,' Fox said.

'She no longer smells of raw fish. Milk and a little cooked rabbit, I fancy. Do you remember where we met her last night?'

'Soon after we began to climb the hill on this side, wasn't it?'

'Yes. We'll have a look over the terrain when we get the chance. Come on.'

They climbed up through Mr Phinn's spinney and finally emerged on the lawn before Jacob's Cottage. 'Though if that's a cottage,' Fox observed, 'Buck House is a bungalow.'

'Case of inverted snobbism, I dare say. It's a nice front, nevertheless. Might have been the dower house to Nunspardon at one time. Rum go, couple of unattached males living side by side in houses that are much too big for them.'

'I wonder how Mr Phinn and the Commander hit it off.'

'I wouldn't mind having a bet that they don't. Look, here he comes.'

'Cripes!' Mr Fox ejaculated. 'What a menagerie!'

Mr Phinn had in fact come out of his house accompanied by an escort of cats and Mrs Twitchett's three fat kittens.

'No more!' he was saying in his curious alto voice. 'All gone! Go and catch micey, you lazy lot of furs.'

He set down the empty dish he had been carrying. Some object fell from his breast pocket and he replaced it in a hurry. Some of his cats pretended alarm and flounced off, the others merely stared at him. The three kittens, seeing their mother, galloped unsteadily towards her with stiff tails and a great deal of conversation. Mr Phinn saw Alleyn and Fox. Staring at them, he clapped his hands like a mechanical toy that had not quite run down.

The tassel of his smoking-cap had swung over his nose but his sudden pallor undid its comic effect. The handle of the concealed object protruded from his breast pocket. He began to walk towards them and his feline escort, with the exception of the Twitchetts, scattered before him.

'Good morning,' Mr Phinn fluted thickly. He swept aside his tassel with a not-quite-steady hand and pulled up a dingy handkerchief, thus concealing the protruding handle. 'To what beneficent constabular breeze do I owe this enchanting surprise? Detectives, emerging from a grove of trees!' he exclaimed, and clasped his hands. 'Like fauns in pursuit of some elusive hamadryad! Armed, I perceive,' he added, with a malevolent glance at Commander Syce's arrow, which Alleyn had retained by the simple expedient of absent-mindedly walking away with it.

'Good morning, Mr Phinn,' Alleyn said. 'I have been renewing my acquaintance with your charming cat.'

'Isn't she sweet?' Mr Phinn moistened his lips with the tip of his tongue. 'Such a devoted mama, you can't think!'

Alleyn sat on his heels beside Mrs Twitchett who gently kicked away one of her too-greedy kittens. 'Her fur's in wonderful condition for a nursing mother,' he said, stroking it. 'Do you give her anything special to eat?'

Mr Phinn began to talk with the sickening extravagance of the feline fanatic. 'A balanced diet,' he explained in a high-pitched voice, 'of her own choosing. Fissy on Mondays and Fridays. Steaky on Tuesdays. Livvy on Wednesdays. Cooked bun on Thursdays and Sundays. Embellished,' he added with a merciless smile, 'by our own clever claws, with micey and birdie.'

'Fish only twice a week,' Alleyn mused and Fox, suddenly feeling that something was expected of him, said: 'Fancy!'

'She is looking forward to tomorrow,' Mr Phinn said, 'with the devoted acquiescence of a good Catholic although, of course theistically, she professes the mysteries of Old Nile.'

'You don't occasionally catch her dinner for her in the Chyne?'

'When I am successful,' Mr Phinn said, 'we share.'

'Did you?' Alleyn asked, fatuously addressing himself to the cat. 'Did you have fresh fissy for your supper last night, my angel?' Mrs Twitchett turned contemptuously to her kittens.

'No!' said Mr Phinn in his natural voice.

'You made no other catch, then, besides the fabulous Old 'Un?'

'No!'

'May we talk?'

Mr Phinn, silent for once, led the way through a side door and down a passage into a sizeable library.

Alleyn's eye for other people's houses unobtrusively explored the room. The Colonel's study had been pleasant, civilized and not lacking in feminine graces. Commander Syce's drawing-room was at once clean, orderly, desolate and entirely masculine. Mr Phinn's library was disorderly, dirty, neglected and ambiguous. It exhibited confused traces of Georgian grace, Victorian pomposity and Edwardian muddle. Cushions that had once been fashionably elaborate were now stained and tarnished. There were yards of dead canvas that had once been acceptable to Burlington House, including the portrait of a fragile-looking lady with a contradictory jaw that was vaguely familiar. There were rows and rows of 'gift' books about cats, cheek-by-jowl with Edwardian novels which, if opened, would be found to contain illustrations of young women in dustcoats and motoring veils making haughty little *moues* at gladiators in Norfolk jackets. But there were also one or two admirable chairs, an unmistakable Lely and a lovely, though filthy, rug. And among the decrepit novels were books of distinction and authority. It was on Mr Phinn's shelves that Alleyn noticed an unexpected link with the Colonel. For here among a collection of books on angling he saw again *The Scaly Breed* by Maurice Cartarette. But what interested Alleyn perhaps more than all these items, was a state of chaos that was to be observed on and near a very nice serpentine-fronted bureau. The choked drawers were half-out, one indeed was on the floor, the top was covered with miscellaneous objects which, to a police-trained eye, had clearly been dragged out in handfuls, while the carpet nearby was littered with a further assortment. A burglar, taken by surprise, could not have left clearer evidence behind him.

'How can I serve you?' asked Mr Phinn. 'A little refreshment, by the way? A glass of sherry? Does Tio Pepe recommend himself to your notice?'

'Not quite so early in the morning, thank you, and I'm afraid this is a duty call.'

'Indeed? How I wish I could be of some help. I have spent a perfectly wretched night – such of it as remained to me – fretting and speculating, you know. A murderer in the Vale! Really, if it wasn't so dreadful there would be a kind of grotesque humour in the thought. We are so very respectable in Swevenings. Not a ripple, one would have thought, on the surface of the Chyne!'

He flinched and made the sort of grimace that is induced by a sudden twinge of toothache.

'Would one not? What,' Alleyn asked, 'about the Battle of the Old 'Un?'

Mr Phinn was ready for him. He fluttered his fingers. '*Nil nisi,*' he said, with rather breathless airiness, 'and all the rest of it but, really, the Colonel was most exasperating as an angler. A monument of integrity in every other respect, I dare say, but as a fly-fisherman I am sorry to say there were some hideous lapses. It is an ethical paradox that so noble a sport should occasionally be wedded to such lamentable malpractices.'

'Such,' Alleyn suggested, 'as casting under a bridge into your neighbour's preserves?'

'I will defend my action before the Judgment Seat and the ghost of the sublime Walton himself will thunder in my defence. It was entirely permissible.'

'Did you and the Colonel,' Alleyn said, 'speak of anything else but this – ah – this ethical paradox?'

Mr Phinn glared at him, opened his mouth, thought perhaps of Lady Lacklander and shut it again. Alleyn for his part, remembered, with exasperation, the law on extrajudicial admissions. Lady Lacklander had told him there had been a further discussion between the two men, but had refused to say what it was about. If Mr Phinn should ever come to trial for the murder of Maurice Cartarette or even if he should merely be called to give evidence against someone else, the use by Alleyn of the first of Lady Lacklander's statements and the concealment of the second, would be held by a court of law to be improper. He decided to take a risk.

'We have been given to understand,' he said, 'that there was in fact a further discussion.'

There was a long silence.

'Well, Mr Phinn?'

'Well. I am waiting.'

'For what?'

'I believe it is known as the Usual Warning,' Mr Phinn said.

'The police are only obliged to give the usual warning when they have decided to make an arrest.'

'And you have not yet arrived at this decision?'

'Not yet.'

'You, of course, have your information from the Lady Gargantua, the Mammoth Châtelaine, the Great, repeat Great, Lady of Nunspardon,' said Mr Phinn, and then surprisingly turned pink. His gaze, oddly fixed, was directed past Alleyn's elbow to some object behind him. It did not waver. 'Not,' Mr Phinn added, 'that, in certain respects, her worth does not correspond by a rough computation with her avoirdupois. Did she divulge the nature of my farther conversation with the Colonel?'

'No.'

'Then neither,' said Mr Phinn, 'shall I. At least, not yet. Not unless I am obliged to do so.'

The direction of his gaze had not shifted.

'Very well,' Alleyn said, and turned away with an air of finality.

He had been standing with his back to a desk. Presiding over an incredibly heaped-up litter were two photographs in tarnished silver frames. One was of the lady of the portrait. The other was of a young man bearing a strong resemblance to her and inscribed in a flowing hand: 'Ludovic'

It was at this photograph that Mr Phinn had been staring.

CHAPTER 8

Jacob's Cottage

Alleyn decided to press home what might or might not be an advantage and so did so with distaste. He had been in the police service for over twenty years. Under slow pressure his outward habit had toughened, but, like an ice cube that under warmth will yield its surface but retain its inward form, so his personality had kept its pattern intact. When an investigation led him, as this did, to take action that was distasteful to him, he imposed a discipline upon himself and went forward. It was a kind of abstinence, however, that prompted him to do so.

He said, looking at the photograph, 'This is your son, sir, isn't it?'

Mr Phinn, in a voice that was quite unlike his usual emphatic alto, said: 'My son, Ludovic.'

'I didn't meet him, but I was in the Special Branch in 1937. I heard about his tragedy, of course.'

'He was a good boy,' Mr Phinn said. 'I think I may have spoiled him. I fear I may have done so.'

'One can't tell about these things.'

'No. One can't tell.'

'I don't ask you to forgive me for speaking of him. In a case of homicide I'm afraid no holds are barred. We have discovered that Sir Harold Lacklander died with the name 'Vic' on his lips and full of concern about the publication of his own memoirs which he had entrusted to Colonel Cartarette. We know that your son was Sir Harold's secretary during a crucial period of his administration in Zlomce and that Sir Harold could hardly avoid mention of the

tragedy of your son's death if he was to write anything like a definitive record of his own career.'

'You need go no further,' said Mr Phinn, with a wave of his hand.
'I see very clearly what is in your mind.' He looked at Fox whose
notebook was in his palm. 'Pray write openly, Inspector. Mr Alleyn,
you wonder, do you not, if I quarrelled with Colonel Cartarette
because he proposed to make public, through Lacklander's memoirs,
the ruin of my boy. Nothing could be farther from the truth.'

'I wonder,' Alleyn said, 'if the discussion that Lady Lacklander
overheard, but doesn't care to reveal, was about some such matter.'

Mr Phinn suddenly beat his pudgy hands together, once. 'If Lady
L. does not care to tell you,' he announced, 'then neither for the
time being do I.'

'I wonder, too,' Alleyn continued, 'if it wouldn't be easy to mis-
judge completely your own motives and those of Lady Lacklander.'

'Ah,' Mr Phinn said, with extraordinary complacency, 'you are on
dangerous ground indeed, my dear Alleyn. Peel away the layers of
motive from the ethical onion and your eyes may well begin to water.
It is no occupation, believe me, for a Chief Detective-Inspector.'

A faint smile played conceitedly about the corners of his mouth.
Alleyn might have supposed him to have completely recovered his
equanimity if it had not been for the slightest possible tic in the
lower lid of his right eye and a movement of the fingers of one hand
across the back of the other.

'I wonder,' Alleyn said, 'if you'd mind showing us your fishing
gear . . . the whole equipment as you took it down yesterday to the
Chyne?'

'And why not?' Mr Phinn rejoined. 'But I demand,' he added
loudly, 'to know if you suspect me of this crime. Do you? Do you?'

'Come now,' Alleyn said, 'you must know very well that you
can't in the same breath refuse to answer our questions and demand
an answer to your own. If we may we would like to see your fishing
gear.'

Mr Phinn stared at him. 'It's not here,' he said. 'I'll get it.'

'Fox will help you.'

Mr Phinn looked as if he didn't much relish this offer, but
appeared to think better of refusing it. He and Fox went out together.
Alleyn moved over to the book-lined wall on his left and took down

Maurice Cartarette's work on *The Scaly Breed*. It was inscribed on the title page: 'January, 1930. For Viccy on his eighteenth birthday with good wishes for many happy castings,' and was signed by the author. The Colonel, Alleyn reflected, had evidently been on better terms with young Phinn than with his father.

He riffled through the pages. The book had been published in 1929 and appeared to be a series of short and pleasantly written essays on the behaviour and eccentricities of freshwater fish. It contained an odd mixture of folkishness, natural history, mild flights of fancy and, apparently, a certain amount of scientific fact. It was illustrated, rather charmingly, with marginal drawings. Alleyn turned back to the title page and found that they were by Geoffrey Syce: another instance, he thought, of the way the people of Swevenings stick together and he wondered if, twenty-six years ago, the Colonel in his regiment, and the Commander in his ship had written to each other about the scaly breed and about how they should fashion their book. His eye fell on a page heading, 'No Two Alike,' and with astonishment he saw what at first he took to be a familiar enough kind of diagram . . . that of two magnified fingerprints, showing the essential dissimilarities. At first glance they might have been lifted from a manual on criminal investigation. When, however, he looked more closely, he found, written underneath: 'Microphotographs. Fig. 1, Scale of brown trout. 6 years. 2½ lbs. Chyne river. Showing 4 years poor growth followed by two years vigorous growth. Fig. 2, Scale of trout. 4 years. 1½ lbs. Chyne river. Note, differences in circuli, winter bands and spawning marks.' With sharpened interest he began to read the accompanying letterpress:

> 'It is not perhaps generally known,' the Colonel had written, 'that the scales of no two trout are alike: I mean, microscopically alike in the sense that no two sets of fingerprints correspond. It is amusing to reflect that in the watery world a rogue-trout may leave incriminating evidence behind him in the form of what might be called scales of justice.'

For the margin Commander Syce had made a facetious picture of a roach with meerschaum and deerstalker hat examining through a lens the scales of a very tough-looking trout.

Alleyn had time to reread the page. He turned back to the frontis-
piece – a drawing of the Colonel himself. Alleyn found in the face a
dual suggestion of soldier and diplomat superimposed, he fancied,
on something that was pure countryman. 'A nice chap, he looks. I
wonder if it would have amused him to know that he himself has
put into my hands the prize piece of information received.'

He replaced the book and turned to the desk with its indescribable litter of pamphlets, brochures, unopened and opened letters,
newspapers and magazines. Having inspected the surface he began,
gingerly, to disturb the top layer and in a moment or two had disclosed a letter addressed to 'Octavius Phinn, Esq.,' in the beautiful
and unmistakable handwriting of Colonel Cartarette.

Alleyn had just had time enough to discover that it contained
about thirty pages of typescript marked on the outside: '7,' when he
heard Fox's voice on the stairs. He turned away and placed himself
in front of the portrait.

Mr Phinn and Fox reappeared with the fishing gear.

'I have,' Alleyn said, 'been enjoying this very charming portrait.'

'My wife.'

'Am I imagining – perhaps I am – a likeness to Dr Mark
Lacklander?'

'There was,' Mr Phinn said shortly, 'a distant connection. Here are
my toys.'

He was evidently one of those anglers who cannot resist the call
of the illustrated catalogue and the lure of the gadget. His creel, his
gaff, his net, his case of flies and his superb rod were supplemented
by every conceivable toy, all of them, Alleyn expected, extremely
expensive. His canvas bag was slotted and pocketed to receive these
mysteries, and Alleyn drew them out one after another to discover
that they were all freshly cleaned and in wonderful order.

'With what fly,' he asked Mr Phinn, 'did you hook the Old 'Un?
It must have been a Homeric struggle, surely?'

'Grant me the bridge,' Mr Phinn shouted excitedly, 'grant me
that, and I'll tell you.'

'Very well,' Alleyn conceded with a grin, 'we'll take the bridge in
our stride. I concede it. Let's have the story.'

Mr Phinn went strongly into action. It appeared that, at the
mention of his prowess, the emotions that had so lately seemed to

grip him were completely forgotten. Fear, if he had known fear, paternal anguish, if he had in fact experienced it, and anger, if it was indeed anger that had occasionally moved him, were all abandoned for the absolute passion of the angler. He led them out of doors, exhibited his retrospective prowess in casting, led them in again and re-enacted in the strangest pantomime his battle with the Old 'Un: how he was played, with breathtaking reverses, up through the waters under the bridge and into Mr Phinn's indisputable preserves. How he was nearly lost and what cunning he displayed and how Mr Phinn countered with even greater cunning of his own. Finally, there was the great capitulation, the landing and the *coup de grace*, this last being administered, as Mr Phinn made clear in spirited pantomime, with a sort of angler's cosh: a short heavily-leaded rod.

Alleyn took this instrument in his hand and balanced it. 'What do you call this thing?' he asked.

'A priest,' Mr Phinn said. 'It is called a priest. I don't know why.'

'Perhaps because of its valedictory function.' He laid it on the desk and placed Commander Syce's arrow beside it. Mr Phinn stared but said nothing.

'I really must return his arrow to Commander Syce,' Alleyn said absently. 'I found it in the spinney, embedded in a tree trunk.'

He might have touched off a high explosive. The colour flooded angrily into Mr Phinn's face and he began to shout of the infamies of Commander Syce and his archery. The death of Thomasina Twitchett's mother at the hands of Commander Syce was furiously recalled. Syce, Mr Phinn said, was a monster, an alcoholic sadist, possessed of a blood-lust. It was with malice aforethought that he had transfixed the dowager Twitchett. The plea of accident was ridiculous: the thing was an obsession. Syce would drink himself into a sagittal fury and fire arrows off madly into the landscape. Only last night, Mr Phinn continued, when he himself was returning from the Chyne after what he now called his little *mésentente* with Colonel Cartarette, the Commander's bow was twanging away on the archery lawn and Mr Phinn had actually heard the tuck of an arrow in a tree trunk dangerously near to himself. The time was a quarter past eight. He remembered hearing his clock chime.

'I think you must be mistaken,' Alleyn put in mildly. 'Nurse Kettle tells us that last evening Commander Syce was completely incapacitated by an acute attack of lumbago.'

Mr Phinn shouted out a rude and derisive word. 'A farrago of nonsense!' he continued. 'Either she is his accomplice or his paramour or possibly,' he amended more charitably, 'his dupe. I swear he was devilishly active last night. I swear it. I trembled lest my Thomasina, who had accompanied me to the Chyne, should share the fate of her mama. She did not join me on my return but had preferred to linger in the evening air. Indeed, the reason for my perhaps slightly dramatic entry into Hammer in the early hours of this morning was my hope of retrieving my errant Fur. The dreadful news with which you met me quite put her out of my head,' Mr Phinn concluded and did not look as if he expected to be believed.

'I see,' Alleyn said, and did not look as if he believed him. 'Quite a chapter of accidents. Do you mind if we take possession of your fishing gear for a short time? Part of a routine check, you know.'

Mr Phinn was at a loss for words. 'But how quite extraordinary!' he at last exclaimed. 'My fishing gear? Well, I suppose one must not refuse.'

'We shan't keep it any longer than is necessary,' Alleyn assured him.

Fox put the kit in order and slung it over his massive shoulder.

'And also, I'm afraid,' Alleyn said apologetically, 'the shoes and suit that you wore on your fishing expedition.'

'My shoes? My suit! But why, why? I don't like this. I don't like it at all.'

'It may be some comfort to you to know that I shall make the same awkward demands of at least four other persons.'

Mr Phinn seemed to brighten a little. 'Blood?' he asked.

'Not necessarily,' Alleyn said coolly. 'This and that, you know, and the other thing. May we have them?'

'A fat lot of use,' Mr Phinn muttered, 'if I said no. And, in any case, you are perfectly welcome to every garment I possess. Homicidally speaking, they are as pure as the driven snow.'

When he saw them Alleyn reflected that although, homicidally speaking, this might be true, from any other point of view it was grossly inaccurate: Mr Phinn's angling garments were exceedingly grubby and smelt quite strongly of fish. Alleyn saw with satisfaction a slimy deposit on the right leg of a pair of old-fashioned knickerbockers. The shoes were filthy and the stockings in holes. With a gesture of defiance, their owner flung on top of them a dilapidated tweed hat with the usual collection of flies in the band.

'Make what you like of them,' he said grandly, 'and see that you let me have them back in the order in which you receive them.'

Alleyn gave him grave assurance to this effect and wrapped up the garments. Fox wrote out a receipt for the unlovely bundle.

'We won't keep you any longer,' Alleyn said, 'unless by any chance you would care to give us a true account of your ramblings in the watches of the night.'

Mr Phinn gaped at him and in doing so resembled for the moment the Old 'Un himself.

'Because,' Alleyn went on, 'you haven't done so yet, you know. I mean your story of seeing lighted windows and calling to tell the Colonel of your catch, was completely blown up by Lady Lacklander. And your latest version . . . that you were on the hunt for your mother-cat . . . really won't do at all. Feline nursing mothers, and you tell us this is a particularly devoted one, do not desert their kittens for six hours on end. Moreover, we came upon Mrs Twitchett last night on her way home about half-past twelve. And why, if the Twitchett story was the true one, did you not produce it in the first instance?' Alleyn waited for some seconds. 'You see,' he said, 'you have no answer to any of these questions.'

'I shall not make any further statements. I prefer to remain silent.'

'Shall I tell you what I think may have happened last night? I think that when you made your first remark as you stood in the french window at Hammer you said something that was near the truth. I think that either then, or perhaps earlier in the evening you had sallied out in search of your great trout. I think you regretted having flung it down on the bridge during your quarrel with Colonel Cartarette. You knew he wouldn't touch it because he had told you so and had gone off, leaving it there. Did you not go down into the valley of the Chyne to retrieve the trout, and did you not find it gone from the bridge when you got there?'

The colour mounted in Mr Phinn's face in uneven patches. He lowered his chin and looked quickly at Alleyn from under his meagre brows. But he said nothing.

'If this is so,' Alleyn went on, 'and I am encouraged by your silence to hope that it may be, I can't help wondering what you did next. Did you come straight back to Hammer and, seeing the lighted windows, make up your mind to accuse the Colonel of having pinched your fish after all? But no. If that had been so, your behaviour would have been different. You would not, before you were aware of his death, have trembled and gone white to the lips. Nor would you have invented your cock-and-bull story of wanting to tell the Colonel all about your catch: a story that was at once disproved when Lady Lacklander told us about your row with the Colonel over that very catch and by the fact that for a long time you have not been on visiting terms with your neighbour.'

Mr Phinn had turned aside, and Alleyn walked round him until they were again face to face.

'How,' he said, 'is one to explain your behaviour of last night? Shall I tell you what I think? I think that when you arrived at Hammer Farm at five past one this morning, you knew already that Colonel Cartarette was dead.'

Still Mr Phinn said nothing.

'Now if this is true,' Alleyn said, 'and again you don't deny it, you have misinformed us about your movements. You let us understand that you returned to the Bottom Meadow just before you came to Hammer Farm at about one o'clock. But your coat was as dry as a chip. So it must have been much earlier in the evening before the rain that you returned to the bridge in the hope of retrieving the fish and found it gone. And knowing that the Colonel was fishing his own waters not far away, would you not seek him out? Now, if you did behave as I have suggested, you did so at a time when nobody saw you. That must have been after Lady Lacklander, Mrs Cartarette and Dr Lacklander had all gone home. Mrs Cartarette reached Hammer Farm at about five past eight and Dr Lacklander went home at eight-fifteen. Neither of them saw the trout. On my working hypothesis, then, you revisited the valley after eight-fifteen and, one would suppose, before a quarter to nine when Nurse Kettle did so. And there, Mr Phinn, in the willow grove you found Colonel Cartarette's dead body with your mammoth trout beside it. And didn't Nurse Kettle very nearly catch you in the willow grove?'

Mr Phinn ejaculated: 'Has she said . . . ' and caught his voice back.

'No,' Alleyn said. 'Not specifically. It is I who suggest that you hid and watched her and crept away when she had gone. I suggest, moreover, that when you bolted for cover, your reading spectacles were snatched from your hat by an envious sliver and that in your panic and your terror of being seen, you dared not look for them. Possibly you did not realize they had gone until you got home. And that's why, after the rain, you stole out again – to try and find your glasses in case they were lost in a place where they might incriminate you. Then you saw the lights of Hammer Farm and dared go no further. You couldn't endure the suspense of not knowing if the Colonel had been found. You drew nearer and Sergeant Oliphant's torchlight shone in your eyes.'

Alleyn turned to the window and looked down at Mr Phinn's spinney, at the upper reaches of the Chyne and at a glimpse, between trees, of the near end of the bridge.

'That,' he said, 'is how I think you moved about the landscape yesterday evening and last night.' Alleyn drew a pair of spectacles from the breast-pocket of his coat and dangled it before Mr Phinn. 'I'm afraid I can't let you have them back just yet. But' – he extended his long finger towards Mr Phinn's breast-pocket – 'isn't that a magnifying glass you have managed to unearth?'

Mr Phinn was silent.

'Well,' Alleyn said. 'There's our view of your activities. It's a picture based on your own behaviour and one or two known facts. If it is accurate, believe me, you will be wise to say so.'

Mr Phinn said in an unrecognizable voice: 'And if I don't choose to speak?'

'You will be within your rights and we shall draw our own conclusions.'

'You still don't give me the famous Usual Warning one hears so much about?'

'No.'

'I suppose,' Mr Phinn said, 'I am a timid man, but I know, in respect of this crime, that I am an innocent one.'

'Well, then,' Alleyn said, and tried to lend the colour of freshness to an assurance he had so often given, 'your innocence should cancel your timidity. You have nothing to fear.'

It seemed to Alleyn as he watched Mr Phinn that he was looking on at the superficial signs of a profound disturbance. It was as if Mr Phinn's personality had been disrupted from below like a thermal pool and in a minute or two would begin to boil.

Some kind of climax was in fact achieved and he began to talk very rapidly in his high voice.

'You are a very clever man. You reason from character to fact and back again. There! I have admitted everything. It's all quite true. I tiffed with Cartarette. I flung my nobel Fin on the bridge. I came home, but did not enter my house. I walked distractedly about my garden. I repented of my gesture and returned. The Fin had gone. I sought out my rival and because of the howl of his dog – a disagreeable canine – I – I found him – ' Here Mr Phinn shut his eyes very tight. 'No, really, it was too disagreeable! Even though his hat was over his face one knew at a glance. And the dog never even looked at one. Howl! Howl! I didn't go near them but I saw my fish! My trout! My Superfin! And then, you know, I heard *her*. Kettle. Stump, stump, stump past the willow grove. I ran, I doubled, I flung myself on my face in the undergrowth and waited until she had gone. And then I came home,' said Mr Phinn, 'and as you have surmised I discovered the loss of my reading glasses which I frequently keep in my hatband. I was afraid. And there you are.'

'Yes,' Alleyn said, 'there we are. How do you feel about making a signed statement to this effect?'

'Another statement. Oh, tedious task! But I am resigned.'

'Good. We'll leave you to write it with the aid of your reading glass. Will you begin with the actual catching of the Old 'Un?'

Mr Phinn nodded.

'And you are still disinclined to tell us the full substance of your discussion with Colonel Cartarette?'

Mr Phinn nodded.

He had his back to the windows and Alleyn faced them. Sergeant Oliphant had come out of the spinney and stood at the foot of the garden. Alleyn moved up to the windows. The sergeant, when he saw him, put his thumb up and turned back into the trees.

Fox picked up the parcel of clothes.

Alleyn said: 'We'll call later for the statement. Or perhaps you would bring it to the police station in Chyning this evening?'

'Very well.' Mr Phinn swallowed and his Adam's apple bobbed in his throat. 'After all,' he said, 'I would hardly desert my Glorious Fin. Would I?'

'You did so before. Why shouldn't you do so again?'

'I am completely innocent.'

'Grand. We mustn't bother you any longer. Goodbye, then, until, shall we say, five o'clock in Chyning.'

They went out by a side door and down the garden to the spinney. The path wound downhill amongst trees to a stile that gave on to the River Path. Here Sergeant Oliphant waited for them. Alleyn's homicide bag, which had been entrusted to the sergeant, rested on the stile. At the sound of their voices he turned and they saw that across his palms there lay a sheet of newspaper.

On the newspaper were the dilapidated remains of a trout.

'I got 'er,' said Sergeant Oliphant.

II

'She was a short piece above the bridge on this side,' explained the sergeant who had the habit of referring to inanimate but recalcitrant objects in the feminine gender. 'Laying in some long grass to which I'd say she'd been dragged. Cat's work, sir, as you can see by the teeth-marks.'

'As we supposed,' Alleyn agreed. 'Mrs Thomasina Twitchett's work.'

'A nice fish, she's been, say two pound, but nothing to the Old 'Un,' said the sergeant.

Alleyn laid the paper and its contents on a step of the stile and hung fondly over it. Mrs Twitchett, if indeed it was she, had made short work of most of the Colonel's trout, if indeed this was his trout. The body was picked almost clean, and some of the smaller bones had been chewed. The head appeared to have been ejected after a determined onslaught and the tail was semi-detached. But from the ribs there still depended some pieces of flesh and rags of skin that originally covered part of the flank and belly of the fish, and it was over an unlovely fragment of skin that Alleyn pored. He laid it out flat, using two pairs of pocket tweezers for the purpose, and with a long finger pointed to something that might have been part of an indented scar. It was about a quarter of an inch wide and had a curved margin. It was pierced in one place as if by a short spike.

'Now blow me down flat,' Alleyn exulted, 'if this isn't the answer to the good little investigating officer's prayer. See here, Fox, isn't this a piece of the sort of scar we would expect to find? And look here.'

Very gingerly he turned the trout over and discovered, clinging to the other flank, a further rag of skin with the apex of a sharp triangular gap in it.

'Sink me if I don't have a look,' Alleyn muttered.

Under Oliphant's enchanted gaze, he opened his case, took from it a flat enamel dish, which he laid on the bottom step of the stile, and a small glass jar with a screw-on lid. Using his tweezers he spread out the piece of skin with the triangular gap on the plate. From the glass jar he took the piece of skin that had been found on the sharp stone under the Old 'Un. Muttering and whistling under his breath, and with a delicate dexterity, he laid the second fragment beside the first, opened it out and pushed and fiddled the one into the other as if they were pieces of a jigsaw puzzle. They fitted exactly.

'And that,' Alleyn said, 'is why Mrs Twitchett met us last night smelling of fresh fish when she should have been stinking of liver. O Fate! O Nemesis! O Something or Another!' he apostrophized. 'Thy hand is here!' And in answer to Oliphant's glassy stare, he added: 'You've done damned handily, Sergeant, to pick this up so quickly. Now, listen and I'll explain.'

The explanation was detailed and exhaustive. Alleyn ended it with an account of the passage he had read in Colonel Cartarette's book. 'We'll send out a signal to some piscatorial pundit,' he said, 'and get a check. But if the Colonel was right, and he seems to have been a conscientious knowledgeable chap, our two trout *cannot* exhibit identical scales. The Colonel's killer, and only his killer, can have handled both fish. We do a round-up of garments, my hearties, and hope for returns.'

Sergeant Oliphant cleared his throat and with an air of modest achievement stooped behind a briar bush. 'There's one other matter, sir,' he said. 'I found this at the bottom of the hill in a bit of underbrush.'

He straightened up. In his hand was an arrow. 'It appears,' he said, 'to have blood on it.'

'Does it, indeed?' Alleyn said, and took it. 'All right, Oliphant. Damn' good show. We're getting on very prettily. And if,' he summarized for the benefit of the gratified and anxious Oliphant, 'if it all tallies up as I believe it must then the pattern will indeed begin to emerge, won't it, Fox?'

'I hope so, Mr Alleyn,' Fox rejoined cheerfully.

'So off you go, Oliphant,' Alleyn said. 'Drive Mr Fox to the station where he will ring the Yard and the Natural History Museum. Deliver your treasure-trove to Dr Curtis. I hope to have the rest of the exhibits before this evening. Come on, chaps, this case begins to ripen.'

He led them back into the valley, saw Oliphant and Fox on their way with an accumulation of gear and objects of interest, and himself climbed up the hill to Nunspardon.

Here, to his surprise, he ran into a sort of party. Shaded from the noontide sun on the terrace before the great house were assembled the three Lacklanders, Kitty Cartarette and Rose. It was now half-past twelve and a cocktail tray gave an appearance of conviviality to a singularly wretched-looking assembly. Lady Lacklander seemed to have retired behind her formidable façade leaving in her wake an expression of bland inscrutability: George stood in a teapot attitude, one hand in his jacket pocket, the other on the back of a chair, one neatly knickered leg straight, one bent. Mark scowled devotedly upon Rose who was pale, had obviously wept a great deal and seemed in addition to her grief to be desperately worried. Kitty, in a tweed suit, high heels and embroidered gloves, was talking to George. She looked exhausted and faintly sulky, as if tragedy had taken her by surprise and let her down. She lent an incongruous note to a conversation piece that seemed only to lack the attendant figures of grooms with hounds in leashes. Her voice was a high-pitched one. Before she noticed Alleyn she had completed a sentence and he had heard it. 'That's right,' she had said. 'Brierley and Bentwood,' and then she saw him and made an abrupt movement that drew all their eyes upon him.

He wondered how many more times he would have to approach these people through their gardens and from an uncomfortable distance. In a way he was beginning to enjoy it. He felt certain that this time, if George Lacklander could have managed it, the waiting group would have been scattered by a vigorous gesture, George himself would have retired to some manly den and Alleyn, in the ripeness of time, would have been admitted by a footman.

As it was, all of them except Lady Lacklander made involuntary movements which were immediately checked. Kitty half-rose as if to beat a retreat, looked disconsolately at George and sank back in her chair.

'They've been having a council of war,' thought Alleyn.

After a moment's further hesitation Mark, with an air of coming to a decision, put his chin up, said loudly: 'It's Mr Alleyn,' and came to meet him. As they approached each other Alleyn saw Rose's face, watchful and anxious, beyond Mark's advancing figure. His momentary relish for the scene evaporated.

'Good morning,' Alleyn said. 'I'm sorry to reappear so soon and to make a further nuisance of myself. I won't keep you long.'

'That's all right,' Mark said pleasantly. 'Who do you want to see?'

'Why, in point of fact, all of you, if I may. I'm lucky to find you in a group like this.'

Mark had fallen into step with him and together they approached the group.

'Well, Rory,' Lady Lacklander shouted as soon as he was within range, 'you don't give us much peace, do you? What do you want this time? The clothes off our backs?'

'Yes,' Alleyn said, 'I'm afraid I do. More or less.'

'And what may that mean? More or less?'

'The clothes off your yesterday-evening backs, if you please.'

'Is this what my sporadic reading has led me to understand as 'a matter of routine'?'

'In a way,' Alleyn said coolly, 'yes. Yes, it is. Routine.'

'And who,' Kitty Cartarette asked in a care-worn voice of nobody in particular, 'said that a policeman's lot is not a happy one?'

This remark was followed by a curious little gap. It was as if her audience had awarded Kitty a point for attempting, under the circumstances, her small joke but at the same time were unable to accept her air of uncertain intimacy which apparently even George found embarrassing. He laughed uncomfortably. Lady Lacklander raised her eyebrows, and Mark scowled at his boots.

'Do you mean,' Lady Lacklander said, 'the clothes that we were all wearing when Maurice Cartarette was murdered?'

'I do, yes.'

'Well,' she said, 'you're welcome to mine. What *was* I wearing yesterday, George?'

'Really, Mama, I'm afraid I don't . . . '

'Nor do I. Mark?'

Mark grinned at her. 'A green tent, I fancy, Gar, darling; a solar topee and a pair of Grandfather's boots.'

'You're perfectly right. My green Harris, it was. I'll tell my maid, Roderick, and you shall have them.'

'Thank you.' Alleyn looked at George. 'Your clothes and boots, please?'

'Ah, spiked shoes and stockings and plus-fours,' George said loudly. 'Very old-fogeyish. Ha-ha.'

'I think they're jolly good,' Kitty said wearily. 'On the right man.' George's hand went to his moustache, but he didn't look at Kitty. He seemed to be exquisitely uncomfortable. 'I,' Kitty added, 'wore a check skirt and a twin set. Madly county, you know,' she added, desperately attempting another joke, 'on account we played golf.' She sounded near to tears.

'And your shoes?' Alleyn asked.

Kitty stuck out her feet. Her legs, Alleyn noted, were good. Her feet, which were tiny, were shod in lizard skin shoes with immensely high heels. 'Not so county,' Kitty said, with the ghost of a grin; 'but the best I had.'

George, apparently in an agony of embarrassment, glanced at the shoes, at his mother and at the distant prospect of the Home Spinney.

Alleyn said: 'If I may, I'll borrow the clothes, gloves, and stockings. We'll pick them up at Hammer Farm on our way back to Chyning.'

Kitty accepted this. She was looking at Alleyn with the eye, however wan, of a woman who spots a genuine Dior in a bargain basement.

'I'll hurry back,' she said, 'and get them ready for you.'

'There's no immediate hurry.'

Mark said: 'I was wearing whites. I put brogues on for going home and carried my tennis shoes.'

'And your racket?'

'Yes.'

'And, after Bottom Bridge, Lady Lacklander's sketching gear and shooting-stick?'

'That's right.'

'By the way,' Alleyn asked him, 'had you gone straight to your tennis party from Nunspardon?'

'I looked in on a patient in the village.'

'And on the gardener's child, didn't you?' Kitty said. 'They told me you'd lanced its gumboil.'

'Yes. An abscess, poor kid,' Mark said cheerfully.

'So you had your professional bag too?' Alleyn suggested.

'It's not very big.'

'Still; quite a load.'

'It was rather.'

'But Lady Lacklander had left it all tidily packed up, hadn't she?'

'Well,' Mark said, with a smile at his grandmother, 'more or less.'

'Nonsense,' Lady Lacklander said, 'there was no more or less about it. I'm a tidy woman and I left everything tidy.'

Mark opened his mouth and shut it again.

'Your paint rag for instance?' Alleyn said, and Mark glanced sharply at him.

'I overlooked the rag, certainly,' said Lady Lacklander rather grandly, 'when I packed up. But I folded it neatly and tucked it under the strap of my haversack. Why have you put on that look, Mark?' she added crossly.

'Well, darling, when I got there, the rag, far from being neatly folded and stowed, was six yards away on a briar bush. I rescued it and put it into your haversack.'

They all looked at Alleyn as if they expected him to make some comment. He was silent, however, and after a considerable pause Lady Lacklander said: 'Well, it couldn't be of less significance, after all. Go indoors and ask them to get the clothes together. Fisher knows what I wore.'

'Ask about mine, old boy, will you?' said George, and Alleyn wondered how many households there were left in England where orders of this sort were still given.

Lady Lacklander turned to Rose. 'And what about you, child?'

But Rose stared out with unseeing eyes that had filled again with tears. She dabbed at them with her handkerchief and frowned at herself.

'Rose?' Lady Lacklander said quietly.

Still frowning, Rose turned and looked at her. 'I'm sorry,' she said.

'They want to know what clothes you wore, my dear.'

'Tennis things, I imagine,' Alleyn said.

Rose said: 'Oh, yes. Of course. Tennis things.'

Kitty said: 'It's the day for the cleaner. I saw your tennis things in the box, didn't I, Rose?'

'I? . . . Yes,' Rose said. 'I'm sorry. Yes, I did put them in.'

'Shall we go and rescue them?' Mark asked.

Rose hesitated. He looked at her for a moment and then said in a level voice: 'OK. I'll come back,' and went into the house. Rose turned away and stood at some distance from the group.

'It's toughest for Rose,' Kitty said, unexpectedly compassionate, and then with a return to her own self-protective mannerisms she sipped her sherry. 'I wish you joy of my skirt, Mr Alleyn,' she added loudly. 'You won't find it very delicious.'

'No?' Alleyn said. 'Why not?'

'It absolutely reeks of fish.'

III

Alleyn observed the undistinguished little face and wondered if his own was equally blank. He then, under the guise of bewilderment, looked at the others. He found that Lady Lacklander seemed about as agitated as a Buddha and that George was in process of becoming startled. Rose was still turned away.

'Are you a fisherman too, then, Mrs Cartarette?' Alleyn asked.

'God forbid!' she said, with feeling. 'No, I tried to take a fish away from a cat last evening.' The others gaped at her.

'My dear Kitty,' Lady Lacklander said, 'I suggest that you consider what you say.'

'Why?' Kitty countered, suddenly common and arrogant. 'Why? It's the truth. What are you driving at?' she added nervously. 'What's the matter with saying I've got fish on my skirt? Here,' she demanded of Alleyn, 'what are they getting at?'

'My good girl . . . ' Lady Lacklander began, but Alleyn cut in:

'I'm sorry, Lady Lacklander, but Mrs Cartarette's perfectly right. There's nothing the matter, I assure you, with speaking the truth.' Lady Lacklander shut her mouth with a snap. 'Where did you meet your cat and fish, Mrs Cartarette?'

'This side of the bridge,' Kitty muttered resentfully.

'Did you, now?' Alleyn said with relish.

'It looked a perfectly good trout to me, and I thought the cat had no business with it. I suppose,' Kitty went on, 'it was one of old Occy Phinn's swarm; the cat, I mean. Anyhow, I tried to get the trout away from it. It hung on like a fury. And then when I did jerk the trout away it turned out to be half-eaten on the other side, sort of. So I let the cat have it back,' Kitty said limply.

Alleyn said: 'Did you notice any particular mark or scar on the trout?'

'Well, hardly. It was half-eaten.'

'Yes, but on the part that was left?'

'I don't think so. Here! What sort of mark?' Kitty demanded, beginning to look alarmed.

'It doesn't matter. Really.'

'It was quite a nice trout. I wondered if Maurice had caught it and then I thought old Occy Phinn must have hooked it and given it to the cat. He's crazy enough on his cats to give them anything, isn't he, George?'

'Good God, yes!' George ejaculated automatically, without looking at Kitty.

'It's a possible explanation,' Alleyn said as if it didn't much matter either way.

Mark came back from the house. 'The clothes,' he said to Alleyn, 'will be packed up and put in your car which has arrived, by the way. I rang up Hammer and asked them to keep back the things for the cleaner.'

'Thank you so much,' Alleyn said. He turned to Lady Lacklander. 'I know you'll understand that in a case like this we have to fuss about and try to get as complete a picture as possible of the days, sometimes even the weeks and months, before the event. It generally turns out that ninety-nine per cent of the information is quite useless and then everybody thinks how needlessly inquisitive and impertinent the police are. Sometimes, however, there is an apparently irrelevant detail that leads, perhaps by accident, to the truth.'

Lady Lacklander stared at him like a basilisk. She had a habit of blinking slowly, her rather white eyelids dropping conspicuously like shutters: a slightly reptilian habit that was disconcerting. She blinked twice in this manner at Alleyn, and said: 'What are you getting at, my dear Roderick? I hope you won't *finesse* too elaborately. Pray, tell us what you want.'

'Certainly. I want to know if, when I arrived, you were discussing Sir Harold Lacklander's memoirs.'

He knew by their very stillness that he had scored. It struck him, not for the first time, that people who have been given a sudden fright tend to look alike; a sort of homogeneous glassiness overtakes them.

Lady Lacklander first recovered from whatever shock they had all received.

'In point of fact we were,' she said. 'You must have extremely sharp ears.'

'I caught the name of my own publishers,' Alleyn said at once. 'Brierley and Bentwood. An admirable firm. I wondered if they are to do the memoirs.'

'I'm glad you approve of them,' she said dryly. 'I believe they are.'

'Colonel Cartarette was entrusted with the publication, wasn't he?'

There was a fractional pause before Mark and Rose together said: 'Yes.'

'I should think,' Alleyn said pleasantly, 'that that would have been a delightful job.'

George, in a strangulated voice, said something about 'Responsibility,' and suddenly offered Alleyn a drink.

'My good George,' his mother said impatiently, 'Roderick is on duty and will have none of your sherry. Don't be an ass.'

George blushed angrily and glanced, possibly for encouragement, at Kitty.

'Nevertheless,' Lady Lacklander said, with a sort of grudging *bonhomie*, 'you may as well sit down, Rory. One feels uncomfortable when you loom. There *is*, after all, a chair.'

'Thank you,' Alleyn said, taking it. 'I don't want to loom any more than I can help, you know, but you can't expect me to be all smiles and prattle when you, as a group, close your ranks with such a deafening clank whenever I approach you.'

'Nonsense,' she rejoined briskly, but a dull colour actually appeared under her weathered skin and for a moment there was a fleeting likeness to her son. Alleyn saw that Rose Cartarette was looking at him with a sort of anguished appeal and that Mark had taken her hand.

'Well,' Alleyn said cheerfully, 'if it's all nonsense I can forget all about it and press on with the no doubt irrelevant details. About the autobiography for instance. I'm glad Mr Phinn is not with us at the moment because I want to ask you if Sir Harold gives a full account of young Phinn's tragedy. He could scarcely, one imagines, avoid doing so, could he?'

Alleyn looked from one blankly staring face to another. 'Or could he?' he added.

Lady Lacklander said: 'I haven't read my husband's memoirs. Nor, I think, has anyone else except Maurice.'

'Do you mean, Lady Lacklander, that you haven't read them in their entirety or that you haven't read or heard a single word of them?'

'We would discuss them. Sometimes I could refresh his memory.'

'Did you discuss the affair of young Ludovic Phinn?'

'Never!' she said very loudly and firmly, and George made a curious noise in his throat.

Alleyn turned to Kitty and Rose.

'Perhaps,' he suggested, 'Colonel Cartarette may have said something about the memoirs?'

'Not to me,' Kitty said, and added: 'Too pukka sahib.'

There was an embarrassed stirring among the others.

'Well,' Alleyn said, 'I'm sorry to labour the point, but I should like to know, if you please, whether either Sir Harold Lacklander or

Colonel Cartarette ever said anything to any of you about the Ludovic Phinn affair in connection with the memoirs.'

'Damned if I see what you're getting at!' George began, to the dismay, Alleyn felt sure, of everybody who heard him. 'Damned if I see how you make out my father's memoirs can have anything to do with Maurice Cartarette's murder. Sorry, Kitty. I beg pardon, Rose. But I mean to say!'

Alleyn said: 'It's eighteen years since young Ludovic Danberry-Phinn committed suicide and a war has intervened. Many people will have forgotten his story. One among those who have remembered it . . . his father . . . must dread above all things any revival.' He leant forward in his chair and, as if he had given some kind of order or exercised some mesmeric influence on his audience, each member of it imitated this movement. George Lacklander was still empurpled, the others had turned very pale, but one expression was common to them all: they looked, all of them, extremely surprised. In Kitty and George and perhaps in Lady Lacklander, Alleyn thought he sensed a kind of relief. He raised his hand. 'Unless, of course,' he said, 'it has come about that in reviving the tragedy through the memoirs, young Phinn's name will be cleared.'

It was as if, out of a cloth that had apparently been wrung dry, an unexpected trickle was induced. George, who seemed to be the most vulnerable of the group, shouted: 'You've no right to assume . . .' and got no farther. Almost simultaneously Mark and Rose, with the occasional unanimity of lovers, said: 'This won't do . . .' and were checked by an imperative gesture from Lady Lacklander.

'Roderick,' Lady Lacklander demanded, 'have you been talking to Octavius Phinn?'

'Yes,' Alleyn said. 'I have come straight here from Jacob's Cottage.'

'Wait a bit, Mama,' George blurted out. 'Wait a bit! Octavius can't have said anything. Otherwise, don't you see, Alleyn wouldn't try to find out from us.'

In the now really deathly silence that followed this speech, Lady Lacklander turned and blinked at her son.

'You ninny, George,' she said, 'you unfathomable fool.'

And Alleyn thought he now knew the truth about Mr Phinn, Colonel Cartarette and Sir Harold Lacklander's memoirs.

CHAPTER 9

Chyning and Uplands

The next observation was made by Mark Lacklander.

'I hope you'll let me speak, Grandmama,' he said. 'And Father,' he added; obviously as a polite afterthought. 'Although, I must confess, most of the virtue had already gone from what I have to say.'

'Then why, my dear boy, say it?'

'Well, Gar, it's really, you know, a matter of principle. Rose and I are agreed on it. We've kept quiet under your orders, but we both have felt, haven't we, Rose, that by far the best thing is to be completely frank with Mr Alleyn. Any other course, as you've seen for yourself, just won't do.'

'I have not changed my mind, Mark. Wait, a little.'

'Oh, *yes*,' Kitty said eagerly, 'I *do* think so, honestly. Wait. I'm sure,' she added, 'it's what he would have said. Maurie, I mean.' Her face quivered unexpectedly, and she fumbled for her handkerchief.

Rose made one of those involuntary movements that are so much more graphic than words, and Alleyn, whom for the moment they all completely disregarded, wondered how the Colonel had enjoyed being called Maurie.

George, with a rebellious glance at his mother, said: 'Exactly what I mean. Wait.'

'By all means, wait,' Alleyn interjected, and stood up. They all jumped slightly. 'I expect,' he suggested to Lady Lacklander, 'you would like, before taking any further steps, to consult with Mr Phinn. As a matter of fact, I think it highly probable that he will suggest it himself.' Alleyn looked very straight at Lady Lacklander. 'I suggest,' he said, 'that you consider just exactly what is at stake in this matter. When a capital crime is committed, you know, all sorts of long-buried secrets are apt to be discovered. It's one of those things about homicide.' She made no kind of response to this and, after a moment, he went on: 'Perhaps when you have all come to a decision you will be kind enough to let me know. They'll always take a message at the Boy and Donkey. And now, if I may, I'll get on with my job.'

He bowed to Lady Lacklander and was about to move off when Mark said: 'I'll see you to your car, sir. Coming, Rose?'

Rose seemed to hesitate, but she went off with him, entirely, Alleyn sensed, against the wishes of the remaining three.

Mark and Rose conducted him round the east wing of the great house to the open platform in front of it. Here Fox waited in the police car. A sports model with a doctor's sticker and a more domestic car, which Alleyn took to be the Cartarettes', waited side by side. The young footman, William, emerged with a suitcase. Alleyn watched him deliver this to Fox and return to the house.

'There goes our dirty washing,' Mark said, and then looked uncomfortable.

Alleyn said: 'But you carried a tennis racket, didn't you, and Sir George, I suppose, a golf bag? May we have them too?'

Mark said: 'Yes, I see. Yes. All right, I'll get them.'

He ran up the steps and disappeared. Alleyn turned to Rose. She stared at the doorway through which Mark had gone and it was as if some kind of threat had overtaken her.

'I'm so frightened,' she said. 'I don't know why, but I'm so frightened.'

'Of what?' Alleyn asked gently.

'I don't know. One of those things, I suppose. I've never felt it before. It's as if my father was the only person that I ever really knew. And now he's gone; someone's murdered him and I feel as if I didn't properly understand anyone at all.'

Mark came back with a bag of clubs and a tennis racket in a press. 'This is it,' he said.

'You didn't have it in one of those waterproof cover things?'

'What? Oh, yes, actually, I did.'

'May I have that too, please?'

Mark made a second trip to get it and was away rather longer. 'I wasn't sure which was the one,' he said, 'but I think this is right.'

Alleyn put it with the bag and racket in the car.

Mark had caught Rose's hand in his. She hung back a little.

'Mr Alleyn,' Mark said, 'Rose and I are in the hell of a spot over this. Aren't we, darling? We're engaged, by the way.'

'You amaze me,' Alleyn said.

'Well, we are. And, of course, wherever it's humanly possible, I'm going to see that Rose is not harried and fussed. She's had a very severe shock and –'

'No, don't,' Rose said. 'Please, Mark, don't.'

Mark gazed at her, seemed to lose the thread of his subject, and then collected himself.

'It's just this,' he said. 'I feel strongly that as far as you and our two families are concerned everything ought to be perfectly straight-forward. We're under promise not to mention this and that and so we can't; but we are both very worried about the way things are going. I mean in respect of Octavius Phinn. You see, sir, we happen to know that poor old Occy Phinn had every possible reason *not* to commit this crime. Every possible reason. And if,' Mark said, 'you've guessed, as I rather think you may have, what I'm driving at, I can't help it.'

'And you agree with all this, Miss Cartarette?' Alleyn asked.

Rose held herself a little aloof now. Tear-stained and obviously exhausted, she seemed to pull herself together and shape her answer with care and difficulty.

'Mr Alleyn, my father would have been appalled if he could have known that, because he and Octavius had a row over the trout, poor Occy might be thought to – to have a motive. They'd had rows over trout for years. It was a kind of joke – nothing. And – whatever else they had to say to each other, and as you know there *was* something else, it would have made Octavius much more friendly. I promise you. You see, I know my father had gone to see Octavius.'

Alleyn said quickly: 'You mean he went to his house? Yesterday afternoon?'

'Yes. I was with him before he went and he said he was going there.'

'Did he say why? I think you spoke of some publishing business.'

'Yes. He – he – had something he wanted to show Occy.'

'What was that, can you tell us?'

'I can't tell you,' Rose said, looking wretchedly unhappy. 'I *do* know actually, but it's private. But I'm sure he went to Occy's because I saw him take the envelope out of the desk and put it in his pocket. . . . ' She put her hand to her eyes. 'But,' she said, 'where is it, then?'

Alleyn said: 'Where exactly was the envelope? In which drawer of his desk?'

'I think the bottom one on the left. He kept it locked, usually.'

'I see. Thank you. And of course Mr Phinn was not at home?'

'No. I suppose, finding him not at home, Daddy followed him down to the stream. Of course I mustn't tell you what his errand was, but if ever,' Rose said in a trembling voice, 'if ever there was an errand of – well, of mercy – Daddy's was one, yesterday afternoon.'

Rose had an unworldly face with a sort of pre-Raphael-iteish beauty; very unmodish in its sorrow and very touching.

Alleyn said gently: 'I know. Don't worry. I can promise we won't blunder.'

'How kind you are,' she said. Mark muttered undistinguishably.

As Alleyn turned away towards the police car her voice halted him. 'It must be somebody mad,' she said. 'Nobody who wasn't mad could possibly do it. Not possibly. There's somebody demented that did it for no reason at all.' She extended her hand towards him a little way, the palm turned up in a gesture of uncertainty and appeal. 'Don't you think so?' she said.

Alleyn said: 'I think you are very shocked and bewildered as well you might be. Did you sleep last night?'

'Not much. I am sorry, Mark, but I didn't take the thing you gave me. I felt I mustn't. I had to wake for him. The house felt as if he was looking for me.'

'I think it might be a good idea,' Alleyn said to Mark, 'if you drove Miss Cartarette to Hammer Farm where perhaps she will be kind enough to hunt up her own and Mrs Cartarette's garments of yesterday. Everything, please, shoes, stockings and all. And treat them, please, like egg-shell china.'

Mark said: 'As important as that?'

'The safety of several innocent persons may depend upon them.'

'I'll take care,' Mark said.

'Good. We'll follow you and collect them.'

'Fair enough,' Mark said. He smiled at Rose. 'And when that's done,' he said, 'I'm going to bring you back to Nunspardon and put my professional foot down about nembutal. Kitty'll drive herself home. Come on.'

Alleyn saw Rose make a small gesture of protest. 'I think perhaps I'll stay at Hammer, Mark.'

'No, you won't, darling.'

'I can't leave Kitty like that.'

'She'll understand. Anyway, we'll be back here before she leaves. Come on.'

Rose turned as if to appeal to Alleyn and then seemed to give up. Mark took her by the elbow and led her away.

Alleyn watched them get into the sports car and shoot off down a long drive. He shook his head slightly and let himself into the front seat beside Fox.

'Follow them, Brer Fox,' he said. 'But sedately. There's no hurry. We're going to Hammer Farm.'

On the way he outlined the general shape of his visit to Nunspardon.

'It's clear enough, wouldn't you agree,' he ended, 'what has happened about the memoirs. Take the facts as we know them. The leakage of information at Zlomce was of such importance that Sir Harold Lacklander couldn't, in what is evidently an exhaustive autobiography, ignore it. At the time of the catastrophe we learnt in the Special Branch from Lacklander himself that after confessing his treachery, young Phinn, as a result of his wigging, committed suicide. We know Lacklander died with young Phinn's name on his lips at the same time showing the greatest anxiety about the memoirs. We know that Cartarette was entrusted with the publication. We know Cartarette took an envelope from the drawer that was subsequently broken open and went to see old Phinn on what Miss Cartarette describes as an errand of mercy. When he didn't find him at home, he followed him into the valley. Finally we know that after they fell out over the poaching they had a further discussion about which, although she admits she heard it, Lady Lacklander will tell us nothing. Now, my dear Brer Fox, why should the Lacklanders or Mr

Phinn or the Cartarettes be so uncommonly touchy about all this? I don't know what you think, but I can find only one answer.'

Fox turned the car sedately into the Hammer Farm drive and nodded his head.

'Seems pretty obvious when you put it like that, Mr Alleyn, I must say. But is there sufficient motive for murder in it?'

'Who the hell's going to say what's a sufficient motive for murder? And, anyway, it may be one of a bunch of motives. Probably is. Stick to *ubi, quibus, auxiliis, quo-modo* and *quando*, Foxkin; let *cur* look after itself and blow me down if *quis* won't walk in when you're least expecting it.'

'So you always tell us, sir,' said Fox.

'All right, all right; I grow to a dotage and repeat myself. There's the lovelorn GP's car. We wait here while they hunt up the garments of the two ladies. Mrs Cartarette's will be brand new extra loud tweeds smelling of Schiaparelli and, presumably, of fish.'

'Must be a bit lonely,' Fox mused.

'Who?'

'Mrs Cartarette. An outsider, you might say, dumped down in a little place where they've known each other's pedigrees since the time they were *all* using bows and arrows. Bit lonely. More she tries to fit in, I dare say, the less they seem to take to her. More polite they get, the more uncomfortable they make her feel.'

'Yes,' Alleyn said, 'true enough. You've shoved your great fat finger into the middle of one of those uncomfortable minor tragedies that the Lacklanders of this world prefer to cut dead. And I'll tell you something else, Fox. Of the whole crowd of them, *not* excluding your girlfriend, there isn't one that wouldn't feel a *kind* of relief if she turned out to have murdered her husband.'

Fox looked startled: 'One, surely?' he ejaculated.

'No,' Alleyn insisted, with a sort of violence that was very rare with him. 'Not one. Not one. For all of them she's the intruder; the disturber; the outsider. The very effort some of them have tried to make on her behalf has added to their secret resentment. I bet you. How did you get on in Chyning?'

'I saw Dr Curtis. He's fixed up very comfortably in the hospital mortuary and was well on with the PM. Nothing new cropped up about the injuries. He says he thinks it's true enough about the fish

scales and will watch out for them and do the microscope job with
all the exhibits. The Yard's going to look up the late Sir Harold's
will and check Commander Syce's activities in Singapore. They say
it won't take long if the Navy List gives them a line on anybody in
the Service who was there at the time and has a shore job now. If
they strike it lucky they may call us back in a couple of hours. I said
the Boy and Donkey and the Chyning station to be sure of catching us.'

'Good,' Alleyn said without much show of interest. 'Hallo, listen
who's coming? Here we go.'

He was out of the car before Fox could reply and with an abrupt
change of speed began to stroll down the drive. His pipe was in his
hands and he busied himself with filling it. The object of this unexpected pantomime now pedalled into Mr Fox's ken; the village postman.

Alleyn, stuffing his pipe, waited until the postman was abreast
with him.

'Good morning,' said Alleyn.

'Morning, sir,' said the postman, braking his bicycle.

'I'll take them, shall I?' Alleyn suggested.

The postman steadied himself with one foot on the ground. 'Well,
ta,' he said, and with a vague suggestion of condolence added: 'Save
the disturbance, like, won't it, sir? Only one, anyway.' He fetched a
long envelope from his bag and held it out. 'For the deceased,' he
said in a special voice. 'Terrible sad, if I may pass the remark.'

'Indeed, yes,' Alleyn said, taking, with a sense of rising excitement the long, and to him familiar, envelope.

'Terrible thing to happen in the Vale,' the postman continued.
'What I mean, the crime, and the Colonel that highly-respected and
never a word that wasn't kindness itself. Everybody's that upset and
that sorry for the ladies. Poor Miss Rose, now! Well, it's terrible.'

The postman, genuinely distressed and at the same time consumed with a countryman's inquisitiveness, looked sideways at
Alleyn. 'You'd be a relative, I dare say, sir.'

'How very kind of you,' Alleyn said, blandly ignoring this
assumption. 'I'll tell them you sent your sympathy, shall I?'

'Ta,' said the postman. 'And whoever done it, what I mean, I'm
sure I hope they get 'em. I hear it's reckoned to be a job for the Yard

and altogether beyond the scope of Bert Oliphant which won't surprise us in the Vale, although the man's active enough when it comes to after hours at the Boy and Donkey. Well, I'll be getting along.'

When he had gone Alleyn returned to Fox.

'Look what I've got,' he said.

Fox contemplated the long envelope and, when Alleyn showed him the reverse side, read the printed legend on the flap. 'From Brierley and Bentwood, St Peter's Place, London, W.1.'

'Publishers?' said Fox.

'Yes. We've got to know what this is, Fox. The flap's very sketchily gummed down. A little tweak and – how easy it would be. Justifiable enough, too, I suppose. However, we'll go the other way round. Here comes Miss Cartarette.'

She came out followed by Mark carrying a suitcase, a tennis racket in a press and a very new golf bag and clubs.

'Here you are, sir,' Mark said. 'We had to fish the clothes out of the dry cleaner's box, but they're all present and correct. Rose said you might want her racket which is absurd, but this is it.'

'Thank you,' Alleyn said, and Fox relieved Mark of his load and put it in the police car. Alleyn showed Rose the envelope.

He said: 'This has come for your father. I'm afraid we may have to ask for all his recent correspondence and certainly for anything that comes now. They will, of course, be returned and, unless used in evidence, will be treated as strictly confidential. I'm so sorry, but that's how it is. If you wish, you may refuse to let me have this one without an official order.'

He was holding it out with the typed superscription uppermost. Rose looked at it without interest.

Mark said: 'Look, darling, I think perhaps you shouldn't – '

'Please take it,' she said to Alleyn. 'It's a pamphlet I should think.'

Alleyn thanked her and watched her go off with Mark in his car.

'Shame to take the money,' said Fox.

Alleyn said: 'I hope, if he knows, the Colonel doesn't think too badly of me.'

He opened the envelope, drew out the enclosure and unfolded it.

Colonel M. C. V. Cartarette, M.V.O., D.S.O.
Hammer Farm
Swevenings

DEAR SIR,

The late Sir Harold Lacklander, three weeks before he died, called upon me for a discussion about his memoirs, which my firm is to publish. A difficulty had arisen in respect of Chapter 7 and Sir Harold informed me that he proposed to take your advice in this matter. He added that if he should not live to see the publication of his memoirs he wished you, if you would accept the responsibility, to edit the work *in toto*. He asked me in the event of his death, to communicate directly with you and with nobody else and stressed the point that your decision in every respect must be considered final.

We have had no further instructions or communications of any kind from Sir Harold Lacklander and I now write, in accordance with his wishes, to ask if you have, in fact, accepted the responsibility of editing the memoirs, if you have received the manuscript and if you have arrived at a decision in the delicate and important matter of Chapter 7.

I shall be most grateful for an early reply. Perhaps you would give me the pleasure of lunching with me when next you are in London. If you would be kind enough to let me know the appropriate date I shall keep it free.

I am, my dear Sir,

Yours truly,
TIMOTHY BENTWOOD

'And I'll give you two guesses, Brer Fox,' Alleyn said, as he refolded the letter and returned it to its envelope, 'what constitues the delicate and important matter of Chapter 7.'

II

When Mark had turned in at the Nunspardon Lodge gates, Rose asked him to stop somewhere on the drive.

'It's no use going on,' she said. 'There's something I've got to say. Please stop.'

'Of course.' Mark pulled into an open space alongside the drive. He stopped his engine and turned to look at her. 'Now,' he said, 'tell me.'

'Mark, he doesn't think it was a tramp.'

'Alleyn?'

'Yes. He thinks it was – one of us. I know he does.'

'What exactly, darling, do you mean by "one of us"?'

Rose made a little faint circling movement of her hand. 'Someone that knew him. A neighbour. Or one of his own family.'

'You can't tell. Honestly. Alleyn's got to do his stuff. He's got to clear the decks.'

'He doesn't think it was a tramp,' Rose repeated, her voice, exhausted and drained of its colour, rose a little. 'He thinks it was one of us.'

Mark said after a long pause: 'Well, suppose, and I don't for a moment admit it – suppose at this stage he does wonder about all of us. After all –'

'Yes,' Rose said, 'after all, he has cause, hasn't he?'

'What do you mean?'

'You see what's happening to us? You're pretending to misunderstand. It's clear enough he's found out about Chapter 7.'

She saw the colour drain out of his face and cried out: 'Oh! What am I doing to us both?'

'Nothing as yet,' Mark said. 'Let's get this straight. You think Alleyn suspects that one of us – me or my father or, I suppose, my grandmother, may have killed your father because he was going to publish the amended version of my grandfather's memoirs. That it?'

'Yes.'

'I see. Well, you may be right. Alleyn may have some such idea. What I want to know now is this: You, yourself, Rose – do you – can it be possible that you, too –? No,' he said. 'Not now. I won't ask you now when you're so badly shocked. We'll wait.'

'We can't wait. I can't go on like this. I can't come back to Nunspardon and pretend the only thing that matters is for me to take a nembutal and go to sleep.'

'Rose, look at me. No, please. Look at me.'

He took her face between his hands and turned it towards him.

'My God,' he said, 'you're afraid of me.'

She did not try to free herself. Her tears ran down between his fingers. 'No,' she cried. 'No, it's not true. I can't be afraid of you, I love you.'

'Are you sure? Are you sure that somewhere in the back of your mind you're not remembering that your father stood between us and that I was jealous of your love for him? And that his death has made you an heiress? Because it has, hasn't it? And that the publication of the memoirs would have set my family against our marriage and brought disrepute upon my name? Are you sure you don't suspect me, Rose?'

'Not you. I promise. Not you.'

'Then – who? Gar? My father? Darling, can you see how fantastic it sounds when one says it aloud?'

'I know it sounds fantastic,' Rose said in despair. 'It's fantastic that anyone should want to hurt my father, but all the same, somebody has killed him. I've got to learn to get used to that. Last night somebody killed my father.'

She pulled his hands away from her face. 'You must admit,' she said, 'that takes a bit of getting used to.'

Mark said: 'What am I to do about this?'

'Nothing, you can't do anything, that's what's so awful, isn't it? You want me to turn to you and find my comfort in you, don't you, Mark? And I want it, too. I long for it. And then, you see, I can't. I can't, because there's no knowing who killed my father.'

There was a long silence. At last she heard Mark's voice. 'I didn't want to say this, Rose, but now I'm afraid I've got to. There are, after all, other people. If my grandmother and my father and I fall under suspicion – oh, yes, and Occy Phinn – isn't there somebody else who can't be entirely disregarded?'

Rose said: 'You mean Kitty, don't you?'

'I do. Yes – equally with us.'

'Don't!' Rose cried out. 'Don't! I won't listen.'

'You've got to. We can't stop now. Do you suppose I enjoy reminding myself – or you – that my father – '

'No! No, Mark! Please!' Rose said, and burst into tears.

Sometimes there exists in people who are attracted to each other a kind of ratio between the degree of attraction and the potential for irritation. Strangely, it is often the unhappiness of one that arouses an equal degree of irascibility in the other. The tear-blotted face, the obstinate misery, the knowledge that this distress is genuine and the feeling of incompetence it induces, all combine to exasperate and inflame.

Rose thought she recognized signs of this exasperation in Mark. His look darkened and he had moved away from her. 'I can't help it, Mark,' she stammered.

She heard his expostulations and reiterated arguments. She thought she could hear, too, a note of suppressed irritation in his voice. He kept saying that the whole thing had better be threshed out between them. 'Let's face it,' he said on a rising note. 'Kitty's *there*, isn't she? And what about Geoffrey Syce or Nurse Kettle? We needn't concentrate exclusively on the Lacklanders, need we?' Rose turned away. Leaning her arm on the ledge of the open window and her face on her arm, she broke down completely.

'Ah, hell!' Mark shouted. He pushed open the door, got out and began to walk angrily to and fro.

It was upon this situation that Kitty appeared, driving herself home from Nunspardon. When she saw Mark's car, she pulled up. Rose made a desperate effort to collect herself. After a moment's hesitation, Kitty got out of her car and came over to Rose. Mark shoved his hands into his pockets and moved away.

'I don't want to butt in,' Kitty said; 'but can I do anything? I mean, just say – I'll get out if I'm no use.'

Rose looked up at her and for the first time saw in her stepmother's face the signs of havoc that Kitty had been at pains to repair. For the first time it occurred to Rose that there are more ways than one of meeting sorrow and for the first time she felt a sense of fellowship for Kitty.

'How kind of you,' she said. 'I'm glad you stopped.'

'That's all right. I was sort of wondering,' Kitty went on, with an unwonted air of hesitation. 'I dare say you'd rather sort of move out. Say if you would. I'm not talking about what you said about the future but of now. I mean I dare say Mark's suggested you stay up at Nunspardon. Do, if you'd like to. I mean, I'll be OK.'

It had never occurred to Rose that Kitty might be lonely if she herself went to Nunspardon. A stream of confused recollections and ideas flooded her thoughts. She reminded herself again that Kitty would now be quite desperately hard up and that she had a responsibility towards her. She wondered if her stepmother's flirtation with Mark's father had not been induced by a sense of exclusion. She looked into the care-worn, over-painted face, and thought: 'After all, we both belonged to him.'

Kitty said awkwardly: 'Well, anyway, I'll push off.'

Suddenly Rose wanted to say: 'I'll come back with you, Kitty. Let's go home.' She fumbled with the handle of the door, but before she could speak or make a move she was aware of Mark. He had come back to the car and had moved round to her side and was speaking to Kitty.

'That's what I've been telling her,' he said. 'In fact, as her doctor, those are my orders. She's coming to Nunspardon. I'm glad you support me.'

Kitty gave him the look that she bestowed quite automatically on any presentable male. 'Well, anyway, she's in good hands,' she said. She gave them a little wave of her own hand and returned to her car.

With a feeling of desolation and remorse Rose watched her drive away.

III

On the way to Chyning Alleyn propounded his theory on Chapter 7.

'Bear in mind,' he said, 'the character of Colonel Cartarette as it emerges from the welter of talk. With the exception of Danberry-Phinn, they are all agreed, aren't they, that Cartarette was a nice chap with uncommonly high standards and a rather tender conscience? All right. For the last time let us remind ourselves that, just before he died, old Lacklander was very much bothered by something to do with Cartarette and the memoirs and that he died with the name Vic on his lips. All right. Whenever the memoirs and/or young Viccy Phinn are mentioned everybody behaves as if they're concealing the fact that they are about to have kittens. Fair enough.

Phinn and Lady Lacklander both agree that there was further discussion, after the row, between Phinn and the Colonel. Lady Lacklander flatly refuses to divulge the subject-matter and Phinn says if she won't neither will he. The Colonel left his house with the intention of calling upon Phinn with whom he had been on bad terms for a long time. Now put all those bits together, remembering the circumstances of young Phinn's death, George Lacklander's virtual admission that the memoirs exonerated young Phinn, Rose Cartarette's statement that her father's visit to old Phinn was an errand of mercy, and the contents of the publisher's letter. Put 'em together and what do you get?'

'Chapter 7 was the bit that exonerated young Phinn. Colonel Cartarette was given the responsibility of including it in this book. He couldn't decide one way or the other and took it to Mr Phinn,' Fox speculated, 'to see which way he felt about it. Mr Phinn was out fishing and the Colonel followed him up. After their dust-up the Colonel – now what does the Colonel do?'

'In effect,' Alleyn said, 'the Colonel says: "All right, you unconscionable old poacher. All right. Look what I'd come to do for you!" And he tells him about Chapter 7. And since we didn't find Chapter 7 on the Colonel we conclude that he gave it there and then to Mr Phinn. This inference is strongly supported by the fact that I saw an envelope with a wad of typescript inside, addressed in the Colonel's hand to Mr Phinn, on Mr Phinn's desk. So what, my old Foxkin, are we to conclude?'

'About Chapter 7?'

'About Chapter 7.'

'You tell me,' said Fox, with a stately smile.

Alleyn told him.

'Well, sir,' Fox said, 'it's possible. It's as good a motive as any for the Lacklanders to do away with the Colonel.'

'Except that if we're right in our unblushing conjectures, Fox, Lady Lacklander overheard the Colonel give Chapter 7 to Mr Phinn, in which case, if any of the Lacklanders were after blood, Mr Phinn's would be the more logical blood to tap.'

'Lady Lacklander may not have heard much of what they said.'

'In which case, why is she so cagey about it all now, and what did she and the Colonel talk about afterwards?'

'Ah, blast!' said Fox in disgust. 'Well, then, it may be that the memoirs and Chapter 7 and Who Stole The Secret Documents in Zlomce? haven't got anything to do with the case.'

'My feeling is that they do belong but are not of the first importance.'

'Well, Mr Alleyn, holding the view you do hold, it's the only explanation that fits.'

'Quite so. And I tell you what, Fox. Motive, as usual, is a secondary consideration. And here is Chyning and a petrol pump and here (hold on to your hat, Fox. Down, down little flutterer) is the Jolly Kettle filling up a newly painted car which I'll swear she calls by a pet name. If you can control yourself we'll pull in for some petrol. Good morning, Miss Kettle.'

'The top of the morning to you, Chief,' said Nurse Kettle turning a beaming face upon them. She slapped the back of her car as if it were a rump. 'Having her elevenses,' she said. 'First time we've met for a fortnight on account she's been having her face lifted. And how *are* you?'

'Bearing up,' Alleyn said, getting out of the car. 'Inspector Fox is turning rather short-tempered.'

Fox ignored him. 'Very nice little car, Miss Kettle,' he said.

'Araminta? She's a good steady girl on the whole,' said Nurse Kettle, remorselessly jolly. 'I'm just taking her out to see a case of lumbago.'

'Commander Syce?' Alleyn ventured.

'That's right.'

'He is completely recovered.'

'You don't say,' Nurse Kettle rejoined, looking rather disconcerted. 'And him tied up in knots last evening. Fancy!'

'He was a cot-case, I understood, when you left him round about eight o'clock last night.'

'*Very* sorry for ourselves, we were, yes.'

'And yet,' Alleyn said, 'Mr Phinn declares that at a quarter past eight, Commander Syce was loosing off arrows from his sixty-pound bow.'

Nurse Kettle was scarlet to the roots of her mouse-coloured hair. Alleyn heard his colleague struggling with some subterranean expression of sympathy.

'Well, fancy!' Nurse Kettle was saying in a high voice. 'There's 'bago for you! Now you see it, now you don't.' And she illustrated this aphorism with sharp snaps of her finger and thumb.

Fox said in an unnatural voice: 'Are you sure, Miss Kettle, that the Commander wasn't having you on? Excuse the suggestion.'

Nurse Kettle threw him a glance that might perhaps be best described as uneasily roguish.

'And why not?' she asked. 'Maybe he was. But not for the reason you mere men suppose.'

She got into her car with alacrity and sounded her horn. 'Home, John, and don't spare the horses,' she cried waggishly and drove away in what was evidently an agony of self-consciousness.

'Unless you can develop a deep-seated and obstinate malady, Brer Fox,' Alleyn said, 'you haven't got a hope.'

'A thoroughly nice woman,' Fox said, and added ambiguously: 'What a pity!'

They got their petrol and drove on to the police station.

Here Sergeant Oliphant awaited them with two messages from Scotland Yard.

'Nice work,' Alleyn said. 'Damn' quick.'

He read aloud the first message. 'Information re trout scales checked with Natural History Museum, Royal Piscatorial Society, Institute for Preservation of British Trout Streams and Dr S. K. M. Solomon, expert and leading authority. All confirm that microscopically your two trout cannot exhibit precisely the same characteristics in scales. Cartarette regarded as authority.'

'Fine!' said Inspector Fox. 'Fair enough!'

Alleyn took up the second slip of paper. 'Report,' he read, 'on the late Sir Harold Lacklander's will.' He read to himself for a minute then looked up. 'Couldn't be simpler,' he said. 'With the exception of the usual group of legacies to dependants the whole lot goes to the widow and to the son, upon whom most of it's entailed.'

'What Miss Kettle told us.'

'Exactly. Now for the third. Here we are. Report on Commander Geoffrey Syce, R.N., retired. Singapore, 1st March, 195–, to 9th April, 195–. Serving in H.M.S. –, based on Singapore. Shore duty. Activities, apart from duties. At first, noticeably quiet tastes and habits. Accepted usual invitations but spent considerable time alone, sketching. Later cohabited with a so-called Miss Kitty de Vere whom he is believed to have met at a taxi-dance. Can follow up history of de Vere if required. Have ascertained that Syce rented apartment occupied by de Vere who subsequently met and married Colonel Maurice Cartarette to whom she is believed to have been introduced by Syce. Sources: . . . '

There followed a number of names, obtained from the Navy List and a note to say that H.M.S. – being now in port it had been possible to obtain information through the appropriate sources at the 'urgent and important' level.

Alleyn dropped the chit on Oliphant's desk.

'Poor Cartarette,' he said with a change of voice, 'and if you like, poor Syce.'

'Or, from the other point of view,' Fox said, 'poor Kitty.'

IV

Before they returned to Swevenings, Alleyn and Fox visited Dr Curtis in the Chyning Hospital mortuary. It was a very small mortuary attached to a sort of pocket hospital and there was a ghastly cosiness in the close proximity of them all to the now irrevocably and dreadfully necrotic Colonel. Curtis, who liked to be thorough in his work, was making an extremely exhaustive autopsy and had not yet completed it. He was able to confirm that there had been an initial blow, followed, it seemed, rather than preceded by a puncture but that neither the blow nor the puncture quite accounted for some of the multiple injuries which were the result, he thought, of pressure. *Contre-coup*, he said, was present in a very marked degree. He would not entirely dismiss Commander Syce's arrows or Lady Lacklander's umbrella spike but he thought her shooting-stick the most likely of the sharp instruments produced. The examination of the shooting-stick for blood traces might bring them nearer to a settlement of this point. The paint rag, undoubtedly, was stained with blood which had not yet been classified. It smelt quite strongly of fish. Alleyn handed over the rest of his treasure trove.

'As soon as you can,' he said, 'do, like a good chap, get on to the fishy side of the business. Find me scales of both trout on one person's article and only on one person's and the rest will follow as the night the day.'

'You treat me,' Curtis said without malice, 'like a tympanist in a jazz band perpetually dodging from one instrument to another. I'll finish my PM, blast you, and Willy Roskill can muck about with your damned scales.' Sir William Roskill was an eminent Home Office analyst.

'I'll ring him up, now,' Alleyn said.

'It's all right, I've rung him. He's on his way. As soon as we know anything we'll ring the station. What's biting you about this case, Rory?' Dr Curtis asked. 'You're always slinging off at the "expeditious" officer and raising your cry of *festina lente*. Why the fuss and hurry? The man was only killed last night.'

'It's a pig of a case,' Alleyn said, 'and on second thoughts I'll keep the other arrow – the bloody one. If it is blood. What the hell can I carry it in? I don't want him to . . . ' He looked at the collection of objects they had brought with them. 'That'll do,' he said. He slung George Lacklander's golf bag over his shoulder, wrapped up the tip of Syce's arrow and dropped it in.

'A pig of a case,' he repeated, 'I hate its guts.'

'Why this more than another?'

But Alleyn did not answer. He was looking at the personal effects of the persons under consideration. They were laid out in neat groups along a shelf opposite the dissecting table, almost as if they were component parts of the autopsy. The Colonel's and Mr Phinn's clothes, boots, fishing gear and hat. Kitty's loud new tweed skirt and twin set. Sir George's plus-fours, stockings and shoes, Mark's and Rose's tennis clothes. Lady Lacklander's tentlike garments, her sketching kit and a pair of ancient but beautifully made brogues. Alleyn stopped, stretched out a hand and lifted one of these brogues.

'Size about four,' he said. 'They were hand-made by the best bootmaker in London in the days when Lady Lacklander still played golf. Here's her name sewn in. They've been cleaned but the soles are still dampish and . . . ' He turned the shoe over and was looking at the heel. It carried minature spikes. Alleyn looked at Fox who, without a word, brought from the end of the shelf a kitchen plate on which were laid out, as if for some starvation diet, the remains of the

Colonel's fish. The flap of skin with its fragment of an impression was carefully spread out. They waited in silence.

'It'll fit all right,' Alleyn said. 'Do your stuff, of course, but it's going to fit. And the better it fits, the less I'm going to like it.'

And with this illogical observation he went out of the mortuary.

'What *is* biting him?' Dr Curtis asked Fox.

'Ask yourself, Doctor,' Fox said. 'It's one of the kind that he's never got, as you might say, used to.'

'Like that, is it?' Dr Curtis, for the moment unmindful of his own terribly explicit job, muttered: 'I often wonder why on earth he entered the Service.'

'I've never liked to inquire,' Fox said in his plain way; 'but I'm sure I'm very glad he did. Well, I'll leave you with your corpse.'

' . . . seeing you,' Dr Curtis said absently and Fox rejoined his principal. They returned to the police station where Alleyn had a word with Sergeant Oliphant. 'We'll leave you here, Oliphant,' Alleyn said. 'Sir William Roskill will probably go straight to the hospital, but as soon as there's anything to report, he or Dr Curtis will ring you up. Here's a list of people I'm going to see. If I'm not at one of these places I'll be at another. See about applying for a warrant; we may be making an arrest before nightfall.'

''T, 't, 't,' Sergeant Oliphant clicked. 'Reely? In what name, sir? Same as you thought?'

Alleyn pointed his long forefinger at a name on the list he had given the sergeant who stared at it for some seconds, his face perfectly wooden.

'It's not positive,' Alleyn said; 'but you'd better warn your tame J.P. about the warrant in case we need it in a hurry. We'll get along with the job now. Put a call through to Brierley and Bentwood, will you, Oliphant? Here's the number. Ask for Mr Timothy Bentwood and give my name.'

He listened while Sergeant Oliphant put the call through and noticed abstractedly that he did this in a quiet and business-like manner.

Alleyn said: 'If Bentwood will play, this should mean the clearing up of Chapter 7.'

Fox raised a massive finger and they both listened to Oliphant.

'Oh yerse?' Oliphant was saying. 'Yerse? Will you hold the line, sir, while I inquire?'

'What is it?' Alleyn demanded sharply.

Oliphant placed the palm of his vast hand over the mouthpiece. 'Mr Bentwood, sir,' he said, 'is in hospital. Would you wish to speak to his secretary?'

'Damnation, blast and bloody hell!' Alleyn said. 'No, I wouldn't. Thank you, Oliphant. Come on, Fox. That little game's gone cold. We'd better get moving. Oliphant, if we can spare the time we'll get something to eat at the Boy and Donkey, but, on the way, we'll make at least one call.' His finger again hovered over the list. The sergeant followed its indication.

'At Uplands?' he said. 'Commander Syce?'

'Yes,' Alleyn said. 'Have everything laid on, and if you get a signal from me come at once with suitable assistance. It'll mean an arrest. Come on, Fox.'

He was very quiet on the way back over Watt's Hill.

As they turned the summit and approached Jacob's Cottage, they saw Mr Phinn leaning over his gate with a kitten on his shoulder.

Alleyn said: 'It might as well be now as later. Let's stop.'

Fox pulled up by the gate and Alleyn got out. He walked over to the gate and Mr Phinn blinked at him.

'Dear me, Chief Inspector,' he said, taking the kitten from his neck and caressing it, 'how very recurrent you are. Quite decimalite, to coin an adjective.'

'It's our job, you know,' Alleyn said mildly. 'You'll find we do tend to crop up.'

Mr Phinn blinked and gave a singular little laugh. 'Am I to conclude then, that I am the subject of your interest? Or are you on your way to fresh fields of surmise and conjecture? Nunspardon, for instance. Do you perhaps envisage my Lady Brobdignagia, the Dowager Tun, the Mammoth Matriarch, stealing a-tiptoe through the daisies? Or George aflame with his newly-acquired dignities, thundering through the willow grove in plus-fours. Or have the injuries a clinical character? Do we suspect the young Aesculapius with scalpel or probe? You are thinking I am a person of execrable taste, but the truth is there *are* other candidates for infamy. Perhaps we should look nearer at hand. At our elderly and intemperate

merryman of the shaft and quiver. Or at the interesting and mysterious widow with the dubious antecedents? Really, how very
footling, if you will forgive me, it all sounds, doesn't it? What can I
do for you?'

Alleyn looked at the pallid face and restless eyes. 'Mr Phinn,' he
said, 'will you let me have your copy of Chapter 7?'

The kitten screamed, opening its mouth and showing its tongue.
Mr Phinn relaxed his fingers, kissed it and put it down.

'Forgive me, my atom,' he said. 'Run to Mother.' He opened the
gate. 'Shall we go in?' he suggested, and they followed him into a
garden dotted about with rustic furniture of an offensive design.

'Of course,' Alleyn said, 'you can refuse. I shall then have to use
some other form of approach.'

'If you imagine,' Mr Phinn said, wetting his hps, 'that as far as I
am concerned this Chapter 7, which I am to suppose you have seen
on my desk but not read, is in any way incriminating, you are entirely mistaken. It constitutes, for me, what may perhaps be described as
a contramotive.'

'So I had supposed,' Alleyn said. 'But don't you think you had
better let me see it?'

There was a long silence. 'Without the consent of Lady
Lacklander,' Mr Phinn said, 'never. Not for all the sleuths in
Christendom.'

'Well,' Alleyn said, 'that's all very correct, I dare say. Would you
suggest, for the sake of argument, that Chapter 7 constitutes a sort
of confession on the part of the author? Does Sir Harold Lacklander,
for instance, perhaps admit that he was virtually responsible for the
leakage of information that tragic time in Zlomce?'

Mr Phinn said breathlessly: 'Pray, what inspires this gush of
unbridled empiricism?'

'It's not altogether that,' Alleyn rejoined with perfect good
humour. 'As I think I told you this morning, I have some knowledge
of the Zlomce affair. You tell us that the new version of Chapter 7
constitutes for you a contramotive. If this is so: if, for instance, it pro-
vides exoneration, can you do anything but welcome its publication?'

Mr Phinn said nothing.

'I think I must tell you,' Alleyn went on, 'that I shall ask the
prospective publishers for the full story of Chapter 7.'

'They have not been informed –'

'On the contrary, unknown to Colonel Cartarette, they were informed by the author.'

'Indeed?' said Mr Phinn, trembling slightly. 'If they possess any vestige of professional rectitude they will refuse to divulge the content.'

'As you do?'

'As I do. I shall refuse any information in this affair, no matter what pressure is put upon me, Inspector Alleyn.'

Mr Phinn had already turned aside when his garden gate creaked and Alleyn said quietly: 'Good morning once again, Lady Lacklander.'

Mr Phinn spun round with an inarticulate ejaculation.

She stood blinking in the sun, without expression and very slightly tremulous.

'Roderick,' said Lady Lacklander, 'I have come to confess.'

CHAPTER 10

Return to Swevenings

Lady Lacklander advanced slowly towards them.

'If that contraption of yours will support my weight, Octavius,' she said, 'I'll take it.'

They stood aside for her. Mr Phinn suddenly began to gabble: 'No, no, no! Not another word! I forbid it.'

She let herself down on a rustic seat.

'For God's sake,' Mr Phinn implored her frantically, 'hold your tongue, Lady L.'

'Nonsense, Occy,' she rejoined, panting slightly. 'Hold yours, my good fool.' She stared at him for a moment and then gave a sort of laugh.

'Good lord, you think I did it myself, do you?'

'No, no, no. What a thing to say!'

She shifted her great torso and addressed herself to Alleyn. 'I'm here, Roderick, virtually on behalf of my husband. The confession I have to offer is his.'

'At last,' Alleyn said. 'Chapter 7.'

'Precisely. I've no idea how much you think you already know or how much you may have been told.'

'By me,' Mr Phinn cried out, 'nothing!'

'Humph!' she said. 'Uncommon generous of you, Octavius.'

Mr Phinn began to protest, threw up his hands and was silent.

'There are, however, other sources,' she went on. 'I understand his wife has been kept posted.' She stared at Alleyn who thought: 'George has told Kitty Cartarette about Chapter 7 and Lady

Lacklander has found out. She thinks Kitty has told me.' He said nothing.

'You may suppose, therefore,' Lady Lacklander continued, 'that I am merely making a virtue of necessity.'

Alleyn bowed.

'It is not altogether that. To begin with, we are, as a family, under a certain obligation to you, Octavius.'

'Stop!' Mr Phinn shouted. 'Before you go on much further, before you *utter* –'

'Mr Phinn,' Alleyn cut in, breaking about three vital items of the police code in one sentence, 'if you don't stop chattering, I shall take drastic steps to make you. Shut up, Mr Phinn.'

'Yes, Occy,' Lady Lacklander said. 'I couldn't agree more. Either shut up or take yourself off, my dear fellow.' She lifted a tiny, fat hand, holding it aloft as if it was one of Mr Phinn's kittens. 'Do me the favour,' she said, 'of believing I have thought things over very carefully and be quiet.'

While Mr Phinn still hesitated, eyeing Alleyn and fingering his lips, Lady Lacklander made a brief comprehensive gesture with her short arms and said: 'Roderick, my husband was a traitor.'

II

They made a strange group, sitting there on uncomfortable rustic benches. Fox took unobtrusive notes, Mr Phinn held his head in his hands, Lady Lacklander, immobile behind the great façade of her fat, talked and talked. Cats came and went gracefully indifferent to the human situation.

'That,' Lady Lacklander said, 'is what you will find in Chapter 7.' She broke off and, after a moment, said: 'This is not going to be easy and I've no wish to make a fool of myself. Will you forgive me for a moment?'

'Of course,' Alleyn said, and they waited while Lady Lacklander, staring before her, beat her puff-ball palms on her knees and got her mouth under control. 'That's better,' she said at last. 'I can manage now.' And she went on steadily. 'At the time of the Zlomce incident my husband was in secret negotiation with a group of Prussian Fascists.

The top group: the men about Hitler a British diplomat whose name' –
her voice creaked and steadied – 'was above reproach in his own country. He was absolutely and traitorously committed to the Nazi
programme.' Alleyn saw that her eyes were bitter with tears. 'They
never found *that* out at your MI5, Roderick, did they?'

'No.'

'And yet this morning I thought that perhaps you knew.'

'I wondered. That was all.'

'So she didn't say anything.'

'She?'

'Maurice's wife. Kitty.'

'No.'

'You never know,' she muttered, 'with that sort of people what
they may do.'

'Nor,' he said, 'with other sorts either, it seems.'

A dark unlovely flush flooded her face.

'The extraordinary thing,' Mr Phinn said suddenly, 'is *why? Why*
did Lacklander do it?'

'The herrenvolk heresy?' Alleyn suggested. 'An aristocratic
Anglo-German alliance as the only alternative to war and commu-
nism and the only hope for the survival of his own class? It was a
popular heresy at that time. He wasn't alone. No doubt he was
promised great things.'

'You don't spare him,' Lady Lacklander said under her breath.

'How can I? In the new Chapter 7, I imagine, he doesn't spare
himself.'

'He repented bitterly. His remorse was frightful.'

'Yes,' Mr Phinn said. 'That is clear enough.'

'Ah, yes!' she cried out. 'Ah, yes, Occy, yes. And most of all for
the terrible injury he did your boy – most of all for that.'

'The injury?' Alleyn repeated, cutting short an attempt on
Mr Phinn's part to intervene. 'I'm sorry, Mr Phinn. We must
have it.'

Lady Lacklander said: 'Why do you try to stop me, Occy? You've
read it. You must want to shout it from the roof-tops.'

Alleyn said: 'Does Sir Harold exonerate Ludovic Phinn?'

'Of everything but carelessness.'

'I see.'

Lady Lacklander put her little fat hands over her face. It was a gesture so out of key with the general tenor of her behaviour, that it was as shocking in its way as a bout of hysteria.

Alleyn said: 'I think I understand. In the business of the railway concessions in Zlomce, was Sir Harold, while apparently acting in accordance with his instructions from the British Government, about to allow the German interest to get control?'

He saw that he was right and went on: 'And at the most delicate stage of these negotiations at the very moment where he desired above all things that no breath of suspicion should be aroused, his private secretary goes out on a Central European bender and lets a German agent get hold of the contents of the vital cable which Sir Harold had left him to decode. Sir Harold is informed by his own government of the leakage. He is obliged to put up a terrific show of Ambassadorial rage. He has no alternative but to send for young Phinn. He accuses him of such things and threatens him with such disastrous exposures, such disgrace and ruin, that the boy goes out and puts an end to it all. Was it like that?'

He looked from one to the other.

'It was like that,' Lady Lacklander said. She raised her voice as if she repeated some intolerable lesson. 'My husband writes that he drove Viccy Phinn to his death as surely as if he had killed him with his own hands. He was instructed to do so by his Nazi masters. It was then that he began to understand what he had done and to what frightful lengths his German associates could drive him. I knew, at that time, he was wretchedly unhappy, but put it down to the shock of Viccy's death and – as I, of course, thought – treachery. But the treachery, Occy, was ours and your Viccy was only a foolish and tragically careless boy.' She looked at Mr Phinn and frowned. 'Yesterday,' she said, 'after your row with Maurice over the trout, he came to me and told me he'd left a copy of the amended Chapter 7 at your house. Why haven't you produced it, Occy? Why just now did you try to stop me? Was it because –'

'Dear me, no,' Mr Phinn said very quietly, 'not from any high-flown scruples, I assure you. It was, if you will believe me, in deference to my boy's wishes. Before he killed himself, Viccy wrote to his mother and to me. He begged us to believe him innocent. He also begged us most solemnly, whatever the future might hold, never to take any action that might injure Sir Harold Lacklander.

You may not have noticed, my dear Lady L., that my foolish boy hero-worshipped your husband. We decided to respect his wishes.'

Mr Phinn stood up. He looked both old and shabby. 'I am not concerned,' he said, 'with the Lacklander conscience, the Lacklander motive, or the Lacklander remorse. I no longer desire the Lacklanders to suffer for my dear boy's death. I do not, I think, believe any more in human expiation. Now, if I may, I shall ask you to excuse me. And if you want to know what I did with Chapter 7, I burnt it to ashes, my dear Chief Inspector, half an hour ago.'

He raised his dreadful smoking-cap, bowed to Lady Lacklander, and walked into his house, followed by his cats.

Lady Lacklander stood up. She began to move towards the gate, seemed to recollect herself and paused. 'I am going to Nunspardon,' she said. Alleyn opened the gate. She went out without looking at him, got into her great car and was driven away.

Fox said: 'Painful business. I suppose the young fellow suspected what was up at the last interview. Unpleasant.'

'Very.'

'Still, as Mr Phinn says, this Chapter 7 really puts him in the clear as far as killing Colonel Cartarette is concerned.'

'Well, no,' Alleyn said.

'No?'

'Not exactly. The Colonel left Chapter 7 at Jacob's Cottage. Phinn, on his own statement, didn't re-enter the house after his row with the Colonel. He returned to the willow grove, found the body and lost his spectacles. He read Chapter 7 for the first time this morning, I fancy, by the aid of a magnifying glass.'

III

'Of course,' Fox said, as they turned into Commander Syce's drive, 'it will have been a copy. The Colonel'd never hand over the original.'

'No. My guess is: he locked the original in the bottom drawer on the left-hand side of his desk.'

'Ah! Now!' Fox said, with relish. 'That might well be.'

'In which case one of his own family or one of the Lacklanders or any other interested person has pinched it and it's probably gone up in smoke like its sister-ship. On the other hand, the bottom drawer may have been empty and the original typescript in Cartarette's bank. It doesn't very much matter, Fox. The publisher was evidently given a pretty sound idea of the alternative version by its author. He could always be called. We may not have to bring the actual text in evidence. I hope we won't.'

'What d'you reckon is the dowager's real motive in coming so remarkably clean all of a sudden?'

Alleyn said crossly: 'I've had my bellyful of motives. Take your choice, Brer Fox.'

'Of course,' Fox said, 'she's a very sharp old lady. She must have guessed we'd find out anyway.'

Alleyn muttered obscurely: 'The mixture as before. And here we go with a particularly odious little interview. Look out for squalls, Brer Fox. Gosh! See who's here!'

It was Nurse Kettle. She had emerged from the front door, escorted by Commander Syce who carried a napkin in his hand. She was about to enter her car and this process was accelerated by Commander Syce who quite obviously drew her attention to the approaching police car and then, limping to her own, opened the door and waited with some evidence of trepidation for her to get in. She did so without glancing at him and started her engine.

'She's told him,' Alleyn said crossly, 'that we've rumbled the 'bago.'

'Acting, no doubt,' Fox rejoined stiffly, 'from the kindest of motives.'

'No doubt.' Alleyn lifted his hat as Nurse Kettle, having engaged her bottom gear with some precipitance, shot past them like a leaping eland. She was extremely red in the face.

Syce waited for them.

Fox pulled up and they both got out. Alleyn slung the golf bag over his shoulder as he addressed himself to Syce.

'May we speak to you indoors somewhere?' Alleyn asked.

Without a word Syce led the way into his living-room where a grim little meal, half-consumed, was laid out on a small table in close proximity to a very dark whisky and water.

The improvised bed was still in commission. A dressing-gown was folded neatly across the foot.

'Sit down?' Syce jerked out but, as he evidently was not going to do so himself, neither Alleyn nor Fox followed his suggestion.

'What's up now?' he demanded.

Alleyn said: 'I've come to ask you a number of questions all of which you will find grossly impertinent. They concern the last occasion when you were in Singapore. The time we discussed this morning, you remember, when you told us you introduced the present Mrs Cartarette to her husband?'

Syce didn't answer. He thrust his hands into the pockets of his coat and stared out of the window.

'I'm afraid,' Alleyn said, 'I shall have to press this a little further. In a word I must ask you if you were not in fact on terms of the greatest intimacy with Miss de Vere, as she was then.'

'Bloody impertinence.'

'Well, yes. But so, when one comes to think of it, is murder.'

'What the hell are you driving at?'

'Ah!' Alleyn exclaimed with one of his very rare gestures, 'how footling all this is! You know damn' well what I'm driving at. Why should we stumble about like a couple of maladroit fencers? See here. I've information from the best possible sources that before she was married you were living with Mrs Cartarette in Singapore. You yourself have told me you introduced her to Cartarette. You came back here and found them man and wife: the last thing, so you told me, that you had intended. All right. Cartarette was murdered last night in the Bottom Meadow and there's a hole in his head that might have been made by an arrow. You gave out that you were laid by with lumbago but you were heard twanging away at your sixty-pound bow when you were supposed to be incapacitated on your bed. Now, send for your solicitor if you like and refuse to talk till he comes, but for the love of Mike don't pretend you don't know what I'm driving at.'

'Great grief!' Syce exclaimed with exactly the same inflection he had used of cats, 'I *liked* Cartarette.'

'You may have liked Cartarette, but did you love his wife?'

'Love,' Syce repeated, turning purple. 'What a word!'

'Well, my dear man – put it this way. Did she love you?'

'Look here, are you trying to make out that she egged me on or – or – I egged her on or any perishing rot of that sort! Thompson,' Commander Syce shouted angrily, 'and Bywaters, by God!'

'What put them into your head, I wonder? The coincidence that he was a seafaring man and she, poor woman, an unfaithful wife?'

'A few more cracks like that and I bloody well will send for a solicitor.'

'You *are* being difficult,' Alleyn said without rancour. 'Will you let me have the clothes you were wearing last evening?'

'What the hell for?'

'For one thing to see if Cartarette's blood is on them.'

'How absolutely piffling.'

'Well, may I have them?'

'I'm wearing them, blast it.'

'Would you mind wearing something else?'

Commander Syce fixed his intensely blue and slightly bloodshot eyes on a distant point in the landscape, and said: 'I'll shift.'

'Thank you. I see you've been using this as a bed-sitting-room during, no doubt, your attack of lumbago. Perhaps for the time being you could shift into your dressing-gown and slippers.'

Syce followed this suggestion. Little gales of whisky were wafted from him and his hands were unsteady, but he achieved his change with the economy of movement practised by sailors. He folded up the garments as they were discarded, passed a line of cord round them, made an appropriate knot and gave the bundle to Fox who wrote out a receipt for it.

Syce tied his dressing-gown cord with a savage jerk.

'No return,' Alleyn remarked, 'of the ailment?'

Syce did not reply.

Alleyn said: 'Why not tell me about it? You must know damn' well that I can't cut all this background stuff dead. Why the devil did you pretend to have lumbago last evening? Was it for the love of a lady?'

It would be inaccurate to say that Commander Syce blushed since his face, throughout the interview, had been suffused. But at this juncture it certainly darkened to an alarming degree.

'Well, *was* it?' Alleyn insisted on a note of exasperation. Fox clapped the bundle of clothes down on a table.

'I know what it's like,' Commander Syce began incomprehensibly. He waved his hand in the direction of Hammer Farm. 'Lonely as hell. Poor little Kit. Suppose she wanted security.

Natural. Ever seen that play? I believe they put it on again a year or two ago. I don't go in for poodle-faking but it was damn' true. In the end she pitched herself out of a top window, poor thing. Frozen out. County.'

'Can you mean *The Second Mrs Tanqueray?*'

'I dare say. And they'd better change their course or she'll do the same thing. Lonely. I know what it's like.'

His gaze travelled to a corner cupboard. 'You have to do something,' he said, and then eyed the tumbler on his luncheon table. 'No good offering you a drink,' he mumbled.

'None in the world, worse luck.'

'Well,' Syce said. He added something that sounded like: 'luck,' and suddenly drained the tumbler.

'As a matter of fact,' he said, 'I'm thinking of giving it up myself. Alcohol.'

'It's a "good familiar creature,"' Alleyn quoted, '"if it be well us'd."'

'That's all right as far as it goes, but what sort of a perisher,' Syce surprisingly observed, 'took the bearings? A nasty little man and a beastly liar into the bargain.'

'True enough. But we're not, after all, discussing Iago and alcohol, but you and lumbago. Why –'

'All right, I heard you before. I'm just thinking what to say.'

He went to the corner cupboard and returned with a half-empty bottle of whisky. 'I've got to think,' he said. 'It's damn' ticklish, I'd have you know.' He helped himself to a treble whisky.

'In that case wouldn't you do better without that snorter you've just poured out?'

'Think so?'

Fox, with his masterly command of the totally unexpected, said: '*She* would.'

'Who?' shouted Commander Syce, looking terrified. He drank half his whisky.

'Miss Kettle.'

'She would what?'

'Think you'd be better without it, sir.'

'She knows what to do,' he muttered, 'if she wants to stop me. Or rather she doesn't. I wouldn't tell *her,*' Commander Syce added in a deeper voice than Alleyn could have imagined him to produce, 'I wouldn't mention it to her on any account whatsoever, never.'

'I'm afraid you really are very tight.'

'It's the last time so early: in future I'm going to wait till the sun's over the yard arm. It happens to be a promise.'

'To Miss Kettle?'

'Who else?' Syce said grandly. 'Why not?'

'An admirable idea. Was it,' Alleyn asked, 'on Miss Kettle's account, by any chance, that you pretended to have lumbago last evening?'

'Who else's,' admitted Syce who appeared to have got into one unchangeable gear. 'Why not?'

'Does she know?'

Fox muttered something undistinguishable, and Syce said: 'She guessed.' He added wretchedly: 'We parted brass rags.'

'You had a row about it?' Alleyn ventured.

'Not about that. About *that.*' He indicated the tumbler. 'So I promised. After today. Yard arm.'

'Good luck to it.'

With the swiftest possible movement Alleyn whisked the arrow from the golf bag and held it under Syce's nose. 'Do you know anything about that?' he asked.

'That's mine. You took it away.'

'No. This is another of your arrows. This was found in Bottom Meadow at the foot of Watt's Hill. If you examine it you'll see there's a difference.'

Alleyn whipped the cover off the tip of the arrow. 'Look,' he said.

Syce stared owlishly at the point.

'Bloody,' he observed.

'Looks like it. What blood? Whose blood?'

Syce thrust his fingers distractedly through his thin hair. 'Cat's blood,' he said.

IV

This was the selfsame arrow, Commander Syce urged, with which some weeks ago he had inadvertently slain the mother of Thomasina Twitchett. He himself had found the body and in his distress had

withdrawn the arrow and qast it from him into the adjacent bushes.
He had taken the body to Mr Phinn who had refused to accept his
explanation and apologies and they had parted, as Commander Syce
again put it, brass rags.

Alleyn asked him if he did not consider it at all dangerous to fire
off arrows at random into his neighbours' spinneys and over them.
The reply was confused and shamefaced. More by surmise and conjecture than by any positive means, Alleyn understood Syce to suggest a close relationship between the degree of his potations and the
incontinence of his archery. At this juncture he became moros and
they could get no more out of him.

'It appears,' Alleyn said as they drove away, 'that when he's completely plastered he gets a sort of cupid fixation and looses off his
shafts blindly into the landscape with a classic disregard for their billets. It's a terrifying thought, but I suppose his immediate neighbours
have learnt to look after themselves.'

'I'm afraid,' Fox said heavily, 'she's bitten off more than she can
chew. I'm afraid so.'

'My dear old Fox, there's no end to the punishment some women
will take.'

'Of course,' Fox said dismally, 'in a manner of speaking, she's
trained for it. There is that.'

'I rather think, you know, that she's one of the sort that has got
to have somebody to cosset.'

'I dare say. Whereas barring the odd bilious turn I'm never out of
sorts. What do we do now, Mr Alleyn?' Fox continued, dismissing
the more intimate theme with an air of finality.

'We can't do anything really conclusive until we get a lead from
Curtis. But we interview George Lacklander all the same, Brer Fox,
and I hope, lay the ghost of young Ludovic Phinn. It's half-past one.
We may as well let them have their luncheon. Let's see what they
can do for us at the Boy and Donkey.'

They ate their cold meat, potato and beetroot with the concentration of men whose meals do not occur as a matter of course, but are
consumed precariously when chances present themselves. Before
they had finished Dr Curtis rang up to give an interim report. He
now plumped unreservedly for a blow on the temple with a blunt
instrument while Colonel Cartarette squatted over his catch.

Subsequent injuries had been inflicted with a pointed instrument after he lay on his side, unconscious or possibly already lifeless. The second injury had all but obliterated the first. He was unable with any certainty to name the first instrument, but the second was undoubtedly the shooting-stick. Sir William Roskill had found traces of recently shed blood under the collar of the disc. He was now checking for the blood group.

'I see,' Alleyn said. 'And the shooting-stick was used –?'

'My dear chap, in the normal way, one must suppose.'

'Yes, one must, mustn't one? Deliberately pushed home and sat on. Horrid-awful behaviour.'

'Brutal,' Dr Curtis said dispassionately.

'All the brutality in the world. Has Willy tackled the fish scales?'

'Give him time. But, yes, he's begun. No report yet?'

'We're going to Nunspardon. Telephone me if there's anything, Curtis, will you? You or Willy?'

'OK.'

Alleyn turned away from the telephone to discover Sergeant Bailey waiting for him with the air of morose detachment that meant he had something of interest to impart. He had, in fact, come from a further detailed overhaul of Colonel Cartarette's study. The bottom drawer on the left of the desk carried an identifiable fingerprint of Sir George Lacklander's.

'I checked it with his grog glass,' Bailey said, looking at his boots. 'The drawer seems to have been wiped over but a dab on the underside must have been missed or something. It's his all right.'

'Very useful,' Alleyn said.

Fox wore that expression of bland inscrutability that always seemed to grow upon him as a case approached its close. He would listen attentively to witnesses, suspects, colleagues or his chief and would presently glance up and move the focus of his gaze to some distant object of complete unimportance. This mannerism had the same effect as a change of conversation. It was as if Mr Fox had become rather pleasurably abstracted. To his associates it was a sign of a peculiar wiliness.

'Remove your attention from the far horizon, Brer Fox,' Alleyn said. 'And bring it to bear on the immediate future. We're going to Nunspardon.'

They were taken there by the Yard driver who was now released from his duties in Bottom Meadow.

As they drove past the long wall that marked the Nunspardon marches Fox began to speculate. 'Do you suppose that they throw it open to the public? They must, mustn't they? Otherwise, how do they manage these days?'

'They manage by a freak. Within the last two generations the Lacklanders have won first prizes in world lotteries. I remember because I was still in the Foreign Service when George Lacklander rang the bell in the Calcutta Sweep. In addition to that they're fantastically lucky racehorse owners and possess one of the most spectacular collections of private jewels in England which I suppose they could use as a sort of lucky dip if they felt the draught. Really, they're one of the few remaining county families who are wealthy through sheer luck.'

'Is that so?' Fox observed mildly. 'And Miss Kettle tells me they've stood high in the county for something like a thousand years. Never a scandal, she says, but then I dare say she's partial.'

'I dare say. A thousand years,' Alleyn said dryly, 'is a tidy reach even for the allegedly blameless Lacklanders.'

'Well, to Miss Kettle's knowledge there's never been the slightest hint of anything past or present.'

'When, for the love of wonder, did you enjoy this cosy chat with Nurse Kettle?'

'Last evening, Mr Alleyn. When you were in the study, you know. Miss Kettle, who was saying at the time that the Colonel was quite one of the old sort, a real gentleman and so on, mentioned that she and her ladyship had chatted on the subject only that afternoon!' Fox stopped, scraped his chin and became abstracted.

'What's up? What subject?'

'Well – er – class obligation and that style of thing. It didn't seem to amount to anything last night because at that stage no connection had been established with the family.'

'Come on.'

'Miss Kettle mentioned in passing that her ladyship had talked about the – er – the – er – as you might say the – er – principle of "*noblesse oblige*," and had let it be known she was very worried.'

'About what?'

'No particular cause was named.'

'And you're wondering now if she was worried about the prospect of an imminent debunking through Chapter 7 of the blameless Lacklanders?'

'Well, it makes you think,' Fox said.

'So it does,' Alleyn agreed as they turned into the long drive to Nunspardon.

'She being a great lady.'

'Are you reminding me of her character, her social position or what Mr Phinn calls her avoirdupois?'

'She must be all of seventeen stone,' Fox mused, 'and I wouldn't mind betting the son'll be the same at her age. Very heavy built.'

'And damn' heavy going into the bargain.'

'Mrs Cartarette doesn't seem to think so.'

'My dear man, as you have already guessed he's the only human being in the district, apart from her husband, who's sent her out any signals of any kind at all and he's sent plenty.'

'You don't reckon she's in love with him, though?'

'You never know – never. I dare say he has his ponderous attractions.'

'Ah, well,' Fox said, and with an air of freshening himself up, stared at a point some distance ahead. It was impossible to guess whether he ruminated upon the tender passion, the character of George Lacklander or the problematical gratitude of Kitty Cartarette. 'You never know,' he sighed, 'he may even be turning it over in his mind how long he ought to wait before it'll be all right to propose to her.'

'I hardly think so, and I must say I hope she's not building on it.'

'You've made up your mind, of course,' Fox said after a pause.

'Well, I have, Fox. I can only see one answer that will fit all the evidence, but unless we get the go-ahead sign from the experts in Chyning, we haven't a case. There we are again.'

They had rounded the final bend in the drive and had come out before the now familiar façade of Nunspardon.

The butler admitted them and contrived to suggest with next to no expenditure of behaviour that Alleyn was a friend of the family and

Fox completely invisible. Sir George, he said, was still at luncheon. If Alleyn would step this way he would inform Sir George. Alleyn, followed by the unmoved Fox, was shown into George Lacklander's study: the last of the studies they were to visit. It still bore, Alleyn recognized, the imprint of Sir Harold Lacklander's personality and he looked with interest at a framed caricaturé of his erstwhile chief made a quarter of a century ago when Alleyn was a promising young man in the Foreign Service. The drawing revived his memories of Sir Harold Lacklander: of his professional charm, his conformation to type, his sudden flashes of wit and his extreme sensitiveness to criticism. There was a large photograph of George on the desk and it was strange to see in it, as Alleyn fancied he could, these elements adulterated and transformed by the addition of something that was either stupidity or indifference. Stupidity? Was George, after all, such an ass? It depended, as usual, on 'what one meant' by an ass.

At this point in Alleyn's meditations, George himself, looking huffily post-prandial, walked in. His expression was truculent.

'I *should* have thought, I *must* say, Alleyn,' he said, 'that one's luncheon hour at least might be left to one.'

'I'm sorry,' Alleyn said, 'I thought you'd finished. Do you smoke between the courses, perhaps?'

Lacklander angrily pitched his cigarette into the fireplace. 'I wasn't hungry,' he said.

'In that case I am relieved that I didn't, after all, interrupt you.'

'What are you driving at? I'm damned if I like your tone, Alleyn. What do you want?'

'I want,' Alleyn said, 'the truth. I want the truth about what you did yesterday evening. I want the truth about what you did when you went to Hammer Farm last night. I want the truth, and I think I have it, about Chapter 7 of your father's memoirs. A man has been murdered. I am a policeman, and I want facts.'

'None of these matters has anything to do with Cartarette's death,' Lacklander said, and wet his lips.

'You won't persuade me of that by refusing to discuss them.'

'Have I said that I refuse to discuss them?'

'All right,' Alleyn sighed. 'Without more ado then, did you expect to find a copy of Chapter 7 when you broke open the drawer in Colonel Cartarette's desk last night?'

'You're deliberately insulting me, by God!'

'Do you deny that you broke open the drawer?'

Lacklander made a small gaping movement with his lips and an ineffectual gesture with his hands. Then, with some appearance of boldness, he said: 'Naturally, I don't do anything of the sort. I did it by – at the desire of his family. The keys seemed to be lost and there were certain things that had to be done – people to be told and all that. She didn't even know the name of his solicitors. And there were people to ring up. They thought his address book might be there.'

'In the locked drawer? The address book?'

'Yes.'

'Was it there?'

He boggled for a moment, and then said: 'No.'

'And you did this job before we arrived?'

'Yes.'

'At Mrs Cartarette's request?'

'Yes.'

'And Miss Cartarette? Was she in the search party?'

'No.'

'Was there, in fact, anything in the drawer?'

'No,' George said hardily. 'There wasn't.' His face had begun to look coarse and blank.

'I put it to you that you did not break open the drawer at Mrs Cartarette's request. It was you, I suggest, who insisted upon doing it because you were in a muck-sweat wanting to find out where the amended Chapter 7 of your father's memoirs might be. I put it to you that your relationship with Mrs Cartarette is such that you were in a position to dictate this manoeuvre.'

'No. You have no right, damn you –'

'I suggest that you are very well aware of the fact that your father wrote an amended version of Chapter 7 which was in effect a confession. In this version he stated firstly, that he himself was responsible for young Ludovic Phinn's suicide and secondly, that he himself had traitorously conspired against his own government with certain elements in the German Government. This chapter, if it were published, would throw such opprobrium upon your father's name that in order to stop its being made public, I suggest, you were prepared to go to the lengths to which you have, in fact, gone. You are an immensely vain man with a confused, indeed a fanatical sense of your family prestige. Have you anything to say to all this?'

A tremor had begun to develop in George Lacklander's hands. He glanced down at them and with an air of covering up a social blunder, thrust them into his pockets. Most unexpectedly he began to laugh, an awkward rocketing sound made on the intake of breath, harsh as a hacksaw.

'It's ridiculous,' he gasped, hunching his shoulder and bending at the waist in a spasm that parodied an ecstasy of amusement. 'No, honestly, it's too much!'

'Why,' Alleyn asked sedately, 'are you laughing?'

Lacklander shook his head and screwed up his eyes. 'I'm so sorry,' he gasped. 'Frightful of me, I know, but really!' Alleyn saw that through his almost sealed eyelids he was peeping out, wary and agitated. 'You don't mean to say you think that I –?' He waved away his uncompleted sentence with a flap of his pink freckled hand.

'– that you murdered Colonel Cartarette, were you going to say?'

'Such a notion! I mean, how? When? With what?'

Alleyn, watching his antics, found them insupportable.

'I know I shouldn't laugh,' Lacklander gabbled. 'But it's so fantastic. How? When? With what?' And through Alleyn's mind dodged a disjointed jingle. 'Quomodo? Quando? Quibus auxiliis?'

'He was killed,' Alleyn said, 'by a blow and a stab. The injuries were inflicted at about five past eight last evening. The murderer stood in the old punt. As for "with what" . . . '

He forced himself to look at George Lacklander whose face, like a bad mask, was still crumpled in a false declaration of mirth.

'The puncture,' Alleyn said, 'was made by your mothers shooting-stick and the initial blow . . . ' He saw the pink hands flex and stretch, flex and stretch. 'By a golf club. Probably a driver.'

At that moment the desk telephone rang. It was Dr Curtis for Alleyn.

He was still talking when the door opened and Lady Lacklander came in followed by Mark. They lined themselves up by George and all three watched Alleyn.

Curtis said: 'Can I talk?'

'Ah, yes,' Alleyn said airily. 'That's all right. I'm afraid I can't do anything to help you, but you can go ahead quietly on your own.'

'I suppose,' Dr Curtis's voice said very softly, 'you're in a nest of Lacklanders?'

'Yes, indeed.'

'All right. I've rung up to tell you about the scales. Willy can't find both types on any of the clothes or gear.'

'No?'

'No. Only on the rag – the paint rag.'

'Both types on that?'

'Yes. And on the punt seat.'

'Yes?'

'Yes. Shall I go on?'

'Do.'

Dr Curtis went on. Alleyn and the Lacklanders watched each other.

CHAPTER 11

Between Hammer and Nunspardon

Nurse Kettle had finished her afternoon jobs in Swevenings but before she returned to Chyning she thought she should visit the child with the abscess in the gardener's cottage at Hammer Farm. She felt some delicacy about this duty because of the calamity that had befallen the Cartarettes. Still, she could slip quietly round the house and down to the cottage without bothering anybody and perhaps the gardener's wife would have a scrap or two of mournful gossip for her about when the funeral was to take place, and what the police were doing and how the ladies were bearing up, and whether general opinion favoured an early marriage between Miss Rose and Dr Mark. She also wondered privately what, if anything, was being said about Mrs Cartarette and Sir George Lacklander, though her loyalty to The Family, she told herself, would oblige her to give a good slap down to any nonsense that was talked in *that* direction.

Perhaps her recent interview with Commander Syce had a little upset her. It had been such a bitter and unexpected disappointment to find him at high noon so distinctly the worse for wear. Perhaps it was disappointment that had made her say such astonishingly snappish things to him; or, more likely, she thought, anxiety. Because, she reflected as she drove up Watt's Hill, she *was* dreadfully anxious about him. Of course she knew very well that he had pretended to be prostrate with lumbago because he wanted her to go on visiting him and this duplicity, she had to admit, gave her a cosy feeling under her diaphragm. But Chief Detective-Inspector Alleyn would have a very different point of view about the deception; perhaps a terrifying point of view. Well, there, she thought, turning in at the Hammer Farm drive, it was no good at her age getting the flutters. In her simple snobbishness she comforted herself with the thought that 'Handsome Alleyn,' as the evening papers called him, was the Right Sort by which Nurse Kettle meant the Lacklander as opposed to the Kettle or Fox or Oliphant sort or, she was obliged to add to herself, the Kitty Cartarette sort. As this thought occurred to her she compressed her generous lips. The memory had arisen of Commander Syce trying half-heartedly to conceal a rather exotic watercolour of Kitty Cartarette. It was a memory that, however much Nurse Kettle might try to shove it out of sight, recurred with unpleasant frequency.

By this time she was out of the car and stumping round the house by a path that ran down to the gardener's cottage. She carried her bag and looked straight before her and she quite jumped when she heard her name called. 'Hallo, there! Nurse Kettle!'

It was Kitty Cartarette sitting out on the terrace with a tea-table in front of her. 'Come and have some,' she called.

Nurse Kettle was dying for a good cup of tea and what was more, she had a bone to pick with Kitty Cartarette. She accepted and presently was seated before the table.

'You pour out,' Kitty said. 'Help yourself.'

She looked exhausted and had made the mistake of over-painting her face. Nurse Kettle asked her briskly if she had had any sleep.

'Oh, yes,' she said, 'doped myself up to the eyebrows last night, but you don't feel so good after it, do you?'

'You certainly do *not*. You want to be careful about that sort of thing, you know, dear.'

'Ah, what the hell!' Kitty said impatiently, and lit a cigarette at the stub of her old one. Her hands shook. She burnt her finger and swore distractedly.

'Now, then,' Nurse Kettle said, making an unwilling concession to the prompting of her professional conscience. 'Steady.' And thinking it might help Kitty to talk, she asked: 'What have you been doing with yourself all day, I wonder?'

'Doing? God, I don't know. This morning for my sins I had to go over to Lacklanders'.'

Nurse Kettle found this statement deeply offensive in two ways. Kitty had commonly referred to the Lacklanders as if they were shopkeepers. She had also suggested that they were bores.

'To Nunspardon?' Nurse Kettle said, with refinement. 'What a lovely old home it is! A show place if ever there was one.' And she sipped her tea.

'The *place* is all right,' Kitty muttered under her breath.

This scarcely veiled slight upon the Lacklanders angered Nurse Kettle still further. She began to wish that she had not accepted tea from Kitty. She replaced her cucumber sandwich on her plate and her cup and saucer on the table.

'Perhaps,' she said, 'you prefer Uplands.'

Kitty stared at her. *'Uplands?'* she repeated, and after a moment's consideration she asked without any great display of interest: 'Here! What are you getting at?'

'I thought,' Nurse Kettle said, with mounting colour, 'you might find the company at Uplands more to your taste than the company at Nunspardon.'

'Geoff Syce?' Kitty gave a short laugh. 'God, that old bit of wreckage! Have a heart!'

Nurse Kettie's face was scarlet. 'If the Commander isn't the man he used to be,' she said, 'I wonder whose fault it is.'

'His own, I should think,' Kitty said indifferently.

'Personally, I've found it's more often a case of *cherchez,*' Nurse Kettle said carefully, *'la femme.'*

'What?'

'When a nice man takes to solitary drinking, it's generally because some woman's let him down.'

Kitty looked at her guest with the momentarily deflected interest of a bitter preoccupation. 'Are you suggesting I'm the woman in this case?' she asked.

'I'm not suggesting anything. But you knew him out in the East, I believe?' Nurse Kettle added, with a spurious air of making polite conversation.

'Oh, yes,' Kitty agreed contemptuously. 'I knew him all right. Did he tell you? Here, what *has* he told you?' she demanded and unexpectedly there was a note of something like desperation in her voice.

'Nothing, I'm sure, that you could take exception to; the Commander, whatever you like to say, *is* a gentleman.'

'How can you be such a fool,' Kitty said drearily.

'Well, really!'

'Don't talk to me about gentlemen. I've had them, thank you. If you ask me it's a case of the higher you go the fewer. Look,' Kitty said with savagery, 'at George Lacklander.'

'Tell me this,' Nurse Kettle cried out, 'did he love you?'

'Lacklander?'

'No.' She swallowed and with dignity corrected Kitty. 'I was referring to the Commander.'

'You talk like a kid. Love!'

'*Honestly!*'

'Look!' Kitty said, 'you don't know anything. Face it: you don't know a single damn' thing. You haven't got a clue.'

'Well, I must say! You can't train for nursing I'll have you know –'

'Oh, well, all right. OK. From that point of view. But from my point of view, honestly, you have no idea.'

'I don't know what we're talking about,' Nurse Kettle said in a worried voice.

'I bet you don't.'

'The Commander . . . ' She stopped short, and Kitty stared at her incredulously.

'Do I see,' Kitty asked, 'what I think I see? You don't tell me you and Geoff Syce . . . God, that's funny!'

Words, phrases, whole speeches suddenly began to pour out of Nurse Kettle. She had been hurt in the most sensitive part of her emotional anatomy and her reflex action was surprising. She scarcely knew herself what she said. Every word she uttered was spoken in defence of something that she would have been unable to define. It is possible that Nurse Kettle, made vulnerable by her feeling for Commander Syce – a feeling that in her cooler moments she would have classed as 'unsuitable' – found in Kitty Cartarette's contempt an implicit threat to what Lady Lacklander had called her belief in degree. In Kitty, over-painted, knowledgeable, fantastically 'Not-quite,' Nurse Kettle felt the sting of implied criticism. It was as if, by her very existence, Kitty Cartarette challenged the hierarchy that was Nurse Kettle's symbol of perfection.

'– so you've no business,' she heard herself saying, 'you've no business to be where you are and behave the way you're behaving. I don't care what's happened. I don't care how *he* felt about you in Singapore or wherever it was. That was *his* business. I don't care.'

Kitty had listened to this tirade without making any sign that she thought it exceptional. Indeed, she scarcely seemed to give it her whole attention but suffered it with an air of brooding discontent. When at last Nurse Kettle ran out of words and breath, Kitty turned and stared abstractedly at her.

'I don't know why you're making such a fuss,' she said. 'Is he game to marry you?'

Nurse Kettle felt dreadful. 'I wish I hadn't said anything,' she muttered. 'I'm going.'

'I suppose he might like the idea of being dry-nursed. *You've* nothing to moan about. Suppose I was friends with him in Singapore? What of it? Go right ahead. Mix in with the bloody county and I hope you enjoy yourself.'

'*Don't* talk about them like that,' Nurse Kettle shouted. 'Don't do it! You know nothing about them. You're ignorant. I always say they're the salt of the earth.'

'Do you!' With methodical care Kitty moved the tea-tray aside as if it prevented her in some way from getting at Nurse Kettle. 'Listen,' she continued, holding the edges of the table and leaning forward, 'listen to me. I asked you to come and sit here because I've got to talk and I thought you might be partly human. I didn't know you were a yes-girl to this gang of fossils. God! You make me sick! What have they got, except money and snob-value, that you haven't got?'

'Lots,' Nurse Kettle declaimed stoutly.

'Like hell, they have! No, listen. Listen! OK, I lived with your boyfriend in Singapore. He was bloody dull but I was in a bit of a jam, and it suited us both. OK, he introduced me to Maurie. OK, he did it like they do: 'look what I've found,' and sailed away in his great big boat and got the shock of his life when he came home and found me next door as Mrs Maurice Cartarette. So what does he do? He couldn't care less what happened to *me*, of course, but could he be just ordinary-friendly and give me a leg up with these survivals from the Ice Age? Not he! He shies off as if I was a nasty smell and takes to the bottle. Not that he wasn't pretty expert at that before.'

Nurse Kettle made as if to rise, but Kitty stopped her with a sharp gesture. 'Stay where you are,' she said. 'I'm talking. So here I was. Married to a – I don't know what – the sort they call a nice chap. Too damn' nice for me. I'd never have pulled it off with him in Singapore if it hadn't been he was lonely and missing Rose. He couldn't bear not to have Rose somewhere about. He was a real baby, though, about other women: more like a mother's darling than an experienced man. You had to laugh sometimes. He wasn't my cup of tea, but I was down to it and, anyway, his sort owed me something.'

'Oh, dear!' Nurse Kettle lamented under her breath. 'Oh, dear, dear, dear!' Kitty glanced at her and went on.

'So how did it go? We married and came here, and he started writing some god-awful book, and Rose and he sat in each other's pockets and the county called. Yes, they called, all right, talking one language to each other and another one to me. Old Occy Phinn, as mad as a meat-axe and doesn't even keep himself clean. The Fat Woman of Nunspardon who took one look at me and then turned polite for the first time in history. Rose, trying so hard to be nice, it's a wonder she didn't rupture something. The parson and his wife and half a dozen women dressed in tweed sacks and felt buckets with faces like the backside of a mule. My God, what have they *got?* They aren't fun, they aren't gay, they don't *do* anything and they look like the wreck of the schooner *Hesperus*. Talk about a living death! And me! Dumped like a sack and meant to be grateful!'

'You don't understand,' Nurse Kettle began and then gave it up. Kitty had doubled her left hand into a fist and was screwing it into the palm of the right, a strangely masculine gesture at odds with her enamelled nails.

'Don't!' Nurse Kettle said sharply. 'Don't do that.'

'Not one of them, not a damn' one was what you might call friendly.'

'Well, dear me, I must say! What about Sir George!' Nurse Kettle cried, exasperated and rattled into indiscretion.

'George! George wanted what they all want and now things have got awkward he doesn't want that. George! George, the umpteenth baronet, is in a muck-sweat. George can't think,' Kitty said in savage mimicry, 'what people might not be saying. He told me so himself! If you knew what I know about George . . . ' Her face, abruptly, was as blank as a shuttered house. 'Everything,' she said, 'has gone wrong. I just don't have the luck.'

All sorts of notions, scarcely comprehensible to herself, writhed about in the mid-region of Nurse Kettle's thoughts. She was remind-ed of seaweed in the depths of a marine pool. Monstrous revelations threatened to emerge and were suppressed by a sort of creaming over of the surface of her mind. She wanted to go away from Kitty Cartarette before any more was done to her innocent idolatries, and yet found herself unable to make the appropriate gestures of depar-ture. She was held in thrall by a convention. Kitty had been talking dismally for some time and Nurse Kettle had not listened. She now caught a desultory phrase.

'Their fault!' Kitty was saying. 'You can say what you like, but whatever has happened is their fault.'

'No, no, no!' Miss Kettle cried out, beating her short scrubbed hands together. 'How can you think that! You terrify me. What are you suggesting?'

II

'What are you suggesting?' George Lacklander demanded as Alleyn at last put down the receiver. 'Who have you been speaking to? What did you mean by what you said to me just now – about –' he looked round at his mother and son an instrument,' he said.

Lady Lacklander said: 'George, I don't know what you and Roderick have been talking about, but I think it's odds on that you'd better hold your tongue.'

'I'm sending for my solicitor.'

She grasped the edge of the desk and let herself down into a chair. The folds of flesh under her chin began to tremble. She pointed at Alleyn.

'Well, Rory,' she demanded, 'what is all this? What are you sug-gesting?'

Alleyn hesitated for a moment, and then said: 'At the moment, I suggest that I see your son alone.'

'No.'

Mark looking rather desperate said: 'Gar, don't you think it might be better?'

'No,' she jabbed her fat finger at Alleyn. 'What have you said and what were you going to say to George?'

'I told him that Colonel Cartarette was knocked out by a golf club. I'll now add for the information of you all, since you choose to stay here, that he was finally killed by a stab through the temple made by your shooting-stick, Lady Lacklander. Your paint rag was used to wipe the scales of two trout from the murderer's hands. The first blow was made from the punt. The murderer in order to avoid being seen from Watt's Hill, got into the punt and slid down the stream using the long mooring rope as you probably did when you yourself sketched from the punt. The punt, borne by the current, came to rest in the little bay by the willow grove and the murderer stood in it idly swinging a club at the daisies growing on the edge of the bank. This enemy of the Colonel's was so well known to him that he paid little attention; said something perhaps about the trout he had caught and went on cutting grass to wrap it in. Perhaps the last thing he saw was the shadow of the club moving swiftly across the ground. Then he was struck on the temple. We think there was a return visit with your shooting-stick, Lady Lacklander, and that the murderer quite deliberately used the shooting-stick on Colonel Cartarette as you used it this morning on your garden path. Placed it over the bruised temple and sat on it. What did you say? Nothing? It's a grotesque and horrible thought, isn't it? We think that on getting up and releasing the shooting-stick there was literally a slip. A stumble, you know. It would take quite a bit of pulling out. There was a backward lunge. A heel came down on the Colonel's trout. The fish would have slid away, no doubt, if it had not been lying on a sharp triangular stone. It was trodden down and, as it were, transfixed on the stone. A flap of skin was torn away and the foot, instead of sliding off, sank in and left an impression. An impression of the spiked heel of a golf shoe.'

George Lacklander said in an unrecognizable voice: 'All this is conjecture!'

'No,' Alleyn said, 'I assure you. Not conjecture.' He looked at Lady Lacklander and Mark. 'Shall I go on?'

Lady Lacklander, using strange uncoordinated gestures, fiddled with the brooches that, as usual, were stuck about her bosom. 'Yes,' she said. 'Go on.'

Mark, who throughout Alleyn's discourse, had kept his gaze fixed on his father, said: 'Go on. By all means. Why not?'

'Right,' Alleyn said. 'Now the murderer was faced with evidence of identity. One imagines the trout glistening with a clear spiked heel mark showing on its hide. It wouldn't do to throw it into the stream or the willow grove and run away. There lay the Colonel with his hands smelling of fish and pieces of cut grass all round him. For all his murderer knew, there might have been a witness to the catch. This, of course, wouldn't matter as long as the murderer's identity was unsuspected. But there is a panic sequel to most crimes of violence and it is under its pressure that the fatal touch of over-cleverness usually appears. I believe that while the killer stood there, fighting down terror, the memory of the Old 'Un lying on Bottom Bridge, arose. Hadn't Danberry-Phinn and the Colonel quarrelled loudly, repeatedly and vociferously – quarrelled that very afternoon over the Old 'Un? Why not replace the Colonel's catch with the fruits of Mr Phinn's poaching tactics and drag, not a red-herring, but a whacking great trout across the trail? Would that not draw attention towards the known enemy and away from the secret one? So there was a final trip in the punt. The Colonel's trout was removed and the Old 'Un substituted. It was at this juncture that Fate, in the person of Mrs Thomasina Twitchett appeared to come to the murderer's aid.'

'For God's sake,' George Lacklander shouted, 'stop talking . . . ' He half-formed an extremely raw epithet, broke off and muttered something indistinguishable.

'Who are you talking about, Rory?' Lady Lacklander demanded. 'Mrs *Who*?'

'Mr Phinn's cat. You will remember Mrs Cartarette told us that in Bottom Meadow she came upon a cat with a half-eaten trout. We have found the remains. There is a triangular gash corresponding with the triangular flap of skin torn off by the sharp stone, and as if justice of nemesis or somebody had assuaged the cat's appetite at the crucial moment, there is also a shred of skin bearing the unmistakable mark of part of a heel and the scar of a spike.'

'But can all this . . . ' Mark began. 'I mean, when you talk of correspondence – '

'Our case,' Alleyn said, 'will, I assure you, rest upon scientific evidence of an unusually precise character. At the moment I'm giving you the sequence of events. The Colonel's trout was bestowed upon the cat. Lady Lacklander's paint rag was used to clean the spike of the shooting-stick and the murderer's hands. You may remember, Dr Lacklander, that your grandmother said she had put all her painting gear tidily away but you, on the contrary, said you found the rag caught up in a briar bush.'

'You suggest then,' Mark said evenly, 'that the murder was done some time between ten to eight when my grandmother went home and a quarter-past eight when I went home.' He thought for a moment and then said: 'I suppose that's quite possible. The murderer might have heard or caught sight of me, thrown down the rag in a panic and taken to the nearest cover only to emerge after I'd picked up the sketching gear and gone on my way.'

Lady Lacklander said after a long pause: 'I find that a horrible suggestion. Horrible.'

'I dare say,' Alleyn agreed dryly. 'It was an abominable business after all.'

'You spoke of scientific evidence,' Mark said.

Alleyn explained about the essential dissimilarities in individual fish scales. 'It's all in Colonel Cartarette's book,' he said, and looked at George Lacklander. 'You had forgotten that perhaps.'

'Matter of fact, I – ah – I don't know that I ever read poor old Maurice's little book.'

'It seems to me to be both charming,' Alleyn said, 'and instructive. In respect of the scales it is perfectly accurate. A trout's scales, the Colonel tells us, are his diary in which his whole life-history is recorded for those who can read them. Only if two fish have identical histories will their scales correspond. Our two sets of scales, luckily, are widely dissimilar. There is Group A; the scales of a nine-or ten-year-old fish who has lived all his life in one environment. And there is Group B, belonging to a smaller fish who, after a slow growth of four years, changed his environment, adopted possibly a sea-going habit, made a sudden spurt of growth and was very likely a newcomer to the Chyne. You will see where this leads us, of course?'

'I'm damned if I do,' George Lacklander said.

'Oh, but, yes, surely. The people who, on their own and other evidence are known to have handled one fish or the other are Mr Phinn, Mrs Cartarette and the Colonel himself. Mr Phinn caught the Old 'Un, Mrs Cartarette tells us she tried to take a fish away from Thomasina Twitchett. The Colonel handled his own catch and refused to touch the Old 'Un. Lady Lacklander's paint rag with the traces of both types of fish-scales, tells us that somebody, we believe the murderer, handled both fish. The further discovery of minute bloodstains tells us that the spike of the shooting-stick was twisted in the rag after being partially cleaned in the earth. If, therefore, with the help of the microscope we could find scales from both fish on the garments of any one of you, that one will be Colonel Cartarette's murderer. That,' Alleyn said, 'was our belief.'

'Was?' Mark said quickly and Fox, who had been staring at a facetious Victorian hunting print, refocused his gaze on his senior officer.

'Yes,' Alleyn said. 'The telephone conversation I have just had was with one of the Home Office men who are looking after the pathological side. It is from him that I got all this expert's stuff about scales. He tells me that on none of the garments submitted are there scales of both types.'

The normal purplish colour flooded back into George Lacklander's face. 'I said from the beginning,' he shouted, 'it was some tramp. Though why the devil you had to – to' (he seemed to hunt for a moderate word) 'to put us through hoops like this . . . ' His voice faded. Alleyn had lifted his hand. 'Well?' Lacklander cried out. 'What is it? What the hell is it? I beg your pardon, Mama.'

Lady Lacklander said automatically: 'Don't be an ass, George.'

'I'll tell you,' Alleyn said, 'exactly what the pathologist has found. He has found traces of scales where we expected to find them: on the Colonel's hands and the edge of one cuff, on Mr Phinn's coat and knickerbockers and, as she warned us, on Mrs Cartarette's skirt. The first of these traces belongs to Group B and the other two to Group A. Yes?' Alleyn said, looking at Mark who had begun to speak and then stopped short.

'Nothing,' Mark said. 'I – no, go on.'

'I've almost finished. I've said that we think the initial blow was made by a golf club probably a driver. I may as well tell you at once that so far none of the clubs has revealed any trace of blood. On the other hand, they have all been extremely well cleaned.'

George said: 'Naturally. My chap does mine.'

'When it comes to shoes, however,' Alleyn went on, 'it's a different story. They, too, have been well cleaned. But in respect of the right foot of a pair of golfing shoes there is something quite definite. The pathologist is satisfied that the scar left on the Colonel's trout was undoubtedly made by the spiked heel of this shoe.'

'It's a bloody lie!' George Lacklander bawled out. 'Who are you accusing? Whose shoe?'

'It's a hand-made job. Size four. Made, I should think, as long as ten years ago. From a very old, entirely admirable and hideously expensive bootmaker in the Burlington Arcade. It's your shoe, Lady Lacklander.'

Her face was too fat to be expressive. She seemed merely to stare at Alleyn in a meditative fashion, but she had gone very pale. At last she said without moving: 'George, it's time to tell the truth.'

'That,' Alleyn said, 'is the conclusion I hoped you would come to.'

III

'What are you suggesting?' Nurse Kettle repeated and then, seeing the look in Kitty's face, she shouted: 'No! Don't tell me!'

But Kitty had begun to tell her. 'It's each for himself in their world,' she said, 'just the same as in anybody else's. If George Lacklander dreams he can make a monkey out of me he's going to wake up in a place where he won't have any more funny ideas. What about the old family name then! Look! Do you know what he gets me to do? Break open Maurice's desk because there's something Maurie was going to make public about old Lacklander and George wants to get in first. And when it isn't there he asks me to find out if it was on the body. Me! And when I won't take that one on, what does he say?'

'I don't know. Don't tell me!'

'Oh, yes, I will. You listen to this and see how you like it. After all the fun and games! Teaching me how to swing . . . ' She made a curious little retching sound in her throat and looked at Nurse Kettle with a kind of astonishment. 'You know,' she said. 'Golf. Well, so what does he do? He says, this morning, when he comes to the car with me, he says he thinks it will be better if we don't see much of each other.' She suddenly flung out a string of adjectives that Nurse Kettle would have considered unprintable. 'That's George Lacklander for you,' Kitty Cartarette said.

'You're a wicked woman,' Nurse Kettle said. 'I forbid you to talk like this. Sir George may have been silly and infatuated. I dare say you've got what it takes, as they say, and he's a widower and I always say there's a trying time for gentlemen just as there is – but that's by the way. What I mean: if he's been silly it's you that's led him on,' Nurse Kettle said, falling back on the inexorable precepts of her kind. 'You caught our dear Colonel and not content with that, you set your cap at poor Sir George. You don't mind who you upset or how unhappy you make other people. I know your sort. You're no good. You're no good at all. I shouldn't be surprised if you weren't responsible for what's happened. Not a scrap surprised.'

'What the hell do you mean?' Kitty whispered. She curled back in her chair and staring at Nurse Kettle she said: 'You with your poor Sir George! Do you know what I think about your poor Sir George? I think he murdered your poor dear Colonel, Miss Kettle.'

Nurse Kettle sprang to her feet. The wrought-iron chair rocked against the table. There was a clatter of china and a jug of milk overturned into Kitty Cartarette's lap.

'How dare you!' Nurse Kettle cried out. 'Wicked! Wicked! *Wicked!*' She heard herself grow shrill and in the very heat of her passion she remembered an important item in her code: Never Raise the Voice. So although she would have found it less difficult to scream like a train she did contrive to speak quietly. Strangely commonplace phrases emerged and Kitty, slant-eyed, listened to them. 'I would advise you,' Nurse Kettle quavered, 'to choose your words. People can get into serious trouble passing remarks like that.' She achieved an appalling little laugh. 'Murdered the Colonel!' she said, and her voice wobbled desperately. 'The idea! If it wasn't so dreadful it'd be funny. With what may I ask? And how?'

Kitty, too, had risen and milk dribbled from her ruined skirt to the terrace. She was beside herself with rage.

'How?' she stammered. 'I'll tell you how and I'll tell you with what. With a golf club and his mother's shooting-stick. That's what. Just like a golf ball it was. Bald and shining. Easy to hit. Or an egg. Easy – '

Kitty drew in her breath noisily. Her gaze was fixed not on Nurse Kettle, but beyond Nurse Kettle's left shoulder. Her face was stretched and stamped with terror. It was as if she had laid back her ears. She was looking down the garden towards the spinney.

Nurse Kettle turned.

The afternoon was far advanced and the men who had come up through the spinney cast long shadows across the lawn, reaching almost to Kitty herself. For a moment she and Alleyn looked at each other and then he came forward. In his right hand he carried a pair of very small old-fashioned shoes: brogues with spikes in the heels.

'Mrs Cartarette,' Alleyn said, 'I am going to ask you if when you played golf with Sir George Lacklander he lent you his mother's shoes. Before you answer me I must warn you – '

Nurse Kettle didn't hear the usual warning. She was looking at Kitty Cartarette in whose face she saw guilt itself. Before this dreadful symptom her own indignation faltered and was replaced as it were professionally by a composed, reluctant and utterly useless compassion.

CHAPTER 12

Epilogue

'George,' Lady Lacklander said to her son, 'we shall, if you please, get this thing straightened out. There must be no reservations before Mark or' – she waved her fat hand at a singularly still figure in a distant chair – 'or Octavius. Everything will come out later on. We may as well know where we are now, among ourselves. There must be no more evasions.'

George looked up, and muttered: 'Very well, Mama.'

'I knew, of course,' his mother went on, 'that you were having one of your elephantine flirtations with this wretched unhappy creature. I was afraid that you had been fool enough to tell her about your father's memoirs and all the fuss over Chapter 7. What I must know, now, is how far your affair with her may be said to have influenced her in what she did.'

'My God!' George said. 'I don't know.'

'Did she hope to marry you, George? Did you say things like: "If only you were free" to her?'

'Yes,' George said, 'I did.' He looked miserably at his mother, and added: 'You see, she wasn't. So it didn't seem to matter.'

Lady Lacklander snorted but not with her usual brio. 'And the memoirs? What did you say to her about them?'

'I just told her about that damned Chapter 7. I just said that if Maurice consulted her I hoped she'd sort of weigh in on our side. And I . . . When that was no use – I – I said – that if he did publish, you know, it'd make things so awkward between the families that we – well –'

'All right. I see. Go on.'

'She knew he had the copy of Chapter 7 when he went out. She told me that – afterwards – this morning. She said she couldn't ask the police about it, but she knew he'd taken it.'

Lady Lacklander moved slightly. Mr Phinn made a noise in his throat.

'Well, Occy?' she said.

Mr Phinn, summoned by telephone and strangely acquiescent, said: 'My dear Lady L., I can only repeat what I've already told you, had you all relied on my discretion, as I must acknowledge Cartarette did, there would have been no cause for anxiety on any of your parts over Chapter 7.'

'You've behaved very handsomely, Occy.'

'No, no,' he said. 'Believe me, no.'

'Yes, you have. You put us to shame. Go on, George.'

'I don't know that there's anything more. Except – '

'Answer me this, George. Did you suspect her?'

George put his great elderly hand across his eyes and said: 'I don't know, Mama. Not at once. Not last night. But this morning. She came by herself, you know. Mark called for Rose. I came downstairs and found her in the hall. It seemed queer. As if she'd been doing something odd.'

'From what Rory tells us she'd been putting my shoes that you'd lent her without my leave, in the downstairs cloakroom,' Lady Lacklander said grimly.

'I am completely at a loss,' Mr Phinn said suddenly.

'Naturally you are, Occy.' Lady Lacklander told him about the shoes. 'She felt of course that she had to get rid of them. They're the ones I wear for sketching when I haven't got a bad toe and my poor fool of a maid packed them up with the other things. Go on, George.'

'Later on, after Alleyn had gone and you went indoors, I talked to her. She was sort of different,' said poor George. 'Well, damned hard. Sort of almost suggesting – well, I mean it wasn't exactly the thing.'

'I wish you would contrive to be more articulate. She suggested that it wouldn't be long before you'd pay your addresses?'

'Er – er – '

'And then?'

'I suppose I looked a bit taken aback. I don't know what I said. And then – it really was pretty frightful – she sort of began, not exactly hinting but – well – '

'Hinting,' Lady Lacklander said, 'will do.'

' – that if the police found Chapter 7 they'd begin to think that I – that we – that – '

'Yes, George. We understand. Motive.'

'It really was frightful. I said I thought it would be better if we didn't sort of meet much. It was just that I suddenly felt I couldn't. Only that, I assure you, Mama. I assure you, Octavius.'

'Yes, yes,' they said. 'All right, George.'

'And then, when I said that, she suddenly looked,' George said this with an unexpected flash, 'like a snake.'

'And you, my poor boy,' his mother added, 'looked, no doubt, like the proverbial rabbit.'

'I feel I've behaved like one, anyway,' George rejoined with a unique touch of humour.

'You've behaved very badly, of course,' his mother said without rancour. 'You've completely muddled your values. Just like poor Maurice himself, only he went still further. You led a completely unscrupulous trollop to suppose that if she was a widow you'd marry her. You would certainly have bored her even more than poor Maurice, but Occy will forgive me if I suggest that your title and your money and Nunspardon offered sufficient compensation. You may, on second thoughts, even have attracted her, George,' his mother added. 'I mustn't, I suppose, underestimate your simple charms.' She contemplated her agonized son for a few minutes and then said: 'It all comes to this, and I said as much to Kettle a few days ago: we can't afford to behave shabbily, George. We've got to stick to our own standards, such as they are, and we daren't muddle our values. Let's hope Mark and Rose between them will pick up the pieces.' She turned to Mr Phinn. 'If any good has come out of this dreadful affair, Occy,' she said, 'it is this. You have crossed the Chyne after I don't know how many years and paid a visit to Nunspardon. God knows we have no right to expect it. We can't make amends, Occy. We can't pretend to try. And there it is. It's over, as they say nowadays, to you.' She held out her hand and Mr Phinn after a moment's hesitation came forward to take it.

II

'You see, Oliphant,' Alleyn said with his customary air of diffidence, 'at the outset it tied up with what all of you told me about the Colonel himself. He was an unusually punctilious man. "Oddly formal," the Chief Constable said, "and devilishly polite, especially with people he didn't like or had fallen out with." He had fallen out with the Lacklanders. One couldn't imagine him squatting on his haunches and going on with his job if Lacklander or his mother turned up in the punt. Or old Phinn with whom he'd had a flaring row. Then, as you and Gripper pointed out, the first injury had been the sort of blow that is struck by a quarryman on a peg projecting from a cliff face at knee-level, or by an underhand service. Or, you might have added, by a golfer. It seemed likely, too, that the murderer knew the habit of the punt and the contra-current of the Chyne, and the fact that where the punt came to rest in the willow grove bay, it was completely masked by trees. You will remember that we found one of Mrs Cartarette's distinctive yellow hairpins in the punt in close association with a number of cigarette butts, some with lipstick and some not.'

'Ah,' Sergeant Oliphant said. 'Dalliance, no doubt.'

'No doubt. When I floated down the stream into the little bay and saw how the daisy heads had been cut off and where they lay, I began to see also, a figure in the punt idly swinging a club: a figure so familiar to the Colonel that after an upward glance and a word of greeting, he went on cutting grass for his fish. Perhaps, urged by George Lacklander, she asked her husband to suppress the alternative version to Chapter 7 and perhaps he refused. Perhaps Lacklander, in his infatuation, had told her that if she was free he'd marry her. Perhaps anger and frustration flooded suddenly up to her savage little brain and down her arms into her hands. There was that bald head, like an immense exaggeration of the golf balls she had swiped at under Lacklander's infatuated tuition. She had been slashing idly at the daisies, now she made a complete back swing and in a moment her husband was curled up on the bank with the imprint of her club on his temple. From that time on she became a murderess fighting down her panic and frantically engaged in the obliteration of evidence. The print of the golf club was completely wiped out by her nightmare performance with the shooting-stick which she had noticed on her way downhill. She tramped on the Colonel's trout and there was the print of her spiked heel on its hide. She grabbed up the trout and was frantic to get rid of it when she saw Mr Phinn's cat. One can imagine her watching to see if Thomasina would eat the fish and her relief when she found that she would. She had seen the Old 'Un on the bridge. No doubt she had heard at least the fortissimo passages of Phinn's quarrel with the Colonel. Perhaps the Old 'Un would serve as false evidence. She fetched it and put it down by the body, but in handling the great trout she let it brush against her skirt. Then she replaced the shooting-stick. Lady Lacklander's painting rag was folded under the strap of her rucksack. Kitty Cartarette's hands were fishy. She used the rag to wipe them. Then, although she was about to thrust the shooting-stick back into the earth, she saw, probably round the collar of the spike, horrible traces of the use she had made of it. She twisted it madly about in the rag which was, of course, already extensively stained with paint. No doubt she would have refolded the rag and replaced it, but she heard, may even have seen, Dr Lacklander. She dropped the rag and bolted for cover. When she emerged she found he had taken away all the painting gear.' Alleyn paused and rubbed his nose. 'I wonder,' he said, 'if it entered her head that Lady Lacklander might be implicated. I wonder exactly when she remembered that she herself was wearing Lady Lacklander's shoes.'

He looked from Fox to Oliphant and the attentive Gripper.

'When she got home,' he said, 'no doubt she at once bathed and changed. She put out her tweed skirt to go to the cleaners. Having attended very carefully to the heel, she then polished Lady Lacklander's shoes. I think that heel must have worried her more than anything else. She guessed that Lacklander hadn't told his mother he'd borrowed the shoes. As we saw this morning, she had no suitable shoes of her own and her feet are much smaller than her stepdaughter's. She drove herself over to Nunspardon this morning and instead of ringing walked in and put the shoes in the downstairs cloakroom. I suppose Lady Lacklander's maid believed her mistress to have worn them and accordingly packed them up with her clothes instead of the late Sir Harold's boots which she had actually worn.'

Fox said: 'When you asked for everybody's clothes, Mrs Cartarette remembered, of course, that her skirt would smell of fish.'

'Yes. She'd put it in the box for the dry cleaning. When she realized we might get hold of the skirt she remembered the great trout brushing against it. With a mixture of bravado and cunning which is, I think, very characteristic, she boldly told me it would smell of fish and had the nerve and astuteness to use Thomasina as a sort of near-the-truth explanation. She only altered one fact. She said she tried to take a fish away from a cat whereas she had given a fish to a cat. If she'd read her murdered husband's book she'd have known that particular cat wouldn't jump and the story was, in fact, a bit too fishy. The scales didn't match.'

Oliphant said suddenly: 'It's a terrible thing to happen in the Vale. Terrible the things that'll come out! How's Sir George going to look?'

'He's going to look remarkably foolish,' Alleyn said with some heat, 'which is no more than he deserves. He's behaved very badly as his mother has no doubt pointed out to him. What's more, he's made things beastly and difficult for his son, who's a good chap, and for Rose Cartarette, who's a particularly nice child. I should say Sir George Lacklander has let his side down. Of course he was no match at all for a woman of her hardihood: he'd have been safer with a puff-adder than Kitty Cartarette, née, heaven help her, de Vere.'

'What, sir, do you reckon – ?' Oliphant began and, catching sight of his superior's face, was silent.

Alleyn said harshly: 'The case will rest on expert evidence of a sort never introduced before. If her counsel is clever and lucky she'll get an acquittal. If he's not so clever and a bit unlucky she'll get a lifer.' He looked at Fox. 'Shall we go?' he said.

He thanked Oliphant and Gripper for their work and went out to the car.

Oliphant said: 'Has something upset the chief, Mr Fox?'

'Don't you worry,' Fox said. 'It's the kind of case he doesn't fancy. Capital charge and a woman. Gets to thinking about what he calls first causes.'

'First causes?' Oliphant repeated dimly.

'Society. Civilization. Or something,' Fox said. 'I mustn't keep him waiting. So long.'

III

'Darling, darling Rose,' Mark said. 'We're in for a pretty ghastly time, I know. But we're in for it together, my dearest love, and I'll watch over you and be with you, and when it's all done with we'll have each other and love each other more than ever before. Won't we? Won't we?'

'Yes,' Rose said, clinging to him. 'We will, won't we?'

'So that something rather wonderful will come out of it all,' Mark said. 'I promise it will. You'll see.'

'As long as we're together.'

'That's right,' Mark said. 'Being together is everything.'

And with one of those tricks that memory sometimes plays upon us, Colonel Cartarette's face as Mark had last seen it in life, rose up clearly in his mind. It wore a singularly compassionate smile.

Together, they drove back to Nunspardon.

IV

Nurse Kettle drove in bottom gear to the top of Watt's Hill and there paused. On an impulse or perhaps inspired by some unacknowledged bit of wishful thinking, she got out and looked down on the village of Swevenings. Dusk had begun to seep discreetly into the valley. Smoke rose in cosy plumes from one or two chimneys; roofs cuddled into their surrounding greenery. It was a circumspect landscape. Nurse Kettle revived her old fancy. 'As pretty as a picture,' she thought, wistfully and was again reminded of an illustrated map. With a sigh, she turned back to her faintly trembling car. She was about to seat herself when she heard a kind of strangulated hail. She looked back and there, limping through the dusk came Commander Syce. The nearer he got to Nurse Kettle, the redder in the face they both became. She lost her head slightly, clambered into her car, turned her engine off and turned it on again. 'Pull yourself together, Kettle,' she said, and leaning out, shouted in an unnatural voice: 'The top of the evening to you.'

Commander Syce came up with her. He stood by the open driving window and even in her flurry, she noticed that he no longer smelt of stale spirits.

'Ha, ha,' he said, laughing hollowly. Sensing perhaps that this was a strange beginning he began again: 'Look here!' he shouted. 'Good lord! Only just heard. Sickening for you. Are you all right? Not too upset and all that? What a thing!'

Nurse Kettle was greatly comforted. She had feared an entirely different reaction to Kitty Cartarette's arrest in Commander Syce.

'What about yourself?' she countered. 'It must be a bit of a shock to *you*, after all.'

He made a peculiar dismissive gesture with the white object he carried.

'Never mind me. Or rather,' Commander Syce amended, dragging feverishly at his collar, 'if you can bear it for a moment . . . '

She now saw that the object was a rolled paper. He thrust it at her. 'There you are,' he said. 'It's nothing, whatever. Don't say a word.'

She unrolled it, peering at it in the dusk. 'Oh,' she cried in an ecstasy, 'how lovely! How lovely! It's my picture-map! Oh, *look!* There's Lady Lacklander, sketching in Bottom Meadow. And the doctor with a stork over his head. Aren't you a *trick?* And there's me – only, you've been much too kind about *me*. ' She leant out of the window turning her lovely map towards the fading light. This brought her closish to Commander Syce, who made a singular little ejaculation and was motionless. Nurse Kettle traced the lively figures through the map – the landlord, the parson, various rustic celebrities. When she came to Hammer Farm, there was the gardener's cottage and his child, and there was Rose bending gracefully in the garden. Nearer the house, one could see even in that light, Commander Syce had used thicker paint.

As if, Nurse Kettle thought with a jolt, there had been an erasure.

And down in the willow grove, the Colonel's favourite fishing haunt, there had been made a similar erasure.

'I started it,' he said, 'some time ago – after your – after your first visit.'

She looked up, and between this oddly-assorted pair a silence fell.

'Give me six months,' Commander Syce said. 'To make sure. It'll be all right. Will you?'

Nurse Kettle assured him that she would.

The Hand in the Sand

The Hand in the Sand was first published
by *American Weekly in* an anthology entitled
My Favourite True Mysteries in 1953

Truth may or may not be stranger than fiction. It is certainly less logical. Consider the affair of the severed hand at Christchurch, New Zealand, in 1885. Late in the afternoon of December 16th of that year, the sergeant on duty at the central police station was visited by two brothers and their respective small sons. They crowded into his office and, with an air of self-conscious achievement, slapped down a parcel, wrapped in newspaper, on his desk. Their name, they said, was Godfrey.

The sergeant unwrapped the parcel. He disclosed, nestling unattractively in folds of damp newsprint, a human hand. It was wrinkled and pallid like the hand of a laundress on washing day. On the third finger, left hand, was a gold ring.

The Godfreys, brothers and sons, made a joint announcement. 'That's Howard's hand,' they said virtually in unison and then added, in explanation, 'bit off by a shark.'

They looked significantly at a poster pasted on the wall of the police office. The poster gave a description of one Arthur Howard and offered a reward for information as to his whereabouts. The Godfreys also produced an advertisement in a daily paper of two months earlier:

Fifty Pounds Reward. Arthur Howard, drowned at Sumner on Saturday last. Will be given for the recovery of the body or the first portion received thereof recognizable. Apply Times Office.

The Godfreys were ready to make a statement. They had spent the day, it seemed, at Taylor's Mistake, a lonely bay not far from the seaside resort of Sumner, where Arthur Rannage Howard had been reported drowned on October 10th. At about two o'clock in the afternoon, the Godfreys had seen the hand lying in the sand below high-water mark.

Elisha, the elder brother, begged the sergeant to examine the ring. The sergeant drew it off the cold, wrinkled finger. On the inside were the initials AH.

The Godfreys were sent away without a reward. From that moment they were kept under constant observation by the police.

A few days later, the sergeant called upon Mrs Sarah Howard. At the sight of the severed hand, she cried out – in tears – that it was her husband's.

Later, a coroner's inquest was held on the hand. Three insurance companies were represented. If the hand was Howard's hand, they were due to pay out, on three life policies, sums amounting to 2,400 pounds. The policies had all been transferred into the name of Sarah Howard.

The circumstances of what the coroner called 'the alleged accident' were gone over at the inquest. On October 10, 1885, Arthur Howard, a railway workshop fitter, had walked from Christchurch to Sumner. On his way he fell in with other foot-sloggers who remembered his clothes and his silver watch on a gold chain and that he had said he meant to go for a swim at Sumner where, in those days, the waters were shark infested.

The next morning a small boy had found Howard's clothes and watch on the end of the pier at Sumner. A few days later insurance had been applied for and refused, the advertisement had been inserted in the paper and, as if in answer to the widow's prayer, the Godfreys, on December 16th, had discovered the hand.

But there also appeared the report of no less than ten doctors who had examined the hand. The doctors, after the manner of experts, disagreed in detail but, in substance, agreed upon three points.

1) The hand had not lain long in the sea.
2) Contrary to the suggestions of the brothers Godfrey, it had not been bitten off by a shark but had been severed by the teeth of a hacksaw.
3) The hand was that of a *woman*.

This damaging report was followed by a statement from an engraver. The initials AH, on the inside of the ring, had not been made by a professional's tool, said this report, but had been scratched by some amateur.

The brothers Godfrey were called in and asked whether, in view of the evidence, they would care to make a further statement.

Elisha Godfrey then made what must have struck the police as one of the most impertinently unlikely depositions in the annals of investigation.

Elisha said that in his former statement he had withheld certain information which he would now divulge. Elisha said that he and his brother had been sitting on the sands when from behind a boulder, there appeared a man wearing blue goggles and a red wig and saying, 'Come here! There's a man's hand on the beach!'

This multi-coloured apparition led Elisha and his brother to the hand, and Elisha had instantly declared, 'That's Howard's hand.'

The goggles and wig had then said, 'Poor fellow . . . poor fellow.'

'Why didn't you tell us before about this chap in the goggles and wig?' the police asked.

'Because,' said Elisha, 'he begged me to promise I wouldn't let anyone know he was there.'

Wearily, a sergeant shoved a copy of this amazing deposition across to Elisha. 'If you've still got the nerve, sign it.'

The Godfreys read it through and angrily signed.

The police, in the execution of their duty, made routine inquiries for information about a gentleman in blue goggles and red wig in the vicinity of Sumner and Taylor's Mistake on the day in question.

To their intense astonishment they found what they were after.

Several persons came forward saying that they had been accosted by this bizarre figure, who excitedly showed them a paper with the Godfreys' name and address on it and told them that the Godfreys had found Howard's hand.

The police stepped up their inquiries and extended them the length and breadth of New Zealand. The result was a spate of information.

The wig and goggles had been seen on the night of the alleged drowning, going north in the ferry steamer. The man who wore them had been run in for insulting a woman, who had afterwards refused to press charges. He had taken jobs on various farms. Most strangely, he had appeared at dawn by the bedside of a fellow worker and had tried to persuade this man to open a grave for him. His name, he had said, was Watt. Finally, and most interesting of all, it appeared that on the 18th of December the goggles and wig had gone for a long walk with Mrs Sarah Howard.

Upon this information, the police arrested the Godfrey brothers and Mrs Howard on a charge of attempting to defraud the insurance companies.

But a more dramatic arrest was made in a drab suburb of the capital city. Here the police ran to earth a strange figure in clothes too big for him, wearing blue goggles and a red wig. It was the missing Arthur Howard.

At the trial, a very rattled jury found the Godfreys and Mrs Howard 'not guilty' on both counts and Howard guilty on the second count of attempting to obtain money by fraud.

So far, everything ties up quite neatly. What won't make sense is that Howard did his best to look like a disguised man, but came up with the most eye-catching 'disguise' imaginable.

No clue has ever been produced as to the owner of the hand. Of eight graves that were subsequently opened in search for the body to match the hand, none contained a dismembered body. But the hand had been hacked off by an amateur. Could Howard have bribed a dissecting-room janitor or enlisted the help of some undertaker's assistant? And if, as seemed certain, it was a woman's hand, where was the rest of the woman?

Then there is Howard's extraordinary masquerade. Why make himself so grotesquely conspicuous? Why blaze a trail all over the country? Did his project go a little to his head? Was he, after all, a victim of the artistic temperament?

The late Mr Justice Alper records that Howard's lawyer told him he knew the answer. But, soon after this, the lawyer died.

I have often thought I would like to use this case as the basis for a detective story, but the material refuses to be tidied up into fiction form. I prefer it as it stands, with all its loose ends dangling. I am loath to concoct the answers. Let this paradoxical affair retain its incredible mystery. It is too good to be anything but true.